Forms
of
Prose Fiction

PRENTICE-HALL ENGLISH LITERATURE SERIES

Maynard Mack, *editor*

"Kinds" are the very life of literature,
and truth and strength come from the
complete recognition of them, from
abounding to the utmost in their
respective senses and sinking deep
into their consistency.

from Preface to *The Awkward Age,* Henry James

Prentice-Hall International, Inc., *London*
Prentice-Hall of Australia, Pty. Ltd., *Sydney*
Prentice-Hall of Canada, Ltd., *Toronto*
Prentice-Hall of India Private Limited, *New Delhi.*
Prentice-Hall of Japan, Inc., *Tokyo*

Forms
of
Prose Fiction

edited by

JAMES L. CALDERWOOD

HAROLD E. TOLIVER

university of california, irvine

Prentice-Hall, Inc.
englewood cliffs, new jersey

ISBN: 0–13–329219–3

Library of Congress Catalog Card Number: 70–167635

Printed in the United States of America

10   9   8   7   6   5   4   3   2   1

Table
of
Contents

Preface

ASSEMBLING REPRESENTATIVE FORMS OF FICTION, in Randall Jarell's words, is like "starting a zoo in a closet: The giraffe alone takes up more space than one has for the collection." Because the size of closets is what it is, we eliminated at the outset verse narratives, novels (which make logical supplements to a basic text in fiction), and kinds of fiction basically unsuitable for formal study. The remainder was still anything but a manageable collection of small and docile creatures; but we could not justify the next step that many anthologies take—the elimination of everything except modern short stories. Fables and parables, romances, satires, fantasies, and realism are but a few of the types and modes that students curious about the nature of fiction will wish to examine; and even readers whose primary interest is modern short fiction cannot isolate it from its ancestors and contemporary kinships without losing perspective on it. Another expediency that deserved not to be repeated as a governing principle was the separation of elements of fiction such as plot, point of view, symbol, and character, though these and other elements are considered in what we hope are appropriate places.

Forms of Prose Fiction therefore assembles as many varieties of short fiction as is feasible given the space and assumes that since one kind of fiction illuminates others, the best arrangement would be by major modes and types. The comparative approach that the introductory materials (and the companion volumes, *Forms of Poetry* and *Forms of Drama*) make explicit the selections and the arrangement reinforce by implication. To assist comparative reading we have aimed for historical depth as well as generic diversity and have tried to make possible the establishing of thematic as well as formal connections among the selections. The instructor is thus provided with several ways of working across the historical and generic spectrums.

We are indebted to Norman Prinsky for assistance with the biographical and critical sketches appended to the text.

JLC
HET
University of California, Irvine

Forms
of
Prose Fiction

.

The Boundaries
and
Modes of Fiction

IF STORIES CAN BE SAID TO HAVE "truth" and "reality," we must mean something special by those words where they refer to created illusions and imaginary events. The entryway to a story leads into a world of imitation objects, fictitious people, and invented happenings that are obviously quite different from their real-life counterparts. Stories sometimes resemble true records to be sure. The beginning of *Robinson Crusoe*, for instance, is as much like autobiography as it is like fiction:

> I was born in the year 1632, in the city of York, of a good family, though not of that country, my father being a foreigner of Bremen who settled first at Hull. He got a good estate by merchandise and, leaving off his trade, lived afterward at York, from whence he had married my mother, whose relations were named Robinson, a very good family in that country, and from whom, I was called Robinson Kreutznaer; but by the usual corruption of words in England we are now called, nay, we call ourselves, and write our name "Crusoe," and so my companions always called me.

The apparently casual way this has of contributing information clause upon clause, as though by afterthought, and the circumstantiality of much of the detail suggest that an unskilled, truthful man is telling his life's story as it occurs to him. We cannot know at this stage of course how important the sense of position, the habits of the mercantile man, and even the methodical carefulness in getting things right in a kind of trial-and-error way will contribute to Crusoe's development. A good deal that will be useful to Defoe's fictional structure is implicit here in the ramshackle style; if the entire paragraph has the look of stumbling autobiography so much the better for the credibility of the fiction.

1

A high incidence of spectacular trouble and adventure soon suggests to us that Defoe is operating as a novelist in this case. But he manages similar effects as a journalist writing of the plague in London as well, and it is finally something more than adventurousness and improbability that distinguishes fiction from fact. The crucial difference lies not in the quality of individual incidents at all but in the coherence and structure of the whole. We expect of the *fictor* (from *fingo*: to invent, imagine, arrange, order) a highly organized narrative. Whereas real life is often merely "one thing after another" in the manner Crusoe strings clauses together, fictional life has a definite beginning, development, and outcome. Its illusions and its imitations are never miscellaneous or accidental; they are composed into "plots," which Aristotle defines as imitations of actions and arrangements of incidents. Fiction manages its special enclosed field, its sequential order, by arranging selected moments as single or multiple actions, each part of which contributes to an organic system of meanings. If any detail of a story is not used or does not make sense eventually, we know where the blame lies—not with "the way things are" in random experience but with either the writer or the reader. It is this highly organic use that Defoe makes of Crusoe's details that finally betrays the fictional nature of the story.

Even the special coherence of stories is not quite sufficient, however, to distinguish them from life or from other kinds of writing. In science and history as well we cross thresholds and discover that the complexities of experience have been composed into organic statements, bounded by logic, hypothesis, and meaningful progression from detail to detail. As opposed to fiction, science sets out to formulate propositions about facts without offering imitative or dramatic images or illusory distortions; it does so sometimes tentatively, in hypotheses, and sometimes more definitively as natural laws. But the difference between "propositions" and the unverifiable statements of imaginative fictions turns out to be less decisive than a purist could wish. Much fact and circumstance adulterates our fictions, the basic materials of which—however fantastic and unlike ordinary experience a given story may seem—come from the writer's experience. Though a fabler may attach a man's head to a lion's body and thus create a mythical entity, all the parts that he assembles are familiar; only the arrangement is unusual.

In turn, much that might be considered "fabrication" creeps into science. It has become commonplace in recent semantics to concede that we cannot describe any phenomenon, even one observed carefully under a microscope, without adding something to it or taking something away; language cannot duplicate reality. Nor can any other medium of expression: Whether we use words, marble, paint, or celluloid transparents, we select, compress, simplify, and rearrange the objects of common perception in ways peculiar to each mode of representation we adopt. Fiction-making is thus virtually synonymous, if not with perception itself, at least with the placing of words and other signs in definite order. The nineteenth-century German philosopher Hans Vaihinger, in a book called *The Philosophy of As If,* lists among ideas that could be considered conveniences or inventions ("as if" arrangements of a purely verbal nature) the idea of zero and infinity, the fixed point, degree, measure, boundary, plurality and number, abstraction, the negative, dichotomy, comparison and contrast, and all "ideal" geometrical shapes such as the circle and the square, nearly all of which we habitually accept as the materials of true science and mathematics.

When we turn from science to history, the purist who would prefer that fiction keep its distance from forms of true statement is even more frustrated. The time-honored distinction between story and history is often difficult to justify. No historical narration in any of its various forms—the chronicle (a narrative account of events in the sequence in which they happened), the personal or autobiographical essay, political history, newspaper reporting, or biography—can make a serious claim to rendering an exact and undistorted account of what has actually happened. For purposes of clarity, we proceed "as if" the Elizabethan period and the Enlightenment existed, but they are clearly conveniences of labeling and organization. (It was not until the "Renaissance" that the "Medieval period" came into existence.) Mark Twain was perhaps more accurate than paradoxical when he wrote, "many things do not happen as they ought, and most things do not happen at all. It is for the conscientious historian to correct these defects."

Confidence in our capacity to distinguish fact from fancy is further undermined when we realize that what one age assumes to be history the next age is likely to attribute to imagination. To Milton the events of Genesis recounted in *Paradise Lost* were literal and sacred truths; since Darwin they have become myths or allegories for most readers. Much of what we now consider fiction was originally told as an elaborated version of fact—including medieval romance, Homeric epic, and ancient myths. On the other hand, not so long ago space travel was considered the ultimate in fantasy; now it has become, in part at least, "reality." Similarly, the wonders of travel literature in the seventeenth and eighteenth centuries must have seemed to many readers pure fabrication, while a largely made-up journey such as Gulliver's travels begins with such circumstantial lifelikeness and detail that we can easily imagine readers being taken in—until Gulliver awakes among the Lilliputians. Many other kinds of books of the past fifty years are also difficult for the librarian to shelve unless he maintains a large space for in-betweens. Hemingway's *Green Hills of Africa,* Truman Capote's *In Cold Blood,* Kurt Vonnegut's *Slaughterhouse Five,* Norman Mailer's *The Armies of the Night: History as a Novel, the Novel as History,* and Wallace Stegner's *Wolf Willow* each in its way combines fiction or fictional techniques with historical narration or journalism. (At the end of this introduction, we have illustrated one kind of mixture of historical narration and fictional elements in Stegner's "The Question Mark in the Circle," an essay that probes sensitively the boundary between them. In other sections, in James' "The Real Thing" and Barth's "Anonymiad," the reader will find fictions concerned with the nature of fiction.)

We stress this confusion of fact and imagination, seemingly so distinct when we cross the threshold of a story, because no comprehensive view of fiction should try to avoid their constant interaction. We should not assume from that entanglement, however, that we must abandon the distinction between them altogether, merely that extreme wariness is called for whenever we use the words "reality" or "truth" in connection with fiction or try to define the nature of its meaning. Imaginative symbol-usage is a uniquely human talent; it allows us to combine the actual and the fanciful meaningfully, weaving together the creative perceptions of mind and imagination and the external materials we find around us. The capacity to fabricate and to arrange is vital to the making of orders that have never existed but might exist, and it is central to the mind's inherent desire to work within enclosed fields, with limited materials that it can manage. It is after all the mixture of verisimilitude and adventure in Robinson Crusoe that intrigues us most; we should not be confused but entertained by it, playing with it as part of the serious game that all worthwhile fictions are. Conceived of in this way fictional orders are one extreme in the spectrum of orders that we make, beginning with simple acts of perception that organize sensory fields and extending to the most elaborate and complex narratives, paintings, symphonies, and other controlled "play" activities. Reality enters these creative fields under the predefined conditions of the game. By making meaningful use of the interplay between imagination and reality, fictions give us a special slant on "truth" that neither science nor history can.

Aristotle begins his *Poetics* with two assumptions that we have implicitly reaffirmed in these observations—that we take a basic pleasure in arranged and fabricated imitations of reality and that we constantly measure them against experience, however fantastic and apparently non-imitative a work may seem. Having suggested some reasons why these assumptions are important to a concept of fiction, we may proceed to ask how and in what degrees works of fiction are comparable to ordinary experience—and also, comparable to other works of fiction that have caused us to see experience differently. Once we have closed off the field of the "game" and arranged its materials according to our wishes, how do we go about relating it to that less organized and unbounded flux of experience that besieges us in daily life?

Relating fiction to life is a matter of comparison in which Aristotle's term "probability" looms large. We constantly measure fictional heroes by men we know and judge fictional deviations from the probable by the norm of ordinary affairs. More specifically, actions and the heroes who perform them can be classified by the kinds of power over chance and circumstance that they exercise. Aristotle distinguishes among heroes larger than life, average, and humbler than ordinary—heroes most likely to be found in epic and tragic modes, normative realism, and ironic or comic modes. In *ironic modes,* a hero is belittled by circumstances that he expects to transcend and cannot, or by circumstances which the context and the literary tradition suggest he ought to transcend. One extreme of irony is sympathetic humor, in which we identify with the hero to some extent; as the other extreme, when the belittling becomes more outrageous and circumstances assault the hero's dignity more successfully, we find burlesque, farce, and other mock-heroic modes. In these the unplanned and the fortuitous continually disrupt the hero's plans and destroy his integrity or his "intactness"—his ability to impose himself on events. If a particular recognizable hero or heroic style is mocked, we have ironic parody, which distorts something familiar, usually from literary history, in such a way as to render it ridiculous and contrived.

The *realistic mode* presents unexceptional, normative experience. It is sometimes distinguished from naturalism by the absence of any claim for absolute objectivity in the author. A naturalist such as the French novelist Zola (1840–1902) claims to offer a slice of life (or *tranche de vie*) more or less as though playing back the products of a camera and taperecorder. The *roman à clef* makes good on the naturalist's claim to literal accuracy in one particular respect, the use of real people as the models for fictional characters so that, to discover the meaning of the work, we require a "key" to equate characters and original models. The autobiographical novel makes good on part of the claim in another way, disguising events of the author's life as fiction. Like these forms of relatively direct imitation, the *roman-fleuve* (chronicle of a family dynasty or social group), the *Bildungsroman* (novel of a young man's growth), the *Künstlerroman* (novel of the artist's life), and the novel of manners (novel of moral behavior, propriety, and social order) adhere to the believable contours of biological, psychic, and social development.

However, they usually have no exact living models and make no pretense to offering uninterpreted slices of reality. The ordinary realist does not consider it out of place to shape the details he selects or to invent what history neglected to supply. Neither naturalists nor realists have managed to do differently. Balzac (1799–1850), for instance, though he considered himself society's "secretary," did not hesitate to offer interpretive essays within the text, heighten dramatic passions and antagonisms, create parallels among characters and actions, invent unnatural and sometimes improbable events, and of course construct unified plots—all of them tasks that no recording historian could perform without destroying his credibility. The historian, too, or course, creates or discovers coherent "careers" in his pursuit of historical logic, from the oldest record of fossils and their evolutionary story to the complex career of a Napoleon or an empire. But he is in no way committed to the law of probability and necessity that Aristotle ascribes to fictional plots and that all narrative realists obey. The historian may give his narration a starting point, a coherent development, and an ending, and he may subordinate all details to a thesis. But he is not obliged to give aesthetic shape to a career or establish a high degree of internal coherence if the record does not establish these for him—as it frequently does not. Also, when the improbable happens in history, it does not usually contribute to a higher or more satisfactory logic, as it should in fiction. If what *has happened* is the subject of the historian in all its untidiness, the subject of the fictional realist is what *usually happens* or *may happen,* in the habits, idiosyncracies, manners, and politics of individuals and societies.

In structure, normative realism tends to follow the "and then and then" sequence of chronicles without a great deal of emphasis on the overlapping periods of time and flashbacks of such novelists as Joyce and Faulkner, for whom the interpenetrating life of the mind and reality are more important than mere events. Such sequentialness does not necessarily result in episodic construction, nor need it fail to generate the parallels, contrasts, and ideas that a work requires if it is to interpret what happens. Unlike the *roman à these* and the *conte philosophique* (novels of ideas), which arrange characters and situations to illustrate matters of opinion, it merely seeks meaning in the logic of natural development itself, either individual development or the development of social groups. The confessional story, the diary, and the epistolary novel usually follow similarly strict chronologies, but in these forms of narrative the emphasis falls on the personal reactions of the writers of confidential documents rather than on the society, action, or processes of development themselves.

As the confessional story illustrates, narrative realism may focus on interior as well as exterior materials. Whereas the "ideal" or extreme of documentary (exterior) realism would be an encyclopaedic coverage of a large society, an environment, or a period, the ideal of interior realism is stream of consciousness, or the uninterpreted flow of thought usually in an ordinary mind. The two kinds are not mutually exclusive. Joyce's *Ulysses,* for instance, documents Leopold Bloom's Dublin and renders also the interior make-up of certain characters, most notably Molly Bloom in a long concluding monologue.

With merely a certain coloring and enlarging of experience, realism may move imperceptibly toward *romance,* which deals with out-of-the-ordinary affairs ranging from the slightly unfamiliar to the grossly improbable. A novel such as *Billy Budd* combines large portions of each: an enormous amount of factual detail concerning whaling and heightened romantic obsessions and adventure. The inner world of a romance character tends to be distorted and dreamlike, and the world outside him is likely to be hospitable to the grotesque and the unusual. Unlike realism, romance often blurs the distinction between exterior and interior, as psychological states are projected into secret sharers, archetypes, and strong contrasts of light and dark, good and evil. The forest in Hawthorne's "Young Goodman Brown," for instance, is both a real forest and a figure for the veiled world of evil projected from the darker areas of the mind. Also, instead of following a strictly sequential arrangement, romance tends to proceed by inexplicable and arbitrary shifts; these gaps in representation suggest mysteries behind the surface illogic of the events. (The marvelous is after all marvelous because the causes of events are invisible and intrude unexpectedly.) But we should distinguish apparent discontinuity from genuinely episodic adventures or such picaresque wandering as *Lazarillo de Tormes* and latter rogues present. Where the picaro gets into and out of one scrape after another in what could easily be a boundless series arranged in virtually any sequence, a typical romance hero like Malory's Lancelot undergoes a voyage of discovery and initiation. Not only are the hidden influences sooner or later clarified, but he himself is "programmed" so that one experince influences others; he is changed by them, and they must therefore happen in a certain sequence.

Romance overlaps other modes besides realism. Voltaire's Candide, for instance, brings together the satiric victim, the utopian seeker, and the romance wanderer: satiric because many episodes juxtapose high expectations with cruel realities that flay the innocent candor and optimism from Candide; utopian because in at least one episode (included in the selections) he is exposed to an ideal state by which other societies may be judged; and romance because he encounters improbabilities in far-flung lands and discovers the same figures and types recurring in a dreamlike manner. Johnson's *Rasselas* is similar but has much less satire; Swift's *Gulliver's Travels* has the same basic ingredients but in different proportions. As outsiders who can both explode the expectations of romance and yet remain distant from normative society, the picaro, the swindler, the naive butt of jokes, and the wandering hero (in *Lazarillo,* Cervantes, Defoe, Swift, Johnson, Fielding, Smollett, and Voltaire) discover society's rules to be a sharp and prickly barrier to his living a normal or average life. They exclude him rather than define and protect him.

But probably the most fruitful combination is romance and realism. Many literary historians in fact find the real beginnings of the novel in the critical spirit generated by the interplay of these two modes, especially as exemplified in Cervantes' *Don Quixote* and eighteenth-century fiction from Defoe to Fielding. The interplay of realism and romance becomes prominent at approximately the end of chivalry and spreads through prose fiction as the pervasive attitude of the realistic middle class toward aristocratic values and literary conventions becomes established. Thus mock-heroic in Fielding, picaresque in Defoe and Smollett, and domestic realism in Richardson form three main strands of the early novel in England. All have residual romance elements even though the leading eighteenth-century novelists again and again disparage romance and contrast to it their own forms of "natural" or normative realism. Unlike the full-fledged picaro or romance wanderer, the hero of the novel with romance elements is not a self-willed outcast or prankster. Sooner or later he finds a way to gain respectability; his adventures, though apparently haphazard and disorganized, lead toward an eventual reconciliation with normal society. Thus when his education is finished, a temporary outcast like Tom Jones abandons the adventures and the indignities he has undergone and discovers the boundaries of realism in property, marriage, and a substantial family heritage. The probable reasserts itself after a last fling at the improbable in the surprising revelation of his parentage. Likewise, both Robinson Crusoe and Moll Flanders shrink into colonial financiers and plantation owners after lives of great hazard and extremity.

By making use of an inherent sense of ordinary experience, we can begin to assess fictional modes by their adherence to or departure from the world of daily experience in this way. We also find it useful at times to focus on the purely formal matters of the "game" or the enclosed field—upon presentation as opposed to representation. A given story may pursue conventions rather than flying horses, dreamlike states, or wizardry away from the commonplace. The anecdote, tale, and short variations of the *roman à these* (story with a moral or governing idea) all have conventional characters whose stock responses are not so much unrealistic as simply convenient for the *fictor*. They also tend to have arbitrary beginnings and endings, as in Thurber's fables, for instance, in disregard for things-as-they-are. At the low or humorous end of the spectrum lies the fabliau (a vulgar anecdote, such as Chaucer's "Miller's Tale") and the beast fable (Thurber's "The Owl Who Was God")—one told mainly for its own sake but sometimes with an implicit lesson, the other told ostensibly for the sake of an explicit *sententia* or moral. Both reveal prearranged and formulaic patterns in the parallelism and symmetry of their narrative incidents; both have a close kinship with stories that come equipped with three bears or seven dwarfs. They usually insist upon poetic justice as the moral aspect of their preference for symmetry and balanced form. Types of humorous tales such as Twain's familiar story of the rigged frog race are "ideally" funny in that nothing fails to happen that will promote a perfect reversal or put down: Whatever makes for a good story simply happens in good stories.

In this cavalier group are many folk tales and tall stories that mix some element of the marvelous or the improbable with circumstantial realism and irony. Rather than consider them romances, we would remain closer to their emphasis if we regarded their romance elements as merely part of the formulaic conveniences by which they work. Once we grant the fabler the right to make frogs boast and hawks stoop at timely moments to swallow them (thus teaching them an appropriate lesson), such moral fables make perfectly good sense. Wit, imagination, and didactic intent often compete for prominence in them. Indeed the moral fable is likely to betray a serious tension between the *sententia* and the story-teller's love of invention. Thurber's mock parables, for instance, stand somewhere between the humorous tale and the didactic fable in this respect, as though written in collaboration by Aesop and Mark Twain, and it is difficult to say whether the concluding moral serves to set off the humor or the humor to reinforce the moral. Whatever their relative weight, however, both elements, humor and *sententia,* clearly impose on the hero a reduction in power that romantic figures escape. Thurber's owl is not allowed to maintain his pompousness or his followers their credulous belief in him. The marvelous, too, when it is permitted in the conventional short tale, is frequently humorous or merely convenient. If the folk hero works a few modest miracles—like the simpleton who counts a room full of lentils with the help of mice—he does so without puzzling very long over how he managed them; he simply accepts whatever comes his way. On the other hand, though the folk tale keeps us involved in a tangible world of chamber pots, rabbits, and cranky princesses, it has few of the constrictions of normality. Realism "salts" the marvelous and the conventional without contradicting them and is itself given the odd twist of a wonderland mirror.

It is not always possible to say whether departures from normative realism are due to convention or to something basic in the way a story sees things. Whereas in humorous folk tales we can clearly identify the story-teller's hand in the fabrication, in fairy tales and myths we are often not intended to separate so readily the qualities of the "good story" from the subject. Is Lancelot's moderate success in the grail quest illustrative of the way-things-are in a Christian view of things or a useful fiction by which Malory's completes his spectrum of illustrative types from the least to the most holy of knights? In myth as in perhaps no other mode of fiction, the world becomes remarkably perfect for aesthetic purposes: No weight of the commonplace and no shapeless factualness drag upon the story: What Lancelot should do to bring the grail quests into shape and fruition Lancelot does. The hero's powers thus enable him to mold events as they should be— and as they never are in recorded history. This is not to say that he molds them for utmost felicity. The hero may be a sacrificial figure whose main value is that of the dying and redeeming god, for instance, and the pattern that he "ideally" fulfills may be a tragic pattern. The point is that no part of the events he engages in is mere meaningless fact; nothing that happens fails to lend significance and heroic dimension to the story. Figures as different as Adonis and Christ have this much in common: Whether taken to be basically human or basically godlike, they perform actions of significant purpose and scope in a world in which what they do, whether tragic or comic, gives shape to all the elements of their stories.

Such figures are likely to be the center of a culture and become surrounded by reinforcing or lesser archetypes. The various archetypal situations of scripture—at least as many interpreters in the past read them, most notably Milton—are grouped around the central figure of the Christ and have as a common purpose the showing forth of God's purposes. In the handling of such writers as Spenser, Milton, and Bunyan, contributing figures and patterns such as the suffering servant, the fall into bondage and release, the golden age and promised land, the sacrifice and the scapegoat, the boastful warrior headed for a fall (Goliath, for instance), and God's champion or God's fool (both illustrated in Samson) may be, at least implicitly, connected in a single "program." All history for a poet like Herbert and an ambitious epic like *Paradise Lost* is the story of a single "author" or artificer whose "book" is history itself, and every subordinate narrative must therefore be read with the entire framework in mind. In commenting on this integration of elements, Northrop Frye cites St. Augustine's axiom that "the Old Testament is revealed in the New and the New concealed in the Old"; the contributory figures of Old Testament narrative are unclear until consummated in the central hero of the culture. Though Greek myth does not have a figure of this organizing scope, any central cultural myth is likely to gather into itself, in its many retellings through the ages, the central values and patterns of heroism that the culture prizes. It will also illustrate many of the conventions and formulaic patterns of "ideal" fictions, with clear beginnings, orderly and logical development, and definite endings.

MEANING IN FICTION

Measuring such mythic patterns against normal reality is never easy, but we do it constantly, at least unconsciously, and the meaning of myth derives in part from that comparsion. But it does not lie in any simple matching of fictional models, drawn to scale, to something exterior; nor does it lie in the imagination's escape into a marvelous and perfectly coherent world apart from the normal one. It lies instead, as we suggested, in the interaction of imitation and imagination, the actual and the fanciful. Without that interaction and without the fusion of fictional pattern and concrete detail no mere accuracy of reporting would be meaningful. We would be much less pleased with the verisimilitude of *Robinson Crusoe* if all Defoe's meticulous detail did not begin to assume some shape and to lead us somewhere. As it is, by the time Crusoe has spent a year or so on his island, it is clear that he is following a meaningful course from primitivism to a relatively sophisticated technology and economy. This and other elements of progression indicate that, however factual the surface of the story, Defoe's imagination and intellect have taken command of the material and shaped it, and the reader in turn may therefore discover a lively interplay of detail and organic pattern.

Most stories contain their own implicit instructions as to how we should approach them and "verify" their statements. They take their direction from an initial situation, follow a course through some variation of complicating cause and effect, and come to an ending that makes sense of all that precedes. Thus Crusoe sets out seeking adventure in defiance of his father's advice, "bent upon seeing the world"; he arouses expectations at every turn and follows up with either confirmations of what we expect or ironic twists that cause us to reinterpret, retroactively, what has happened before. This progression is the essence of "plot," which is the key to fiction's command over its materials, and it dictates the method of nearly all fictional interpretation. The first few sentences of a story indicate what kind of world we are entering, whether comic or tragic, heroic or humorous, detailed and fully documented or having gaps and intervals. As we are led forward, subsequent phases unfold either as confirmed knowledge or more likely as both new knowledge and unexpected complication. Eventually all parts of the fictional work form a system, teased by mystery and delay, in the light of which every detail must be read. No part of Crusoe's adventures can be interpreted finally without reference to the dynamic whole enclosed between the covers of the book.

The same can be said for the details of a poem or play, but prose fiction depends more heavily on the temporal sequence of events, the linear career of the story. In contrast, poems emphasize the interaction of words and the metrical movement of lines, and plays emphasize the dramatic exchange of characters as the cause of action. The general movement of stories is an imitation of historical succession rather than that of a verbal event or dramatic event, though it may include these. Story logic is causational logic: Crusoe's island adventure happens because of, as well as after, the preceding adventures.

Consider, for instance, the anxious moment when Crusoe rescues Friday from the cannibals (below, p. 108). We note first that Friday comes to this stage in the island's developing economy when a servant is especially appropriate and that, as usual, Crusoe absorbs every new challenge into a "household" way of looking at things that has formed the governing logic of his development. All things are economic objects for him. (He is given to itemized lists and inventories, for instance.) We will fail to understand why Defoe chooses the details he does and why he arranges them in this particular order unless we see the technology of Crusoe's household operation. Crusoe is preoccupied in the rescue of Friday with how to go about the rescue, how it can be managed—not we notice, with psychological repercussions, the ultimate significance such a providential blessing might portend, or the strange culture the intruders might have. When he has time to reflect, he devotes his attention to Friday's impact on the household—on food production, tool-making, and practical and religious education. Beyond this social and economic level we could no doubt find ample materials in the passage for psychological analysis and the traumas of racial relations, but whatever we decided to do ultimately with all the details of the passage, we can not escape the weight of the on-going narrative and the pressure brought to bear upon the episode by the rest of the novel. Every element that we single out is part of a successive continuity.

The shorter and less detailed a story is, the more completely its meaning can be paraphrased and generalized. We would have little luck trying to put the meaning of *War and Peace* in a few sentences or even a single book. But in a brief didactic fable such as Johnson's "Fable of the Vultures," the details serve mainly as illustration for a moral that we can generalize very easily. Beyond the outer margin of fiction but similar to such fables are epigrams, adages, and proverbs, which use very brief narrative metaphors or concrete vehicles to make a simple point. We can easily imagine these being expanded into small didactic stories, and they often are incorporated into moral fables as nuggets of generalized meaning. For instance, Bion's observation that "boys throw stones at frogs in sport, but the frogs die not in sport but in earnest" could be expanded into a brief narrative without losing the germ; or it could be appended to a beast fable as a summary. Gloucester's remark in *King Lear*, "As flies to wanton boys are we to th' Gods;/They kill us for their sport," though more ambitious in context, is not yet a story, merely an illustrative metaphor that squeezes a large part of the "story of mankind" into a nutshell. Such statements often serve as points of recognition in fiction that crystalize the meaning of events necessarily strung out in the telling.

Many stories, in fact, have special moments of recognition that may be called epiphanies, in which certain characters and the reader discover what the cumulative evidence demonstrates ("The Grave" and "The Wall," for instance). The detective story is par excellence a riddle construction whose details make sense in the light of a single revelation—the culprit and his motives and means. Even quite long and detailed stories may give us some proverbial gathering points that bring scattered narrative events into focus. It is a common practice in the eighteenth-century novel, for instance, for the author to intrude with interpretive essays and generalized comment. Such commentary may be interleaved with the incidents at any point or placed at the beginning, as in Jane Austen's axiomatic introduction to *Pride and Prejudice:*

> It is a truth universally acknowledged, that a single man in possession of a good fortune must be in want of a wife. However little known the feelings or views of such a man may be on his first entering a neighbourhood, this

truth is so well fixed in the minds of the surrounding families, that he is considered as the rightful property of someone or other of their daughters.

We accept such generalizations readily if they pertain directly to the fictional matters in hand.

In fables like Johnson's "Fable of the Vultures" and in satiric works such as *Gulliver's Travels,* the manipulative hand of the author is sometimes more obviously exposed in didactic comments on the action, and "meaning" becomes to some extent equivalent to the author's "intent." Thus when Swift has Gulliver say of an illustrious professor who has invented a wonderful book-writing mechanism, "I told him, although it were the custom of our learned in Europe to steal inventions from each other...I would take such caution, that he should have the honour entire without a rival," we know that it is partly Swift who is speaking. Though Gulliver means the word "honor" straightforwardly, Swift intends it ironically because such inventions are obviously not worth stealing—and neither in all probability are those promoted for self-interest by the learned men of Europe. We accept Swift's use of Gulliver as a puppet without great difficulty because the fiction is well-established and Gulliver is not entirely sacrificed to his author. The essayist or anatomist is a perfectly valid part of the *fictor,* who must, however, provide a fiction worthy of his interpretation.

At times we can distinguish more categorically between fictional and nonfictional commentary and meaning than the overlapping of Swift's didactic intent and Gulliver's fictional biography allow. We can do so partly on the grounds that in purely expository uses of narrative illustration the writer either speaks in his own voice throughout, vouching for the material he presents, or indicates clearly his uses of make-believe voices, while in fictional uses of expository material the author remains masked and vouches for nothing. Swift reserves the right to turn ironic expositor when he wishes, but if he were to do so too often and too blantantly, failing to remember the fiction of the presenter Gulliver, we would soon lose confidence in the logic of the narrative. As it is, even when we sense the author's presence behind a passage such as the one just cited, we sense it "playfully." A truly discursive, non-fiction writer, on the other hand, clearly marks the beginning and ending of whatever hypothetical or fictional elements he incorporates. He must make propositional statements and generalizations primary or we will lose confidence in him as an expositor. His truthful statements call forth and control all narrative illustrations, which he presents as models to capture the essential features of something too large, scattered, or intangible to present otherwise. In contrast, Jane Austen's opening paragraph merely pretends to offer a "truth universally acknowledged" as it pretends to offer historical facts; the observation is elicited by the invented people of the book and their situation. That it could well apply to society in general only tells us that we are entering a world much like the ordinary one, where the same social customs and moral laws apply.

When we enter another kind of world we may find the logic of progression quite different. Consider, for instance, the opening of Kafka's story "Metamorphosis":

> As Gregor Samsa awoke one morning from uneasy dreams he found himself transformed in his bed into a gigantic insect. He was lying on his hard, as it were armour-plated, back and when he lifted his head a little he could see his dome-like brown belly divided into stiff arched segments on top of which the bed-quit could hardly keep in position and was about to slide off completely. His numerous legs, which were pitifully thin compared to the rest of his bulk, waved helplessly before his eyes.

So bewildering and irrational is the initial presupposition of the story that any valid generalization or prediction about what will follow would be difficult to make. Kafka is understandably not given to axioms of Jane Austen's kind. At the same time, "Metamorphosis" makes its own kind of fictional, narrative sense. The strange metamorphoses of the dream world invade the world of waking and there take on the solidity and articulation that distinct phenomena have before our waking eyes. Once he has taken the incredible first step, Kafka subsequently follows its implications with relentless logic and offers no more surprises of that kind. Gregor Samsa's bugness becomes a test of the strengths and weaknesses of his family, which are revealed in a new light by the strain the family labors under.

Actually, at least four kinds of presentation bear upon the use of generalization and the discovery of meaning in fiction: discursive or oratorical, historical, dramatic or mimetic, and fictional. (The singer-presenter of ballads and lyrics might conceivably make a fifth.) The presenter of the first is an anatomist of ideas and of natural or social phenomena; he is basically a philosopher, scientist, or sociologist, and his statements can be checked against recurrent events and summarized in thesis statements. The second is also a *histor* or "knower" but he presents information as past and completed—also as arranged, selected, and no doubt distorted as we suggested earlier. The third is a *hister* or "actor" who enacts a role. (Thus the player of Hamlet helps Shakespeare present the play *Hamlet* without Shakespeare's needing to interfere in person.) Finally, the *fictor,* unlike the others, offers pretended narrative information, seen as completed and past, at least some of which is invented. His examples are more "philosophical" than history is, as Aristotle says, because they may be reprentative and universal; but they are also more concrete than the precepts of philosophy. The *fictor,* too, may present the story through a role-playing narrator or *hister,* either as an imagined first person who is part of the story he tells, as in Gulliver's case, or as a fictive "historian" speaking in third person and pretending that his fiction is truth, as Fielding does for the most part in *Tom Jones*. A historical novelist mixes the *fictor* and the *histor,* as any documentary realist does. The historian in turn may pretend to be a fictionalist: When George Gissing retired to the English countryside to write his memoirs, for instance, he pretended that he had discovered a "life and opinions" of someone else. He pretended to be a *fictor* rather than an autobiographer.

From these modes of presentation we can anticipate that essay materials and generalizations will have a special function in fiction's plotted movement. As part of the narrative stages of knowledge, they are entangled in the changing condition of characters, who are themselves necessarily kept from realizing the complete significance of what is happening. Though generalizations look outward to the reader and involve his expectations from point to point in the story and though nothing can prevent an author from offering an explicit interpretation of events, the many details through which the story extends itself resist easy summary. Generalizations scarcely fill time in the saying. They refer not to particular times and incidents but to universals. Stories, on the other hand, are partly dramatic enactments that require all their details, the essence of which is to fill time with specific happenings. Like music, they convey to us a sense of the rhythm and arrangement of their materials and of paced discovery. Perhaps in no form of art outside of music, in fact, is temporal process so important as it is in fictional narration. Hence, whatever universal principles a generalization may propose, they are articulated also through events and objects, through linear careers. They contribute to, but do not substitute for, episodic development and drama.

Awareness of that principle in determining the meaning of fiction returns us to our original distinction between the enclosed fields of a story and the openly referential constructions of science and history. In non-fiction writing, discovery precedes presentation and concerns events already finished or reducible to laws and opinions before they are introduced. The expository manner of science and history introduces a general thesis, usually at the outset, and presents its examples under the command of sufficient reason throughout. But fictional statements are resisted as well as forwarded by narrative complication; they are part of an agonized, suspenseful discovery whose meaning is embedded in concrete objects, paced sequences, and dramatic encounter. Rather than beginning with a general thesis, a story may well begin with a Gregor Samsa waving his insect legs before his unbelieving eyes.

The balancing of dramatically embodied meaning and generalizations is only one element of coherent form by which stories establish the rules of their particular games. In reading the stories that follow, one should try to discover the range and function of those rules in order to play by them himself and remember that though no two stories ask quite the same things of us, an approach to one will gain from the experience of others of its general kind. After an excursion across the boundaries of fiction into historical narration with Wallace Stegner, we will turn our attention to a selection of fiction that entrusts much of its meaning to types and archetypes as devices to organize and interpret a particular kind of world.

The Question Mark
in the Circle

wallace stegner

AN ORDINARY ROAD MAP of the United States, one that for courtesy's sake includes the first hundred miles on the Canadian side of the Line, will show two roads, graded but not paved, reaching up into western Saskatchewan to link U.S. 2 with Canada 1, the Trans-Canada Highway. One of these little roads leads from Havre, on the Milk River, to Maple Creek; the other from Malta, also on the Milk, to Swift Current. The first, perhaps a hundred and twenty miles long, has no towns on it big enough to show on a map of this scale. The second, fifty miles longer, has two, neither of which would be worth comment except that one of them, Val Marie, is the site of one of the few remaining prairie-dog towns anywhere. The rest of that country is notable primarily for its weather, which is violent and prolonged; its emptiness, which is almost frighteningly total; and its wind, which blows all the time in a way to stiffen your hair and rattle the eyes in your head.

This is no safety valve for the population explosion, no prize in a latter-day land rush. It has had its land rush, and recovered. If you owned it, you might be able to sell certain parts of it at a few dollars an acre; many parts you couldn't give away. Not many cars raise dust along its lonely roads—it is country people do not much want to cross, much less visit. But that block of country between the Milk River and the main line of the Canadian Pacific, and between approximately the Saskatchewan-Alberta line and Wood Mountain, is what this book is about. It is the place where I spent my childhood. It is also the place where the Plains, as an ecology, as a native Indian culture, and as a process of white settlement, came to their climax and their end. Viewed personally and historically, that almost featureless prairie glows with more color than it reveals to the appalled and misdirected tourist. As memory, as experience, those Plains are unforgettable; as history, they have the lurid explosiveness of a prairie fire, quickly dangerous, swiftly over.

I have sometimes been tempted to believe that I grew up on a gun-toting frontier. This temptation I trace to a stagecoach ride in the spring of 1914, and to a cowpuncher named Buck Murphy.

The stagecoach ran from Gull Lake, Saskatchewan, on the main line of the Canadian Pacific, to the town I shall call Whitemud, sixty miles southwest in the valley of the Whitemud or Frenchman River. The grade from Moose Jaw already reached to Whitemud, and steel was being laid, but no trains were yet running when the stage brought in my mother, my brother, and myself, plus a red-faced cowpuncher with a painful deference to ladies and a great affection for little children. I rode the sixty miles on Buck Murphy's lap, half anesthetized by his whiskey breath, and during the ride I confounded both my mother and Murphy by fishing from under his coat a six-shooter half as big as I was.

A little later Murphy was shot and killed by a Mountie in the streets of Shaunavon, up the line. As I heard later, the Mountie was scared and trigger-happy, and would have been in real trouble for an un-Mountie-like killing if Murphy had not been carrying a gun. But instead of visualizing it as it probably was—Murphy coming down the street in a buckboard, the Mountie on the corner, bad blood between them, a suspicious move, a shot, a scared team, a crowd collecting—I have been led by a lifetime of horse opera to imagine that death in standard walk-down detail. For years, growing up in more civilized places, I got a comfortable sense of status out of recalling that in my youth I had been a friend of badmen and an eyewitness to gunfights in wide streets between false-fronted saloons. Not even the streets and saloons, now that I test them, were authentic, for I don't think I was ever in Shaunavon in my boyhood, and I could not have reconstructed an image from Whitemud's streets because at the time of Murphy's death Whitemud didn't have any. It hardly even had houses: We ourselves were living in a derailed dining car.

Actually Murphy was an amiable, drunken, sentimental, perhaps dishonest, and generally harmless Montana cowboy like dozens of others. He may have been in Canada for reasons that would have interested Montana sheriffs, but more likely not; and if he had been, so were plenty of others who never thought of themselves as badmen. The Cypress Hills had always made a comfortable retiring place just a good day's ride north of the Line. Murphy would have carried a six-shooter mainly for reasons of brag; he would have worn it inside his coat because Canadian law forbade the carrying of sidearms.

When Montana cattle outfits worked across the Line they learned to leave their guns in their bedrolls. In the American West men came before law, but in Saskatchewan the law was there before settlers, before even cattlemen, and not merely law but law enforcement. It was not characteristic that Buck Murphy should die in a gunfight, but if he had to die by violence it was entirely characteristic that he should be shot by a policeman.

The first settlement in the Cypress Hills country was a village of *métis* winterers, the second was a short-lived Hudson's Bay Company post on Chimney Coulee, the third was the Mounted Police headquarters at Fort Walsh, the fourth was a Mountie outpost erected on the site of the burned Hudson's Bay Company buildings to keep an eye on Sitting Bull and other Indians who congregated in that country in alarming numbers after the big troubles of the 1870's. The Mountie post on Chimney Coulee, later moved down onto the river, was the predecessor of the town of Whitemud. The overgrown foundation stones of its cabins remind a historian why there were no Boot Hills along the Frenchman. The place was too well policed.

So as I have learned more I have had to give up the illusion of a romantic gun-toting past, and it is hardly glamour that brings me back, a middle-aged pilgrim, to the village I last saw in 1920. Neither do I come back with the expectation of returning to a childhood wonderland—or I don't think I do. By most estimates, including most of the estimates of memory, Saskatchewan can be a pretty depressing country.

The Frenchman, a river more American than Canadian since it flows into the Milk and thence into the Missouri, has changed its name since my time to conform with American maps. We always called it the Whitemud, from the stratum of pure white kaolin exposed along its valley. Whitemud or Frenchman, the river is important in my memory, for it conditioned and contained the town. But memory, though vivid, is imprecise, without sure dimensions, and it is as much to test memory against adult observation as for any other reason that I return. What I remember are low bars overgrown with wild roses, cutbank bends, secret paths through the willows, fords across the shallows, swallows in the clay banks, days of indolence and adventure where space was as flexible as the mind's cunning and where time did not exist. That was at the heart of it, the sunken and sanctuary river valley. Out around, stretching in all directions from the benches to become coextensive with the disk of the world, went the uninterrupted prairie.

The geologist who surveyed southern Saskatchewan in the 1870's called it one of the most desolate and forbidding regions on earth. I can remember plenty of times when it seemed so to me and my family. Yet as I poke the car tentatively eastward into it from Medicine Hat, returning to my childhood through a green June, I look for desolation and can find none.

The plain spreads southward below the Trans-Canada Highway, an ocean of wind-troubled grass and grain. It has its remembered textures: winter wheat heavily headed, scoured and shadowed as if schools of fish move in it; spring wheat with its young seed-rows as precise as combings in a boy's wet hair; gray-brown summer fallow with the weeds disked under; and grass, the marvelous curly prairie wool tight to the earth's skin, straining the wind as the wheat does, but in its own way, secretly.

Prairie wool blue-green, spring wheat bright as new lawn, winter wheat gray-green at rest and slaty when the wind flaws it, roadside primroses as shy as prairie flowers are supposed to be, and as gentle to the eye as when in my boyhood we used to call them wild tulips, and by their coming date the beginning of summer.

On that monotonous surface with its occasional ship-like farm, its atolls of shelter-belt trees, its level ring of horizon, there is little to interrupt the eye. Roads run straight between parallel lines of fence until they intersect the circle of the horizon. It is a landscape of circles, radii, perspective exercises —a country of geometry.

Across its empty miles pours the pushing and shouldering wind, a thing you tighten into as a trout tightens into fast water. It is a grassy, clean, exciting wind, with the smell of distance in it, and in its search for whatever it is looking for it turns over every wheat blade and head, every pale prim- rose, even the ground-hugging grass. It blows yellow-headed blackbirds and hawks and prairie sparrows around the air and ruffles the short tails of meadowlarks on fenceposts. In collaboration with the light, it makes lovely and changeful what might otherwise be characterless.

It is a long way from characterless; "overpowering" would be a better word. For over the segmented circle of earth is domed the biggest sky any- where, which on days like this sheds down on range and wheat and summer fallow a light to set a painter wild, a light pure, glareless, and transparent. The horizon a dozen miles away is as clean a line as the nearest fence. There is no haze, neither the woolly gray of humid countries nor the blue atmos- phere of the mountain West. Across the immense sky move navies of cumuli, fair-weather clouds, their bottoms as even as if they had scraped themselves flat against the flat earth.

The drama of this landscape is in the sky, pouring with light and always moving. The earth is passive. And yet the beauty I am struck by, both as present fact and as revived memory, is a fusion: This sky would not be so spectacular without this earth to change and glow and darken under it. And whatever the sky may do, however the earth is shaken or darkened, the Euclidean perfection abides. The very scale, the hugeness of simple forms, emphasizes stability. It is not hills and mountains which we should call eternal. Nature abhors an elevation as much as it abhors a vacuum; a hill is no sooner elevated than the forces of erosion begin tearing it down. These prairies are quiescent, close to static; looked at for any length of time, they begin to impose their awful perfection on the observer's mind. Eternity is a peneplain.

In a wet spring such as this, there is almost as much sky on the ground as in the air. The country is dotted with sloughs, every depression is full of water, the roadside ditches are canals. Grass and wheat grow to the water's edge and under it; they seem to grow right under the edges of the sky. In deep sloughs tules haves rooted, and every such pond is dignified with mating mallards and the dark little automata that glide after them as if on strings.

The nesting mallards move in my memory, too, pulling after them shadowy, long-forgotten images. The picture of a drake standing on his head with his curly tailfeathers sticking up from a sheet of wind-flawed slough is tangled in my remembering senses with the feel of the grassy edge under my bare feet, the smell of mud, the push of the traveler wind, the weight of the sun, the look of the sky with its level-floored clouds made for the penetration of miraculous Beanstalks.

Desolate? Forbidding? There was never a country that in its good moments was more beautiful. Even in drouth or dust storm or blizzard it is the reverse of monotonous, once you have submitted to it with all the senses. You don't get out of the wind, but learn to lean and squint against it. You don't escape sky and sun, but wear them in your eyeballs and on your back. You become acutely aware of yourself. The world is very large, the sky even larger, and you are very small. But also the world is flat, empty, nearly abstract, and in its flatness you are a challenging upright thing, as sudden as an exclamation mark, as enigmatic as a question mark.

It is a country to breed mystical people, egocentric people, perhaps poetic people. But not humble ones. At noon the total sun pours on your single head; at sunrise or sunset you throw a shadow a hundred yards long. It was not prairie dwellers who invented the indifferent universe or impotent man. Puny you may feel there, and vulnerable, but not unnoticed. This is a land to mark the sparrow's fall.

Our homestead lay south of here, right on the Saskatchewan-Montana border—a place so ambiguous in its affiliations that we felt as uncertain as the drainage about which way to flow. It would be no more than thirty or forty miles out of my way, now, and yet I do not turn south to try to find it, and I know very well why. I am afraid to. In the Dust Bowl years all that country was returned to range by the Provincial Farm Rehabilitation Administration. I can imagine myself bumping across burnouts and cactus clumps, scanning the dehumanized waste for some mark—shack or wind-leaned chickencoop, wagon ruts or abandoned harrow with its teeth full of Russian thistle—to reassure me that people did once live there. Worse, I can imagine actually

finding the flat on which our house stood, the coulee that angled up the
pasture, the dam behind which the spring thaw created our "rezavoy"—
locating the place and standing in it ringed by emptiness and silence, while
the wind fingered my face and whispered to itself like an old blind woman,
and a burrowing owl, flustered by the unfamiliar visitor, bowed from the
dirt mound of its doorstep, saying, "Who? Who?"

I do not want that. I don't want to find, as I know I will if I go down
there, that we have vanished without trace like a boat sunk in mid-ocean. I
don't want our shack to be gone, as I know it is; I would not enjoy hunting
the ground around it for broken crockery and rusty nails and bits of glass.
I don't want to know that our protective pasture fence has been pulled down
to let the prairie in, or that our field, which stopped at the Line and so
defined a sort of identity and difference, now flows southward into Montana
without a break as restored grass and burnouts. Once, standing alone under
the bell-jar sky gave me the strongest feeling of personal singularity I shall
ever have. That was because it was all new, we were taking hold of it to
make it ours. But to return hunting relics, to go down there armed only
with memory and find every trace of our passage wiped away—that would be
to reduce my family, myself, the hard effort of years, to solipsism, to make us
as fictive as a dream.

If I say to the owl, "Your great-grandfather lived in my house, and
could turn his head clear around and look out between his shoulder blades,"
I know he will bow, being polite, and then turn *his* head clear around and look
out between his shoulder blades, and seeing only unbroken grass, will cough
and say, "What house? Whose?" I know the very way the wind will ruffle
his feathers as he turns; I can hear the dry silence that will resume as soon
as he stops speaking. With the clarity of hallucination I can see my mother's
weathered, rueful, half-laughing face, and hear the exact tone, between
regretful and indomitable, in which she says the words with which she
always met misfortune or failure: "Well," she will say, "better luck next
time!"

I had much better let it alone. The town is safer. I turn south only far
enough to come up onto the South Bench, and then I follow a dirt road
eastward so as to enter Whitemud from the old familiar direction. That much
I will risk.

It is a far more prosperous country than I remember, for I return at the
crest of a wet cycle. The farms that used to jut bleakly from the prairie
are bedded in cottonwoods and yellowflowering caragana. Here and there
the horizontal land is broken by a new verticality more portentous than
windmills or elevators—the derricks of oil rigs. Farther north, prosperity
rides on the uranium boom. Here it rides on wheat and oil. But though the
country is no longer wild, this section within reach of town is even emptier,
more thinly lived in, than in our time. Oil crews create no new towns and

do not enlarge the old ones more than briefly. Even if they hit oil, they erect a Christmas tree on the well and go away. As for wheat, fewer and fewer farmers produce more and more of it.

To us, a half section was a farm. With modern machinery, a man by himself can plow, seed, and harvest a thousand or twelve hundred acres. The average Saskatchewan farm is at least a section; two sections, or even more, are not uncommon. And that is the good land, not the submarginal land such as ours which has been put back to grass. Even such a duchy of a farm is only a part-time job. A man can seed a hundred acres a day. Once the crop is in there is little to do until harvest. Then a week or two on the combine, a week or two of hauling, a week or two of working the summer fallow and planting winter wheat, and he is all done until May.

This is a strange sort of farming, with its dangers of soil exhaustion, drouth, and wind erosion, and with highly specialized conditions. Only about half of the farmhouses on the prairie are lived in any more, and some of those are lived in only part time, by farmers who spend all but the crop season in town, as we did. Many a farmer miles from town has no farmhouse at all, but commutes to work in a pickup. There is a growing class of trailer farmers, suitcase farmers, many of them from the United States, who camp for three or four months beside the field and return to Minneapolis or Bismarck when the crop is in.

Hence the look of extensive cultivation and at the same time the emptiness. We see few horses, few cattle. Saskatchewan farmers could go a long way toward supplying the world's bread, but they are less subsistence farmers than we were in 1915. They live in towns that have the essential form and function of medieval towns, or New England country towns, or Mormon villages in irrigated land: clusters of dwellings surrounded by the cultivated fields. But here the fields are a mile or two miles square and may be forty miles from the home of the man who works them.

So it is still quiet earth, big sky. Human intrusions seem as abrupt as the elevators that leap out of the plain to announce every little hamlet and keep it memorable for a few miles. The countryside and the smaller villages empty gradually into the larger centers; in the process of slow adaptation to the terms the land sets, the small towns get smaller, the larger ones larger. Whitemud, based strategically on railroad and river, is one of the ones that will last.

In the fall it was always a moment of pure excitement, after a whole day on the trail, to come to the rim of the South Bench. More likely than not I would be riding with my mother in the wagon while my father had my brother with him in the Ford. The horses would be plodding with their noses nearly to their knees, the colt would be dropping tiredly behind. We would be choked with dust, cranky and headachy with heat, our joints loosened with fifty miles of jolting. Then miraculously the land fell away below us, I would lift my head from my mother's lap and push aside the straw hat that had been protecting my face from the glare, and there below, looped in its green coils of river, snug and protected in its sanctuary valley, lay town.

The land falls away below me now, the suddenness of my childhood town is the old familiar surprise. But I stop, looking, for adult perception has in ten seconds clarified a childhood error. I have always thought of the Whitemud as running its whole course in a deeply sunken valley. Instead, I see that the river has cut deeply only through the uplift of the hills; that off to the southeast, out on the prairie, it crawls disconsolately flat across the land. It is a lesson in how peculiarly limited a child's sight is: He sees only what he can see. Only later does he learn to link what he sees with what he already knows, or has imagined or heard or read, and so come to make perception serve inference. During my childhood I kept hearing about the Cypress Hills, and knew that they were somewhere nearby. Now I see that I grew up in them. Without destroying the intense familiarity, the flooding recognition of the moment, that grown-up understanding throws things a little out of line, and so it is with mixed feelings of intimacy and strangeness that I start down the dugway grade. Things look the same, surprisingly the same, and yet obscurely different. I tick them off, easing watchfully back into the past.

There is the Frenchman's stone barn, westward up the river valley a couple of miles. It looks exactly as it did when we used to go through the farmyard in wagon or buckboard and see the starlted kids disappearing around every corner, and peeking out at us from hayloft door and cowshed after we passed. Probably they were *métis*, halfbreeds; to us, who had never heard the word *métis*, they were simply Frenchmen, part of the vague and unknown past that had given our river one of its names. I bless them for their permanence, and creep on past the cemetery, somewhat larger and somewhat better kept than I remember it, but without disconcerting changes. Down below me is the dam, with its wide lake behind it. It takes me a minute to recollect that by the time we left Whitemud Pop Martin's dam had long since washed out. This is a new one, therefore, but in approximately the old place. So far, so good.

The road I bump along is still a dirt road, and it runs where it used to run, but the wildcat oil derrick that used to be visible from the turn at the foot of the grade is not there any longer. I note, coming in toward the edge of town, that the river has changed its course somewhat, swinging closer to the southern hills and pinching the road space. I see a black iron bridge, new, that evidently leads some new road off into the willow bottoms westward, toward the old Carpenter ranch. I cannot see the river, masked in willows and alders, and anyway my attention is taken by the town ahead of me, which all at once reveals one element of the obscure strangeness that has been making me watchful. Trees.

My town used to be as bare as a picked bone, with no tree anywhere around it larger than a ten-foot willow or alder. Now it is a grove. My memory gropes uneasily, trying to establish itself among fifty-foot cotton-woods, lilac and honeysuckle hedges, and flower gardens. Searched for, plenty of familiarities are there: the Pastime Theater, identical with the one that sits across Main Street from the firehouse in my mind; the lumber yard where we used to get cloth caps advertising De Laval Cream Sepa-rators; two or three hardware stores (a prairie wheat town specializes in hardware stores), though each one now has a lot full of farm machinery next to it; the hotel, just as it was rebuilt after the fire; the bank, now remodeled into the office; the Presbyterian church, now United, and the *Leader* office, and the square brick prison of the school, now with three smaller prisons added to it. These are old acquaintances that I can check against their replicas in my head and take satisfaction from. But among them are the evidences of Progress—hospital, Masonic Lodge, at least one new elevator, a big quonset-like skating rink—and all tree-shaded, altered and distorted and made vaguely disturbing by greenery. In the old days we all used to try to grow trees, transplanting them from the Hills or getting them free with any two-dollar purchase from one of the stores, but they always dried up and died. To me, who came expecting a dusty hamlet, the change is charming, but memory has been fixed by time as photographs fix the faces of the dead, and this reality is dreamlike. I cannot find myself or my family or my companions in it.

My progress up Main Street, as wide and empty and dusty as I remember it, has taken me to another iron bridge across the eastern loop of the river, where the flume of Martin's irrigation ditch used to cross, and from the bridge I get a good view of the river. It is disappointing, a quiet creek twenty yards wide, the color of strong tea, its banks a tangle of willow and wild rose. How could adventure ever have inhabited those willows, or won-der, or fear, or the other remembered emotions? Was it along here I shot at the lynx with my brother's .25–.20? And out of what log (there is no possibility of a log in these brakes, but I distinctly remember a log) did my bullet knock chips just under the lynx's bobtail?

A muddy little stream, a village grown unfamiliar with time and trees. I turn around and retrace my way up Main Street and park and have a Coke in the confectionery store. It is run by a Greek, as it used to be, but whether the same Greek or another I would not know. He does not recognize me, nor I him. Only the smell of his place is familiar, syrupy with old delights, as if the ghost of my first banana split had come close to breathe on me. Still in search of something or someone to make the town fully real to me, I get the telephone book off its nail by the wall telephone and run

through it, sitting at the counter. There are no more than seventy or eighty
names in the Whitemud section. I look for Huffman—none. Bickerton—none.
Fetter—none. Orullian—none. Stenhouse—none. Young—one, but not by a
first name I remember. There are a few names I do remember—Harold Jones
and William Christenson and Nels Sieverud and Jules LaPlante. (That last
one startles me. I always thought his name was Jewell.) But all of the names
I recognize are those of old-timers, pioneers of the town. Not a name that I
went to school with, not a single person who would have shared as a contemporary my own experience of this town in its earliest years, when the river
still ran clear and beaver swam in it in the evenings. Who in town remembers
Phil Lott, who used to run coyotes with wolfhounds out on the South Bench?
Who remembers in the way I do the day he drove up before Leaf's store in
his democrat wagon and unloaded from it two dead hounds and the lynx
that had killed them when they caught him unwarily exposed out on the
flats? Who remembers in *my* way that angry and disgusted scene, and
shares my recollection of the stiff, half-disemboweled bodies of the hounds
and the bloody grin of the lynx? Who feels it or felt it, as I did and do, as a
parable, a moral lesson for the pursuer to respect the pursued?

Because it is not shared, the memory seems fictitious, and so do other
memories: the blizzard of 1916 that marooned us in the schoolhouse for a
night and a day, the time the ice went out and brought both Martin's dam
and the CPR bridge in kindling to our doors, the games of fox-and-geese in
the untracked snow of a field that is now a grove, the nights of skating with
a great fire leaping from the river ice and reflecting red from the cutbanks. I
have used those memories for years as if they really happened, have made
stories and novels of them. Now they seem uncorroborated and delusive.
Some of the pioneers still in the telephone book would remember, but
pioneers' memories are no good to me. Pioneers would remember the making
of the town; to me, it was made, complete, timeless. A pioneer's child is what
I need now, and in this town the pioneers' children did not stay, but went on,
generally to bigger places farther west, where there was more opportunity.

Sitting in the sticky-smelling, nostalgic air of the Greek's confectionery
store, I am afflicted with the sense of how many whom I have known are
dead, and how little evidence I have that I myself have lived what I remember. It is not quite the same feeling I imagined when I contemplated driving
out to the homestead. That would have been absolute denial. This, with its
tantalizing glimpses, its hints and survivals, is not denial but only doubt.
There is enough left to disturb me, but not to satisfy me. So I will go a
little closer. I will walk on down into the west bend and take a look at
our house.

In the strange forest of the school yard the boys are friendly, and their
universal air of health, openness, and curiosity reassures me. This is still a
good town to be a boy in. To see a couple of them on the prowl with air

rifles (in my time we would have been carrying .22's or shotguns, but we would have been of the same tribe) forces me to readjust my disappointed estimate of the scrub growth. When one is four feet high, ten-foot willows are a sufficient cover, and ten acres are a wilderness.

By now, circling and more than half unwilling, I have come into the west end of town, have passed Corky Jones's house (put off till later that meeting) and the open field beside Downs's where we used to play run-sheep-run in the evenings, and I stand facing the four-gabled white frame house that my father built. It ought to be explosive with nostalgias and bright with recollections, for this is where we lived for five or six of my most impressionable years, where we all nearly died with the flu in 1918, where my grandmother "went crazy" and had to be taken away by a Mountie to the Provincial asylum because she took to standing silently in the door of the room where my brother and I slept—just hovered there for heaven knows how long before someone discovered her watching and listening in the dark. I try to remember my grandmother's face and cannot; only her stale old-woman's smell after she became incontinent. I can summon up other smells, too—it is the smells that seem to have stayed with me: baking paint and hot tin and lignite smoke behind the parlor heater; frying scrapple, which we called headcheese, on chilly fall mornings after the slaughtering was done; the rich thick odor of doughnuts frying in a kettle of boiling lard (I always got to eat the "holes"). With effort, I can bring back Christmases, birthdays, Sunday School parties in that house, and I have not forgotten the licking I got when, aged about six, I was caught playing with my father's loaded .30–.30 that hung above the mantel just under the Rosa Bonheur painting of three white horses in a storm. After that licking I lay out behind the chopping block all one afternoon watching my big dark heavy father as he worked at one thing and another, and all the time I lay there I kept aiming an empty cartridge case at him and dreaming murder.

Even the dreams of murder, which were bright enough at the time, have faded; he is long dead, and if not forgiven, at least propitiated. My mother too, who saved me from him so many times, and once missed saving me when he clouted me with a chunk of stove wood and knocked me over the woodbox and broke my collarbone: She too has faded. Standing there looking at the house where our lives entangled themselves in one another, I am infuriated that of that episode I remember less her love and protection and anger than my father's inept contrition. And walking all around the house trying to pump up recollection, I notice principally that the old barn is gone. What I see, though less changed than the town in general, still has power to disturb me; it is all dreamlike, less real than memory, less convincing than the recollected odors.

Whoever lives in the house now is a tidy housekeeper; the yard is neat, the porch swept. The corner where I used to pasture my broken-legged colt is a bed of flowers, the yard where we hopefully watered our baby spruces is a lawn enclosed by a green hedge. The old well with the hand pump is still in the side yard. For an instant my teeth are on edge with the memory of the dry screech of that pump before a dipperful of priming water took hold, and an instant later I feel the old stitch in my side from an even earlier time, the time when we still carried water from the river, and I dipped a bucket down into the hole in the ice and toted it, staggering and with the other arm stuck stiffly out, up the dugway to the kitchen door.

Those instants of memory are persuasive. I wonder if I should knock on the door and ask the housewife to let me look around, go upstairs to our old room in the west gable, examine the ceiling to see if the stains from the fire department's chemicals are still there. My brother and I used to lie in bed and imagine scenes and faces among the blotches, giving ourselves inadvertent Rorschach tests. I have a vivid memory, too, of the night the stains were made, when we came out into the hard cold from the Pastime Theater and heard the firehouse bell going and saw the volunteer fire department already on the run, and followed them up the ditch toward the glow of the fire, wondering whose house, until we got close and it was ours.

It is there, and yet it does not flow as it should, it is all a pumping operation. I half suspect that I am remembering not what happened but something I have written. I find that I am as unwilling to go inside that house as I was to try to find the old homestead in its ocean of grass. All the people who once shared the house with me are dead; strangers would have effaced or made doubtful the things that might restore them in my mind.

Behind our house there used to be a footbridge across the river, used by the Carpenters and others who lived in the bottoms, and by summer swimmers from town. I pass by the opaque and troubling house to the cutbank. The twin shanties that through all the town's life have served as men's and women's bath houses are still there. In winter we used to hang our frozen beef in one of them. I remember iron evenings when I went out with a lantern and sawed and haggled steaks from a rocklike hind quarter. But it is still an academic execise; I only remember it, I do not feel the numb fingers and the fear that used to move just beyond the lantern's glow.

Then I walk to the cutbank edge and look down, and in one step the past comes closer than it has yet been. There is the gray curving cutbank, not much lower than I remember it when we dug cave holes in it or tunneled down its drifted cliff on our sleds. The bar is there at the inner curve of the bend, and kids are wallowing in a quicksandy mudhole and shrieking on an otter slide. They chase each other into the river and change magically from black to white. The water has its old quiet, its whirpools spin lazily into deep water. On the footbridge, nearly exactly where it used to be, two little girls lie staring down into the water a foot below their noses. Probably they are watching suckers that lie just as quietly against the bottom. In my time we used to snare them from the bridge with nooses of copper wire.

It is with me all at once, what I came hoping to re-establish, an ancient, unbearable recognition, and it comes partly from the children and the footbridge and the river's quiet curve, but much more from the smell. For here, pungent and pervasive, is the smell that has always meant my childhood. I have never smelled it anywhere else, and it is as evocative as Proust's madeleine and tea.

But what is it? Somehow I have always associated it with the bath house, with wet bathing suits and damp board benches, heaps of clothing, perhaps even the seldom rinsed corners where desperate boys had made water. I go into the men's bath house, and the smell is there, but it does not seem to come from any single thing. The whole air smells of it, outside as well as in. Perhaps it is the river water, or the mud, or something about the float and footbridge. It is the way the old burlap-tipped diving board used to smell; it used to remain in the head after a sinus-flooding dive.

I pick up a handful of mud and sniff it. I step over the little girls and bend my nose to the wet rail of the bridge. I stand above the water and sniff. On the other side I strip leaves off wild rose and dogwood. Nothing doing. And yet all around me is that odor that I have not smelled since I was eleven, but have never forgotten—have *dreamed,* more than once. Then I pull myself up the bank by a gray-leafed bush, and I have it. The tantalizing and ambiguous and wholly native smell is no more than the shrub we called wolf willow, now blooming with small yellow flowers.

It is wolf willow, and not the town or anyone in it, that brings me home. For a few minutes, with a handful of leaves to my nose, I look across at the clay bank and the hills beyond where the river loops back on itself, enclosing the old sports and picnic ground, and the present and all the years between are shed like a boy's clothes dumped on the bath-house bench. The perspective is what it used to be, the dimensions are restored, the senses are as clear as if they had not been battered with sensation for forty alien years. And the queer adult compulsion to return to one's beginnings is assuaged. A contact has been made, a mystery touched. For the moment, reality is made exactly equivalent with memory, and a hunger is satisfied. The sensuous little savage that I once was is still intact inside me.

Later, looking from the North Bench hills across my restored town, I can see the river where it shallows and crawls southeastward across the prairie toward the Milk, the Missouri, and the Gulf, and I toy with the notion that a man is like the river or the clouds, that he can be constantly moving and yet steadily renewed. The sensuous little savage, at any rate, has not been rubbed away or dissolved; he is as solid a part of me as my skeleton.

And he has a fixed and suitably arrogant relationship with his universe, a relationship geometrical and symbolic. From his center of sensation and question and memory and challenge, the circle of the world is measured, and in that respect the years of experience I have loaded upon my savage have not altered him. Lying on a hillside where I once sprawled among the crocuses, watching the town herd and snaring May's emerging gophers, I feel how the world still reduces me to a point and then measures itself from me. Perhaps the meadowlark singing from a fence post—a meadowlark whose dialect I recognize—feels the same way. All points on the circumference are equidistant from him; in him all radii begin; all diameters run through him; if he moves, a new geometry creates itself around him.

No wonder he sings. It is a good country that can make anyone feel so.

And it is a fact that once I have, so to speak, recovered myself as I used to be, I can look at the town, whose childhood was exactly contemporary with my own, with more understanding. It turns out to have been a special sort of town—special not only to me, in that it provided the indispensable sanctuary to match the prairie's exposure, but special in its belated concentration of Plains history. The successive stages of the Plains frontier flowed like a pageat through these Hills, and there are men still alive who remember almost the whole of it. My own recollections cover only a fragment; and yet it strikes me that this is *my* history. My disjunct, uprooted, cellular family was more typical than otherwise on the frontier. But more than we knew, we had our place in a human movement. What this town and its surrounding prairie grew from, and what they grew into, is the record of my tribe. If I am native to anything, I am native to this.

Modes of the
Typical and Archetypical

Introduction to
the Typical
and
Archetypical

THE HISTORICAL RELATIONSHIP between myth, folklore, saga, and romance is not always clear, and we cannot be sure if one derives from another or what specific purposes they might once have served. Did the various sub-mythic and heroic modes from romance to the fairy-story, for instance, progressively reduce the materials of myth—until in folklore we have the small scale adventures of diminutive creatures—or have all of these forms always existed side by side? Were stories of Greek gods that animate aspects of nature from thunder (Jove) to earth (Cybele) and fire (Vulcan) meant as modes of expression, or were they thought to describe actual deities? Was the opening of Genesis written to "classify" elements of the creation (water, earth, light, and creatures) and arrange them in order of priority, or was it accepted as sacred and literal from the beginning?

Whatever the historical relationships and purposes of these forms of narrative, when we consider them as analogous modes each assumes a place in the spectrum of types; each helps us understand the others. The *märchen* or folk tale, the tale of adventure, sophisticated fairy romance (Spenser's *Faerie Queene* or Tolkien's *Fellowship of the Ring*, for instance) Arthurian legend, saga, and fairy tale contain many similar patterns and depend to some extent on the typical and the archetypical for their meaning. Though all fiction has something of the typical in it, realistic modes are more dominated by texture, detail and plausible characterization; myths, fables, romances, parables, and allegories by recurrent patterns. An archetype is usually defined as the original of a pattern, of which, in Webster's words, all things of the same type are representations or copies. Archetypes are usually found either in sacred writings or in a body of literature based on them, such as biblical literature and stories like Malory's grail quests. The first chapters of Genesis, for instance, proceed through a model of law-giving order and make Adam and Eve both the fullest image of the creator and the founding image of subsequent "types." The Garden of Eden is an archetype of the golden place; the Fall is an archetype of disobedience and lost innocence; the wilderness is an archetype of the place of search and exile. The pattern of the six day's creation and the subsequent events in the fall and exile are thereafter imitated by the days and weeks of the historical world as it spins out its typical repetitions of the archetype.

The events of human history that occur between Genesis and the apocalypse in the biblical "completion myth" have frequently been interpreted in the light of the entire story, with its before-which-nothing-happened beginning and its after-which-nothing-happens ending. The motives and purposes of the creation are found to carry through history and give it significance. In those who make of biblical literature a "supreme fiction" (such as Milton), a deeply historical view backward and a prophetic view forward to the end of history influences every episode in the interim. One way of bringing that influence to bear traditionally is to read historical events "typologically." Typology is a special branch of the typical in which historical figures, primarily in the Old Testament, are interpreted as veiled copies of an archetype. Thus in Medieval and Renaissance readings of the Old Testament, events are considered "prefigurations" of an ultimate reality summed up in Christ. In this framework, we can see the distinction between the type and the archetype clearly, as basically a distinction between recurrent historical patterns and a summary reality to which they point, an "eschatological" end. Such a view of history as Milton and others of his time held obviously allows no hard and fast distinctions between history and myth, or between the ordinary and the sacred, because every literal or historical happening is subject to allegorization.

We select the Hebraic-Christian example because it is the most available and most central to western fictions, but other cultures illustrate a similar participation of archetypes and types in each other. Hesiod's "Works and Days" also starts with a Golden Age followed by lesser ages. Egyptian chronology passes from an age of gods or mythic age through an age of heroes, for whom romance would be appropriate, to an age of men, appropriate material for realism. In whatever culture we find them, archetypes are either more grandly heroic or more grandly terrible than types, which are closer to normal human dimensions. A list of recurrent types in western literature would include a large number of comic figures like the miser, the clown, the fool, the cuckhold, the simpleton, the cheat, the plotting servant, and so forth, all of whom tend to be entangled in the mechanics of everyday embarrassments. Only when the type touches upon the sacred or the demonic, as in the sacrificial hero of tragedy, the saint, or the devil, do we begin to want to consider him an archetype.

But more important for our purposes than the distinction between archetypes and types or their interaction are the kinds of narrative procedure and structure associated with them. The key to their function in fictional construction is their *reduplication*. Recurrence is not limited to romance or myth, of course; it is evident in any form of narrative "return"—a summary, a reflection or recollection, an echo, an allusion to a former moment in the narrative—and as such it is very helpful to any writer committed to a linear form. Whereas a lyric poem by its very brevity, its rhyme, repeated line length, stanzas, and other devices of shape and sound has a built in unity and means of aesthetic self-enclosure, fiction may be descriptively very ample and very complex in plot. The amount of sheer matter in Conrad's *Nostromo* or Dostoyevsky's *The Brothers Karamazov* is immense. Echoes, parallels, secret sharers, image patterns, and moments of recollection are therefore useful to counterbalance what might otherwise become a multiplicity of episodes and plot complications. Myths and romances simply make a more prominent and frequent use of such devices. Structural reduplication and the mirroring of one character in another contributes in them to a sense of design and often of a mysterious and marvelous fate. Their echoes make one episode or image implicitly the product of a general source or central pattern even though that source may remain hidden and enigmatic.

Romance, fable, allegory, and fairy tale all share a special concern with repeatable events, but despite this important similarity they also have notable differences. In fairy-stories, miraculous favors and coincidences are granted not to heroes of great stature but to common swineherds, poor maidens, and poverty-stricken lads who discover that the meek shall be amusing as well blessed. Their marvelous transformations seem to happen by lucky accident rather than by design. When Jack trades a perfectly good cow for a bag of beans and awakens to a blessed reversal of fortunes, he has merely stumbled into good fortune: He remains essentially the comic swain he has always been, perhaps favored by destiny in some odd way but not by some hidden sentient power. Such "eucatastrophes," as Tolkien calls them (or "happy reversals" reminiscent of Gospel's "high and joyous" conclusion), occur without benefit of anything so elevated as an apocalyptic goal that rewards good and punishes evil: Jack's good fortune happens because the story-teller decrees it and because it satisfies our recurrent wish to pass through tribulations and on to extraordinary conclusions. Though fairy tales often deal with familiar objects such as bean stalks, the sun, moon, and animals of the forest, the simplicity of their surfaces is made luminous by their setting in the land of faery. Under the magic of that setting any given object may be singled out as the key that unlocks good fortune; the power of blessedness lies in the talisman itself. One of the most typical patterns of the fairy-story, in fact, is the magical opening of a doorway to wonder that enables the hero to pass from the ordinary world to the land of dream fulfillment, where everything is both marvelous and ultimately coherent. The "doom" of the fairy tale forbids that anything be left undone which a complete and final ending requires.

As we move further from high archetypes into mixed modes, the sacred and the commonplace become more evenly balanced. Romances usually fall midway in the spectrum. Malory's version of the grail story, for instance, follows the careers of several kinds of knights between Galahad, the most holy, and Gawain, the least holy of knights. The story of the quester seeking illumination intersects the secular (mainly erotic and political) story of the court. As both a typical exemplar of courtly love and as a seeker of high vision, Lancelot is caught between these competing systems of value and between levels of the typical and the archetypal. His progress on the quest forces him to see one plane continually in terms of the other. Previously, despite the occasional marvels that his secular adventures have put in his path, things have always been much as they seem. Now, in the grail world, he is caught in a bewildering allegorical pageant in which things that appear to mean one thing turn out to mean another, and all surfaces suggest ranges of meaning beyond his comprehension. His progress comes under obscure commandments whose origins go far back—eventually to Christ's instructions to the apostles, which in turn are rooted in the plan that links history to Genesis and the apocalypse. Lancelot's hasty and partial vision of the grail indicates his ambiguous position above Gawain but well below knights like Galahad, Sir Bors, and Percival, who learn to imitate the archetype closely.

Wherever we find divine powers in romance, their demonic counterparts are seldom far off, and as sacred patterns become invested in human heroes such as Lancelot or Young Goodman Brown, demonic powers are usually invested in matching antagonists. This is especially true in the peculiar branch of romance that flowered in the eighteenth century, Gothic fiction, the center of which is usually held by a demonic figure seeking to dominate others and blindly devoted to sensual delights. In romances that lean toward realism, the dimensions of the hero and the willful strength of his antagonists are naturally scaled down somewhat. Conrad's "Heart of Darkness" and Hawthorne's "Young Goodman Brown," to take two well-known examples, are versions of demonic romance. The historical instruments of Conrad's darkness are imperialism and African savagery, both explainable social elements, and the demonic powers that haunts Goodman Brown are a concealed part of the Puritan township itself. Brown thus lives in a world sharply divided between warring forces that have both mythic dimensions and a relatively ordinary village surface. Part of the meaning of Conrad and Hawthorne is that the demonic element lies at the heart of the commercial and the social world.

The heroes of Kafka likewise find normal expectations juxtaposed traumatically with obscure and powerful forces. In the "Parable of the Bridge," for instance, the bridge's suppositions about itself and its logical reading of its condition are completely reversed by an unknown assailant. Instead of performing a meaningful action or demonstrating what bridges are destined to be (why bridges if not to provide safe passage over abysses?), the assailant violates its formal dress and destroys its logic. Far from granting safe passage to helpless travelers, the bridge itself collapses. "Meaning" as the sequential logic of details thereby crumbles. The enigmatic jab of the sharp stick, administered by a creature without apparent motives, represents an intrusion of the absurd in what proves to be a world of bottomless conjecture. Like the "Parable of the Law," the "Parable of the Bridge" overturns the normal pattern of narrative expectation: Appearances do not prove to be the veiled expression of meaningful intelligences, but neither are they merely themselves and nothing more. In Conrad's "The Secret Sharer," we again find an obscure and divided world. However, in this case the surface of life aboard ship remains logical and well-ordered despite the underground reality that haunts it. The secret sharer both collaborates with and contrasts to the surface life of the captain: He does not destroy it. The psychological doubles eventually assist each other in resuming their separate courses.

As we trace the influence of the typical and archetypical further into the realm of realism, we discover the principles of dramatic contrast between good and evil, divine and demonic forces, surface and dark underside, still working but less prominently. Myth and realism in works like Joyce's *Ulysses* and Barth's *Giles Goat-Boy* produce constant "perspectives by incongruity" (to borrow Kenneth Burke's apt term) in which the ample dimensions of the world of myth and heroic pattern are exploited to reveal the limitations of circumstantial realism; and realism in turn causes us to make certain judgments of myth. A recent cartoon in Punch reveals graphically the ironic effect of such contrasts. In it a modern version of the apocalypse is juxtaposed with dingy normality as a shaggy-looking couple in a run-down room awaken to merely another dawn. Beside their iron bed is a hand-printed sign "The End of the World is at Hand," which they have obviously been carrying about with them. As the wife admonishes her groggy mate, "Rise and shine Benjamin. It's still here," their unmarvelous "awakening" to the same old routine passes a certain comment on the grandeur of their expectations; and in return the dream of a grand ending-of-all-endings passes judgment on their unflattering daily "progress." In a similar way, the spirit of realism and the spirit of myth and romance have collided freely in prose fiction since Cervantes' Quixote first rode out to test the values of romantic chivalry against the thieves and cheating innkeepers of an unmagical world. In the novel, their battle has been somewhat unequal since Defoe, Richardson, and Fielding, who converted the potentially romantic adventures of their wandering heroes and heroines into the detailed substance of a more and more predictable daily life. But they continue their fruitful interaction in works as diverse as Eliot's *Middlemarch* and Faulkner's *Light in August,* as well as in Poe, Hawthorne, Conrad, Kafka, and Barth, whose portrayal of surfaces still contains a sense of potentially powerful forces underneath.

Equally likely to combine the typical and the realistic is allegory, in which pattern dominates detail—often, however, the pattern of ideas rather than of types or archetypes. The allegorist offers definite indications of a figure's significance, especially in personification allegory, which assigns animated characteristics to abstractions like Error and Duplicity. Slightly different from personified abstractions are figures like Everyman who stand symbolically for a class or species rather than an idea. In a story like "Young Goodman Brown," as the title suggests the protagonist represents a youthful, initially innocent good man who grows gloomy and sullen when he discovers the nature of his townsmen. Though he is made complex by this psychological change, he remains something of an everyman figure throughout. In "The Portable Phonograph," the well-articulated surface of the story makes more use of symbolic detail than allegory normally does. In this modern version of apocalyptic, the world ends not with a bang or whimper but with a rediscovery of the cave, as four rather ordinary men slip backward into primitivism. This general human progress from an original barbarism through an interim culture and back to basic fire, food, and shelter is symbolized by the phonograph and all the circumstances of its use, as meaning arises constantly and naturally in details and their elaboration. We are not meant to translate those details into ideas or make the four men representative of, say, four vices or virtues or even of social classes. No object in the story can be said to "stand for" a particular, explicit idea beyond the inherent meaning of the men in their odd situation. Yet the men are themselves carefully chosen to illustrate the general possibilities of culture under the stress of a final warfare. In such a story it is impossible to separate the method of realistic portrayal from the generalizing effect of the typical and the symbolic: Each narrative element from descriptive setting to action reinforces the others and becomes both concrete and universal, typical and particular.

Parables, too, hover frequently between the two extremes, the typical and the particular, but they naturally have less scope for detail than either allegory or symbolic stories. Christ's parables amplify a single symbol or metaphor—an exchange of talents between lord and servant, the sowing of seed, the spreading of light. Plato's allegory of the cave is a Platonist version of a similar search for absolutes; it accomplishes for Plato's philosophical system what Christ's parables accomplish in the exposition of a fundamental view of the end. Into a single amplified metaphor, Socrates (the narrator) compresses the essential matters of his view of temporal illusion and truth. However, by contrast to Christ's narrative method, with its implicit concern with historical process and ultimate outcome, Plato stresses a static polarity between light and shadow, illusion and reality, becoming and being. This difference reminds us that for Plato the contrasts between the two realms are a standing metaphysical contrast, and that "truth" for him is unvarying and atemporal. Though the movement of the parable imitates the process of illumination as Socrates expounds to his pupil Glaucon the meaning of the image he has presented, Glaucon's own reiterated "Very true" proves that Truth is in fact innate and need only be recollected. The details of the parable are thus merely convenient instruments to bring back to consciousness truths already in our possession; nothing uniquely "real" is contained in temporal objects or actions themselves.

In ironic allegories and parables such as William March's "White and Yellow Corn" and Samuel Johnson's fable of the vultures, expected truth or conventional generality and what the narrative illustration actually shows to be the case are discrepant. For Johnson, "man" is the self-slaying animal, suitably discussed by vultures. For March, "truth" is a wizened, unvisited old creature who is easily stretched and virtually unknown. In "The Saga of Grettir the Strong" we find the heroic and archetypical similarly tempered with irony. Although in his best moments Grettir is larger than ordinary and will fight three men unassisted, he listens to prudence when confronted by four or more. Except for the trolls and spirits that he fights, the doom that haunts him, and the witchcraft that eventually subdues him, he has little commerce with the supernatural: His main encounters are not with gods, wizards, or shape-changers but with other men as boisterous and as muscular as he. Even the trolls he meets are humanized and muscular. As a robber, outlaw, and frequent committer of manslaughter, he sometimes resembles the picaresque rogue and at other times the satiric protagonists of Rabelais, Swift, and Voltaire. He also recalls Samson in his love of riddles and practical jokes, but in place of the sacred law that Samson champions and then violates, he is upheld and condemned by a strictly civil law. He is exiled from a purely human society according to codes of conduct that are by and large reasonable. In structure, too, the northland saga of Grettir's type hovers between episodic adventure, historical chronicle, and a quasimagical sense of ritual balance, parallelism, and prophecies of doom. The marvelous is mixed with the skeptical and the ironic.

As we might expect when Mark Twain turns to Genesis, "Eve's Diary" also contains a mixture of ironic realism, the marvelous, and the typical. Read against the background of *Paradise Lost,* Twain's version of the discovery and loss of paradise is somewhat directionless—perhaps because it is too much captivated by its own devices. But it nonetheless makes use of the latent interest of the myth and holds them to its own purposes, working constantly against the high expectations of the story it humanizes. Eve's diary is thus both myth and confession. As Cecily remarks about the diaries of a young girl in *The Importance of Being Earnest,* it is the record of her own thoughts and impressions, and "consequently meant for publication." In taking an inside view of Eve's first few days, Twain balances humor, lyricism, pathos, and the implicit wonder of a radical beginning. Exploiting the basic enchantment of her first exposure to the moon, fire, and man he makes them merely one aspect of her feminine nature, which also includes vanity, talkativeness, and flirtation. The story ends where stories of Eden must, at Adam's discovery of a new dimension of knowledge in the Fall. At that point myth touches upon those everyday disappointments and sorrows of transiency for which Adam and Eve are conveniently blameable, and the archetype of paradise blends into the typicality of Everyman confronting the facts of the daily struggle.

Biblical Narrative

chapter i

IN THE BEGINNING God created the Heaven, and the Earth. And the earth was without forme, and voyd, and darkenesse was upon the face of the deepe: and the Spirit of God mooved upon the face of the waters. And God said, Let there be light: and there was light. And God saw the light, that it was good: and God divided the light from the darknesse. And God called the light, Day, and the darknesse he called Night: and the evening and the morning were the first day.

And God said, Let there be a firmament in the midst of the waters: and let it divide the waters from the waters. And God made the firmament; and divided the waters, which were under the firmament, from the waters, which were above the firmament: and it was so. And God called the firmament, Heaven: and the evening and the morning were the second day.

And God said, Let the waters under the heaven be gathered together unto one place, and let the dry land appeare: and it was so. And God called the drie land, Earth, and the gathering together of the waters called hee, Seas: and God saw that it was good. And God said, Let the Earth bring foorth grasse, the herbe yeelding seed, and the fruit tree, yeelding fruit after his kinde, whose seed is in it selfe, upon the earth: and it was so. And the earth brought foorth grasse, and herbe yeelding seed after his kinde, and the tree yeelding fruit, whose seed was in it selfe, after his kinde: and God saw that it was good. And the evening and the morning were the third day.

And God said, Let there be lights in the firmament of the heaven, to divide the day from the night: and let them be for signes and for seasons, and for dayes and yeeres. And let them be for lights in the firmament of the heaven, to give light upon the earth: and it was so. And God made two great lights: the greater light to rule the day, and the lesser light to rule the night: he made the starres also. And God set them in the firmament of the heaven, to give light upon the earth: and to rule over the day, and over the night, and to divide the light from the darkness: and God saw that it was good. And the evening and the morning were the fourth day.

And God said, Let the waters bring foorth aboundantly the moving creature that hath life, and foule that may flie above the earth in the open firmament of heaven. And God created great whales, and every living creature that moveth, which the waters brought forth aboundantly after their kinde, and every winged foule after his kinde: and God saw that it was good. And God blessed them, saying, Be fruitfull, and multiply, and fill the waters in the Seas, and let foule multiply in the earth. And the evening and the morning were the fift day.

And God said, Let the earth bring forth the living creature after his kinde, cattell, and creeping thing, and beast of the earth after his kinde: and it was so. And God made the beast of the earth after his kinde, and cattell after their kinde, and every thing that creepeth upon the earth, after his kinde: and God saw that it was good.

And God said, Let us make man in our Image, after our likenesse: and let them have dominion over the fish of the sea, and over the foule of the aire, and over the cattell, and over all the earth, and over every creeping thing that creepeth upon the earth. So God created man in his owne Image, in the Image of God created hee him; male and female created hee them. And God blessed them, and God said unto them, Be fruitfull, and multiply, and replenish the earth, and subdue it, and have dominion over the fish of the sea, and over the foule of the aire, and over every living thing that mooveth upon the earth.

And God said, Behold I have given you every herbe bearing seede, which is upon the face of all the earth, and every tree, in the which is the fruit of a tree yeelding seed, to you it shall be for meat: and to every beast of the earth, and to every foule of the aire, and to every thing that creepeth upon the earth, wherein there is life, I have given every greene herbe for meat: and it was so. And God saw every thing that hee had made: and behold, it was very good. And the evening and the morning were the sixth day.

chapter ii

Thus the heavens and the earth were finished, and all the hoste of them. And on the seventh day God ended his worke, which hee had made: And he rested on the seventh day from all his worke, which he had made. And God blessed the seventh day, and sanctified it: because that in it he had rested from all his worke, which God created and made.

These are the generations of the heavens, and of the earth, when they were created; in the day that the LORD God made the earth, and the heavens, and every plant of the field, before it was in the earth, and every herbe of the field, before it grew: for the LORD God had not caused it to raine upon the earth, and there was not a man to till the ground. But there went up a mist from the earth, and watered the whole face of the ground. And the LORD God formed man of the dust of the ground, and breathed into his nostrils the breath of life; and man became a living soule.

And the LORD God planted a garden Eastward in Eden; and there he put the man whom he had formed. And out of the ground made the LORD God to grow every tree that is pleasant to the sight, and good for food: the tree of life also in the midst of the garden, and the tree of knowledge of good and evil. And a river went out of Eden to water the garden, and from thence it was parted, and became into foure heads. The name of the first is Pison: that is it which compasseth the whole land of Havilah, where there is gold. And the gold of that land is good: There is Bdellium and the Onix stone. And the name of the second river is Gihon: the same is it that compasseth the whole land of Ethiopia. And the name of the third river is Hiddekel; that is it which goeth toward the East of Assyria: and the fourth river is Euphrates. And the LORD God tooke the man, and put him into the garden of Eden, to dresse it, and to keepe it. And the LORD God commanded the man, saying, Of every tree of the garden thou mayest freely eate. But of the tree of the knowledge of good and evil, thou shalt not eate of it: for in the day that thou eatest hereof, thou shalt surely die.

And the LORD God said, It is not good that the man should be alone: I will make him an helpe meet for him. And out of the ground the LORD God formed every beast of the field, and every foule of the aire, and brought them unto Adam, to see what he would call them: and whatsoever Adam called every living creature, that was the name thereof. And Adam gave names to all cattell, and to the foule of the aire, and to every beast of the fielde: but for Adam there was not found an helpe meete for him. And the LORD God caused a deepe sleepe to fall upon Adam, and hee slept; and he tooke one of his ribs, and closed up the flesh in stead thereof. And the rib which the LORD God had taken from man, made hee a woman, and brought her unto the man. And Adam said, This is now bone of my bones, and flesh of my flesh: she shalbe called woman, because shee was taken out of man. Therefore shall a man leave his father and his mother, and shall cleave unto his wife: and they shalbe one flesh. And they were both naked, the man and his wife, and were not ashamed.

chapter iii

Now the serpent was more subtill then any beast of the field, which the
LORD God had made, and he said unto the woman, Yea, hath God said, Ye
shall not eat of every tree of the garden? And the woman said unto the
serpent, Wee may eate of the fruite of the trees of the garden: but of the
fruit of the tree, which is in the midst of the garden, God hath said, Ye shal
not eate of it, neither shall ye touch it, lest ye die. And the Serpent said
unto the woman, Ye shall not surely die. For God doeth know, that in the
day ye eate thereof, then your eyes shalbee opened: and yee shall bee as
Gods, knowing good and evill. And when the woman saw, that the tree was
good for food, and that it was pleasant to the eyes, and a tree to be desired
to make one wise, she tooke of the fruit thereof, and did eate, and gave also
unto her husband with her, and hee did eate. And the eyes of them both
were opened, and they knew that they were naked, and they sewed figge
leaves together, and made themselves aprons. And they heard the voyce of
the LORD God, walking in the garden in the coole of the day: and Adam and
his wife hid themselves from the presence of the LORD God, amongst the trees
of the garden. And the LORD God called unto Adam, and said unto him,
Where art thou? And he said, I heard thy voice in the garden: and I was
afraid, because I was naked, and I hid my selfe. And he said, Who told
thee, that thou wast naked? Hast thou eaten of the tree, whereof I commanded thee, that thou shouldest not eate? And the man said, The woman
whom thou gavest to be with mee, shee gave me of the tree, and I did eate.
And the LORD God said unto the woman, What is this that thou hast done?
And the woman said, The Serpent beguiled me, and I did eate. And the
LORD God said unto the Serpent, Because thou hast done this, thou art cursed
above all cattel, and above every heast of the field: upon thy belly shalt thou
goe, and dust shalt thou eate, all the dayes of thy life. And I will put enmitie
betweene thee and the woman, and betweene thy seed and her seed: it shal
bruise thy head, and thou shalt bruise his heele. Unto the woman he said, I
will greatly multiply thy sorowe and thy conception. In sorow thou shalt
bring forth children: and thy desire shall be to thy husband, and hee shall
rule over thee. And unto Adam he said, Because thou hast hearkened unto
the voyce of thy wife, and hast eaten of the tree, of which I commaunded
thee, saying, Thou shalt not eate of it: cursed is the ground for thy sake:
in sorow shalt thou eate of it all the dayes of thy life. Thornes also and
thistles shall it bring forth to thee: and thou shalt eate the herbe of the
field. In the sweate of thy face shalt thou eate bread, till thou returne unto
the ground: for out of it wast thou taken, for dust thou art, and unto dust
shalt thou returne. And Adam called his wives name Eve, because she was
the mother of all living. Unto Adam also, and to his wife, did the LORD God
make coates of skinnes, and cloathed them.

And the Lord God said, Behold, the man is become as one of us, to know good and evill. And now lest hee put forth his hand, and take also of the tree of life, and eate and live for ever: therefore the Lord God sent him foorth from the garden of Eden, to till the ground, from whence he was taken. So he drove out the man: and he placed at the East of the garden of Eden, Cherubims, and a flaming sword, which turned every way, to keepe the way of the tree of life.

chapter iiii

And Adam knew Eve his wife, and shee conceived, and bare Cain, and said, I have gotten a man from the Lord. And she againe bare his brother Abel, and Abel was a keeper of sheep, but Cain was a tiller of the ground. And in processe of time it came to passe, that Cain brought of the fruite of the ground, an offering unto the Lord. And Abel, he also brought of the firstlings of his flocke, and of the fat thereof: and the Lord had respect unto Abel, and to his offering. But unto Cain, and to his offring he had not respect: and Cain was very wroth, and his countenance fell. And the Lord said unto Cain, Why art thou wroth? And why is thy countenance fallen? If thou doe well, shalt thou not be accepted? and if thou doest not well, sinne lieth at the doore: And unto thee shall be his desire, and thou shalt rule over him. And Cain talked with Abel his brother: and it came to passe when they were in the field, that Cain rose up against Abel his brother, and slew him.

And the Lord said unto Cain, Where is Abel thy brother? And hee said, I know not: Am I my brothers keeper? And he said, What hast thou done? the voyce of thy brothers blood cryeth unto me, from the ground. And now art thou cursed from the earth, which hath opened her mouth to receive thy brothers blood from thy hand. When thou tillest the ground, it shall not henceforth yeeld unto thee her strength: A fugitive and a vagabond shalt thou be in the earth. And Cain said unto the Lord, My punishment is greater, then I can beare. Behold, thou hast driven me out this day from the earth, and from thy face shall I be hid, and I shall be a fugitive, and a vagabond in the earth: and it shall come to passe, that every one that findeth me, shall slay me. And the Lord said unto him, Therefore whosoever slayeth Cain, vengeance shalbe taken on him seven fold. And the Lord set a marke upon Cain, lest any finding him, should kill him.

Parables

matthew

chapter xiii

THE SAME DAY WENT IESUS out of the house, and sate by the sea side. And great multitudes were gathered together unto him, so that hee went into a ship, and sate, and the whole multitude stood on the shore. And hee spake many things unto them in parables, saying, Behold, a sower went foorth to sow. And when he sowed, some seedes fell by the wayes side, and the foules came, and devoured them up. Some fell upon stony places, where they had not much earth: and foorthwith they sprung up, because they had no deepenesse of earth. And when the Sunne was up, they were scorched: and because they had not root, they withered away. And some fell among thorns: and the thornes sprung up, and choked them. But other fell into good ground, and brought foorth fruit, some an hundred folde, some sixtie folde, some thirty folde. Who hath eares to heare, let him heare. And the disciples came, and sayd unto him, Why speakest thou unto them in parables? He answered, and said unto them, Because it is given unto you to know the mysteries of the kingdome of heaven, but to them it is not given. For whosoever hath, to him shall be given, and he shall have more abundance: but whosoever hath not, from him shall be taken away, even that hee hath. Therefore speake I to them in parables: because they seeing, see not: and hearing, they heare not, neither doe they understand. And in them is fulfilled the prophecie of Esaias, which saith,

By hearing ye shall heare, and shall not understand:
And seeing yee shall see, and shall not perceive.

> *For this peoples heart is waxed grosse,*
> *And their eares are dull of hearing,*
> *And their eyes they have closed,*
> *Lest at any time they should see with their eyes,*
> *And heare with their eares,*
> *And should understand with their heart,*
> *And should be converted,*
> *And I should heale them.*

But blessed are your eyes, for they see: and your eares, for they heare. For verely I say unto you, that many Prophets, and righteous men have desired to see those things which yee see, and have not seene them: and to heare those things which ye heare, and have not heard them.

Heare ye therefore the parable of the sower. When any one heareth the word of the kingdome, and understandeth it not, then commeth the wicked one, and catcheth away that which was sowen in his heart: this is hee which received seede by the way side. But he that received the seed into stony places, the same is he that heareth the word, and anon with ioy receiveth it: yet hath hee not root in himselfe, but dureth for a while: for when tribulation or persecution ariseth because of the word, by and by he is offended. He also that received seed among the thorns, is he that heareth the word, and the care of this world, and the deceitfulnesse of riches choke the word, and he becommeth unfruitfull. But he that received seed into the good ground, is hee that heareth the word, and understandeth it, which also beareth fruit, and bringeth foorth, some an hundred fold, some sixtie, some thirty.

Another parable put he forth unto them, saying; The kingdome of heaven is likened unto a man which sowed good seed in his field: but while men slept, his enemy came and sowed tares among the wheat, and went his way. But when the blade was sprung up, and brought forth fruit, then appeared the tares also. So the servants of the housholder came, and said unto him, Sir, didst not thou sow good seede in thy field? from whence then hath it tares? He said unto them, An enemy hath done this. The servants said unto him, Wilt thou then that we goe and gather them up? But he said, Nay: lest while yee gather up the tares, ye root up also the wheat with them. Let both grow together until the harvest: and in the time of harvest, I will say to the reapers, Gather ye together first the tares, and binde them in bundels to burne them: but gather the wheat into my barne.

Another parable put he foorth unto them, saying, The kingdome of heaven is like to a graine of mustard seed, which a man tooke, and sowed in his field. Which indeed is the least of al seeds: but when it is growen, it is the greatest among herbes, and becommeth a tree: to that the birds of the aire come and lodge in the branches thereof.

Another parable spake he unto them, The kingdome of heaven is like unto leaven, which a woman tooke, and hid in three measures of meale, till the whole was leavened. All these things spake Iesus unto the multitude in parables, and without a parable spake hee not unto them: that it might bee fulfilled which was spoken by the Prophet, saying,

I will open my mouth in parables,
I will utter things which have bin kept secret from the foundation of the world.

Then Iesus sent the multitude away, and went into the house: and his disciples came unto him, saying, Declare unto us the parable of the tares of the field. He answered, and said unto them, Hee that soweth the good seed, is the sonne of man. The field is the world. The good seed, are the children of the kingdome: but the tares are the children of the wicked one. The enemie that sowed them, is the devill. The harvest, is the ende of the world. And the reapers are the Angels. As therefore the tares are gathered and burnt in the fire: so shall it be in the end of this world. The Sonne of man shall send forth his Angels, and they shall gather out of his kingdome all things that offend, and them which doe iniquitie: and shall cast them into a furnace of fire: there shall be wayling and gnashing of teeth. Then shall the righteous shine foorth as the Sunne, in the kingdome of their father. Who hath eares to heare, let him heare.

Againe, the kingdome of heaven is like unto treasure hid in a field: the which when a man hath found, hee hideth, and for joy thereof goeth and selleth all that hee hath, and buyeth that field.

Againe, the kingdome of heaven is like unto a marchant man, seeking goodly pearles: who when hee had found one pearle of great price, he went and solde all that he had, and bought it.

Againe, the kingdome of heaven is like unto a net that was cast into the sea, and gathered of every kind, which, when it was full, they drew to shore, and sate downe, and gathered the good into vessels, but cast the bad away. So shall it be at the ende of the world: the Angels shal come forth, and sever the wicked from among the iust, and shal cast them into the furnace of fire: there shall be wailing, and gnashing of teeth. Iesus saith unto them, Have ye understood all these things? They say unto him, Yea, Lord. Then said he unto them, Therefore every Scribe which is instructed unto the kingdome of heaven, is like unto a man that is an housholder, which bringeth foorth out of his treasure things new and old.

And it came to passe, that when Iesus had finished these parables, hee departed thence.

chapter xxv

Then shall the kingdome of heaven be likened unto ten Virgins, which tooke their lamps, and went forth to meet the bridegrome. And five of them were wise, and five were foolish. They that were foolish tooke their lampes, and tooke no oyle with them: but the wise tooke oyle in their vessels with their lampes. While the bridegrome taried, they all slumbred and slept. And at midnight there was a cry made, Behold, the bridegrome commeth, goe ye out to meet him. Then all those virgins arose, and trimmed their lampes. And the foolish said unto the wise, Give us of your oyle, for our lampes are gone out. But the wise answered, saying, Not so, lest there be not ynough for us and you, but goe ye rather to them that sell, and buy for your selves. And while they went to buy, the bridegrome came, and they that were ready, went in with him to the marriage, and the doore was shut. Afterward came also the other virgines, saying, Lord, Lord, open to us. But he answered, and said, Verely I say unto you, I know you not. Watch therefore, for ye know neither the day, nor the houre, wherein the Sonne of man commeth.

For the kingdome of heaven is as a man travailing into a farre countrey, who called his owne servants, and delivered unto them his goods: and unto one he gave five talents, to another two, and to another one, to every man according to his severall ability, and straightway tooke his iourney. Then hee that had received the five talents, went and traded with the same, and made them other five talents. And likewise he that had received two, he also gained other two. But hee that had received one, went and digged in the earth, and hid his lordes money. After a long time, the lord of those servants commeth, and reckoneth with them. And so hee that had received five talents, came and brought other five talents, saying, Lord, thou deliveredst unto me five talents, behold, I have gained besides them, five talents moe. His lord said unto him, Well done, thou good and faithful servant, thou hast been faithful over a few things, I will make thee ruler over many things: enter thou into the ioy of thy lord. He also that had received two talents, came and said, Lord, thou deliveredst unto me two talents: behold, I have gained two other talents besides them. His lord said unto him, Well done, good and faithfull servant, thou hast beene faithfull over a few things, I will make thee ruler over many things: enter thou into the ioy of thy lord. Then he which had received the one talent, came and said, Lord, I knew thee that thou art an hard man, reaping where thou hast not sowen, and gathering where thou hast not strawed: and I was afraid, and went and hidde thy talent in the earth: loe, there thou hast that is thine. His lord answered, and said unto him, Thou wicked and slouthfull servant, thou knewest that I reape where I sowed not, and gather where I have not strawed: thou oughtest therefore to have put my money to the exchangers, and then at my comming I should have received mine owne with usurie. Take therefore the talent from him, and give it unto him which hath ten talents. For unto every one that hath shall be given, and he shall have abundance: but from him that hath not, shal be taken away, even that which he hath. And cast yee the unprofitable servant into outer darkenesse, there shall be weeping and gnashing of teeth.

When the Sonne of man shall come in his glory, and all the holy Angels with him, then shall hee sit upon the throne of his glory: and before him shall be gathered all nations, and he shall separate them one from another, as a shepheard divideth his sheepe from the goats. And he shall set the sheepe on his right hand, but the goats on the left. Then shall the King say unto them on his right hand, Come ye blessed of my Father, inherit the kingdome prepared for you from the foundation of the world. For I was an hungred, and yee gave me meate: I was thirstie, and ye gave me drinke: I was a stranger, and ye tooke me in: naked, and ye clothed me: I was sicke, any yee visited me: I was in prison, and ye came unto me. Then shall the righteous answere him, saying, Lord, when saw we thee an hungred, and fedde thee? or thirstie, and gave thee drinke? When saw wee thee a stranger, and tooke thee in? or naked, and clothed thee? Or when saw we thee sicke, or in prison, and came unto thee? And the King shall answere, and say unto them, Verely I say unto you, in as much as ye have done it unto one of the least of these my brethren, ye have done it unto me. Then shall he say also unto them on the left hand, Depart from me, ye cursed, into everlasting fire, prepared for the devill and his angels. For I was an hungred, and yee gave me no meat: I was thirstie, and ye gave me no drinke: I was a stranger, and yee tooke me not in: naked, and ye clothed mee not: sicke, and in prison, and yee visited me not. Then shall they also answere him, saying, Lord, when saw we thee an hungred, or athirst, or a stranger, or naked, or sicke, or in prison, and did not minister unto thee? Then shall he answere them, saying, Verely, I say unto you, in as much as ye did it not to one of the least of these, ye did it not to me. And these shall goe away into everlasting punishment: but the righteous into life eternall.

ABRAHAM AND ISAAC

And it came to passe after these things, that God did tempt Abraham, and said unto him, Abraham. And hee said, Beholde, heere I am. And he said, Take now thy sonne, thine only sonne Isaac, whom thou lovest, and get thee into the land of Moriah: and offer him there for a burnt offering upon one of the Mountaines which I will tell thee of.

And Abraham rose up earely in the morning, and sadled his asse, and tooke two of his yong men with him, and Isaac his sonne, and clave the wood for the burnt offering, and rose up, and went unto the place of which God had told him. Then on the third day Abraham lift up his eyes, and saw the place afarre off. And Abraham said unto his yong men, Abide you here with the asse, and I and the lad will goe yonder and worship, and come againe to you. And Abraham tooke the wood of the burnt offering, and layd it upon Isaac his sonne: and he tooke the fire in his hand, and a knife: and they went both of them together. And Isaac spake unto Abraham his father, and said, My father: and he said, Here am I, my sonne. And hee said, Behold the fire and wood: but where is the lambe for a burnt offring? And Abraham

said, My sonne, God will provide himselfe a lambe for a burnt offering: so
they went both of them together. And they came to the place which God
had tolde him of, and Abraham built an Altar there, and layd the wood in
order, and bound Isaac his sonne, and layde him on the Altar upon the
wood. And Abraham stretched foorth his hand, and tooke the knife to slay
his sonne. And the Angel of the LORD called unto him out of heaven, and
said, Abraham, Abraham. And he said, Here am I. And he said, Lay not
thine hand upon the lad, neither do thou any thing unto him: for now I
know that thou fearest God, seeing thou hast not withhelde thy sonne, thine
onely sonne from mee. And Abraham lifted up his eyes, and looked, and
beholde, behinde him a Ramme caught in a thicket by his hornes: And
Abraham went and tooke the Ramme, and offered him up for a burnt offering,
in the stead of his sonne. And Abraham called the name of that place
Iehovah-ijreh,[1] as it is said to this day, In the Mount of the Lord it shalbe
seene.

And the Angel of the LORD called unto Abraham out of heaven the
second time, and said, By my selfe have I sworne, saith the LORD, for because
thou hast done this thing, and hast not withheld thy sonne, thine onely
sonne, that in blessing I will blesse thee, and in multiplying, I will multiply
thy seed as the starres of the heaven, and as the sand which is upon the sea
shore, and thy seed shall possesse the gate of his enemies. And in thy seed
shall all the nations of the earth be blessed, because thou hast obeyed my
voice.

---

[1] That is, The LORD will see, or, provide.

Eve's Diary

mark twain

translated from the original

SATURDAY.—I AM ALMOST A WHOLE DAY OLD, NOW. I arrived yesterday. That is as it seems to me. And it must be so, for if there was a day-before-yesterday I was not there when it happened, or I should remember it. It could be, of course, that it did happen, and that I was not noticing. Very well; I will be very watchful now, and if any day-before-yesterdays happen I will make a note of it. It will be best to start right and not let the record get confused, for some instinct tells me that these details are going to be important to the historian some day. For I feel like an experiment, I feel exactly like an experiment; it would be impossible for a person to feel more like an experiment than I do, and so I am coming to feel convinced that that is what I *am*—an experiment; just an experiment, and nothing more.

Then if I am an experiment, am I the whole of it? No, I think not; I think the rest of it is part of it. I am the main part of it, but I think the rest of it has its share in the matter. Is my position assured, or do I have to watch it and take care of it? The latter, perhaps. Some instinct tells me that eternal vigilance is the price of supremacy. [That is a good phrase, I think, for one so young.]

Everything looks better to-day than it did yesterday. In the rush of finishing up yesterday, the mountains were left in a ragged condition, and some of the plains were so cluttered with rubbish and remnants that the aspects were quite distressing. Noble and beautiful works of art should not be subjected to haste; and this majestic new world is indeed a most noble and beautiful work. And certainly marvelously near to being perfect, notwithstanding the shortness of the time. There are too many stars in some places and not enough in others, but that can be remedied presently, no doubt. The moon got loose last night, and slid down and fell out of the scheme —a very great loss; it breaks my heart to think of it. There isn't another thing among the ornaments and decorations that is comparable to it for beauty and finish. It should have been fastened better. If we can only get it back again——

But of course there is no telling where it went to. And besides, whoever gets it will hide it; I know it because I would do it myself. I believe I can be honest in all other matters, but I already begin to realize that the core and center of my nature is love of the beautiful, a passion for the beautiful, and that it would not be safe to trust me with a moon that belonged to another person and that person didn't know I had it. I could give up a moon that I found in the daytime, because I should be afraid some one was looking; but if I found it in the dark, I am sure I should find some kind of an excuse for not saying anything about it. For I do love moons, they are so pretty and so romantic. I wish we had five or six; I would never go to bed; I should never get tired lying on the moss-bank and looking up at them.

Stars are good, too. I wish I could get some to put in my hair. But I suppose I never can. You would be surprised to find how far off they are, for they do not look it. When they first showed, last night, I tried to knock some down with a pole, but it didn't reach, which astonished me; then I tried clods till I was all tired out, but I never got one. It was because I am left-handed and cannot throw good. Even when I aimed at the one I wasn't after I couldn't hit the other one, though I did make some close shots, for I saw the black blot of the clod sail right into the midst of the golden clusters forty or fifty times, just barely missing them, and if I could have held out a little longer maybe I could have got one.

So I cried a little, which was natural, I suppose, for one of my age, and after I was rested I got a basket and started for a place on the extreme rim of the circle, where the stars were close to the ground and I could get them with my hands, which would be better, anyway, because I could gather them tenderly then, and not break them. But it was farther than I thought, and at last I had to give it up; I was so tired I couldn't drag my feet another step; and besides, they were sore and hurt me very much.

I couldn't get back home; it was too far and turning cold; but I found some tigers and nestled in among them and was most adorably comfortable, and their breath was sweet and pleasant, because they live on strawberries. I had never seen a tiger before, but I knew them in a minute by the stripes. If I could have one of those skins, it would make a lovely gown.

To-day I am getting better ideas about distances. I was so eager to get hold of every pretty thing that I giddily grabbed for it, sometimes when it

was too far off, and sometimes when it was but six inches away but seemed a foot—alas, with thorns between! I learned a lesson; also I made an axiom, all out of my own head—my very first one: *The scratched Experiment shuns the thorn*. I think it is a very good one for one so young.

I followed the other Experiment around, yesterday afternoon, at a distance, to see what it might be for, if I could. But I was not able to make out. I think it is a man. I had never seen a man, but it looked like one, and I feel sure that that is what it is. I realize that I feel more curiosity about it than about any of the other reptiles. If it is a reptile, and I suppose it is; for it has frowsy hair and blue eyes, and looks like a reptile. It has no hips; it tapers like a carrot; when it stands, it spreads itself apart like a derrick; so I think it is a reptile, though it may be architecture.

I was afraid of it at first, and started to run every time it turned around, for I thought it was going to chase me; but by and by I found it was only trying to get away, so after that I was not timid any more, but tracked it along, several hours, about twenty yards behind, which made it nervous and unhappy. At last it was a good deal worried, and climbed a tree. I waited a good while, then gave it up and went home.

To-day the same thing over. I've got it up the tree again.

Sunday.—It is up there yet. Resting, apparently. But that is a subterfuge: Sunday isn't the day of rest; Saturday is appointed for that. It looks to me like a creature that is more interested in resting than in anything else. It would tire me to rest so much. It tires me just to sit around and watch the tree. I do wonder what it is for; I never see it do anything.

They returned the moon last night, and I was *so* happy! I think it is very honest of them. It slid down and fell off again, but I was not distressed; there is no need to worry when one has that kind of neighbors; they will fetch it back. I wish I could do something to show my appreciation. I would like to send them some stars, for we have more than we can use. I mean I, not we, for I can see that the reptile cares nothing for such things.

It has low tastes, and is not kind. When I went there yesterday evening in the gloaming it had crept down and was trying to catch the little speckled fishes that play in the pool, and I had to clod it to make it go up the tree again and let them alone. I wonder if *that* is what it is for? Hasn't it any heart? Hasn't it any compassion for those little creatures? Can it be that it was designed and manufactured for such ungentle work? It has the look of it. One of the clods took it back of the ear, and it used language. It gave me a thrill, for it was the first time I had ever heard speech, except my own. I did not understand the words, but they seemed expressive.

When I found it could talk I felt a new interest in it, for I love to talk; I talk, all day, and in my sleep, too, and I am very interesting, but if I had another to talk to I could be twice as interesting, and would never stop, if desired.

If this reptile is a man, it isn't an *it*, is it? That wouldn't be grammatical, would it? I think it would be *he*. I think so. In that case one would parse it thus: nominative, *he;* dative, *him;* possessive, *his'n*. Well, I will consider it a man and call it he until it turns out to be something else. This will be handier than having so many uncertainties.

Next week Sunday.—All the week I tagged around after him and tried to get acquainted. I had to do the talking, because he was shy, but I didn't mind it. He seemed pleased to have me around, and I used the sociable "we" a good deal, because it seemed to flatter him to be included.

Wednesday.—We are getting along very well indeed, now, and getting better and better acquainted. He does not try to avoid me any more, which is a good sign, and shows that he likes to have me with him. That pleases me, and I study to be useful to him in every way I can, so as to increase his regard. During the last day or two I have taken all the work of naming things off his hands, and this has been a great relief to him, for he has not gift in that line, and is evidently very grateful. He can't think of a rational name to save him, but I do not let him see that I am aware of his defect. Whenever a new creature comes along I name it before he has time to expose himself by an awkward silence. It this way I have saved him many embarrassments. I have no defect like his. The minute I set eyes on an animal I know what it is. I don't have to reflect a moment; the right name comes out instantly, just as if it were an inspiration, as no doubt it is, for I am sure it wasn't in me half a minute before. I seem to know just by the shape of the creature and the way it acts what animal it is.

When the dodo came along he thought it was a wildcat—I saw it in his eye. But I saved him. And I was careful not to do it in a way that could hurt his pride. I just spoke up in a quite natural way of pleased surprise, and not as if I was dreaming of conveying information, and said, "Well, I do declare, if there isn't the dodo!" I explained—without seeming to be explaining—how I knew it for a dodo, and although I thought maybe he was a little piqued that I knew the creature when he didn't, it was quite evident that he admired me. That was very agreeable, and I thought of it more than once with gratification before I slept. How little a thing can make us happy when we feel that we have earned it!

Thursday.—My first sorrow. Yesterday he avoided me and seemed to wish I would not talk to him. I could not believe it, and thought there was some mistake, for I loved to be with him, and loved to hear him talk, and so how could it be that he could feel unkind toward me when I had not done anything? But at last it seemed true, so I went away and sat lonely in the place where I first saw him the morning that we were made and I did not know what he was and was indifferent about him; but now it was a mournful place, and every little thing spoke of him, and my heart was very sore. I did not know why very clearly, for it was a new feeling; I had not experienced it before, and it was all a mystery, and I could not make it out.

But when night came I could not bear the lonesomeness, and went to the

new shelter which he has built, to ask him what I had done that was wrong and how I could mend it and get back his kindness again; but he put me out in the rain, and it was my first sorrow.

Sunday.—It is pleasant again, now, and I am happy; but those were heavy days; I do not think of them when I can help it.

I tried to get him some of those apples, but I cannot learn to throw straight. I failed, but I think the good intention pleased him. They are forbidden, and he says I shall come to harm; but so I come to harm through pleasing him, why shall I care for that harm?

Monday.—This morning I told him my name, hoping it would interest him. But he did not care for it. It is strange. If he should tell me his name, I would care. I think it would be pleasanter in my ears than any other sound.

He talks very little. Perhaps it is because he is not bright, and is sensitive about it and wishes to conceal it. It is such a pity that he should feel so, for brightness is nothing; it is in the heart that the values lie. I wish I could make him understand that a loving good heart is riches, and riches enough, and that without it intellect is poverty.

Although he talks so little, he has quite a considerable vocabulary. This morning he used a surprisingly good word. He evidently recognized, himself, that it was a good one, for he worked it in twice afterward, casually. It was not good casual art, still it showed that he possesses a certain quality of perception. Without a doubt that seed can be made to grow, if cultivated.

Where did he get that word? I do not think I have ever used it.

No, he took no interest in my name. I tried to hide my disappointment, but I suppose I did not succeed. I went away and sat on the moss-bank with my feet in the water. It is where I go when I hunger for companionship, some one to look at, some one to talk to. It is not enough—that lovely white body painted there in the pool—but it is something, and something is better than utter loneliness. It talks when I talk; it is sad when I am sad; it comforts me with its sympathy; it says, "Do not be downhearted, you poor friendless girl; I will be your friend." It *is* a good friend to me, and my only one; it is my sister.

That first time that she forsook me! ah, I shall never forget that—never, never. My heart was lead in my body! I said, "She was all I had, and now she is gone!" In my despair I said, "Break, my heart; I cannot bear my life any more!" and hid my face in my hands, and there was no solace for me. And when I took them away, after a little, there she was again, white and shining and beautiful, and I sprang into her arms!

That was perfect happiness; I had known happiness before, but it was not like this, which was ecstasy. I never doubted her afterward. Sometimes she stayed away—maybe an hour, maybe almost the whole day, but I waited and did not doubt; I said, "She is busy, or she is gone a journey, but she will come." And it was so: she always did. At night she would not come if it was

dark, for she was a timid little thing; but if there was a moon she would come. I am not afraid of the dark, but she is younger than I am; she was born after I was. Many and many are the visits I have paid her; she is my comfort and my refuge when my life is hard—and it is mainly that.

Tuesday.—All the morning I was at work improving the estate; and I purposely kept away from him in the hope that he would get lonely and come. But he did not.

At noon I stopped for the day and took my recreation by flitting all about with the bees and the butterflies and reveling in the flowers, those beautiful creatures that catch the smile of God out of the sky and preserve it! I gathered them, and made them into wreaths and garlands and clothed myself in them while I ate my luncheon—apples, of course; then I sat in the shade and wished and waited. But he did not come.

But no matter. Nothing would have come of it, for he does not care for flowers. He calls them rubbish, and cannot tell one from another, and thinks it is superior to feel like that. He does not care for me, he does not care for flowers, he does not care for the painted sky at eventide—is there anything he does care for, except building shacks to coop himself up in from the good clean rain, and thumping the melons, and sampling the grapes, and fingering the fruit on the trees, to see how those properties are coming along?

I laid a dry stick on the ground and tried to bore a hole in it with another one, in order to carry out a scheme that I had, and soon I got an awful fright. A thin, transparent bluish film rose out of the hole, and I dropped everything and ran! I thought it was a spirit, and I *was* so frightened! But I looked back, and it was not coming; so I leaned against a rock and rested and panted, and let my limbs go on trembling until they got steady again; then I crept warily back, alert, watching, and ready to fly if there was occasion; and when I was come near, I parted the branches of a rose-bush and peeped through—wishing the man was about, I was looking so cunning and pretty—but the sprite was gone. I went there, and there was pinch of delicate pink dust in the hole. I put my finger in, to feel it, and said *ouch!* and took it out again. It was a cruel pain. I put my finger in my mouth; and by standing first on one foot and then the other, and grunting, I presently eased my misery; then I was full of interest, and began to examine.

I was curious to know what the pink dust was. Suddenly the name of it occurred to me, though I had never heard of it before. It was *fire!* I was as certain of it as a person could be of anything in the world. So without hesitation I named it that—fire.

I had created something that didn't exist before; I had added a new thing to the world's uncountable properties; I realized this, and was proud of my achievement, and was going to run and find him and tell him about it, thinking to raise myself in his esteem—but I reflected, and did not do it. No—he would not care for it. He would ask what it was good for, and what could I answer? for if it was not *good* for something, but only beautiful, merely beautiful——

So I sighed, and did not go. For it wasn't good for anything; it could not build a shack, it could not improve melons, it could not hurry a fruit crop; it was useless, it was a foolishness and a vanity; he would despise it and say cutting words. But to me it was not despicable; I said, "Oh, you fire, I love you, you dainty pink creature, for you are *beautiful*—and that is enough!" and was going to gather it to my breast. But refrained. Then I made another maxim out of my own head, though it was so nearly like the first one that I was afraid it was only a plagiarism: *"The burnt Experiment shuns the fire."*

I wrought again; and when I had made a good deal of fire-dust I emptied it into a handful of dry brown grass, intending to carry it home and keep it always and play with it; but the wind struck it and it sprayed up and spat out at me fiercely, and I dropped it and ran. When I looked back the blue spirit was towering up and stretching and rolling away like a cloud, and instantly I thought of the name of it—*smoke!*—though, upon my word, I had never heard of smoke before.

Soon, brilliant yellow and red flares shot up through the smoke, and I named them in an instant—*flames*—and I was right, too, though these were the very first flames that had ever been in the world. They climbed the trees, they flashed splendidly in and out of the vast and increasing volume of tumbling smoke, and I had to clap my hands and laugh and dance in my rapture, it was so new and strange and so wonderful and so beautiful!

He came running, and stopped and gazed, and said not a word for many minutes. Then he asked what it was. Ah, it was too bad that he should ask such a direct question. I had to answer it, of course, and I did. I said it was fire. If it annoyed him that I should know and he must ask; that was not my fault; I had no desire to annoy him. After a pause he asked:

"How did it come?"

Another direct question, and it also had to have a direct answer.

"I made it."

The fire was traveling farther and farther off. He went to the edge of the burned place and stood looking down, and said:

"What are these?"

"Fire-coals."

He picked up one to examine it, but changed his mind and put it down again. Then he went away. *Nothing* interests him.

But I was interested. There were ashes, gray and soft and delicate and pretty—I knew what they were at once. And the embers; I knew the embers, too. I found my apples, and raked them out, and was glad; for I am very young and my appetite is active. But I was disappointed; they were all burst open and spoiled. Spoiled apparently; but it was not so; they were better than raw ones. Fire is beautiful; some day it will be useful, I think.

Friday.—I saw him again, for a moment, last Monday at nightfall, but only for a moment. I was hoping he would praise me for trying to improve the estate, for I had meant well and had worked hard. But he was not pleased, and turned away and left me. He was also displeased on another account: I tried once more to persuade him to stop going over the Falls. That was because the fire had revealed to me a new passion—quite new, and distinctly different from love, grief, and those others which I had already discovered—*fear.* And it is horrible!—I wish I had never discovered it; it gives me dark moments, it spoils my happiness, it makes me shiver and tremble and shudder. But I could not persuade him, for he has not discovered fear yet, and so he could not understand me.

extract from adam's diary

Perhaps I ought to remember that she is very young, a mere girl, and make allowances. She is all interest, eagerness, vivacity, the world is to her a charm, a wonder, a mystery, a joy; she can't speak for delight when she finds a new flower, she must pet it and caress it and smell it and talk to it, and pour out endearing names upon it. And she is color-mad: brown rocks, yellow sand, gray moss, green foliage, blue sky; the pearl of the dawn, the purple shadows on the mountains, the golden islands floating in crimson seas at sunset, the pallid moon sailing through the shredded cloud-rack, the star-jewels glittering in the wastes of space—none of them is of any practical value, so far as I can see, but because they have color and majesty, that is enough for her, and she loses her mind over them. If she could quiet down and keep still a couple of minutes at a time, it would be a reposeful spectacle. In that case I think I could enjoy looking at her; indeed I am sure I could, for I am coming to realize that she is a quite remarkably comely creature— lithe, slender, trim, rounded, shapely, nimble, graceful; and once when she was standing marble-white and sun-drenched on a boulder, with her young head tilted back and her hand shading her eyes, watching the flight of a bird in the sky, I recognized that she was beautiful.

Monday noon.—If there is anything on the planet that she is not interested in it is not in my list. There are animals that I am indifferent to, but it is not so with her. She has no discrimination, she takes to all of them, she thinks they are all treasures, every new one is welcome.

When the mighty brontosaurus came striding into camp, she regarded it as an acquisition, I considered it a calamity; that is a good sample of the lack of harmony that prevails in our views of things. She wanted to domesticate it, I wanted to make it a present of the homestead and move out. She believed it could be tamed by kind treatment and would be a good pet; I said a pet twenty-one feet high and eighty-four feet long would be no proper think to have about the place, because, even with the best intentions and without meaning any harm, it could sit down on the house and mash it, for any one could see by the look of its eye that it was absent-minded.

Still, her heart was set upon having that monster, and she couldn't give it up. She thought we could start a dairy with it, and wanted me to help her milk it; but I wouldn't; it was too risky. The sex wasn't right, and we hadn't any ladder anyway. Then she wanted to ride it, and look at the scenery. Thirty or forty feet of its tail was lying on the ground, like a fallen tree, and she thought she could climb it, but she was mistaken; when she got to the steep place it was too slick and down she came, and would have hurt herself but for me.

Was she satisfied now? No. Nothing ever satisfies her but demonstration; untested theories are not in her line, and she won't have them. It is the right spirit, I concede it; it attracts me; I feel the influence of it; if I were with her more I think I should take it up myself. Well, she had one theory remaining about this colossus: she thought that if we could tame him and make him friendly we could stand him in the river and use him for a bridge. It turned out that he was already plenty tame enough—at least as far as she was concerned—so she tried her theory, but it failed: every time she got him properly placed in the river and went ashore to cross over on him, he came out and followed her around like a pet mountain. Like the other animals. They all do that.

Friday.—Tuesday—Wednesday—Thursday—and to-day: all without seeing him. It is a long time to be alone; still, it is better to be alone than unwelcome.

I *had* to have company— I was made for it, I think—so I made friends with the animals. They are just charming, and they have the kindest disposition and the politest ways; they never look sour, they never let you feel that you are intruding, they smile at you and wag their tail, if they've got one, and they are always ready for a romp or an excursion or anything you want to propose. I think they are perfect gentlemen. All these days we have had such good times, and it hasn't been lonesome for me, ever. Lonesome! No, I should say not. Why, there's always a swarm of them around— sometimes as much as four or five acres—you can't count them; and when you stand on a rock in the midst and look out over the furry expanse it is so mottled and splashed and gay with color and frisking sheen and sun-flash, and so rippled with stripes, that you might think it was a lake, only you know it isn't; and there's storms of sociable birds, and hurricanes of whirring wings; and when the sun strikes all that feathery commotion, you have a blazing up of all the colors you can think of, enough to put your eyes out.

We have made long excursions, and I have seen a great deal of the world; almost all of it, I think; and so I am the first traveler, and the only one. When we are on the march, it is an imposing sight—there's nothing like it anywhere. For comfort I ride a tiger or a leopard, because it is soft and has a round back that fits me, and because they are such pretty animals; but for long distance or for scenery I ride the elephant. He hoists me up with his trunk, but I can get off myself; when we are ready to camp, he sits and I slide down the back way.

The birds and animals are all friendly to each other, and there are no disputes about anything. They all talk, and they all talk to me, but it must be a foreign language, for I cannot make out a word they say; yet they often understand me when I talk back, particularly the dog and the elephant. It makes me ashamed. It shows that they are brighter than I am, and are therefore my superiors. It annoys me, for I want to be the principal Experiment myself—and I intend to be, too.

I have learned a number of things, and am educated, now, but I wasn't at first. I was ignorant at first. At first it used to vex me because, with all my watching, I was never smart enough to be around when the water was running uphill; but now I do not mind it. I have experimented and experimented until now I know it never does run uphill, except in the dark. I know it does in the dark, because the pool never goes dry, which it would, of course, if the water didn't come back in the night. It is best to prove things by actual experiment; then you *know*; whereas if you depend on guessing and supposing and conjecturing, you will never get educated.

Some things you *can't* find out; but you will never know you can't by guessing and supposing: no, you have to be patient and go on experimenting until you find out that you can't find out. And it is delightful to have it that way, it makes the world so interesting. If there wasn't anything to find out, it would be dull. Even trying to find out and not finding out is just as interesting as trying to find out and finding out, and I don't know but more so. The secret of the water was a treasure until I *got* it; then the excitement all went away, and I recognized a sense of loss.

By experiment I know that wood swims, and dry leaves, and feathers, and plenty of other things; therefore by all that cumulative evidence you know that a rock will swim; but you have to put up with simply knowing it, for there isn't any way to prove it—up to now. But I shall find a way—then *that* excitement will go. Such things make me sad; because by and by when I have found out everything there won't be any more excitements, and I do love excitements so! The other night I couldn't sleep for thinking about it.

At first I couldn't make out what I was made for, but now I think it was to search out the secrets of this wonderful world and be happy and thank the Giver of it all for devising it. I think there are many things to learn yet —I hope so; and by economizing and not hurrying too fast I think they will last weeks and weeks. I hope so. When you cast up a feather it sails away on the air and goes out of sight; then you throw up a clod and it doesn't. It comes down, every time. I have tried it and tried it, and it is always so. I wonder why it is? Of course it *doesn't* come down, but why should it *seem* to? I suppose it is an optical illusion. I mean, one of them is. I don't know which one. It may be the feather, it may be the clod; I can't prove which it is, I can only demonstrate that one or the other is a fake, and let a person take his choice.

By watching, I know that the stars are not going to last. I have seen some of the best ones melt and run down the sky. Since one can melt, they can all melt; since they can all melt, they can all melt the same night. That sorrow will come—I know it. I mean to sit up every night and look at them as long as I can keep awake; and I will impress those sparkling fields on my memory, so that by and by when they are taken away I can by my fancy restore those lovely myriads to the black sky and make them sparkle again, and double them by the blur of my tears.

after the fall

When I look back, the Garden is a dream to me. It was beautiful, surpassingly beautiful, enchantingly beautiful; and now it is lost, and I shall not see it any more.

The Garden is lost, but I have found *him,* and am content. He loves me as well as he can; I love him with all the strength of my passionate nature, and this, I think, is proper to my youth and sex. If I ask myself why I love him, I find I do not know, and do not really much care to know; so I suppose that this kind of love is not a product of reasoning and statistics, like one's love for other reptiles and animals. I think that this must be so. I love certain birds because of their song; but I do not love Adam on account of his singing—no, it is not that; the more he sings the more I do not get reconciled to it. Yet I ask him to sing, because I wish to learn to like everything he is interested in. I am sure I can learn, because at first I could not stand it, but now I can. It sours the milk, but it doesn't matter; I can get used to that kind of milk.

It is not on account of his brightness that I love him—no, it is not that. He is not to blame for his brightness, such as it is, for he did not make it himself; he is as God made him, and that is sufficient. There was a wise purpose in it, *that* I know. In time it will develop, though I think it will not be sudden; and besides, there is no hurry; he is well enough just as he is.

It is not on account of his gracious and considerate ways and his delicacy that I love him. No, he has lacks in these regards, but he is well enough just so, and is improving.

It is not on account of his industry that I love him—no, it is not that. I think he has it in him, and I do not know why he conceals it from me. It is my only pain. Otherwise he is frank and open with me, now. I am sure he keeps nothing from me but this. It grieves me that he should have a secret from me, and sometimes it spoils my sleep, thinking of it, but I will put it out of my mind; it shall not trouble my happiness, which is otherwise full to overflowing.

It is not on account of his education that I love him—no, it is not that. He is self-educated, and does really know a multitude of things, but they are not so.

It is not on account of his chivalry that I love him—no, it is not that. He told on me, but I do not blame him; it is a peculiarity of sex, I think, and he did not make his sex. Of course I would not have told on him, I would have perished first; but that is a peculiarity of sex, too, and I do not take credit for it, for I did not make my sex.

Then why is it that I love him? *Merely because he is masculine,* I think.

At bottom he is good, and I love him for that, but I could love him without it. If he should beat me and abuse me, I should go on loving him. I know it. It is a matter of sex, I think.

He is strong and handsome, and I love him for that, and I admire him and am proud of him, but I could love him without those qualities. If he were plain, I should love him; if he were a wreck, I should love him; and I would work for him, and slave over him, and pray for him, and watch by his bedside until I died.

Yes, I think I love him merely because he is *mine* and is *masculine*. There is no other reason, I suppose. And so I think it is as I first said: that this kind of love is not a product of reasonings and statistics. It just *comes*— none knows whence—and cannot explain itself. And doesn't need to.

It is what I think. But I am only a girl, and the first that has examined this matter, and it may turn out that in my ignorance and inexperience I have not got it right.

forty years later

It is my prayer, it is my longing, that we may pass from this life together —a longing which shall never perish from the earth, but shall have place in the heart of every wife that loves, until the end of time; and it shall be called by my name.

But if one of us must go first, it is my prayer that it shall be I; for he is strong, I am weak, I am not so necessary to him as he is to me—life without him would not be life; how could I endure it? This prayer is also immortal, and will not cease from being offered up while my race continues. I am the first wife; and in the last wife I shall be repeated.

at eve's grave

ADAM: Wheresoever she was, *there* was Eden.

Works and Days

hesiod

MUSES OF PIERIA who give glory through song, come hither, tell of Zeus your father and chant his praise. Through him mortal men are famed or unfamed, sung or unsung alike, as great Zeus wills. For easily he makes strong, and easily he brings the strong man low; easily he humbles the proud and raises the obscure, and easily he straightens the crooked and blasts the proud,— Zeus who thunders aloft and has his dwelling most high. Attend thou with eye and ear, and make judgements straight with righteousness. And I, Perses, would tell of true things.

So, after all, there was not one kind of Strife alone, but all over the earth there are two. As for the one, a man would praise her when he came to understand her; but the other is blameworthy: and they are wholly different in nature. For one fosters evil war and battle, being cruel: Her no man loves; but perforce, through the will of the deathless gods, men pay harsh Strife her honour due. But the other is the elder daughter of dark Night, and the son of Cronos who sits above and dwells in the aether, set her in the roots of the earth: and she is far kinder to men. She stirs up even the shiftless to toil; for a man grows eager to work when he considers his neighbour, a rich man who hastens to plough and plant and put his house in good order; and neighbour vies with his neighbour as he hurries after wealth. This Strife is wholesome for men. And potter is angry with potter, and craftsman with craftsman, and beggar is jealous of beggar, and minstrel of minstrel.

Reprinted by permission of the publisher and the Loeb Classical Library from Hugh G. Evelyn-White, translator Hesoid THE HOMERIC HYMNS Cambridge, Mass.: Harvard University Press.

Perses, lay up these things in your heart, and do not let that Strife who delights in mischief hold your heart back from work, while you peep and peer and listen to the wrangles of the court-house. Little concern has he with quarrels and courts who has not a year's victuals laid up betimes, even that which the earth bears, Demeter's grain. When you have got plenty of that, you can raise disputes and strive to get another's goods. But you shall have no second chance to deal so again: Nay, let us settle our dispute here with true judgement which is of Zeus and is perfect. For we had already divided our inheritance, but you seized the greater share and carried it off, greatly swelling the glory of our bribe-swallowing lords who love to judge such a cause as this. Fools! They know not how much more the half is than the whole, nor what great advantage there is in mallow and asphodel.[1]

For the gods keep hidden from men the means of life. Else you would easily do work enough in a day to supply you for a full year even without working; soon would you put away your rudder over the smoke, and the fields worked by ox and sturdy mule would run to waste. But Zeus in the anger of his heart hid it, because Prometheus the crafty deceived him; therefore he planned sorrow and mischief against men. He hid fire; but that the noble son of Iapetus stole again for men from Zeus the counsellor in a hollow fennel-stalk, so that Zeus who delights in thunder did not see it. But afterwards Zeus who gathers the clouds said to him in anger:

"Son of Iapetus, surpassing all in cunning, you are glad that you have outwitted me and stolen fire—a great plague to you yourself and to men that shall be. But I will give men as the price for fire an evil thing in which they may all be glad of heart while they embrace their own destruction."

So said the father of men and gods, and laughed aloud. And he bade famous Hephaestus[2] make haste and mix earth with water and to put in it the voice and strength of human kind, and fashion a sweet, lovely maiden-shape, like to the immortal goddesses in face; and Athene to teach her needlework and the weaving of the varied web; and golden Aphrodite to shed grace upon her head and cruel longing and cares that weary the limbs. And he charged Hermes the guide, the Slayer of Argus, to put in her a shameless mind and a deceitful nature.

So he ordered. And they obeyed the lord Zeus the son of Cronos. Forthwith the famous Lame God moulded clay in the likeness of a modest maid, as the son of Cronos purposed. And the goddess bright-eyed Athene girded and clothed her, and the divine Graces and queenly Persuasion put necklaces of gold upon her, and the rich-haired Hours crowned her head with spring flowers. And Pallas Athene bedecked her form with all manner of finery. Also the Guide, the Slayer of Argus, contrived within her lies and crafty words and a deceitful nature at the will of loud thundering Zeus, and

1 That is, the poor man's face, like "bread and cheese."
2 The lame god of fire.

the Herald of the gods put speech in her. And he called this woman Pandora,[3] because all they who dwelt on Olympus gave each a gift, a plague to men who eat bread.

But when he had finished the sheer, hopeless snare, the Father sent glorious Argus-Slayer, the swift messenger of the gods, to take it to Epimetheus as a gift. And Epimetheus did not think on what Prometheus had said to him, bidding him never take a gift of Olympian Zeus, but to send it back for fear it might prove to be something harmful to men. But he took the gift, and afterwards, when the evil thing was already his, he understood.

For ere this the tribes of men lived on earth remote and free from ills and hard toil and heavy sicknesses which bring the Fates upon men; for in misery men grow old quickly. But the woman took off the great lid of the jar[4] with her hands and scattered all these and her thought caused sorrow and mischief to men. Only Hope remained there in an unbreakable home within under the rim of the great jar, and did not fly out at the door; for ere that, the lid of the jar stopped her, by the will of Aegis-holding Zeus who gathers the clouds. But the rest, countless plagues, wander amongst men; for earth is full of evils and the sea is full. Of themselves diseases come upon men continually by day and by night, bringing mischief to mortals silently; for wise Zeus took away speech from them. So is there no way to escape the will of Zeus.

Or if you will, I will sum you up another tale well and skilfully—and do you lay it up in your heart,—how the gods and mortal men sprang from one source.

First of all the deathless gods who dwell on Olympus made a golden race of mortal men who lived in the time of Cronos when he was reigning in heaven. And they lived like gods without sorrow of heart, remote and free from toil and grief: miserable age rested not on them; but with legs and arms never failing they made merry with feasting beyond the reach of all evils. When they died, it was as though they were overcome with sleep, and they had all good things; for the fruitful earth unforced bare them fruit abundantly and without stint. They dwelt in ease and peace upon their lands with many good things, rich in flocks and loved by the blessed gods.

But after the earth had covered this generation—they are called pure spirits dwelling on the earth, and are kindly, delivering from harm, and guardians of mortal men; for they roam everywhere over the earth, clothed in mist and keep watch on judgements and cruel deeds, givers of wealth; for this royal right also they received;—then they who dwell on Olympus made a second generation which was of silver and less noble by far. It was like the golden race neither in body nor in spirit. A child was brought up at his good

---

[3] The All-endowed.

[4] The jar or casket contained the gifts of the gods mentioned in 1. 82.

mother's side an hundred years, an utter simpleton, playing childishly in his own home. But when they were full grown and were come to the full measure of their prime, they lived only a little time and that in sorrow because of their foolishness, for they could not keep from sinning and from wronging one another, nor would they serve the immortals, nor sacrifice on the holy altars of the blessed ones as it is right for men to do wherever they dwell. Then Zeus the son of Cronos was angry and put them away, because they would not give honour to the blessed gods who live on Olympus.

But when earth had covered this generation also—they are called blessed spirits of the underworld by men, and, though they are of second order, yet honour attends them also—Zeus the Father made a third generation of mortal men, a brazen race, sprung from ash-trees[5]; and it was in no way equal to the silver age, but was terrible and strong. They loved the lamentable works of Ares and deeds of violence; they ate no bread, but were hard of heart like adamant, fearful men. Great was their strength and unconquerable the arms which grew from their shoulders on their strong limbs. Their armour was of bronze, and their houses of bronze, and of bronze were their implements: There was no black iron. These were destroyed by their own hands and passed to the dank house of chill Hades, and left no name: Terrible though they were, black Death seized them, and they left the bright light of the sun.

But when earth had covered this generation also, Zeus the son of Cronos made yet another, the fourth, upon the fruitful earth, which was nobler and more righteous, a god-like race of hero-men who are called demi-gods, the race before our own, throughout the boundless earth. Grim war and dread battle destroyed a part of them, some in the land of Cadmus at seven-gated Thebe when they fought for the flocks of Oedipus, and some, when it had brought them in ships over the great sea gulf to Troy for rich-haired Helen's sake: There death's end enshrouded a part of them. But to the others father Zeus the son of Cronos gave a living and an abode apart from men, and made them dwell at the ends of earth. And they live untouched by sorrow in the islands of the blessed along the shore of deep swirling Ocean, happy heroes for whom the grain-giving earth bears honey-sweet fruit flourishing thrice a year, far from the deathless gods, and Cronos rules over them; for the father of men and gods released him from his bonds. And these last equally have honour and glory.

And again far-seeing Zeus made yet another generation, the fifth, of men who are upon the bounteous earth.

Thereafter, would that I were not among the men of the fifth generation,

---

5 Eustathius refers to Hesiod as stating that men sprung "from oaks and stones and ashtrees." Proclus believed that the Nymphs called Meliae (*Theogony,* 187) are intended. Goettling would render: "A race terrible because of their (ashen) spears."

but either had died before or been born afterwards. For now truly is a race
of iron, and men never rest from labour and sorrow by day, and from
perishing by night; and the gods shall lay sore trouble upon them. But, notwithstanding, even these shall have some good mingled with their evils. And
Zeus will destroy this race of mortal men also when they come to have grey
hair on the temples at their birth.[6] The father will not agree with his
children, nor the children with their father, nor guest with his host, nor
comrade with comrade; nor will brother be dear to brother as aforetime.
Men will dishonour their parents as they grow quickly old, and will carp at
them, childing them with bitter words, hard-hearted they, not knowing the
fear of the gods. They will not repay their aged parents the cost of their
nurture, for might shall be their right: And one man will sack another's city.
There will be no favour for the man who keeps his oath or for the just for
good; but rather men will praise the evil-doer and his violent dealing.
Strength will be right and reverence will cease to be; and the wicked will
hurt the worthy man, speaking false words against him, and will swear an
oath upon them. Envy, foul-mouthed, delighting in evil, with scowling face,
will go along with wretched men one and all. And then Aidôs and Nemesis,[7]
with their sweet forms wrapped in white robes, will go from the wide-pathed
earth and forsake mankind to join the company of the deathless gods: And
bitter sorrows will be left for mortal men, and there will be no help against
evil.

6 *i.e.* the race will so degenerate that at the last even a new-born child will show the
marks of old age.

7 Aidôs, as a quality, is that feeling of reverence or shame which restrains men from
wrong: Nemesis is the feeling of righteous indignation aroused especially by the sight of
the wicked in undeserved prosperity (*cf. Psalms,* lxxii. 1–19).

The Allegory of the Cave

plato

And now, I said, let me show in a figure how far our nature is enlightened or unenlightened: Behold! human beings living in an underground den, which has a mouth open towards the light and reaching all along the den; here they have been from their childhood, and have their legs and necks chained so that they cannot move, and can only see before them, being prevented by the chains from turning round their heads. Above and behind them a fire is blazing at a distance, and between the fire and the prisoners there is a raised way; and you will see, if you look, a low wall built along the way, like the screen which marionette players have in front of them, over which they show the puppets.

I see.

And do you see, I said, men passing along the wall carrying all sorts of vessels, and statues and figures of animals made of wood and stone and various materials, which appear over the wall? Some of them are talking, others silent.

You have shown me a strange image, and they are strange prisoners.

Like ourselves, I replied; and they see only their own shadows, or the shadows of one another, which the fire throws on the opposite wall of the cave?

True, he said; how could they see anything but the shadows if they were never allowed to move their heads?

And of the objects which are being carried in like manner they would only see the shadows?

From *The Republic,* trans. B. Jowett (New York: The Macmillan Co., 1892).

Yes, he said.

And if they were able to converse with one another, would they not suppose that they were naming what was actually before them?

Very true.

And suppose further that the prison had an echo which came from the other side, would they not be sure to fancy when one of the passers-by spoke that the voice which they heard came from the passing shadow?

No question, he replied.

To them, I said, the truth would be literally nothing but the shadows of the images.

That is certain.

And now look again, and see what will naturally follow if the prisoners are released and disabused of their error. At first, when any of them is liberated and compelled suddenly to stand up and turn his neck round and walk and look towards the light, he will suffer sharp pains; the glare will distress him and he will be unable to see the realities of which in his former state he had seen the shadows; and then conceive some one saying to him, that what he saw before was an illusion, but that now, when he is approaching nearer to being and his eye is turned towards more real existence, he has a clearer vision—what will be his reply? And you may further imagine that his instructor is pointing to the objects as they pass and requiring him to name them—will he not be perplexed? Will he not fancy that the shadows which he formerly saw are truer than the objects which are now shown to him?

Far truer.

And if he is compelled to look straight at the light, will he not have a pain in his eyes which will make him turn away to take refuge in the objects of vision which he can see, and which he will conceive to be in reality clearer than the things which are now being shown to him?

True, he said.

And suppose once more, that he is reluctantly dragged up a steep and rugged ascent, and held fast until he is forced into the presence of the sun himself, is he not likely to be pained and irritated? When he approaches the light his eyes will be dazzled and he will not be able to see anything at all of what are now called realities.

Not all in a moment, he said.

He will require to grow accustomed to the sight of the upper world. And first he will see the shadows best, next the reflections of men and other objects in the water, and then the objects themselves; then he will gaze upon the light of the moon and the stars and the spangled heaven; and he will see the sky and the stars by night better than the sun or the light of the sun by day?

Certainly.

Last of all he will be able to see the sun, and not mere reflections of him in the water, but he will see him in his own proper place, and not in another; and he will contemplate him as he is.

Certainly.

He will then proceed to argue that this is he who gives the season and the years, and is the guardian of all that is in the visible world, and in a certain way the cause of all things which he and his fellows have been accustomed to behold?

Clearly, he said, he would first see the sun and then reason about him.

And when he remembered his old habitation, and the wisdom of the den and his fellow-prisoners, do you not suppose that he would felicitate himself on the change, and pity them?

Certainly, he would.

And if they were in the habit of conferring honors among themselves on those who were quickest to observe the passing shadows and to remark which of them went before, and which followed after, and which were together; and who were therefore best able to draw conclusions as to the future, do you think that he would care for such honors and glories, or envy the possessors of them? Would he not say with Homer,

Better to be the poor servant of a poor master,

and to endure anything, rather than think as they do and live after their manner?

Yes, he said, I think that he would rather suffer anything than entertain these false notions and live in this miserable manner.

Imagine once more, I said, such an one coming suddenly out of the sun to be replaced in his old situation; would he not be certain to have his eyes full of darkness?

To be sure, he said.

And if there were a contest, and he had to compete in measuring the shadows with the prisoners who had never moved out of the den, while his sight was still weak, and before his eyes had become steady (and the time which would be needed to acquire this new habit of sight might be very considerable) would he not be ridiculous? Men would say of him that up he went and down he came without his eyes; and that it was better not even to think of ascending; and if any one tried to loose another and lead him up to the light, let them only catch the offender, and they would put him to death.

No question, he said.

This entire allegory, I said, you may now append, dear Glaucon, to the previous argument; the prison-house is the world of sight, the light of the fire is the sun, and you will not misapprehend me if you interpret the journey upwards to be the ascent of the soul into the intellectual world according to my poor belief, which, at your desire, I have expressed—whether rightly or wrongly God knows. But, whether true or false, my opinion is that in the world of knowledge the idea of good appears last of all, and is seen only with an effort; and, when seen, is also inferred to be the universal author of all things beautiful and right, parent of light and of the lord of light in this visible world, and the immediate source of reason and truth in the intellectual; and that this is the power upon which he who would act rationally either in public or private life must have his eye fixed.

I agree, he said, as far as I am able to understand you.

Moreover, I said, you must not wonder that those who attain to this beatific vision are unwilling to descend to human affairs; for their souls are ever hastening into the upper world where they desire to dwell; which desire of theirs is very natural, if our allegory may be trusted.

Yes, very natural.

And is there anything surprising in one who passes from divine contemplations to the evil state of man, misbehaving himself in a ridiculous manner; if, while his eyes are blinking and before he has become accustomed to the surrounding darkness, he is compelled to fight in courts of law, or in other places, about the images or the shadows of images of justice, and is endeavouring to meet the conceptions of those who have never yet seen absolute justice?

Anything but surprising, he replied.

Any one who has common sense will remember that the bewilderments of the eyes are of two kinds, and arise from two causes, either from coming out of the light or from going into the light, which is true of the mind's eye, quite as much as of the bodily eye; and he who remembers this when he sees any one whose vision is perplexed and weak, will not be too ready to laugh; he will first ask whether that soul of man has come out of the brighter life, and is unable to see because unaccustomed to the dark, or having turned from darkness to the day is dazzled by excess of light. And he will count the one happy in his condition and state of being, and he will pity the other; or, if he have a mind to laugh at the soul which comes from below into the light, there will be more reason in this than in the laugh which greets him who returns from above out of the light into the den.

That, he said, is a very just distinction.

But then, if I am right, certain professors of education must be wrong when they say that they can put a knowledge into the soul which was not there before, like sight into blind eyes.

They undoubtedly say this, he replied.

Whereas, our argument shows that the power and capacity of learning exists in the soul already; and that just as the eye was unable to turn from darkness to light without the whole body, so too the instrument of knowledge can only by the movement of the whole soul be turned from the world of becoming into that of being, and learn by degrees to endure the sight of being, and of the brightest and best of being, or in other words, of the good.

Very true.

From The Saga of Grettir the Strong

anonymous

chapter xvii

GRETTIR SAILS FOR NORWAY
AND IS WRECKED ON HARAMARSEY

THERE DWELT AT REYDARFELL on the banks of the Hvita a man named
Haflidi, a mariner, owning a ship of his own which was lying in dock in the
Hvita river. He had as his mate a man named Bard who had a young and
petty wife. Asmund sent a man to Haflidi asking him to take Grettir and
look after him. Haflidi answered that he had heard that Grettir was very
difficult to get on with, but out of friendship for Asmund he took him. Grettir,
therefore, prepared to go to sea. His father would not give him any outfit for
his voyage beyond his bare provisions and a little wadmal. Grettir asked
him to give him some sort of weapon. Asmund answered: "You have never
been obedient to me. Nor do I know what you would do with a weapon that
would be of any profit. I shall not give you any."

Grettir said: *"Work not done needs no reward."*

Father and son parted with little love between them. Many wished him
a good voyage, but few a safe return. His mother went with him along the
road. Before they parted she said: "You have not been sent off in the way
that I should have wished, my son, or in a way befitting your birth. The

From THE SAGA OF GRETTIR THE STRONG, translated by G. A. Hight. Everyman's
Library. Reprinted by permission of E. P. Dutton & Co., Inc. © Introduction and
editorial matter, J. M. Dent & Sons, Ltd. 1965.

most cruel thing of all, I think, is that you have not a weapon which you can use. My heart tells me that you will want one."

Then she took from under her mantle a sword all ready for use, a valuable possession. She said: "This was the sword of Jokull, my father's father and of the ancient Vatnsdal men, in whose hands it was blessed with victory. I give it to you; use it well."

Grettir thanked her warmly and said it would be more precious to him than any other possession though of greater value. Then he went on his way and Asdis wished him all possible happiness. He rode South over the heath and did not stop till he reached his ship. Haflidi received him well and asked him about his outfit for the voyage. Grettir spoke a verse:

> *"Oh trimmer of sails! my father is wealthy,*
> *but poorly enough he sent me from home.*
> *My mother it was who gave me this sword.*
> *True is the saying:* The mother is best."

Haflidi said it was evident that she had most thought for him.

Directly they were ready and had a wind they got under way. When they were out of shallow water they hoisted their sail. Grettir made himself a corner under the ship's boat, whence he refused to stir either to bale or to trim the sails or to do any work in the ship, as it was his duty to do equally with the other men; nor would he buy himself off. They sailed to the South, rounded Reykjanes and left the land behind them, when they met with stormy weather. The ship was rather leaky and became very uneasy in the gale; the crew were very much exhausted. Grettir only let fly satirical verses at them, which angered them sorely. One day when it was very stormy and very cold the men called out to Grettir to get up and work; they said their claws were quite frozen. He answered:

> *" 'Twere well if every finger were froze*
> *on the hands of such a lubberly crew."*

They got no work out of him and liked him even worse than before, and said they would pay him out on his person for his squibs and his mutinous behaviour.

"You like better," they said, "to pat the belly of Bard the mate's wife than to bear a hand in the ship. But we don't mean to stand it."

The weather grew steadily worse; they had to bale night and day, and they threatened Grettir. Haflidi when he heard them went up to Grettir and said: "I don't think your relations with the crew are very good. You are mutinous and make lampoons about them, and they threaten to pitch you overboard. This is most improper."

"Why cannot they mind their own business?" Grettir rejoined. "But I should like one or two to remain behind with me before I go overboard."

"That is impossible," said Haflidi. "We shall never get on upon those terms. But I will make you a proposal about it."

"What is that?"

"The thing which annoys them is that you make lampoons about them. Now I suggest that you make a lampoon about me. Then, perhaps, they will become better disposed towards you."

"About you I will never utter anything but good," said he. "I am not going to compare you with the sailors."

"But you might compose a verse which should at first appear foul, but on closer view prove to be fair."

"That," he answered, "I am quite equal to."

Haflidi then went to the sailors and said: "You have much toil; and it seems that you don't get on with Grettir."

"His lampoons," they answered, "annoy us more than anything else."

Then Haflidi, speaking loud, said: "It will be the worse for him some day."

Grettir, when he heard himself being denounced, spoke a verse:

> *"Other the words that Haflid spake*
> *when he dined on curds at Reydarfell.*
> *But now two meals a day he takes*
> *in the steed of the bays mid foreland shores."*

The sailors were very angry and said he should not lampoon Haflidi for nothing. Haflidi said: "Grettir certainly deserves that you should take him down a little, but I am not going to risk my good name because of his ill-temper and caprice. This is not the time to pay him out, when we are all in such danger. When you get on shore you can remember it if you like."

"Shall we not endure what you can endure?" they said. "Why should a lampoon hurt us more than it does you?"

Haflidi said so it should be, and after that they cared less about Grettir's lampoons.

The voyage was long and fatiguing. The ship sprung a leak, and the men began to be worn out. The mate's young wife was in the habit of stitching Grettir's sleeves for him, and the men used to banter him about it. Haflidi went up to Grettir where he was lying and said:

> *"Arise from thy den! deep furrows we plough!*
> *Remember the word thou didst speak to the fair.*
> *Thy garment she sewed; but now she commands*
> *that thou join in the toil while the land is afar."*

Grettir got up at once and said:

> *"I will rise, though the ship be heavily rolling.*
> *The woman is vexed that I sleep in my den.*
> *She will surely be wrath if here I abide*
> *while others are toiling at work that is mine."*

Then he hurried aft where they were baling and asked what they wanted him to do. They said he would do little good. He replied: "A man's help is something." Haflidi told them not to refuse his help. "Maybe," he said, "he is thinking of loosening his hands if he offers his services."

In those days in sea-going ships there were no scuppers for baling; they only had what is called *bucket* or *pot-baling,* a very troublesome and fatiguing process. There were two buckets, one of which went down while the other came up. The men told Grettir to take the buckets down, and said they would try what he could do. He said the less tried the better, and went below and filled his bucket. There were two men above to empty the buckets as he handed them. Before long they both gave in from fatigue. Then four others took their places, but the same thing happened. Some say that before they were done eight men were engaged in emptying the buckets for him. At last the ship was baled dry. After this, the seamen altered their behaviour towards Grettir, for they realised the strength which was in him. From that time on he was ever the forwardest to help wherever he was required.

They now held an easterly course out to sea. It was every dark. One night when they least expected it, they struck a rock and the lower part of the ship began to fill. The boats were got out and the women put into them with all the loose property. There was an island a little way off, whither they carried as much of their property as they could get off in the night. When the day broke, they began to ask where they were. Some of them who had been about the country before recognised the coast of Sunnmøre in Norway. There was an island lying a little off the mainland called Haramarsey, with a large settlement and a farm belonging to the Landman on it.

chapter xviii

ADVENTURE IN THE
HOWE OF KAR THE OLD

The name of the Landman who lived in the island was Thorfinn. He was a son of Kar the Old, who had lived there for a long time. Thorfinn was a man of great influence.

When the day broke, the people on the island saw that there were some sailors there in distress and reported it to Thorfinn, who at once set about to launch his large sixteen-oared boat. He put out as quickly as possible with some thirty men to save the cargo of the trader, which then sank and was lost, along with much property. Thorfinn brought all the men off her to his house, where they stayed for a week drying their goods. Then they went away to the South, and are heard of no more in this story.

Grettir stayed behind with Thorfinn, keeping very quiet and speaking little. Thorfinn gave him his board, but took little notice of him. Grettir held rather aloof, and did not accompany him when he went abroad every day. This annoyed Thorfinn, but he did not like to refuse Grettir his hospitality; he was a man who kept open house, enjoyed life and liked to see other men happy. Grettir liked going about and visiting the people in the other farms on the island. There was a man named Audun, who dwelt at Vindheim. Grettir went to see him daily and became very intimate with him, sitting there all day long.

One evening very late when Grettir was preparing to return home, he saw a great fire shoot up on the headland below Audun's place, and asked what new thing that might be. Audun said there was no pressing need for him to know.

"If they saw such a thing in our country," said Grettir, "they would say the fire came from some treasure."

"He who rules that fire," answered the man, "is one whom it will be better not to inquire about."

"But I want to know," Grettir said.

"On that headland," said Audun, "there is a howe, wherein lies Kar the Old, the father of Thorfinn. Once upon a time father and son had a farm-property on the island; but ever since Kar died his ghost has been walking and has scared away all the other farmers, so that now the whole island belongs to Thorfinn, and no man who is under Thorfinn's protection suffers any injury."

"You have done right to tell me," said Grettir. "Expect me here to-morrow morning, and have tools ready for digging."

"I won't allow you to have anything to do with it," said Audun, "because I know that it will bring Thorfinn's wrath down upon you."

Grettir said he would risk that.

The night passed; Grettir appeared early the next morning, and the bondi, who had got all the tools for digging ready, went with Grettir to the howe. Grettir broke open the grave, and worked with all his might, never stopping until he came to wood, by which time the day was already spent. He tore away the woodwork; Audun implored him not to go down, but Grettir bade him attend to the rope, saying that he meant to find out what it was that dwelt there. Then he descended into the howe. It was very dark and the odour was not pleasant. He began to explore how it was arranged, and found the bones of a horse. Then he knocked against a sort of throne in which he was aware of a man seated. There was much treasure of gold and silver collected together, and a casket under his feet, full of silver. Grettir took all the treasure and went back towards the rope, but on his way he felt himself seized by a strong hand. He left the treasure to close with his aggressor and the two engaged in a merciless struggle. Everything about them was smashed. The howe-dweller made a ferocious onslaught. Grettir for some time gave way, but found that no holding back was possible. They did not spare each other. Soon they came to the place where the horse's bones were lying, and here they struggled for long, each in turn being brought to his knees. At last it ended in the howe-dweller falling backwards with a horrible crash, whereupon Audun above bolted from the rope, thinking that Grettir was killed. Grettir then drew his sword Jokulsnaut, cut off the head of the howe-dweller and laid it between his thighs. Then he went with the treasure to the rope, but finding Audun gone he had to swarm up the rope with his hands. First he tied the treasure to the lower end of the rope, so that he could haul it up after him. He was very stiff from his struggle with Kar, but he turned his steps towards Thorfinn's house, carrying the treasure along with him. He found them all at supper. Thorfinn cast a severe glance at him and asked what he had found so pressing to do that he could not keep proper hours like other men.

"*Many a trifle happens at eve,*" he replied.

Then he brought out all the treasure which he had taken from the howe and laid it on the table. One thing there was upon which more than anything else Grettir cast his eyes, a short sword, which he declared to be finer than any weapon which he had ever seen. It was the last thing that he showed. Thorfinn opened his eyes when he saw the sword, for it was an heirloom of his family and had never been out of it.

"Whence came this treasure?" he asked.

Grettir then spake a verse:

> "*Scatterer of gold! 'twas the lust of wealth*
> *that urged my hand to ravish the grave.*
> *This know; but none hereafter, I ween,*
> *will be fain to ransack Fafnir's lair.*"

Thorfinn said: "You don't seem to take it very seriously; no one ever before had any wish to break open the howe. But since I know that all treasure which is hidden in the earth or buried in a howe is in a wrong place I hold you guilty of no misdeed, especially since you have brought it to me."

Grettir answered:

> "*The monster is slain! in the dismal tomb*
> *I have captured a sword, dire wounder of men.*

> *Would it were mine! a treasure so rare*
> *I never would suffer my hand to resign."*

"You have spoken well," Thorfinn answered. "But before I can give you the sword you must display your prowess in some way. I never got it from my father whilst he lived."

Grettir said: "No one knows to whom the greatest profit will fall ere all is done."

Thorfinn took the treasure and kept the sword in his own custody near his bed. The winter came on bringing Yule-tide, and nothing more happened that need be told of.

chapter xix

BERSERKS AT HARAMARSEY

The following summer jarl Eirik the son of Hakon was preparing to leave his country and sail to the West to join his brother-in-law King Knut the Great in England, leaving the government of Norway in the hands of Hakon his son, who, being an infant, was placed under the government and regency of Eirik's bother, jarl Sveinn. Before leaving Eirik summoned all his Land-men and the larger bondis to meet him. Eirik the jarl was an able ruler, and they had much discussion regarding the laws and their administration. It was considered a scandal in the land that pirates and berserks should be able to come into the country and challenge respectable people to the *holmgang* for their money or their women, no weregild being paid whichever fell. Many had lost their money and been put to shame in this way; some indeed had lost their lives. For this reason jarl Eirik abolished all *holmgang* in Norway and declared all robbers and berserks who disturbed the peace outlaws. Thorfinn the son of Kar of Haramarsey, being a man of wise counsel and a close friend of the jarl, was present at the meeting.

The worst of these ruffians were two brothers named Thorir Paunch and Ogmund the Bad. They came from Halogaland and were bigger and stronger than other men. When angry they used to fall into the berserk's fury, and nothing escaped that was before them. They used to carry off men's wives, keep them for a week or two and then send them back. Wherever they came they committed robberies and other acts of violence. Jarl Eirik had declared them outlaws throughout Norway. The man who had been most active in getting them outlawed was Thorfinn, and they were determined to pay him out in full for his hostility.

The jarl's expedition is told of in his saga, and the government of Norway was left in the hands of jarl Sveinn, with the regency. Thorfinn returned home and remained there until about Yule-tide, as has already been told. Towards Yule-tide he made ready to go on a journey to his farm called Slysfjord on the mainland, whither he had invited a number of his friends. He could not take his wife with him, because their grown-up daughter was lying sick, so they both had to stay at home. Grettir and eight of the serving men remained with them. Thorfinn went with thirty freemen to the Yule festival, at which there was much gladness and merriment.

Yule-eve set in with bright and clear weather. Grettir, who was generally abroad in the daytime, was watching the vessels which came along the coast, some from the North, some from the South, meeting at the places agreed upon for their drinking-bouts. The bondi's daughter was then better and could go out with her mother. So the day passed. At last Grettir noticed a ship rowing up to the island, not large, covered with shields amidships and painted above the water-line. They were rowing briskly and making for Thorfinn's boat-houses. They ran the boat on to the beach and all sprang ashore. Grettir counted the men; there were twelve in all, and their aspect did not look peaceful. After hauling up their boat out of the water they all made for the boat-house where Thorfinn's great boat, mentioned already, was stowed. She always required thirty men to put her to sea, but the twelve shoved her along the beach at once. Then they brought their own boat into the boat-house. It was very evident to Grettir that they did not mean to wait for an invitation, so he went up to them, and greeting them in a friendly way asked who they were and who was their captain. The man whom he addressed answered him at once, saying his name was Thorir, called Paunch; the others were his brother Ogmund with their companions. "I think," he added, "that your master Thorfinn has heard our names mentioned. But is he at home?"

"You must be men who have luck," said Grettir, "you have come most opportunely, if you are the people I take you for. The bondi has gone from home with all his freedmen and will not be back until after Yule. The good-wife is at home with her daughter, and if I had any grudge to repay, I would come just as you do, for there is everything here which you want, ale to drink and other delights."

Thorir was silent while Grettir went on talking. Then he turned to Ogmund and said: "Has anything not happened as I said it would? I should not be sorry to punish Thorfinn for having got us outlawed. This man seems ready to tell us everything; we don't have to drag the words out of his mouth."

"Every one is master of his own words," said Grettir. "If you will come home with me I will give you what entertainment I can."

They thanked him and said they would accept his invitation. When they reached the house Grettir took Thorir by the hand and led him into the hall. He was very talkative. The mistress was in the hall decorating it and putting all in order. On hearing what Grettir said, she came to the door and asked who it was that Grettir was welcoming so warmly.

Grettir answered: "It will be advisable, mistress, to be civil to these men who have come. They are the bondi Thorir Paunch and his followers, and have come, all twelve of them, to spend Yule-tide here. It is fortunate for us, for we have had little company till now."

She said: "I don't call them bondis, nor are they decent men, but arrant robbers and malefactors. I would gladly pay a large portion of my property for them not to have come just at this time. It is an ill return that you make to Thorfinn for having saved you from shipwreck and kept you this winter like a free man, destitute as you were."

"You would do better," said Grettir, "if you first took off the wet clothes from your guests instead of casting reproaches upon me. You will have plenty of time for that."

Then Thorir said: Don't be angry, mistress! You shall lose nothing by your husband being away, for you shall have a man in his place and so shall your daughter and all the other women."

"That is spoken like a man," said Grettir. "The women shall be quite contented with what they get."

Then all the women fled and began to weep, being overcome by terror. Grettir said to the berserks: "Give me all the things which you want to lay aside, your weapons and your wet clothes, for the men will not obey us while they are frightened."

Thorir said he cared little for the women's whining. "But," he said, "we mean to treat you in a different way from the other men of the house. It seems to me that we may make a comrade of you."

"See to that yourselves," said Grettir. "But I do not look upon all men alike."

Then they laid aside most of their weapons. Grettir said: "I think now you had better sit down at the table and have some drink. You must be thirsty after your rowing."

They said they were quite ready for a drink, but did not know where the cellar was. Grettir asked whether they would let him arrange for their entertainment, which they willingly agreed to. So Grettir went and fetched some ale which he gave them to drink. They were very tired and drank enormously. He kept them well plied with the strongest ale there was, and they sat there for a long time whilst he told them funny stories. There was a tremendous din amongst them all, and the servants had no wish to approach them.

Thorir said: "I never yet met with a stranger who treated me like this man. What reward shall we give you for all that you have done, Grettir?"

Grettir replied: "I don't expect any reward for my services at present. But if when you depart we are still as good friends as we seem to be now, I should very much like to join your company, and though I may not be able to do as much work as any of you, I will not be a hindrance in any doughty undertaking."

They were delighted, and wanted to swear fellowship with him at once. Grettir said that could not be, "for," he added, "there is truth in the saying that ale is another man, and such a thing should not be done hastily, so let it remain at what I said; we are both little in the habit of restraining ourselves.

They declared that they did not mean to go back. The night was now coming on and it was getting very dark. Grettir noticed that they were rather fuddled, and asked whether they did not think it was time to go to bed. Thorir said: "So it is; but I have to fulfil my promise to the mistress." Grettir then went out and called out loud: "Go to bed, women! Such is the will of Thorir the bondi."

The women execrated him and could be heard howling like wolves. The berserks then left the room. Grettir said: "Let us go outside; I will show you the room in which Thorfinn keeps his clothes."

They were agreeable and all went out to an enormous outhouse, which was very strongly built, and had a strong lock on the outer door. Adjoining it was a large and well-built privy, with only a wooden partition between it and the room of the outhouse, which was raised above the ground and had to be reached by steps. The berserks then began skylarking and pushing Grettir about. He fell down the steps, as if in sport and in a moment was out of the house, had pulled the bolt, slammed the door to, and locked it. Thorir and his mates thought at first that the door had swung to of itself, and paid little attention; they had a light with them by which Grettir had been showing them all Thorfinn's treasures, and they continued looking at them for some time.

Grettir went off to the homestead, and on reaching the door cried out very loud, asking where the mistress was. She was silent, being afraid to answer. He said: "Here is rather good sport to be had. Are there any arms which are good for anything?"

"There are arms," she said; "but I don't know for what purpose you want them."

"We will talk about that afterwards; but now let each do what he can; it is the last chance."

"Now indeed were God in the dwelling," she said, "if anything should happen to save us. Over Thorfinn's bed there hangs the great halberd which belonged to Kar the Old; there, too, is a helmet and a corselet and a good short sword. The weapons will not fail if your heart holds firm."

Grettir took the helmet and spear, girt the sword about him and went quickly out. The mistress called to her men and bade them follow their brave champion. Four of them rushed to their arms, but the other four durst not go near them.

Meantime the berserks thought that Grettir was a long time away and began to suspect some treachery. They rushed to the door and found it locked. They strained at the woodwork till every timber groaned. At last they tore down the wooden partition and so gained the passage where the privy was, and thence the steps. Then the berserks' fury fell upon them and they howled like dogs. At that moment Grettir returned, and taking his halberd in both hands he thrust it right through Thorir's body just as he was about to descend the steps. The blade was very long and broad. Ogmund the Bad was just behind pushing him on, so that the spear passed right up to the hook, came out at his back between the shoulderblades and entered the breast of Ogmund. They both fell dead, pierced by the spear. Then all the others dashed down as they reached the steps. Grettir tackled them each in turn, now thrusting with the spear, now hewing with the sword, while they defended themselves with logs lying on the ground or with anything else which they could get. It was a terrible trial of a man's prowess to deal with men of their strength, even unarmed.

Grettir slew two of the Halogaland men there in the enclosure. Four of the serving-men then came up. They had not been able to agree upon which arms each should take, but they came out to the attack directly the berserks were running away; when these turned against them they fell back on the house. Six of the ruffians fell, all slain by Grettir's own hand; the other six then fled towards the landing place and took refuge in the boat-house, where they defended themselves with oars. Grettir received a severe blow from one of them and narrowly escaped a serious hurt.

The serving-men all went home and told great stories of their own exploits. The lady wanted to know what had become of Grettir, but they could not tell her. Grettir slew two men in the boat-house, but the other four got away, two in one direction, two in another. He pursued those who were nearest to him. The night was very dark. They ran to Vindheim, the place spoken of before, and took refuge in a barn, where they fought for a long time until at last Grettir killed them. By this time he was terribly stiff and exhausted. The night was far spent; it was very cold and there were driving snow-storms. He felt little inclination to go after the two who yet remained, so he went back home. The goodwife kindled a light and put it in a window in the loft at the top of the house, where it served him as a guide, and he was able to find his way home by the light. When he came to the door the mistress came to meet him and bade him welcome.

"You have earned great glory," she said, "and have saved me and my household from a disgrace never to be redeemed if you had not delivered us."

"I think I am much the same person as I was last evening when you spoke so roughly to me," said Grettir.

"We knew not then the might that was in you," she said, "as we know it now. Everything in the house shall be yours, so far as it is fitting for me to bestow and right for you to receive. I doubt not that Thorfinn will reward you in a better way when he comes home."

"There is little that I want as a reward at present," said Grettir. "But I accept your offer until your husband returns. I think now that you will be able to sleep in peace undisturbed by the berserks."

Grettir drank little before he retired and lay all night in his armour. In the morning, directly the day broke, all the men of the island were called together to go forth and search for the two berserks who had escaped. They were found at the end of the day lying under a rock, both dead from cold and from their wounds; they were carried away and buried in a place on the shore beneath the tide, with some loose stones over them, after which the islanders returned home, feeling that they could live in peace. When Grettir came back to the house and met the mistress he spoke a verse:

> "Near the surging sea the twelve lie buried.
> I stayed not my hand but slew them alone.
> Great lady! what deed that is wrought by a man
> shall be sung of as worthy if this be deemed small?"

She answered: "Certainly you are very unlike any other man now living." She set him in the high seat and gave him the best of everything. So it remained until Thorfinn returned.

chapter xxxiv

GRETTIR VISITS HIS UNCLE JOKULL

We have now to return to Grettir, who was at home in Bjarg during the autumn which followed his meeting with Warrior-Bardi at Thoreyjargnup. When the winter was approaching, he rode North across the neck to Vididal and stayed at Audunarstad. He and Audun made friends again; Grettir gave him a valuable battle-axe and they agreed to hold together in friendship. Audun had long lived there, and had many connections. He had a son named Egill, who married Ulfheid the daughter of Eyjolf, the son of Gudmund; their son Eyjolf, who was killed at the All-Thing, was the father of Orm the chaplain of Bishop Thorlak.

Grettir rode to the North to Vatnsdal and went on a visit to Tunga, where dwelt his mother's brother, Jokull the son of Bard, a big strong man and exceedingly haughty. He was a mariner, very cantankerous, but a person of much consideration. He welcomed Grettir, who stayed three nights with him. Nothing was talked about but Glam's walking, and Grettir inquired minutely about all the particulars. Jokull told him that no more was said than had really happened.

"Why, do you want to go there?" he asked.

Grettir said that it was so. Jokull told him not to do it.

"It would be a most hazardous undertaking," he said. "Your kinsmen incur a great risk with you as you are. There does not seem to be one of the younger men who is your equal. It is ill dealing with such a one as Glam. Much better with human men than with goblins of that sort."

Grettir said he had a mind to go to Thorhallsstad and see how things were. Jokull said: "I see there is no use in dissuading you. The saying is true that *Luck is one thing, brave deeds another*."

"*Woe stands before the door of one but enters that of another*," answered Grettir. "I am thinking how it may fare with you yourself before all is done."

"It may be," said Jokull, "that we both see what is before us, and yet we may not alter it."

Then they parted, neither of them well pleased with the other's prophetic saying.

chapter xxxv

THE FIGHT WITH GLAM'S GHOST

Grettir rode to Thorhallsstad where he was welcomed by the bondi. He asked Grettir whither he was bound, and Grettir said he wished to spend the night there if the bondi permitted. Thorhall said he would indeed be thankful to him for staying there.

"Few," he said, "think it a gain to stay here for any time. You must have heard tell of the trouble that is here, and I do not want you to be inconvenienced on my account. Even if you escape unhurt yourself, I know for certain that you will lose your horse, for no one can keep his beast in safety who comes here."

Grettir said there were plenty more horses to be had if anything happened to this one.

Thorhall was delighted at Grettir's wishing to remain, and received him with both hands. Grettir's horse was placed securely under lock and key and they both went to bed. The night passed without Glam showing himself.

"Your being here has already done some good," said Thorhall. "Glam has always been in the habit of riding on the roof or breaking open the doors every night, as you can see from the marks."

"Then," Grettir said, "either he will not keep quiet much longer, or he will remain so more than one night. I will stay another night and see what happens."

Then they went to Grettir's horse and found it had not been touched. The bondi thought that all pointed to the same thing. Grettir stayed a second night and again the thrall did not appear. The bondi became hopeful and went to see the horse. There he found the stable broken open, the horse dragged outside and every bone in his body broken. Thorhall told Grettir what had occurred and advised him to look to himself, for he was a dead man if he waited for Glam.

Grettir answered: "I must not have less for my horse than a sight of the thrall."

The bondi said there was no pleasure to be had from seeing him: "He is not like any man. I count every hour a gain that you are here."

The day passed, and when the hour came for going to bed Grettir said he would not take off his clothes, and lay down on a seat opposite to Thorkell's sleeping apartment. He had a shaggy cloak covering him with one end of it fastened under his feet and the other drawn over his head so that he could see through the neck-hole. He set his feet against a strong bench which was in front of him. The frame-work of the outer door had been all broken away and some bits of wood had been rigged up roughly in its place. The partition which had once divided the hall from the entrance passage was all broken, both above the cross-beam and below, and all the bedding had been upset. The place looked rather desolate. There was a light burning in the hall by night.

When about a third part of the night had passed Grettir heard a loud noise. Something was going up on to the building, riding above the hall and kicking with its heels until the timbers cracked again. This went on for some time, and then it came down towards the door. The door opened and Grettir saw the thrall stretching in an enormously big and ugly head. Glam moved slowly in, and on passing the door stood upright, reaching to the roof. He turned to the hall, resting his arms on the cross-beam and peering along the hall. The bondi uttered no sound, having heard quite enough of what had gone on outside. Grettir lay quite still and did not move. Glam saw a heap of something in the seat, came farther into the hall and seized the cloak tightly with his hand. Grettir pressed his foot against the plank and the cloak held firm. Glam tugged at it again still more violently, but it did not give way. A third time he pulled, this time with both hands and with such force that he pulled Grettir up out of the seat, and between them the cloak was torn in two. Glam looked at the bit which he held in his hand and wondered much who could pull like that against him. Suddenly Grettir sprang under his arms, seized him round the waist and squeezed his back with all his might, intending in that way to bring him down, but the thrall wrenched his arms till he staggered from the violence. Then Grettir fell back to another bench. The benches flew about and everything was shattered around them. Glam wanted to get out, but Grettir tried to prevent him by stemming his foot against anything he could find. Nevertheless Glam succeeded in getting him outside the hall. Then a terrific struggle began, the thrall trying to drag him out of the house, and Grettir saw that however hard he was to deal with in the house, he would be worse outside, so he strove with all his might to keep him from getting out. Then Glam made a desperate effort and gripped Grettir tightly towards him, forcing him to the porch. Grettir saw that he could not put up any resistance, and with a sudden movement he dashed into the thrall's arms and set both his feet against a stone which was fastened in the ground at the door. For that Glam was not prepared, since he had been tugging to drag Grettir towards him; he reeled backwards and tumbled hind-foremost out of the door, tearing away the lintel with his shoulder and shattering the roof, the rafters and the frozen thatch. Head over heels he fell out of the house and Grettir fell on top of him. The moon was shining very brightly outside, with light clouds passing over it and hiding it now and again. At the moment when Glam fell the moon shone forth, and Glam turned his eyes up towards it. Grettir himself has related that that sight was the only one which ever made him tremble. What with fatigue and all else that he had endured, when he saw the horrible rolling of Glam's eyes his heart sank so utterly that he had not strength to draw his sword, but lay there wellnigh betwixt life and death. Glam possessed more malignant power than most fiends, for he now spoke in this wise:

"You have expended much energy, Grettir, in your search for me. Nor is that to be wondered at, if you should have little joy thereof. And now I tell you that you shall possess only half the strength and firmness of heart that were decreed to you if you had not striven with me. The might which was yours till now I am not able to take away, but it is in my power to ordain that never shall you grow stronger than you are now. Nevertheless your might is sufficient, as many shall find to their cost. Hitherto you have earned fame through your deeds, but henceforward there shall fall upon you exile and battle; your deeds shall turn to evil and your guardian-spirit shall forsake you. You will be outlawed and your lot shall be to dwell ever alone. And this I lay upon you, that these eyes of mine shall be ever before your vision. You will find it hard to live alone, and at last it shall drag you to death."

When the thrall had spoken the faintness which had come over Grettir left him. He drew his short sword, cut off Glam's head and laid it between his thighs. Then the bondi came out, having put on his clothes while Glam was speaking, but he did not venture to come near until he was dead. Thorhall praised God and thanked Grettir warmly for having laid this unclean spirit. Then they set to work and burned Glam to cold cinders, bound the ashes in a skin and buried them in a place far away from the haunts of man or beast. Then they went home, the day having nearly broken. Grettir was very stiff and lay down to rest. Thorhall sent for some men from the next farms and let them know how things had fared. They all realised the importance of Grettir's deed when they heard of it; all agreed that in the whole country side for strength and courage and enterprise there was not the equal of Grettir the son of Asmund.

Thorhall bade a kindly farewell to Grettir and dismissed him with a present of a fine horse and proper clothes, for all that he had been wearing were torn to pieces. They parted in friendship. Grettir rode to Ass in

Vatnsdal and was welcomed by Thorvald, who asked him all about his encounter with Glam. Grettir told him everything and said that never had his strength been put to trial as it had been in their long struggle. Thorvald told him to conduct himself discreetly; if he did so he might prosper, but otherwise he would surely come to disaster. Grettir said that his temper had not improved, that he had even less discretion than before, and was more impatient of being crossed. In one thing a great change had come over him; he had become so frightened of the dark that he dared not go anywhere alone at night. Apparitions of every kind came before him. It has since passed into an expression, and men speak of "Glam's eyes" or "Glam visions" when things appear otherwise than as they are.

Having accomplished his undertaking Grettir rode back to Bjarg and spent the winter at home.

Lancelot and the
Grail Quest

sir thomas malory

...THAN ANONE THEY HARDE CRAKYNGE AND CRYYNGE OF THUNDIR, that
hem thought the palyse sholde all to-dryve. So in the myddys of the blast
entyrde a sonnebeame, more clerer by seven tymys than ever they saw day,
and all they were alyghted of the grace of the Holy Goste. Then began
every knyght to beholde other, and eyther saw other, by their semynge,
fayrer than ever they were before. Natforthan there was no knyght that
myght speke one worde a grete whyle, and so they loked every man on other
as they had bene doome.

Than entird into the halle the Holy Grayle coverde with whyght samyte,
but there was none that myght se hit nother whom that bare hit. And there
was all the halle fulfylled with good odoures, and every knyght had such
metis and drynkes as he beste loved in thys worlde.

And whan the Holy Grayle had bene borne thorow the hall, than the
holy vessell departed suddeynly, that they wyst [knew] nat where hit becam.
Than had they all breth to speke, and than the kyng yelded thankynges to
God of Hys good grace that He had sente them.

'Sertes,' seyde the kynge, 'we ought to thanke oure Lorde Jesu Cryste
gretly that he hath shewed us thys day at the reverence of thys hyghe feste
of Pentecost.'

'Now,' seyde sir Gawayne, 'we have bene servyd thys day of what metys
and drynkes we thought on. But one thyng begyled us, that we myght nat
se the Holy Grayle: hit was so preciously coverde. Wherefore I woll make

From THE WORKS OF SIR THOMAS MALORY, ed. Eugene Vinaver. By permission of
Oxford University Press.

here a vow that to-morne, withoute longer abydynge, I shall laboure in the queste of the Sankgreall, and that I shall holde me oute a twelve-month and a day or more if nede be, and never shall I returne unto the courte agayne tylle I have sene hit more opynly than hit hath bene shewed here. And iff I may nat spede I shall returne agayne as he that may nat be ayenst the wylle of God.

So whan they of the Table Rounde harde sir Grawayne sey so, they arose up the moste party and made such avowes as sir Gawayne hathe made. Anone as kynge Arthur harde thys he was gretly dysplesed, for he wyst well he myght nat agaynesey their avowys.

'Alas!' seyde kynge Arthure unto sir Gawayne, 'ye have nygh slayne me for the avow that ye have made, for thorow you ye have berauffte me the fayryst and the trewyst of knyghthode that ever was sene togydir in ony realme of the worlde. For whan they departe frome hense I am sure they all shall never mete more togydir in thys worlde, for they shall dye many in the queste. And so hit forthynkith nat me a litill, for I have loved them as well as my lyff. Wherefore hit shall greve me ryght sore, the departicion of thys felyship, for I have had an olde custom to have hem in my felyship.'

And therewith the teerys felle in hys yen, and than he seyde,

'Sir Gawayne, Gawayne! Ye have sette me in grete sorow, for I have grete doute that my trew felyshyp shall never mete here more agayne.'

'A, sir,' seyde sir Launcelot, 'comforte yourself! For hit shall be unto us a grete honoure, and much more than we dyed in other placis, for of dethe we be syker.'

'A, Launcelot!' seyde the kynge, 'the grete love that I have had unto you all the dayes of my lyff makith me to sey such dolefull wordis! For there was never Crysten kynge that ever had so many worthy men at hys table as I have had thys day at the Table Rounde. And that ys my grete sorow.'

When the quene, ladyes, and jantillwomen knew of thys tydyng they had such sorow and hevynes that there myght no tunge telle, for tho knyghtes had holde them in honoure and charité. But aboven all othir quene Gwenyver made grete sorow.

'I mervayle,' seyde she, 'that my lorde woll suffir hem to departe fro hym.'

Thus was all the courte trowbled for the love of the departynge of these knyghtes, and many of tho ladyes that loved knyghtes wolde have gone with hir lovis. And so had they done, had nat an olde knyght com amonge them in relygious clothynge and spake all on hyght and seyde,

'Fayre lordis whych have sworne in the queste of the Sankgreall, thus sendith you Nacien the eremyte [hermit] worde that none in thys queste lede lady nother jantillwoman with hym, for hit ys nat to do in so hyghe a servyse as they laboure in. For I warne you playne, he that ys nat clene of hys synnes he shall nat se the mysteryes of oure Lorde Jesu Cryste'.... [the knights set out on their separate adventures.]

Syr Launcelot rode overthwarte and endelonge a wylde foreyst and hylde no patthe but as wylde adventure lad hym. And at the last he com to a stony crosse whych departed two wayes in waste londe, and by the crosse was a stone that was a marble, but hit was so durke that sir Launcelot myght nat wete what hyt was. Than sir Launcelot loked bysyde hym and saw an olde chapell, and there he wente to have founde people.

And anone sir Launcelot fastenyd hys horse tylle a tre, and there he dud of hys sylde and hynge hyt uppon a tre, and than he wente to the chapell dore and founde hit waste and brokyn. And within he founde a fayre awter full rychely arayde with clothe of clene sylke, and there stoode a clene fayre candyllstykke whych bare six grete candyls therein, and the candilstyk was of sylver; and whan sir Launcelot saw thys lyght he had grete wylle for to entir into the chapell, but he coude fynde no place where he myght entir. Than was he passyng hevy and dysmayed, and returned ayen and cam to hys horse, and dud of hys sadyll and brydyll and leete hym pasture hym, and unlaced hys helme and ungerde hys swerde and layde hym downe to slepe uppon hys shylde tofore the crosse.

And so he felle on slepe; and half wakyng and half slepynge he saw commyng by hym two palfreyes, all fayre and whyght, whych bare a lytter, and therein lyyng a syke knyght. And whan he was nyghe the crosse he there abode stylle. All thys sir Launcelot sye and behylde hit, for he slepte nat veryly, and he herde hym sey,

'A, sweete Lorde! Whan shall thys sorow leve me, and whan shall the holy vessell com by me wherethorow I shall be be heled? For I have endured thus longe for litill trespasse, a full grete whyle!'

Thus complayned the knyght and allways sir Launcelot harde hit. So with that sir Launcelot sye the candyllstyk with the six tapirs cam before the crosse, and he saw nobody that brought hit. Also there cam a table of sylver and the holy vessell of the Sankgreall which sir Launcelot had sene toforetyme [before] in kynge Pescheors house. And therewith the syke knyght sette hym up, and hylde up both hys hondys, and seyde,

'Fayre swete Lorde whych ys here within the holy vessell, take hede unto me, that I may be hole of thys malody!'

And therewith on hys hondys and kneys he wente so nyghe that he towched the holy vessell and kyst hit, and anone he was hole. And than he seyde,

'Lorde God, I thanke The, for I am helyd of thys syknes!'

So whan the holy vessell had bene there a grete whyle hit went unto the chapell with the chaundeler and the lyght, so that sir Launcelot wyst nat where hit was becom; for he was overtakyn with synne, that he had no power to ryse agayne the holy vessell. Wherefore aftir that many men seyde hym shame, but he toke repentaunce aftir that.

Than the syke knyght dressed hym up and kyssed the crosse. Anone hys squyre brought hym hys armys and asked hys lorde how he ded.

'Sertes,' seyde he, 'I thanke God, ryght well! Thorow the holy vessell I am heled. But I have mervayle of thys slepyng knyght that he had no power to awake whan thys holy vessell was brought hydir.'

'I dare well sey,' seyde the squyre, 'that he dwellith in som dedly synne whereof he was never confessed.'

'Be my fayth,' seyde the knyght, 'whatsomever he be, he ys unhappy. For as I deme he ys of the felyship of the Rounde Table whych ys entird in the queste of the Sankgreall.'

'Sir,' seyde the squyre, 'here I have brought you all youre armys save youre helme and youre swerde, and therefore, be myne assente, now may ye take thys knyghtes helme and his swerde.'

And so he dud. And whan he was clene armed he toke there sir Launce-lottis horse, for he was bettir than hys, and so departed they frome the crosse.

Than anone sir Launcelot waked and sett hym up and bethought hym what he had sene there and whether hit were dremys or nat. Ryght so harde he a voyse that seyde,

'Sir Launcelot, more harder than ys the stone, and more bitter than ys the woode, and more naked and barer than ys the lyeff of the fygge-tre! Therefore go thou from hens, and withdraw the from thys holy places!'

And whan sir Launcelot herde thys he was passyng hevy and wyst nat what to do. And so departed sore wepynge and cursed the tyme that he was borne, for than he demed never to have worship more. For tho wordis wente to hys herte, tylle that he knew wherefore he was called so.

Than sir Launcelot wente to the crosse and founde hys helme, hys swerde, and hys horse away. And than he called hymselff a verry wrecch and moste unhappy of all knyghtes, and there he seyde,

'My synne and my wychednes hath brought me unto grete dishonoure! For whan I sought worldly adventures for worldely desyres I ever encheved them and had the bettir in every place, and never was I discomfite in no quarell, were hit ryght were hit wronge. And now I take uppon me the adventures to seke of holy thynges, now I se and undirstonde that myne olde synne hyndryth me and shamyth me, that I had no power to stirre nother speke when the holy bloode appered before me.'

So thus he sorowed tyll hit was day, and harde the fowlys synge; than somwhat he was comforted. But whan sir Launcelot myssed his horse and hys harneyse than he wyst well God was displesed with hym. And so he departed frome the crosse on foote into a fayre foreyste, and so by pryme he cam to an hyghe hylle and founde an ermytage and an ermyte therein whych was goyng unto masse.

And than sir Launcelot kneled downe and cryed on oure Lorde mercy for hys wycked workys. So whan masse was done sir Launcelot called hym, and prayde hym for seynte charité for to hyre hys lyff.

'With a good wylle,' seyde the good man, and asked hym whethir he was of kyng Arthurs and of the felyship of the Table Rounde.

'Ye, forsoth, sir, and my name ys sir Launcelot du Lake, that hath bene ryght well seyde off. And now my good fortune ys chonged, for I am the moste wrecch of the worlde.'

The ermyte behylde hym and had mervayle whye he was so abaysshed.

'Sir,' seyde the ermyte, 'ye ought to thanke God more than ony knyght lyvynge, for He hath caused you to have more worldly worship than ony knyght that ys now lyvynge. And for youre presumpcion to take uppon you in dedely synne for to be in Hys presence, where Hys flessh and Hys blood was, which caused you ye myght nat se hyt with youre worldely yen, for He woll nat appere where such synners bene but if hit be unto their grete hurte other unto their shame. And there is no knyght now lyvynge that ought to yelde God so grete thanke os ye [as you], for He hath yevyn you beauté, bownté, semelynes, and grete strengthe over all other knyghtes. And therefore ye ar the more beholdyn unto God than ony other man to love Hym and drede Hym, for youre strengthe and your manhode woll litill avayle you and God be agaynste you.'

Than sir Launcelot wepte with hevy harte and seyde,

'Now I know well ye sey me sothe [truth].'

'Sir,' seyde the good man, 'hyde none olde synne frome me.'

'Truly,' seyde sir Launcelot, 'that were me full lothe to discover, for thys fourtene yere I never discoverde one thynge that I have used, and that may I now wyghte [know] my shame and my disadventures.'

And than he tolde there the good man all hys lyff, and how he had loved a quene unmesurabely and oute of mesure longe.

'And all my grete dedis of armys that I have done for the moste party was for the quenys sake, and for hir sake wolde I do batayle were hit ryght other wronge. And never dud I batayle all only for Goddis sake, but for to wynne worship and to cause me the bettir to be beloved, and litill or nought I thanked never God of hit.' Than sir Launcelot seyde, 'Sir, I pray you counceyle me.'

'Sir, I woll counceyle you,' seyde the ermyte, 'yf ye shall ensure me by youre knyghthode ye shall no more com in that quenys felyship as much as ye may forbere.'

And than sir Launcelot promysed hym that he nolde, by the faythe of hys body.

'Sir, loke that your harte and youre mowth accorde,' seyde the good man, 'and I shall ensure you ye shall have the more worship than ever ye had.'

'Holy fadir,' seyde sir Launcelot, 'I mervayle of the voyce that seyde to me mervayles wordes, as ye have herde toforehonde [before].'

'Have ye no mervayle,' seyde the good man, 'thereoff, for hit semyth well God lovith you. For men may undirstonde a stone ys harde of kynde, and namely one more than another, and that ys to undirstonde by the, sir Launcelot, for thou wolt nat leve thy synne for no goodnes that God hath sente the. Therefore thou arte more harder than ony stone, and woldst never be made neyssh nother by watir nother by fyre, and that ys the hete of the Holy Goste may nat entir in the.

'Now take hede, in all the worlde men shall nat fynde one knyght to whom oure Lorde hath yevyn so much of grace as He hath lente the, for He hathe yeffyn the fayrenes with semelynes; also He hath yevyn the wytte and discression to know good frome ille. He hath also yevyn prouesse and hardinesse, and gevyn the to worke so largely that thou hast had the bettir all thy dayes of thy lyff wheresomever thou cam. And now oure Lorde wolde suffir the no lenger but that thou shalt know Hym whether thou wolt other nylt. And why the voyce called the bitterer than the woode, for wheresomever much synne dwellith there may be but lytyll swettnesse; wherefore thou art lykened to an olde rottyn tre.

'Now have I shewed the why thou art harder than the stone and bitterer than the tre; now shall I shew the why thou art more naked and barer than the fygge-tre. Hit befelle that oure Lorde on Palme Sonday preched in Jerusalem, and there He founde in the people that all hardnes was herberowd in them, and there He founde in all the towne nat one that wolde herberow Hym. And than He wente oute of the towne and founde in myddis the way a fygge-tre which was ryght fayre and well garnysshed of levys, but fruyte had hit none. Than oure Lorde cursed the tre that bare no fruyte; that betokenyth the fyg-tre unto Jerusalem that had levys and no fruyte. So thou, sir Launcelot, whan the Holy Grayle was brought before the, He founde in the no fruyte, nother good thought nother good wylle, and defouled with lechory.'

'Sertes,' seyde sir Launcelot, 'all that ye have seyde ys trew, and frome hensforewarde I caste me, by the grace of God, never to be so wycked as I have bene but as to sew knyghthode and to do fetys of armys.'

Than thys good man joyned sir Launcelot suche penaunce as he myght do and to sew knyghthode, and so assoyled hym, and prayde hym to abyde with hym all that day.

'I woll well,' seyde sir Launcelot, 'for I have nother helme, horse, ne swerde.'

'As for that,' seyde the good man, 'I shall helpe you or to-morne at evyn of an horse and all that longith unto you.'

And than sir Launcelot repented hym gretly of hys myssedeys. . . .

[Lancelot leaves the hermit and continues on his search for the grail.] As he loked before hym he sye a fayre playne, and besyde that a fayre castell, and before the castell were many pavelons of sylke and of dyverse hew. And hym semed that he saw there fyve hondred knyghtes rydnge on horsebacke, and there was two partyes: they that were of the castell were all on black horsys and their trappoures black, and they that were withoute were all on whyght horsis and trappers. So there began a grete turnemente, and everyche hurteled with other, that hit mervayled sir Launcelot gretly. And at the laste hym thought they of the castell were putt to the wars.

Than thought sir Launcelot for to helpe there the wayker party in increasyng of his shevalry. And so sir Launcelot threste in amonge the party of the castell and smote downe a knyght, horse and man, to the erthe, and then he russhed here and there and ded many mervaylous dedis of armys. And than he drew oute hys swerde and strake many knyghtes to the earth, that all that saw hym mervayled that ever one knyght myght do so grete dedis of armys.

But allwayes the whyght knyghtes hylde them nyghe aboute sir Launcelot for to tire hym and wynde hym, and at the laste, as a man may not ever endure sir Launcelot waxed so faynt of fyghtyng and travaillyng, and was so wery of hys grete dedis, that he myght nat lyffte up hys armys for to gyff one stroke, that he wente never to have borne armys.

And than they all toke and ledde hym away into a foreyste and there made hym to alyght to reeste hym. And than all the felyship of the castell were overcom for the defaughte of hym. Than they seyd all unto sir Launcelot.

'Blessed be God that ye be now of oure felyship, for we shall holde you in oure preson.'

And so they leffte hym with few wordys, and than sir Launcelot made grete sorowe: 'For never or now was I never at turnemente nor at justes but I had the beste. And now I am shamed, and am sure that I am more synfuller than ever I was.'

Thus he rode sorowyng halff a day oute of dispayre, tyll that he cam into a depe valey. And whan sir Launcelot sye he myght nat ryde up unto the mountayne, he there alyght undir an appyll-tre. And there he leffte hys helme and hys shylde, and put hys horse unto pasture, and than he leyde hym downe to slepe.

And than hym thought there com an olde man afore hym whych seyde, 'A, Launcelot, of evill, wycked fayth and poore beleve! Wherefore ys thy wyll turnd so lyghtly toward dedly synne?'

And whan he had seyde thus he vanysshed away, and sir Launcelot wyst nat where he becom. Than he toke hys horse and armed hym. And as he rode by the hygheway he saw a chapell where was a recluse, which had a wyndow, that she myght se up to the awter. And all aloude she called sir Launcelot for that he semed a knyght arraunte.

And than he cam, and she asked hym what he was, and of what place, and where aboute he wente to seke. And than he tolde hir alltogydir worde by worde, and the trouth how hit befelle hym at the turnemente, and aftir that he tolde hir hys avision that he had that nyght hys slepe, and prayd her to telle hym what hit myght mene.

'A, Launcelot,' seyde she, 'as longe as ye were knyght of erthly knyghthode ye were the moste mervayloust man of the worlde, and moste adventurest. Now,' seyde the lady, 'sitthen ye be sette amonge the knyghtis of hevynly adventures, if adventure falle thee contrary have thou no mervayle; for that turnamente yestirday was but a tokenynge of oure Lorde. And natforethan there was none enchauntemente, for they at the turnemente were erthely knyghtes. The turnamente was tokyn to se who sholde have moste knyghtes of Eliazar, the sonne of kynge Pelles, or Argustus, the sonne of kynge Harlon. But Eliazar was all clothed in whyght, and Argustus were coverde in blacke. And what thys betokenyth I shal telle you.

'The day of Pentecoste, whan kynge Arthure hylde courte, hit befelle that erthely kynges and erthely knyghtes toke a turnemente togydirs, that ys to sey the queste of the Sankgreall. Of thes the erthely knyghtes were they which were clothed all in blake, and the coveryng betokenyth the synnes whereof they be nat confessed. And they with the coverynge of whyght betokenyth virginité, and they that hath chosyn chastité. And thus was the queste begonne in them. Than thou behelde the synners and the good men. And whan thou saw the synners overcom thou enclyned to that party for bobbaunce [boasting] and pryde of the worlde, and all that muste be leffte in that queste; for in thys queste thou shalt have many felowis and thy bettirs, for thou arte so feble of evyll truste and good beleve. Thys made hit whan thou were where they toke the, and ladde the into the foreyste.

'And anone there appered the Sankgreall unto the whyght knyghtes, but thou were so fyeble of good beleve and fayth that thou myght nat abyde hit for all the techyng of the good man before. But anone thou turned to the synners, and that caused thy mysseaventure, that thou sholde know God frome vayneglory of the worlde; hit ys nat worth a peare. And for grete pryde thou madist grete sorow that thou haddist nat overcom all the whyght knyghtes. Therefore God was wrothe with you, for in thys queste God lovith no such dedis. And that made the avision to say to the that thou were of evyll faythe and of poore belyeve, the which woll make the to falle into the depe pitte of helle, if thou kepe the nat the bettir.

'Now have I warned the of thy vayneglory and of thy pryde, that thou haste many tyme arred ayenste thy Maker. Beware of everlastynge payne, for of all erthly knyghtes I have moste pité of the, for I know well thou haste nat thy pere of ony erthly synfull man.'

And so she commaunded sir Launcelot to dyner. And aftir dyner he toke hys horse and commaunde her to God, and so rode into a depe valey. And there he saw a ryver that hyght Mortays. And thorow the watir he muste nedis passe, the whych was hedyous. And than in the name of God he toke hit with good herte.

And whan he com over he saw an armed knyght, horse and man all black as a beré. Withoute ony worde he smote sir Launcelottis horse to the dethe. And so he paste on and wyst nat where he was becom.

And than he toke hys helme and hys shylde, and thanked God of hys adventure.

Now seyth the tale that whan sir Launcelot was com to the watir of Mortays as hit ys reherced before, he was in grete perell. And so he leyde hym downe and slepte, and toke the adventure that God wolde sende hym. So whan he was aslepe there cam a vision unto hym that seyde,

'Sir Launcelot, aryse up and take thyne armour, and entir into the firste shippe that thou shalt fynde!'

And whan he herde thes wordys he sterte up and saw grete clerenesse aboute hym, and than he lyffte up hys honde and blyssed hym. And so toke hys armys and made hym redy.

And at the laste he cam by a stronde and founde a shippe withoute sayle other ore. And as sone as he was within the shippe, there he had the moste swettness that ever he felte, and he was fulfylled with all thynge that he thought on other desyred. Than he seyde,

'Swete Fadir, Jesu Cryste! I wote natt what joy I am in, for thys passith all erthely joyes that ever I was in.'

And so in thys joy he leyde hym downe to the shippe-bourde and slepte tyll day. And whan he awooke he founde there a fayre bed, and therein lyynge a jantillwoman dede, which was sir Percivalles sister. And as sir Launcelot avised her, he aspyed in hir ryght honde a wrytte whych he rad, that tolde hym all the aventures that ye have herde before, and of what lynayge she was com.

So with thys jantillwoman sir Launcelot was a moneth and more. If ye wold aske how he lyved, for He that fedde the peple of Israel with manna in deserte, so was he fedde; for every day, whan he had seyde hys prayers, he was susteyned with the grace of the Holy Goste.

And so on a nyght he wente to play hym by the watirs syde, for he was somwhat wery of the shippe. And than he lystened and herde an hors com and one rydyng uppon hym, and whan he cam nyghe hym semed a knyght, and so he late hym passe and wente thereas the ship was. And there he alyght and toke the sadyll and the brydill, and put the horse frome hym, and so wente into the shyppe.

And than sir Launcelot dressed hym unto the shippe and seyde,

'Sir, ye be wellcom!'

And he answerd, and salewed hym agayne and seyde,

'Sir, what ys youre name? For much my herte gevith unto you.'

'Truly,' seyde he, 'my name ys sir Launcelot du Lake.'

'Sir,' seyde he, 'than be ye wellcom! For ye were the begynner of me in thys worlde.'

'A, sir, ar ye sir Galahad?

'Ye, forsothe.'

And so he kneled downe and askyd hym hys blyssynge. And aftir that toke of hys helme and kyssed hym, and there was grete joy betwyxte them, for no tunge can telle what joy was betwyxte them.

And there every of them tolde othir the aventures that had befalle them syth that they departed frome the courte. And anone as sir Galahad saw the jantillwoman dede in the bedde he knew her well, and seyde grete worship of hir, that she was one of the beste maydyns lyvyng and hit was grete pité of hir dethe.

But whan sir Launcelot herde how the mervayles swerde was gotyn and who made hit, and all the mervayles rehersed afore, than he prayd sir Galahad that he wolde shew hym the swerde. And so he brought hit forth and kyssed the pomell and the hiltis and the scawberde.

'Truly,' seyde sir Launcelot, 'never arste knew I of so hyghe adventures done, and so mervalous stronge.'

So dwelled sir Launcelot and Galahad within that shippe halff a yere, and served God dayly and nyghtly with all their power. And often they aryved in yles ferre frome folke, where there repayred none but wylde beestes, and ther they founde many straunge adventures and peryllous which they brought to an end. But for tho adventures were with wylde beestes and nat in the quest of the Sancgreal, therfor the tale makith here no mencyon therof; for it wolde be to longe to telle of alle tho adventures that befelle them.

So aftir, on a Mondaye, hit befelle that they aryved in the edge of a foreyste tofore a crosse. And thenne sawe they a knyghte armed all in whyte, and was rychely horsed, and ledde in his ryght hond a whyte hors. And so he cam to the shyp and salewed the two knyghtes in the Hyghe Lordis behalff, and seyde unto sir Galahad,

'Sir, ye have bene longe inowe with youre fadir. Therefore com oute of the shippe, and take thys horse, and go where the aventures shall lede you in the queste of the Sankgreall.'

Than he wente to hys fadir and kyste hym swetely and seyde,

'Fayre swete fadir, I wote nat whan I shall se you more tyll I se the body of Jesu Cryste.'

'Now, for Goddis love,' seyde sir Launcelot, 'pray to the Fadir that He holde me stylle in Hys servyse.'

And so he toke hys horse, and there they hard a voyce that seyde,

'Every of you thynke for to do welle, for nevermore shall one se another off you before the dredefull day of doome.'

'Now, my sonne, sir Galahad, sith we shall departe and nother of us se other more, I pray to that Hyghe Fadir, conserve me and you bothe.'

'Sir,' seyde sir Galahad, 'no prayer avaylith so much as youres.'

And therewith sir Galahad entird into the foreyste. And the wynde arose and drove sir Launcelot more than a moneth thorow the se, where he sleped but litill, but prayde to God that he myght se som tydynges of the Sankgreall.

So hit befelle on a nyght, at mydnyght, he aryved before a castell, on the backe syde whiche was ryche and fayre, and there was a posterne opened toward the see, and was open withoute ony kepynge, save two lyons kept the entré; and the moone shone ryght clere. Anone sir Launcelot herd a voyce that seyde,

'Launcelot, go oute of this shyp, and entre into the castel where thou shalte see a grete parte of thy desyre.'

Thenne he ran to hys armys and so armed hym, and so wente to the gate and saw the lyons. Thenne sette he hand to his suerd and drewe hit. So there cam a dwerf sodenly and smote hym the arme so sore that the suerd felle oute of his hand. Then herde he a voice say,

'O, man of evylle feyth and poure byleve! Wherefore trustist thou more on thy harneyse than in thy Maker? For He myght more avayle the than thyne armour, in what servyse that thou arte sette in.'

Than seyde sir Launcelot, 'Fayre Fadir, Jesu Cryste! I thanke The of Thy grete mercy that Thou reprevyst me of my myssedede Now se I that Thou holdiste me for one of Thy servauntes.'

Than toke he hys swerde agyne and put hit up in hys sheethe, and made a crosse in hys forehede, and cam to the lyons. And they made sembelaunte to do hym harme. Natwithstondynge he passed by them withoute hurte, and entird into the castell to the chyeff fortresse. And there were they all at reste.

Than sir Launcelot entred so armed, for he founde no gate nor doore but hit was opyn. And at the laste he founde a chambir whereof the doore was shutte, and he sett hys honde thereto to have opened hit, but he myght nat. Than he enforced hym myckyll to undo the doore. Than he lystened and herde a voice whych sange so swetly that hit semede none erthely thynge, and hym thought the voice seyde,

'Joy and honoure be to the Fadir of Hevyn.'

Than sir Launcelot kneled adowne tofore the chambir dore, for well wyst he that there was the Sankgreall within that chambir. Than seyde he,

'Fayre swete Fadir, Jesu Cryste! If ever I dud thynge that plesed The, Lorde, for Thy pité ne have me nat in dispite for my synnes done byforetyme, and that Thou shew me somthynge of that I seke.'

And with that he saw the chambir dore opyn, and there cam oute a grete clerenesse, that the house was as bryght as all the tourcheis of the worlde had bene there. So cam he to the chambir doore and wolde have entird. And anone a voice seyde unto hym,

'Sir Launcelot, flee and entir nat, for thou ought nat to do hit! For and if thou entir thou shalt forthynke [regret] hit.'

Than he withdrew hym aback ryght hevy. Than loked he up into the myddis of the chambir and saw a table of sylver, and the holy vessell coverde with rede samyte, and many angels aboute hit, whereof one hylde a candyll of wexe brennynge, and the other hylde a crosse and the ornementis of an awter. And before the holy vessell he saw a good man clothed as a pryste, and hit semed that he was at the sakerynge of the masse. And hit semed to sir Launcelot that above the prystis hondys were three men, whereof the two put the yongyste by lyknes betwene the prystes hondis; and so he lyffte hym up ryght hyghe, and hit semed to shew so to the peple.

And than sir Launcelot mervayled nat a litill, for hym thought the pryste was so gretly charged of the vygoure that hym semed that he sholde falle to the erth. And whan he saw none aboute hym that wolde helpe hym, than cam he to the dore a grete pace and seyde,

'Fayre Fadir, Jesu Cryste, ne take hit for no synne if I helpe the good man whych hath grete nede of helpe.'

Ryght so entird he into the chambir and cam toward the table of sylver, and whan he cam nyghe hit he felte a breeth that hym thought hit was entromedled with fyre, which smote hym so sore in the vysayge that hym thought hit brente hys vysayge. And therewith he felle to the erthe and had no power to aryse, as he that was so araged that had loste the power of hys body and hys hyrynge and syght. Than felte he many hondys whych toke hym up and bare hym oute of the chambir doore and leffte hym there semynge dede to all people.

So uppon the morrow, whan hit was fayre day, they within were rysen and founde sir Launcelot lyynge before the chambir doore. All they mervayled how that he com in. And so they loked uppon hym, and felte hys powse to wete whethir were ony lyff in hym. And so they founde lyff in hym, but he myght nat stonde nother stirre no membir that he had.

And so they toke hym by every parte of the body and bare hym into a chambir and leyde hym in a rych bedde farre frome folke. And so he lay four dayes.

Than one seyde he was on lyve, and another seyde nay, he was dede.

'In the name of God,' seyde an olde man, 'I do you veryly to wete he ys nat dede, but he ys as fulle of lyff as the strengyst of you all. Therefore I rede you all that he bewell kepte tylle God sende lyff in hym agayne.'

So in such maner they kepte sir Launcelot four-and-twenty dayes and also many nyghtis, that ever he lay stylle as a dede man. And at the twenty-fifth day befylle hym aftir mydday that he opened hys yen. And whan he saw folke he made grete sorow and seyde,

'Why have ye awaked me? For I was more at ease than I am now. A, Jesu Cryste, who myght be so blyssed that myght se opynly Thy grete mervayles of secretnesse there where no synner may be?'

'What have ye sene?' seyde they aboute hym.

'I have sene', seyde he, 'grete mervayles that no tunge may telle, and more than ony herte can thynke. And had nat my synne bene beforetyme, ellis I had sene muche more.'

Than they tolde hym how he had layne there four-and-twenty dayes and nyghtes. Than hym thought hit was ponyshemente for the four-and-twenty yere that he had bene a synner, wherefore oure Lorde put hym in penaunce the four-and-twenty dayes and nyghtes. Than loked Launcelot tofore hym and saw the hayre whych he had borne nyghe a yere; for that he forthoughte hym ryght muche that he ad brokyn his promyse unto the ermyte whych he had avowed to do.

Than they asked how hit stood with hym.

'Forsothe,' seyde he, 'I am hole of body, thanked be oure Lorde. Therefore, for Goddis love, telle me where I am.'

Than seyde they all that he was in the castell of Carbonek.

Therewith com a jantillwoman and brought hym a shirte of small lynen clothe; but he chaunged nat there, but toke the hayre to hym agayne.

'Sir,' seyde they, 'the queste of the Sankgreall ys encheved now ryght in you, and never shall ye se of Sankgreall more than ye have sene.'

'Now I thanke God,' seyde sir Launcelot, 'for Hys grete mercy of that I have sene, for hit suffisith me. For, as I suppose, no man in thys worlde have lyved bettir than I have done to enchyeve that I have done.'

And therewith he toke the hayre and clothed hym in hit, and aboven that he put a lynen shirte, and aftir that a roobe of scarlet, freyssh and new. And whan he was so arayed they mervayled all, for they knew hym well that he was sir Launcelot, the good knyght. And than they seyde all,

'A, my lorde sir Launcelott, ye be he?'

And he seyde, 'Yee truly, I am he.'

Than came worde to the kynge Pelles that the knyght that had layne so longe dede was the noble knyght sir Launcelot. Than was the kynge ryght glad and wente to se hym, and whan sir Launcelot saw hym com he dressed hym ayenste hym, and than made the kynge grete joy of hym. And there the kynge tolde hym tydynges how his fayre doughter was dede. Than sir Launcelot was ryght hevy and seyde,

'Me forthynkith of the deth of youre doughter, for she was a full fayre lady, freyshe and yonge. And well I wote she bare the beste knyght that ys now on erthe, or that ever was syn God was borne.'

So the kynge hylde hym there four dayes, and on the morow he toke hys leve at kynge Pelles and at all the felyship, and thanked them of the grete laboure.

Ryght so as they sate at her dyner in the chyff halle, hit befylle that the Sangreall had fulfylled the table with all metis that ony harte myght thynke. And as they sate they saw all the doorys of the paleyse and wyndowes shutte withoute mannys honde. So were they all abaysshed. So a knyght whych was all armed cam to the chyeff dore, and knocked and cryed,

'Undo!'

But they wolde nat, and ever he cryed,

'Undo!'

So hit noyed hem so much that the kynge hymselff arose and cam to a wyndow there where the knyght called. Than he seyde,

'Sir knyght, ye shall nat enter at thys tyme, whyle the Sankgreall ys hyre. And therefore go ye into anothir fortresse, for ye be none of the knyghtes of the Quest, but one of them whych have servyd the fyende, and haste leffte the servyse of oure Lorde.'

Than was he passynge wroth at the kynges wordis.

'Sir knyght,' seyde the kynge, 'syn ye wolde so fayne entir, telle me of what contrey ye be.'

'Sir,' he seyde, 'I am of the realme of Logrys, and my name ys sir Ector de Marys, brother unto my lorde sir Launcelot.'

'In the name of God,' seyde the kynge, 'me forthynkis sore of that I have seyde, for youre brother ys hereinne.'

Whan sir Ector undirstood that hys brother was there, for he was the man in the worlde that he moste drad and loved, than he seyde,

'A, good lorde, now dowblith my sorow and shame! Full truly seyde the good man of the hylle unto sir Gawayne and to me of oure dremys.'

Than wente he oute of the courte as faste as hys horse myght, and so thorowoute the castell.

Than kyng Pelles cam to sir Launcelot and tolde hym tydynges of hys brothir. Anone he was sory therefore that he wyst nat what to do. So sir Launcelot departed and toke hys armys and seyde he wold go se the realme of Logris whych he had nat sene afore in a yere, and therewith commaunded the kynge of God.

And so rode thorow many realmys, and at the laste he com to a whyght abbay, and there they made hym that nyght grete chere. And on the morne he arose and hard masse, and afore an awter he founde a ryche tombe which was newly made. And than he toke hede and saw the sydys wryten with golde which seyde,

'Here lyeth kyng Bagdemagus of Gore, which kynge Arthurs nevew slew,' and named hym sir Gawayne.

Than was nat he a litill sory, for sir Launcelot loved hym muche more than ony other and had hit bene ony other than sir Gawayne he sholde nat ascape frome the dethe, and seyde to hymselff,

'A, lorde God! Thys ys a grete hurte unto kynge Arthurs courte, the losse of suche a man!'

And than he departed and cam to the abbey where sir Galahad dud the aventure of the tombis and wan the whyght shylde with the rede crosse. And there had he grete chere all that nyght, and on the morne he turned to Camelot where he founde kynge Arthure and the quene.

But many of the knyghtes of Rounde Table were slayne and destroyed, more than halff; and so three of them were com home, sir Ector, Gawayne, and Lyonell, and many other that nedith nat now to reherce. And all the courte were passyng glad of sir Launcelot, and the kynge asked hym many tydyngis of hys sonne sir Galahad.

And there sir Launcelot tolde the kynge of hys aventures that befelle hym syne he departed. And also he tolde hym of the aventures of sir Galahad, sir Percivale, and sir Bors whych that he knew by the lettir of the ded mayden, and also as sir Galahad had tolde hym.

'Now God wolde,' seyde the kynge, 'that they were all three here!'

'That shall never be,' seyde sir Launcelot, 'for two of hem shall ye never se. But one of them shall com home agayne.'

From Robinson Crusoe
"Friday"

daniel defoe

I NEVER SO MUCH AS TROUBLED MYSELF to consider what I should do with myself when I came thither; what would become of me, if I fell into the hands of the savages; or how I should escape from them, if they attempted me; no, nor so much as how it was possible for me to reach the coast and not be attempted by some or other of them, without any possibility of delivering myself; and if I should not fall into their hands, what I should do for provision, or whither I should bend my course; none of these thoughts, I say, so much as came in my way; but my mind was wholly bent upon the notion of my passing over in my boat to the mainland. I looked back upon my present condition as the most miserable that could possibly be; that I was not able to throw myself into anything but death that could be called worse; that if I reached the shore of the main, I might perhaps meet with relief, or I might coast along, as I did on the shore of Africa, till I came to some inhabited country, and where I might find some relief; and after all, perhaps I might fall in with some Christian ship that might take me in; and if the worse came to the worst, I could but die, which would put an end to all these miseries at once. Pray note, all this was the fruit of a disturbed mind, an impatient temper, made, as it were, desperate by the long continuance of my troubles and the disappointments I had met in the wreck I had been on board of, and where I had been so near the obtaining what I so earnestly longed for, viz., somebody to speak to and to learn some knowledge from of the place where I was and of the probable means of my deliverance; I say, I was agitated wholly by these thoughts. All my calm of mind in my resignation to Providence, and waiting the issue of the dispositions of Heaven, seemed to be suspended; and I had, as it were, no power to turn my thoughts to anything but to the project of a voyage to the main, which came upon me with such force and such an impetuosity of desire that it was not to be resisted.

When this had agitated my thoughts for two hours or more, with such violence that it set my very blood into a ferment, and my pulse beat as high as if I had been in a fever merely with the extraordinary fervor of my mind about it, Nature, as if I had been fatigued and exhausted with the very thought of it, threw me into a sound sleep. One would have thought I should have dreamed of it; but I did not, nor of anything relating to it; but I dreamed that as I was going out in the morning as usual from my castle, I saw upon the shore two canoes and eleven savages coming to land, and that they brought with them another savage, whom they were going to kill, in order to eat him; when on a sudden, the savage that they were going to kill jumped away, and ran for his life; and I thought in my sleep that he came running into my little thick grove, before my fortification, to hide himself; and that I, seeing him alone and not perceiving that the other sought him that way, showed myself to him, and smiling upon him, encouraged him; that he kneeled down to me, seeming to pray me to assist him; upon which I showed my ladder, made him go up, and carried him into my cave, and he became my servant; and that as soon as I had gotten this man, I said to myself, "Now I may certainly venture to the mainland; for this fellow will serve me as a pilot, and will tell me what to do and whither to go for provisions; and whither not to go for fear of being devoured; what places to venture into, and what to escape." I waked with this thought and was under such inexpressible impressions of joy at the prospect of my escape in my dream that the disappointments which I felt upon coming to myself and finding it was no more than a dream were equally extravagant the other way, and threw me into a very great dejection of spirit.

Upon this, however, I made this conclusion, that my only way to go about an attempt for an escape was, if possible, to get a savage into my possession; and if possible, it should be one of their prisoners who they had condemned to be eaten and should bring hither to kill; but these thoughts still were attended with this difficulty, that it was impossible to effect this without attacking a whole caravan of them and killing them all; and this was not only a very desperate attempt and might miscarry, but on the other hand, I had greatly scrupled the lawfulness of it to me; and my heart trembled at the thoughts of shedding so much blood, though it was for my deliverance. I need not repeat the arguments which occurred to me against this, they being the same mentioned before; but though I had other reasons to offer now, viz., that those men were enemies to my life and would devour me if they could; that it was self-preservation, in the highest degree, to deliver myself from this death of a life, and was acting in my own defense as much as if they were actually assaulting me, and the like;

I say, though these things argued for it, yet the thoughts of shedding human blood for my deliverance were very terrible to me, and such as I could by no means reconcile myself to a great while.

However, at last, after many secret disputes with myself and after great perplexities about it, for all these arguments, one way and another, struggled in my head a long time, the eager prevailing desire of deliverance at length mastered all the rest, and I resolved, if possible, to get one of those savages into my hands, cost what it would. My next thing then was to contrive how to do it, and this indeed was very difficult to resolve on. But as I could pitch upon no probable means for it, so I resolved to put myself upon the watch, to see them when they came on shore, and leave the rest to the event, taking such measures as the opportunity should present, let be what would be.

With these resolutions in my thoughts, I set myself upon the scout, as often as possible, and indeed so often till I was heartily tired of it; for it was above a year and half that I waited, and for a great part of that time went out to the west end and to the southwest corner of the island almost every day to see for canoes, but none appeared. This was very discouraging, and began to trouble me much; though I cannot say that it did in this case, as it had done some time before that, viz., wear off the edge of my desire to the thing. But the longer it seemed to be delayed, the more eager I was for it; in a word, I was not at first so careful to shun the sight of these savages and avoid being seen by them as I was now eager to be upon them.

Besides, I fancied myself able to manage one, nay, two or three savages, if I had them, so as to make them entirely slaves to me, to do whatever I should direct them and to prevent their being able at any time to do me any hurt. It was a great while that I pleased myself with this affair, but nothing still presented; all my fancies and schemes came to nothing, for no savages came near me for a great while.

About a year and half after I had entertained these notions and, by long musing, had as it were resolved them all into nothing, for want of an occasion to put them in execution, I was surprised one morning early with seeing no less than five canoes all on shore together on my side the island; and the people who belonged to them all landed, and out of my sight. The number of them broke all my measures, for seeing so many and knowing that they always came four or six, or sometimes more in a boat, I could not tell what to think of it, or how to take my measures, to attack twenty or thirty men singlehanded; so I lay still in my castle, perplexed and discomforted. However, I put myself into all the same postures for an attack that I had formerly provided and was just ready for action if anything had presented; having waited a good while, listening to hear if they made any noise, at length being very impatient, I set my guns at the foot of my ladder and clambered up to the top of the hill by my two stages as usual; standing so, however, that my head did not appear above the hill, so that they could not perceive me by any means; here I observed by the help of my perspective-glass that they were no less than thirty in number, that they had a fire kindled, that they had had meat dressed. How they had cooked it, that I knew not, or what it was; but they were all dancing in I know not how many barbarous gestures and figures, their own way, round the fire.

While I was thus looking on them, I perceived by my perspective two miserable wretches dragged from the boats, where, it seems, they were laid by, and were now brought out for the slaughter, I perceived one of them immediately fell, being knocked down, I suppose, with a club or wooden sword, for that was their way, and two or three others were at work immediately, cutting him open for their cookery, while the other victim was left standing by himself, till they should be ready for him. In that very moment, this poor wretch seeing himself a little at liberty, Nature inspired him with hopes of life, and he started away from them, and ran with incredible swiftness along the sands directly towards me, I mean towards that part of the coast where my habitation was.

I was dreadfully frighted (that I must acknowledge) when I perceived him to run my way; and especially, when, as I thought, I saw him pursued by the whole body; and now I expected that part of my dream was coming to pass, and that he would certainly take shelter in my grove; but I could not depend by any means upon my dream for the rest of it, viz., that the other savages would not pursue him thither, and find him there. However, I kept my station, and my spirits began to recover when I found that there was not above three men that followed him; and still more was I encouraged when I found that he outstripped them exceedingly in running and gained ground of them; so that if he could but hold it for half an hour, I saw easily he would fairly get away from them all.

There was between them and my castle the creek which I mentioned often at the first part of my story, when I landed my cargoes out of the ship; and this I saw plainly he must necessarily swim over, or the poor wretch would be taken there. But when the savage escaping came thither, he made nothing of it, though the tide was then up, but plunging in, swam through in about thirty strokes or thereabouts, landed, and ran on with exceeding strength and swiftness; when the three persons came to the creek, I found that two of them could swim, but the third could not, and that standing on the other side, he looked at the other, but went no further; and soon after went softly back again; which, as it happened, was very well for him in the main.

I observed that the two who swam were yet more than twice as long swimming over the creek as the fellow was that fled from them. It came now very warmly upon my thoughts, and indeed irresistibly, that now was my time to get me a servant, and perhaps a companion, or assistant; and that I was called plainly by Providence to save this poor creature's life; I immediately run down the ladders with all possible expedition, fetched my two guns, for they were both but at the foot of the ladders, as I observed above; and getting up again, with the same haste, to the top of the hill, I crossed toward the sea; and having a very short cut, and all down hill, clapped myself in the way between the pursuers and the pursued; hallooing aloud to him that fled, who, looking back, was at first perhaps as much frighted at me as at them; but I beckoned with my hand to him to come back; and in the meantime, I slowly advanced towards the two that followed; then rushing at once upon the foremost, I knocked him down with the stock of my piece; I was loath to fire, because I would not have the rest hear; though at that distance, it would not have been easily heard, and being out of sight of the smoke too, they would not have easily known what to make of it. Having knocked this fellow down, the other who pursued with him stopped, as if he had been frighted; and I advanced apace towards him; but as I came nearer, I perceived presently he had a bow and arrow and was fitting it to shoot at me; so I was then necessitated to shoot at him first, which I did, and killed him at the first shoot; the poor savage who fled, but had stopped, though he saw both his enemies fallen and killed, as he thought, yet was so frighted with the fire and noise of my piece, that he stood stock still and neither came forward or went backward, though he seemed rather inclined to fly still than to come on; I hallooed again to him, and made signs to come forward, which he easily understood and came a little way, then stopped again and then a little further and stopped again, and I could then perceive that he stood trembling, as if he had been taken prisoner, and had just been to be killed, as his two enemies were; I beckoned him again to come to me and gave him all the signs of encouragement that I could think of, and he came nearer and nearer, kneeling down every ten or twelve steps in token of acknowledgment for my saving his life. I smiled at him and looked pleasantly and beckoned to him to come still nearer; at length he came close to me, and then he kneeled down again, kissed the ground, and laid his head upon the ground, and, taking me by the foot, set my foot upon his head; this, it seems, was in token of swearing to be my slave forever; I took him up, and made much of him, and encouraged him all I could. But there was more work to do yet, for I perceived the savage who I knocked down was not killed, but stunned with the blow, and began to come to himself; so I pointed to him, and showing him the savage, that he was not dead; upon this he spoke some words to me, and though I could not understand them, yet I thought they were pleasant to hear, for they were the first sound of a man's voice that I had heard, my own excepted, for about twenty-five years. But there was no time for such reflections now; the savage who was knocked down recovered himself so far as to sit up upon the ground, and I perceived that my savage began to be afraid; but when I saw that, I presented my other piece at the man as if I would shoot him; upon this my savage, for so I call him now, made a motion to me to lend him my sword, which hung naked in a belt by my side; so I did. He no sooner had it, but he runs to his enemy, and at one blow cut off his head as cleverly, no executioner in Germany could have done it sooner or better; which I thought very strange for one who I had reason to believe never saw a sword in his life before, except their own wooden swords; however, it seems, as I learned afterwards, they make their wooden swords so sharp, so heavy, and the wood is so hard, that they will cut off heads even with them, ay, and arms, and that at one blow too; when he had done this, he comes laughing to me in sign of triumph and brought me the sword again, and with abundance of gestures which I did not understand, laid it down, with the head of the savage that he had killed, just before me.

But that which astonished him most was to know how I had killed the other Indian so far off; so pointing to him, he made signs to me to let him go to him; so I bade him go, as well as I could; when he came to him, he stood like one amazed, looking at him, turned him first on one side, then on t' other, looked at the wound the bullet had made, which, it seems, was just in his breast, where it had made a hole, and no great quantity of blood had followed, but he had bled inwardly, for he was quite dead. He took up his bow and arrows, and came back; so I turned to go away and beckoned to him to follow me, making signs to him that more might come after them.

Upon this he signed to me that he should bury them with sand, that they might not be seen by the rest if they followed; and so I made signs again to him to do so; he fell to work, and in an instant he had scraped a hole in the sand with his hands big enough to bury the first in, and then dragged him into it and covered him and did so also by the other; I believe he had buried them both in a quarter of an hour; then calling him away, I carried him, not to my castle, but quite away to my cave, on the farther part of the island; so I did not let my dream come to pass in that part, viz., that he came into my grove for shelter.

Here I gave him bread and a bunch of raisins to eat, and a draught of water, which I found he was indeed in great distress for, by his running; and having refreshed him, I made signs for him to go lie down and sleep, pointing to a place where I had laid a great parcel of rice-straw and a blanket upon it, which I used to sleep upon myself sometimes; so the poor creature laid down and went to sleep.

He was a comely, handsome fellow, perfectly well made, with straight strong limbs, not too large; tall and well-shaped, and, as I reckon, about twenty-six years of age. He had a very good countenance, not a fierce and surly aspect; but seemed to have something very manly in his face, and yet he had all the sweetness and softness of an European in his countenance too, especially when he smiled. His hair was long and black, not curled like wool; his forehead very high and large; and a great vivacity and sparkling sharpness in his eyes. The color of his skin was not quite black, but very tawny; and yet not of an ugly, yellow, nauseous tawny, as the Brazilians and Virginians, and other natives of America are; but of a bright kind of a dun olive color that had in it something very agreeable, though not very easy to describe. His face was round and plump; his nose small, not flat like the Negroes; a very good mouth, thin lips, and his fine teeth well set, and white as ivory. After he had slumbered, rather than slept, about half an hour, he waked again, and comes out of the cave to me; for I had been milking my goats, which I had in the enclosure just by. When he espied me, he came running to me, laying himself down again upon the ground, with all the possible signs of an humble, thankful disposition, making a many antic gestures to show it. At last he lays his head flat upon the ground, close to my foot, and sets my other foot upon his head, as he had done before; and after this, made all the signs to me of subjection, servitude, and submission imaginable, to let me know how he would serve me as long as he lived; I understood him in many things and let him know I was very well pleased with him; in a little time I began to speak to him and teach him to speak to me; and first, I made him know his name should be *Friday,* which was the day I saved his life; I called him so for the memory of the time; I likewise taught him to say *Master,* and then let him know that was to be my name; I likewise taught him to say *Yes* and *No* and to know the meaning of them; I gave him some milk in an earthen pot and let him see me drink it before him and sop my bread in it; and I gave him a cake of bread to do the like, which he quickly complied with, and made signs that it was very good for him.

I kept there with him all that night; but as soon as it was day, I beckoned to him to come with me, and let him know I would give him some clothes, at which he seemed very glad, for he was stark naked. As we went by the place where he had buried the two men, he pointed exactly to the place and showed me the marks that he had made to find them again, making signs to me that we should dig them up again and eat them; at this I appeared very angry, expressed my abhorrence of it, made as if I would vomit at the thoughts of it, and beckoned with my hand to him to come away, which he did immediately, with great submission. I then led him up to the top of the hill, to see if his enemies were gone; and pulling out my glass, I looked, and saw plainly the place where they had been, but no appearance of them or of their canoes; so that it was plain they were gone and had left their two comrades behind them, without any search after them.

But I was not content with this discovery; but having now more courage, and consequently more curiosity, I takes my man Friday with me, giving him the sword in his hand, with the bow and arrows at his back, which I found he could use very dexterously, making him carry one gun for me, and I two for myself, and away we marched to the place where these creatures had been; for I had a mind now to get some fuller intelligence of them. When I came to the place, my very blood ran chill in my veins and my heart sunk within me at the horror of the spectacle. Indeed it was a dreadful sight, at least it was so to me, though Friday made nothing of it. The place was covered with human bones, the ground dyed with their blood, great pieces of flesh left here and there, half eaten, mangled and scorched; and in short, of all the tokens of the triumphant feast they had been making there, after a victory over their enemies. I saw three skulls, five hands, and the bones of three or four legs and feet, and abundance of other parts of the bodies; and Friday, by his signs, made me understand that they brought over four prisoners to feast upon; that three of them were eaten up and that he, pointing to himself, was the fourth; that there had been a great battle between them and their next king, whose subjects it seems he had been one of; and that they had taken a great number of prisoners, all which were carried to several places by those that had taken them in the fight, in order to feast upon them, as was done here by these wretches upon those they brought hither.

I caused Friday to gather all the skulls, bones, flesh, and whatever remained, and lay them together on a heap and make a great fire upon it and burn them all to ashes. I found Friday had still a hankering stomach after some of the flesh, and was still a cannibal in his nature; but I discovered so much abhorrence at the very thoughts of it and at the least appearance of it that he durst not discover it; for I had by some means let him know that I would kill him if he offered it.

When we had done this, we came back to our castle, and there I fell to work for my man Friday; and first of all, I gave him a pair of linen drawers, which I had out of the poor gunner's chest I mentioned, and which I found in the wreck; and which with a little alteration fitted him very well; then I made him a jerkin of goat's skin, as well as my skill would allow, and I was grown a tolerable good tailor; and I gave him a cap, which I had made of a hare-skin, very convenient and fashionable enough; and thus he was clothed for the present tolerably well; and was mighty well pleased to see himself almost as well clothed as his master. It is true, he went awkwardly in these things at first; wearing the drawers was very awkward to him, and the sleeves of the waistcoat galled his shoulders and the inside of his arms; but a little easing them where he complained they hurt him and using himself to them, at length he took to them very well.

The next day after I came home to my hutch with him, I began to consider where I should lodge him; and that I might do well for him and yet be perfectly easy myself, I made a little tent for him in the vacant place between my two fortifications, in the inside of the last and in the outside of the first; and as there was a door or entrance there into my cave, I made a formal framed door-case, and a door to it of boards, and set it up in the passage, a little within the entrance; and causing the door to open on the inside, I barred it up in the night, taking in my ladders too; so that Friday could no way come at me in the inside of my innermost wall without making so much noise in getting over that it must needs waken me; for my first wall had now a complete roof over it of long poles, covering all my tent and leaning up to the side of the hill, which was again laid across with smaller sticks instead of laths, and then thatched over a great thickness with the rice-straw, which was strong like reeds; and at the hole or place which was left to go in or out by the ladder I had placed a kind of trapdoor, which, if it had been attempted on the outside, would not have opened at all, but would have fallen down and made a great noise; and as to weapons, I took them all into my side every night.

But I needed none of all this precaution; for never man had a more faithful, loving, sincere servant than Friday was to me; without passions, sullenness, or designs, perfectly obliged and engaged; his very affections were tied to me, like those of a child to a father; and I dare say he would have sacrificed his life for the saving mine upon any occasion whatsoever; the many testimonies he gave me of this put it out of doubt and soon convinced me that I needed to use no precautions as to my safety on his account.

This frequently gave me occasion to observe, and that with wonder, that however it had pleased God, in His providence, and in the government of the works of His hands, to take from so great a part of the world of His creatures the best uses to which their faculties and the powers of their souls are adapted, yet that He has bestowed upon them the same powers, the same reason, the same affections, the same sentiments of kindness and obligation, the same passions and resentments of wrongs, the same sense of gratitude, sincerity, fidelity, and all the capacities of doing good and receiving good that He has given to us; and that when He pleases to offer to them occasions of exerting these, they are as ready, nay, more ready apply them to the right uses for which they were bestowed than we are. And this made me very melancholy sometimes, in reflecting, as the several occasions presented, how mean a use we make of all these, even though we have these powers enlightened by the great lamp of instruction, the Spirit of God, and by the knowledge of His Word, added to our understanding; and why it has pleased God to hide the like saving knowledge from so many millions of souls, who, if I might judge by this poor savage, would make a much better use of it than we did.

From hence, I sometimes was led too far to invade the sovereignty of Providence and, as it were, arraign the justice of so arbitrary a disposition of things that should hide that light from some and reveal it to others, and yet expect a like duty from both. But I shut it up and checked my thoughts with this conclusion; first, that we did not know by what light and law these should be condemned; but that as God was necessarily, and by the nature of His being, infinitely holy and just, so it could not be but that if these creatures were all sentenced to absence from Himself, it was on account of sinning against that light which, as the Scripture says, was a law to themselves, and by such rules as their consciences would acknowledge to be just, though the foundation was not discovered to us. And second, that still, as we are all the clay in the hand of the Potter, no vessel could say to Him, "Why hast Thou formed me thus?"

But to return to my new companion: I was greatly delighted with him and made it my business to teach him everything that was proper to make him useful, handy, and helpful; but especially to make him speak and understand me when I spake; and he was the aptest scholar that ever was, and particularly was so merry, so constantly diligent, and so pleased when he could but understand me or make me understand him that it was very pleasant to me to talk to him; and now my life began to be so easy that I began to say to myself that could I but have been safe from more savages, I cared not if I was never to remove from the place while I lived.

After I had been two or three days returned to my castle, I thought that, in order to bring Friday off from his horrid way of feeding and from the relish of a cannibal's stomach, I ought to let him taste other flesh; so I took him out with me one morning to the woods. I went, indeed, intending to kill a kid out of my own flock and bring him home and dress it. But as I was going, I saw a she-goat lying down in the shade and two young kids sitting by her; I catched hold of Friday. "Hold," says I, "stand still"; and made signs to him not to stir; immediately I presented my piece, shot and killed one of the kids. The poor creature, who had at a distance, indeed, seen me kill the savage, his enemy, but did not know or could imagine how it was done, was sensibly surprised, trembled and shook, and looked so amazed that I thought he would have sunk down. He did not see the kid I had shot at, or perceive I had killed it, but ripped up his waistcoat to feel if he was not wounded, and, as I found presently, thought I was resolved to kill him; for he came and kneeled down to me and, embracing my knees, said a great many things I did not understand; but I could easily see that the meaning was to pray me not to kill him.

I soon found a way to convince him that I would do him no harm and, taking him up by the hand, laughed at him and pointed to the kid which I had killed, beckoned to him to run and fetch it, which he did; and while he was wondering and looking to see how the creature was killed, I loaded my gun again, and by and by I saw a great fowl, like a hawk, sit upon a tree, within shot; so, to let Friday understand a little what I would do, I called him to me again, pointed at the fowl, which was indeed a parrot, though I thought it had been a hawk; I say, pointing to the parrot and to my gun and to the ground under the parrot, to let him see I would make it fall, I made him understand that I would shoot and kill that bird; accordingly I fired and bade him look, and immediately he saw the parrot fall, he stood like one frighted again, notwithstanding all I had said to him; and I found he was the more amazed because he did not see me put anything into the gun; but thought that there must be some wonderful fund of death and destruction in that thing, able to kill man, beast, bird, or anything near or far off; and the astonishment this created in him was such as could not wear off for a long time; and I believe, if I would have let him, he would have worshiped me and my gun. As for the gun itself, he would not so much as touch it for several days after; but would speak to it and talk to it as if it had answered him, when he was by himself; which, as I afterwards learned of him, was to desire it not to kill him.

Well, after his astonishment was a little over at this, I pointed to him to run and fetch the bird I had shot, which he did, but stayed some time; for the parrot, not being quite dead, was fluttered away a good way off from the place where she fell; however, he found her, took her up, and brought her to me; and as I had perceived his ignorance about the gun before, I took this advantage to charge the gun again and not let him see me do it, that I might be ready for any other mark might present; but nothing more offered at that time; so I brought home the kid, and the same evening I took the skin off and cut it out as well as I could; and having a pot for that purpose, I boiled, or stewed, some of the flesh, and made some very good broth; and after I had begun to eat some, I gave some to my man, who seemed very glad of it and liked it very well; but that which was strangest to him was to see me eat salt with it; he made a sign to me that the salt was not good to eat, and putting a little into his own mouth, he seemed to nauseate it, and would spit and sputter at it, washing his mouth with fresh water after it; on the other hand, I took some meat in my mouth without salt, and I pretended to spit and sputter for want of salt, as fast as he had done at the salt; but it would not do; he would never care for salt with his meat or in his broth; at least, not a great while, and then but a very little.

Having thus fed him with boiled meat and broth, I was resolved to feast him the next day with roasting a piece of the kid; this I did by hanging it before the fire in a string, as I had seen many people do in England, setting two poles up, one on each side the fire, and one cross on the top, and tying the string to the cross-stick, letting the meat turn continually. This Friday admired very much; but when he came to taste the flesh, he took so many ways to tell me how well he liked it that I could not but understand him; and at last he told me he would never eat man's flesh any more, which I was very glad to hear.

The next day I set him to work to beating some corn out, and sifting it in the manner I used to do, as I observed before, and he soon understood how to do it as well as I, especially after he had seen what the meaning of it was, and that it was to make bread of; for after that I let him see me make my bread and bake it too, and in a little time Friday was able to do all the work for me, as well as I could do it myself.

I began now to consider that having two mouths to feed instead of one, I must provide more ground for my harvest and plant a larger quantity of corn than I used to do; so I marked out a larger piece of land and began the fence in the same manner as before, in which Friday not only worked very willingly and very hard but did it very cheerfully; and I told him what it was for, that it was for corn to make more bread, because he was now with me, and that I might have enough for him and myself too. He appeared very sensible of that part and let me know that he thought I had much more labor upon me on his account than I had for myself; and that he would work the harder for me, if I would tell him what to do.

Young
Goodman Brown

nathaniel hawthorne

YOUNG GOODMAN BROWN CAME FORTH AT SUNSET into the street at Salem village; but put his head back, after crossing the threshold, to exchange a parting kiss with his young wife. And Faith, as the wife was aptly named, thrust her own pretty head into the street, letting the wind play with the pink ribbons of her cap while she called to Goodman Brown.

"Dearest heart," whispered she, softly and rather sadly, when her lips were close to his ear, "prithee put off your journey until sunrise and sleep in your own bed to-night. A lone woman is troubled with such dreams and such thoughts that she's afeared of herself sometimes. Pray tarry with me this night, dear husband, of all nights in the year."

"My love and my Faith," replied young Goodman Brown, "of all nights in the year, this one night must I tarry away from thee. My journey, as thou callest it, forth and back again, must needs be done 'twixt now and sunrise. What, my sweet, pretty wife, dost thou doubt me already, and we but three months married?"

"Then God bless you!" said Faith, with the pink ribbons; "and may you find all well when you come back."

"Amen!" cried Goodman Brown. "Say thy prayers, dear Faith, and go to bed at dusk, and no harm will come to thee."

So they parted; and the young man pursued his way until, being about to turn the corner by the meeting-house, he looked back and saw the head of Faith still peeping after him with a melancholy air, in spite of her pink ribbons.

"Poor little Faith!" thought he, for his heart smote him. "What a wretch am I to leave her on such an errand! She talks of dreams, too. Methought as she spoke there was trouble in her face, as if a dream had warned her what work is to be done to-night. But no, no; 'twould kill her to think of it. Well, she's a blessed angel on earth; and after this one night I'll cling to her skirts and follow her to heaven."

With this excellent resolve for the future, Goodman Brown felt himself justified in making more haste on his present evil purpose. He had taken a dreary road, darkened by all the gloomiest trees of the forest, which barely stood aside to let the narrow path creep through, and closed immediately behind. It was all as lonely as could be; and there is this peculiarity in such a solitude, that the traveller knows not who may be concealed by the innumerable trunks and the thick boughs overhead; so that with lonely footsteps he may yet be passing through an unseen multitude.

"There may be a devilish Indian behind every tree," said Goodman Brown to himself; and he glanced fearfully behind him as he added, "What if the devil himself should be at my very elbow!"

His head being turned back, he passed a crook of the road, and, looking forward again, beheld the figure of a man, in grave and decent attire, seated at the foot of an old tree. He arose at Goodman Brown's approach and walked onward side by side with him.

"You are late, Goodman Brown," said he. "The clock of the Old South was striking as I came through Boston, and that is full fifteen minutes agone."

"Faith kept me back a while," replied the young man, with a tremor in his voice, caused by the sudden appearance of his companion, though not wholly unexpected.

It was now deep dusk in the forest, and deepest in that part of it where these two were journeying. As nearly as could be discerned, the second traveller was about fifty years old, apparently in the same rank of life as Goodman Brown, and bearing a considerable resemblance to him, though perhaps more in expression than features. Still they might have been taken for father and son. And yet, though the elder person was as simply clad as the younger, and as simple in manner too, he had an indescribable air of one who knew the world, and who would not have felt abashed at the governor's dinner table or in King William's court, were it possible that his affairs should call him thither. But the only thing about him that could be fixed upon as remarkable was his staff, which bore the likeness of a great black snake, so curiously wrought that it might almost be seen to twist and wriggle itself like a living serpent. This, of course, must have been an ocular deception, assisted by the uncertain light.

"Come, Goodman Brown," cried his fellow-traveller, "this is a dull place for the beginning of a journey. Take my staff, if you are so soon weary."

"Friend," said the other, exchanging his slow pace for a full stop, "having kept covenant by meeting thee here, it is my purpose now to return whence I came. I have scruples touching the matter thou wot'st of."

"Sayest thou so?" replied he of the serpent, smiling apart. "Let us walk on, nevertheless, reasoning as we go; and if I convince thee not thou shalt turn back. We are but a little way in the forest yet."

"Too far! too far!" exclaimed the goodman, unconsciously resuming his walk, "My father never went into the woods on such an errand, nor his father before him. We have been a race of honest men and good Christians since the days of the martyrs; and shall I be the first of the name of Brown that ever took this path and kept——"

"Such company, thou wouldst say," observed the elder person, interpreting his pause. "Well said, Goodman Brown! I have been as well acquainted with your family as with ever a one among the Puritans; and that's no trifle to say. I helped your grandfather, the constable, when he lashed the Quaker woman so smartly through the streets of Salem; and it was I that brought your father a pitch-pine knot, kindled at my own hearth, to set fire to an Indian village, in King Philip's war. They were my good friends, both; and many a pleasant walk have we had along this path, and returned merrily after midnight. I would fain be friends with you for their sake."

"If it be as thou sayest," replied Goodman Brown, "I marvel they never spoke of these matters; or, verily, I marvel not, seeing that the least rumor of the sort would have driven them from New England. We are a people of prayer, and good works to boot, and abide no such wickedness."

"Wickedness or not," said the traveller with the twisted staff, "I have a very general acquaintance here in New England. The deacons of many a church have drunk the communion wine with me; the selectmen of divers towns make me their chairman; and a majority of the Great and General Court are firm supporters of my interest. The governor and I, too—— But these are state secrets."

"Can this be so?" cried Goodman Brown, with a stare of amazement at his undisturbed companion. "Howbeit, I have nothing to do with the governor and council; they have their own ways, and are no rule for a simple husbandman like me. But, were I to go on with thee, how should I meet the eye of that good old man, our minister, at Salem village? Oh, his voice would make me tremble both Sabbath day and lecture day."

Thus far the elder traveller had listened with due gravity; but now burst into a fit of irrepressible mirth, shaking himself so violently that his snakelike staff actually seemed to wriggle in sympathy.

"Ha! ha! ha!" shouted he again and again; then composing himself, "Well, go on, Goodman Brown, go on; but, prithee, don't kill me with laughing."

"Well, then, to end the matter at once," said Goodman Brown, considerably nettled, "there is my wife, Faith. It would break her dear little heart; and I'd rather break my own."

"Nay, if that be the case," answered the other, "e'en go thy ways, Goodman Brown. I would not for twenty old women like the one hobbling before us that Faith should come to any harm."

As he spoke he pointed his staff at a female figure on the path, in whom Goodman Brown recognized a very pious and exemplary dame, who had taught him his catechism in youth, and was still his moral and spiritual adviser, jointly with the minister and Deacon Gookin.

"A marvel, truly, that Goody Cloyse should be so far in the wilderness at nightfall," said he. "But with your leave, friend, I shall take a cut through the woods until we have left this Christian woman behind. Being a stranger to you, she might ask whom I was consorting with and whither I was going."

"Be it so." said his fellow-traveller. "Betake you to the woods, and let me keep the path."

Accordingly the young man turned aside, but took care to watch his companion, who advanced softly along the road until he had come within a staff's length of the old dame. She, meanwhile, was making the best of her way, with singular speed for so aged a woman, and mumbling some indistinct words—a prayer, doubtless—as she went. The traveller put forth his staff and touched her withered neck with what seemed the serpent's tail.

"The devil!" screamed the pious old lady.

"Then Goody Cloyse knows her old friend?" observed the traveller, confronting her and leaning on his writhing stick.

"Ah, forsooth, and is it your worship indeed?" cried the good dame. "Yea, truly is it, and in the very image of my old gossip, Goodman Brown, the grandfather of the silly fellow that now is. But—would your worship believe it—my broomstick hath strangely disappeared, stolen, as I suspect, by that unhanged witch, Goody Cory, and that, too, when I was all anointed with the juice of smallage, and cinquefoil, and wolf's bane—"

"Mingled with fine wheat and the fat of a new-born babe," said the shape of old Goodman Brown.

"Ah, your worship knows the recipe," cried the old lady, cackling aloud. "So, as I was saying, being all ready for the meeting, and no horse to ride on, I made up my mind to foot it; for they tell me there is a nice young man to be taken into communion tonight. But now your good worship will lend me your arm, and we shall be there in a twinkling."

"That can hardly be," answered her friend, "I may not spare you my arm, Goody Cloyse; but here is my staff, If you will."

So saying, he threw it down at her feet, where, perhaps, it assumed life, being one of the rods which its owner had formerly lent to the Egyptian magi. Of this fact, however, Goodman Brown could not take cognizance. He had cast up his eyes in astonishment, and, looking down again, beheld neither

Goody Cloyse nor the serpentine staff, but his fellow-traveller alone, who waited for him as calmly as if nothing had happened.

"That old woman taught me my catechism," said the young man; and there was a world of meaning in this simple comment.

They continued to walk onward, while the elder traveller exhorted his companion to make good speed and persevere in the path, discoursing so aptly that his arguments seemed rather to spring up in the bosom of his auditor than to be suggested by himself. As they went, he plucked a branch of maple to serve for a walking stick, and began to strip it of the twigs and little boughs, which were wet with evening dew. The moment his fingers touched them they became strangely withered and dried up as with a week's sunshine. Thus the pair proceeded, at a good free pace, until suddenly, in a gloomy hollow of the road, Goodman Brown sat himself down on the stump of a tree and refused to go any farther.

"Friend," said he, stubbornly, "my mind is made up. Not another step will I budge on this errand. What if a wretched old woman do choose to go to the devil when I thought she was going to heaven: is that any reason why I should quit my dear Faith and go after her?"

"You will think better of this by and by." said his acquaintance, composedly. "Sit here and rest yourself a while; and when you feel like moving again, there is my staff to help you along."

Without more words, he threw his companion the maple stick, and was as speedily out of sight as if he had vanished into the deepening gloom. The young man sat a few moments by the roadside, applauding himself greatly, and thinking with how clear a conscience he should meet the minister in his morning walk, nor shrink from the eye of good old Deacon Gookin. And what calm sleep would be his that very night, which was to have been spent so wickedly, but so purely and sweetly now, in the arms of Faith! Amidst these pleasant and praiseworthy meditations, Goodman Brown heard the tramp of horses along the road, and deemed it advisable to conceal himself within the verge of the forest, conscious of the guilty purpose that had brought him thither, though now so happily turned from it.

On came the hoof tramps and the voices of the riders, two grave old voices, conversing soberly as they drew near. These mingled sounds appeared to pass along the road, within a few yards of the young man's hiding-place; but, owing doubtless to the depth of the gloom at that particular spot, neither the travellers nor their steeds were visible. Though their figures brushed the small boughs by the wayside, it could not be seen that they intercepted, even for a moment, the faint gleam from the strip of bright sky athwart which they must have passed. Goodman Brown alternately crouched and stood on tiptoe, pulling aside the branches and thrusting forth his head as far as he durst without discerning so much as a shadow. It vexed him the more, because he could have sworn, were such a thing possible, that he recognized the voices of the minister and Deacon Gookin, jogging along quietly, as they were wont to do, when bound to some ordination or ecclesiastical council. While yet within hearing, one of the riders stopped to pluck a switch.

"Of the two, reverend sir," said the voice like the deacon's, "I had rather miss an ordination dinner than to-night's meeting. They tell me that some of our community are to be here from Falmouth and beyond, and others from Connecticut and Rhode Island, besides several of Indian powwows, who, after their fashion, know almost as much deviltry as the best of us. Moreover, there is a goodly young woman to be taken into communion."

"Mighty well, Deacon Gookin!" replied the solemn old tones of the minister. "Spur up, or we shall be late. Nothing can be done you know until I get on the ground."

The hoofs clattered again; and the voices, talking so strangely in the empty air, passed on through the forest, where no church had ever been gathered or solitary Christian prayed. Whither, then, could these holy men be journeying so deep into the heathen wilderness? Young Goodman Brown caught hold of a tree for support, being ready to sink down on the ground, faint and overburdened with the heavy sickness of his heart. He looked up to the sky, doubting whether there really was a heaven above him. Yet there was the blue arch, and the stars brightening in it.

"With heaven above and Faith below, I will yet stand firm against the devil!" cried Goodman Brown.

While he still gazed upward into the deep arch of the firmament and had lifted his hands to pray, a cloud, though no wind was stirring, hurried across the zenith and hid the brightening stars. The blue sky was still visible, except directly overhead, where this black mass of cloud was sweeping swiftly northward. Aloft in the air, as if from the depths of the cloud, came a confused and doubtful sound of voices. Once the listener fancied that he could distinguish the accents of towns-people of his own, men, and women, both pious and ungodly, many of whom he had met at the communion table, and had seen others rioting at the tavern. The next moment, so indistinct were the sounds, he doubted whether he had heard aught but the murmur of the old forest, whispering without a wind. Then came a stronger swell of those familiar tones, heard daily in the sunshine at Salem village, but never until now from a cloud of night. There was one voice of a young woman, uttering lamentations, yet with an uncertain sorrow, and entreating for some favor, which, perhaps, it would grieve her to obtain; and all the unseen multitude, both saints and sinners, seemed to encourage her onward.

"Faith!" shouted Goodman Brown, in a voice of agony and desperation; and the echoes of the forest mocked him, crying, "Faith! Faith!" as if bewildered wretches were seeking her all through the wilderness.

The cry of grief, rage, and terror was yet piercing the night, when the unhappy husband held his breath for a response. There was a scream, drowned immediately in a louder murmer of voices, fading into far-off laughter, as the dark cloud swept away, leaving the clear and silent sky above Goodman Brown. But something fluttered lightly down through the air and caught on the branch of a tree. The young man seized it, and beheld a pink ribbon.

"My Faith is gone!" cried he, after one stupefied moment. "There is no good on earth; and sin is but a name. Come, devil; for to thee is this world given."

And, maddened with despair, so that he laughed loud and long, did Goodman Brown grasp his staff and set forth again, at such a rate that he seemed to fly along the forest path rather than to walk or run. The road grew wilder and drearier and more faintly traced, and vanished at length, leaving him in the heart of the dark wilderness, still rushing onward with the instinct that guides mortal man to evil. The whole forest was peopled with frightful sounds—the creaking of the trees, the howling of wild beasts, and the yell of Indians; while sometimes the wind tolled like a distant church bell, and sometimes gave a broad roar around the traveller, as if all Nature were laughing him to scorn. But he was himself the chief horror of the scene, and shrank not from its other horrors.

"Ha! ha! ha!" roared Goodman Brown when the wind laughed at him. "Let us hear which will laugh loudest. Think not to frighten me with your deviltry. Come witch, come wizard, come Indian pow-wow, come devil himself, and here comes Goodman Brown. You may as well fear him as he fear you."

In truth, all through the haunted forest there could be nothing more frightful than the figure of Goodman Brown. On he flew among the black pines, brandishing his staff with frenzied gestures, now giving vent to an inspiration of horrid blasphemy, and now shouting forth such laughter as set all the echoes of the forest laughing like demons around him. The fiend in his own shape is less hideous than when he rages in the breast of man. Thus sped the demoniac on his course, until, quivering among the trees, he saw a red light before him, as when the felled trunks and branches of a clearing have been set on fire, and throw up their lurid blaze against the sky, at the hour of midnight. He paused, in a lull of the tempest that had driven him onward, and heard the swell of what seemed a hymn, rolling solemnly from a distance with the weight of many voices. He knew the tune; it was a familiar one in the choir of the village meeting-house. The verse died heavily away, and was lengthened by a chorus, not of human voices, but of all the sounds of the benighted wilderness pealing in awful harmony together. Goodman Brown cried out, and his cry was lost to his own ear by its unison with the cry of the desert.

In the interval of silence he stole forward until the light glared full upon his eyes. At one extremity of an open space, hemmed in by the dark wall of the forest arose a rock, bearing some rude, natural resemblance either to an altar or a pulpit, and surrounded by four blazing pines, their tops aflame, their stems untouched, like candles at an evening meeting. The mass of foliage that had overgrown the summit of the rock was all on fire, blazing high into the night and fitfully illuminating the whole field. Each pendent twig and leafy festoon was in a blaze. As the red light arose and fell, a numerous congregation alternately shone forth, then disappeared in shadow, and again grew, as it were, out of the darkness, peopling the heart of the solitary woods at once.

"A grave and dark-clad company," quoth Goodman Brown.

In truth they were such. Among them, quivering to and fro between gloom and splendor, appeared faces that would be seen next day at the council board of the province, and others which, Sabbath after Sabbath, looked devoutly heavenward, and benignantly over the crowded pews, from the holiest pulpits in the land. Some affirm that the lady of the governor was there. At least there were high dames well known to her, and wives of honored husbands, and widows, a great multitude, and ancient maidens, all of excellent repute, and fair young girls, who trembled lest their mothers should espy them. Either the sudden gleams of light flashing over the obscure field bedazzled Goodman Brown, or he recognized a score of the church members of Salem village famous for their especial sanctity. Good old Deacon Gookin had arrived, and waited at the skirts of that venerable saint, his revered pastor. But irreverently consorting with these grave, reputable, and pious people, these elders of the church, these chaste dames and dewy virgins, there were men of dissolute lives and women of spotted fame, wretches given over to all mean and filthy vice, and suspected even of horrid crimes. It was strange to see that the good shrank not from the wicked, nor were the sinners abashed by the saints. Scattered also among their pale-faced enemies were the Indian priests, or pow-wows, who had often scared their native forest with more hideous incantations than any known to English witchcraft.

"But where is Faith?" thought Goodman Brown; and, as hope came into his heart, he trembled.

Another verse of the hymn arose, a slow and mounrnful strain, such as the pious love, but joined to words which expressed all that our nature can conceive of sin, and darkly hinted at far more. Unfathomable to mere mortals is the lore of fiends. Verse after verse was sung; and still the chorus of the desert swelled between like the deepest tone of a mighty organ; and with the final peal of that dreadful anthem there came a sound, as if the roaring wind, the rushing streams, the howling beasts, and every other voice of the unconcerted wilderness were mingling and according with the voice of guilty man in homage to the prince of all. The four blazing pines threw up a loftier flame, and obscurely discovered shapes and visages of horror on the smoke wreaths above the impious assembly. At the same moment the fire on the rock shot redly forth and formed a glowing arch above its base, where now appeared a figure. With reverence be it spoken, the figure bore no slight similitude, both in garb and manner, to some grave divine of the New England churches.

"Bring forth the converts!" cried a voice that echoed through the field and rolled into the forest.

At the word, Goodman Brown stepped forth from the shadow of the trees and approached the congregation, with whom he felt a loathful brotherhood by the sympathy of all that was wicked in his heart. He could have well-nigh sworn that the shape of his own dead father beckoned him to advance, looking downward from a smoke wreath, while a woman, with dim features of despair, threw out her hand to warn him back. Was it his mother? But he had no power to retreat one step, nor to resist, even in thought, when the minister and good old Deacon Gookin seized his arms and led him to the blazing rock. Thither came also the slender form of a veiled female, led between Goody Cloyse, that pious teacher of the catechism, and Martha Carrier, who had received the devil's promise to be queen of hell. A rampant hag was she. And there stood the proselytes beneath the canopy of fire.

"Welcome, my children," said the dark figure, "to the communion of your race. Ye have found thus young your nature and your destiny. My children, look behind you!"

They turned; and flashing forth, as it were, in a sheet of flame, the fiend worshippers were seen; the smile of welcome gleamed darkly on every visage.

"There," resumed the sable form, "are all whom ye have reverenced from youth. Ye deemed them holier than yourselves, and shrank from your own sin, contrasting it with their lives of righteousness and prayerful aspirations heavenward. Yet here are they all in my worshipping assembly. This night it shall be granted you to know their secret deeds: how hoary-bearded elders of the church have whispered wanton words to the young maids of their households; how many a woman, eager for widows' weeds has given her husband a drink at bedtime and let him sleep his last sleep in her bosom; how beardless youths have made haste to inherit their fathers' wealth; and how fair damsels—blush not, sweet ones—have dug little graves in the garden, and bidden me, the sole guest to an infant's funeral. By the sympathy of your human hearts for sin ye shall scent out all the places—whether in church, bedchamber, street, field, or forest—where crime has been committed, and shall exult to behold the whole earth one stain of guilt, one mighty blood spot. Far more than this. It shall be yours to penetrate, in every bosom, the deep mystery of sin, the fountain of all wicked arts, and which inexhaustibly supplies more evil impulses than human power—than my power at its utmost—can make manifest in deeds. And now, my children, look upon each other."

They did so; and, by the blaze of the hell-kindled torches, the wretched man beheld his Faith, and the wife her husband, trembling before that unhallowed altar.

"Lo, there ye stand, my children," said the figure, in a deep and solemn tone, almost sad with its despairing awfulness, as if his once angelic nature could yet mourn for our miserable race. "Depending upon one another's hearts, ye had still hoped that virtue were not all a dream. Now are ye undeceived. Evil is the nature of mankind. Evil must be your only happiness. Welcome again, my children, to the communion of your race."

"Welcome," repeated the fiend worshippers, in one cry of despair and triumph.

And there they stood, the only pair, as it seemed, who were yet hesitating on the verge of wickedness in this dark world. A basin was hollowed, naturally, in the rock. Did it contain water, reddened by the lurid light? or was it blood? or, perchance, a liquid flame? Herein did the shape of evil dip his hand and prepare to lay the mark of baptism upon their foreheads, that they might be partakers of the mystery of sin, more conscious of the secret guilt of others, both in deed and thought, than they could now be of their own. The husband cast one look at his pale wife, and Faith at him. What polluted wretches would the next glance show them to each other, shuddering alike at what they disclosed and what they saw!

"Faith! Faith!" cried the husband, "Look up to heaven, and resist the wicked one."

Whether Faith obeyed he knew not. Hardly had he spoken when he found himself amid calm night and solitude, listening to a roar of the wind which died heavily away through the forest. He staggered against the rock, and felt it chill and damp; while a hanging twig, that had been all on fire, besprinkled his cheek with the coldest dew.

The next morning young Goodman Brown came slowly into the street of Salem village, staring around him like a bewildered man. The good old minister was taking a walk along the graveyard to get an appetite for breakfast and meditate on his sermon, and bestowed a blessing, as he passed, on Goodman Brown. He shrank from the venerable saint as if to avoid an anathema. Old Deacon Gookin was at domestic worship, and the holy words of his prayer were heard through the open window. "What God doth the wizard pray to?" quoth Goodman Brown. Goody Cloyse, that excellent old Christian, stood in the early sunshine at her own lattice, catechizing a little girl who had brought her a pint of morning's milk. Goodman Brown snatched away the child as from the grasp of the fiend himself. Turning the corner by the meeting-house, he spied the head of Faith, with the pink ribbons, gazing anxiously forth, and bursting into such joy at sight of him that she skipped along the street and almost kissed her husband before the whole village. But Goodman Brown looked sternly and sadly into her face, and passed on without a greeting.

Had Goodman Brown fallen asleep in the forest and only dreamed a wild dream of a witch-meeting?

Be it so if you will; but, alas! it was a dream of evil omen for young Goodman Brown. A stern, a sad, a darkly meditative, a distrustful, if not a desperate man did he become from the night of that fearful dream. On the Sabbath day, when the congregation were singing a holy psalm, he could not listen because an anthem of sin rushed loudly upon his ear and drowned all the blessed strain. When the minister spoke from the pulpit with power and fervid eloquence, and, with his hand on the open Bible, of the sacred truths of our religion, and of saint-like lives and triumphant deaths, and of future bliss or misery unutterable, then did Goodman Brown turn pale, dreading lest the roof should thunder down upon the gray blasphemer and his hearers. Often, waking suddenly at midnight, he shrank from the bosom of Faith; and at morning or eventide, when the family knelt down at prayer, he scowled and muttered to himself, and gazed sternly at his wife, and turned away. And when he had lived long, and was borne to his grave a hoary corpse, followed by Faith, an aged woman, and children and grandchildren, a goodly procession, besides neighbors not a few, they carved no hopeful verse upon his tombstone, for his dying hour was gloom.

The Secret Sharer

joseph conrad

ON MY RIGHT HAND there were lines of fishing-stakes resembling a mysterious system of half-submerged bamboo fences, incomprehensible in its division of the domain of tropical fishes, and crazy of aspect as if abandoned forever by some nomad tribe of fishermen now gone to the other end of the ocean; for there was no sign of human habitation as far as the eye could reach. To the left a group of barren islets, suggesting ruins of stone walls, towers, and blockhouses, had its foundations set in a blue sea that itself looked solid, so still and stable did it lie below my feet; even the track of light from the westering sun shone smoothly, without that animated glitter which tells of an imperceptible ripple. And when I turned my head to take a parting glance at the tug which had just left us anchored outside the bar, I saw the straight line of the flat shore joined to the stable sea, edge to edge, with a perfect and unmarked closeness, in one leveled floor half brown, half blue under the enormous dome of the sky. Corresponding in their insignificance to the islets of the sea, two small clumps of trees, one on each side of the only fault in the impeccable joint, marked the mouth of the river Meinam we had just left on the first preparatory stage of our homeward journey; and, far back on the inland level, a larger and loftier mass, the grove surrounding the great Paknam pagoda, was the only thing on which the eye could rest from the vain task of exploring the monotonous sweep of the horizon. Here and there gleams as of a few scattered pieces of silver marked the windings of the great river; and on the nearest of them, just within the bar, the tug steaming right into the land became lost to my sight, hull and funnel and

Joseph Conrad, *The Secret Sharer*. Reprinted by permission of J. M. Dent & Sons Ltd. and of the Trustees of the Joseph Conrad Estate.

masts, as though the impassive earth had swallowed her up without an effort, without a tremor. My eye followed the light cloud of her smoke, now here, now there, above the plain, according to the devious curves of the stream, but always fainter and farther away, till I lost it at last behind the miter-shaped hill of the great pagoda. And then I was left alone with my ship, anchored at the head of the Gulf of Siam.

She floated at the starting-point of a long journey, very still in an immense stillness, the shadows of her spars flung far to the eastward by the setting sun. At that moment I was alone on her decks. There was not a sound in her—and around us nothing moved, nothing lived, not a canoe on the water, not a bird in the air, not a cloud in the sky. In this breathless pause at the threshold of a long passage we seemed to be measuring our fitness for a long and arduous enterprise, the appointed task of both our existences to be carried out, far from all human eyes, with only sky and sea for spectators and for judges.

There must have been some glare in the air to interfere with one's sight, because it was only just before the sun left us that my roaming eyes made out beyond the highest ridge of the principal islet of the group something which did away with the solemnity of perfect solitude. The tide of darkness flowed on swiftly; and with tropical suddenness a swarm of stars came out above the shadowy earth, while I lingered yet, my hand resting lightly on my ship's rail as if on the shoulder of a trusted friend. But, with all that multitude of celestial bodies staring down at one, the comfort of quiet communion with her was gone for good. And there were also disturbing sounds by this time—voices, footsteps forward; the steward flitted along the main deck, a busily ministering spirit; a hand-bell tinkled urgently under the poop-deck. . . .

I found my two officers waiting for me near the supper table, in the lighted cuddy. We sat down at once, and as I helped the chief mate, I said:

"Are you aware that there is a ship anchored inside the islands? I saw her mastheads above the ridge as the sun went down."

He raised sharply his simple face, overcharged by a terrible growth of whisker, and emitted his usual ejaculations: "Bless my soul, sir! You don't say so!"

My second mate was a round-cheeked, silent young man, grave beyond his years, I thought; but as our eyes happened to meet I detected a slight quiver on his lips. I looked down at once. It was not my part to encourage sneering on board my ship. It must be said, too, that I knew very little of my officers. In consequence of certain events of no particular significance, except to myself, I had been appointed to the command only a fortnight before. Neither did I know much of the hands forward. All these people had been together for eighteen months or so, and my position was that of the only stranger on board. I mention this because it has some bearing on what is to follow. But what I felt most was my being a stranger to the ship; and if all the truth must be told, I was somewhat of a stranger to myself. The youngest man on board (barring the second mate), and untried as yet by a position of the fullest responsibility, I was willing to take the adequacy of the others for granted. They had simply to be equal to their tasks; but I wondered how far I should turn out faithful to that ideal conception of one's own personality every man sets up for himself secretly.

Meantime the chief mate, with an almost visible effect of collaboration on the part of his round eyes and frightful whiskers, was trying to evolve a theory of the anchored ship. His dominant trait was to take all things into earnest consideration. He was of a painstaking turn of mind. As he used to say, he "liked to account to himself" for practically everything that came in his way, down to a miserable scorpion he had found in his cabin a week before. The why and the wherefore of that scorpion—how it got on board and came to select his room rather than the pantry (which was a dark place and more what a scorpion would be partial to), and how on earth it managed to drown itself in the inkwell of his writing-desk—had exercised him infinitely. The ship within the islands was much more easily accounted for; and just as we were about to rise from table he made his pronouncement. She was, he doubted not, a ship from home lately arrived. Probably she drew too much water to cross the bar except at the top of spring tides. Therefore she went into that natural harbor to wait for a few days in preference to remaining in an open roadstead.

"That's so," confirmed the second mate, suddenly, in his slightly hoarse voice. "She draws over twenty feet. She's the Liverpool ship *Sephora* with a cargo of coal. Hundred and twenty-three days from Cardiff."

We looked at him in surprise.

"The tugboat skipper told me when he came on board for your letters, sir," explained the young man. "He expects to take her up the river the day after tomorrow."

After thus overwhelming us with the extent of his information he slipped out of the cabin. The mate observed regretfully that he "could not account for that young fellow's whims." What prevented him telling us all about it at once, he wanted to know.

I detained him as he was making a move. For the last two days the crew had had plenty of hard work, and the night before they had very little sleep. I felt painfully that I—a stranger—was doing something unusual when I directed him to let all hands turn in without setting an anchor-watch. I proposed to keep on deck myself till one o'clock or thereabouts. I would get the second mate to relieve me at that hour.

"He will turn out the cook and the steward at four," I concluded, "and then give you a call. Of course at the slightest sign of any sort of wind we'll have the hands up and make a start at once."

He concealed his astonishment. "Very well, sir." Outside the cuddy he put his head in the second mate's door to inform him of my unheard-of caprice to take a five hours' anchor-watch on myself. I heard the other raise his voice incredulously—"What? The Captain himself?" Then a few more murmurs, a door closed, then another. A few moments later I went on deck.

My strangeness, which had made me sleepless, had prompted that unconventional arrangement, as if I had expected in those solitary hours of the night to get on terms with the ship of which I knew nothing, manned by men of whom I knew very little more. Fast alongside a wharf, littered like any ship in port with a tangle of unrelated things, invaded by unrelated shore people, I had hardly seen her yet properly. Now, as she lay cleared for sea, the stretch of her main-deck seemed to me very fine under the stars. Very fine, very roomy for her size, and very inviting. I descended the poop and paced the waist, my mind picturing to myself the coming passage through the Malay Archipelago, down the Indian Ocean, and up the Atlantic. All its phases were familiar enough to me, every characteristic, all the alternatives which were likely to face me on the high seas—everything! ... except the novel responsibility of command. But I took heart from the reasonable thought that the ship was like other ships, the men like other men, and that the sea was not likely to keep any special surprises expressly for my discomfiture.

Arrived at that comforting conclusion, I bethought myself of a cigar and went below to get it. All was still down there. Everybody at the after end of the ship was sleeping profoundly. I came out again on the quarterdeck, agreeably at ease in my sleeping-suit on that warm breathless night, barefooted, a glowing cigar in my teeth, and, going forward, I was met by the profound silence of the fore end of the ship. Only as I passed the door of the forecastle I heard a deep, quiet, trustful sigh of some sleeper inside. And suddenly I rejoiced in the great security of the sea as compared with the unrest of the land, in my choice of that untempted life presenting no disquieting problems, invested with an elementary moral beauty by the absolute straightforwardness of its appeal and by the singleness of its purpose.

The riding-light in the fore-rigging burned with a clear, untroubled, as if symbolic, flame, confident and bright in the mysterious shades of the night. Passing on my way aft along the other side of the ship, I observed that the rope side-ladder, put over, no doubt, for the master of the tug when he came to fetch away our letters, had not been hauled in as it should have been. I became annoyed at this, for exactitude in small matters is the very soul of discipline. Then I reflected that I had myself peremptorily dismissed my officers from duty, and by my own act had prevented the anchor-watch being formally set and things properly attended to. I asked myself whether it was wise ever to interfere with the established routine of duties even from the kindest of motives. My action might have made me appear eccentric. Goodness only knew how that absurdly whiskered mate would "account" for my conduct, and what the whole ship thought of that informality of their new captain. I was vexed with myself.

Not from compunction certainly, but, as it were mechanically, I proceeded to get the ladder in myself. Now a side-ladder of that sort is a light affair and comes in easily, yet my vigorous tug, which should have brought it flying on board, merely recoiled upon my body in a totally unexpected jerk. What the devil!...I was so astounded by the immovableness of that ladder that I remained stock-still, trying to account for it to myself like that imbecile mate of mine. In the end, of course, I put my head over the rail.

The side of the ship made an opaque belt of shadow on the darkling glassy shimmer of the sea. But I saw as once something elongated and pale floating very close to the ladder. Before I could form a guess a faint flash of phosphorescent light, which seemed to issue suddenly from the naked body of a man, flickered in the sleeping water with the elusive, silent play of summer lightning in a night sky. With a gasp I saw revealed to my stare a pair of feet, the long legs, a broad livid back immersed right up to the neck in a greenish cadaverous glow. One hand, awash, clutched the bottom rung of the ladder. He was complete but for the head. A headless corpse! The cigar dropped out of my gaping mouth with a tiny plop and a short hiss quite audible in the absolute stillness of all things under heaven. At that I suppose he raised up his face, a dimly pale oval in the shadow of the ship's side. But even then I could only barely make out down there the shape of his black-haired head. However, it was enough for the horrid, frost-bound sensation which had gripped me about the chest to pass off. The moment of vain exclamations was past, too. I only climbed on the spare and leaned over the rail as far as I could, to bring my eyes nearer to that mystery floating alongside.

As he hung by the ladder, like a resting swimmer, the sea-lightning played about his limbs at every stir; and he appeared in it ghastly, silvery, fish-like. He remained as mute as fish, too. He made no motion to get out of the water, either. It was inconceivable that he should not attempt to come on board, and strangely troubling to suspect that perhaps he did not want to. And my first words were prompted by just that troubled incertitude.

"What's the matter?" I asked in my ordinary tone, speaking down to the face upturned exactly under mine.

"Cramp," it answered, no louder. Then slightly anxious, "I say, no need to call anyone."

"I was not going to," I said.

"Are you alone on deck?"

"Yes."

I had somehow the impression that he was on the point of letting go the ladder to swim away beyond my ken—mysterious as he came. But, for the moment, this being appearing as if he had risen from the bottom of the sea (it was certainly the nearest land to the ship) wanted only to know the time. I told him. And he, down there, tentatively:

"I suppose your captain's turned in?"

"I am sure he isn't," I said.

He seemed to struggle with himself, for I heard something like the low, bitter murmur of doubt. "What's the good?" His next words came out with a hesitating effort.

"Look here, my man. Could you call him out quietly?"

I thought the time had come to declare myself.

"*I* am the captain."

I heard a "By Jove!" whispered at the level of the water. The phosphorescence flashed in the swirl of the water all about his limbs, his other hand seized the ladder.

"My name's Leggatt."

The voice was calm and resolute. A good voice. The self-possession of that man had somehow induced a corresponding state in myself. It was very quietly that I remarked:

"You must be a good swimmer."

"Yes. I've been in the water practically since nine o'clock. The question for me now is whether I am to let go this ladder and go on swimming till I sink from exhaustion, or—to come on board here."

I felt this was no mere formula of desperate speech, but a real alternative in the view of a strong soul. I should have gathered from this that he was young; indeed, it is only the young who are ever confronted by such clear issues. But at the time it was pure intuition on my part. A mysterious communication was established already between us two—in the face of that silent, darkened tropical sea. I was young, too; young enough to make no comment. The man in the water began suddenly to climb up the ladder, and I hastened away from the rail to fetch some clothes.

Before entering the cabin I stood still, listening in the lobby at the foot of the stairs. A faint snore came through the closed door of the chief mate's room. The second mate's door was on the hook, but the darkness in there was absolutely soundless. He, too, was young and could sleep like a stone. Remained the steward, but he was not likely to wake up before he was called. I got a sleeping-suit out of my room and, coming back on deck, saw the naked man from the sea sitting on the mainhatch, glimmering white in the darkness, his elbows on his knees and his head in his hands. In a moment he had concealed his damp body in a sleeping-suit of the same gray-stripe pattern as the one I was wearing and followed me like my double on the poop. Together we moved right aft, barefooted, silent.

"What is it?" I asked in a deadened voice, taking the lighted lamp out of the binnacle, and raising it to his face.

"An ugly business."

He had rather regular features: a good mouth; light eyes under somewhat heavy, dark eyebrows; a smooth, square forehead; no growth on his cheeks; a small, brown mustache, and a well-shaped, round chin. His expression was concentrated, mediative, under the inspecting light of the lamp I held up to his face; such as a man thinking hard in solitude might wear. My sleeping-suit was just right for his size. A well-knit young fellow of twenty-five at most. He caught his lower lip with the edge of white, even teeth.

"Yes," I said, replacing the lamp in the binnacle. The warm, heavy tropical night closed upon his head again.

"There's a ship over there," he murmured.

"Yes, I know. The *Sephora*. Did you know of us?"

"Hadn't the slightest idea. I am the mate of her—" He paused and corrected himself. "I should say I *was*."

"Aha! Something wrong?"

"Yes. Very wrong indeed. I've killed a man."

"What do you mean? Just now?"

"No, on the passage. Weeks ago. Thirty-nine south. When I say a man—"

"Fit of temper," I suggested, confidently.

The shadowy, dark head, like mine, seemed to nod imperceptibly above the ghostly gray of my sleeping-suit. It was, in the night, as though I had been faced by my own reflection in the depths of a somber and immense mirror.

"A pretty thing to have to own up to for a Conway boy," murmured my double, distinctly.

"You're a Conway boy?"

"I am," he said, as if startled. Then, slowly..."Perhaps you too—"

It was so; but being a couple of years older I had left before he joined. After a quick interchange of dates a silence fell; and I thought suddenly of my absurd mate with his terrific whiskers and the "Bless my soul—you don't say so" type of intellect. My double gave me an inkling of his thoughts by saying: "My father's a parson in Norfolk. Do you see me before a judge and jury on that charge? For myself I can't see the necessity. There are fellows that an angel from heaven—And I am not that. He was one of those creatures that are just simmering all the time with a silly sort of wickedness. Miserable devils that have no business to live at all. He wouldn't do his duty and wouldn't let anybody else do theirs. But what's the good of talking! You know well enough the sort of ill-conditioned snarling cur—"

He appealed to me as if our experiences had been as identical as our clothes. And I knew well enough the pestiferous danger of such a character where there are no means of legal repression. And I knew well enough also that my double there was no homicidal ruffian. I did not think of asking him for details, and he told me the story roughly in brusque, disconnected sentences. I needed no more. I saw it all going on as though I were myself inside that other sleeping-suit.

"It happened while we were setting a reefed foresail, at dusk. Reefed foresail! You understand the sort of weather. The only sail we had left to keep the ship running; so you may guess what it had been like for days. Anxious sort of job, that. He gave me some of his cursed insolence at the sheet. I tell you I was overdone with this terrific weather that seemed to have no end to it. Terrific, I tell you—and a deep ship. I believe the fellow himself was half crazed with funk. It was no time for gentlemanly reproof, so I turned round and felled him like an ox. He up and at me. We closed just as an awful sea made for the ship. All hands saw it coming and took to the rigging, but I had him by the throat, and went on shaking him like a rat, the men above us yelling, 'Look out! look out!' Then a crash as if the sky had fallen on my head. They say that for over ten minutes hardly anything was to be seen of the ship—just the three masts and a bit of the forecastle head and of the poop all awash driving along in a smother of foam. It was a miracle that they found us, jammed together behind the forebits. It's clear that I meant business, because I was holding him by the throat still when they picked us up. He was black in the face. It was too much for them. It seems they rushed us aft together, gripped as we were, screaming 'Murder!' like a lot of lunatics, and broke into the cuddy. And the ship running for her life, touch and go all the time, any minute her last in a sea fit to turn your hair gray only a-looking at it. I understand that the skipper, too, started raving like the rest of them. The man had been deprived of sleep for more than a week, and to have this sprung on him at the height of a furious gale nearly drove him out of his mind. I wonder they didn't fling me overboard after getting the carcass of their precious ship-mate out of my fingers. They had rather a job to separate us, I've been told. A sufficiently fierce story to make an old judge and a respectable jury sit up a bit. The first thing I heard when I came to myself was the maddening howling of that endless gale, and on that the voice of the old man. He was hanging on to my bunk, staring into my face out of his sou'wester.

" 'Mr. Leggatt, you have killed a man. You can act no longer as chief mate of this ship.' "

His care to subdue his voice made it sound monotonous. He rested a hand on the end of the skylight to steady himself with, and all that time did not stir a limb, so far as I could see. "Nice little tale for a quiet tea-party," he concluded in the same tone.

One of my hands, too, rested on the end of the skylight; neither did I stir a limb, so far as I knew. We stood less than a foot from each other. It occurred to me that if old "Bless my soul—you don't say so" were to put his head up the companion and catch sight of us, he would think he was seeing double, or imagine himself come upon a scene of weird witchcraft; the strange captain having a quiet confabulation by the wheel with his own gray ghost. I became very much concerned to prevent anything of the sort. I heard the other's soothing undertone.

"My father's a parson in Norfolk," it said. Evidently he had forgotten he had told me this important fact before. Truly a nice little tale.

"You had better slip down into my stateroom now," I said, moving off stealthily. My double followed my movements; our bare feet made no sound; I let him in, closed the door with care, and, after giving a call to the second mate, returned on deck for my relief.

"Not much sign of any wind yet," I remarked when he approached.

"No, sir. Not much," he assented, sleepily, in his hoarse voice, with just enough deference, no more, and barely suppressing a yawn.

"Well, that's all you have to look out for. You have got your orders."

"Yes, sir."

I paced a turn or two on the poop and saw him take up his position face forward with his elbow in the ratlines of the mizzen-rigging before I went below. The mate's faint snoring was still going on peacefully. The cuddy lamp was burning over the table on which stood a vase with flowers, a polite attention from the ship's provision merchant—the last flowers we should see for the next three months at the very least. Two bunches of bananas hung from the beam symmetrically, one on each side of the rudder-casing. Everything was as before in the ship—except that two of her captain's sleeping-suits were simultaneously in use, one motionless in the cuddy, the other keeping very still in the captain's stateroom.

It must be explained here that my cabin had the form of the capital letter L, the door being within the angle and opening into the short part of the letter. A couch was to the left, the bed-place to the right; my writing-desk and the chronometers' table faced the door. But anyone opening it, unless he stepped right inside, had no view of what I call the long (or vertical) part of the letter. It contained some lockers surmounted by a bookcase; and a few clothes, a thick jacket or two, caps, oilskin coat, and such like, hung on hooks. There was at the bottom of that part a door opening into my bath-room, which could be entered also directly from the saloon. But that way was never used.

The mysterious arrival had discovered the advantage of this particular shape. Entering my room, lighted strongly by a gift bulkhead lamp swung on gimbals above my writing-desk, I did not see him anywhere till he stepped out quietly from behind the coats hung in the recessed part.

"I heard somebody moving about, and went in there at once," he whispered.

I, too, spoke under my breath.

"Nobody is likely to come in here without knocking and getting permission."

He nodded. His face thin and the sunburn faded, as though he had been ill. And no wonder. He had been, I heard presently, kept under arrest in his cabin for nearly seven weeks. But there was nothing sickly in his eyes or in his expression. He was not a bit like me, really; yet, as we stood leaning over my bed-place, whispering side by side, with our dark heads together and our backs to the door, anybody bold enough to open it stealthily would have been treated to the uncanny sight of a double captain busy talking in whispers with his other self.

"But all this doesn't tell me how you came to hang on to our sideladder," I inquired, in the hardly audible murmurs we used, after he had told me something more of the proceedings on board the *Sephora* once the bad weather was over.

"When we sighted Java Head I had had time to think all those matters out several times over. I had six weeks of doing nothing else, and with only an hour or so every evening for a tramp on the quarter-deck."

He whispered, his arms folded on the side of my bed-place, staring through the open port. And I could imagine perfectly the manner of this thinking out—a stubborn if not a steadfast operation; something of which I should have been perfectly incapable.

"I reckoned it would be dark before we closed with the land," he continued, so low that I had to strain my hearing, near as we were to each other, shoulder touching shoulder almost. "So I asked to speak to the old man. He always seemed very sick when he came to see me—as if he could not look me in the face. You know, that foresail saved the ship. She was too deep to have run long under bare poles. And it was I that managed to set it for him. Anyway, he came. When I had him in my cabin—he stood by the door looking at me as if I had the halter round my reck already—I asked him right away to leave my cabin door unlocked at night while the ship was going through Sunda Straits. There would be the Java coast within two or three miles, off Angier Point. I wanted nothing more. I've had a prize for swimming my second year in the Conway."

"I can believe it," I breathed out.

"God only knows why they locked me in every night. To see some of their faces you'd have thought they were afraid I'd go about at night stangling people. Am I a murdering brute? Do I look it? By Jove! if I had been he wouldn't have trusted himself like that into my room. You'll say I might have chucked him aside and and bolted out, there and then—it was dark already. Well, no. And for the same reason I wouldn't think of trying to smash the door. There would have been a rush to stop me at the noise, and I did not mean to get into a confounded scrimmage. Somebody else might have got killed—for I would not have broken out only to get chucked back, and I did not want any more of that work. He refused, looking more sick than ever. He was afraid of the men, and also of that old second mate of his who had been sailing with him for years—a grayheaded old humbug; and his steward, too, had been with him devil knows how long—seventeen years or more—a dogmatic sort of loafer who hated me like poison, just because I was the chief mate. No chief mate ever made more than one voyage in the *Sephora*, you know. Those two old chaps ran the ship. Devil only knows what the skipper wasn't afraid of (all his nerve went to pieces altogether in that hellish spell of bad weather we had)—of what the law would do to him—of his wife, perhaps. Oh, yes! she's on board. Though I don't think she would have meddled. She would have been only too glad to have me out of the ship in any way. The 'brand of Cain' business, don't you see. That's all right. I was ready enough to go off wandering on the face of the earth—and that was price enough to pay for an Abel of that sort. Anyhow, he wouldn't listen to me. 'This thing must take its course. I represent the law here.' He was shaking like a leaf. 'So you won't?' 'No!' 'Then I hope you will be able to sleep on that,' I said, and turned my back on him. 'I wonder that *you* can,' cries he, and locks the door.

"Well, after that, I couldn't. Not very well. That was three weeks ago. We have had a slow passage through the Java Sea; drifted about Carimata for ten days. When we anchored here they thought, I suppose, it was all right. The nearest land (and that's five miles) is the ship's destination; the consul would soon set about catching me; and there would have been no object in bolting to these islets there. I don't suppose there's a drop of water on them. I don't know how it was, but tonight that steward, after bringing me my supper, went out to let me eat it, and left the door unlocked. And I ate it—all there was, too. After I had finished I strolled out on the quarter-deck. I don't know that I meant to do anything. A breath of fresh air was all I wanted, I believe. Then a sudden temptation came over me. I kicked off my slippers and was in the water before I had made up my mind fairly. Somebody heard the splash and they raised an awful hullabaloo. 'He's gone! Lower the boats! He's committed suicide! No, he's swimming.' Certainly I was swimming. It's not so easy for a swimmer like me to commit suicide by drowning. I landed on the nearest islet before the boat left the ship's side. I heard them pulling about in the dark, hailing, and so on, but after a bit they gave up. Everything quieted down and the anchorage became as still as death. I sat down on a stone and began to think. I felt certain they would start searching for me at daylight. There was no place to hide on those stony things—and if there had been, what would have been the good? But now I was clear of that ship, I was not going back. So after a while I took off all my clothes, tied them up in a bundle with a stone inside, and dropped them in the deep water on the outer side of that islet. That was suicide enough for me. Let them think what they liked, but I didn't mean to drown myself. I meant to swim till I sank—but that's not the same thing. I struck out for another of these little islands, and it was from that one that I first saw your riding-light. Something to swim for. I went on easily, and on the way I came upon a flat rock a foot or two above water. In the daytime, I dare say, you might make it out with a glass from your poop. I scrambled up on it and rested myself for a bit. Then I made another start. That last spell must have been over a mile."

His whisper was getting fainter and fainter, and all the time he stared straight out through the port-hole, in which there was not even a star to be seen. I had not interrupted him. There was something that made comment impossible in his narrative, or perhaps in himself; a sort of feeling, a quality, which I can't find a name for. And when he ceased, all I found was a futile whisper: "So you swam for our light?"

"Yes—straight for it. It was something to swim for. I couldn't see any stars low down because the coast was in the way, and I couldn't see the land, either. The water was like glass. One might have been swimming in a confounded thousand-feet deep cistern with no place for scrambling out anywhere; but what I didn't like was the notion of swimming round and round like a crazed bullock before I gave out; and as I didn't mean to go back...No. Do you see me being hauled back, stark naked, off one of these little islands by the scruff of the neck and fighting like a wild beast? Somebody would have got killed for certain, and I did not want any of that. So I went on. Then your ladder—"

"Why didn't you hail the ship?" I asked, a little louder.

He touched my shoulder lightly. Lazy footsteps came right over our heads and stopped. The second mate had crossed from the other side of the poop and might have been hanging over the rail, for all we knew.

"He couldn't hear us talking—could he?" My double breathed into my very ear, anxiously.

His anxiety was an answer, a sufficient answer, to the question I had put to him. An answer containing all the difficulty of that situation. I closed the port-hole quietly, to make sure. A louder word might have been overheard.

"Who's that?" he whispered then.

"My second mate. But I don't know much more of the fellow than you do."

And I told him a little about myself. I had been appointed to take charge while I least expected anything of the sort, not quite a fortnight ago. I didn't know either the ship or the people. Hadn't had the time in port to look about me or size anybody up. And as to the crew, all they knew was that I was appointed to take the ship home. For the rest, I was almost as much of a stranger on board as himself, I said. And at the moment I felt it most acutely. I felt that it would take very little to make me a suspect person in the eyes of the ship's company.

He had turned about meantime; and we, the two strangers in the ship, faced each other in identical attitudes.

"Your ladder—" he murmured, after a silence. "Who'd thought of finding a ladder hanging over at night in a ship anchored out here! I felt just then a very unpleasant faintness. After the life I've been leading for nine weeks, anybody would have got out of condition. I wasn't capable of swimming round as far as your rudder-chains. And, lo and behold! there was a ladder to get hold of. After I gripped it I said to myself, 'What's the good?' When I saw a man's head looking over I thought I would swim away presently and leave him shouting—in whatever language it was. I didn't mind being looked at. I—I liked it. And then you speaking to me so quietly —as if you had expected me—made me hold on a little longer. It had been a confounded lonely time—I don't mean while swimming. I was glad to talk a little to somebody that didn't belong to the *Sephora*. As to asking for the captain, that was a mere impulse. It could have been no use, with all the ship knowing about me and the other people pretty certain to be round here in the morning. I don't know—I wanted to be seen, to talk with some-body, before I went on. I don't know what I would have said.... 'Fine night, isn't it?' or something of the sort."

"Do you think they will be round here presently?" I asked with some incredulity.

"Quite likely," he said, faintly.

He looked extremely haggard all of a sudden. His head rolled on his shoulders.

"H'm. We shall see then. Meantime get into that bed," I whispered. "Want help? There."

It was a rather high bed-place with a set of drawers underneath. This amazing swimmer really needed the lift I gave him by seizing his leg. He tumbled in, rolled over on his back, and flung one arm across his eyes. And then, with his face nearly hidden, he must have looked exactly as I used to look in that bed. I gazed upon my other self for a while before drawing across carefully the two green serge curtains which ran on a brass rod. I thought for a moment of pinning them together for greater safety, but I sat down on the couch, and once there I felt unwilling to rise and hunt for a pin. I would do it in a moment. I was extremely tired, in a peculiarly intimate way, by the strain of stealthiness, by the effort of whispering and the general secrecy of this excitement. It was three o'clock by now and I had been on my feet since nine, but I was not sleepy; I could not have gone to sleep. I sat there, fagged out, looking at the curtains, trying to clear my mind of the confused sensation of being in two places at once, and greatly bothered by an exasperating knocking in my head. It was a relief to discover suddenly that it was not in my head at all, but on the outside of the door. Before I could collect myself the words "Come in" were out of my mouth, and the steward entered with a tray, bringing in my morning coffee. I had slept, after all, and I was so frightened that I shouted, "This way! I am here, steward," as though he had been miles away. He put down the tray on the table next the couch and only then said, very quietly, "I can see you are here, sir." I felt him give me a keen look, but I dared not meet his eyes just then. He must have wondered why I had drawn the curtains of my bed before going to sleep on the couch. He went out, hooking the door open as usual.

I heard the crew washing decks above me. I knew I would have been told at once if there had been any wind. Calm, I thought, and I was doubly vexed. Indeed, I felt dual more than ever. The steward reappeared suddenly in the doorway. I jumped up from the couch so quickly that he gave a start.

"What do you want here?"

"Close your port, sir—they are washing decks."

"It is closed," I said, reddening.

"Very well, sir." But he did not move from the doorway and returned my stare in an extraordinary, equivocal manner for a time. Then his eyes wavered, all his expression changed, and in a voice unusually gentle, almost coaxingly:

"May I come in to take the empty cup away, sir?"

"Of course!" I turned my back on him while he popped in and out. Then I unhooked and closed the door and even pushed the bolt. This sort of thing could not go on very long. The cabin was as hot as an oven, too. I took a peep at my double, and discovered that he had not moved, his arm was still over his eyes; but his chest heaved; his hair was wet; his chin glistened with perspiration. I reached over him and opened the port.

"I must show myself on deck," I reflected.

Of course, theoretically, I could do what I liked, with no one to say nay to me within the whole circle of the horizon; but to lock my cabin door and take the key away I did not dare. Directly I put my head out of the companion I saw the group of my two officers, the second mate barefooted, the chief mate in long india-rubber boots, near the break of the poop, and the steward half-way down the poop-ladder talking to them eagerly. He happened to catch sight of me and dived, the second ran down on the main-deck shouting some order or other, and the chief mate came to meet me, touching his cap.

There was a sort of curiosity in his eye that I did not like. I don't know whether the steward had told them that I was "queer" only, or downright drunk, but I know the man meant to have a good look at me. I watched him coming with a smile which, as he got into point-blank range, took effect and froze his very whiskers. I did not give him time to open his lips.

"Square the yards by lifts and braces before the hands go to breakfast."

It was the first particular order I had given on board that ship; and I stayed on deck to see it executed, too. I had felt the need of asserting myself without loss of time. That sneering young cub got taken down a peg or two on that occasion, and I also seized the opportunity of having a good look at the face of every foremast man as they filed past me to go to the after braces. At breakfast time, eating nothing myself, I presided with such frigid dignity that the two mates were only too glad to escape from the cabin as soon as decency permitted; and all the time the dual working of my mind distracted me almost to the point of insanity. I was constantly watching myself, my secret self, as dependent on my actions as my own personality, sleeping in that bed, behind that door which faced me as I sat at the head of the table. It was very much like being mad, only it was worse because one was aware of it.

I had to shake him for a solid minute, but when at last he opened his eyes it was in the full possession of his senses, with an inquiring look.

"All's well so far," I whispered. "Now you must vanish into the bath-room."

He did so, as noiseless as a ghost, and then I rang for the steward, and facing him boldly, directed him to tidy up my stateroom while I was having my bath—"and be quick about it." As my tone admitted of no excuses, he said, "Yes, sir," and ran off to fetch his dust-pan and brushes. I took a bath and did most of my dressing, splashing, and whistling softly for the steward's edification, while the secret sharer of my life stood drawn up bolt upright in that little space, his face looking very sunken in daylight, his eyelids lowered under the stern, dark line of his eyebrows drawn together by a slight frown.

When I left him there to go back to my room the steward was finishing dusting. I sent for the mate and engaged him in some insignificant conversation. It was, as it were, trifling with the terrific character of his whiskers; but my object was to give him an opportunity for a good look at my cabin. And then I could at last shut, with a clear conscience, the door of my stateroom and get my double back into the recessed part. There was nothing else for it. He had to sit still on a small folding stool, half smothered by the heavy coats hanging there. We listened to the steward going into the bath-room out of the saloon, filling the water-bottles there, scrubbing the bath, setting things to rights, whisk, bang, clatter—out again into the saloon—turn the key—click. Such was my scheme for keeping my second self invisible. Nothing better could be contrived under the circumstances. And there we sat; I at my writing-desk ready to appear busy with some papers, he behind me out of sight of the door. It would not have been prudent to talk in daytime; and I could not have stood the excitement of that queer sense of whispering to myself. Now and then, glancing over my shoulder, I saw him far back there, sitting rigidly on the low stool, his bare feet close together, his arms folded, his head hanging on his breast—and perfectly still. Anybody would have taken him for me.

I was fascinated by it myself. Every moment I had to glance over my shoulder. I was looking at him when a voice outside the door said:

"Beg pardon, sir."

"Well!"...I kept my eyes on him, and so when the voice outside the door announced, "There's a ship's boat coming our way, sir," I saw him give a start—the first movement he had made for hours. But he did not raise his bowed head.

"All right. Get the ladder over."

I hesitated. Should I whisper something to him? But what? His immobility seemed to have been never disturbed. What could I tell him he did not know already?... Finally I went on deck.

ii

The skipper of the *Sephora* had a thin red whisker all round his face, and the sort of complexion that goes with hair of that color; also the particular, rather smeary shade of blue in the eyes. He was not exactly a showy figure; his shoulders were high, his stature but middling—one leg slightly more bandy than the other. He shook hands, looking vaguely around. A spiritless tenacity was his main characteristic, I judged. I behaved with a politeness which seemed to disconcert him. Perhaps he was shy. He mumbled to me as if he were ashamed of what he was saying; gave his name (it was something like Archbold—but at this distance of years I hardly am sure), his ship's name, and a few other particulars of that sort, in the manner of a criminal making a reluctant and doleful confession. He had had terrible weather on the passage out—terrible—terrible—wife aboard, too.

By this time we were seated in the cabin and the steward brought in a tray with a bottle and glasses. "Thanks! No." Never took liquor. Would have some water, though. He drank two tumblerfuls. Terrible thirsty work. Ever since daylight had been exploring the islands round his ship.

"What was that for—fun?" I asked, with an appearance of polite interest.

"No!" He sighed. "Painful duty."

As he persisted in his mumbling and I wanted my double to hear every word, I hit upon the notion of informing him that I regretted to say I was hard of hearing.

"Such a young man, too!" he nodded, keeping his smeary blue, unintelligent eyes fastened upon me. "What was the cause of it—some disease?" he inquired, without the least sympathy and as if he thought that, if so, I'd got no more than I deserved.

"Yes; disease," I admitted in a cheerful tone which seemed to shock him. But my point was gained, because he had to raise his voice to give me his tale. It is not worth while to record that version. It was just over two months since all this had happened, and he had thought so much about it that he seemed completely muddled as to its bearings, but still immensely impressed.

"What would you think of such a thing happening on board your own ship? I've had the *Sephora* for these fifteen years. I am a well-known shipmaster."

He was densely distressed—and perhaps I should have sympathized with him if I had been able to detach my mental vision from the unsuspected sharer of my cabin as though he were my second self. There he was on the other side of the bulkhead, four or five feet from us, no more, as we sat in the saloon. I looked politely at Captain Archbold (if that was his name), but it was the other I saw, in a gray sleeping-suit, seated on a low stool, his bare feet close together, his arms folded, and every word said between us falling into the ears of his dark head bowed on his chest.

"I have been at sea now, man and boy, for seven-and-thirty years, and I've never heard of such a thing happening in an English ship. And that it should be my ship. Wife on board, too."

I was hardly listening to him.

"Don't you think," I said, "that the heavy sea which, you told me, came aboard just then might have killed the man? I have seen the sheer weight of a sea kill a man very neatly, by simply breaking his neck."

"Good God!" he uttered, impressively, fixing his smeary blue eyes on me. "The sea! No man killed by the sea ever looked like that." He seemed positively scandalized at my suggestion. And as I gazed at him, certainly not prepared for anything original on his part, he advanced his head close to mine and thrust his tongue out at me so suddenly that I couldn't help starting back.

After scoring over my calmness in this graphic way he nodded wisely. If I had seen the sight, he assured me, I would never forget it as long as I lived. The weather was too bad to give the corpse a proper set burial. So next day at dawn they took it up on the poop, covering its face with a bit of bunting; he read a short prayer, and then, just as it was, in its oilskins and long boots, they launched it amongst those mountainous seas that seemed ready every moment to swallow up the ship herself and the terrified lives on board of her.

"That reefed foresail saved you," I threw in.

"Under God—it did," he exclaimed fervently. "It was by a special mercy, I firmly believe, that it stood some of those hurricane squalls."

"It was the setting of that sail which—" I began.

"God's own hand in it," he interrupted me. "Nothing less could have done it. I don't mind telling you that I hardly dared give the order. It seemed impossible that we could touch anything without losing it, and then our last hope would have been gone."

The terror of that gale was on him yet. I let him go on for a bit, then said, casually—as if returning to a minor subject:

"You were very anxious to give up your mate to the shore people, I believe?"

He was. To the law. His obscure tenacity on that point had in it something incomprehensible and a little awful; something, as it were, mystical, quite apart from his anxiety that he should not be suspected of "countenancing and doings of that sort." Seven-and-thirty virtuous years at sea, of which over twenty of immaculate command, and the last fifteen in the *Sephora*, seemed to have laid him under some pitiless obligation.

"And you know," he went on, groping shamefacedly amongst his feelings, "I did not engage that young fellow. His people had some interest with my owners. I was in a way forced to take him on. He looked very smart, very gentlemanly, and all that. But do you know—I never liked him, somehow. I am a plain man. You see, he wasn't exactly the sort for the chief mate of a ship like the *Sephora*."

I had become so connected in thoughts and impressions with the secret sharer of my cabin that I felt as if I, personally, were being given to understand that I, too, was not the sort that would have done for the chief mate of a ship like the *Sephora*. I had no doubt of it in my mind.

"Not at all the style of man. You understand," he insisted, superfluously, looking hard at me.

I smiled urbanely. He seemed at a loss for a while.

"I suppose I must report a suicide."

"Beg pardon?"

"Sui-cide! That's what I'll have to write to my owners directly I get in."

"Unless you manage to recover him before tomorrow," I assented, dispassionately. . . . "I mean, alive."

He mumbled something which I really did not catch, and I turned my ear to him in a puzzled manner. He fairly bawled:

"The land—I say, the mainland is at least seven miles off my anchorage."

"About that."

My lack of excitement, of curiosity, of surprise, of any sort of pronounced interest, began to arouse his distrust. But except for the felicitous pretense of deafness I had not tried to pretend anything. I had felt utterly incapable of playing the part of ignorance properly, and therefore was afraid to try. It is also certain that he had brought some ready-made suspicions with him, and that he viewed my politeness as a strange and unnatural phenomenon. And yet how else could I have received him? Not heartily! That was impossible for psychological reasons, which I need not state here. My only object was to keep off his inquiries. Surlily? Yes, but surliness might have provoked a point-blank question. From its novelty to him and from its nature, punctilious courtesy was the manner best calculated to restrain the man. But there was the danger of his breaking through my defense bluntly. I could not, I think, have met him by a direct lie, also for psychological (not moral) reasons. If he had only known how afraid I was of his putting my feeling of identity with the other to the test! But, strangely enough—(I thought of it only afterwards)—I believe that he was not a little disconcerted by the reverse side of that weird situation, by something in me that reminded him of the man he was seeking—suggested a mysterious similitude to the young fellow he had distrusted and disliked from the first.

However that might have been, the silence was not very prolonged. He took another oblique step.

"I reckon I had no more than a two-mile pull to your ship. Not a bit more."

"And quite enough, too, in this awful heat," I said.

Another pause full of mistrust followed. Necessity, they say, is mother of invention, but fear, too, is not barren of ingenious suggestions. And I was afraid he would ask me point-blank for news of my other self.

"Nice little saloon, isn't it?" I remarked, as if noticing for the first time the way his eyes roamed from one closed door to the other. "And very well fitted out, too. Here, for instance," reaching over the back of my seat negligently and flinging the door open, "is my bath-room."

He made an eager movement, but hardly gave it a glance. I got up, shut the door of the bath-room, and invited him to have a look round, as if I were very proud of my accommodation. He had to rise and be shown round, but he went through the business without any raptures whatever.

"And now we'll have a look at my stateroom," I declared, in a voice as loud as I dared to make it, crossing the cabin to the starboard side with purposely heavy steps.

He followed me in and gazed around. My intelligent double had vanished. I played my part.

"Very convenient—isn't it?"

"Very nice. Very comf..." He didn't finish and went out brusquely as if to escape from some unrighteous wiles of mine. But it was not to be. I had been too frightened not to feel vengeful; I felt I had him on the run, and I meant to keep him on the run. My polite insistence must have had something menacing in it, because he gave in suddenly. And I did not let him off a single item; mate's room, pantry, storerooms, the very saillocker which was also under the poop—he had to look into them all. When at last I showed him out on the quarter-deck he drew a long, spiritless sigh, and mumbled dismally that he must really be going back to his ship now. I desired my mate, who had joined us, to see to the captain's boat.

The man of whiskers gave a blast on the whistle which he used to wear hanging round his neck, and yelled, "*Sephora's* away!" My double down there in my cabin must have heard, and certainly could not feel more relieved than I. Four fellows came running out from somewhere forward and went over the side, while my own men, appearing on deck too, lined the rail. I escorted my visitor to the gangway ceremoniously, and nearly overdid it. He was a tenacious beast. On the very ladder he lingered, and in that unique, guiltily conscientious manner of sticking to the point:

"I say...you...you don't think that—"

I covered his voice loudly:

"Certainly not.... I am delighted. Good-by."

I had an idea of what he meant to say, and just saved myself by the privilege of defective hearing. He was too shaken generally to insist, but my mate, close witness of that parting, looked mystified and his face took on a thoughtful cast. As I did not want to appear as if I wished to avoid all communication with my officers, he had the opportunity to address me.

"Seems a very nice man. His boat's crew told our chaps a very extraordinary story, if what I am told by the steward is true. I suppose you had it from the captain, sir?"

"Yes. I had a story from the captain."

"A very horrible affair—isn't it, sir?"

"It is."

"Beats all these tales we hear about murders in Yankee ships."

"I don't think it beats them. I don't think it resembles them in the least."

"Bless my soul—you don't say so! But of course I've no acquaintance whatever with American ships, not I, so I couldn't go against your knowledge. It's horrible enough for me. . . . But the queerest part is that those fellows seemed to have some idea the man was hidden aboard here. They had really. Did you ever hear of such a thing?"

"Preposterous—isn't it?"

We were walking to and fro athwart the quarter-deck. No one of the crew forward could be seen (the day was Sunday), and the mate pursued:

"There was some little dispute about it. Our chaps took offense. 'As if we would harbor a thing like that,' they said. 'Wouldn't you like to look for him in our coal-hole?' Quite a tiff. But they made it up in the end. I suppose he did drown himself. Don't you, sir?"

"I don't suppose anything."

"You have no doubt in the matter, sir?"

"None whatever."

I left him suddenly. I felt I was producing a bad impression, but with my double down there it was most trying to be on deck. And it was almost as trying to be below. Altogether a nerve-trying situation. But on the whole I felt less torn in two when I was with him. There was no one in the whole ship whom I dared take into my confidence. Since the hands had got to know his story, it would have been impossible to pass him off for anyone else, and an accidental discovery was to be dreaded now more than ever. . . .

The steward being engaged in laying the table for dinner, we could talk only with our eyes when I first went down. Later in the afternoon we had a cautious try at whispering. The Sunday quietness of the ship was against us; the stillness of air and water around her was against us; the elements, the men were against us—everything was against us in our secret partnership; time itself—for this could not go on forever. The very trust in Providence was, I suppose, denied to his guilt. Shall I confess that this thought cast me down very much? And as to the chapter of accidents which counts for so much in the book of success, I could only hope that it was closed. For what favorable accident could be expected?

"Did you hear everything?" were my first words as soon as we took up our position side by side, leaning over my bed-place.

He had. And the proof of it was his earnest whisper. "The man told you he hardly dared to give the order."

I understood the reference to be to that saving foresail.

"Yes. He was afraid of it being lost in the setting."

"I assure you he never gave the order. He may think he did, but he never gave it. He stood there with me on the break of the poop after the maintopsail blew away, and whimpered about our last hope—positively whimpered about it and nothing else—and the night coming on! To hear one's skipper go on like that in such weather was enough to drive any fellow out of his mind. It worked me up into a sort of desperation. I just took it into my own hands and went away from him, boiling, and— But what's the use telling you? *You* know! . . . Do you think that if I had not been pretty fierce with them I should have got the men to do anything? Not it! The bo's'n perhaps? Perhaps! It wasn't a heavy sea—it was a sea gone mad! I suppose the end of the world will be something like that; and a man may have the heart to see it coming once and be done with it—but to have to face it day after day— I don't blame anybody. I was precious little better than the rest. Only—I was an officer of that old coal-wagon, anyhow—"

"I quite understand," I conveyed that sincere assurance into his ear. He was out of breath with whispering; I could hear him pant slightly. It was all very simple. The same strung-up force which had given twenty-four men a chance, at least, for their lives, had, in a sort of recoil, crushed an unworthy mutinous existence.

But I had no leisure to weigh the merits of the matter—footsteps in the saloon, a heavy knock. "There's enough wind to get under way with, sir." Here was the call of a new claim upon my thoughts and even upon my feelings.

"Turn the hands up, " I cried through the door. "I'll be on deck directly."

I was going out to make the acquaintance of my ship. Before I left the cabin our eyes met—the eyes of the only two strangers on board. I pointed to the recessed part where the little campstool awaited him and laid my finger on my lips. He made a gesture—somewhat vague—a little mysterious, accompanied by a faint smile, as if of regret.

This is not the place to enlarge upon the sensations of a man who feels for the first time a ship move under his feet to his own independent word. In my case they were not unalloyed. I was not wholly alone with my command; for there was that stranger in my cabin. Or rather, I was not completely and wholly with her. Part of me was absent. That mental feeling of being in two places at once affected me physically as if the mood of secrecy had penetrated my very soul. Before an hour had elapsed since the ship had begun to move, having occasion to ask the mate (he stood by my side) to take a compass bearing of the Pagoda, I caught myself reaching up to his ear in whispers. I say I caught myself, but enough had escaped to startle the man. I can't describe it otherwise than by saying that he shied. A grave, preoccupied manner, as though he were in possession of some perplexing intelligence, did not leave him henceforth. A little later I moved away from the rail to look at the compass with such a stealthy gait that the helmsman noticed it—and I could not help noticing the unusual roundness of his eyes. These are trifling instances, though it's to no commander's advantage to be suspected of ludicrous eccentricities. But I was also more seriously affected. There are to a seaman certain words, gestures, that should in given conditions come as naturally, as instinctively as the winking of a menaced eye. A certain order should spring on to his lips without thinking; a certain sign should get itself made, so to speak, without reflection. But all unconscious alertness had abandoned me. I had to make an effort of will to recall myself back (from the cabin) to the conditions of the moment. I felt that I was appearing an irresolute commander to those people who were watching me more or less critically.

And, besides, there were the scares. On the second day out, for instance, coming off the deck in the afternoon (I had straw slippers on my bare feet) I stopped at the open pantry door and spoke to the steward. He was doing something there with his back to me. At the sound of my voice he nearly jumped out of his skin, as the saying is, and incidentally broke a cup.

"What on earth's the matter with you?" I asked, astonished.

He was extremely confused. "Beg your pardon, sir. I made sure you were in your cabin."

"You see I wasn't."

"No, sir. I could have sworn I had heard you moving in there not a moment ago. It's most extraordinary...very sorry, sir."

I passed on with an inward shudder. I was so identified with my secret double that I did not even mention the fact in those scanty, fearful whispers we exchanged. I suppose he had made some slight noise of some kind or other. It would have been miraculous if he hadn't at one time or another. And yet, haggard as he appeared, he looked always perfectly self-controlled, more than calm—almost invulnerable. On my suggestion he remained almost entirely in the bath-room, which, upon the whole, was the safest place. There could be really no shadow of an excuse for anyone ever wanting to go in there, once the steward had done with it. It was a very tiny place. Sometimes he reclined on the floor, his legs bent, his head sustained on one elbow. At others I would find him on the camp-stool, sitting in his gray sleeping-suit and with his cropped dark hair like a patient, unmoved convict. At night I would smuggle him into my bedplace, and we would whisper together, with the regular footfalls of the officer of the watch passing and repassing over our heads. It was an infinitely miserable time. It was lucky that some tins of fine preserves were stowed in a locker in my stateroom; hard bread I could always get hold of; and so he lived on stewed chicken, paté de foie gras, asparagus, cooked oysters, sardines—on all sorts of abominable sham delicacies out of tins. My early morning coffee he always drank; and it was all I dared do for him in that respect.

Every day there was the horrible maneuvering to go through so that my room and then the bath-room should be done in the usual way. I came to hate the sight of the steward, to abhor the voice of that harmless man. I felt that it was he who would bring on the disaster of discovery. It hung like a sword over our heads.

The fourth day out, I think (we were then working down the east side of the Gulf of Siam, tack for tack, in light winds and smooth water)—the fourth day, I say, of this miserable juggling with the unavoidable, as we sat at our evening meal, that man, whose slightest movement I dreaded, after putting down the dishes ran up on deck busily. This could not be dangerous. Presently he came down again; and then it appeared that he had remembered a coat of mine which I had thrown over a rail to dry after having been wetted in a shower had passed over the ship in the afternoon. Sitting stolidly at the head of the table I became terrified at the sight of the garment on his arm. Of course he made for my door. There was no time to lose.

"Steward," I thundered. My nerves were so shaken that I could not govern my voice and conceal my agitation. This was the sort of thing that made my terrifically whiskered mate tap his forehead with his forefinger. I had detected him using that gesture while talking on deck with a confidential air to the carpenter. It was too far to hear a word, but I had no doubt that this pantomime could only refer to the strange new captain.

"Yes, sir," the pale-faced steward turned resignedly to me. It was this maddening course of being shouted at, checked without rhyme or reason, arbitrarily chased out of my cabin, suddenly called into it, sent flying out of his pantry on incomprehensible errands, that accounted for the growing wretchedness of his expression.

"Where are you going with that coat?"

"To your room, sir."

"Is there another shower coming?"

"I'm sure I don't know, sir. Shall I go up again and see, sir?"

"No! never mind."

My object was attained, as of course my other self in there would have heard everything that passed. During this interlude my two officers never raised their eyes off their respective plates; but the lip of that confounded cub, the second mate, quivered visibly.

I expected the steward to hook my coat on and come out at once. He was very slow about it; but I dominated my nervousness sufficiently not to shout after him. Suddenly I became aware (it could be heard plainly enough) that the fellow for some reason or other was opening the door of the bathroom. It was the end. The place was literally not big enough to swing a cat in. My voice died in my throat and I went stony all over. I expected to hear a yell of surprise and terror, and made a movement, but had not the strength to get on my legs. Everything remained still. Had my second self taken the poor wretch by the throat? I don't know what I could have done next moment if I had not seen the steward come out of my room, close the door, and then stand quietly by the sideboard.

"Saved," I thought. "But, no! Lost! Gone! He was gone!"

I laid my knife and fork down and leaned back in my chair. My head swam. After a while, when sufficiently recovered to speak in a steady voice, I instructed my mate to put the ship round at eight o'clock himself.

"I won't come on deck," I went on. "I think I'll turn in, and unless the wind shifts I don't want to be disturbed before midnight. I feel a bit seedy."

"You did look middling bad a little while ago," the chief mate remarked without showing any great concern.

They both went out, and I stared at the steward clearing the table. There was nothing to be read on that wretched man's face. But why did he avoid my eyes I asked myself. Then I thought I should like to hear the sound of his voice.

"Steward!"

"Sir!" Startled as usual.

"Where did you hang up that coat?"

"In the bath-room, sir." The usual anxious tone. "It's not quite dry yet, sir."

For some time longer I sat in the cuddy. Had my double vanished as he had come? But of his coming there was an explanation, whereas his disappearance would be inexplicable.... I went slowly into my dark room, shut the door, lighted the lamp, and for a time dared not turn round. When at last I did I saw him standing bolt-upright in the narrow recessed part. It would not be true to say I had a shock, but an irresistible doubt of his bodily existence flitted through my mind. Can it be, I asked myself, that he is not visible to other eyes than mine? It was like being haunted. Motionless, with a grave face, he raised his hands slightly at me in a gesture which meant clearly, "Heavens! what a narrow escape!" Narrow indeed. I think I had come creeping quietly as near insanity as any man who has not actually gone over the border. That gesture restrained me, so to speak.

The mate with the terrific whiskers was now putting the ship on the other tack. In the moment of profound silence which follows upon the hands going to their stations I heard on the poop his raised voice: "Hard alee!" and the distant shout of the order repeated on the maindeck. The sails, in that light breeze, made but a faint fluttering noise. It ceased. The ship was coming round slowly; I held my breath in the renewed stillness of expectation; one wouldn't have thought that there was a single living soul on her decks. A sudden brisk shout, "Mainsail haul!" broke the spell, and in the noisy cries and rush overhead of the men running away with the main-brace we two, down in my cabin, came together in our usual position by the bed-place.

He did not wait for my question. "I heard him fumbling here and just managed to squat myself down in the bath," he whispered to me. "The fellow only opened the door and put his arm in to hang the coat up. All the same—"

"I never thought of that," I whispered back, even more appalled than before at the closeness of the shave, and marveling at that something un-yielding in his character which was carrying him through so finely. There was no agitation in his whisper. Whoever was being driven distracted, it was not he. He was sane. And proof of his sanity was continued when he took up the whispering again.

"It would never do for me to come to life again."

It was something that a ghost might have said. But what he was alluding to was his old captain's reluctant admission of the theory of suicide. It would obviously serve his turn—if I had understood at all the view which seemed to govern the unalterable purpose of his action.

"You must maroon me as soon as ever you can get amongst these islands off the Cambodge shore," he went on.

"Maroon you! We are not living in a boy's adventure tale," I protested. His scornful whispering took me up.

"We aren't indeed! There's nothing of a boy's tale in this. But there's nothing else for it. I want no more. You don't suppose I am afraid of what can be done to me? Prison or gallows or whatever they may please. But you don't see me coming back to explain such things to an old fellow in a wig and twelve respectable tradesmen, do you? What can they know whether I am guilty or not—or of *what* I am guilty, either? That's my affair. What does the Bible say? 'Driven off the face of the earth.' Very well. I am off the face of the earth now. As I came at night so I shall go."

"Impossible!" I murmured. "You can't."

"Can't?...Not naked like a soul on the Day of Judgment. I shall freeze on to this sleeping-suit. The Last Day is not yet—and...you have understood thoroughly. Didn't you?"

I felt suddenly ashamed of myself. I may say truly that I understood—and my hesitation in letting that man swim away from my ship's side had been a mere sham sentiment, a sort of cowardice.

"It can't be done now till next night," I breathed out. "The ship is on the off-shore tack and the wind may fail us."

"As long as I know that you understand," he whispered. "But of course you do. It's a great satisfaction to have got somebody to understand. You seem to have been there on purpose." And in the same whisper, as if we two whenever we talked had to say things to each other which were not fit for the world to hear, he added, "It's very wonderful."

We remained side by side talking in our secret way—but sometimes silent or just exchanging a whispered word or two at long intervals. And as usual he stared through the port. A breath of wind came now and again into our faces. The ship might have been moored in dock, so gently and on an even keel she slipped through the water, that did not murmur even at our passage, shadowy and silent like a phantom sea.

At midnight I went on deck, and to my mate's great surprise put the ship round on the other tack. His terrible whiskers flitted round me in silent criticism. I certainly should not have done it if it had been only a question of getting out of that sleepy gulf as quickly as possible. I believe he told the second mate, who relieved him, that it was a great want of judgment. The other only yawned. That intolerable cub shuffled about so sleepily and lolled against the rails in such a slack, improper fashion that I came down on him sharply.

"Aren't you properly awake yet?"

"Yes, sir! I am awake."

"Well, then, be good enough to hold yourself as if you were. And keep a look-out. If there's any current we'll be closing with some islands before daylight."

The east side of the gulf is fringed with islands, some solitary, others in groups. On the blue background of the high coast they seem to float on silvery patches of calm water, arid and gray, or dark green and rounded like clumps of evergreen bushes, with the larger ones, a mile or two long, showing the outlines of ridges, ribs of gray rock under the dank mantle of matted leafage. Unknown to trade, to travel, almost to geography, the manner of life they harbor is an unsolved secret. There must be villages— settlements of fishermen at least—on the largest of them, and some communication with the world is probably kept up by native craft. But all that forenoon, as we headed for them, fanned along by the faintest of breezes, I saw no sign of man or canoe in the field of the telescope I kept on pointing at the scattered group.

At noon I gave no orders for a change of course, and the mate's whiskers became much concerned and seemed to be offering themselves unduly to my notice. At last I said:

"I am going to stand right in. Quite in—as far as I can take her."

The stare of extreme surprise imparted an air of ferocity also to his eyes, and he looked truly terrific for a moment.

"We're not doing well in the middle of the gulf," I continued, casually. "I am going to look for the land breezes tonight."

"Bless my soul! Do you mean, Sir, in the dark amongst the lot of all them islands and reefs and shoals?"

"Well—if there are any regular land breezes at all on this coast one must get close inshore to find them, mustn't one?"

"Bless my soul!" he exclaimed again under his breath. All that afternoon he wore a dreamy, contemplative appearance which in him was a mark of perplexity. After dinner I went into my stateroom as if I meant to take some rest. There we two bent our dark heads over a half-unrolled chart lying on my bed.

"There," I said. "It's got to be Koh-ring. I've been looking at it ever since sunrise. It has got two hills and a low point. It must be inhabited. And on the coast opposite there is what looks like the mouth of a biggish river—with some town, no doubt, not far up. It's the best chance for you that I can see."

"Anything. Koh-ring let it be."

He looked thoughtfully at the chart as if surveying chances and distances from a lofty height—and following with his eyes his own figure wandering on the blank land of Cochin-China, and then passing off that piece of paper clean out of sight into uncharted regions. And it was as if the ship had two captains to plan her course for her. I had been so worried and restless running up and down that I had not had the patience to dress that day. I had remained in my sleeping-suit, with straw slippers and a soft floppy hat. The closeness of the heat in the gulf had been most oppressive, and the crew were used to see me wandering in that airy attire.

"She will clear the south point as she heads now," I whispered into his ear. "Goodness only knows when, though, but certainly after dark. I'll edge her in to half a mile, as far as I may be able to judge in the dark—"

"Be careful," he murmured, warningly—and I realized suddenly that all my future, the only future for which I was fit, would perhaps go irretrievably to pieces in any mishap to my first command.

I could not stop a moment longer in the room. I motioned him to get out of sight and made my way on the poop. That unplayful cub had the watch. I walked up and down for a while thinking things out, then beckoned him over.

"Send a couple of hands to open the two quarter-deck ports," I said, mildly.

He actually had the impudence, or else so forgot himself in his wonder at such an incomprehensible order, as to repeat:

"Open the quarter-deck ports! What for, sir?"

"The only reason you need concern yourself about is because I tell you to do so. Have them opened wide and fastened properly."

He reddened and went off, but I believe made some jeering remark to the carpenter as to the sensible practice of ventilating a ship's quarterdeck. I know he popped into the mate's cabin to impart the fact to him because the whiskers came on deck, as it were by chance, and stole glances at me from below—for signs of lunacy or drunkenness, I suppose.

A little before supper, feeling more restless than ever, I rejoined, for a moment, my second self. And to find him sitting so quietly was surprising, like something against nature, inhuman.

I developed my plan in a hurried whisper.

"I shall stand in as close as I dare and then put her round. I will presently find means to smuggle you out of here into the sail-locker, which communicates with the lobby. But there is an opening, a sort of square for hauling the sails out, which gives straight on the quarter-deck and which is never closed in fine weather, so as to give air to the sails. When the ship's way is deadened in stays and all the hands are aft at the mainbraces you will have a clear road to slip out and get overboard through the open quarter-deck port. I've had them both fastened up. Use a rope's end to lower yourself into the water so as to avoid a splash—you know. It could be heard and cause some beastly complication."

He kept silent for a while, then whispered, "I understand."

"I won't be there to see you go," I began with an effort. "The rest... I only hope I have understood, too."

"You have. From first to last"—and for the first time there seemed to be a faltering, something strained in his whisper. He caught hold of my arm, but the ringing of the supper bell made me start. He didn't, though; he only released his grip.

After supper I didn't come below again till well past eight o'clock. The faint, steady breeze was loaded with dew; and the wet, darkened sails held all there was of propelling power in it. The night, clear and starry, sparkled darkly, and the opaque, lightless patches shifting slowly against the low stars were the drifting islets. On the port bow there was a big one more distant and shadowily imposing by the great space of sky it eclipsed.

On opening the door I had a back view of my very own self looking at a chart. He had come out of the recess and was standing near the table.

"Quite dark enough," I whispered.

He stepped back and leaned against my bed with a level, quiet glance. I sat on the couch. We had nothing to say to each other. Over our heads the officer of the watch moved here and there. Then I heard him move quickly. I knew what that meant. He was making for the companion; and presently his voice was outside my door.

"We are drawing in pretty fast, sir. Land looks rather close."

"Very well," I answered. "I am coming on deck directly."

I waited till he was gone out of the cuddy, then rose. My double moved too. The time had come to exchange our last whispers, for neither of us was ever to hear each other's natural voice.

"Look here!" I opened a drawer and took out three sovereigns. "Take this anyhow. I've got six and I'd give you the lot, only I must keep a little money to buy some fruit and vegetables for the crew from native boats as we go through Sunda Straits."

He shook his head.

"Take it," I urged him, whispering desperately. "No one can tell what—"

He smiled and slapped meaningly the only pocket of the sleeping-jacket. It was not safe, certainly. But I produced a large old silk handkerchief of mine, and tying the three pieces of gold in a corner, pressed it on him. He was touched, I suppose, because he took it at last and tied it quickly round his waist under the jacket, on his bare skin.

"Our eyes met; several seconds elapsed, till, our glances still mingled, I extended my hand and turned the lamp out. Then I passed through the cuddy, leaving the door of my room wide open. . . . "Steward!"

He was still lingering in the pantry in the greatness of his zeal, giving a rub-up to plated cruet stand the last thing before going to bed. Being careful not to wake up the mate, whose room was opposite, I spoke in an undertone.

He looked round anxiously, "Sir!"

"Can you get me a little hot water from the galley?"

"I am afraid, sir, the galley fire's been out for some time now."

"Go and see."

He flew up the stairs.

"Now," I whispered, loudly, into the saloon—too loudly, perhaps, but I was afraid I couldn't make a sound. He was by my side in an instant—the double captain slipped past the stairs—through a tiny dark passage . . . a sliding door. We were in the sail-locker, scrambling on our knees over the sails. A sudden thought struck me. I saw myself wandering barefooted, bareheaded, the sun beating on my dark poll. I snatched off my floppy hat and tried hurriedly in the dark to ram it on my other self. He dodged and fended off silently. I wonder what he thought had come to me before he understood and suddenly desisted. Our hands met gropingly, lingered united in a steady, motionless clasp for a second. . . . No word was breathed by either of us when they separated.

I was standing quietly by the pantry door when the steward returned.

"Sorry, sir. Kettle barely warm. Shall I light the spirit-lamp?"

"Never mind."

I came out on deck slowly. It was now a matter of conscience to shave the land as close as possible—for now he must go overboard whenever the ship was put in stays. Must! There could be no going back for him. After a moment I walked over to leeward and my heart flew into my mouth at the nearness of the land on the bow. Under any other circumstances I would not have held on a minute longer. The second mate had followed me anxiously.

I looked on till I felt I could command my voice.

"She will weather," I said then in a quiet tone.

"Are you going to try that, sir?" he stammered out incredulously.

I took no notice of him and raised my tone just enough to be heard by the helmsman.

"Keep her good full."

"Good full, sir."

The wind fanned my cheek, the sails slept, the world was silent. The strain of watching the dark loom of the land grow bigger and denser was too much for me. I had shut my eyes—because the ship must go closer. She must! The stillness was intolerable. Were we standing still?

When I opened my eyes the second view started my heart with a thump. The black southern hill of Koh-ring seemed to hang right over the ship like a towering fragment of the everlasting night. On that enormous mass of blackness there was not a gleam to be seen, not a sound to be heard. It was gliding irresistibly towards us and yet seemed already within reach of the hand. I saw the vague figures of the watch grouped in the waist, gazing in awed silence.

"Are you going on, sir?" inquired an unsteady voice at my elbow.

I ignored it. I had to go on.

"Keep her full. Don't check her way. That won't do now," I said, warningly.

"I can't see the sails very well," the helmsman answered me, in strange, quavering tones.

Was she close enough? Already she was, I won't say in the shadow of the land, but in the very blackness of it, already swallowed up as it were, gone too close to be recalled, gone from me altogether.

"Give the mate a call," I said to the young man who stood at my elbow as still as death. "And turn all hands up."

My tone had a borrowed loudness reverberated from the height of the land. Several voices cried out together: "We are all on deck, sir."

Then stillness again, with the great shadow gliding closer, towering higher, without a light, without a sound. Such a hush had fallen on the ship that she might have been a bark of the dead floating in slowly under the very gate of Erebus.

"My God! Where are we?"

It was the mate moaning at my elbow. He was thunderstruck, and as it were deprived of the moral support of his whiskers. He clapped his hands and absolutely cried out, "Lost!"

"Be quiet," I said, sternly.

He lowered his tone, but I saw the shadowy gesture of his despair. "What are we doing here?"

"Looking for the land wind."

He made as if to tear his hair, and addressed me recklessly.

"She will never get out. You have done it, sir. I knew it'd end in something like this. She will never weather, and you are too close now to stay. She'll drift ashore before she's round. O my God!"

I caught his arm as he was raising it to batter his poor devoted head, and shook it violently.

"She's ashore already," he wailed, trying to tear himself away.

"Is she?...Keep good full there!"

"Good full, sir," cried the helmsman in a frightened, thin, child-like voice.

I hadn't let go the mate's arm and went on shaking it. "Ready about, do you hear? You go forward"—shake—"and stop there"—shake—"and hold your noise"—shake—"and see these head-sheets properly overhauled"—shake, shake—shake.

And all the time I dared not look towards the land lest my heart should fail me. I released my grip at last and he ran forward as if fleeing for dear life.

I wondered what my double there in the sail-locker thought of this commotion. He was able to hear everything—and perhaps he was able to understand why, on my conscience, it had to be thus close—no less. My first order "Hard alee!" re-echoed ominously under the towering shadow of Koh-ring as if I had shouted in a mountain gorge. And then I watched the land intently. In that smooth water and light wind it was impossible to feel the ship coming-to. No! I could not feel her. And my second self was making now ready to slip out and lower himself overboard. Perhaps he was gone already...?

The great black mass brooding over our very mastheads began to pivot away from the ship's side silently. And now I forgot the secret stranger ready to depart, and remembered only that I was a total stranger to the ship. I did not know her. Would she do it? How was she to be handled?

I swung the mainyard and waited helplessly. She was perhaps stopped, and her very fate hung in the balance, with the black mass of Koh-ring like the gate of the everlasting night towering over her taffrail. What would she do now? Had she way on her yet? I stepped to the side swiftly, and on the shadowy water I could see nothing except a faint phosphorescent flash revealing the glassy smoothness of the sleeping surface. It was impossible to tell—and I had not learned yet the feel of my ship. Was she moving? What I needed was something easily seen, a piece of paper, which I could throw overboard and watch. I had nothing on me. To run down for it I didn't dare. There was no time. All at once my strained, yearning state distinguished a white object floating within a yard of the ship's side. White on the black water. A phosphorescent flash passed under it. What was that thing?...I recognized my own floppy hat. It must have fallen off his head...and he didn't bother. Now I had what I wanted—the saving mark for my eyes. But I hardly thought of my other self, now gone from the ship, to be hidden forever from all friendly faces, to be a fugitive and a vagabond on the earth, with no brand of the curse on his sane forehead to stay a slaying hand... too proud to explain.

And I watched the hat—the expression of my sudden pity for his mere flesh. It had been meant to save his homeless head from the dangers of the sun. And now—behold—it was saving the ship, by serving me for a mark to help out the ignorance of my strangeness. Ha! It was drifting forward, warning me just in time that the ship had gathered sternway.

"Shift the helm," I said in a low voice to the seaman standing still like a statue.

The man's eyes glistened wildly in the binnacle light as he jumped round to the other side and spun round the wheel.

I walked to the break of the poop. On the overshadowed deck all hands stood by the forebraces waiting for my order. The stars ahead seemed to be gliding from right to left. And all was so still in the world that I heard the quiet remark, "She's round," passed in a tone of intense relief between two seamen.

"Let go and haul."

The foreyards ran round with a great noise, amidst cheery cries. And now the frightful whiskers made themselves heard giving various orders. Already the ship was drawing ahead. And I was alone with her. Nothing! no one in the world should stand now between us, throwing a shadow on the way of silent knowledge and mute affection, the perfect communion of a seaman with his first command.

Walking to the taffrail, I was in time to make out, on the very edge of a darkness thrown by a towering black mass like the very gateway of Erebus —yes, I was in time to catch an evanescent glimpse of my white hat left behind to mark the spot where the secret sharer of my cabin and of my thoughts, as though he were my second self, had lowered himself into the water to take his punishment: a free man, a proud swimmer striking out for a new destiny.

The
Portable Phonograph

walter van tilburg clark

THE RED SUNSET, with narrow, black cloud strips like threats across it, lay on the curved horizon of the prairie. The air was still and cold, and in it settled the mute darkness and greater cold of night. High in the air there was wind, for through the veil of the dusk the clouds could be seen gliding rapidly south and changing shapes. A queer sensation of torment, of two-sided, unpredictable nature, arose from the stillness of the earth air beneath the violence of the upper air. Out of the sunset, through the dead, matted grass and isolated weed stalks of the prairie, crept the narrow and deeply rutted remains of a road. In the road, in places, there were crusts of shallow, brittle ice. There were little islands of an old oiled pavement in the road too, but most of it was mud, now frozen rigid. The frozen mud still bore the toothed impress of great tanks, and a wanderer on the neighboring undulations might have stumbled, in this light, into large, partially filled-in and weed-grown cavities, their banks channelled and beginning to spread into badlands. These pits were such as might have been made by falling meteors, but they were not. They were the scars of gigantic bombs, their rawness already made a little natural by rain, seed, and time. Along the road, there were rakish remnants of fence. There was also, just visible, one portion of tangled and multiple barbed wire still erect, behind which was a shelving ditch with small caves, now very quiet and empty, at intervals in its back wall. Otherwise there was no structure or remnant of a structure visible over the dome of the darkling earth, but only, in sheltered hollows, the darker shadows of young trees trying again.

Under the wuthering arch of the high wind a V of wild geese fled south. The rush of their pinions sounded briefly, and the faint, plaintive notes of their expeditionary talk. Then they left a still greater vacancy. There was the smell and expectation of snow, as there is likely to be when the wild geese fly south. From the remote distance, towards the red sky, came faintly the protracted howl and quick yap-yap of a prairie wolf.

North of the road, perhaps a hundred yards, lay the parallel and deeply intrenched course of a small creek, lined with leafless alders and willows. The creek was already silent under ice. Into the bank above it was dug a sort of cell, with a single opening, like the mouth of a mine tunnel. Within the cell there was a little red of fire, which showed dully through the opening, like a reflection or a deception of the imagination. The light came from the chary burning of four blocks of poorly aged peat, which gave off a petty warmth and much acrid smoke. But the precious remnants of wood, old fence posts and timbers from the long-deserted dugouts, had to be saved for the real cold, for the time when a man's breath blew white, the moisture in his nostrils stiffened at once when he stepped out, and the expansive blizzards paraded for days over the vast open, swirling and settling and thickening, till the dawn of the cleared day when the sky was thin blue-green and the terrible cold, in which a man could not live for three hours unwarmed, lay over the uniformly drifted swell of the plain.

Around the smoldering peat, four men were seated crosslegged. Behind them, traversed by their shadows, was the earth bench, with two old and dirty army blankets, where the owner of the cell slept. In a niche in the opposite wall were a few tin utensils which caught the glint of the coals. The host was rewrapping in a piece of daubed burlap four fine, leather-bound books. He worked slowly and very carefully, and at last tied the boundle securely with a piece of grass-woven cord. The other three looked intently upon the process, as if a great significance lay in it. As the host tied the cord, he spoke. He was an old man, his long, matted beard and hair gray to nearly white. The shadows made his brows and cheekbones appear gnarled, his eyes and cheeks deeply sunken. His big hands, rough with frost and swollen by rheumatism, were awkward but gentle at their task. He was like a prehistoric priest performing a fateful ceremonial rite. Also his voice had in it a suitable quality of deep, reverent despair, yet perhaps at the moment, a sharpness of selfish satisfaction.

"When I perceived what was happening," he said, "I told myself, 'It is the end. I cannot take much; I will take these.'

"Perhaps I was impractical," he continued. "But for myself, I do not regret, and what do we know of those who will come after us? We are the doddering remnant of a race of mechanical fools. I have saved what I love; the soul of what was good in us is here; perhaps the new ones will make a strong enough beginning not to fall behind when they become clever."

He rose with slow pain and placed the wrapped volumes in the niche with his utensils. The others watched him with the same ritualistic gaze.

"Shakespeare, the Bible, *Moby Dick, The Divine Comedy,*" one of them said softly. "You might have done worse, much worse."

"You will have a little soul left until you die," said another harshly. "That is more than is true of us. My brain becomes thick, like my hands." He held the big, battered hands, with their black nails, in the glow to be seen.

"I want paper to write on," he said. "And there is none."

The fourth man said nothing. He sat in the shadow farthest from the fire, and sometimes his body jerked in its rags from the cold. Although he was still young, he was sick and coughed often. Writing implied a greater future than he now felt able to consider.

The old man seated himself laboriously, and reached out, groaning at the movement, to put another block of peat on the fire. With bowed heads and averted eyes, his three guests acknowledged his magnanimity.

"We thank you, Doctor Jenkins, for the reading," said the man who had named the books.

They seemed then to be waiting for something. Doctor Jenkins understood, but was loath to comply. In an ordinary moment he would have said nothing. But the words of *The Tempest,* which he had been reading, and the religious attention of the three made this an unusual occasion.

"You wish to hear the phonograph," he said grudgingly.

The two middle-aged men stared into the fire, unable to formulate and expose the enormity of their desire.

The young man, however, said anxiously, between suppressed coughs, "Oh, please," like an excited child.

The old man rose again in his difficult way, and went to the back of the cell. He returned and placed tenderly upon the packed floor, where the firelight might fall upon it, an old portable phonograph in a black case. He smoothed the top with his hand, and then opened it. The lovely green-felt-covered disk became visible.

"I have been using thorns as needles," he said. "But tonight, because we have a musician among us"—he bent his head to the young man, almost invisible in the shadow—"I will use a steel needle. There are only three left."

The two middle-aged men stared at him in speechless adoration. The one with the big hands, who wanted to write, moved his lips, but the whisper was not audible.

"Oh, don't!" cried the young man, as if he were hurt. "The thorns will do beautifully."

"No," the old man said. "I have become accustomed to the thorns, but they are not really good. For you, my young friend, we will have good music tonight."

"After all," he added generously, and beginning to wind the phonograph, which creaked, "they can't last forever."

"No, nor we," the man who needed to write said harshly. "The needle, by all means."

"Oh, thanks," said the young man. "Thanks," he said again in a low, excited voice, and then stifled his coughing with a bowed head.

"The records, though," said the old man when he had finished winding, "are a different matter. Already they are very worn. I do not play them more than once a week. One, once a week, that is what I allow myself.

"More than a week I cannot stand it; not to hear them," he apologized.

"No, how could you?" cried the young man. "And with them here like this."

"A man can stand anything," said the man who wanted to write, in his harsh, antagonistic voice.

"Please, the music," said the young man.

"Only the one," said the old man. "In the long run, we will remember more that way."

He had a dozen records with luxuriant gold and red seals. Even in that light the others could see that the threads of the records were becoming worn. Slowly he read out the titles and the tremendous dead names of the composers and the artists and the orchestras. The three worked upon the names in their minds, carefully. It was difficult to select from such a wealth what they would at once most like to remember. Finally, the man who wanted to write named Gershwin's "New York."

"Oh, no," cried the sick young man, and then could say nothing more because he had to cough. The others understood him, and the harsh man withdrew his selection and waited for the musician to choose.

The musician begged Doctor Jenkins to read the titles again, very slowly, so that he could remember the sounds. While they were read, he lay back against the wall, his eyes closed, his thin, horny hand pulling at his light beard, and listened to the voices and the orchestras and the single instruments in his mind.

When the reading was done he spoke despairingly. "I have forgotten," he complained; "I cannot hear them clearly."

"There are things missing," he explained.

"I know," said Doctor Jenkins. "I thought that I knew all of Shelley by heart. I should have brought Shelley."

"That's more soul than we can use," said the harsh man. *"Moby Dick* is better.

"By God, we can understand that," he emphasized.

The Doctor nodded.

"Still," said the man who had admired the books, "we need the absolute if we are keep a grasp on anything.

"Anything but these sticks and peat clods and rabbit snares," he said bitterly.

"Shelley desired an ultimate absolute," said the harsh man. "It's too much," he said. "It's no good; no earthly good."

The musician selected a Debussy nocturne. The others considered and approved. They rose to their knees to watch the Doctor prepare for the playing, so that they appeared to be actually in an attitude of worship. The peat glow showed the thinness of their bearded faces, and the deep lines in them, and revealed the condition of their garments. The other two continued to kneel as the old man carefully lowered the needle onto the spinning disk, but the musician suddenly drew back against the wall again, with his knees up, and buried his face in his hands.

At the first notes of the piano the listeners were startled. They stared at each other. Even the musician lifted his head in amazement, but then quickly bowed in again, strainingly, as if he were suffering from a pain he might not be able to endure. They were all listening deeply, without movement. The wet, blue-green notes tinkled forth from the old machine, and were individual, delectable presences in the cell. The individual, delectable presences swept into a sudden tide of unbearably beautiful dissonance, and then continued fully the swelling and ebbing of that tide, the dissonant inpourings, and the resolutions, and the diminishments, and the little, quiet wavelets of interlude lapping between. Every sound was piercing and singularly sweet. In all the men except the musician, there occurred rapid sequences of tragically heightened recollection. He heard nothing but what was there. At the final, whispering disappearance, but moving quietly so that the others would not hear him and look at him, he let his head fall back in agony, at if it were drawn there by the hair, and clenched the fingers of one hand over his teeth. He sat that way while the others were silent, and until they began to breathe again normally. His drawn-up legs were trembling violently.

Quickly Doctor Jenkins lifted the needle off, to save it and not to spoil the recollection with scraping. When he had stopped the whirling of the sacred disk, he courteously left the phonograph open and by the fire, in sight.

The others, however, understood. The musician rose last, but then abruptly, and went quickly out at the door without saying anything. The others stopped at the door and gave their thanks in low voices. The Doctor nodded magnificently.

"Come again," he invited, "in a week. We will have the 'New York.'"

When the two had gone together, out towards the rimed road, he stood in the entrance, peering and listening. At first, there was only the resonant boom of the wind overhead, and then far over the dome of the dead, dark plain, the wolf cry lamenting. In the rifts of clouds the Doctor saw four stars flying. It impressed the Doctor that one of them had just been obscured by the beginning of a flying cloud at the very moment he heard what he had been listening for, a sound of suppressed coughing. It was not near-by, however. He believed that down against the pale alders he could see the moving shadow.

With nervous hands he lowered the piece of canvas which served as his door, and pegged it at the bottom. Then quickly and quietly, looking at the piece of canvas frequently, he slipped the records into the case, snapped the lid shut, and carried the phonograph to his couch. There, pausing often to stare at the canvas and listen, he dug earth from the wall and disclosed a piece of board. Behind this there was a deep hole in the wall, into which he put the phonograph. After a moment's consideration, he went over and reached down his bundle of books and inserted it also. Then, guardedly, he once more sealed up the hole with the board and the earth. He also changed his blankets, and the grass-stuffed sack which served as a pillow, so that he could lie facing the entrance. After carefully placing two more blocks of peat upon the fire, he stood for a long time watching the stretched canvas, but it seemed to billow naturally with the first gusts of a lowering wind. At last he prayed, and got in under his blankets, and closed his smoke-smarting eyes. On the inside of the bed, next the wall, he could feel with his hand the comfortable piece of lead pipe.

Parable of
the Law

franz kafka

K. WAITED FOR HIM at the foot of the steps. The priest stretched out his
hand to K. while he was still on the way down from a higher level. 'Have
you a little time for me?' asked K. 'As much time as you need,' said the
priest, giving K. the small lamp to carry. Even close at hand he still wore
a certain air of solemnity. 'You are very good to me,' said K. They paced side
by side up and down the dusky aisle. 'But you are an exception among those
who belong to the Court. I have more trust in you than in any of the others,
though I know many of them. With you I can speak openly.' 'Don't be
deluded,' said the priest. 'How am I being deluded?' asked K. 'You are delud-
ing yourself about the Court,' said the priest. 'In the writings which preface
the Law that particular delusion is described thus: Before the Law stands
a door-keeper on guard. To this door-keeper there comes a man from the
country who begs for admittance to the Law. But the door-keeper says that
he cannot admit the man at the moment. The man, on reflection, asks if he
will be allowed, then, to enter later. "It is possible," answers the doorkeeper,
"but not at this moment." Since the door leading into the Law stands open
as usual and the door-keeper steps to one side, the man bends down to peer
through the entrance. When the door-keeper sees that, he laughs and says:
"If you are so strongly tempted, try to get in without my permission. But
note that I am powerful. And I am only the lowest door-keeper. From hall
to hall, keepers stand at every door, one more powerful than the other. Even

the third of these has an aspect that even I cannot bear to look at." These
are difficulties which the man from the country has not expected to meet,
the Law, he thinks, should be accessible to every man and at all times, and
when he looks more closely at the door-keeper in his furred robe, with his
huge pointed nose and long thin, Tartar beard, he decides that he had better
wait until he gets permission to enter. The door-keeper gives him a stool and
lets him sit down at the side of the door. There he sits waiting for days and
years. He makes many attempts to be allowed in and wearies the door-
keeper with his importunity. The door-keeper often engages him in brief
conversation, asking him about his home and about other matters, but the
questions are put quite impersonally, as great men put questions, and always
conclude with the statement that the man cannot be allowed to enter yet.
The man, who has equipped himself with many things for his journey, parts
with all he has, however valuable, in the hope of bribing the door-keeper.
The door-keeper accepts it all, saying, however, as he takes each gift: "I
take this only to keep you from feeling that you have left something undone."
During all these long years the man watches the door-keeper almost inces-
santly. He forgets about the other door-keepers, and this one seems to him
the only barrier between himself and the Law. In the first years he curses his
evil fate aloud; later, as he grows old, he only mutters to himself. He grows
childish, and since in his prolonged watch he has learned to know even the
fleas in the door-keeper's fur collar, he begs the very fleas to help him and
to persuade the door-keeper to change his mind. Finally his eyes grow dim
and he does not know whether the world is really darkening around him or
whether his eyes are only deceiving him. But in the darkness he can now
perceive a radiance that streams immortally from the door of the Law. Now
his life is drawing to a close. Before he dies, all that he has experienced
during the whole time of his sojourn condenses in his mind into one question,
which he has never yet put to the door-keeper. He beckons the door-keeper,
since he can no longer raise his stiffening body. The door-keeper has to bend
far down to hear him, for the difference in size between them has increased
very much to the man's disadvantage. "What do you want to know now?"
asks the door-keeper, "you are insatiable." "Everyone strives to attain the
Law," answers the man, "how does it come about, then, that in all these years
no one has come seeking admittance but me?" The door-keeper perceives
that the man is at the end of his strength and his hearing is failing, so he
bellows in his ear: "No one but you could gain admittance through this door,
since this door was intended only for you. I am now going to shut it." '

'So the door-keeper deluded the man,' said K. immediately, strongly
attracted by the story. 'Don't be too hasty,' said the priest, 'don't take over
an opinion without testing it. I have told you the story in the very words of
the scriptures. There's no mention of delusion in it.' 'But it's clear enough,'
said K., 'and your first interpretation of it was quite right. The door-keeper

gave the message of salvation to the man only when it could no longer help him.' 'He was not asked the question any earlier,' said the priest, 'and you must consider, too, that he was only a door-keeper, and as such fulfilled his duty.' 'What makes you think he fulfilled his duty?' asked K. 'He didn't fulfil it. His duty might have been to keep all strangers away, but this man, for whom the door was intended, should have been let in.' 'You have not enough respect for the written word and you are altering the story,' said the priest. 'The story contains two important statements made by the door-keeper about admission to the Law, one at the beginning, the other at the end. The first statement is: that he cannot admit the man at the moment, and the other is: that this door was intended only for the man. If there were a contradiction between the two, you would be right and the door-keeper would have deluded the man. But there is no contradiction. The first statement, on the contrary, even implies the second. One could almost say that in suggesting to the man the possibility of future admittance the door-keeper is exceeding his duty. At that moment his apparent duty is to refuse admittance and indeed many commentators are surprised that the suggestion should be made at all, since the door-keeper appears to be a precisian with a stern regard for duty. He does not once leave his post during these many years, and he does not shut the door until the very last minute; he is conscious of the importance of his office, for he says: "I am powerful"; he is respectful to his superiors, for he says: "I am only the lowest door-keeper"; he is not garrulous, for during all these years he puts only what are called "impersonal questions"; he is not to be bribed, for he says in accepting a gift: "I take this only to keep you from feeling that you have left something undone"; where his duty is concerned he is to be moved neither by pity nor rage, for we are told that the man "wearied the door-keeper with his importunity"; and finally even his external appearance hints at a pedantic character, the large, pointed nose and the long, thin, black, Tartar beard. Could one imagine a more faithful door-keeper? Yet the door-keeper has other elements in his character which are likely to advantage anyone seeking admittance and which make it comprehensible enough that he should somewhat exceed his duty in suggesting the possibility of future admittance. For it cannot be denied that he is a little simple-minded and consequently a little conceited. Take the statements he makes about his power and the power of the other door-keepers and their dreadful aspect which even he cannot bear to see—I hold that these statements may be true enough, but that the way in which he brings them out shows that his perceptions are confused by simpleness of mind and conceit. The commentators note in this connexion: "The right perception of any matter and a misunderstanding of the same matter do not wholly exclude each other." One must at any rate assume that such simpleness and conceit, however sparingly indicated, are likely to weaken his defence of the door; they are breaches in the character of the door-keeper. To this must be added the fact that the door-keeper seems to be a friendly creature by nature, he is by no means always on his official dignity. In the very first moments he allows himself the jest of inviting the man to enter in spite of the strictly maintained veto against entry; then he does not, for instance, send the man away, but gives him, as we are told, a stool and lets him sit down beside the door. The patience with which he endures the man's appeals during so many years, the brief conversations, the acceptance of the gifts, the politeness with which he allows the man to curse loudly in his presence the fate for which he himself is responsible—all this lets us deduce certain motions of sympathy. Not every door-keeper would have acted thus. And finally, in answer to a gesture of the man's he stoops low down to give him the chance of putting a last question. Nothing but mild impatience—the door-keeper knows that this is the end of it all—is discernible in the words: "You are insatiable." Some push this mode of interpretation even further and hold that these words express a kind of friendly admiration, though not without a hint of condescension. At any rate the figure of the door-keeper can be said to come out very differently from what you fancied.' 'You have studied the story more exactly and for a longer time than I have,' said K. They were both silent for a little while. Then K. said: 'So you think the man was not deluded?' 'Don't misunderstand me,' said the priest, 'I am only showing you the various opinions concerning that point. You must not pay too much attention to them. The scriptures are unalterable and the comments often enough merely express the commentator's bewilderment. In this case there even exists an interpretation which claims that the deluded person is really the door-keeper.' 'That's a far-fetched interpretation,' said K. 'On what is it based?' 'It is based,' answered the priest, 'on the simple-mindedness of the door-keeper. The argument is that he does not know the Law from inside, he knows only the way that leads to it, where he patrols up and down. His ideas of the interior are assumed to be childish, and it is supposed that he himself is afraid of the other guardians whom he holds up as bogies before the man. Indeed, he fears them more than the man does, since the man is determined to enter after hearing about the dreadful guardians of the interior, while the door-keeper has no desire to enter, at least not so far as we are told. Others again say that he must have been in the interior already, since he is after all engaged in the service of the Law and can only have been appointed from inside. This is countered by arguing that he may have been appointed by a voice calling from the interior, and that anyhow he cannot have been far inside, since the aspect of the third door-keeper is more than he can endure. Moreover, no indication is given that during all these years he ever made any remarks showing a knowledge of the interior, except for the one remark about the door-keepers. He may have been forbidden to do so, but there is no mention of that either. On these grounds the conclusion is reached that he knows nothing about the aspect and significance of the interior, so that he is in a state of delusion. But he is deceived also about his relation to the man from the country, for he is subject to the man and does not know it. He treats the man instead as his own subordinate, as can be recognized from many details that must be still fresh in your mind. But, according to this view of the story, it is just as clearly indicated that he is really subordinated to the man. In the first place, a bondman is always subject to a free man. Now the man from the country is really free, he can go where he likes, it is only the Law that is closed to him, and access to the Law is forbidden him only by one individual, the door-keeper. When he sits down on the stool by the side of the door and stays there for the rest of his life, he does it of his own free will; in the story there is no mention of any compulsion. But the door-keeper is bound to his post by his very office, he does not dare strike out into the country, nor apparently may he go into the interior of the Law, even should he wish to. Besides, although he is in the service of the Law, his service is confined to this one entrance; that is to say, he serves only this man for whom alone the entrance is intended. On that ground too he is subject to the man. One must assume that for many years, for as long as it takes a man to grow up to the prime of life, his service was in a sense an empty formality, since he had to wait for a man to come, that is to say someone in the prime of life, and so had to wait a long time before the purpose of his service could be fulfilled, and, moreover, had to wait on the man's pleasure, for the man came of his own free will. But the termination of his service also depends on the man's term of life, so that to the very end he is subject to the man. And it is emphasized throughout that the door-keeper apparently realizes nothing of all this. That is not in itself remarkable, since according to this interpretation the door-keeper is deceived in a much more important issue, affecting his very office. At the end, for example, he says regarding the entrance to the Law: "I am now going to shut it," but at the beginning of the story we are told that the door leading into the Law stands always open, and if it stands open always, that is to say at all times, without reference to the life or death of the man, then the door-keeper is incapable of closing it. There is some difference of opinion about the motive behind the door-keeper's statement, whether he said he was going to close the door merely for the sake of giving an answer, or to emphasize his devotion to duty, or to bring the man into a state of grief and regret in his last moments. But there is no lack of agreement that the door-keeper will not be able to shut the door. Many indeed profess to find that he is subordinate to the man even in wisdom, towards the end, at least, for the man sees the radiance that issues from the door of the Law while the door-keeper in his official position must stand with his back to the door, nor does he say anything to show that he has perceived the change.' 'That is well argued,' said K., after repeating to himself in a low voice several passages from the priest's exposition. 'It is well argued, and I am inclined to agree that the door-keeper is deluded. But that has not made me abandon my former opinion, since both conclusions are to some extent compatible. Whether the door-keeper is clear-sighted or deluded does not dispose of the matter. I said the man is deluded. If the door-keeper is clear-sighted, one might have doubts about that, but if the door-keeper himself is deluded, then his delusion must of necessity be communicated to the man. That makes the door-keeper not, indeed, a swindler, but a creature so simple-minded that he ought to be dismissed at once from his office. You mustn't forget that the door-keeper's delusions do himself no harm but do infinite harm to the man.' 'There are objections to that,' said the priest. 'Many aver that the story confers no right on anyone to pass judgement on the door-keeper. Whatever he may seem to us, he is yet a servant of the Law; that is, he belongs to the Law and as such is set beyond human judgement. In that case one dare not believe that the door-keeper is subordinate to the man. Bound as he is by his service, even at the door of the Law, he is incomparably freer than anyone at large in the world. The man is only seeking the Law, the door-keeper is already attached to it. It is the Law that has placed him at his post; to doubt his integrity is to doubt the Law itself.' 'I don't agree with that point of view,' said K. shaking his head, 'for if one accepts it, one must accept as true everything the door-keeper says. But you yourself have sufficiently proved how impossible it is to do that.' 'No,' said the priest, 'it is not necessary to accept everything as true, one must only accept it as necessary.' 'A melancholy conclusion,' said K. 'It turns lying into a universal principle.'

K. said that with finality, but it was not his final judgement. He was too tired to survey all the conclusions arising from the story, and the trains of thought into which it was leading him were unfamiliar, dealing with impalpabilities better suited to a theme for discussion among Court officials than for him. The simple story had lost its clear outline, he wanted to put it out of his mind, and the priest, who now showed great delicacy of feeling, suffered him to do so and accepted his comment in silence, although undoubtedly he did not agree with it.

The Parable of
the Bridge

franz kafka

I WAS STIFF AND COLD, I was a bridge. Over an abyss I lay. The points of my feet bored in on one side, my hands on the other. I had clamped myself fast in the crumbling clay. My coattails fluttered at my sides. In the depths the icy trout stream sounded. No tourist strayed to this pathless height, the bridge was not yet traced on any map. So I lay and waited; I could only wait. Without falling no bridge, once spanned, can cease to be a bridge.

Once, toward evening it was—was it the first, was it the thousandth, I do not know—my thoughts were always in confusion and went round and round. Toward evening in summer, the brook rustled darkly, I heard a human step! To me, to me.—Extend yourself, bridge, prepare you railless beam, hold the one entrusted to you. Compensate unnoticeably for the uncertainty of his step, but if he stumbles, then let yourself be known and like a mountain god hurl him onto the land.

He came, with the iron point of his stick he tapped me, then with it he lifted my coattails and arranged them on me. He plunged the point into my bushy hair and kept it there for a long time, no doubt while he wildly gazed round him. Then, however, I was following him in my dream over mountain and valley—he sprang with both feet onto the middle of my body. I shuddered with wild pain, completely unknowing. Who was it? A child? A dream? A highwayman? A suicide? A tempter? A destroyer? And I turned round so that I could see him.—A bridge to turn around! I had not yet turned round, when I was falling, I was falling and I was torn to pieces and impaled on the pointed rocks, which had always stared up at me so peacefully from the rushing water.

Ironic Modes

fantastic satire
humor
fable
utopian fiction
parody

Introduction to
Ironic Modes

RATHER THAN INVENTING wonderful or terrible incidents as the writer of romance does, the satirist normally exaggerates common eccentricities, vices, and foibles in the manner of the caricaturist who departs from mimetic accuracy in the enlargement of a nose or an ear. Mock romance, mock epic, parody, mock argument, and verbal caricature are combinations simultaneously of an implicit concept of propriety or decorum and a magnified greed, gullibility, knavery, or other human defect. However, satire may add to its normal spirit of ironic criticism certain elements of romance, such as the heroic journey or the marvelous incident. Rabelais, Swift, and Voltaire, for instance, expose degeneracy and foolishness with different combinations of the fantastic and the deformed. By having Gargantua and his son Pantagruel suffer all the conceivable ailments to which the human body is suceptible, Rabelais exposes the romanticism of the hero-making process. The adventurous protagonists of Swifts and Voltaire are less lusty and more easily shocked than Rabelais', but they too travel through a cankered, illogical world that flails body and spirit with sublime disregard for personal dignity and a liking for fabled adventure.

As any of these examples will illustrate, narrative satire makes a special use of fable and chronological sequence. Ordinarily, satirists require hypothetical or "ideal" instances of evils and either an argumentative line of development, like that of Erasmus' *Praise of Folly*, or a great many hard-core cases of folly, usually arranged episodically. Their method of canvasing the plentiful field of human vice is not always compatible with the consistent, sequential logic of narrative. Also, more often than most fablers the narrative satirist lifts the fictional mask, as Swift does in the passage quoted below, and reinforces narrative with didactic elements contributed by a speaker free to generalize from the incidents he has invented. He "sermonizes" the text in much the same way that many modern plays break the barrier between play and audience in order to appeal more directly to the audience's moral sense. Fantastic satire is therefore often a curiously mixed narrative-didactic mode; it entices us into a fictional world that is both elaborate in detail and highly manipulated to make its point clear.

The friction between narrative logic and satiric intent is perhaps still more evident in characterization. Minor characters in satire tend to become static humorous types described for their own sakes rather than contributors to an evolving plot—as with "Dr. Goat" in the Spanish picaresque novel *The Swindler*:

> He was in holy orders, as skinny as a peashooter, generous only in height, with a small head and ginger hair. I need say no more, if you remember that Judas had red hair. His eyes were sunk so deep in his head that they were like lamps at the end of a cave; so sunken and dark that they looked like a draper's window. His nose was partly Roman and partly French, because it was poxy with cold sores (not the real pox of course; it costs money to catch that). His whiskers were pale, scared stiff of his starving mouth which was threatening to gnaw them. I don't know how many of his teeth he had missing: I suppose he had dismissed them as there was never any work for them to do. His neck was as long as an ostrich's and his Adam's apple looked as if it had been forced to go and look for food.[1]

Because the protagonist provides the lens through which we see each adventure, satire ordinarily changes incidents, supporting characters, and situations freely, as the illustration of such vices as the "Goat's" penury demands, without developing the central character. The Swindler, Gulliver, Candide, or Gargantua must remain incurable if he is to receive and register new shock and indignation at each exposure to folly and knavery. Hence as long as Voltaire requires Candide's inexperience and naïveté, Candide resists discarding the optimism that his teachers have instilled in him.

Hence in place of the psychological development of narrative characters, satiric plots offer a special kind of continuity, often closer to that of a catalogue or to an encyclopedia of follies than to continuous narrative. Picaresque satire, especially, passes from incident to incident as though through categories of vice. Each new crowd that the Swindler joins has its own specialists in knavery, like the professional confidence men of Madrid, some of them "gentlemen without funds," as one of them explains to him, "others empty-bellied, half-baked, scabby, skinny and wolfish," but all of then devoted to their particular rackets. The arts and dodges of each swindle

---

[1] *Two Spanish Picaresque Novels: Lazarillo de Tormes and The Swindler*, trans. Michael Alpert (Baltimore: Penguin Books, 1969), p. 93.

are described with meticulous care, and then the Swindler moves on to new territory. Satire like *Gulliver's Travels* and *Candide*—the heroes of which are not themselves illustrations of vice—are usually strung together along a similar line of adventures but without the direct participation of the protagonist himself in the hunger, scatology, flogging, cheating, and obtuseness that he finds on his travels through the fringes of society.

The name of satire itself gives us a clue to the special function of narrative in it: Satire assembles a "satura" or assorted mixture, a "full plate," of examples in whatever order seems best for their moral exposure, which may not be the best order for the development of a continuing character. By the device of enumeration, the satirist often includes evils too numerous for narrative illustration. Thus when Gulliver (in the fourth book of the *Travel*) counts over European habits happily missing from the better life of the Houyhnhnms, he suggests further sequences to which Swift might have exposed him had he wished to elaborate. Satisfied with the list itself in this instance, Swift makes a ventriloquist's presentation through Gulliver of a plenty that even the most inventive of fables would have difficulty illustrating:

> I had no occasion of bribing, flattering or pimping to procure the favour of any great man or of his minion. I wanted no fence against fraud or oppression; here was neither physician to destroy my body, nor lawyer to ruin my fortune; no informer to watch my words and actions, or forge accusations against me for hire: here were no gibers, censurers, backbiters, pickpockets, highwaymen, housebreakers, attorneys, bawds, buffoons, gamesters, politicians, wits, splenetics, tedious talkers, controvertists, ravishers, murderers, robbers, virtuosos: no leaders or followers of party and faction: no encouragers to vice, by seducement or examples: no dungeon, axes, gibbets, whipping-posts, or pillories: no cheating shopkeepers or mechanics: no pride, vanity, or affectation: no fops, bullies, drunkards, strolling whores, or poxes: no ranting, lewd, expensive wives.

Like several others of its kind in the *Travels*, the list is miscellaneous as well as plentiful in types, and randomness is part of its effect: All system and logic fail before the abundance of men's vices. The touch of organization that the list has merely reinforces the shock to normal expectation: Physicians destroy rather than improve health; attorneys are listed between housebreakers and bawds, and like politicians are impugned by the company they keep.

When narrative structure and the anatomy of moral defects combine, the sequential logic of an unfolding, accumulative experience has to yield something to the "full plate" miscellany and the sermonizing use of illustration in this manner. At the same time, however, hypothetical models and lists of follies in turn concede something to the temporal development of fable and character. Though Gulliver and the narrative progress in which he participates may be set aside to accommodate the local effects of Swift's wit and satiric purpose and though Candide remains naive despite a multitude of nerve-shattering encounters with villainy and folly, both principal characters threaten eventually to cease being authorial puppets. The forward-moving continuity of narrative demands that if a character carries the same name from incident to incident he must also carry memory and trained reflexes. By maintaining a delicate balance between narrative episodes as illustrations of itemized vices and as stages of development, and by manipulating constantly the collision of ideals and realities, Voltaire manages eventually to fuse satiric anatomy, narrative, the roman à these, utopian fiction, and parody. Candide's career ends as a logical outcome both of accumulated experience and of the satiric thesis of the work: He outgrows the flat type of the naive optimist and from a plateau of new awareness becomes a saddened, nearly three-dimensional man. The critical debate over the character of Gulliver, especially in the final book of the *Travels,* stems in part from a similar tension between narrative logic and satiric plenty, but in this case Gulliver proves less easily transformable into a consistent character. Readers must finally judge for themselves whether or not Swift allows him to emerge from the world of satiric fantasy and become a character who conceivably might dwell in historical England. The material for such an emergence from puppetdom is present in both Voltaire and Swift in the exposure of both protagonists, especially Gulliver, to meticulously exact ordinary details and facts. So firmly grounded in circumstantial evidence is the fantasy that realistic psychological growth can easily be imagined in the entanglement of character and environment, especially since character in fiction is so often revealed in the mirror of concrete objects and incidents that correspond in some way to it.

As *Candide* and the *Travels* suggest, we frequently find in satire not only mixtures of narrative technique, fantastic medlies of folly, and moral theses but also utopian elements and their parody. An arrangement of "perfect" follies in a never-never land is inherently utopian. Beyond that, works like Butler's *Erehwon* and Orwell's *1984* enlarge upon the clash between the imaginary good place and the perfect nightmare, in which governments and citizenry become bad enough to tempt the satirist. Like other forms of satire, utopian narrative satire involves a continuous though implicit view of normality; but it compares exceptionally high expectations for a good life with exceptionally grotesque distortions of it and thus widens the gap between the two components of ironic statement. In utopian modes satire frequently touches upon romance and demonstrates that one may find an inversion for nearly every mode. In straightforward high or mythic modes, the good place is a natural paradise or a sacred court such as that of St. John's revelations or the New Jerusalem of Spenser and Blake. Hypothetical good places range downward from there through degrees of perfection to the opposite extreme, the infernal city. Near the first extreme is the romance utopia located in an out-of-the-way place, an Arcadia, for instance, that is something less than celestial but more than ordinary. Such a place combines idyllic nature with a peaceful and non-competitive society. Near the other extreme is the demonic city such as the London of Conrad's *Secret Agent* or the nighttime Dublin of Joyce's *Ulysses*. Somewhere near the center is the purely historical city— Paris, London, New York. This temporal city is the main locality of most novels and of realistic fiction generally; it may contain shades of utopia or Pandaemonium, but for the most part it displays merely the ordinary pleasures, muddled citizenry, and bureaucracy to which we have grown accustomed. Rather than the fixed and unchanging archetypes of hell or heaven or the relatively fixed types of virtue and vice in utopian and demonic places, it illustrates a world of process, where experience is always changing, people grow and decline, and all things flow from others without final boundaries.

Each of these locations may have its ironic versions or inversions. Since one man's utopia is likely to be another man's nightmare, the perfect city or court reveals new possibilities as soon as the satirist discovers it; it reminds him quickly both of man's capacity to believe in any illusion and of less ideal places where inept government combines with foolishness to make a Vanity Fair of all social arrangements. Such a place is less perfect in evil than outright Pandaemonium and of course very far from the celestial city, but it may suggest these extremes to the satirist, whose use of fantasy often juxtaposes vices and follies with products of the mythic imagination. In the satirist's inversion of utopia, a protagonist like Voltaire's Candide is constantly threatened with outrages to mind and body and is lucky to escape assault, dismemberment, or burning; at the same time, the very location of his trials suggest what ought to be, in a dimension somewhat beyond his usual simple expectations. In the city of the clouds, Gulliver finds stupidity prevailing despite pretenses to a higher scientific order and wisdom; even among the Houyhnhnms the greatest reason sometimes leads to the most inhumane policy. (In any case, Gulliver himself is not fit to live there.) Candide's best hope, finally, is not utopia at all but some small, obscure garden—the nearest thing to paradise he can manage—to which he retires while still mentally and physically intact. Whereas Candide seeks that retirement before he is hopelessly embittered, Gulliver waits too long and retires already an incurable misanthropist, disillusioned by too frequent and too violent a contrast between ideals and their grotesque distortion.

A mode as promiscuous as satiric fantasy, with its catalogues of vice, its mock arguments, its narrative examples, its utopian elements, and its marvels of bizarre and perverted behavior, will not hesitate to draw upon other generic elements as well if they will augment its "full plate." One element that has recently become more prominent in satire is science fiction, perhaps because an ideal place, language, perpetual motion machine, or whatever one may conceive, is always about to be built by science and make its contribution to utopia. Swift anticipates the flirtation between science fiction and satire in the Grand Academy of Lagado, where pure reason is given a long enough tether to destroy itself. Unfortunately, those who propose to use science as a means to the perfect life are usually captured by one facet of a fixed idea and blinded to its other implications—like ardent exponents of a miracle drug that expertly cures one disease but just as efficiently kills patients with its "side effects." If science fiction and utopian satire have come to rub elbows more frequently since Swift's time, it is partly because science has come even more to the forefront as a special kind of progress. But its projected dreams of an ideal planetary (or interplanetary) life are undercut—in the satirist's jaundiced eye—by a continuous degeneration of the environment, as in fulfillment of Swiftean and Orwellean prophecies it produces destructive weapons on the way to peacefully harnessed power; insecticides that kill birds, fish, and people as well as twelve-spotted beetles; and automobiles that devour oxygen and wreck easily.

Utopian or pastoral good places, "science," heroic modes, and satire thus collaborate frequently in a special kind of fiction that mixes their different expectations for didactic effectiveness. The ironies of their mixture are by no means a new discovery, nor are they limited to prose fiction. For Milton in *Paradise Lost,* for instance, the initiator of all ambitious science and self-improving quests for knowledge and power is Satan, whose Faustian idea for the improvement of Heaven and whose eventual demonic city are products of the most advanced discoveries in munitions, propaganda, and enginering. It is no accident that the forbidden apple hangs from the tree of "science" ("knowledge"), which Milton associates with unprincipled self-advancement and with an experiment in mind-expanding chemistry. Epic ambition, romantic aspiration, utopian thought, and satire touch briefly in Eve's scheme to remake her own nature and achieve a magnificent, godlike vision. When her plan backfires, innocent knowledge is converted into tragic experience. The ironist in Milton reacts to that acid transformation of dreams as the subordinate partner to the visionary in him, who sees the emergence eventually of a further good and a higher paradise from the fall. Though for a moment Satan brings fantasy and sacred parody into the poem and causes dreams and ideals to break loose from their containing order, the primacy of the creator's plan is reasserted and with it the higher strain of the religious epic. (Note a similar combination of romance and irony in Twain's diary of Eve.)

Whether or not the heroic has precisely the implications it has in utopian works or Milton's epic, it frequently does contribute one side to irony's double awareness. In *Don Quixote,* Cervantes presents a constant interplay between high expectations, derived from chivalric romance, and undignified realities. Even brief ironic parables like Dr. Johnson's, James Thurber's, and

William March's obviously play upon a similar discrepancy and use fantasy to reinforce the playfulness of their indirection. When vultures are made to talk we can expect an oblique angle on what they consider. In a work like *Tristram Shandy* the standards of expectation are set not so much by normal reality as by customary novelistic procedure, and the constant disruption of that procedure strikes us as itself fantastic. Sterne attacks the logic of causal sequence at its root. We cannot identify in any simple way with a character whose every motion is blocked by an interfering incident because heroic achievement is inseparable from sequential growth and the exercise of will against a resisting environment.

As we suggest in *Forms of Poetry,* "satire's most natural form...seems to be 'mock-form,' or parody, just as its most natural kind of meaning seems to be irony, or 'mock-meaning.' " Eve and Satan succeed in constructing parodies of spiritual progress; Swift's academicians, of scientific discovery; and Sterne's household, of continuous logic and causal sequence. In these examples of the ironic mode, parody is subordinate to a more general aim. But parody may be a distinctive kind in its own right when it caricatures a particular style. As continuous ironic comparison, it hearkens back to the origins of satire in the hex or charm in which a model of an enemy is transfixed with a pin or a ritual formula; it takes its value both from accurate imitation and from a distorting discrepancy between it and the original. Max Beerbohm's parody of Henry James's involved style is a good example. It calls the main values of that style into question—the heightened sensibility, the victory of nuance over plain sense, the indirectness of statement, the odd twist of syntax or placement of an adverb that carries a sentence outside ordinary speech by giving it a precious turn. As with all particular parodies, awareness of the thing parodied is necessary to complete its metaphoric comparison; a "take off" is basically an act of distorting mimicry, a flight of inventive imagination over a subject already familiar, the effect of which is to make us regard the subject from a new and more critical perspective. Parody is also sportive as well as critical, however. If the parodist can perform in the style of James or Hemingway and still have reserves of wit to mock that style, it cannot be so difficult to be the original. But such a claim can only be made in a light-hearted manner: Max Beerbohm is not after all Henry James; he merely plays a certain kind of game that demonstrates his mastery of the difference.

In this he is typical of both the parodist in particular and ironists in general, because whatever the object of criticism, the essence of irony is playfulness. Satiric fantasy, mock parables, and the mock-heroic all require an established form or set of values as the other half of the statement they make; in a perfect world, there would presumably be no irony. At one periphery of the mode, where playfulness begins to be missing, is the dark humor of a John Hawkes or Peter Matthiessen, or the relatively humorless warp of Kafka. At the other periphery, where the critical spirit weakens and humor dominates, we have comedies of situation such as Evelyn Waugh's. In between, modern texts and authors such as Abram Tertz (*The Makepeace Experiment*), Ray Bradbury, Kurt Vonnegut, Samuel Beckett, Saul Bellow (in *Henderson the Rain King*), John Barth, and Nathanael West still combine the fable or heroic voyage with the continuously dashed expectations of satire, much in the manner of Rabelais, Swift, and Voltaire, though usually with less gusto and multiplicity of detail. In the tradition that emphasizes social matter more than fable and fantasy, Kingsley Amis, Henry Green, and E. M. Forster continue in the critical spirit of *Tristram Shandy* and *Vanity Fair*. The following selections given an idea of that abiding ironic spirit and its fruitful combinations with heroic and utopian fictions and other narrative forms.

Gargantua and Panurge

rabelais

AFTER WHAT MANNER GARGANTUA HAD HIS NAME GIVEN HIM;
AND HOW HE TIPELED, BIBBED, AND CURRIED THE CAN

THE GOOD MAN GRANGOUSIER, drinking and making merry with the rest, heard the horrible noise which his son had made as he entered into the light of this world, when he cried out, "Drink, drink, drink"; whereupon he said in French, *"Que* GRAND TU AS & *souple le gousier";* that is to say, "How great and nimble a throat thou hast"; which the company hearing, said, that verily the child ought to be called Gargantua, because it was the first word that, after his birth, his father had spoke, in imitation, and at the example, of the ancient Hebrews; whereunto he condescended, and his mother was very well pleased therewith: in the meanwhile, to quiet the child, they gave him to drink a *tirelarigot,* that is, till his throat was like to crack with it; then was he carried to the font, and there baptized, according to the manner of good Christians.

Immediately thereafter were appointed for him seventeen thousand nine hundred and thirteen cows, of the towns of Pautille and Breemond, to furnish him with milk in ordinary; for it was impossible to find a nurse sufficient for him in all the country, considering the great quantity of milk that was requisite for his nourishment; although there were not wanting some doctors of the opinion of Scotus, who affirmed that his own mother gave him suck, and that she could draw out of her breasts one thousand four hundred two pipes and nine pails of milk at every time: which, indeed, is not probable;

From THE WORKS OF RABELAIS, trans. Ives Washburn. Reprinted by permission of the Tudor Publishing Company, New York. © 1930 by Ives Washburn.

and this point hath been found duggishly scandalous and offensive to tender ears, for that it savoured a little of heresy. Thus was he handled for one year and ten months; after which time, by the advice of physicians, they began to carry him abroad, and then was made for him a fine little cart, drawn with oxen, of the invention of Jan Denio, wherein they led him hither and thither with great joy; and he was worth the seeing, for he was a fine boy, had a burly physiognomy, and almost ten chins; he cried very little, but beshit himself every hour; for, to speak truly of him, he was wonderfully phlegmatic in his posteriors, both by reason of his natural complexion, and the accidental disposition which had befallen him by his too much quaffing of the Septembral juice. Yet without a cause did not he sip one drop; for if he happened to be vexed, angry, displeased, or sorry; if he did fret, if he did weep, if he did cry, and what grievous quarter soever he kept, bring him some drink, he would be instantly pacified, come to his own temper, be in a good humour again, and as still and quiet as ever. One of his governesses told me (swearing by her fig) how he was so accustomed to this kind of way, that at the sound of pints and flaggons, he would on a sudden fall into an ecstasy, as if he had then tasted of the joys of Paradise; so that they, upon consideration of this his divine complexion, would every morning, to cheer him up, play with a knife upon the glasses, on the bottles with their stopples, and on the pottle-pots with their lids and covers, at the sound whereof he become gay, would leap for joy, would loll and rock himself in the cradle, then nod with his head, *monocordizing* his fingers, and *barytonizing* with his tail.

HOW PANURGE BELATED THE MANNER HOW HE ESCAPED OUT OF THE HANDS OF THE TURKS

The great wit and judgment of Pantagruel was immediately after this made known to all the world, by seting forth his praises in print, and putting upon record this late wonderful proof he had given thereof amongst the rolls of the crown, and registers of the palace; in such sort, that everybody began to say that Solomon, who by a probable guess only, without any further certainty, caused the child to be delivered to his own mother, shewed never in his time such a masterpiece of wisdom, as the good Pantagruel had done: happy are we therefore that have him in our country. And indeed they would have made him thereupon master of the requests, and president in the court; but he refused all, very graciously thanking them for their offer; "for," said he, "there is too much slavery in these offices, and very hardly can they be saved that do exercise them, considering the great corruption that is amongst men; which makes me believe, if the empty seats of angels be not filled with other kind of people than those, we shall not have the final judgment these seven thousand sixty and seven jubilees yet to come: and so Cusanus will be deceived in his conjecture. Remember that I have told you of it, and given you fair advertisement in time and place convenient. But if you have any hogsheads of good wine, I willingly will accept of a present of that." Which they very heartily did do, in sending him of the best that was in the city; and he drank reasonably well. But poor Panurge bibbed and bowsed of it most villainously: for he was as dry as a red-herring, as lean as a rake, and like a poor lank slender cat, walked gingerly as if he had trod upon eggs; so that by some one being admonished, in the midst of his draught of a large deep bowl, full of excellent claret, with these words: "Fair and softly, gossip, you suck up as if you were mad"; "I give thee to the devil," said he; "thou hast not found here thy tippling sippers of Paris, that drink no more than the chaffinch, and never take in their beak full of liquor, till they be bobbed on the tails after the manner of the sparrows. O companion, if I could mount up as well as I can get down, I had been long ere this above the sphere of the moon with Empedocles. But I cannot tell what a devil this means. This wine is so good and delicious, that the more I drink thereof, the more I am athirst. I believe the shadow of my master Pantagruel maketh men a-thirsty, as the moon makes the catarrhs and defluxions." At which word the company began to laugh; which Pantagruel perceiving, said: "Panurge, what is that which moves you to laugh so?" "Sir," said he, "I was telling them that those devilish Turks are very unhappy, in that they never drink one drop of wine; and that though there were no other harm in all Mahomet's alcoran, yet for this one base point of abstinence from wine, which therein is commanded, I would not submit myself unto their law." "But now tell me," said Pantagruel, "how you escaped out of their hands." "By G—, sir," said Panurge, "I will not lie to you in one word.

"The rascally Turks had broached me upon a spit, all larded like a rabbit: for I was so dry and meagre, that otherwise of my flesh they would have made but very bad meat: and in this manner began to roast me alive. As they were thus roasting me, I recommended myself unto the divine grace, having in my mind the good St. Lawrence, and always hoped in God that he would deliver me out of this torment; which came to pass, and that very strangely; for as I did commit myself with all my heart to God, crying, 'Lord God, help me! Lord God, save me! Lord God, take me out of this pain and hellish torture, wherein these traitorous dogs detain me for my sincerity in the maintenance of thy law!' the turnspit fell asleep by the divine will, or else by the virtue of some good Mercury, who cunningly brought Argus into a sleep for all his hundred eyes. When I saw that he did no longer turn me in roasting, I looked upon him, and perceived that he was fast asleep: then took I up in my teeth a firebrand, by the end where it was not burnt, and cast it into the lap of my roaster; and another did I throw as well as I could under a field bed, that was placed near to the chimney, wherein was the straw-bed of my master turnspit. Presently the fire took hold in the straw, and from the straw to the bed, and from the bed to

the loft, which was planked and cieled with fir, after the fashion of the
foot of a lamp. But the best was that the fire, which I had cast into the
lap of my paltry roaster, burnt all his groin, and was beginning to seize upon
his cullions, when he became sensible of the danger: for his smelling was not
so bad, but that he felt it sooner than he could have seen daylight. Then
suddenly getting up, and in great amazement running to the window, he
cried out to the streets as high as he could, 'Dal-baroth! dal-baroth! dal-
baroth!' which is as much to say, fire! fire! fire! Incontinently turning
about, he came straight towards me, to throw me quite into the fire; and, to
that effect, had already cut the ropes wherewith my hands were tied, and was
doing the cords from off my feet, when the master of the house hearing him
cry fire, and smelling the smoke from the very street where he was walking
with some other bashaws and mustaphas, ran with all the speed he had to
save what he could, and to carry away his jewels; yet such was his rage,
before he could well resolve how to go about it, that he caught the broach
whereon I was spitted, and therewith killed my roaster stark dead, of which
wound he died there for want of regimen, or otherwise: for he ran him in with
the spit a little above the navel, towards the right flank, till he pierced the
third lappet of his liver, and the blow slanting upwards from the diaphragm,
through which it had made penetration, the spit pass'd athwart the peri-
cardium, and came out above at his shoulders, betwixt the spondyls and the
left homoplat.

"True it is, for I will not lie, that in drawing the spit out of my body,
I fell to the ground near unto the andirons, and so by the fall took some hurt;
which indeed had been greater, but that the lardons, or little slices of
bacon wherewith I was stuck, kept off the blow. My bashaw then seeing the
case to be desperate, his house burnt without remission, and all his goods
lost, gave himself over unto all the devils in hell, calling upon some of them
by their names, Grilgoth, Astarot, Rappalus, and Gribouillis, nine several
times; which when I saw, I had above five pennyworth of fear, dreading that
the devils would come even then to carry away this fool, and seeing me so
near him would perhaps snatch me up too. I am ready, thought I, half
roasted, and my lardons will be the cause of my mischief; for these devils
are very lickorous of lardons, according to the authority which you have of
the philosopher Jamblicus and Murmault, in the apology of Bossutis,
adulterated *pro magistros nostros:* but for my better security I made the sign
of the cross; crying, *'Hagios, athanatos ho theos!'* and none came. At
which, my rogue bashaw, being very much aggrieved, would in transpiercing
his heart with my spit have killed himself; and to that purpose had set it
against his breast, but it could not enter, because it was not sharp enough.
Whereupon I, perceiving that he was not like to work upon his body the
effect which he intended, although he did not spare all the force he had to
thrust it forward, came up to him, and said, 'Master Bugrino, thou dost

here but trifle away thy time, for thou wilt never kill thyself thus as thou dost. Well, thou may'st hurt or bruise somewhat within thee, so as to make thee languish all thy life time most pitifully amongst the hands of the chirurgeons: but if thou wilt be counselled by me, I will kill thee clear outright, so that thou shalt not so much as feel it; and trust me, for I have killed a great many others, who never have complained afterward.' 'Ha, my friend,' said he, 'I prythee do so, and for thy pains I will give thee my codpiece: take, here it is, there are six hundred seraphs in it, and some fine diamonds, and most excellent rubies.' " "And where are they?" said Epistemon. "By St. John!" said Panurge, "they are a good way hence, if they always keep going: but where is the last year's snow? This was the greatest care that Villon the Parision poet took." "Make an end," said Pantagruel, "that we may know how thou didst dress thy bashaw." "By the faith of an honest man," said Panurge, "I do not lie in one word; I swaddled him in a scurvy swathel-binding, which I found lying there half-burnt, and with my cords tied him royster-like both hand and foot, in such sort that he was not able to wince; then past my spit through his throat, and hanged him thereon, fastening the end thereof at two great hooks, or cramp-irons, upon which they did hang their halberds; and then, kindling a fire under him, did flame you up my milourt, as they use to dry herrings in a chimney: with this, taking his budget, and a little javelin that was upon the foresaid hooks, I ran away a fair gallop-rake, and God he knows how I did smell my shoulder of mutton.

"When I was come down into the street, I found everybody come to put out the fire with store of water, and seeing me so half-roasted, they did naturally pity my case, and threw all their water upon me, which by a most joyful refreshing of me, did me very much good. Then did they present me with some victuals; but I could not eat much, because they gave me nothing to drink but water, after their fashion. Other hurt they did me none; only one little villainous Turkey knob-breasted rogue came to snatch away some of my lardons; but I gave him such a sturdy thump, and sound rap on the fingers, with all the weight of my javelin, that he came no more the second time. Shortly this, there came towards me a pretty young Corinthian wench, who brought me a box full of conserves, of round Myrabolan plums, called emblicks, and looked upon my poor Roger with an eye of great compassion, as it was flea-bitten and pinked with the sparkles of the fire from whence it came; for it reached no further in length, believe me, than my knees. But note, that this roasting cured me entirely of a sciatica, whereunto I had been subject above seven years before, upon that side which my roaster, by falling asleep, suffered to be burnt.

"Now whilst they were thus busy about me, the fire triumphed; never ask, how? for it took hold on above two thousand houses; which one of them espying, cried out, saying, 'By Mahoom's belly all the city is on fire,

and we do nevertheless stand gazing here, without offering to bring any relief.'
Upon this, every one ran to save his own. For my part, I took my way
towards the gate. When I was got upon the knap of a little hillock, not far
off, I turned me about as did Lot's wife, and looking back, saw all the
city burning in a fair fire: whereat I was so glad, that I had almost beshit
myself for joy; but God punished me well for it." "How?" said Pantagruel.
"Thus," said Panurge; "for when with pleasure I beheld this jolly fire,
jesting with myself, and saying, 'Ha poor fleas, ha poor mice, you will
have a bad winter of it this year; the fire is in your reeks, it is in your
bedstraw'; out came more than six, yea more than thirteen hundred and
eleven dogs, great and small, all together out of the town, flying away from
the fire. At the first approach they ran all upon me, being carried on by the
scent of my leacherous half-roasted flesh, and had even then devoured me in
a trice, if my good angel had not then inspired me with the instruction of a
remedy, very sovereign against the pain of the teeth." "And wherefore," said
Pantagruel, "wert thou afraid of the pain of the teeth? wert thou not
cured of thy rheums?" "By Palm-Sunday," said Panurge, "is there any
greater pain of the teeth than when the dogs' have you by the legs? But on a
sudden, as my good angel directed me, I thought upon my lardons, and
threw them into the midst of the field amongst them: then did the dogs
run, and fight with one another at fair teeth, which should have the lardons;
by this means they left me, and I left them also bustling with, and haring
one another. Thus did I escape frolic and lively, grammercy roast-meat and
cookery."

From Don Quixote
"The Windmills"

miguel de cervantes

...AT THAT MOMENT they caught sight of some thirty or forty windmills, which stand on that plain, and as soon as Don Quixote saw them he said to his squire: 'Fortune is guiding our affairs better than we could have wished. Look over there, friend Sancho Panza, where more than thirty monstrous giants appear. I intend to do battle with them and take all their lives. With their spoils we will begin to get rich, for this is a fair war, and it is a great service to God to wipe such a wicked brood from the face the earth.'

'What giants?' asked Sancho Panza.

'Those you see there,' replied his master, 'with tneir long arms. Some giants have them about six miles long.'

'Take care, your worship,' said Sancho; 'those things over there are not giants but windmills, and what seem to be their arms are the sails, which are whirled round in the wind and make the millstone turn.'

'It is quite clear,' replied Don Quixote, 'that you are not experienced in this matter of adventures. They are giants, and if you are afraid, go away and say your prayers, whilst I advance and engage them in fierce and unequal battle.'

As he spoke, he dug his spurs into steed Rocinante, paying no attention to his squire's shouted warning that beyond all doubt they were windmills and no giants he was advancing to attack. But he went on, so positive that they were giants that he neither listened to Sancho's cries nor noticed what

From Cervantes' DON QUIXOTE, trans. by J. M. Cohen. Reprinted by permission of Penguin Books Ltd.

they were, even when he got near them. Instead he went on shouting in a loud voice: 'Do not fly, cowards, vile creatures, for it is one knight alone who assails you.'

At that moment a slight wind arose, and the great sails began to move. At the sight of which Don Quixote shouted: 'Though you wield more arms than the giant Briareus, you shall pay for it!' Saying this, he commended himself with all his soul to his Lady Dulcinea, beseeching her aid in his great peril. Then, covering himself with his shield and putting his lance in the rest, he urged Rocinante forward at a full gallop and attacked the nearest windmill, thrusting his lance into the sail. But the wind turned it with such violence that it shivered his weapon in pieces, dragging the horse and his rider with it, and sent the knight rolling badly injured across the plain. Sancho Panza rushed to his assistance as fast as his ass could trot, but when he came up he found that the knight could not stir. Such a shock had Rochinante given him in their fall.

'O my goodness!' cried Sancho. 'Didn't I tell your worship to look what you were doing, for they were only windmills? Nobody could mistake them, unless he had windmills on the brain.'

'Silence, friend Sancho,' replied Don Quixote. 'Matters of war are more subject than most to continual change. What is more, I think—and that is the truth—that the same sage Friston who robbed me of my room and my books has turned those giants into windmills, to cheat me of the glory of conquering them. Such is the enmity he bears me; but in the very end his black arts shall avail him little against the goodness of my sword.'

'God send it as He will,' replied Sancho Panza, helping the knight to get up and remount Rocinante, whose shoulders were half dislocated.

As they discussed this last adventure they followed the road to the pass of Lapice where, Don Quixote said, they could not fail to find many and various adventures, as many travellers passed that way. He was much concerned, however, at the loss of his lance, and, speaking of it to his squire, remarked: 'I remember reading that a certain Spanish knight called Diego Perez de Vargas, having broken his sword in battle, tore a great bough or limb from an oak, and performed such deeds with it that day, and pounded so many Moors, that he earned the surname of the Pounder, and thus he and his descendants from that day onwards have been called Vargas y Machuca. I mention this because I propose to tear down just such a limb from the first oak we meet, as big and as good as his; and I intend to do such deeds with it that you may consider yourself most fortunate to have won the right to see them. For you will witness things which will scarcely be credited.'

'With God's help,' replied Sancho, 'and I believe it all as your worship says. But sit a bit more upright, sir, for you seem to be riding lop-sided. It must be from the bruises you got when you fell.'

'That is the truth,' replied Don Quixote. 'And if I do not complain of the pain, it is because a knight errant is not allowed to complain of any wounds, even though his entrails may be dropping out through them.'

'If that's so, I have nothing more to say,' said Sancho, 'but God knows I should be glad if your worship would complain if anything hurt you. I must say, for my part, that I have to cry out at the slightest twinge, unless this business of not complaining extends to knights errants' squires as well.'

Don Quixote could not help smiling at his squire's simplicity, and told him that he could certainly complain how and when he pleased, whether he had cause or no, for up to that time he had never read anything to the contrary in the law of chivalry.

Sancho reminded him that it was time for dinner, but his master replied that he had need of none, but that his squire might eat whenever he pleased. With this permission Sancho settled himself as comfortably as he could on his ass and, taking out what he had put into the saddle-bags, jogged very leisurely along behind his master, eating all the while; and from time to time he raised the bottle with such relish that the best-fed publican in Malaga might have envied him. Now, as he went along like this, taking repeated gulps, he entirely forgot the promise his master had made him, and reckoned that going in search of adventures, however dangerous, was more like pleasure than hard work.

They passed that night under some trees, from one of which our knight tore down a dead branch to serve him as some sort of lance, and stuck into it the iron head of the one that had been broken. And all night Don Quixote did not sleep but thought about his Lady Dulcinea, to conform to what he had read in his books about knights errant spending many sleepless nights in woodland and desert dwelling on the memory of their ladies. Not so Sancho Panza; for, as his stomach was full, and not of chicory water, he slept right through till morning. And, if his master had not called him, neither the sunbeams, which struck him full on the face, nor the song of the birds, who in great number and very joyfully greeted the dawn of the new day, would have been enough to wake him. As he got up he made a trial of his bottle, and found it rather limper than the night before; whereat his heart sank, for he did not think they were taking the right road to remedy this defect very quickly. Don Quixote wanted no breakfast for, as we have said, he was determined to subsist on savoury memories. Then they turned back on to the road they had been on before, towards the pass of Lapice, which they sighted about three in the afternoon.

'Here,' exclaimed Don Quixote on seeing it, 'here, brother Sancho Panza, we can steep our arms to the elbows in what they call adventures. But take note that though you see me in the greatest danger in the world, you must not put your hand to your sword to defend me, unless you know that my assailants are rabble and common folk; in which case you may come to my aid. But should they be knights, on no account will it be legal or permissible, by the laws of chivalry, for you to assist me until you are yourself knighted.'

'You may be sure, sir,' replied Sancho, 'that I shall obey your worship perfectly there. Especially as I am very peaceable by nature and all against shoving myself into brawls and quarrels. But as to defending myself, sir, I shan't take much notice of those rules, because divine law and human law allow everyone to defend himself against anyone who tries to harm him.'

'I never said otherwise,' replied Don Quixote, 'but in the matter of aiding me against knights, you must restrain your natural impulses.'

'I promise you I will,' replied Sancho, 'and I will observe this rule as strictly as the Sabbath.'

In the middle of this conversation two monks of the order of St. Benedict appeared on the road, mounted on what looked like dromedaries; for the two mules they were riding were quite as big. They were wearing riding-masks against the dust and carrying sunshades. And behind them came a coach, with four or five horsemen escorting it, and two muleteers on foot.

In the coach, as it afterwards turned out, was a Basque lady travelling to Seville to join her hushband, who was going out to take up a very important post in the Indies. The monks were not of her company, but merely journey-ing on the same road.

Now no sooner did Don Quixote see them in the distance than he said to his squire: 'Either I am much mistaken, or this will prove the most famous adventure ever seen. For those dark shapes looming over there must, beyond all doubt, be enchanters bearing off in that coach some princess they have stolen; and it is my duty to redress this wrong with all my might.'

'This will be a worse job than the windmills,' said Sancho. 'Look, sir, those are Benedictine monks, and the coach must belong to some travellers. Listen to me, sir. Be careful what you do, and don't let the Devil deceive you.'

'I have told you,' replied Don Quixote, 'that you know very little of this subject of adventures. What I say is true, and now you will see it.'

So saying, he rode forward and took up his position in the middle of the road along which the monks were coming; and when they got so near that he thought they could hear him, he called out in a loud voice: 'Monstrous and diabolical crew! Release immediately the noble princesses whom you are forcibly carrying off in that coach, or prepare to receive instant death as the just punishment for your misdeeds.'

The monks reined in their mules, and stopped in astonishment at Don Quixote's appearance and at his speech.

'Sir Knight,' they replied, 'we are neither monstrous nor diabolical, but two monks of St Benedict travelling about our business, nor do we know whether there are any princesses being carried off in that coach or not.'

'No fair speeches for me, for I know you, perfidious scoundrels!' cried Don Quixote. Then, without waiting for their reply, he spurred Rocinate and, with his lance lowered, charged at the foremost monk with such vigour and fury that, if he had not slid from his mule, he would have been thrown to the ground and badly hurt, if not killed outright. The second monk, on seeing his companion so treated, struck his heels into his stout mule's flanks and set her galloping over the plain fleeter than the wind itself. When Sancho Panza saw the monk on the ground, he got down lightly from his ass, ran up and started to strip him of his clothes. Upon this, two servants of the monks arrived and asked him why he was stripping their master. Sancho replied that the clothes fell rightly to his share as spoils of the battle which his master, Don Quixote, had won. The lads, who did not get the joke nor understand this talk of spoils and battles, saw that Don Quixote had gone off and was talking with the ladies in the coach, and so fell upon Sancho and knocked him down. And, pulling every hair from his beard, they kicked him mercilessly, and left him stretched on the ground, breathless and stunned. Then, without a moment's hesitation, the monk remounted his mule, trembling, terrified and as white as a sheet; and as soon as he was up he spurred after his comrade, who was waiting for him some distance off, watching to see the upshot of this sudden attack. But without caring to wait for the end of the adventure, they went on their way, crossing themselves more often than if they had had the Devil himself at their backs.

Don Quixote, as we have said, was talking with the lady in the coach: 'Your fair ladyship may now dispose of yourself as you desire, for now the pride of your ravishers lies in the dust, overthrown by this strong arm of mine. And lest your be racked with doubt as to the name of your deliverer, know that I am Don Quixote de la Mancha, knight errant, adventurer and captive to the peerless and beautiful lady, Dulcinea del Toboso. And in requital of the benefit you have received from me, I would ask no more of you than to go to El Toboso and present yourself on my behalf before that lady, telling her what I have done for your deliverance.'

All that Don Quixote said was overheard by one of the squires accompanying the coach, a Basque. And when he saw that the knight would not let them pass, but was talking of their turning back at once to El Toboso, he went up to Don Quixote and, grasping his lance, addressed him in bad Castilian and worse Basque.

'Get along, you ill-gotten knight. By God who made me, if you do not leave coach I kill you, sure as I be Basque.'

Don Quixote understood him very well, and replied with great calm: 'If you were a knight, as you are not, I should have punished your rash insolence by now, you slavish creature.'

'I not gentleman? I swear you liar, as I am a Christian. You throw down lance and draw sword, and you will see you are carrying the water to the cat. Basque on land, gentleman at sea. A gentleman, by the devil, and you lie if you say otherwise!'

' "Now you shall see," said Agrages,' quoted Don Quixote, and threw his lance down on the ground. Then, drawing his sword and grasping his shield, he rushed at his antagonist, determined to take his life. When the Basque saw him coming he would have liked to get down from his mule, as it was a poor sort of hired beast and not to be trusted, but there was nothing for it but to draw his sword. He was, however, lucky enough to be near the coach, from which he was able to snatch a cushion to serve as a shield; whereupon they immediately fell to, as if they had been two mortal enemies. The rest of the party tried to pacify them, but could not; for the Basque swore in his uncouth language that if they did not let him finish the battle, he would himself kill his mistress and all who hindered him.

The lady in the coach, amazed and terrified at the sight, made the coachman drive off a little way, and sat watching the deadly struggle from a distance. In the course of the fight the Basque dealt Don Quixote a mighty blow on one shoulder, thrusting above his shield, and had our knight been without defence he would have been cleft to the waist. When Don Quixote felt the weight of that tremendous stroke he cried out aloud: 'O lady of my soul, Dulcinea, flower of beauty, come to the aid of this your knight, who for the sake of your great goodness is now in this dire peril!'

To speak, to raise his sword, to cover himself with his shield and attack the Basque: All this was the work of a moment. For he had resolved to risk everything upon a single stroke. The Basque, seeing him come on, judged Don Quixote's courage by his daring, and decided to do the same as he. So he covered himself well with his cushion and waited, unable to turn his mule in either direction, for the beast was now dead weary, and not being made for such games, could not budge a step.

Don Quixote, as we have said, rushed at the wary Basque with sword aloft, determined to cleave him to the waist; and the Basque watched, with his sword also raised and well guarded by his cushion; while all the by-standers trembled in terrified suspense, hanging upon the issue of the dreadful blows with which they threatened one another. And the lady of the coach and her waiting-women offered a thousand vows and prayers to all the images and places of devotion in Spain, that God might deliver their squire and them from the great peril they were in.

But the unfortunate thing is that the author of this history left the battle in suspense at this critical point, with the excuse that he could find no more records of Don Quixote's exploits than those related here. It is true that the second author of this work would not believe that such a curious history could have been consigned to oblivion, or that the learned of La Mancha could have been so incurious as not to have in their archives or in their registries some documents relating to this famous knight. So, strong in this opinion, he did not despair of finding the conclusion of this delightful story and, by the favour of Heaven, found it, as shall be told in our second part.

In the first part of this history we left the valiant Basque and the famous Don Quixote with naked swords aloft, on the point of dealing two such furious downward strokes as, had they struck true, would have cleft both knights asunder from head to foot, and split them like pomegranates. At this critical point our delightful history stopped short and remained mutilated, our author failing to inform us where to find the missing part. This caused me great annoyance, for my pleasure from the little I had read turned to displeasure at the thought of the small chance there was of finding the rest of this delightful story. For it seemed to me that the greater part was missing. It appeared to my mind impossible, and contrary to all sound custom, that so good a knight should have lacked a sage to undertake the writing of his unparalleled achievements, since there never was one of those knights errant who—as the people say—go out on their adventures, that ever lacked one. For every one of them had one or two sages ready at hand, not only to record their deeds, but to describe their minutest thoughts and most trivial actions, however much concealed; and so good a knight could not have been so unfortunate as to lack what Platir and the like had in such abundance. I really could not bring myself to believe that such a gallant history could have been left maimed and mutilated, and laid the blame on the malice of time, the devourer and consumer of all things, for either concealing or destroying the sequel. On the other hand, I thought that, as there had been found among Don Quixote's books some as modern as *The Unveiling of Jealousy* and *Nymphs and Shepherds of Henares,* his history must be modern too, and that, though it might not be written down, it would be remembered by the people of his village and of the neighbourhood. This thought made me anxious and eager for real and authentic knowledge of the whole life and marvels of our famous Spaniard, Don Quixote de la Mancha, the light and mirror of Manchegan chivalry, and the first man of our times, of these calamitous times of ours, to devote himself to the toils and exercise of knight errantry; to redress wrongs, aid widows and protect maidens, such as roam up-hill and down-dale with their whips and palfreys and their whole virginities about them. For there were virgins in the olden days who, unless ravished by some rogue or by a boor with his steel cap and axe or by some monstrous giant, never slept a night under a roof all their lives, and at the age of eighty went to their graves as spotless virgins as the mothers that bore them. Now I say that for this, and for many other reasons our gallant Quixote deserves continuous and immemorial praise; and even I should have my share, for my toil and pains in searching for the end of this delightful history. Though well I know that if Heaven, chance, and good fortune had not aided me, the world would have remained without the amusement and pleasure which an attentive reader may now enjoy for as much as two hours on end.

This is how the discovery occurred:—One day I was in the Alcana at Toledo, when a lad came to sell some parchments and old papers to a silk merchant. Now as I have a taste for reading even torn papers lying in the streets, I was impelled by my natural inclination to take up one of the parchment books the lad was selling, and saw in it characters which I recognized as Arabic. But though I could recognize them I could not read them, and looked around to see if there was not some Spanish-speaking Moor about, to read them to me; and it was not difficult to find such as interpreter there. For, even if I had wanted one for a better and older language, I should have found one. In short, chance offered me one, to whom I explained what I wanted, placing the book in his hands. He opened it in the middle, and after reading a little began to laugh. I asked him what he was laughing at, and he answered that it was at something written in the margin of the book by way of a note. I asked him to tell me what it was and, still laughing, he answered: 'This is what is written in the margin: "They say that Dulcinea del Toboso, so often mentioned in this history, was the best hand at salting pork of any woman in all La Mancha." '

When I heard the name of Dulcinea del Toboso I was surprised and astonished, for I immediately surmised that these books must contain the story of Don Quixote. With this idea I pressed him to read the beginning, and when he did so, making an extempore translation from the Arabic into Castilian, he said that the heading was: History of Don Quixote de la Mancha, written by Cide Hamete Benengeli, Arabic historian. I needed great caution to conceal the joy I felt when the title of the book reached my ears. Running to the silk merchant, I bought all the lad's parchments and papers for half a *real*, but if he had had any sense and known how much I wanted them, he might very well have demanded and got more than six *reals* from the sale. I then went off with the Moor into the cloister of the cathedral, and asked him to translate for me into Castilian everything in those books that dealt with Don Quixote, adding nothing and omitting nothing; and I offered to pay him whatever he asked. He was satisfied with fifty pounds of raisins and three bushels of wheat, and promised to translate them well, faithfully, and very quickly. But, to make the business easier and not to let such a prize out of my hands, I took him to my house; and there in little more than six weeks he translated it all just as it is set down here.

On the first sheet was a very life-like picture of Don Quixote's fight with the Basque. Both were shown in the very postures the story describes, with swords aloft, the one covered by his shield, the other by his cushion, and the Basque's mule so life-like that you could tell from a mile off that it was a hired one.

At the feet of the Basque was a scroll that read: '*Don Sancho de Azpeitia*', which no doubt was his name: and at Rocinante's was another which read: '*Don Quixote*'. Rocinante was marvellously painted, so long and lank, so hollow and lean, with such a sharp backbone, and so far wasted in consumption that it was quite clear at a glance how wisely and rightly he had been called Rocinante. Beside him stood Sancho Panza, holding his ass by the halter, and at his feet was another label which read: '*Sancho Zancas*'; and according to the picture he must have had a big belly, a short body, and long shanks; which must be what gave him the names of Panza and Zancas, for he is called by both these names at different times in the history. There were some other details to be seen, but they are none of them of great importance, and have no concern with the faithful telling of this story;—and no story is bad if it is truthful.

Now, if any objection can be made against the truth of this history, it can only be that its narrator was an Arab—men of that nation being ready liars, though as they are so much our enemies he might be thought rather to have fallen short of the truth than to have exaggerated. So it seems to me; for when he could and should have let himself go in praise of so worthy a knight he seems deliberately to have passed on in silence; an ill deed and malicious, since historians are bound by right to be exact, truthful, and absolutely unprejudiced, so that neither interest nor fear, dislike nor affection, should make them turn from the path of truth, whose mother is history, rival of time, storehouse of great deeds, witness of the past, example and lesson to the present, warning to the future. In this history I know that you will find all the entertainment you can desire; and if any good quality is missing, I am certain that it is the fault of its dog of an author rather than any default in the subject. To conclude, the second part, according to the translator, began thus:

The trenchant swords of the two valorous and furious combatants, brandished aloft, seemed to threaten the heavens, the earth, and the pit of hell, such was their courageous aspect. The first to strike his blow was the choleric Basque; and he struck with such force and fury that if the edge of his sword had not turned in its descent, that one blow would have been enough to finish the dire conflict and all our knight's adventures. But good fortune was preserving him for greater things, and twisted his enemy's sword, so that, although it struck him on his left shoulder, it did him no other injury than to disarm all that side, taking with it a great piece of his helmet with half an ear, all of which fell to the ground in hideous ruin, leaving our knight in a very evil plight.

God help me, who is there could worthily describe the rage which now entered the heart of our Manchegan on finding himself thus treated? All that can be said is that he rose once more in his stirrups and, grasping his sword tighter in both his hands, brought it down with such fury full on the

Basque's cushion and on his head, that despite that protection he began to spout blood out of his nostrils, his mouth, and his ears, as if a mountain had fallen on him. He looked as if he was going to tumble off his mule, which he would no doubt have done if he had not clung round her neck. But even so he lost his stirrups and then let go with his arms; while the beast, terrified by the weight of the blow, began to gallop about the field, and with a plunge or two threw her master on to the ground.

Don Quixote was looking on most composedly. But, when he saw the squire fall, he jumped down from his horse and, running very nimbly up to him, put the point of his sword between his enemy's eyes, bidding him surrender or he would cut off his head. The Basque was so stunned that he could not answer a word, and things would have gone badly with him, so blind with rage was Don Quixote, if the ladies in the coach, who till then had been watching the fight in dire dismay, had not run to the spot, and begged him very earnestly to do them the great kindness and favour of sparing their squire's life. To which request Don Quixote replied very haughtily and gravely:

'Certainly, fair ladies; I am most willing to do what you ask. But there must be one condition agreed, which is that this knight shall promise to go to the town of El Toboso, and present himself from me before the peerless Lady Dulcinea, so that she may deal with him according to her pleasure.'

The terrified and distessed ladies did not consider what Don Quixote required nor ask who Dulcinea was, but promised him that the squire should carry out the knight's command.

'Then, upon your word,' said Don Quixote, 'I will do him no other hurt, though he richly deserves it at my hands.'

From Gulliver's Travels

jonathan swift

THE GRAND ACADEMY OF LAGADO

[AFTER DISCOVERING AND VISITING for awhile the flying island of Laputa, Lemuel Gullier is conveyed to Balnibarbi, where he is received by a "great Lord" named Munodi and on the following morning given a tour of the principal city of Balnibarbi, Lagado.]

The next morning after my arrival, he took me in his chariot to see the town, which is about half the bigness of London, but the houses very strangely built, and most of them out of repair. The people in the streets walked fast, looked wild, their eyes fixed, and were generally in rags. We passed through one of the town gates, and went about three miles into the country, where I saw many labourers working with several sorts of tools in the ground, but was not able to conjecture what they were about; neither did I observe any expectation either of corn or grass, although the soil appeared to be excellent. I could not forbear admiring at these odd appearances both in town and country, and I made bold to desire my conductor, that he would be pleased to explain to me what could be meant by so many busy heads, hands, and faces, both in the streets and the fields, because I did not discover any good effects they produced; but on the contrary, I never knew a soil so unhappily cultivated, houses so ill contrived and so ruinous, or a people whose countenances and habit expressed so much misery and want.

This Lord Munodi was a person of the first rank, and had been some years Governor of Lagado; but by a cabal of ministers was discharged for insufficiency. However, the King treated him with tenderness, as a well-meaning man, but of a low contemptible understanding.

When I gave that free censure of the country and its inhabitants, he made no further answer than by telling me, that I had not been long enough among them to form a judgment; and that the different nations of the world had different customs, with other common topics to the same purpose. But when we returned to his palace, he asked me how I liked the building, what absurdities I observed, and what quarrel I had with the dress or looks of his domestics. This he might safely do, because every thing about him was magnificent, regular, and polite. I answered that his Excellency's prudence, quality, and fortune, had exempted him from those defects, which folly and beggary had produced in others. He said if I would go with him to his country house, about twenty miles distant, where his estate lay, there would be more leisure for this kind of conversation. I told his Excellency that I was entirely at his disposal; and accordingly we set out next morning.

During our journey, he made me observe the several methods used by farmers in managing their lands, which to me were wholly unaccountable; for, except in some very few places, I could not discover one ear of corn or blade of grass. But, in three hours travelling the scene was wholly altered; we came into a most beautiful country; farmers' houses at small distances, neatly built; the fields enclosed, containing vineyards, corn-grounds, and meadows. Neither do I remember to have seen a more delightful prospect. His Excellency observed my countenance to clear up; he told me, with a sigh, that there his estate began, and would continue the same, till we should come to his house. That his countrymen ridiculed and despised him for managing his affairs no better, and for setting so ill an example to the kingdom, which however was followed by very few, such as were old, and wilful, and weak like himself.

We came at length to the house, which was indeed a noble structure, built according to the best rules of ancient architecture. The fountains, gardens, walks, avenues, and groves, were all disposed with exact judgment and taste. I gave due praises to every thing I saw, whereof his Excellency took not the least notice till after supper, when, there being no third companion, he told me with a very melancholy air, that he doubted he must throw down his houses in town and country, to rebuild them after the present mode, destroy all his plantations, and cast others into such a form as modern usage required, and give the same directions to all his tenants, unless he would submit to incur the censure of pride, singularity, affectation, ignorance, caprice, and perhaps increase his Majesty's displeasure.

That the admiration I appeared to be under would cease or diminish when he had informed me of some particulars, which probably I never heard of at court, the people there being too much taken up in their own speculations, to have regard to what passed here below.

The sum of his discourse was to this effect. That about forty years ago, certain persons went up to Laputa, either upon business or diversion, and, after five months continuance, came back with a very little smattering in mathematics, but full of volatile spirits acquired in that airy region. That these persons upon their return began to dislike the management of every thing below, and fell into schemes of putting all arts, sciences, languages, and mechanics upon a new foot. To this end they procured a royal patent for erecting an Academy of Projectors in Lagado; and the humour prevailed so strongly among the people, that there is not a town of any consequence in the kingdom without such an academy. In these colleges, the professors contrive new rules and methods of agriculture and building, and new instruments and tools for all trades and manufactures, whereby, as they undertake, one man shall do the work of ten; a palace may be built in a week, of materials so durable as to last for ever without repairing. All the fruits of the earth shall come to maturity at whatever season we think fit to choose, and increase an hundred fold more than they do at present, with innumerable other happy proposals. The only inconvenience is, that none of these projects are yet brought to perfection, and in the mean time, the whole country lies miserably waste, the houses in ruins, and the people without food or clothes. By all which, instead of being discouraged, they are fifty times more violently bent upon prosecuting their schemes, driven equally on by hope and despair: that as for himself, being not of an enterprising spirit, he was content to go on in the old forms, to live in the houses his ancestors had built, and act as they did in every part of life without innovation. That some few other persons of quality and gentry had done the same, but were looked on with an eye of contempt and ill will, as enemies to art, ignorant, and ill commonwealth's-men, preferring their own ease and sloth before the general improvement of their country.

His Lordship added, that he would not by any further particulars prevent the pleasure I should certainly take in viewing the grand Academy, whither he was resolved I should go. He only desired me to observe a ruined building upon the side of a mountain about three miles distant, of which he gave me this account. That he had a very convenient mill within half a mile of his house, turned by a current from a large river, and sufficient for his own family as well as a great number of his tenants. That about seven years ago, a club of those projectors came to him with proposals to destroy this mill, and build another on the side of that mountain, on the long ridge whereof a long canal must be cut for a repository of water, to be conveyed up by pipes and engines to supply the mill: because the wind and air upon a height agitated the water, and thereby made it fitter for motion: and because the water descending down a declivity would turn the mill with half the current of a river whose course is more upon a level. He said, that being then not very well with the court, and pressed by many of his friends, he complied with the proposal; and after employing an hundred men for two years, the work miscarried, the projectors went off, laying the blame entirely upon him, railing at him ever since, and putting others upon the same experiment, with equal assurance of success, as well as equal disappointment.

In a few days we came back to town, and his Excellency, considering the bad character he had in the Academy, would not go with me himself, but recommended me to a friend of his to bear me company thither. My lord was pleased to represent me as a great admirer of projects, and a person of much curiosity and easy belief; which, indeed, was not without truth; for I had myself been a sort of projector in my younger days.

chapter v

This Academy is not an entire single building, but a continuation of several houses on both sides of a street, which growing waste was purchased and applied to that use.

I was received very kindly by the Warden, and went for many days to the Academy. Every room hath in it one or more projectors, and I believe I could not be in fewer than five hundred rooms.

The first man I saw was of a meagre aspect, with sooty hands and face, his hair and beard long, ragged and singed in several places. His clothes, shirt, and skin, were all of the same colour. He had been eight years upon a project for extracting sun-beams out of cucumbers, which were to be put into vials hermetically sealed, and let out to warm the air in raw inclement summers. He told me, he did not doubt in eight years more he should be able to supply the Governor's gardens with sunshine at a reasonable rate; but he complained that his stock was low, and entreated me to give him something as an encouragement to ingenuity, especially since this had been a very dear season for cucumbers. I made him a small present, for my lord had furnished me with money on purpose, because he knew their practice of begging from all who go to see them.

I went into another chamber, but was ready to hasten back, being almost overcome with a horrible stink. My conductor pressed me forward, conjuring me in a whisper to give no offence, which would be highly resented, and therefore I durst not so much as stop my nose. The projector of this cell was the most ancient student of the Academy; his face and beard were of a pale yellow; his hands and clothes daubed over with filth. When I was presented to him, he gave me a closes embrace (a compliment I could well have excused). His employment from his first coming into the Academy, was an operation to reduce human excrement to its original food, by separating the several parts, removing the tincture which it received from the gall, making the odour exhale, and scumming off the saliva. He had a weekly allowance from the society, of a vessel filled with human ordure, about the bigness of a Bristol barrel.

I saw another at work to calcine ice into gunpowder, who likewise showed me a treatise he had written concerning the malleability of fire, which he intended to publish.

There was a most ingenious architect who had contrived a new method for building houses, by beginning at the roof, and working downwards to the foundation, which he justified to me by the like practice of those two prudent insects, the bee and the spider.

There was a man born blind, who had several apprentices in his own condition: their employment was to mix colours for painters, which their master taught them to distinguish by feeling and smelling. It was indeed my misfortune to find them at that time not very perfect in their lessons, and the professor himself happened to be generally mistaken: this artist is much encouraged and esteemed by the whole fraternity.

In another apartment I was highly pleased with a projector, who had found a device for ploughing the ground with hogs, to save the charges of ploughs, cattle, and labour. The method is this: in an acre of ground you bury, at six inches distance and eight deep, a quantity of acorns, dates, chestnuts, and other mast or vegetables whereof these animals are fondest; then you drive six hundred or more of them into the field, where in a few days they will root up the whole ground in search of their food, and make it fit for sowing, at the same time manuring it with their dung. It is true, upon experiment they found the charge and trouble very great, and they had little or no crop. However, it is not doubted that this invention may be capable of great improvement.

I went into another room, where the walls and ceiling were all hung round with cobwebs, except a narrow passage for the artist to go in and out. At my entrance he called aloud to me not to disturb his webs. He lamented the fatal mistake the world had been so long in of using silk-worms, while we had such plenty of domestic insects, who infinitely excelled the former, because they understood how to weave as well as spin. And he proposed farther, that by employing spiders, the charge of dyeing silks should be wholly saved, whereof I was fully convinced when he showed me a vast number of flies most beautifully coloured, wherewith he fed his spiders, assuring us, that the webs would take a tincture from them; and as he had them in all hues, he hoped to fit everybody's fancy, as soon as he could find proper food for the flies, of certain gums, oils, and other glutinous matter to give a strength and consistence to the threads.

There was an astronomer who had undertaken to place a sundial upon the great weathercock on the town-house, by adjusting the annual and diurnal motions of the earth and sun, so as to answer and coincide with all accidental turnings by the wind.

I was complaining of a small fit of colic, upon which my conductor led me into a room, where a great physician resided, who was famous for curing that disease by contrary operations from the same instrument. He had a large pair of bellows with a long slender muzzle of ivory. This he conveyed eight inches up the anus, and drawing in the wind, he affirmed he could make the guts as lank as a dried bladder. But when the disease was more stubborn and violent, he let in the muzzle while the bellows were full of wind, which he discharged into the body of the patient, then withdrew the instrument to replenish it, clapping his thumb strongly against the orifice of the fundament; and this being repeated three or four times, the adventitious wind would rush out, bringing the noxious along with it (like water put into a pump), and the patient recover. I saw him try both experiments upon a dog, but could not discern any effect from the former. After the latter, the animal was ready to burst, and made so violent a discharge, as was very offensive to me and my companions. The dog died on the spot, and we left the doctor endeavouring to recover him by the same operation.

I visited many other apartments, but shall not trouble my reader with all the curiosities I observed, being studious of brevity.

I had hitherto seen only one side of the Academy, the other being appropriated to the advancers of speculative learning, of whom I shall say something when I have mentioned one illustrious person more, who is called among them *the universal artist*. He told us he had been thirty years employing his thoughts for the improvement of human life. He had two large rooms full of wonderful curiosities, and fifty men at work. Some were condensing air into a dry tangible substance, by extracting the nitre, and letting the aqueous or fluid particles percolate; others softening marble for pillows and pincushions; others petrifying the hoofs of a living horse to preserve them from foundering. The artist himself was at that time busy upon two great designs; the first, to sow land with chaff, wherein he affirmed the true seminal virtue to be contained, as he demonstrated by several experiments which I was not skilful enough to comprehend. The other was, by a certain composition of gums, minerals, and vegetables outwardly applied, to prevent the growth of wool upon two young lambs; and he hoped in a reasonable time to propagate the breed of naked sheep all over the kingdom.

We crossed a walk to the other part of the Academy, where, as I have already said, the projectors in speculative learning resided.

The first professor I saw was in a large room, with forty pupils about him. After salutation, observing me to look earnestly upon a frame, which took up the greatest part of both the length and breadth room, he said perhaps I might wonder to see him employed in a project for improving speculative knowledge by practical and mechanical operations. But the world would soon be sensible of its usefulness, and he flattered himself that a more noble exalted thought never sprang in any other man's head. Every one knew how laborious the usual method is of attaining to arts and sciences; whereas, by his contrivance, the most ignorant person at a reasonable charge, and with a little bodily labour, may write books in philosophy, poetry, politics, law, mathematics, and theology, without the least assistance from genius or study. He then led me to the frame, about the sides whereof all his pupils stood in ranks. It was twenty foot square, placed in the middle of the room. The superficies was composed of several bits of wood, about the bigness of a die, but some larger than others. They were all linked together by slender wires. These bits of wood were covered on every square with paper pasted on them, and on these papers were writen all the words of their language, in their several moods, tenses, and declensions, but without any order. The professor then desired me to observe, for he was going to set his engine at work. The pupils at his command took each of them hold of an iron handle, whereof there were forty fixed round the edges of the frame, and giving them a sudden turn, the whole disposition of the words was entirely changed. He

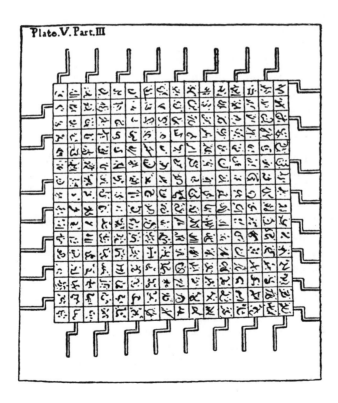

then commanded six and thirty of the lads to read the several lines softly
as they appeared upon the frame; and where they found three or four words
together that might make part of a sentence, they dictated to the four
remaining boys who were scribes. This work was repeated three or four times,
and at every turn the engine was so contrived, that the words shifted into new
places, as the square bits of wood moved upside down.

Six hours a day the young students were employed in this labour, and
the professor showed me several volumes in large folio already collected,
of broken sentences, which he intended to piece together, and out of those rich
materials to give the world a complete body of all arts and sciences; which,
however, might be still improved, and much expedited, if the public would
raise a fund for making and employing five hundred such frames in Lagado,
and oblige the managers to contribute in common their several collections.

He assured me, that this invention had employed all his thoughts from
his youth, that he had emptied the whole vocabulary into his frame, and
made the strictest computation of the general proportion there is in books
between the numbers of particles, nouns, and verbs, and other parts of speech.

I made my humblest acknowledgment to this illustrious person for his
great communicativeness, and promised if ever I had the good fortune to
return to my native country, that I would do him justice, as the sole inventor
of this wonderful machine; the form and contrivance of which I desired
leave to delineate upon paper, as in the figure here annexed. I told him,
although it were the custom of our learned in Europe to steal inventions
from each other, who had thereby at least this advantage, that it became
a controversy which was the right owner, yet I would take such caution, that
he should have the honour entire without a rival.

We next went to the school of languages, where three professors sat in
consultation upon improving that of their own country.

The first project was to shorten discourse by cutting polysyllables into
one, and leaving out verbs and participles, because in reality all things
imaginable are but nouns.

The other project was a scheme for entirely abolishing all words whatsoever; and this was urged as a great advantage in point of health as well
as brevity. For it is plain, that every word we speak is in some degree a
diminution of our lungs by corrosion, and consequently contributes to the
shortening of our lives. An expedient was therefore offered, that since
words are only names for *things*, it would be more convenient for all men
to carry about them such things as were necessary to express the particular
business they are to discourse on. And this invention would certainly have
taken place, to the great ease as well as health of the subject, if the women,
in conjunction with the vulgar and illiterate, had not threatened to raise
a rebellion, unless they might be allowed the liberty to speak with their
tongues, after the manner of their ancestors; such constant irreconcilable

enemies to science are the common people. However, many of the most learned and wise adhere to the new scheme of expressing themselves by things, which hath only this inconvenience attending it, that if a man's business be very great, and of various kinds, he must be obliged in proportion to carry a greater bundle of things upon his back, unless he can afford one or two strong servants to attend him. I have often beheld two of those sages almost sinking under the weight of their packs, like pedlars among us; who, when they met in the streets, would lay down their loads, open their sacks, and hold conversation for an hour together; then put up their implements, help each other to resume their burthens, and take their leave.

But for short conversations a man may carry implements in his pockets and under his arms, enough to supply him, and in his house he cannot be at a loss. Therefore the room where company meet who practice this art is full of all things ready at hand, requisite to furnish matter for this kind of artificial converse.

Another great advantage proposed by this invention, was that it would serve as an universal language to be understood in all civilised nations, whose goods and utensils are generally of the same kind, or nearly resembling, so that their uses might easily be comprehended. And thus ambassadors would be qualified to treat with foreign princes or ministers of state, to whose tongues they were utter strangers.

I was at the mathematical school, where the master taught his pupils after a method scarce imaginable to us in Europe. The proposition and demonstration were fairly written on a thin wafer, with ink composed of a cephalic tincture. This the student was to swallow upon a fasting stomach, and for three days following eat nothing but bread and water. As the wafer digested, the tincture mounted to his brain, bearing the proposition along with it. But the success hath not hitherto been answerable, partly by some error in the *quantum* or composition, and partly by the perverseness of lads, to whom this bolus is so nauseous, that they generally steal aside, and discharge it upwards before it can operate; neither have they been yet persuaded to use so long an abstinence as the prescription requires.

chapter vi

A FURTHER ACCOUNT OF THE ACADEMY. THE AUTHOR PROPOSES SOME IMPROVEMENTS WHICH ARE HONOURABLY RECEIVED.

In the school of political projectors I was but ill entertained, the professors appearing in my judgment wholly out of their senses, which is a scene that never fails to make me melancholy. These unhappy people were proposing schemes for persuading monarchs to choose favourites upon the score of their wisdom, capacity and virtue; of teaching ministers to consult the public good; of rewarding merit, great abilities and eminent services; of instructing princes to know their true interest by placing it on the same foundation with that of their people: of choosing for employments persons qualified to exercise them; with many other wild impossible chimeras, that never entered before into the heart of man to conceive, and confirmed in me the old observation, that there is nothing so extravagant and irrational which some philosophers have not maintained for truth.

But, however, I shall so far do justice to this part of the Academy, as to acknowledge that all of them were not so visionary. There was a most ingenious doctor who seemed to be perfectly versed in the whole nature and system of government. This illustrious person had very usefully employed his studies in finding out effectual remedies for all diseases and corruptions to which the several kinds of public administration are subject by the vices or infirmities of those who govern, as well as by the licentiousness of those who are to obey. For instance: whereas all writers and reasoners have agreed, that there is a strict universal resemblance between the natural and the political body; can there be any thing more evident, than that the health of both must be preserved, and the diseases cured, by the same prescriptions? It is allowed that senates and great councils are often troubled with redundant, ebullient, and other peccant humours, with many diseases of the head, and more of the heart; with strong convulsions, with grievous contractions of the nerves and sinews in both hands, but especially the right; with spleen, flatus, vertigos and deliriums; with scrofulous tumours full of fœtid purulent matter; with sour frothy ructations, with canine appetites and crudeness of digestion, besides many others needless to mention. This doctor therefore proposed that upon the meeting of a senate, certain physicians should attend at the three first days of their sitting, and, at the close of each day's debate, feel the pulses of every senator; after which, having maturely considered, and consulted upon the nature of the several maladies, and the methods of cure, they should on the fourth day return to the senate house, attended by their apothecaries stored with proper medicines, and before the members sat, administer to each of them lenitives, aperitives, abstersives, corrosives, restringents, palliatives, laxatives, cephalalgics, icterics, apophlegmatics, acoustics, as their several cases required; and according as these medicines should operate, repeat, alter, or omit them at the next meeting.

This project could not be of any great expense to the public, and might, in my poor opinion, be of much use for the dispatch of business in those countries where senates have any share in the legislative power, beget unanimity, shorten debates, open a few mouths which are now closed, and close many more which are now open; curb the petulancy of the young, and correct the positiveness of the old; rouse the stupid, and damp the pert.

Again, because it is a general complaint that the favourites of princes are troubled with short and weak memories, the same doctor proposed, that whoever attended a first minister, after having told his business with the utmost brevity, and in the plainest words, should at his departure give the said minister a tweak by the nose, or a kick in the belly, or tread on his corns, or lug him thrice by both ears, or run a pin into his breech, or pinch his arm black and blue, to prevent forgetfulness: and at every levee day repeat the same operation, till the business were done or absolutely refused.

He likewise directed, that every senator in the great council of a nation, after he had delivered his opinion, and argued in the defence of it, should be obliged to give his vote directly contrary; because if that were done, the result would infallibly terminate in the good of the public.

When parties in a state are violent, he offered a wonderful contrivance to reconcile them. The method is this. You take an hundred leaders of each party, you dispose them into couples of such whose heads are nearest of a size; then let two nice operators saw off the occiput of each couple at the same time, in such a manner that the brain may be equally divided. Let the occiputs thus cut off be interchanged, applying each to the head of his opposite party-man. It seems indeed to be a work that requireth some exactness, but the professor assured us, that if it were dextrously performed the cure would be infallible. For he argued thus; that the two half brains being left to debate the matter between themselves within the space of one skull, would soon come to a good understanding, and produce that moderation, as well as regularity of thinking, so much to be wished for in the heads of those who imagine they came into the world only to watch and govern its motion: and as to the difference of brains in quantity or quality, among those who are directors in faction, the doctor assured us from his own knowledge, that it was a perfect trifle.

I heard a very warm debate between two professors, about the most commodious and effectual ways and means of raising money without grieving the subject. The first affirmed the justest method would be to lay a certain tax upon vices and folly, and the sum fixed upon every man to be rated after the fairest manner by a jury of his neighbours. The second was of an opinion directly contrary, to tax those qualities of body and mind for which men chiefly value themselves, the rate to be more or less according to the degrees of excelling, the decision whereof should be left entirely to their own breast. The highest tax was upon men who are the greatest favourites of the other sex, and the assessments according to the number and natures of the favours they have received; for which they are allowed to be their own vouchers. Wit, valour, and politeness were likewise proposed to be largely taxed, and collected in the same manner, by every person's giving his own word for the quantum of what he possessed. But as to honour, justice, wisdom and learning, they should not be taxed at all, because they are qualifications of so singular a kind, that no man will either allow them in his neighbour, or value them in himself.

The women were proposed to be taxed according to their beauty and skill in dressing, wherein they had the same privilege with the men, to be determined by their own judgment. But constancy, chastity, good sense, and good nature were not rated, because they would not bear the charge of collecting.

To keep senators in the interest of the crown, it was proposed that the members should raffle for employments, every man first taking an oath, and giving security that he would vote for the court, whether he won or no, after which the losers had in their turn the liberty of raffling upon the next vacancy. Thus hope and expectation would be kept alive, none would complain of broken promises, but impute their disappointments wholly to Fortune, whose shoulders are broader and stronger than those of a ministry.

Another professor showed me a large paper of instructions for discovering plots and conspiracies against the government. He advised great statesmen to examine into the diet of all suspected persons; their times of eating; upon which side they lay in bed; with which hand they wiped their posteriors, to take a strict view of their excrements, and from the colour, the odour, the taste, the consistence, the crudeness or maturity of digestion, form a judgment of the thoughts and designs. Because men are never so serious, thoughtful, and intent, as when they are at stool, which he found by frequent experiment: for in such conjunctures, when he used merely as a trial to consider which was the best way of murdering the King, his ordure would have a tincture of green, but quite different when he thought only of raising an insurrection or burning the metropolis.

The whole discourse was written with great acuteness, containing many observations both curious and useful for politicians, but as I conceived not altogether complete. This I ventured to tell the author, and offered if he pleased to supply him with some additions. He received my proposition with more compliance than is usual among writers, especially those of the projecting species, professing he would be glad to receive farther information.

I told him, that in the kingdom of Tribnia, by the natives called Langden, where I had long sojourned, the bulk of the people consisted wholly of discoverers, witnesses, informers, accusers, prosecutors, evidences, swearers, together with their several subservient and subaltern instruments, all under the colours, the conduct, and pay of ministers and their deputies. The plots in that kingdom are usually the workmanship of those persons who desire to raise their own characters of profound politicians, to restore new vigour to a crazy administration, to stifle or divert general discontents, to fill their coffers with forfeitures, and raise or sink the opinion of public credit, as either shall best answer their private advantage. It is first agreed and settled among them what suspected persons shall be accused of a plot: then effectual care is taken to secure all their letters and other papers, and put the owners in chains. These papers are delivered to a set of artists, very dextrous in finding out the mysterious meanings of words, syllables, and letters. For instance, they can decipher a close-stool to signify a privy-council, a flock of geese a senate, a lame dog an invader, a codshead a————, the plague a standing army, a buzzard a prime minister, the gout a high priest, a gibbet a secretary of state, a chamber-pot a committee of grandees, a sieve a court lady, a broom a revolution, a mousetrap an employment, a bottomless pit the treasury, a sink a court, a cap and bells a favourite, a broken reed a court of justice, an empty tun a general, a running sore the administration.

When this method fails, they have two others more effectual, which the learned among them call acrostics and anagrams. First they can decipher all initial letters into political meanings. Thus N shall signify a plot, B a regiment of horse, L a fleet at sea. Or secondly by transposing the letters of the alphabet in any suspected paper, they can lay open the deepest designs of a discontented party. So, for example, if I should say in a letter to a friend, Our brother Tom has just got the piles, a man of skill in this art would discover how the same letters which compose that sentence may be analysed into the following words: Resist—a plot is brought home—the tour. And this is the anagrammatic method.

The professor made me great acknowledgments for communicating these observations, and promised to make honourable mention of me in his treatise.

I saw nothing in this country that could invite me to a longer continuance, and began to think of returning home to England.

From The Life and Opinions of Tristram Shandy, Gentleman

laurence sterne

chapter i

I WISH EITHER MY FATHER OR MY MOTHER, or indeed both of them, as they were in duty both equally bound to it, had minded what they were about when they begot me; had they duly consider'd how much depended upon what they were then doing;—that not only the production of a rational Being was concern'd in it, but that possibly the happy formation and temperature of his body, perhaps his genius and the very cast of his mind;— and, for aught they knew to the contrary, even the fortunes of his whole house might take their turn from the humours and dispositions which were then uppermost:——Had they duly weighed and considered all this, and proceeded accordingly,——I am verily persuaded I should have made a quite different figure in the world, from that, in which the reader is likely to see me.—Believe me, good folks, this is not so inconsiderable a thing as many of you may think it;—you have all, I dare say, heard of the animal spirits, as how they are transfused from father to son, &c. &c.—and a great deal to that purpose:—Well, you may take my word, that nine parts in ten of a man's sense or his nonsense, his successes and miscarriages in this world depend upon their motions and activity, and the different tracks and trains you put them into; so that when they are once set a-going, whether right or wrong, 'tis not a halfpenny matter,—away they go cluttering like hey-go-mad; and by treading the same steps over and over again, they presently make a road of it, as plain and as smooth as a garden-walk, which, when they

The Riverside edition of THE LIFE AND OPINIONS OF TRISTRAM SHANDY, GENTLEMAN is reprinted by courtesy of Houghton Mifflin Co.

214

are once used to, the Devil himself sometimes shall not be able to drive them off it.

Pray, my dear, quoth my mother, *have you not forgot to wind up the clock?*——*Good G—!* cried my father, making an exclamation, but taking care to moderate his voice at the same time,——*Did ever woman, since the creation of the world, interrupt a man with such a silly question?* Pray, what was your father saying?——Nothing.

chapter ii

—Then, positively, there is nothing in the question, that I can see, either good or bad.——Then let me tell you, Sir, it was a very unseasonable question at least,—because it scattered and dispersed the animal spirits, whose business it was to have escorted and gone hand-in-hand with the HOMUN-CULUS,[1] and conducted him safe to the place destined for his reception.

The HOMUNCULUS, Sir, in how-ever low and ludicrous a light he may appear, in this age of levity, to the eye of folly or prejudice;—to the eye of reason in scientifick research, he stands confess'd—a BEING guarded and circumscribed with rights:——The minutest philosophers, who by the bye, have the most enlarged understandings, (their souls being inversely as their enquiries) shew us incontestably, That the HOMUNCLUS is created by the same hand,—engender'd in the same course of nature,—endowed with the same loco-motive powers and faculties with us:——That he consists, as we do, of skin, hair, fat, flesh, veins, arteries, ligaments, nerves, cartilages, bones, marrow, brains, glands, genitals, humours, and articulations;——is a Being of as much activity,——and, in all senses of the word, as much and as truly our fellow-creature as my Lord Chancellor of England.—He may be benefited, he may be injured,—he may obtain redress;—in a word, he has all the claims and rights of humanity, which *Tully,*[2] *Puffendorff,*[3] or the best ethick writers allow to arise out of that state and relation.

Now, dear Sir, what if any accident had befallen him in his way alone? ——or that, thro' terror of it, natural to so young a traveller, my little gentleman had got to his journey's end miserably spend;——his muscular strength and virility worn down to a thread;—his own animal spirits ruffled beyond description,—and that in this sad disorder'd state of nerves, he had laid down a prey to sudden starts, or a series of melancholy dreams and fancies for nine long, long months together.——I tremble to think what a foundation had been laid for a thousand weaknesses both of body and mind, which no skill of the physician or the philosopher could ever afterwards have set thoroughly to rights.

[1] Spermatazoon.
[2] Cicero.
[3] Samuel Pufendorf, German philosopher.

chapter iii

To my uncle Mr. *Toby Shandy* do I stand indebted for the preceding anecdote, to whom my father, who was an excellent natural philosopher, and much given to close reasoning upon the smallest matters, had oft, and heavily, complain'd of the injury; but once more particularly, as my uncle *Toby* well remember'd, upon his observing a most unaccountable obliquity, (as he call'd it) in my manner of setting up my top, and justifying the principles upon which I had done it,—the old gentleman shook his head, and in a tone more expressive by half of sorrow than reproach,—he said his heart all along foreboded, and he saw it verified in this, and from a thousand other observations he had made upon me, That I should neither think nor act like any other man's child:——*But alas!* continued he, shaking his head a second time, and wiping away a tear which was trickling down his cheeks, *My Tristram's misfortunes began nine months before ever he came into the world.*

——My mother, who was sitting by, look'd up,—but she knew no more than her backside what my father meant,—but my uncle, Mr. *Toby Shandy,* who had been often informed of the affair,—understood him very well.

chapter iv

I know there are readers in the world, as well as many other good people in it, who are no readers at all,—who find themselves ill at ease, unless they are let into the whole secret from first to las, of every thing which concerns you.

It is in pure compliance with this humour of theirs, and from a backwardness in my nature to disappoint any one soul living, that I have been so very particular already. As my life and opinions are likely to make some noise in the world, and, if I conjecture right, will take in all ranks, professions, and denominations of men whatever,—be no less read than the *Pilgrim's Progress* itself—and, in the end, prove the very thing which *Montaigne* dreaded his essays should turn out, that is, a book for a parlour-window;—I find it necessary to consult every one a little in his turn; and therefore must beg pardon for going on a little further in the same way: For which cause, right glad I am, that I have begun the history of myself in the way I have done; and that I am able to go on tracing every thing in it, as *Horace* says, *ab Ovo.*[4]

Horace, I know, does not recommend this fashion altogether: But that gentleman is speaking only of an epic poem or a tragedy;—(I forget which)

[4] From the egg (beginning).

—besides, if it was not so, I should beg Mr. *Horace's* pardon;—for in writing what I have set about, I shall confine myself neither to his rules, nor to any man's rules that ever lived.

To such, however, as do not choose to go so far back into these things, I can give no better advice, than that they skip over the remaining part of this Chapter; for I declare before hand, 'tis wrote only for the curious and inquisitive.

—————————Shut the door.—————

I was begot in the night, betwixt the first *Sunday* and the first *Monday* in the month of *March*, in the year of our Lord one thousand seven hundred and eighteen. I am positive I was.—But how I came to be so very particular in my account of a thing which happened before I was born, is owing to another small anecdote known only in our own family, but now made publick for the better clearing up this point.

My father, you must know, who was originally a *Turky* merchant, but had left off business for some years, in order to retire to, and die upon, his paternal estate in the county of——, was, I believe, one of the most regular men in every thing he did, whether 'twas matter of business, or matter of amusement, that ever lived. As a small specimen of this extreme exactness of his, to which he was in truth a slave,—he had made it a rule for many years of his life,—on the first *Sunday night* of every month through-out the whole year,—as certain as ever the *Sunday night* came,—to wind up a large house-clock which we had standing upon the back-stairs head, with his own hands:—And being somewhere between fifty and sixty years of age, at the time I have been speaking of,—he had likewise gradually brought some other little family concernments to the same period, in order, as he would often say to my uncle *Toby*, to get them all out of the way at one time, and be no more plagued and pester'd with them the rest of the month.

It was attended but with one misfortune, which, in a great measure, fell upon myself, and the effects of which I fear I shall carry with me to my grave; namely, that, from an unhappy association of ideas which have no connection in nature, it so fell out at length, that my poor mother could never hear the said clock wound up,—but the thoughts of some other things unavoidably popp'd into her head,—*& vice versâ*:—which strange combi-nation of ideas, the sagacious *Locke*, who certainly understood the nature of these things better than most men, affirms to have produced more wry actions than all other sources of prejudice whatsoever.

But this by the bye.

Now it appears, by a memorandum in my father's pocket-book, which now lies upon the table, "That on *Lady-Day*, which was on the 25th of the same month in which I date my geniture,—my father set out upon his journey to *London* with my eldest brother *Bobby*, to fix him at *Westminster* school;" and, as it appears from the same authority, "That he did not get down to his wife and family till the *second week* in *May* following,"—it brings the thing almost to a certainty. However, what follows in the beginning of the next chapter puts it beyond all possibility of doubt.

————But pray, Sir, What was your father doing all *December*,—*January*, and *February?*—Why, Madam,—he was all that time afflicted with a Sciatica.

chapter v

On the fifth day of *November*, 1718, which to the æra fixed on, was as near nine kalendar months as any husband could in reason have expected,—was I *Tristram Shandy,* Gentleman, brought forth into this scurvy and disasterous world of ours.—I wish I had been born in the Moon, or in any of the planets, (except *Jupiter* or *Saturn,* because I never could bear cold weather) for it could not well have fared worse with me in any of them (tho' I will not answer for *Venus*) than it has in this vile, dirty planet of ours,—which o' my conscience, with reverance be it spoken, I take to be made of the shreds and clippings of the rest;————not but the planet is well enough, provided a man could be born in it to a great title or to a great estate; or could any how contrive to be called up to publick charges, and employments of dignity or power;—but that is not my case;————and therefore every man will speak of the fair as his own market has gone in it;—for which cause I affirm it over again to be one of the vilest worlds that ever was made;—for I can truly say, that from the first hour I drew my breath in it, to this, that I can now scarce draw it at all, for an asthma I got in scating against the wind in *Flanders*;—I have been the continual sport of what the world calls Fortune; and though I will not wrong her by saying, She ever made me feel the weight of any great or signal evil;—yet with all the good temper in the world, I affirm it of her, that in every stage of my life, and at every turn and corner where she could get fairly at me, the ungracious Duchess has pelted me with a set of as pitiful misadventures and cross accidents as ever small HERO sustained.

chapter vi

In the beginning of the last chapter, I inform'd you exactly *when* I was born;—but I did not inform you, *how. No*; that particular was reserved entirely for a chapter by itself;—besides, Sir, as you and I are in a manner perfect strangers to each other, it would not have been proper to have let you into too many circumstances relating to myself all at once.—You must have a little patience. I have undertaken, you see, to write not only my life, but my opinions also; hoping and expecting that your knowledge of my character, and of what kind of a mortal I am, by the one, would give you a better relish for the other. As you proceed further with me, the slight acquaintance which is now beginning betwixt us, will grow into familiarity; and that, unless one of us is in fault, will terminate in friendship.——*O diem præclarum!*[5]——then nothing which has touched me will be thought trifling in its nature, or tedious in its telling. Therefore, my dear friend and companion, if you should thing me somewhat sparing of my narrative on my first setting out,—bear with me,—and let me go on, and tell my story my own way:——or if I should seem now and then to trifle upon the road,——or should sometimes put on a fool's cap with a bell to it, for a moment or two as we pass along,—don't fly off,—but rather courteously give me credit for a little more wisdom than appears upon my outside;—and as we jog on, either laugh with me, or at me, or in short, do any thing,—only keep your temper.

chapter vii

In the same village where my father and my mother dwelt, dwelt also a thin, upright, motherly, notable, good old body of a midwife, who, with the help of a little plain good sense, and some years full employment in her business, in which she had all along trusted little to her own efforts, and a great deal to those of dame nature,—had acquired, in her way, no small degree of reputation in the world;—by which word *world,* need I in this place inform your worship, that I would be understood to mean no more of it, than a small circle described upon the circle of the great world, of four *English* miles diameter, or thereabouts, of which the cottage where the good old woman lived; is supposed to be the centre.——She had been left, it seems, a widow in great distress, with three or four small children, in her forty-seventh year; and as she was at the time a person of decent carriage,— grave deportment,——a woman moreover of few words, and withall an object of compassion, whose distress and silence under it call'd out the louder for a friendly lift: the wife of the parson of the parish was touch'd with pity; and having often lamented an inconvenience, to which her husband's flock had for many years been exposed, inasmuch, as there was no such thing as a midwife, of any kind or degree to be got at, let the case have been never so urgent, within less than six or seven long miles riding; which said seven long miles in dark nights and dismal roads, the country thereabouts being nothing but a deep clay, was almost equal to fourteen; and that in effect was sometimes next to having no midwife at all; it came into her head, that it would be doing as seasonable a kindness to the whole parish, as to the poor creature herself, to get her a little instructed in some of the plain principles of the business, in order to set her up in it. As no woman thereabouts was better qualified to execute the plan she had formed than herself, the Gentlewoman very charitably undertook it; and having great influence over the female part of the parish, she found no difficulty in effecting it to the

---

[5] O day of glory!

utmost of her wishes. In truth, the parson join'd his interest with his wife's in the whole affair; and in order to do things as they should be, and give the poor soul as good a title by law to practise, as his wife had given by institution,——he chearfully paid the fees for the ordinary's licence himself, amounting, in the whole, to the sum of eighteen shillings and fourpence; so that, betwixt them both, the good woman was fully invested in the real and corporal possession of her office, together with all its *rights, members, and appurtenances whatsoever.*

These last words, you must know, were not according to the old form in which such licences, faculties, and powers usually ran, which in like cases had heretofore been granted to the sisterhood. But it was according to a neat *Formula* of *Didius*[6] his own devising, who having a particular turn for taking to pieces, and new framing over again, all kind of instruments in that way, not only hit upon this dainty amendment, but coax'd many of the old licensed matrons in the neighbourhood, to open their faculties afresh, in order to have this whim-wham of his inserted.

I own I never could envy *Didius* in these kinds of fancies of his:—But every man to his own taste.—Did not Dr. *Kunastrokius,*[7] that great man, at his leisure hours, take the greatest delight imaginable in combing of asses tails, and plucking the dead hairs out with his teeth, though he had tweezers always in his pocket? Nay, if you come to that, Sir, have not the wisest of men in all ages, not excepting *Solomon* himself,—have they not had their HOBBY-HORSES;—their running horses,—their coins and their cockle-shells, their drums and their trumpets, their fiddles, their pallets,—their maggots and their butterflies?—and so long as a man rides his HOBBY-HORSE peaceably and quitely along the King's highway, and neither compels you or me to get up behind him,——pray, Sir, what have either you or I to do with it?

chapter viii

—*De gustibus non est disputandum;*[8]—that is, there is no disputing against HOBBY-HORSES; and, for my part, I seldom do; nor could I with any sort of grace, had I been an enemy to them at the bottom; for happening, at certain intervals and changes of the Moon, to be both fiddler and painter, according as the fly stings:—Be it known to you, that I keep a couple of pads myself, upon which, in their turns, (nor do I care who knows it) I frequently ride out and take the air;—tho' sometimes, to my shame be it spoken, I take somewhat longer journies than what a wise man would think altogether right.—But the truth is,—I am not a wise man;——and besides am a mortal of so little consequence in the world, it is not much matter

---

6 Second century Roman.

7 Coined from cunnus, Latin for female genitals.

8 Concerning taste, there is no dispute.

what I do; so I seldom fret or fume at all about it: Nor does it much disturb my rest when I see such great Lords and tall Personages as hereafter follow;—such, for instance, as my Lord A, B, C, D, E, F, G, H, I, K, L, M, N, O, P, Q, and so on, all of a row, mounted upon their several horses;—some with large stirrups, getting on in a more grave and sober pace;——others on the contrary, tuck'd up to their very chins, with whips across their mouths, scouring and scampering it away like so many little party-colour'd devils astride a mortgage,—and as if some of them were resolved to break their necks.—So much the better—say I to myself;—for in case the worst should happen, the world will make a shift to do excellently well without them;—and for the rest,——why,——God speed them,——e'en let them ride on without any opposition from me; for were their lordships unhorsed this very night,——'tis ten to one but that many of them would be worse mounted by one half before to-morrow morning.

Not one of these instances therefore can be said to break in upon my rest.—But there is an instance, which I own puts me off my guard, and that is, when I see one born for great actions, and, what is still more for his honour, whose nature ever inclines him to good ones;——when I behold such a one, my Lord, like yourself, whose principles and conduct are as generous and noble as his blood, and whom, for that reason, a corrupt world cannot spare one moment;—when I see such a one, my Lord, mounted, though it is but for a minute beyond the time which my love to my country has prescribed to him, and my zeal for his glory wishes,—then, my Lord, I cease to be a philosopher, and in the first transport of an honest impatience, I wish the HOBBY-HORSE, with all his fraternity, at the Devil.

> My Lord,
> I maintain this to be a dedication, notwithstanding its singularity in the three great essentials of matter, form, and place: I beg, therefore, you will accept it as such, and that you will permit me to lay it, with the most respectful humility, at your Lordship's feet,—when you are upon them,—which you can be when you please;—and that is, my Lord, whenever there is occasion for it, and I will add, to the best purposes too. I have the honour to be,
>
> *My Lord,*
> *Your Lordship's most obedient,*
> *and most devoted,*
> *and most humble servant,*
>
> TRISTRAM SHANDY

chapter ix

I solemnly declare to all mankind, that the above dedication was made for no one Prince, Prelate, Pope, or Potentate,—Duke, Marquis, Earl, Viscount, or Baron of this, or any other Realm in Christendom;——nor has it yet been hawk'd about, or offered publickly or privately, directly or indirectly, to any one person or personage, great or small; but is honestly a true Virgin-Dedication untried on, upon any soul living.

I labour this point so particularly, merely to remove any offence or objection which might arise against it from the manner in which I propose to make the most of it;—which is the putting it up fairly to publick sale; which I now do.

——Every author has a way of his own, in bringing his points to bear—for my own part, as I hate chaffering and higgling for a few guineas in a dark entry;—I resolved within myself, from the very beginning, to deal squarely and openly with your Great Folks in this affair, and try whether I should not come off the better by it.

If therefore there is any one Duke, Marquis, Earl, Viscount, or Baron, in these his Majesty's dominions, who stands in need of a tight, genteel dedication, and whom the above will suit, (for by the bye, unless it suits in some degree, I will not part with it)——it is much at his service for fifty guineas;——which I am positive is twenty guineas less than it ought to be afforded for, by any man of genius.

My Lord, if you examine it over again, it is far from being a gross piece of daubing, as some dedications are. The design, your Lordship sees, is good, the colouring transparent,—the drawing not amiss;—or to speak more like a man of science,—and measure my piece in the painter's scale, divided into 20,—I believe, my Lord, the out-lines will turn out as 12,—the composition as 9,—the colouring as 6,—the expression 13 and a half,—and the design,—if I may be allowed, my Lord, to understand my own *design*, and supposing absolute perfection in designing, to be as 20,—I think it cannot well fall short of 19. Besides all this,—there is keeping in it, and the dark strokes in the HOBBY-HORSE, (which is a secondary figure, and a kind of background to the whole) give great force to the principal lights in your own figure, and makes it come off wonderfully;——and besides, there is an air of originality in the *tout ensemble*.[9]

Be pleased, my good Lord, to order the sum to be paid into the hands of Mr. *Dodsley*,[10] for the benefit of the author; and in the next edition care shall be taken that this chapter be expunged, and your Lorship's titles, distinctions, arms and good actions, be placed at the front of the preceding chapter: All which, from the words, *De gustibus non est disputandum*, and whatever else in this book relates to HOBBY-HORSES, but no more, shall stand dedicated to your Lordship.—The rest I dedicate to the MOON, who, by the

[9] Entire construction.
[10] Sterne's publisher.

bye, of all the PATRONS or MATRONS I can think of, has most power to set my book a-going, and make the world run mad after it.

> Bright Goddess,
> *If thou art not too busy with* CANDID *and Miss* CUNEGUND'S[11] *affairs,*
> *—take* Tristram Shandy's *under thy protection also.*

chapter x

Whatever degree of small merit, the act of benignity in favour of the midwife, might justly claim, or in whom that claim truly rested,—at first sight seems not very material to this history;——certain however it was, that the gentlewoman, the parson's wife, did run away at that time with the whole of it: And yet, for my life, I cannot help thinking but that the parson himself, tho' he had not the good fortune to hit upon the design first,—yet, as he heartily concurred in it the moment it was laid before him, and as heartily parted with his money to carry it into execution, had a claim to some share of it,—if not to a full half of whatever honour was due to it.

The world at that time was pleased to determine the matter otherwise.

Lay down the book, and I will allow you half a day to give a probable guess at the grounds of this procedure.

Be it known then, that, for about five years before the date of the midwife's licence, of which you have had so circumstantial an account,—the parson we have to do with, had made himself a country-talk by a breach of all decorum, which he had committed against himself, his station, and his office;——and that was, in never appearing better, or otherwise mounted, than upon a lean, sorry, jack-ass of a horse, value about one pound fifteen shillings; who, to shorten all description of him, was full brother to *Rosinante*,[12] as far as similitude congenial could make him; for he answered his description to a hair-breadth in ever thing,—except that I do not remember 'tis any where said, that *Rosinante* was broken winded; and that, moveover, *Rosinante,* as is the happiness of most *Spanish* horses, fat or learn,—was undoubtedly a horse at all points.

I know very well that the HERO's horse was a horse of chaste deportment, which may have given grounds for a contrary opinion: But it is certain at the same time, that *Rosinante's* continency (as may be demonstrated from the adventure of the *Yanguesian* carriers) proceeded from no bodily defect or cause whatsoever, but from the temperance and orderly current of his blood.—And let me tell you, Madam, there is a great deal of very good

11 Characters in Voltaire's *Candide.*
12 Don Quixote's horse; see above pp. 198–99.

chastity in the world, in behalf of which you could not say more for your life.

Let that be as it may, as my purpose is to do exact justice to every creature brought upon the stage of this dramatic work,—I could not stifle this distinction in favour of Don *Quixote*'s horse;——in all other points the parson's horse, I say, was just such another,—for he was as lean, and as lank, and as sorry a jade, as HUMILITY herself could have bestrided.

In the estimation of here and there a man of weak judgment, it was greatly in the parson's power to have helped the figure of this horse of his,— for he was master of a very handsome demi-peak'd saddle, quilted on the seat with green plush, garnished with a noble row of silver-headed studs, and a noble pair of shining brass stirrups, with a housing altogether suitable, of grey superfine cloth, with an edging of black lace, terminating in a deep, black, silk fringe, *poudré d'or*,[13]—all which he had purchased in the pride and prime of his life, together with a grand embossed bridle, ornamented at all points as it should be.——But not caring to banter his beast, he had hung all these up behind his study door;—and, in lieu of them, had seriously befitted him with just such a bridle and such a saddle, as the figure and value of such a steed might well and truly deserve.

In the several sallies about his parish, and in the neighbouring visits to the gentry who lived around him,——you will easily comprehend, that the parson, so appointed, would both hear and see enough to keep his philosophy from rusting. To speak the truth, he never could enter a village, but he caught the attention of both old and young.——Labour stood still as he pass'd,—the bucket hung suspended in the middle of the well,——the spinning-wheel forgot its round,—even chuck-farthing and shuffle-cap[14] themselves stood gaping till he had got out of sight; and as his movement was not of the quickest, he had generally time enough upon his hands to make his observations,—to hear the groans of the serious,——and the laughter of the lighthearted;—all which he bore with excellent tranquillity.—His character was,——he loved a jest in his heart—and as he saw himself in the true point of ridicule, he would say, he could not be angry with others for seeing him in a light, in which he so strongly saw himself: So that to his friends, who knew his foible was not the love of money, and who therefore made the less scruple in bantering the extravagance of his humour,—instead of giving the true cause,——he chose rather to join in the laugh against himself; and as he never carried one single ounce of flesh upon his own bones, being altogether as spare a figure as his beast,—he would sometimes insist upon it, that the horse was as good as the rider deserved;—that they were, centaur-like,— both of a piece. At other times, and in other moods, when his spirits were above the temptation of false wit,—he would say, he found himself going

[13] Powdered with gold.
[14] Country games.

off fast in a consumption; and, with great gravity, would pretend, he could not bear the sight of a fat horse without a dejection of heart, and a sensible alteration in his pulse; and that he had made choice of the lean one he rode upon, not only to keep himself in countenance, but in spirits.

At different times he would give fifty humorous and opposite reasons for riding a meek-spirited jade of a broken-winded horse, preferably to one of mettle;—for on such a one he could sit mechanically, and meditate as delightfully *de vanitate mundi et fugâ sæculi*,[15] as with the advantage of a death's head before him;—that, in all other exercitations, he could spend his time, as he rode slowly along,——to as much account as in his study; ——that he could draw up an argument in his sermon,—or a hole in his breeches, as steadily on the one as in the other;—that brisk trotting and slow argumentation, like wit and judgment, were two incompatible movements.—But that, upon his steed—he could unite and reconcile every thing, —he could compose his sermon,—he could compose his cough,—and, in case nature gave a call that way, he could likewise compose himself to sleep.—In short, the parson upon such encounters would assign any cause, but the true cause,—and he withheld the true one, only out of a nicety of temper, because he thought it did honour to him.

But the truth of the story was as follows: In the first years of this gentleman's life, and about the time when the superb saddle and bridle were purchased by him, it had been his manner, or vanity, or call it what you will,—to run into the opposite extream.—In the language of the county where he dwelt, he was to have loved a good horse, and generally had one of the best in the whole parish standing in his stable always ready for saddling; and as the nearest midwife, as I told you, did not live nearer to the village than seven miles, and in a vile country,——it so fell out that the poor gentleman was scarce a whole week together without some piteous application for his beast; and as he was not an unkind-hearted man, and every case was more pressing and more distressful than the last,—as much as he loved his beast, he had never a heart to refuse him; the upshot of which was generally this, that his horse was either clapp'd, or spavin'd, or greaz'd;—or he was twitter-bon'd, or broken-winded, or something, in short, or other had befallen him which would let him carry no flesh;—so that he had every nine or ten months a bad horse to get rid of,—and a good horse to purchase in his stead.

What the loss in such a balance might amount to, *communibus annis*,[16] I would leave to a special jury of sufferers in the same traffic, to determine;— but let it be what it would, the honest gentleman bore it for many years without a murmur, till at length, by repeated ill accidents of the kind, he found it necessary to take the thing under consideration; and upon weighing

15 On the world's vanity and time's haste.
16 In common years.

the whole, and summing it up in his mind, he found it not only disproportion'd to his other expences, but withall so heavy an article in itself, as to disable him from any other act of generosity in his parish: Besides this he considered, that, with half the sum thus galloped away, he could do ten times as much good;——and what still weighed more with him than all other considerations put together, was this, that it confined all his charity into one particular channel, and where, as he fancied, it was the least wanted, namely to the child-bearing and child-getting part of his parish; reserving nothing for the impotent,—nothing for the aged,—nothing for the many comfortless scenes he was hourly called forth to visit, where poverty, and sickness, and affliction dwelt together.

For these reasons he resolved to discontinue the expence; and there appeared but two possible ways to extricate him clearly out of it;—and these were, either to make it an irrevocable law never more to lend his steed upon any application whatever,—or else be content to ride the last poor devil, such as they had made him, with all his aches and infirmities, to the very end of the chapter.

As he dreaded his own constancy in the first,——he very chearfully betook himself to the second; and tho' he could very well have explain'd it, as I said, to his honour,—yet, for that very reason, he had a spirit above it; choosing rather to bear the contempt of his enemies, and the laughter of his friends, than undergo the pain of telling a story, which might seem a panegyric upon himself.

I have the highest idea of the spiritual and refined sentiments of this reverend gentleman, from this single stroke in his character, which I think comes up to any of the honest refinements of the peerless knight of *La Mancha*,[17] whom, by the bye, with all his follies, I love more, and would actually have gone further to have paid a visit to, than the greatest hero of antiquity.

But this is not the moral of my story: The thing I had in view was to shew the temper of the world in the whole of this affair.—For you must know, that so long as this explanation would have done the parson credit,—the devil a soul could find it out,—I suppose his enemies would not, and that his friends could not.——But no sooner did he bestir himself in behalf of the midwife, and pay the expences of the ordinary's licence to set her up,—but the whole secret came out; every horse he had lost, and two horses more than ever he had lost, with all the circumstances of their destruction, were known and distinctly remembered.—The story ran like wild-fire.—"The parson had a returning fit of pride which had just seized him; and he was going to be well mounted once again in his life; and if it was so, 'twas plain as the sun at noon-day, he would pocket the expence of the licence, ten times

17 Don Quixote.

told the very first year:——So that every body was left to judge what were his views in this act of charity."

What were his views in this, and in every other action of his life,—or rather what were the opinions which floated in the brains of other people concerning it, was a thought which too much floated in his own, and too often broke in upon his rest, when he should have been sound asleep.

About ten years ago this gentleman had the good fortune to be made entirely easy upon that score,—it being just so long since he left his parish, ——and the whole world at the same time behind him,—and stands accountable to a judge of whom he will have no cause to complain.

But there is a fatality attends the actions of some men: Order them as they will, they pass thro' a certain medium which so twists and refracts them from their true directions——that, with all the titles to praise which a rectitude of heart can give, the doers of them are nevertheless forced to live and die without it.

Of the truth of which this gentleman was a painful example.——But to know by what means this came to pass,—and to make that knowledge of use to you, I insistupon it that you read the two following chapters, which contain such a sketch of his life and conversation, as will carry its moral along with it.—When this is done, if nothing stops us in our way, we will go on with the midwife.

chapter xi

Yorick was this parson's name, and, what is very remarkable in it, (as appears from a most ancient account of the family, wrote upon strong vellum, and now in perfect preservation) it had been exactly so spelt for near,——I was within an ace of saying nine hundred years;——but I would not shake my credit in telling an improbable truth, however indisputable in itself;—— and therefore I shall content myself with only saying,—It had been exactly so spelt, without the least variation or transposition of a single letter, for I do not know how long; which is more than I would venture to say of one half of the best surnames in the kingdom; which, in a course of years, have generally undergone as many chops and changes as their owners.—Has this been owing to the pride, or to the shame of the respective proprietors?— In honest truth, I think, sometimes to the one, and sometimes to the other, just as the temptation has wrought. But a villainous affair it is, and will one day so blend and confound us all together, that no one shall be able to stand up and swear, "That his own great grandfather was the man who did either this or that."

This evil had been sufficiently fenced against by the prudent care of the *Yorick's* family, and their religious preservation of these records I quote, which do further inform us, That the family was originally of *Danish* extraction, and had been transplanted into *England* as early as in the reign of *Horwendillus,* king of *Denmark,* in whose court it seems, an ancestor of this Mr. *Yorick's,* and from whom he was lineally descended, held a considerable post to the day of his death. Of what nature this considerable post was, this record saith not;—it only adds, That, for near two centuries, it had been totally abolished as altogether unnecessary, not only in that court, but in every other court of the Christian world.

It has often come into my head, that this post could be no other than that of the king's chief Jester;—and that *Hamlet's Yorick,* in our *Shakespeare,* many of whose plays, you know, are founded upon authenticated facts,—was certainly the very man.

I have not the time to look into *Saxo-Grammaticus's Danish* history, to know the certainty of this;—but if you have leisure, and can easily get at the book, you may do it full as well yourself.

I had just time, in my travels through *Denmark* with Mr. *Noddy's* eldest son, whom, in the year 1741, I accompanied as governor, riding along with him at a prodigious rate thro' most parts of *Europe,* and of which original journey perform'd by us two, a most delectable narrative will be given in the progress of this work. I had just time, I say, and that was all, to prove the truth of an observation made by a long sojourner in that country;—— namely, "That nature was neither very lavish, nor was she very stingy in her gifts of genius and capacity to its inhabitants;—but, like a discreet parent, was moderately kind to them all; observing such an equal tenor in the distribution of her favours, as to bring them, in those points, pretty near to a level with each other; so that you will meet with few instances in that kingdom of refin'd parts; but a great deal of good plain household understanding amongst all ranks of people, of which every body has a share;" which is, I think, very right.

With us, you see, the case is quite different;—we are all ups and downs in this matter;—you are a great genius;—or 'tis fifty to one, Sir, you are a great dunce and a blockhead;—not that there is a total want of intermediate steps,—no,—we are not so irregular as that comes to;—but the two extremes are more common, and in a greater degree in this unsettled island, where nature, in her gifts and dispositions of this kind, is most whimsical and capricious; fortune herself not being more so in the bequest of her goods and chattels than she.

This is all that ever stagger'd my faith in regard to *Yorick's* extraction, who, by what I can remember of him, and by all the accounts I could ever get of him, seem'd not to have had one single drop of *Danish* blood in his whole crasis; in nine hundred years, it might possibly have all run out:——I will not philosophize one moment with you about it; for happen how it would, the fact was this:—That instead of that cold phlegm and exact regularity of sense and humours, you would have look'd for, in one so extracted;—he was, on the contrary, as mercurial and sublimated a composition,—as heteroclite a creature in all his declensions;———with as much life and whim, and *gaité de cœur*[18] about him, as the kindliest climate could have engendered and put together. With all this sail, poor *Yorick* carried not one ounce of ballast; he was utterly unpractised in the world; and, at the age of twenty-six, knew just about as well how to steer his course in it, as a romping, unsuspicious girl of thirteen: So that upon his first setting out, the brisk gale of his spirits, as you will imagine, ran him foul ten times in a day of some body's tackling; and as the grave and more slow-paced were oftenest in his way, ———you may likewise imagine, 'twas with such he had generally the ill luck to get the most entangled. For aught I know there might be some mixture of unlucky wit at the bottom of such *Fracas:*—For, to speak the truth, *Yorick* had an invincible dislike and opposition in his nature to gravity;———not to gravity as such;———for where gravity was wanted, he would be the most grave and serious of mortal men for days and weeks together;—but he was an enemy to the affectation of it, and declared open war against it, only as it appeared a cloak for ignorance, or for folly; and then, whenever it fell in his way, however sheltered and protected, he seldom gave it much quarter.

Sometimes, in his wild way of talking, he would say, That gravity was an errant scoundrel; and he would add,—of the most dangerous kind too,— because a sly one; and that, he verily believed, more honest, well-meaning people were bubbled out of their goods and money by it in one twelve-month, than by pocket-picking and shop-lifting in seven. In the naked temper which a merry heart discovered, he would say, There was no danger,— but to itself;—whereas the very essence of gravity was design, and conse-quently deceit;—'twas a taught trick to gain credit of the world for more sense and knowledge than a man was worth; and that, with all its pretensions, —it was no better, but often worse, than what a *French* wit had long ago defined it,—*viz. A mysterious carriage of the body to cover the defects of the mind;*—which definition of gravity, *Yorick,* with great imprudence, would say, deserved to be wrote in letters of gold.

But, in plain truth, he was a man unhackneyed and unpractised in the world, and was altogether as indiscreet and foolish on every other subject of discourse where policy is wont to impress restraint. *Yorick* had no impres-sion but one, and that was what arose from the nature of the deed spoken of; which impression he would usually translate into plain *English* without any periphrasis,———and too oft without much distinction of either personage, time, or place;—so that when mention was made of a pitiful or an ungenerous proceeding,—he never gave himself a moment's time to reflect who was the Hero of the piece,———what his station,———or how far he had power to hurt him hereafter;—but if it was a dirty action,———without more ado,———The man was a dirty fellow,—and so on:—And as his comments had usually the ill fate to be terminated either in a *bon mot,* or to be enliven'd throughout

---

[18] Gaiety of heart.

with some drollery or humour of expression, it gave wings to *Yorick's* indiscretion. In a word, tho' he never sought, yet, at the same time, as he seldom shun'd occasions of saying what came uppermost, and without much ceremony;——he had but too many temptations in life, of scattering his wit and his humour,—his gibes and his jests about him.——They were not lost for want of gathering.

What were the consequences, and what was *Yorick's* catastrophe thereupon, you will read in the next chapter.

chapter xii

The *Mortgager and Mortgagée* differ the one from the other, not more in length of purse, than the *Jester* and *Jestée* do, in that of memory. But in this the comparison between them runs, as the scholiasts call it, upon all-four;[19] which, by the bye, is upon one or two legs more, than some of the best of *Homer's can pretend to;*——namely, That the one raises a sum and the other a laugh at your expence, and think no more about it. Interest, however, still runs on in both cases;—the periodical or accidental payments of it, just serving to keep the memory of the affair alive; till, at length, in some evil hour,—pop comes the creditor upon each, and by demanding principal upon the spot, together with full interest to the very day, makes them both feel the full extent of their obligations.

As the reader (for I hate your *ifs*) has a thorough knowledge of human nature, I need say more to satisfy him, that my Hero could not go on at this rate without some slight experience of these incidental mementos. To speak the truth, he had wantonly involved himself in a multitude of small book-debts of this stamp, which, notwithstanding *Eugenius's* frequent advice, he too much disregarded; thinking, that as not one of them was contracted thro' any malignancy;—but, on the contrary, from an honesty of mind, and a mere jocundity of humour, they would all of them be cross'd out in course.

Eugenius would never admit this; and would often tell him, that one day or other he would certainly be reckoned with; and he would often add, in an accent of sorrowful apprehension,—to the uttermost mite. To which *Yorick*, with his usual carelessness of heart, would as often answer with a pshaw!—and if the subject was started in the fields,—with a hop, skip, and a jump, at the end of it; but if close pent up in the social chimney corner, where the culprit was barricado'd in, which a table and a couple of arm chairs, and could not so readily fly off in a tangent,—*Eugenius* would then go on with his lecture upon discretion, in words to this purpose, though somewhat better put together.

Trust me, dear *Yorick,* this unwary pleasantry of thine will sooner or

---

[19] The comparison, unlike some of Homer's similes, corresponds in all points, as marginal commentators (scholiasts) would say.

later bring thee into scrapes and difficulties, which no after-wit can extricate thee out of.——In these sallies, too oft, I see, it happens, that a person laugh'd at, considers himself in the light of a person injured, with all the rights of such a situation belonging to him; and when thou viewest him in that light too, and reckons up his friends, his family, his kindred, and allies, ——and musters up with them the many recruits which will list under him from a sense of common danger;—'tis no extravagant arithmetic to say, that for every ten jokes,—thou hast got a hundred enemies; and till thou hast gone on, and raised a swarm of wasps about thy ears, and art half stung to death by them, thou wilt never be convinced it is so.

I cannot suspect it in the man whom I esteem, that there is the least spur from spleen or malevolence of intent in these sallies.——I believe and know them to be truly honest and sportive:—But consider, my dear lad, that fools cannot distinguish this,—and that knaves will not; and thou knowest not what it is, either to provoke the one, or to make merry with the other,— whenever they associate for mutual defence, depend upon it, they will carry on the war in such a manner against thee, my dear friend, as to make thee heartily sick of it, and of thy life too.

REVENGE from some baneful corner shall level a tale of dishonour at thee, which no innocence of heart or integrity of conduct shall set right.——The fortunes of thy house shall totter,—thy character, which led the way to them, shall bleed on every side of it,—thy faith questioned,—thy works belied,—thy wit forgotten,—thy learning trampled on. To wind up the last scene of thy tragedy, CRUELTY and COWARDICE, twin ruffians, hired and set on by MALICE in the dark, shall strike together at all thy infirmities and mistakes:—The best of us, my dear lad, lie open there,—and trust me,— trust me, *Yorick, When to gratify a private appetite, it is once resolved upon, that an innocent and an helpless creature shall be sacrificed, 'tis an easy matter to pick up sticks enew from any thicket where it has strayed, to make a fire to offer it up with.*

Yorick scarce ever heard this sad vaticination of his destiny read over to him, but with a tear stealing from his eye, and a promissory look attending it, that he was resolved, for the time to come, to ride his tit[20] with more sobriety.——But, alas, too late!—a grand confederacy, with * * * * * and * * * * * at the head of it, was form'd before the first prediction of it.—The whole plan of the attack, just as *Eugenius* had foreboded, was put in execution all at once,—with so little mercy on the side of the allies,—and so little suspicion in *Yorick,* of what was carrying on against him,—that when he thought, good easy man! full surely prefement was o'ripening,—they had smote his root, and then he fell, as many a worthy man had fallen before him.

Yorick, however, fought it out with all imaginable gallantry for some

20 A small horse.

time; till over-power'd by numbers, and worn out at length by the calamities of the war,—but more so, by the ungenerous manner in which it was carried on,—he threw down the sword; and though he kept up his spirits in appearance to the last, he died, nevertheless, as was generally thought, quite broken hearted.

What inclined *Eugenius* to the same opinion, was as follows:

A few hours before *Yorick* breath'd his last, *Eugenius* stept in with an intent to take his last sight and last farewell of him: Upon his drawing *Yorick's* curtain, and asking how he felt himself, *Yorick,* looking up in his face, took hold of his hand,—and, after thanking him for the many tokens of his friendship to him, for which, he said, if it was their fate to meet hereafter, —he would thank him again and again.—He told him, he was within a few hours of giving his enemies the slip for ever.—I hope not, answered *Eugenius,* with tears trickling down his cheeks, and with the tenderest tone that ever man spoke,—I hope not, *Yorick,* said he.—*Yorick* replied, with a look up, and a gentle squeeze of *Eugenius's* hand, and that was all,—but it cut *Eugenius* to his heart.—Come,—come, *Yorick,* quoth *Eugenius,* wiping his eyes, and summoning up the man within him,—my dear lad, be comforted,— let not all thy spirits and fortitude forsake thee at this crisis when thou most wants them;——who knows what resources are in store, and what the power of God may yet do for thee?——*Yorick* laid his hand upon his heart, and gently shook his head;—for my part, continued *Eugenius,* crying bitterly as he uttered the words,—I declare I know not, *Yorick,* how to part with thee, ——and would gladly flatter my hopes, added *Eugenius,* chearing up his voice, that there is still enough left of thee to make a bishop,—and that I may live to see it.——I beseech thee, *Eugenius,* quoth *Yorick,* taking off his nightcap as well as he could with his left hand,——his right being still grasped in that of *Eugenius,*——I beseech thee to take a view of my head.—I see nothing that ails it, replied *Eugenius.* Then, alas! my friend, said *Yorick,* let me tell you, that 'tis so bruised and mis-shapen'd with the blows which * * * * * and * * * * *, and some others have so unhandsomely given me in the dark, that I might say with *Sancho Pança,* that should I recover, and "Mitres thereupon he suffer'd to rain down from heaven as thick as hail, not one of 'em would fit it."——*Yorick's* last breath was hanging upon his trembling lips ready to depart as he uttered this;—yet still it was utter'd with something of a *Cervantick* tone;—and as he spoke it, *Eugenius* could perceive a stream of lambent fire lighted up for a moment in his eyes:— faint picture of those flashes of his spirit, which (as *Shakespeare* said of his ancestor) were wont to set the table in a roar!

Eugenius was convinced from this, that the heart of his friend was broke; he squeez'd his hand,——and then walk'd softly out of the room, weeping as he walk'd. *Yorick* followed *Eugenius* with his eyes to the door,—he then closed them,—and never opened them more.

He lies buried in a corner of his church-yard, in the parish of——,
under a plain marble slab, which his friend *Eugenius,* by leave of his
executors, laid upon his grave, with no more than these three words of
inscription serving both for his epitaph and elegy.

> Alas, poor YORICK!

Ten times in a day has *Yorick's* ghost the consolation to hear his
monumental inscription read over with such a variety of plaintive tones, as
denote a general pity and esteem for him;——a foot-way crossing the church-
yard close by the side of his grave,—not a passenger goes by without stopping
to cast a look upon it,——and sighing as he walks on,

Alas, poor YORICK!

chapter xiii

It is so long since the reader of this rhapsodical work has been parted
from the midwife, that it is high time to mention her again to him, merely to
put him in mind that there is such a body still in the world, and whom, upon
the best judgment I can form upon my own plan at present,—I am going to
introduce to him for good and all: But as fresh matter may be started, and
much unexpected business fall out betwixt the reader and myself, which may
require immediate dispatch;——'twas right to take care that the poor woman
should not be lost in the mean time;—because when she is wanted we can
no way do without her.

I think I told you that this good woman was a person of no small note
and consequence throughout our whole village township;—that her fame
had spread itself to the very out-edge and circumference of that circle of
importance, of which kind every soul living, whether he has a shirt to his
back or no,——has one surrounding him;—which said circle, by the way,
whenever 'tis that such a one is of great weight and importance in the *world,*
——I desire may be enlarged or contracted in your worship's fancy, in a
compound-ratio of the station, profession, knowledge, abilities, and depth
(measuring both ways) of the personage brought before you.

In the present case, if I remember, I fixed it at about four or five miles,
which not only comprehended the whole parish, but extended itself to two
or three of the adjacent hamlets in the skirts of the next parish; which made
a considerable thing of it. I must add, That she was, moreover, very well
looked on at one large grange-house and some other odd houses and farms
within two or three miles, as I said, from the smoke of her own chimney:——
But I must here, once for all, inform you, that all this will be more exactly
delineated and explain'd in a map, now in the hands of the engraver, which,

with many other pieces and developments to this work, will be added to the end of the twentieth volume,—not to swell the work,—I detest the thought of such a thing;——but by way of commentary, scholium, illustration, and key to such passages, incidents, or inuendos as shall be thought to be either of private interpretation, or of dark or doubtful meaning after my life and my opinions shall have been read over, (now don't forget the meaning of the word) by all the *world;*—which, betwixt you and me, and in spite of all the gentlemen reviewers in *Great-Britain,* and of all that their worships shall undertake to write or say to the contrary,——I am determined shall be the case.——I need not tell your worship, that all this is spoke in confidence.

chapter xiv

Upon looking into my mother's marriage settlement, in order to satisfy myself and reader in a point necessary to be clear'd up, before we could proceed any further in this history;—I had the good fortune to pop upon the very thing I wanted before I had read a day and a half straightforwards, —it might have taken me up a month;—which shews plainly, that when a man sits down to write a history,—tho' it be but the history of *Jack Hickathrift* or *Tom Thumb,* he knows no more than his heels what lets and confounded hinderances he is to meet with in his way,—or what a dance he may be led, by one excursion or another, before all is over. Could a historiographer drive on his history, as a muleteer drives on his mule,—straight forward;——for instance, from *Rome* all the way to *Loretto,* without ever once turning his head aside either to the right hand or to the left,—he might venture to foretell you to an hour when he should get to his journey's end;——but the thing is, morally speaking, impossible: For, if he is a man of the least spirit, he will have fifty deviations from a straight line to make with this or that party as he goes along, which he can no ways avoid. He will have views and prospects to himself perpetually soliciting his eye, which he can no more help standing still to look at than he can fly; he will moreover have various

> Accounts to reconcile:
> Anecdotes to pick up:
> Inscriptions to make out:
> Stories to weave in:
> Traditions to sift:
> Personages to call upon:
> Panegyricks to paste up at this door:

Pasquinades[21] at that:——All which both the man and his mule are quite

[21] Satires.

exempt from. To sum up all; there are archives at every stage to be look'd into, and rolls, records, documents, and endless genealogies, which justice ever and anon calls him back to stay the reading of:—In short, there is no end of it;——for my own part, I declare I have been at it these six weeks, making all the speed I possibly could,—and am not yet born:—I have just been able, and that's all, to tell you *when* it happen'd, but not *how*;—so that you see the thing is yet for from being accomplished.

These unforeseen stoppages, which I own I had no conception of when I first set out;—but which, I am convinced now, will rather increase than diminish as I advance,—have struck out a hint which I am resolved to follow;—and that is,—not to be in a hurry;—but to go on leisurely, writing and publishing two volumes of my life every year;—which, if I am suffered to go on quietly, and can make a tolerable bargain with my bookseller, I shall continue to do as long as I live.

The Fable
of the Vultures

samuel johnson

MANY NATURALISTS ARE OF OPINION that the animals which we commonly consider as mute have the power of imparting their thoughts to one another. That they can express general sensations is very certain; every being that can utter sounds has a different voice for pleasure and for pain. The hound informs his fellows when he scents his game; the hen calls her chickens to their food by her cluck, and drives them from danger by her scream.

Birds have the greatest variety of notes; they have indeed a variety which seems almost sufficient to make a speech adequate to the purposes of a life, which is regulated by instinct, and can admit little change or improvement. To the cries of birds, curiosity or superstition has been always attentive; many have studied the language of the feathered tribes, and some have boasted that they understood it.

The most skillful or most confident interpreters of the sylvan dialogues have been commonly found among the philosophers of the East, in a country where the calmness of the air and the mildness of the seasons allow the student to pass a great part of the year in groves and bowers. But what may be done in one place by peculiar opportunities may be performed in another by peculiar diligence. A shepherd of Bohemia has, by long abode in the forests, enabled himself to understand the voice of birds; at least he relates with great confidence a story, of which the credibility is left to be considered by the learned.

"As I was sitting," said he, "within a hollow rock, and watching my sheep that fed in the valley, I heard two vultures interchangeable crying on

From *The Idler*, No. 22, Sept. 16, 1758.

the summit of the cliff. Both voices were earnest and deliberate. My curiosity prevailed over my care of the flock; I climbed slowly and silently from crag to crag, concealed among the shrubs till I found a cavity where I might sit and listen without suffering, or giving disturbance.

"I soon perceived that my labor would be well repaid; for an old vulture was sitting on a naked prominence with her young about her, whom she was instructing in the arts of a vulture's life, and preparing by the last lecture for their final dismission to the mountains and the skies.

" 'My children,' said the old vulture, 'you will the less want my instructions because you have had my practice before your eyes; you have seen me snatch from the farm the household fowl; you have seen me seize the leveret[1] in the bush, and the kid in the pasture; you know how to fix your talons, and how to balance your flight when you are laden with your prey. But you remember the taste of more delicious food; I have often regaled you with the flesh of man.' 'Tell us,' said the young vultures, 'where man may be found, and how he may be known; his flesh is surely the natural food of a vulture. Why have you never brought a man in your talons to the nest?' 'He is too bulky,' said the mother; 'when we find a man, we can only tear away his flesh and leave his bones upon the ground.' 'Since man is so big,' said the young ones, 'how do you kill him? You are afraid of the wolf and of the bear; by what power are vultures superior to man? Is man more defenseless than a sheep?' 'We have not the strength of man,' returned the mother; 'and I am sometimes in doubt whether we have the subtilty; and the vultures would seldom feast upon his flesh, had not nature, that devoted him to our uses, infused into him a strange ferocity which I have never observed in any other being that feeds upon the earth. Two herds of men will often meet and shake the earth with noise, and fill the air with fire. When you hear noise and see fire, with flashes along the ground, hasten to the place with your swiftest wing, for men are surely destroying one another; you will then find the ground smoking with blood, and covered with carcasses, of which many are dismembered and mangled for the convenience of the vulture.' 'But when men have killed their prey,' said the pupil, 'why do they not eat it? When the wolf has killed a sheep, he suffers not the vulture to touch it till he has satisfied himself. Is not man another kind of wolf?' 'Man,' said the mother, 'is the only beast who kills that which he does not devour, and this quality makes him so much a benefactor to our species.' 'If men kill our prey and lay it in our way,' said the young one, 'what need shall we have of laboring for ourselves?' 'Because man will, sometimes,' replied the mother, 'remain for a long time quiet in his den. The old vultures will tell you when you are to watch his motions. When you see men in great numbers moving close together like a flight of storks, you may conclude that they are hunting,

---

1 young hare.

and that you will soon revel in human blood.' 'But still,' said the young one, 'I would gladly know the reason of this mutual slaughter. I could never kill what I could not eat.' 'My child,' said the mother, 'this is a question which I cannot answer, though I am reckoned the most subtile bird of the mountain. When I was young, I used frequently to visit the aerie of an old vulture who dwelt upon the Carpathian rocks; he had many observations; he knew the places that afforded prey round his habitation as far in every direction as the strongest wing can fly between the rising and setting of the summer sun; he had fed year after year on the entrails of men. His opinion was that men had only the appearance of animal life, being really vegetables with a power of motion; and that as the boughs of an oak are dashed together by the storm that swine may fatten upon the falling acorns, so men are by some unaccountable power driven one against another till they lose their motion that vultures may be fed. Others think they have observed something of contrivance and policy among these mischievous beings; and those that hover more closely round them, pretend that there is in every herd one that gives directions to the rest, and seems to be more eminently delighted with a wide carnage. What it is that entitles him to such pre-eminence we know not; he is seldom the biggest or the swiftest, but he shows by his eagerness and diligence that he is, more than any of the others, a friend to vultures.' "

From Candide

voltaire

ARRIVAL OF CANDIDE AND HIS VALET
IN THE COUNTRY OF ELDORADO
AND WHAT THEY SAW THERE

WHEN THEY REACHED THE FRONTIERS of the Oreillons, Cacambo said to Candide: "You see this hemisphere is no better than the other; take my advice, let us go back to Europe by the shortest road." "How can we go back," said Candide, "and where can we go? If I go to my own country, the Bulgarians and the Abares are murdering everybody; if I return to Portugal I shall be burned; if we stay here, we run the risk of being spitted at any moment. But how can I make up my mind to leave that part of the world where Mademoiselle Cunegonde is living?" "Let us go to Cayenne," said Cacambo, "we shall find Frenchmen there, for they go all over the world; they might help us. Perhaps God will have pity on us." It not easy to go to Cayenne. They knew roughly the direction to take, but mountains, rivers, precipices, brigands and savages were everywhere terrible obstacles. Their horses died of fatigue; their provisions were exhausted; for a whole month they lived on wild fruits and at last found themselves near a little river fringed with cocoanut-trees which supported their lives and their hopes. Cacambo, who always gave advice as prudent as the old woman's, said to Candide: "We can go no farther, we have walked far enough; I can see an empty canoe in the bank, let us fill it with cocoanuts, get into the little boat and drift with the current; a river always leads to some inhabited place. If we do not find anything pleasant, we shall at least find something new." "Come on then," said Candide, "and let us trust to Providence." They drifted for some leagues between banks which were sometimes flowery, sometimes bare, sometimes flat, sometimes steep. The river continually became wider; finally it disappeared under an arch of frightful rocks which towered up to the very sky. The two travelers were bold enough to trust themselves to the current under this arch. The stream, narrowed between walls, carried them with horrible rapidity and noise. After twenty-four hours they saw daylight again; but their canoe was wrecked on reefs; they had to crawl from rock to rock for a whole league and at last they discovered an immense horizon, bordered by inaccessible mountains. The country was cultivated for pleasure as well as for necessity; everywhere the useful was agreeable. The roads were covered or rather ornamented with carriages of brilliant material and shape, carrying men and women of singular beauty, who were rapidly drawn along by large red sheep whose swiftness surpassed that of the finest horses of Andalusia, Tetuan, and Mequinez. "This country," said Candide, "is better than Westphalia." He landed with Cacambo near the first village he came to. Several children of the village, dressed in torn gold brocade, were playing horseshoes outside the village. Our two men from the other world amused themselves by looking on; their horseshoes were large round pieces, yellow, red and green which shone with peculiar lustre. The travellers were curious enough to pick up some of them; they were of gold, emeralds and rubies, the least of which would have been the greatest ornament in the Mogul's throne. "No doubt," said Cacambo, "these children are the sons of the King of this country playing horseshoes." At that moment the village schoolmaster appeared to call them into school. "This," said Candide, "is the tutor of the Royal Family." The little beggars immediately left their game, abandoning their horseshoes and everything with which they had been playing. Candide picked them up, ran to the tutor, and presented them to him humbly, giving him to understand by signs that their Royal Highnesses had forgotten their gold and their precious stones. The village schoolmaster smiled, threw them on the ground, gazed for a moment at Candide's face with much surprise and continued on his way. The travelers did not fail to pick up the gold, the rubies and the emeralds. "Where are we?" cried Candide. "The children of the King must be well brought up, since they are taught to despise gold and precious stones." Cacambo was as much surprised as Candide. At last they reached the first house in the village, which was built like a European palace. There were crowds of people round the door and still more inside; very pleasant music could be heard and there was a delicious smell of cooking. Cacambo went up to the door and heard them speaking Peruvian; it was his maternal tongue, for everyone knows that Cacambo was born in a village of Tucuman where nothing else is spoken. "I will act as your interpreter," he said to Candide, "this is an inn, let us enter." Immediately two boys and two girls of the inn, dressed in cloth of gold, whose hair was bound up with ribbons, invited them to sit down to the table d'hôte. They served four soups each garnished with two parrots, a boiled condor which weighed two hundred pounds, two roast monkeys of excellent flavor, three hundred colibris in one dish and six hundred humming-birds in another, exquisite ragouts and delicious pastries, all in dishes of a sort of rock-crystal. The boys and girls brought several sorts of drinks made of sugar-cane. Most of the guests were merchants and coachmen, all extremely polite, who asked Cacambo a few questions with the most delicate discretion and answered his in a satisfactory manner. When the meal was over, Cacambo, like Candide, thought he could pay the reckoning by throwing on the table two of the large pieces of gold he had picked up; the host and hostess laughed until they had to hold their sides. At last they recovered themselves. "Gentlemen," said the host, "we perceive you are strangers; we are not accustomed to seeing them. Forgive us if we began to laugh when you offered us in payment the stones from our highways. No doubt you have none of the money of this country, but you do not need any to dine here. All the hotels established for the utility of commerce are paid for by the government. You have been ill-entertained here because this is a poor village; but everywhere else you will be received as you deserve to be." Cacambo explained to Candide all that the host had said, and Candide listened in the same admiration and disorder with which his friend Cacambo interpreted. "What can this country be," they said to each other, "which is unknown to the rest of the world and where all nature is so different from ours? Probably it is the country where everything is for the best; for there must be one country of that sort. And, in spite of what Dr. Pangloss said, I often noticed that everything went very ill in Westphalia."

WHAT THEY SAW
IN THE LAND OF ELDORADO

Cacambo informed the host of his curiosity, and the host said. "I am a very ignorant man and am all the better for it; but we have here an old man who has retired from the court and who is the most learned and most communicative man in the kingdom." And he at once took Cacambo to the old man. Candide now played only the second part and accompanied his valet. They entered a very simple house, for the door was only of silver and the paneling of the apartments in gold, but so tastefully carved that the richest decorations did not surpass it. The antechamber indeed was only encrusted with rubies and emeralds; but the order with which everything was arranged atoned for this extreme simplicity. The old man received the two strangers on a sofa padded with colibri feathers, and presented them with drinks in diamond cups; after which he satisfied their curiosity in these words: "I am a hundred and seventy-two years old and I heard from my late father, the King's equerry, the astonishing revolutions of Peru of which he had been an eyewitness. The kingdom where we now are is the ancient country of the Incas, who most imprudently left it to conquer part of the world and were at last destroyed by the Spaniards. The princes of their family who remained in their native country had more wisdom; with the consent of the nation, they ordered that no inhabitants should ever leave our little kingdom, and this it is that has preserved our innocence and our felicity. The Spaniards had some vague knowledge of this country, which they called Eldorado, and about a hundred years ago an Englishman named Raleigh came very near to it; but, since we are surrounded by inaccessible rocks and precipices, we have hitherto been exempt from the rapacity of the nations of Europe who have an inconceivable lust for the pebbles and mud of our land and would kill us to the last man to get possession of them." The conversation was long; it touched upon the form of the government, manners, women, public spectacles and the arts. Finally Candide, who was always interested in metaphysics, asked through Cacambo whether the country had a religion. The old man blushed a little. "How can you doubt it?" said he "Do you think we are ingrates?" Cacambo humbly asked what was the religion of Eldorado. The old man blushed again. "Can there be two religions?" said he. "We have, I think, the religion of every one else; we adore God from evening until morning." "Do you adore only one God?" said Canambo, who continued to act as the interpreter of Candide's doubts. "Manifestly," said the old man, "there are not two or three or four. I must confess that the people of your world ask very extraordinary questions." Candide continued to press the old man with questions; he wished to know how they prayed to God in Eldorado. "We do not pray," said the good and respectable sage, "we have nothing to ask from him; he has given us everything necessary and we continually give him thanks." Candide was curious to see the priests; and asked where they were. The good old man smiled. "My friends," said he, "we are all priests; the King and all the heads of families solemnly sing praises every morning, accompanied by five or six thousand musicians." "What! Have you no monks to teach, to dispute, to govern, to intrigue and to burn people who do not agree with them?" "For that, we should have to become fools," said the old man; "here we are all of the same opinion and do not understand what you mean with your monks." At all this Candide was in an ecstasy and said to himself: "This is very different from West-phalia and the castle of His Lordship the Baron; if our friend Pangloss had seen Eldorado, he would not have said that the castle of Thunder-ten-tronckh was the best of all that exists on the earth; certainly, a man should travel." After this long conversation the good old man ordered a carriage to be harnessed with six sheep and gave the two travelers twelve of his servants to take them to court. "You will excuse me," he said, "if my age deprives me of the honor of accompanying you. The King will receive you in a manner which will not displease you and doubtless you will pardon the customs of the country if any of them disconcert you." Candide and Cacambo entered the carriage; the six sheep galloped off and in less than four hours they reached the King's palace, which was situated at one end of the capital. The portal was two hundred and twenty feet high and a hundred feet wide; it is impossible to describe its material. Anyone can see the prodigious superiority it must have over the pebbles and sand we call *gold* and *gems*. Twenty beautiful maidens of the guard received Candide and Cacambo as they alighted from the carriage, conducted them to the baths and dressed them in robes woven from the down of colibris; after which the principal male and female officers of the Crown led them to his Majesty's apartment through two files of a thousand musicians each, according to the usual custom. As they approached the throne-room, Cacambo asked one of the chief officers how they should behave in his Majsety's presence; whether they should fall on their knees or flat on their faces, whether they should put their hands on their heads or on their backsides; whether they should lick the dust of the throne-room; in a word, what was the ceremony? "The custom," said the chief officer, "is to embrace the King and to kiss him on either cheek." Candide and Cacambo threw their arms round his Majesty's neck; he received them with all imaginable favor and politely asked them to supper. Meanwhile they were carried to see the town, the public buildings rising to the very skies, the market-places ornamented with thousands of columns, the fountains of rose-water and of liquors distilled from sugar-cane, which played continually in the public squares paved with precious stones which emitted a perfume like that of cloves and cinnamon. Candide asked to see the law courts; he was told there were none, and that nobody ever went to law. He asked if there were prisons and was told there were none. He was still more surprised and pleased by the palace of sciences, where he saw a gallery two thousand feet long, filled with instruments of mathematics and physics. After they had explored all the afternoon about a thousandth part of the town, they were taken back to the King. Candide sat down to table with his Majesty, his valet Cacambo and several ladies. Never was there a better supper, and never was anyone wittier at supper than his Majesty. Cacambo explained the King's witty remarks to Candide and even when translated they still appeared witty. Among all the things which amazed Candide, this did not amaze him the least. They enjoyed this hospitality for a month. Candide repeatedly said to Cacambo: "Once again, my friend, it is quite true that the castle where I was born cannot be compared with this country; but then Mademoiselle Cunegonde is not here and you probably have a mistress in Europe. If we remain here, we shall only be like everyone else; but if we return to our own world with only twelve sheep laden with Eldorado pebbles, we shall be richer than all the kings put together; we shall have no more Inquisitors to fear and we can easily regain Mademoiselle

Cunegonde." Cacambo agreed with this; it is so pleasant to be on the move, to show off before friends, to make a parade of the things seen on one's travels, that these two happy men resolved to be so no longer and to ask his Majesty's permission to depart. "You are doing a very silly thing," said the King. "I know my country is small; but when we are comfortable anywhere we should stay there; I certainly have not the right to detain foreigners, that is a tyranny which does not exist either in our manners or our laws; all men are free, leave when you please, but the way out is very difficult. It is impossible to ascend the rapid river by which you miraculously came here and which flows under arches of rock. The mountains which surround the whole of my kingdom are ten thousand feet high and are perpendicular like walls; they are more than ten leagues broad, and you can only get down them by way of precipices. However, since you must go, I will give orders to the directors of machinery to make a machine which will carry you comfortably. When you have been taken to the other side of the mountains, nobody can proceed any farther with you; for my subjects have sworn never to pass this boundary and they are too wise to break their oath. Ask anything else of me you wish." "We ask nothing of your Majesty," said Cacambo, "except a few sheep laden with provisions, pebbles and the mud of this country." The King laughed. "I cannot understand," said he, "the taste you people of Europe have for our yellow mud; but take as much as you wish, and much good may it do you." He immediately ordered his engineers to make a machine to hoist these two extraordinary men out of his kingdom. Three thousand learned scientists worked at it; it was ready in a fortnight and only cost about twenty million pounds sterling in the money of that country. Candide and Cacambo were placed on the machine; there were two large red sheep saddled and bridled for them to ride on when they had passed the mountains, twenty pack sheep laden with provisions, thirty carrying presents of the most curious productions of the country and fifty laden with gold, precious stones and diamonds. The King embraced the two vagabonds tenderly. Their departure was a splendid sight and so was the ingenious manner in which they and their sheep were hoisted on to the top of the mountains. The scientists took leave of them after having landed them safely, and Candide's only desire and object was to go and present Mademoiselle Cunegonde with his sheep. "We have sufficient to pay the governor of Buenos Ayres," said he, "if Mademoiselle Cunegonde can be bought. Let us go to Cayenne, and take ship, and then we will see what kingdom we will buy."

CONCLUSION

At the bottom of his heart Candide had not the least wish to marry Cunegonde. But the Baron's extreme impertinence determined him to complete the marriage, and Cunegonde urged it so warmly that he could not retract. He consulted Pangloss, Martin and the faithful Cacambo. Pangloss wrote an excellent memorandum by which he proved that the Baron had no rights over his sister and that by all the laws of the empire she could make a left-handed marriage with Candide. Martin advised that the Baron should be thrown into the sea; Cacambo decided that he should be returned to the Levantine captain and sent back to the galleys, after which he would be returned by the first ship to the Vicar-General Rome. This was though to be very good advice; the old woman approved it; they said nothing to the sister; the plan was carried out with the aid of a little money and they had the pleasure of duping a Jesuit and punishing the pride of a German Baron.

It would be natural to suppose that when, after so many disasters, Candide was married to his mistress, and living with the philosopher Pangloss, the philosopher Martin, the prudent Cacambo and the old woman, having brought back so many diamonds from the country of the ancient Incas, he would lead the most pleasant life imaginable. But he was so cheated by the Jews that he had nothing left but his little farm; his wife, growing uglier every day, became shrewish and unendurable; the old woman was ailing and even more bad-tempered than Cunegonde. Cacambo, who worked in the garden and then went to Constantinople to sell vegetables, was overworked and cursed his fate. Pangloss was in despair because he did not shine in some German university. As for Martin, he was firmly convinced that people are equally uncomfortable everywhere; he accepted things patiently. Candide, Martin and Pangloss sometimes argued about metaphysics and morals. From the windows of the farm they often watched the ships going by, filled with effendis, pashas, and cadis, who were being exiled to Lemnos, to Mitylene and Erzerum. They saw other cadis, other pashas and other effendis coming back to take the place of the exiles and to be exiled in their turn. They saw the neatly impaled heads which were taken to the Sublime Porte. These sights redoubled their discussions; and when they were not arguing, the boredom was so excessive that one day the old woman dared to say to them: "I should like to know which is worse, to be raped a hundred times by Negro pirates, to have a buttock cut off, to run the gauntlet among the Bulgarians, to be whipped and flogged in an *auto-da-fé*, to be dissected, to row in a galley, in short, to endure all the miseries through which we have passed, or to remain here doing nothing?"

" 'Tis a great question," said Candide.

These remarks led to new reflections, and Martin especially concluded that man was born to live in the convulsions of distress or in the lethargy of boredom. Candide did not agree, but he asserted nothing. Pangloss confessed that he had always suffered horribly; but, having once maintained that everything was for the best, he had continued to maintain it without believing it.

One thing confirmed Martin in his detestable principles, made Candide hesitate more than ever, and embarrassed Pangloss. And it was this. One day there came to their farm Paquette and Friar Giroflée, who were in the most extreme misery; they had soon wasted their three thousand piastres, had left each other, made up, quarrelled again, been put in prison, escaped, and finally Friar Giroflée had turned Turk. Paquette continued her occupation everywhere and now earned nothing by it. "I foresaw," said Martin to Candide, "that your gifts would soon be wasted and would only make them the more miserable. You and Cacambo were once bloated with millions of piastres and you are no happier than Friar Giroflée and Paquette." "Ah! Ha!" said Pangloss to Paquette, "so Heaven brings you back to us, my dear child? Do you know that you cost me the end of my nose, an eye and an ear! What a plight you are in! Ah! What a world this is!" This new occurrence caused them to philosophize more than ever.

In the neighborhood there lived a very famous Dervish, who was supposed to be the best philosopher in Turkey; they went to consult him; Pangloss was the spokesman and said: "Master, we have come to beg you to tell us why so strange an animal as man was ever created." "What has it to do with you?" said the Dervish. "Is it your business?" "But, reverend father," said Candide, "there is a horrible amount of evil in the world." "What does it matter," said the Dervish, "whether there is evil or good? When his highness sends a ship to Egypt, does he worry about the comfort or discomfort of the rats in the ship?" "Then what should we do?" said Pangloss. "Hold your tongue," said the Dervish. "I flattered myself," said Pangloss, "that I should discuss with you effects and causes, this best of all possible worlds, the origin of evil, the nature of the soul and pre-established harmony." At these words the Dervish slammed the door in their faces.

During this conversation the news went round that at Constantinople two viziers and the mufti had been strangled and several of their friends impaled. This catastrophe made a prodigious noise everywhere for several hours. As Pangloss, Candide and Martin were returning to their little farm, they came upon an old man who was taking the air under a bower of orange-trees at his door. Pangloss, who was as curious as he was argumentative, asked him what was the name of the mufti who had just been strangled. "I do not know," replied the old man. "I have never known the name of any mufti or of any vizier. I am entirely ignorant of the occurrence you mention; I presume that in general those who meddle with public affairs sometimes perish miserably and that they deserve it; but I never inquire what is going on in Constantinople; I content myself with sending there for sale the produce of the garden I cultivate." Having spoken thus, he took the strangers into his house. His two daughters and his two sons presented them with several kinds of sherbet which they made themselves, caymac flavored with candied citron peel, oranges, lemons, limes, pineapples, dates, pistachios and Mocha coffee which had not been mixed with the bad coffee of Batavia and the Isles. After which this good Mussulman's two daughters perfumed the beards of Candide, Pangloss and Martin. "You must have a vast and magnificent estate?" said Candide to the Turk. "I have only twenty acres," replied the Turk. "I cultivate them with my children; and work keeps at bay three great evils: boredom, vice and need."

As Candide returned to his farm he reflected deeply on the Turk's remarks. He said to Pangloss and Martin: "That good old man seems to me to have chosen an existence preferable by far to that of the six kings with whom we had the honor to sup." "Exalted rank," said Pangloss, "is very dangerous, according to the testimony of all philosophers; for Eglon, King of the Moabites, was murdered by Ehud; Absalon was hanged by the hair and pierced by three darts; King Nadab, son of Jeroboam, was killed by Baasha; King Elah by Zimri; Ahaziah by Jehu; Athaliah by Jehoiada; the Kings Jehoiakim, Jeconiah and Zedekiah were made slaves. You know in what manner died Crœsus, Astyages, Darius, Denys of Syrause, Pyrrhus, Perseus, Hannibal, Jugurtha, Ariovistus, Cæsar, Pompey, Nero, Otho, Vitellius, Domitian, Richard ii of England, Edward ii, Henry vi, Richard iii, Mary Stuart, Charles i, the three Henrys of France, the Emperor Henry iv. You know..." "I also know," said Candide, "that we should cultivate our garden." "You are right," said Pangloss, "for, when man was placed in the Garden of Eden, he was placed there *ut operaretur eum,* to dress it and to keep it; which proves that man was not born for idleness." "Let us work without theorizing," said Martin; " 'tis the only way to make life endurable."

The whole small fraternity entered into this praiseworthy plan, and each started to make use of his talents. The little farm yielded well. Cunegonde was indeed very ugly, but she became an excellent pastry-cook; Paquette embroidered; the old woman took care of the linen. Even Friar Giroflée performed some service; he was a very good carpenter and even became a man of honor; and Pangloss sometimes said to Candide: "All events are linked up in this best of all possible worlds; for, if you had not been expelled from the noble castle, by hard kicks in your backside for love of Mademoiselle Cunegonde, if you had not been clapped into the Inquisition, if you had not wandered about America on foot, if you not stuck your sword in the Baron, if you had not lost all your sheep from the land of Eldorado, you would not be eating candied citrons and pistachios here." "That's well said," replied Candide, "but we must cultivate our garden."

The Mote in the Middle Distance

max beerbohm

IT WAS WITH THE SENSE of a, for him, very memorable something that he peered now into the immediate future, and tried, not without compunction, to take that period up where he had, prospectively, left it. But just where the deuce *had* he left it? The consciousness of dubiety was, for our friend, not, this morning, quite yet clean-cut enough to outline the figures on what she had called his "horizon," between which and himself the twilight was indeed of a quality somewhat intimidating. He had run up, in the course of time, against a good number of "teasers"; and the function of teasing them back—of, as it were, giving them, every now and then, "what for"—was in him so much a habit that he would have been at a loss had there been, on the face of it, nothing to lose. Oh, he always had offered rewards, of course— had ever so liberally pasted the windows of his soul with staring appeals, minute descriptions, promises that knew no bounds. But the actual recovery of the article—the business of drawing and crossing the cheque, blotched though this were with tears of joy—had blankly appeared to him rather in the light of a sacrilege, casting, he sometimes felt, a palpable chill on the fervour of the next quest. It was just this fervour that was threatened as, raising himself on his elbow, he stared at the foot of his bed. That his eyes refused to rest there for more than the fraction of an instant, may be taken —*was*, even then, taken by Keith Tantalus—as a hint of his recollection that after all the phenomenon wasn't to be singular. Thus the exact repetition, at the foot of Eva's bed, of the shape pendulous at the foot of *his*

From the book A CHRISTMAS GARLAND by Max Beerbohm. Reprinted by permission of E. P. Dutton & Co., Inc., and of William Heinemann Ltd.

was hardly enough to account for the fixity with which he envisaged it, and for which he was to find, some years later, a motive in the (as it turned out) hardly generous fear that Eva had already made the great investigation "on her own." Her very regular breathing presently reassured him that, if she *had* peeped into "her" stocking, she must have done so in sleep. Whether he should wake her now, or wait for their nurse to wake them both in due course, was a problem presently solved by a new development. It was plain that his sister was now watching him between her eyelashes. He had half expected that. She really was—he had often told her that she really was—magnificent; and her magnificence was never more obvious than in the pause that elapsed before she all of a sudden remarked, "They so very indubitably *are,* you know!"

It occurred to him as befitting Eva's remoteness, which was a part of Eva's magnificence, that her voice emerged somewhat muffled by the bedclothes. She was ever, indeed, the most telephonic of her sex. In talking to Eva you always had, as it were, your lips to the receiver. If you didn't try to meet her fine eyes, it was that you simply couldn't hope to: there were too many dark, too many buzzing and bewildering and all frankly not negotiable leagues in between. Snatches of other voices seemed often to intertrude themselves in the parley; and your loyal effort not to overhear these was complicated by your fear of missing what Eva might be twittering. "Oh, you certainly haven't, my dear, the trick of propinquity!" was a thrust she had once parried by saying that, in that case, *he* hadn't—to which his unspoken rejoinder that she had caught her tone from the peevish young women at the Central seemed to him (if not perhaps in the last, certainly in the last but one, analysis) to lack finality. With Eva, he had found, it was always safest to "ring off." It was with a certain sense of his rashness in the matter, therefore, that he now, with an air of feverishly "holding the line," said, "Oh, as to that!"

Had *she,* he presently asked himself, "rung off"? It was characteristic of our friend—was indeed "him all over"—that his fear of what she was going to say was as nothing to his fear of what she might be going to leave unsaid. He had, in his converse with her, been never so conscious as now of the intervening leagues; they had never so insistently beaten the drum of his ear; and he caught himself in the act of awfully computing, with a certain statistical passion, the distance between Rome and Boston. He had never been able to decide which of these points he was psychically the nearer to at the moment when Eva, replying, "Well, one does, anyhow, leave a margin for the pretext, you know!" made him, for the first time in his life, wonder whether she were not more magnificent than even he had ever given her credit for being. Perhaps it was to test this theory, or perhaps merely to gain time, that he now raised himself to his knees, and, leaning with outstretched arm towards the foot of his bed, made as though to touch the stocking which Santa Claus had, overnight, left dangling there. His posture, as he stared obliquely at Eva, with a sort of beaming defiance, recalled to him something seen in an "illustration." This reminiscence, however—if such it was, save in the scarred, the poor dear old woebegone and so very beguilingly *not* refractive mirror of the moment—took a peculiar twist from Eva's behaviour. She had, with startling suddenness, sat bolt upright, and looked to him as if she were overhearing some tragedy at the other end of the wire, where, in the nature of things, she was unable to arrest it. The gaze she fixed on her extravagant kinsman was of a kind to make him wonder how he contrived to remain, as he beautifully did, rigid. His prop was possibly the reflection that flashed on him that, if *she* abounded in attenuations, well, hang it all, so did *he*! It was simply a difference of plane. Readjust the "values," as painters say, and there you were! He was to feel that he was only too crudely "there" when, leaning further forward, he laid a chubby forefinger on the stocking, causing that receptacle to rock ponderously to and fro. This effect was more expected than the tears which started to Eva's eyes and the intensity with which "Don't you," she exclaimed, "see?"

"The mote in the middle distance?" he asked. "Did you ever, my dear, know me to see anything else? I tell you it blocks out everything. It's a cathedral, it's a herd of elephants, it's the whole habitable globe. Oh, it's, believe me, of an obsessiveness!" But his sense of the one thing it *didn't* block out from his purview enabled him to launch at Eva a speculation as to just how far Santa Claus had, for the particular occasion, gone. The gauge, for both of them, of this seasonable distance seemed almost blatantly suspended in the silhouettes of the two stockings. Over and above the basis of (presumably) sweetmeats in the toes and heels, certain extrusions stood for a very plenary fulfilment of desire. And since Eva *had* set her heart on a doll of ample proportions and practicable eyelids—*had* asked that most admirable of her sex, their mother, for it with not less directness than he himself had put into his demand for a sword and helmet—her coyness now struck Keith as lying near to, at indeed a hardly measurable distance from, the border line of his patience. If she didn't *want* the doll, why the deuce had she made such a point of getting it? He was perhaps on the verge of putting this question to her, when, waving her hand to include both stockings, she said, "Of course, my dear, you *do* see. There they are, and you know I know you know we wouldn't, either of us, dip a finger into them." With a vibrancy of tone that seemed to bring her voice quite close to him, "One doesn't," she added, "violate the shrine—pick the pearl from the shell!"

Even had the answering question "Doesn't one just?" which for an instant hovered on the tip of his tongue, been uttered, it could not have obscured for Keith the change which her magnificence had wrought in him. Something, perhaps, of the bigotry of the convert was already discernible in the way that, averting his eyes, he said, "One doesn't even peer." As to whether, in the years that have elapsed since he said this, either of our friends (now adult) has, in fact, "peered," is a question which, whenever I call at the house, I am tempted to put to one or other of them. But any regret I may feel in my invariable failure to "come up to the scratch" of yielding to this temptation is balanced, for me, by my impression—my sometimes all but throned and anointed certainty—that the answer, if vouchsafed, would be in the negative.

The Owl Who Was God

james thurber

ONCE UPON A STARLESS MIDNIGHT there was an owl who sat on the branch of an oak tree. Two ground moles tried to slip quietly by, unnoticed. "You!" said the owl. "Who?" they quavered, in fear and astonishment, for they could not believe it was possible for anyone to see them in that thick darkness. "You two!" said the owl. The moles hurried away and told the other creatures of the field and forest that the owl was the greatest and wisest of all animals because he could see in the dark and because he could answer any question. "I'll see about that," said a secretary bird, and he called on the owl one night when it was again very dark. "How many claws am I holding up?" said the secretary bird. "Two," said the owl, and that was right. "Can you give me another expression for 'that is to say' or 'namely'?" asked the secretary bird. "To wit," said the owl. "Why does a lover call on his love?" asked the secretary bird. "To woo," said the owl.

The secretary bird hastened back to the other creatures and reported that the owl was indeed the greatest and wisest animal in the world because he could answer any question. "Can he see in the daytime, too?" asked a red fox. "Yes," echoed a dormouse and a French poodle. "Can he see in the daytime, too?" All the other creatures laughed loudly at this silly question, and they set upon the red fox and his friends and drove them out of the region. Then they sent a messenger to the owl and asked him to be their leader.

When the owl appeared among the animals it was high noon and the sun was shining brightly. He walked very slowly, which gave him an appearance of great dignity, and he peered about him with large, staring eyes, which gave him an air of tremendous importance. "He's God!" screamed a Plymouth Rock hen. And the others took up the cry "He's God!" So they followed him wherever he went and when he began to bump into things they began to bump into things, too. Finally he came to a concrete highway and he started up the middle of it and all the other creatures followed him. Presently a hawk, who was acting as outrider, observed a truck coming toward them at fifty miles an hour, and he reported to the secretary bird and the secretary bird reported to the owl. "There's danger ahead," said the secretary bird. "To wit?" said the owl. The secretary bird told him. "Aren't you afraid?" he asked. "Who?" said the owl calmly, for he could not see the truck. "He's God!" cried all the creatures again, and they were still crying "He's God!" when the truck hit them and ran them down. Some of the animals were merely injured, but most of them, including the owl, were killed.

Moral: You can fool too many of the people too much of the time.

The Green Isle in the Sea

james thurber

ONE SWEET MORNING in the Year of Our Lord, Nineteen hundred and thirty-nine, a little old gentleman got up and threw wide the windows of his bedroom, letting in the living sun. A black widow spider, who had been dozing on the balcony, slashed at him, and although she missed, she did not miss very far. The old gentleman went downstairs to the dining-room and was just sitting down to a spendid breakfast when his grandson, a boy named Burt, pulled the chair from under him. The old man's hip was strained but it was fortunately not broken.

Out in the street, as he limped toward a little park with many trees, which was to him a green isle in the sea, the old man was tripped up by a gaily-colored hoop sent rolling at him, with a kind of disinterested deliberation, by a grim little girl. Hobbling on a block farther, the old man was startled, but not exactly surprised, when a bold daylight robber stuck a gun in his ribs. "Put 'em up, Mac," said the robber, "and come across." Mac put them up and came across with his watch and money and a gold ring his mother had given him when he was a boy.

When at last the old gentleman staggered into the little park, which had been to him a fountain and a shrine, he saw that half the trees had been killed by a blight, and the other half by a bug. Their leaves were gone and they no longer afforded any protection from the skies, so that the hundred planes which appeared suddenly overhead had an excellent view of the little old gentleman through their bombing-sights.

Moral: The world is so full of a number of things. I am sure we should all be as happy as kings, and you know how happy kings are.

The Unique Quality
of Truth

william march

WHEN THE OLD SCHOLAR heard that Truth was in the country, he decided to find her, as he had devoted his life to studying her in all her forms. He set out immediately, and at last he came upon the cottage in the mountains where Truth lived alone. He knocked on the door, and Truth asked what he wanted. The scholar explained who he was, adding that he had always wanted to know her and had wondered a thousand times what she really was like.

Truth came to the door soon afterwards, and the scholar saw that the pictures he had formed of her in his imagination were wrong. He had thought of Truth as a gigantic woman with flowing hair who sat nobly on a white horse, or, at the very least, as a sculptured heroic figure with a wide white brow and untroubled eyes. In reality, Truth was nothing at all like that; instead, she was merely a small, shapeless old woman who seemed made of some quivering substance that resembled india rubber.

"All right,' said the old lady in a resigned voice. "What do you want to know?"

"I want to know what you are."

The old lady thought, shook her head, and answered, "That I don't know. I couldn't tell you to save my life."

"Then have you any special quality that makes you an individual?" asked the scholar. "Surely you must have some characteristic that is uniquely yours."

"As a matter of fact, I have," said the old lady; then, seeing the question on the scholar's lips, she added, "I'll show you what I mean. It's easier than trying to explain."

The shapeless old woman began to bounce like a rubber ball, up and down on her doorstep, getting a little higher each time she struck the floor. When she was high enough for her purpose, she seized the woodwork above her door and held on; then she said, "Take hold of my legs and walk back the way you came, and when you know what my unique quality is, shout and let me know."

The old scholar did as he was told, racking his brains in an effort to determine what quality it was that distinguished Truth. When he reached the road, he turned around, and there in the distance was Truth still clinging to the woodwork above her door.

"Don't you see by this time?" she shouted. "Don't you understand now what my particular quality is?"

"Yes," said the old scholar. "Yes, I do."

"Then turn my legs loose and go on home," said Truth in a small petulant voice.

From The Day of the Locust

nathanael west

WHAT TOD REACHED THE STREET, he saw a dozen great violet shafts of light moving across the evening sky in wide crazy sweeps. Whenever one of the fiery columns reached the lowest point of its arc, it lit for a moment the rose-colored domes and delicate minarets of Kahn's Persian Palace Theatre. The purpose of this display was to signal the world premiere of a new picture.

Turning his back on the searchlights, he started in the opposite direction, toward Homer's place. Before he had gone very far, he saw a clock that read a quarter past six and changed his mind about going back just yet. He might as well let the poor fellow sleep for another hour and kill some time by looking at the crowds.

When still a block from the theatre, he saw an enormous electric sign that hung over the middle of the street. In letters ten feet high he read that—

"MR. KAHN A PLEASURE DOME DECREED"

Although it was still several hours before the celebrities would arrive, thousands of people had already gathered. They stood facing the theatre with their backs toward the gutter in a thick line hundreds of feet long. A big squad of policemen was trying to keep a lane open between the front rank of the crowd and the façade of the theatre.

Tod entered the lane while the policeman guarding it was busy with a woman whose parcel had torn open, dropping oranges all over the place. Another policeman shouted for him to get the hell across the street, but he took a chance and kept going. They had enough to do without chasing him. He noticed how worried they looked and how careful they tried to be. If they had to arrest someone, they joked good-naturedly with the culprit, making light of it until they got him around the corner, then they whaled him with their clubs. Only so long as the man was actually part of the crowd did they have to be gentle.

Tod had walked only a short distance along the narrow lane when he began to get frightened. People shouted, commenting on his hat, his carriage, and his clothing. There was a continuous roar of catcalls, laughter and yells, pierced occasionally by a scream. The scream was usually followed by a sudden movement in the dense mass and part of it would surge forward wherever the police line was weakest. As soon as that part was rammed back, the bulge would pop out somewhere else.

The police force would have to be doubled when the stars started to arrive. At the sight of their heroes and heroines, the crowd would turn demoniac. Some little gesture, either too pleasing or too offensive, would start it moving and then nothing but machine guns would stop it. Individually the purpose of its members might simply to be to get a souvenir, but collectively it would grab and rend.

A young man with a portable microphone was describing the scene. His rapid, hysterical voice was like that of a revivalist preacher whipping his congregation toward the ecstasy of fits.

"What a crowd, folks! What a crowd! There must be ten thousand excited, screaming fans outside Kahn's Persian tonight. The police can't hold them. Here, listen to them roar."

He held the microphone out and those near it obligingly roared for him.

"Did you hear it? It's a bedlam, folks. A veritable bedlam! What excitement! Of all the premières I've attended, this is the most...the most... stupendous, folks. Can the police hold them? Can they? It doesn't look so, folks..."

Another squad of police came charging up. The sergeant pleaded with the announcer to stand further back so the people couldn't hear him. His men threw themselves at the crowd. It allowed itself to be hustled and shoved out of habit and because it lacked an objective. It tolerated the police, just as a bull elephant does when he allows a small boy to drive him with a light stick.

Tod could see very few people who looked tough, nor could he see any working men. The crowd was made up of the lower middle classes, every other person one of his torchbearers.

Just as he came near the end of the lane, it closed in front of him with a heave, and he had to fight his way through. Someone knocked his hat off and when he stooped to pick it up, someone kicked him. He whirled around angrily and found himself surrounded by people who were laughing at him. He knew enough to laugh with them. The crowd became sympathetic. A stout woman slapped him on the back, while a man handed him his hat, first brushing it carefully with his sleeve. Still another man shouted for a way to be cleared.

By a great deal of pushing and squirming, always trying to look as though he were enjoying himself, Tod finally managed to break into the open. After rearranging his clothes, he went over to a parking lot and sat down on the low retaining wall that ran along the front of it.

New groups, whole families, kept arriving. He could see a change come over them as soon as they had become part of the crowd. Until they reached the line, they looked diffident, almost furtive, but the moment they had become part of it, they turned arrogant and pugnacious. It was a mistake to think them harmless curiosity seekers. They were savage and bitter, especially the middle-aged and the old, and had been made so by boredom and disappointment.

All their lives they had slaved at some kind of dull, heavy labor, behind desks and counters, in the fields and at tedious machines of all sorts, saving their pennies and dreaming of the leisure that would be theirs when they had enough. Finally that day came. They could draw a weekly income of ten or fifteen dollars. Where else should they go but California, the land of sunshine and oranges?

Once there, they discover that sunshine isn't enough. They get tired of oranges, even of avocado pears and passion fruit. Nothing happens. They don't know what to do with their time. They haven't the mental equipment for leisure, the money nor the physical equipment for pleasure. Did they slave so long just to go to an occasional Iowa picnic? What else is there? They watch the waves come in at Venice. There wasn't any ocean where most of them came from, but after you've seen one wave you've seen them all. The same is true of the airplanes at Glendale. If only a plane would crash once in a while so that they could watch the passengers being consumed in a "holocaust of flame," as the newspapers put it. But the planes never crash.

Their boredom becomes more and more terrible. They realize that they've been tricked and burn with resentment. Every day of their lives they read the newspapers and went to the movies. Both fed them on lynchings, murder, sex crimes, explosions, wrecks, love nests, fires, miracles, revolutions, wars. This daily diet made sophisticates of them. The sun is a joke. Oranges can't titillate their jaded palates. Nothing can ever be violent enough to make taut their slack minds and bodies. They have been cheated and betrayed. They have slaved and saved for nothing.

Tod stood up. During the ten minutes he had been sitting on the wall, the crowd had grown thirty feet and he was afraid that his escape might be cut off if he loitered much longer. He crossed to the other side of the street and started back.

He was trying to figure what to do if he were unable to wake Homer when, suddenly he saw his head bobbing above the crowd. He hurried toward him. From his appearance, it was evident that there was something definitely wrong.

Homer walked more than ever like a badly made automaton and his features were set in a rigid, mechanical grin. He had his trousers on over his nightgown and part of it hung out of his open fly. In both of his hands were suitcases. With each step, he lurched to one side then the other, using the suitcases for balance weights.

Tod stopped directly in front of him, blocking his way.

"Where're you going?"

"Wayneville," he replied, using an extraordinary amount of jaw movement to get out this single word.

"That's fine. But you can't walk to the station from here. It's in Los Angeles."

Homer tried to get around him, but he caught his arm.

"We'll get a taxi. I'll go with you."

The cabs were all being routed around the block because of the preview. He explained this to Homer and tried to get him to walk to the corner.

"Come on, we're sure to get one on the next street."

Once Tod got him into a cab, he intended to tell the driver to go to the nearest hospital. But Homer wouldn't budge, no matter how hard he yanked and pleaded. People stopped to watch them, others turned their heads curiously. He decided to leave him and get a cab.

"I'll come right right back," he said.

He couldn't tell from either Homer's eyes or expression whether he heard, for they both were empty of everything, even annoyance. At the corner he looked around and saw that Homer had started to cross the street, moving blindly. Brakes screeched and twice he was almost run over, but he didn't swerve or hurry. He moved in a straight diagonal. When he reached the other curb, he tried to get on the sidewalk at a point where the crowd was very thick and was shoved violently back. He made another attempt and this time a policeman grabbed him by the back of the neck and hustled him to the end of the line. When the policeman let go of him, he kept on walking as though nothing had happened.

Tod tried to get over to him, but was unable to cross until the traffic lights changed. When he reached the other side, he found Homer sitting on a bench, fifty or sixty feet from the outskirts of the crowd.

He put his arm around Homer's shoulder and suggested that they walk a few blocks further. When Homer didn't answer, he reached over to pick up one of the valises. Homer held on to it.

"I'll carry it for you," he said, tugging gently.

"Thief!"

Before Homer could repeat the shout, he jumped away. It would be extremely embarrassing if Homer shouted thief in front of a cop. He thought of phoning for an ambulance. But then, after all, how could he be sure that Homer was crazy? He was sitting quietly on the bench, minding his own business.

Tod decided to wait, then try again to get him into a cab. The crowd was growing in size all the time, but it would be at least half an hour before it over-ran the bench. Before that happened, he would think of some plan. He moved a short distance away and stood with his back to a store window so that he could watch Homer without attracting attention.

About ten feet from where Homer was sitting grew a large eucalyptus tree and behind the trunk of the tree was a little boy. Tod saw him peer around it with great caution, then suddenly jerk his head back. A minute later he repeated the maneuver. At first Tod thought he was playing hide and seek, then noticed that he had a string in his hand which was attached to an old purse that lay in front of Homer's bench. Every once in a while the child would jerk the string, making the purse hop like a sluggish toad. Its torn lining hung from its iron mouth like a furry tongue and a few uncertain flies hovered over it.

Tod knew the game the child was playing. He used to play it himself when he was small. If Homer reached to pick up the purse, thinking there was money in it, he would yank it away and scream with laughter.

When Tod went over to the tree, he was surprised to discover that it was Adore Loomis, the kid who lived across the street from Homer. Tod tried to chase him, but he dodged around the tree, thumbing his nose. He gave up and went back to his original position. The moment he left, Adore got busy with his purse again. Homer wasn't paying any attention to the child, so Tod decided to let him alone.

Mrs. Loomis must be somewhere in the crowd, he thought. Tonight when she found Adore, she would give him a hiding. He had torn the pocket of his jacket and his Buster Brown collar was smeared with grease.

Adore had a nasty temper. The completeness with which Homer ignored both him and his pocketbook made him frantic. He gave up dancing it at the end of the string and approached the bench on tiptoes, making ferocious faces, yet ready to run at Homer's first move. He stopped when about four feet away and stuck his tongue out. Homer ignored him. He took another step forward and ran through a series of insulting gestures.

If Tod had known that the boy held a stone in his hand, he would have interfered. But he felt sure that Homer wouldn't hurt the child and was waiting to see if he wouldn't move because of his pestering. When Adore raised his arm, it was too late. The stone hit Homer in the face. The boy

turned to flee, but tripped and fell. Before he could scramble away, Homer
landed on his back with both feet, then jumped again.

Tod yelled for him to stop and tried to yank him away. He shoved
Tod and went on using his heels. Tod hit him as hard as he could, first in
the belly, then in the face. He ignored the blows and continued to stamp
on the boy. Tod hit him again and again, then threw both arms around
him and tried to pull him off. He couldn't budge him. He was like a stone
column.

The next thing Tod knew, he was torn loose from Homer and sent to his
knees by a blow in the back of the head that spun him sideways. The
crowd in front of the theatre had charged. He was surrounded by churning
legs and feet. He pulled himself erect by grabbing a man's coat, then let
himself be carried along backwards in a long, curving swoop. He saw Homer
rise above the mass for a moment, shoved against the sky, his jaw hanging
as though he wanted to scream but couldn't. A hand reached up and caught
him by his open mouth and pulled him forward and down.

There was another dizzy rush. Tod closed his eyes and fought to keep
upright. He was jostled about in a hacking cross surf of shoulders and
backs, carried rapidly in one direction and then in the opposite. He kept
pushing and hitting out at the people around him, trying to face in the
direction he was going. Being carried backwards terrified him.

Using the eucalyptus tree as a landmark, he tried to work toward it by
slipping sideways against the tide, pushing hard when carried away from
it and riding the current when it moved toward his objective. He was within
only a few feet of the tree when a sudden, driving rush carried him far past
it. He struggled desperately for a moment, then gave up and let himself be
swept along. He was the spearhead of a flying wedge when it collided with
a mass going in the opposite direction. The impact turned him around. As
the two forces ground against each other, he was turned again and again, like
a grain between millstones. This didn't stop until he became part of the
opposing force. The pressure continued to increase until he thought he must
collapse. He was slowly pushed into the air. Although relief for his cracking
ribs could be gotten by continuing to rise, he fought to keep his feet on the
ground. Not being able to touch was an even more dreadful sensation than
being carried backwards.

There was another rush, shorter this time, and he found himself in a dead
spot where the pressure was less and equal. He became conscious of a terrible
pain in his left leg, just above the ankle, and tried to work it into a more
comfortable position. He couldn't turn his body, but managed to get his
head around. A very skinny boy, wearing a Western Union cap, had his back
wedged against his shoulder. The pain continued to grow and his whole leg as
high as the groin throbbed. He finally got his left arm free and took the
back of the boy's neck in his fingers. He twisted as hard as he could. The

boy began to jump up and down in his clothes. He managed to straighten his elbow, by pushing at the back of the boy's head, and so turn half way around and free his leg. The pain didn't grow less.

There was another wild surge forward that ended in another dead spot. He now faced a young girl who was sobbing steadily. Her silk print dress had been torn down the front and her tiny brassiere hung from one strap. He tried by pressing back to give her room, but she moved with him every time he moved. Now and then, she would jerk violently and he wondered if she was going to have a fit. One of her thighs was between his legs. He struggled to get free of her, but she clung to him, moving with him and pressing against him.

She turned her head and said, "Stop, stop," to someone behind her.

He saw what the trouble was. An old man, wearing a Panama hat and horn-rimmed glasses, was hugging her. He had one of his hands inside her dress and was biting her neck.

Tod freed his right arm with a heave, reached over the girl and brought his fist down on the man's head. He couldn't hit very hard but managed to knock the man's hat off, also his glasses. The man tried to bury his face in the girl's shoulder, but Tod grabbed one of his ears and yanked. They started to move again. Tod held on to the ear as long he could, hoping that it would come away in his hand. The girl managed to twist under his arm. A piece of her dress tore, but she was free of her attacker.

Another spasm passed through the mob and he was carried toward the curb. He fought toward a lamp-post, but he was swept by before he could grasp it. He saw another man catch the girl with the torn dress. She screamed for help. He tried to get to her, but was carried in the opposite direction. This rush also ended in a dead spot. Here his neighbors were all shorter than he was. He turned his head upward toward the sky and tried to pull some fresh air into his aching lungs, but it was all heavily tainted with sweat.

In this part of the mob no one was hysterical. In fact, most of the people seemed to be enjoying themselves. Near him was a stout woman with a man pressing hard against her from in front. His chin was on her shoulder, and his arms were around her. She paid no attention to him and went on talking to the woman at her side.

"The first thing I knew," Tod heard her say, "there was a rush and I was in the middle."

"Yeah. Somebody hollered, 'Here comes Gary Cooper,' and then wham!"

"That ain't it," said a little man wearing a cloth cap and pullover sweater. "This is a riot you're in."

"Yeah," said a third woman, whose snaky gray hair was hanging over her face and shoulders. "A pervert attacked a child."

"He ought to be lynched."

Everybody agreed vehemently.

"I come from St. Louis," announced the stout woman, "and we had one of them pervert fellers in our neighborhood once. He ripped up a girl with a pair of scissors."

"He must have been crazy," said the man in the cap. "What kind of fun is that?"

Everybody laughed. The stout woman spoke to the man who was hugging her.

"Hey, you," she said. "I ain't no pillow."

The man smiled beatifically but didn't move. She laughed, making no effort to get out of his embrace.

"A fresh guy," she said.

The other woman laughed.

"Yeah," she said, "this is a regular free-for-all."

The man in the cap and sweater thought there was another laugh in his comment about the pervert.

"Ripping up a girl with scissors. That's the wrong tool."

He was right. They laughed even louder than the first time.

"You'd done it different, eh, kid?" said a young man with a kidney-shaped head and waxed mustaches.

The two women laughed. This encouraged the man in the cap and he reached over and pinched the stout woman's friend. She squealed.

"Lay off that," she said good-naturedly.

"I was shoved," he said.

An ambulance siren screamed in the street. Its wailing moan started the crowd moving again and Tod was carried along in a slow, steady push. He closed his eyes and tried to protect his throbbing leg. This time, when the movement ended, he found himself with his back to the theatre wall. He kept his eyes closed and stood on his good leg. After what seemed like hours, the pack began to loosen and move again with a churning motion. It gathered momentum and rushed. He rode it until he was slammed against the base of an iron rail which fenced the driveway of the theatre from the street. He had the wind knocked out of him by the impact, but managed to cling to the rail. He held on desperately, fighting to keep from being sucked back. A woman caught him around the waist and tried to hang on. She was sobbing rhythmically. Tod felt his fingers slipping from the rail and kicked backwards as hard as he could. The woman let go.

Despite the agony in his leg, he was able to think clearly about his picture, "The Burning of Los Angeles." After his quarrel with Faye, he had worked on it continually to escape tormenting himself, and the way to it in his mind had become almost automatic.

As he stood on his good leg, clinging desperately to the iron rail, he could see all the rough charcoal strokes with which he had blocked it out on the big canvas. Across the top, parallel with the frame, he had drawn the burning city, a great bonfire of architectural styles, ranging from Egyptian to Cape Cod colonial. Through the center, winding from left to right, was a long hill street and down it, spilling into the middle foreground, came the mob carrying baseball bats and torches. For the faces of its members, he was using the innumerable sketches he had made of the people who come to California to die; the cultists of all sorts, economic as well as religious, the wave, airplane, funeral and preview watchers—all those poor devils who can only be stirred by the promise of miracles and then only to violence. A super "Dr. Know-All Pierce-All" had made the necessary promise and they were marching behind his banner in a great united front of screwballs and screwboxes to purify the land. No longer bored, they sang and danced joyously in the red light of the flames.

In the lower foreground, men and women fled wildly before the vanguard of the crusading mob. Among them were Faye, Harry, Homer, Claude and himself. Faye ran proudly, throwing her knees high. Harry stumbled along behind her, holding on to his beloved derby hat with both hands. Homer seemed to be falling out of the canvas, his face half-asleep, his big hands clawing the air in anguished pantomime. Claude turned his head as he ran to thumb his nose at his pursuers. Tod himself picked up a small stone to throw before continuing his flight.

He had almost forgotten both his leg and his predicament, and to make his escape still more complete he stood on a chair and worked at the flames in an upper corner of the canvas, modeling the tongues of fire so that they licked even more avidly at a corinthian column that held up the palmleaf roof of a nutburger stand.

He had finished one flame and was starting on another when he was brought back by someone shouting in his ear. He opened his eyes and saw a policeman trying to reach him from behind the rail to which he was clinging. He let go with his left hand and raised his arm. The policeman caught him by the wrist, but couldn't lift him. Tod was afraid to let go until another man came to aid the policeman and caught him by the back of his jacket. He let go of the rail and they hauled him up and over it.

When they saw that he couldn't stand, they let him down easily to the ground. He was in the theatre driveway. On the curb next to him sat a woman crying into her skirt. Along the wall were groups of other disheveled people. At the end of the driveway was an ambulance. A policeman asked him if he wanted to go to the hospital. He shook his head no. He then offered him a lift home. Tod had the presence of mind to give Claude's address.

He was carried through the exit to the back street and lifted into a police car. The siren began to scream and at first he thought he was making the noise himself. He felt his lips with his hands. They were clamped tight. He knew then it was the siren. For some reason this made him laugh and he began to imitate the siren as loud as he could.

Anonymiad

john barth

headpiece

When Dawn rose, pink as peerless Helen's teat,

which in fact swung wineskinlike between her hind legs and was piebald
as her pelt, on which I write,

> *The salty minstrel oped his tear-brined eye,*
> *And remarking it was yet another day...*

Ended his life. Commenced his masterpiece. Returned to sleep.
  Invoked the muse:

> *Twice-handled goddess! Sing through me the boy*
> *Whom Agamemnon didn't take to Troy,*
> *But left behind to see his wife stayed chaste.*
> *Tell, Muse, how Clytemnestra maced*
> *Her warden into song, made vain his heart*
> *With vision of renown; musick the art*
> *Wherewith was worked self-ruin by a youth*
> *Who'd sought in his own art some music truth*
> *About the world and life, of which he knew*
> *Nothing. Tell how ardent his wish grew*
> *To autograph the future, wherefore he*

> *Let sly Aegisthus ship him off to see*
> *The Wide Real World. Sing of the guile*
> *That fetched yours truly to a nameless isle,*
> *By gods, men, and history forgot,*
> *To sing his sorry self.*

And die. And rot. And feed his silly carcass to the birds.

> *But not before he'd penned a few last words,*

inspired by the dregs and lees of the muse herself, at whom, Zeus willing, he'll have a final go before he corks her for good and casts her adrift, vessel of his hopeless hope. The Minstrel's Last Lay.

> *Once upon a time*
> *I composed in witty rhyme*
> *And poured libations to the muse Erato.*
>
> *Merope would croon,*
> *"Minstrel mine, a lay! A tune!"*
> *"From bed to verse," I'd answer; "that's my motto."*
>
> *Stranded by my foes,*
> *Nowadays I write in prose,*
> *Forsaking measure, rhyme, and honeyed diction;*
>
> Amphora's *my muse:*
> *When I finish off the booze,*
> *I hump the jug and fill her up with fiction.*

I begin in the middle—where too I'll end, there being alas to my arrested history as yet no dénouement. God knows how long I'd been out of writing material until this morning, not to mention how long altogether I've been marooned upon this Zeus-forsaken rock, in the middle of nowhere. There, I've begun, in the middle of nowhere, tricked ashore in manhood's forenoon with nine amphorae of Mycenaean red and abandoned to my own devisings. After half a dozen years of which more later I was down to the last of them, having put her sisters to the triple use aforesung: one by one I broke their seals, drank the lovelies dry, and, fired by their beneficence, not only made each the temporary mistress of my sole passion but gave back in the form of art what I'd had from them. Me they nourished and inspired; them I fulfilled to the top of my bent, and launched them worldward fraught with our joint conceits. Their names are to me now like the memory of old songs: Euterpe! Polyhymnia! I recall Terpsichore's lovely neck, Urania's matchless shoulders; in dreams I hear Melpomene singing yet in the wet west wind, her voice ever deeper as our romance waned; I touch again Erato's ears, too delicate for mortal clay, surely the work of Aphrodite! I smile at Clio's gravity, who could hold more wine than any of her sisters without growing tipsy; I shake my head still at the unexpected passion of saucy Thalia, how she clung to me even when broken by love's hard knocks. Fair creatures. Often I wonder where the tides of life have fetched them, whether they're undone by age and the world or put on the shelf by some heartless new master. What lovers slake themselves now at those fragile mouths? Do they still bear my charge in them, or is it jettisoned and lost, or brought to light?

With anticipation of Calliope, the last, I consoled me for their casting off. Painful state for a lover, to have always before him the object of his yen—naked, cool, serene—and deny his parchèd sense any slake but the lovely sight of her! No less a regimen I imposed upon myself—imperfectly, imperfectly, I'm not made of stone, and there she stood, brimful of spirit, heavy with what I craved, sweating delicately where the sun caressed her flank, and like her sisters infinitely accessible! A night came, I confess it, when need overmastered me; I broke my vow and her seal; other nights followed (never many in a season, but blessed Zeus, most blest Apollo, how many empty seasons have gone by!) when, despite all new resolve and cursing my weak-willedness even as I tipped her to my will, I eased my burden with small increase of hers. But take her to me altogether I did not, or possess myself of the bounty I thirsted for, and which freely she would yield. Until last night! Until the present morn! For in that measureless drear interval, now to be exposed, I had nothing to write upon, no material wherewith to fashion the work I'd vowed she must inspire me to, and with which, in the last act of our loveship and my life, I'd freight her.

Calliope, come, refresh me; it's the hour for exposition!

> *I'll bare at last my nameless tale, and then...*
> *Hie here, sweet Muse: your poet must dip his pen!*

i

Ink of the squid, his obscure cloak; blood of my heart; wine of my inspiration: record on Helen's hide, in these my symbols, the ills her namesake wrought what time, forsaking the couch of fairhaired Menelaus, she spread her legs for Paris et cetera.

My trouble was, back home in 'prentice days, I never could come out straight-faced with "Daughter of Zeus, eggborn Clytemnestra" and the rest, or in general take seriously enough the pretensions of reality. Youngster though I was, nowise sophisticated, I couldn't manage the correct long face when Agamemnon hectored us on Debts of Honor, Responsibility to Our Allies, and the like. But I don't fool myself: if I never took seriously the world and its tiresome concerns, it's because I was never able to take myself seriously; and the reason for that, I've known for some while, is the fearsomeness of the facts of life. Merope's love, Helen's whoring, Menelaus's noise, Agamemnon's slicing up his daughter for the weatherman—all the large and deadly passions of men and women, wolves, frogs, nightingales; all this business of seizing life, grabbing hold with both hands—it must've scared the daylights out of me from the first. While other fellows played with their spears, I learned to play the lyre. I wasn't the worst-looking man in Argolis; I had a ready wit and a good ear, and knew how to amuse the ladies. A little more of those virtues (and a lot more nerve, and better luck in the noble-birth way), I might have been another Paris; it's not your swaggerers like Menelaus the pretty girls fall for, or even your bully-boys like Agamemnon: it's the tricky chaps like Paris, graceful as women themselves almost, with their mischief eyes and honey tongues and nimble fingers, that set maiden hearts a-flutter and spit maidenheads like squablings. Aphrodite takes care of her own. Let that one have his Helen; this musicked to him in his eighteenth year milkmaid Merope, fairest-formed and straightest-hearted that ever mused goatherd into minstrelsy.

Daily then I pastured with that audience, two-score nans and my doe-eye nymph, to whom I sang songs perforce original, as I was ignorant of the common store. Innocent, I sang of innocence, thinking I sang of love and fame. Merope put down her jug, swept back her hair, smiled and listened. In modes of my own invention, as I supposed, I sang my vow to make a name for myself in the world at large.

"Many must wish the same," my honeyhead would murmur. But could she've shown me that every browsy hill in Greece had its dappled nans and famestruck twanger, I'd've not been daunted. My dreams, like my darling, perched light but square on a three-leg seat: first, while I scoffed at them myself, and at the rube their dreamer, I sucked them for life; the world was wide, as my songs attested, its cities flocked with brilliant; I was a nameless rustic plucker, unschooled, unmannered, late finding voice, innocent of fashion, uneasy in the world and my own skin—so much so, my crazy hope of shedding it was all sustained me. Fair as the country was and the goatboy life my fellows' lot, if I could not've imagined my music's one day whisking me Orionlike to the stars, I'd have as well flung myself into the sea. No other fate would even faintly do; an impassioned lack of alternatives moved my tongue; what for another might be heartfelt wish was for me an absolute condition. Second, untutored as I was and narrow my acquaintance, I knew none whose fancy so afflicted him as mine me. Especially when I goated it alone, the world's things took a queer sly aspect: it was as if the olive hillside hummed, not with bees, but with some rustle secret; the placid goats were in on it; asphodels winked and nodded behind my back; the mountain took broody note; the very sunlight trembled; I was a stranger to my hands and feet. Merope herself, when these humors gripped me, was alien and horrific as a sphinx: her perfect body, its pulse and breath, smote me with dismay: ears! toes! What creature did it wrap, that was not I, that claimed to love me? My own corse was a rude anthropophage that had swallowed me whole at birth and suffered indigestion ever since; could Merope see what I couldn't, who it was spoke from his gripèd bowels? When she and I, the goats our original, invented love—romped friggly in the glens and found half a hundred pretty pathways to delight, each which we thought ourselves the first to tread—some I as foreign to the me that pleasured as goatherd to goats stood by, tight-lipped, watching, or aswoon at the entire strangeness of the world.

And yet, third prop of revery, there *was* Merope, realer than myself though twice my dreams: the ardent fact of her, undeniable as incredible, argued when all else failed that the gods had marked me for no common fate. That a spirit so fresh and unaffected, take my word, no space for details, in a form fit to warm the couch of kings, should elect to give not only ear but heart and dainty everything to a lad the contrary of solipsistic, who felt the world and all its contents real except himself. . . . Perched astride me in a wild-rosemary-patch, her gold skin sweating gently from our sport, her gold hair tenting us, Merope'd say: "I love you"; and while one of me inferred: "Therefore I am," and another wondered whether she was nymph doing penance for rebuffing Zeus or just maid with unaccountable defect of good sense, a third exulted: "Then nothing is impossible!" and set out to scale Parnassus blithely as he'd peaked the mount of Love.

Had I known what cloak of climbers mantles that former hill, so many seasoneder and cleverer than I, some schooled for the ascent from earliest childhood, versed in the mountain's every crag and col, rehearsed in the lore of former climbers. . . . But I didn't, except in that corner of my fancy that imaged all possible discouragements and heeded none. As a farm boy, innocent of the city's size, confidently expects on his first visit there to cross paths with the one inhabitant he knows among its scores of thousands, and against all reason does, so when at market-time I took goats to golden Mycenae to be sold at auction, I wasn't daunted as I should've been by the pros who minstrelled every wineshop, but leaned me on the Lion's Gate, took up my lyre, and sang a sprightly goat-song, fully expecting that the Queen herself would hear and call for me.

The song, more or less improvised, had to do with a young man who announces himself, in the first verse, to be a hickly swain new-come from the bosky outback: he sings what a splendid fellow he is, fit consort for a queen. In the second verse he's accosted by an older woman who declares that while she doubtless appears a whore, she is in fact the Queen disguised; she takes the delighted singer to a crib in the common stews, which she asserts to be a wing of the palace reconstructed, at her order, to resemble a brothel: the trulls and trollops thereabout, she explains, are gentlewomen at their sport, the pimps and navvies their disguisèd noble lovers. Did the masquerade strike our minstrel as excessive? He was to bear in mind that the whims of royalty are like the gods', mighty in implementation and consequence. Her pleasure, she discloses in the third verse, is that he should lie with her as with a woman of the streets, the newest fashion among great ladies: she's chosen him for her first adventure of this sort because, while obviously not of noble birth, he's of somewhat gentler aspect than the lot of commoners; to make the pretense real, he's to pay her a handsome love-price, which she stipulates. The fellow laughs and agrees, but respectfully points out that her excessive fee betrays her innocence of prostitution; if verisimilitude is her object, she must accept the much lower wage he names. Not without expressions of chagrin the lady acquiesces, demanding only the right to earn a bonus for meritorious performance. In the fifth and sixth verses they set to, in manner described in salacious but musically admirable cadenzas; in the seventh the woman calls for fee and bonus, but her minstrel love politely declines: to her angry protests he replies, in the eighth verse, that despite herself she makes love like a queen; her excellency shows through the cleverest disguise. How does he know? Because, he asserts, he's not the rustic he has feigned, but an exile prince in flight from the wrath of a neighbor king, whose queen had been his mistress until their amour came to light. Begging the amazed and skeptic lady not to betray him to the local nobility so well masked, he pledges in return to boast to no one that he has lain with Her Majesty. As I fetched him from the stews wondering mellifluously whether his partner was a queen disguised as a prostitute or a prostitute disguised as a queen disguised et cetera, I was seized by two armored guards and fetched myself to a room above a nearby wineshop. The premises were squalid; the room was opulent; beside a window overlooking the Lion's Gate sat a regal dame ensconced in handmaids.

What about the minstrel, she wanted to know: Was he a prince in mufti or a slickering rustic? Through my tremble I saw bright eyes in her sharp-bone countenance. I struck a chord to steady my hand, wrung rhymes from alarmèd memory, took a breath, and sang in answer:

> "As Tyrian role may cloak a bumpkin heart,
> So homespun hick may play the royal part.
> Men may be kings in spirit or in mien.
> Which make more kingly lovers? Ask a queen!

But don't ask me which sort of queen to ask," I added quickly; "I haven't been in town long enough to learn the difference."

The maids clapped hands to mouths; the lady's eyes flashed, whether with anger or acknowledgment I couldn't judge. "See he goes to school on the matter," she ordered a plumpish gentleman across the room, eunuch by the look of him. Then she dismissed us, suddenly fretsome, and turned to the window, as one waiting for another to appear.

On with the story, cut corners: Clytemnestra herself it was, wont to rest from her market pleasures in that apartment. Her eunuch—Chief Minstrel, it turned out—gave me a gold piece and bade me report to him in Agamemnon's scullery when I came to town, against the chance the whim should take Her Majesty to hear me again. Despite the goldhair wonder that rested on my chest as I reported this adventure next day, I was astonished after all that dreams come true.

"The King and Queen are real!" I marveled. "They want *me* to minstrel them!"

Fingering my forearm Merope said: "Because you're the best." I must go to town often, we agreed, perhaps even live there; on the other hand, it would be an error to put by my rustic origins and speech, as some did: in song, at least (where dwelt the only kings and courtiers we knew), such pretense always came a cropper. Though fame and clever company no doubt would change me in some ways, I should not change myself for them, it being on the one hand Merope's opinion that worldliness too ardently pursued becomes affectation, mine on the other that innocence artificially preserved becomes mere crankhood.

"We'll come back here often," I told her, "to remind us who we are."

She stroked my fingers, in those days scarcely calloused by the lyre. "Was the Queen very beautiful?"

I promised to notice next time. Soon after, we bid the goats goodbye and moved to Mycenae. Merope was frightened by the din of so many folk and wagons and appalled by everyone's bad manners, until I explained that these were part of the excitement of city life. Every day, all day, in our mean little flat, I practiced my art, which before I'd turned to only when the mood was on me; eveningly I reported to the royal kitchen, where lingered a dozen other mountebanks and minstrels just in favor. Ill at ease in their company, I kept my own, but listened amazed to their cynic jokes about the folk they flattered in their lays, and watched with dismay the casual virtuosity with which they performed for one another's amusement while waiting the royal pleasure. I hadn't half their skill and wit! Yet the songs I made from my rural means—of country mouse and city mouse, or the war between the ants and the mice—were well enough received; especially when I'd got the knack of subtly mocking in such conceits certain figures in the court— those who, like the King, were deaf to irony—I'd see Clytemnestra's eyes flash over her wine, as if to say, "Make asses of *them* all you please, but don't think you're fooling me!" and a coin or two would find their way meward. Flattering it was, for a nameless country lad, to hear the Queen herself praise his songs and predict a future for him in the minstrel way. When I got home, often not till sunup, I'd tell my sleepish darling all I'd seen and done, and there'd be love if the day hadn't spent me, which alas it sometimes had. That first gold piece I fetched to a smith and caused to be forged into a ring, gift to the gods' gift to me; but I misguessed the size, and fearing she'd lose it, Merope bade me wear it in her stead.

i½

Once upon a time I told tales stright out, alternating summary and dramatization, developing characters and relationships, laying on bright detail and rhetorical flourish, et cetera. I'm not that amateur at the Lion's Gate; I know my trade. But I fear we're too far gone now for such luxury, Helen and I; I must get to where I am; the real drama, for yours truly, is whether he can trick this tale out at all—not the breath-batingest plot in the world, but there we are. It's an old story anyhow, this part of it; the corpus bloats with its like; I'll throw you the bones, to flesh out or pick at as you will.

What I had in mind was an *Anonymiad* in nine parts, reflecting (so you were to've nudged your neighbor and observed) the nine amphorae and ditto muses; or seven parts plus head- and tailpiece: the years of my maroonment framed by its causes and prognosis. The prologue was to've established, hopefully has done, the ground-conceit and the narrative voice and viewpoint: a minstrel stuck on some Aegean clinker commences his story, in the process characterizing himself and hinting at the circumstances leading to his plight. Parts One through Four were to rehearse those circumstances, Five through Seven the stages of his island life vis-à-vis his minstrelling—innocent garrulity, numb silence, and terse self-knowledge, respectively—and fetch the narrative's present time up to the narrator's. The epilogue's a sort of envoi to whatever eyes, against all odds, may one day read it. But though you're to go through the several parts in order, they haven't been set down that way: after writing the headpiece I began to fear that despite my planning I mightn't have space enough to get the tale told; since it pivots about Part Four (the headpiece and three parts before, three parts and the tailpiece after), I divided Helen's hide in half to insure the right narrative proportions; then, instead of proceeding with the exposition heralded at the tail of the headpiece, I took my cue from a remark I'd made earlier on, began in the middle, and wrote out Parts Five, Six, and Seven. Stopping at the head of the tailpiece, which I'm leaving blank for my last words, I returned to compose Parts One, Two, and Three, and the pivotal Part Four. But alas, there's more to my matter and less to my means than I'd supposed; for a while at least I'll have to tell instead of showing; if you must have dialogue and dashing about, better go to the theater.

So, so: the rest of Part One would've shown the minstrel, under the eunuch's tutelage, becoming more and more a professional artist until he's Clytemnestra's pet entertainer. A typical paragraph runs: *We got on, the Queen and I, especially when the Paris-thing blew up and Agamemnon started conscripting his sister-in-law's old boyfriends. Clytemnestra wasn't impressed by all the spearrattling and the blather of National Honor, any more than I, and couldn't've cared less what happened to Helen. She'd been ugly duckling in the house of Tyndareus, Clytie, second prize in the house of Atreus; she knew Agamemnon envied his brother, and that plenty of Trojan slave-girls would see more of the Family Jewels, while he was avenging the family honor, than she'd seen in some while. Though she'd got a bit hard-boiled by life in Mycenae, she was still a Grade-A figure of a woman; it's a wonder she didn't put horns on him long before the war....*

In addition to their expository function, this and like passages establish the minstrel's growing familiarity and preoccupation with affairs of court. His corresponding professional sophistication, at expense of his former naive energy, was to be rendered as a dramatical correlative to the attrition of his potency with Merope (foreshadowed by the earlier ring-business and the Chief Minstrel's eunuchhood), or vice versa. While still proud of her lover's success, Merope declares in an affecting speech that she preferred the simple life of the goat pasture and the ditto songs he sang there, which now seem merely to embarrass him. The minstrel himself wonders whether the changes in his life and work are for the better: the fact is—as he makes clear on the occasion of their revisiting the herd—that having left country but never, despite his success, quite joined the court, he feels out of place now in both. Formerly he sang of bills and nans as Daphnises and Chloes; latterly he sings of courtly lovers as bucks and does. His songs, he fears, are growing in some instances merely tricksy, in others crankish and obscure; moreover, the difficulties of his position in Mycenae have increased with his reputation: Agamemnon presses on the one hand for anti-Trojan songs in the national interest, Clytemnestra on the other for anti-Iliads to feed her resentment. Thus far he's contrived a precarious integrity by satirizing his own dilemma, for example—but arthritis is retiring the old eunuch, and our narrator has permitted himself to imagine that he's among the candidates for the Chief-Minstrelship, despite his youth: should he be so laureled, the problem of quid pro quo might become acute. All these considerations notwithstanding (he concludes), one can't pretend to an innocence outgrown or in other wise retrace one's steps, unless by coming full circle. Merope doesn't reply; the minstrel attempts to entertain her with a new composition, but neither she nor the goats (who'd used to gather when he sang) seem much taken by it. The rest of the visit goes badly.

ii

Part Two opens back in Mycenae, where all is a-bustle with war preparations. The minstrel, in a brilliant trope which he predicts will be as much pirated by later bards as his device of beginning in the middle, compares the scene to a beehive; he then apostrophizes on the war itself:

The war, the war! To be cynical of its warrant was one thing—bloody madness it was, whether Helen or Hellespont was the prize—and my own patriotism was nothing bellicose: dear and deep as I love Argolis, Troy's a fine place too, I don't doubt, and the Trojan women as singable as ours. To Hades with war and warriors: I had no illusions about the expedition.

Yet I wanted to go along! Your dauber, maybe, or your marble-cracker, can hole up like a sybil in a cave, just him and the muse, and get a lifework done; even Erato's boys, if they're content to sing twelve-liners all their days about Porphyria's eyebrow and Althea's navel, can forget the world outside their bedchambers. But your minstrel who aspires to make and people worlds of his own had better get to know the one he's in, whether he cares for it or not. I believe I understood from the beginning that a certain kind of epic was my fate: that the years I was to spend, in Mycenae and here [i.e., here, this island, where we are now], *turning out clever lyrics, satires, and the like, were as it were apprenticeships in love, flirtation-trials to fit me for master-husbandhood and the siring upon broad-hipped Calliope, like Zeus upon Alcmena, of a very Heracles of fictions. "First fact of our generation,"* Agamemnon called the war in his recruitment speeches; how should I, missing it, speak to future times as the voice of ours?

He adds: *Later I was to accept that I wasn't of the generation of Agamemnon, Odysseus, and those other giant brawlers (in simple truth I was too young to sail with the fleet), nor yet of Telemachus and Orestes, their pale shadows. To speak for the age, I came to believe, was less achievement than to speak for the ageless; my membership in no particular generation I learned to treasure as a passport out of history, or exemption from the drafts of time. But I begged the King to take me with him, and was crestfallen when he refused. No use Clytemnestra's declaring (especially when the news came in from Aulis that they'd cut up Iphigenia) it was my clearsightedness her husband couldn't stick, my not having hymned the bloody values of his crowd; what distressed me as much as staying home from Troy was a thing I couldn't tell her of: Agamemnon's secret arrangement with me...* his reflections upon and acceptance of which end the episode—or *chapter,* as I call the divisions of my unversed fictions. Note that no mention is made of Merope in this excursus, which pointedly develops a theme (new to literature) first touched on in Part One: the minstrel's yen for a broader range of life-experience. His feeling is that having left innocence behind, he must pursue its opposite; though his conception of "experience" in this instance is in terms of travel and combat, the metaphor with which he figures his composing-plans is itself un-innocent in a different sense.

The truth is that he and his youthful sweetheart find themselves nightly more estranged. Merope is unhappy among the courtiers and musicians, who speak of nothing but Mycenaean intrigues and Lydian minors; the minstrel ditto among everyone else, now that his vocation has become a passion—though he too considers their palace friends mostly fops and bores, not by half so frank and amiable as the goats. The "arrangement" he refers to is concluded just before the King's departure for Aulis; Agamemnon calls for the youth and without preamble offers him the title of Acting Chief Minstrel, to be changed to Chief Minstrel on the fleet's return. Astonished, the young man realizes, as after his good fortune at the Lion's Gate, how much his expectations have in fact been desperate dream:

"*I . . .I accept* [I have him cry gratefully, thus becoming the first author in the world to reproduce the stammers and hesitations of actual human speech. But the whole conception of a literature faithful to daily reality is among the innovations of this novel opus] *!*"—whereupon the King asks "one small favor in return." Even as the minstrel protests, in hexameters, that he'll turn his music to no end beyond itself, his heart breaks at the prospect of declining the title after all:

Whereto, like windfall wealth, he had at once got used.

Tut, Agamemnon replies: though he personally conceives it the duty of every artist not to stand aloof from the day's great issues, he's too busy coping with them to care, and has no ear for music anyhow. All he wants in exchange for the proffered title is that the minstrel keep a privy eye on Clytemnestra's activities, particularly in the sex and treason way, and report any infidelities on his return.

Unlikeliest commission [the minstrel exclaims to you at this point, leaving ambiguous which commission is meant]! *The King and I were nowise confidential; just possibly he meant to console me for missing the fun in Troy* (he'd *see it so*) *by giving me to feel important on the home front. But chances are he thought himself a truly clever fellow for leaving a spy behind to watch for horns on the royal brow, and what dismayed me was less the ingenuousness of that plan—I knew him no Odysseus—as his assumption that from me he had nothing to fear! As if I were my gelded predecessor, or some bugger of my fellow man* (*no shortage of* those *in the profession*), *or withal so unattractive Clytemnestra'd never give me a tumble! And I a lyric poet, Aphrodite's very barrister, the Queen's Chief Minstrel!*

No more is said on this perhaps surprising head for the present; significantly, however, his reluctance to compromise his professional integrity is expressed as a concern for what Merope will think. On the other hand, he reasons, the bargain has nothing to do with his art; he'll compose what he'll compose whether laureled or un, and a song fares well or ill irrespective of its maker. In the long run Chief-Minstrelships and the like are meaningless; precisely therefore their importance in the short. Muse willing, his name will survive his lifetime; he will not, and had as well seize what boon the meanwhile offers. He accepts the post on Agamemnon's terms.

Part Three, consequently, will find the young couple moved to new lodgings in the palace itself, more affluent and less happy. Annoyance at what he knows would be her reaction has kept the minstrel from confiding to his friend the condition of his Acting Chief Minstrelship; his now nearly-constant attendance on the

No use, this isn't working either, we're halfway through, the end's in sight; I'll never get to where I am; Part Three, Part Three, my crux, my core, I'm cutting you out; ———; there, at the heart, never to be filled, a mere lacuna.

iv

The trouble with us minstrels is, when all's said and done we love our work more than our women. More, indeed, than we love ourselves, else I'd have turned me off long since instead of persisting on this rock, searching for material, awaiting inspiration, scrawling out in nameless numbhood futile notes...for an *Anonymiad,* which herefort, having made an Iphigenia of Chapter Three, I can transcribe directly to the end of my skin. To be moved to art instead of to action by one's wretchedness may preserve one's life and sanity; at the same time, it may leave one wretcheder yet.

My mad commission from Agamemnon, remember, was not my only occupation in that blank chapter; I was also developing my art, by trial, error, and industry, with more return than that other project yielded. I examined our tongue, the effects wrought in it by minstrels old and new and how it might speak eloquentest for me. I considered the fashions in art and ideas, how perhaps to enlist their aid in escaping their grip. And I studied myself, musewise at least: who it was spoke through the bars of my music like a prisoner from the keep; what it was he strove so laboriously to enounce, if only his name; and how I might accomplish, or at least abet, his unfettering. In sum I schooled myself in all things pertinent to master-minstrelling—save one, the wide world, my knowledge whereof remained largely secondhand. Alas: for where Fancy's springs are unlevee'd by hard Experience they run too free, flooding every situation with possibilities until Prudence and even Common Sense are drowned.

Thus when it became apparent that Clytemnestra was indeed considering an affair—but with Agamemnon's cousin, and inspired not by the passion of love, which was out of her line, but by a resolve to avenge the sacrifice of Iphigenia—and that my folly had imperiled my life, my title, and my Merope, I managed to persuade myself not only that the Queen might be grateful after all for my confession and declaration, but that Merope's playing up to coarse Aegisthus in the weeks that followed might be meant simply to twit me for having neglected her and to spur my distracted ardor. A worldlier wight would've fled the *polis:* I hung on.

And composed! Painful irony, that anguish made my lyre speak ever eloquenter; that the odes on love's miseries I sang nightly may have not only fed Clytemnestra's passions and inspired Aegisthus's, but brought Merope's untimely into play as well, and wrought my downfall! He was no Agamemnon, Thyestes's son, nor any matchwit for the Queen, but he was no fool, either; he assessed the situation in a hurry, and whether his visit to Mycenae had been innocent or not to begin with, he saw soon how the land lay, and stayed on. Ingenuous, aye, dear Zeus, I was ingenuous, but jealousy sharpens a man's eyes: I saw his motive early on, as he talked forever of Iphigenia, and slandered Helen, and teased Merope, and deplored the war, and spoke as if jestingly of the power his city and Clytemnestra's would have, joined under one ruler—all the while deferring to the Queen's judgments, flattering her statecraft, asking her counsel on administrative matters...and smacking lips loudly whenever Merope, whom he'd demanded as his table-servant at first sight of her, went 'round with the wine.

Me too he flattered, I saw it clear enough, complimenting my talent, repeating Clytemnestra's praises, marveling that I'd made so toothsome a conquest as Merope. By slyly pretending to assume that I was the Queen's gigolo and asking me with a wink how she was in bed, he got from me a hot denial I'd ever tupped her; by acknowledging then that a bedmate like Merope must indeed leave a man itchless for other company, he led me to hints of my guiltful negligence in that quarter. Thereafter he grew bolder at table, declaring he'd had five hundred women in his life and inviting Clytemnestra to become the five hundred first, if only to spite Agamemnon, whom he frankly loathed, and Merope the five hundred second, after which he'd seduce whatever other women the palace offered. Me, to sure, he laughed, he'd have to get rid of, or geld like certain other singers; why didn't I take a trip somewhere, knock about the world a bit, taste foreign cookery and foreign wenches, fight a few fist-fights, sire a few bastards? 'Twould be the making of me, minstrelwise! He and the Queen meanwhile would roundly cuckold Agamemnon, just for sport of it, combine their two kingdoms, and, if things worked out, give hubby the ax and make their union permanent: Clytemnestra could rule the roost, and he'd debauch himself among the taverns and Meropes of their joint domain.

All this, mind, in a spirit of raillery; Clytemnestra would chuckle, and Merope chide him for overboldness. But I saw how the Queen's eyes flashed, no longer at my cadenzas; and Merope'd say later, "At least he can talk about something besides politics and music." I laughed too at his sallies, however anxioused by Merope's pleasure in her new role, for the wretch was sharp, and though it sickened me to picture him atop the Queen—not to mention my frustrate darling!—heaving his paunch upon her and grinning through his whiskers, I admired his brash way with them and his gluttony for life's delights, so opposite to my poor temper. Aye, aye, there was my ruin: I *liked* the scoundrel after all, as I liked Clytemnestra and even Agamemnon; as I liked Merope, quite apart from loving or desiring her, whose impish spirit and vivacity reblossomed, in Aegisthus's presence, for the first time since we'd left the goats, and quite charmed the Mycenaean court. Most of all I was put down by the sheer energy of the lot of them: sackers of cities, breakers of vows, scorners of minstrels—admirable, fearsome! Watching Clytemnestra's eyes, I could hear her snarl with delight beneath the gross usurper, all the while she contemned his luxury and schemed her schemes; I could see herself take ax to Agamemnon, laugh with Aegisthus at their bloody hands, draw him on her at the corpse's side—smile, even, as she dirked him at the moment of climax! Him too I could hear laugh at her guile as his life pumped out upon her: bloody fine trick, Clytie girl, and enjoy your kingdom! And in Merope, my gentle, my docile, my honey: in her imperious new smile, in how she smartly snatched and bit the hand Aegisthus pinched her with, there began to stir a woman more woman than the pair of Leda's hatchlings. No, no, I was not up to them, I was not up to life—but it was myself I despised therefor, not the world.

Weeks passed; Clytemnestra made no reference to my *gaffe;* Merope grew by turns too silent with me, too cranky, or too sweet. I began to imagine them both Aegisthus's already; indeed, for aught I knew in dismalest moments they might be whoring it with every man in the palace, from Minister of Trade to horse-groom, and laughing at me with all Mycenae. Meanwhile, goat-face Aegisthus continued to praise my art (not without discernment for all his coarseness, as he had a good ear and knew every minstrel in the land) even as he teased my timid manner and want of experience. No keener nose in Greece for others' weaknesses: he'd remark quite seriously, between jests, that with a little knowledge of the world I might become in fact its chief minstrel; but if I tasted no more of life than Clytemnestra's dinner parties, of love no more than Merope's favors however extraordinary, perforce I'd wither in the bud while my colleagues grew to fruition. Let Athens, he'd declare, be never so splendid; nonetheless, of a man whose every day is passed within its walls one says, not that he's been to Athens, but that he's been nowhere. Every song I composed was a draught from the wine jug of my experience, which if not replenished must anon run dry....

"Speaking of wine," he added one evening, "two of Clytie's boats are sailing tomorrow with a cargo of it to trade along the coast, and I'm shipping aboard for the ride. Ten ports, three whorehouses each, home in two months. Why not go too?"

At thought of his departure my heart leaped up; I glanced at Merope, standing by with her flagon, and found her coolly smiling meward, no stranger to the plan. Aegisthus read my face and roared.

"She'll keep, Minstrel! And what a lover you'll be when you get back!"

Clytemnestra, too, arched brows and smiled. Under other circumstances I might've found some sort of voyage appealing, since I'd been nowhere; as was I wanted only to see Aegisthus gone. But those smiles—on the one hand of the queen of my person, on the other of that queen of my heart whom I would so tardily recrown—altogether unnerved me. I'd consider the invitation overnight, I murmured, unless the Queen ordered one course or the other.

"I think the voyage is a good idea," Clytemnestra said promptly, and added in Aegisthus's teasing wise: "With you two out of the palace, Merope and I can get some sleep." My heart was stung by their new camaraderie and the implication, however one took it, that their sleep had been being disturbed. The Queen asked for Merope's opinion.

"He's often said a minstrel has to see the world," my darling replied. Was it spite or sadness in the steady eyes she turned to me? "Go see it. It's all the same to me."

Prophetic words! How they mocked the siren Experience, whose song I heeded above the music of my own heart! To perfect the irony of my foolishness, Aegisthus here changed strategy, daring me, as it were, to believe the other, bitter meaning of her words, which I was to turn upon my tongue for many a desolated year.

"Don't forget," he reminded me with a grin: "I might be out to trick you! Maybe I'll heave you overboard one night, or maroon you on a rock and have Merope to myself! For all you know, Minstrel, she might want to be rid of you; this trip might be *her* idea. . . ."

Limply I retorted, his was a sword could cut both ways. My accurst and heart-hurt fancy cast up reasons now for sailing in despite of all: my position in Mycenae was hot, and might be cooled by a sea journey; Agamemnon could scarcely blame me for his wife's misconduct if I was out of town on her orders; perhaps there were Chief-Minstrelships to be earned in other courts; I'd achieve a taintless fame and send word for Merope to join me. At very least she would be safe from his predations while we were at sea; my absence, not impossibly, would make her heart fonder; I'd find some way to get us out of Mycenae when I returned, et cetera. Meantime. . . I shivered. . .the world, the world! My breath came short, eyes teared; we laughed, Aegisthus and I, and at Clytemnestra's smiling hest drank what smiling Merope poured.

And next day we two set sail, and laughed and drank across the wine-dark sea to our first anchorage: a flowered, goated, rockbound isle. Nor did Aegisthus's merry baiting cease when we put ashore with nine large amphorae: the local maidens, he declared, were timid beauties whose wont it was to spy from the woods when a ship came by; nimble as goddesses they were at the weaving of figured tapestries, which they bartered for wine, the island being grapeless; but so shy they'd not approach till the strangers left, whereupon they'd issue from their hiding places and make off with the amphorae, leaving in exchange a fair quantity of their ware. Should a man be clever enough to lay hold of them, gladly they'd buy their liberty with love; but to catch them was like catching at rainbows or the chucklings of the sea. What he proposed therefore was that we conceal us in a ring of wine jugs on the beach, bid the crew stand by offshore, snatch us each a maiden when they came a-fetching, and enjoy the ransom. Better yet, I could bait them with music, which he'd been told was unknown on this island.

"Unless you think I'm inventing all this to trick you," he added with a grin. "Wouldn't you look silly jumping out to grab an old wine merchant, or squatting there hot and bothered while I sail back to Mycenae!"

He *dared* me to think him honest; dared me to commit myself to delicious, preposterous fantasy. Ah, he played me like a master lyrist his instrument, with reckless inspiration, errless art.

"The bloody world's a dare!" he went so far as to say, elbowing my arm as we ringed the jugs. "Your careful chaps never look foolish, but they never taste the best of it, either!" Think how unlikely the prospect was, he challenged me, that anything he'd said was true; think how crushinger it would be to be victim of my own stupendous gullibility more than of his guile; how bitterer my abandonment in the knowledge that he and Merope and Clytemnestra were not only fornicating all over the palace but laughing at my innocence, as they'd done from the first, till their sides ached. "On the other hand," he concluded fiercely, and squeezed my shoulder, "think what you'll miss if it turns out I was telling you the truth and you were too sensible to believe it! Young beauties, Minstrel, shy as yourself and sweet as a dream! That's what we're here for, isn't it? Meropes by the dozen, ours for the snatching! Oh my gods, what the world can be, if you dare grab hold! And what a day!"

The last, at least, was real enough: never such a brilliant forenoon, sweet beach, besplendored sea! My head ached with indecision; the rough crew grinned by the boat, leaning on their oars. Life roared oceanlike with possibility: outrageous risks! outrageous joys! I stood transfixed, helpless to choose; Aegisthus snatched my lyre, clubbed me with a whang among the amphorae, sprang into the boat. I lay where felled, in medias res, and wept with relief to be destroyed at last; the sailors' guffaws as they pulled away were like a music.

v

Long time I lay a-beachèd, even slept, and dreamed a dream more real than the itch that had marooned me. My privy music drew the island girls: smooth-limbed, merry-eyed Meropes; I seized the first brown wrist that came in reach; her sisters fled. Mute, or too frightened to speak, my victim implored me with her eyes. She was evolly, slender, delicate, and (farewell, brute dreams) real: a human person, sense and flesh, undeniable as myself and for aught I knew as lonely. A real particular history had fetched her to that time and place, as had fetched me; she too, not impossibly, was gull of the wily world, a trickèd innocent and hapless self-deceiver. Perhaps she had a lover, or dreamed of one; might be she was fond of singing, balmed fragile sense with art. She was in my power; I let her go; she stood a moment rubbing her wrist. I begged her pardon for alarming her; it was loneliness, I said, made my fancy cruel. My speech was no doubt foreign to her; no doubt she expected ravishment, having been careless enough to get caught; perhaps she'd *wanted* a tumbling, been slow a-purpose, what did I know of such matters? It would not have surprised me to see her sneer at a man not man enough to force her; perhaps I would yet, it was not too late; I reached out my hand, she caught it up with a smile and kissed it, I woke to my real-life plight.

In the days thereafter, I imagined several endings to the dream: she fled with a laugh or hoot; I pursued her or did not, caught her or did not, or she returned. In my favorite ending we became friends: gentle lovers, affectionate and lively. I called her by the name of that bee-sweet form I'd graced her with, she me my own in the clover voice that once had crooned it. I tried imagining her mad with passion for me, as women in song were for their beloveds—but the idea of my inspiring such emotion made me smile. No, I would settle for a pastoral affection spiced with wild seasons, as I'd known; I did not need adoring. We would wed, get sons and daughters; why hadn't I Merope? We would even be faithful, a phenomenon and model to the faithless world. . . .

Here I'd break off with a groan, not that my bedreamèd didn't exist (or any other life on my island, I presently determined, except wild goats and birds), but that she did, and I'd lost her. The thought of Merope in the swart arms of Aegisthus, whether or not she mocked my stranding, didn't drive me to madness or despair, as I'd expected it would; only to rue that I'd not been Aegisthus enough to keep her in my own. Like him, like Agamemnon, like Iphigenia for all I knew, I had got my character's desert.

Indeed, when I'd surveyed the island and unstoppered the first of the crocks, I was able to wonder, not always wryly, whether the joke wasn't on my deceivers. It was a perfumed night; the sea ran hushed beneath a gemmèd sky; there were springs of fresh water, trees of wild fruit, vines of wild grape; I could learn to spear fish, snare birds, milk goats. My lyre was unstrung forever, but I had a voice to sing with, an audience once more of shaggy nans and sea birds—and my fancy to recompense for what it had robbed me of. There was all the world I needed; let the real one clip and tumble, burn and bleed; let Agamemnon pull down towns and rape the widows of the slain; let Menelaus shake the plain with war-shouts and Helen take on all comers; let maids grow old, princes rich, poets famous—I had imagination for realm and mistress, and her dower language! Isolated from

one world by Agamemnon, from another by my own failings, I'd make
Mycenaes of which I was the sole inhabitant, and sing to myself from their
golden towers the one tale I knew.

Crockèd bravery; I smile at it now, but for years it kept me off the
rocks, and though my moods changed like the sea-face, I accomplished much.
Now supposing I'd soon be rescued I piled up beacons on every headland;
now imagining a lengthy tenure, in fits of construction I raised me a house,
learned to trap and fish, cultivated fruits and berries, made goatsmilk cheese
and wrappings of hide—and filled jar after jar with the distillations of my
fancy. Then would come sieges of despair, self-despisal, self-pity; gripped as
by a hand I would gasp with wretchedness on my pallet, unable to muster
resolve enough to leap into the sea. Impossible to make another hexameter,
groan at another sundown, weep at another rosy-fingered dawn! But down the
sun went, and re-rose; anon the wind changed quarter; I'd fetch me up, wash
and stretch, and with a sigh prepare a fresh batch of ink, wherein I was soon
busily aswim.

It was this invention saved me, for better or worse. I had like my fellow
been used to composing in verse and committing the whole to memory, along
with the minstrel repertoire. But that body of song, including my Mycenaean
productions, rang so hollow in my stranded ears I soon put it out of mind.
What are Zeus's lecheries and Hera's revenge, to a man on a rock? No past
musings seemed relevant to my new estate, about which I found such a deal
to say, memory couldn't keep pace. Moreover, the want of any audience
but asphodel, goat, and tern played its part after all in the despairs that
threatened me: a man sings better to himself if he can imagine someone's
listening. In time therefore I devised solutions to both problems. Artist
through, I'd been wont since boyhood when pissing on beach or bank to
make designs and clever symbols with my water. From this source, as from
Pegasus's idle hooftap on Mount Helicon, sprang now a torrent of inspiration: using tanned skins in place of a sand-beach, a seagull-feather for
my tool, and a mixture of wine, blood, and squid-ink for a medium, I
developed a kind of coded markings to record the utterance of mind and
heart. By drawing out these chains of symbols I could so preserve and
display my tale, it was unnecessary to remember it. I could therefore compose
more and faster; I came largely to exchange song for written speech, and
when the gods vouchsafed me a further great idea, that of launching my
productions worldward in the empty amphorae, they loosed from my dammèd
soul a Deucalion-flood of literature.

For eight jugsworth of years thereafter, saving the spells of inclement
weather aforementioned, I gloried in my isolation and seeded the waters
with its get, what I came to call *fiction*. That is, I found that by pretending
that things had happened which in fact had not, and that people existed
who didn't, I could achieve a lovely truth which actuality obscures—especial-

ly when I learned to abandon myth and pattern my fabrications on actual people and events: Menelaus, Helen, the Trojan War. It was *as if* there were this minstrel and this milkmaid, et cetera; one could I believe draw a whole philosophy from that *as if*.

Two vessels I cargoed with rehearsals of traditional minstrelsy, bringing it to bear in this novel mode on my current circumstances. A third I freighted with imagined versions, some satiric, of "the first fact of our generation": what was going on at Troy and in Mycenae. To the war and Clytemnestra's treachery I worked out various dénouements: Trojan victories, Argive victories, easy and arduous homecomings, consequences tragical and comic. I wrote a version wherein Agamemnon kills his brother, marries Helen, and returns to Lacedemon instead of to Mycenae; another in which he himself is murdered by Clytemnestra, who arranges as well the assassination of the other expeditionary princes and thus becomes empress of both Hellas and Troy, with Paris as her consort and Helen as her cook—until all are slain by young Orestes, who then shares the throne with Merope, adored by him since childhood despite the difference in their birth. I was fonder of that one than of its less likely variants—such as that, in cuckold fury, Agamemnon butchers Clytemnestra's whole ménage except Merope, who for then rejecting his advances is put ashore to die on the island where everyone supposes I've perished long since. We meet; she declares it was in hopes of saving me she indulged Aegisthus; I that it was the terror of her love and beauty drove me from her side. We embrace, sweetly as once in rosemaryland. . . . But I could only smile at such notions, for in my joy at having discovered the joy of writing, the world might've offered me Mycenae and got but a shrug from me. Indeed, one night I fancied I heard a Meropish voice across the water, calling the old name she called me by—and I ignored that call to finish a firelit chapter. Had Merope—aye, Trojan Helen herself—trespassed on my island in those days, I'd have flayed her as soon as I'd laid her, and on that preciousest of parchments scribed the little history of our love.

By the seventh jug, after effusions of religious narrative, ribald tale-cycles, verse-dramas, comedies of manners, and what-all, I had begun to run out of world and material—though not of ambition, for I could still delight in the thought of my amphorae floating to the wide world's shores, being discovered by who knew whom, salvaged from the deep, their contents deciphered and broadcast to the ages. Even when, in black humors, I imagined my *opera* sinking undiscovered (for all I could tell, none might've got past the rocks of my island), or found but untranslated, or translated but ignored, I could yet console myself that Zeus at least, or Poseidon, read my heart's record. Further, further: should the Olympians themselves prove but dreams of our minstrel souls (I'd changed my own conception of their nature several times), still I could soothe me with the thought that somewhere outside myself my enciphered spirit drifted, realer than the gods, its significance as objective and undecoded as the stars'.

Thus I found strength to fill two more amphorae: the seventh with long prose fictions of the realistical, the romantical, and the fantastical kind, the eighth with comic histories of my spirit, such of its little victories, defeats, insights, blindnesses, et cetera as I deemed might have impersonal resonation or pertinence to the world; I'm no Narcissus. But if I had lost track of time, it had not of me: I was older and slower, more careful but less concerned; as my craft improved, my interest waned, and my earlier zeal seemed hollow as the jugs it filled. Was there any new thing to say, new way to say the old? The memory of literature, my own included, gave me less and less delight; the "immortality" of even the noblest works I knew seemed a paltry thing. It appeared as fine a lot to me, and as poor, to wallow like Aegisthus in the stews as to indite the goldenest verses ever and wallow in the ages' admiration. As I had used to burn with curiosity to know how it would be to be a Paris or Achilles, and later to know which of my imagined endings to the war would prove the case, but came not to care, so now I was no longer curious even about myself, what I might do next, whether anyone would find me or my scribbles. My last interest in that subject I exhausted with the dregs of Thalia, my eighth muse and mistress. It was in a fit of self-disgust I banged her to potsherds; her cargo then I had to add to Clio's, and as I watched that stately dame go under beneath her double burden, my heart sank likewise into the dullest deep.

vi

A solipsist had better get on well with himself, successfullier than I that ensuing season. Time was when I dreamed of returning to the world; time came when I scattered my beacons lest rescue interrupt me; now I merely sat on the beach, sun-dried, seasalted: a survival-expert with no will to live. My very name lost sense; anon I forgot it; had "Merope" called again I'd not have known whom she summoned. Once I saw a ship sail by, unless I dreamed it, awfully like Agamemnon's and almost within hail; I neither hid nor hallooed. Had the King put ashore, I wouldn't have turned my head. The one remaining amphora stood untapped. Was I thirty? Three thousand thirty? I couldn't care enough to shrug.

Then one noon, perhaps years later, perhaps that same day, another object hove into my view. Pot-red, bobbing, it was an amphora, barnacled and sea-grown from long voyaging. I watched impassive while wind and tide fetched it shoreward, a revenant of time past; nor was I stirred to salvage when the surf broke it up almost at my feet. Out washed a parchment marked with ink, and came to rest on the foreshore—whence, finally bemused,

I retrieved it. The script was run, in places blank; I couldn't decipher it, or if I did, recognize it as my own, though it may have been.

No matter: a new notion came, as much from the lacunae as from the rest, that roused in me first an echo of my former interest in things, in the end a resolve which if bone-cool was ditto deep: I had thought myself the only stranded spirit, and had survived by sending messages to whom they might concern; now I began to imagine that the world contained another like myself. Indeed, it might be astrew with islèd souls, become minstrels perforce, and the sea a-clink with literature! Alternatively, one or several of my measages may have got through: the document I held might be no ciphered call for aid but a reply, whether from the world or some maroonèd fellow-inksman: that rescue was on the way; that there was no rescue, for anyone, but my SOS's had been judged to be not without artistic merit by some who'd happened on them; that I should forget about my plight, a mere scribblers' hazard, and sing about the goats and flowers instead, the delights of island life, or the goings-on among the strandees of that larger isle the world.

I never ceased to allow the likelihood that the indecipherable ciphers were my own; that the sea had fertilized me as it were with my own seed. No matter, the principle was the same: that I could be thus messaged, even by that stranger my former self, whether or not the fact tied me to the world, inspired me to address it once again. That night I broke Calliope's aging seal, and if I still forwent her nourishment, my abstinence was rather now prudential or strategic than indifferent.

vii

That is to say, I began to envision the possibility of a new work, hopefully surpassing, in any case completing, what I'd done theretofore, my labor's fulfillment and vindication. I was obliged to plan with more than usual care: not only was there but one jug to sustain my inspiration and bear forth its vintage; there remained also, I found to my dismay, but one goat in the land to skin for writing material. An aging nan she was, lone survior of the original herd, which I'd slaughtered reckless in my early enthusiasm, supposing them inexhaustible and only later begun to conserve, until in my late dumps I'd let husbandry go by the board with the rest. That she had no mate, and so I no future vellum, appalled me now; I'd've bred her myself hadn't bigot Nature made love between the species fruitless, for my work in mind was no brief one. But of coming to terms with circumstance I was grown a master: very well, I soon said to myself, it must be managed by the three of us, survivors all: one old goat, one old jug, one old minstrel, we'd expend ourselves in one new song, and then an end to us!

First, however, the doe had to be caught; it was no accident she'd outlived the others. I set about constructing snares, pitfalls, blind mazes, at the same time laying groundplans for the masterwork in my head. For a long time both eluded me, though vouchsafing distant glimpses of themselves. I'd named the doe *Helen,* so epic fair she seemed to me in my need, and cause of so great vain toil, but her namesake had never been so hard to get: *Artemis* had fit her cold fleetness better; *Iphigenia* my grim plants for her, to launch with her life the expedition of my fancy. *Tragedy* and *satire* both deriving, in the lexicon of my inventions, from *goat,* like the horns from Helen's head, I came to understand that the new work would combine the two, which I had so to speak kept thitherto in their separate amphorae. For when I reviewed in my imagination the goings-on in Mycenae, Lacedemon, Troy, the circumstances of my life and what they had disclosed to me of capacity and defect, I saw too much of pity and terror merely to laugh; yet about the largest hero, gravest catastrophe, sordidest deed there was too much comic, one way or another, to sustain the epical strut or tragic frown. In the same way, the piece must be no Orphic celebration of the unknowable; time had taught me too much respect for men's intelligence and resourcefulness, not least my own, and too much doubt of things transcendent, to make a mystic hymnist of me. Yet neither would it be a mere discourse or logic preachment; I was too sensible of the great shadow that surrounds our lights, like the sea my island shore. Whimsic fantasy, grub fact, pure senseless music—none in itself would do; to embody *all* and rise above each, in a work neither longfaced nor idiotly grinning, but adventuresome, passionately humored, merry with the pain of insight, wise and smiling in the terror of our life—that was my calm ambition.

And to get it all out of and back into one jug, on a single skin! Every detail would need be right, if I was to achieve the effects of epic amplitude and lyric terseness, the energy of innocence and experience's restraint. Adversity generates guileful art: months I spent considering and rejecting forms, subjects, viewpoints, and the rest, while I fashioned trap after trap for Helen and sang bait-songs of my plans—both in vain. Always she danced and bleated out of reach, sometimes so far away I confused her with the perchèd gulls or light-glints on the rock, sometimes so near I saw her black eyes' sparkle and the gray-pink cartography of her udder. Now and then she'd vanish for days together; I'd imagine her devoured by birds, fallen to the fishes, or merely uncapturable, and sink into despondencies more sore than any I'd known. My "Anonymiad," too, I would reflect then (so I began to think of it, as lacking a subject and thus a name), was probably impossible, or, what was worse, beyond my talent. Perhaps, I'd tell myself bitterly, it had been written already, even more than once; for all I knew the waters were clogged with its like, a menace to navigation and obstruction on the wide world's littoral.

I myself may already have written it; cast it forth, put it out of mind, and then picked it up where it washed back to me, having circuited Earth's countries or my mere island. I yearned to be relieved of myself: by heart failure, bolt from Zeus, voice from heaven. None forthcoming, I'd relapse into numbness, as if, having abandoned song for speech, I meant now to give up language altogether and float voiceless in the wash of time like an amphora in the sea, my vision bottled. This anesthesia proved my physician, gradually curing me of self-pity. Anon Helen's distant call would put off torpor; I resumed the pursuit, intently, thoughtfully—but more and more detached from final concern for its success.

For just reason, maybe, I came at last one evening to my first certainty about the projected work: that it would be written from my only valid point of view, first person anonymous. At that moment *Anonymiad* became its proper name. At that moment also, singing delightedly my news, I stumbled into one of the holes I'd dug for Helen. With the curiosity of her species she returned at once down the path wherealong I'd stalked her, to see why I'd abandoned the hunt. Indeed, as if to verify that I was trapped or dead, she peered into my pit. But I was only smiling, and turning on my finger Merope's ring; when she came to the edge I seized her by the pastern, pulled her in. A shard of deceasèd Thalia, long carried on me, ended her distress, which whooped deaf-heavenward like glee.

tailpiece

It had been my plan, while the elements cured her hide, to banquet on Helen's carcass and drink my fill of long-preserved Calliope. And indeed, for some days after my capture I sated every hunger and slaked every thirst, got drunk and glutted, even, as this work's headpiece attests. But it was not as it would have been in callower days. My futile seed had soured Calliope, and long pursuit so toughened Helen I'd as well made a meal of my writing-hand. Were it not too late for doubts—and I not flayed and cured myself, by sun, salt, and solitude, past all but the memory of tenderness —I'd wonder whether I should after all have skinned and eaten her, whom too I saw I had misnamed. We could perhaps have been friends, once she overcame her fright; I'd have had someone to talk to when Calliope goes, and with whom to face the unwritable postscript, fast approaching, of my *Anonymiad*.

Whereto, as I forewarned, there's no dénouement, only a termination or ironical coda. My scribbling has reached the end of Helen; I've emptied Calliope upon the sand. It was my wish to elevate maroonment into a minstrel masterpiece; instead, I see now, I've spent my last resources contrariwise, reducing the masterpiece to a chronicle of minstrel misery. Even so, much is left unsaid, much must be blank.

No matter. It is finished, Apollo be praised; there remains but to seal and launch Calliope. Long since I've ceased to care whether this is found and read or lost in the belly of a whale. I have no doubt that by the time any translating eyes fall on it I'll be dust, along with Clytemnestra, Aegisthus, Agamemnon...and Merope, if that was your name, if I haven't invented you as myself. I could do well by you now, my sweet, to whom this and all its predecessors are a continuing, strange love letter. I wish you were here. The water's fine; in the intervals of this composition I've taught myself to swim, and if some night your voice recalls me, by a new name, I'll commit myself to it, paddling and resting, drifting like my amphorae, to attain you or to drown.

There, my tale's afloat. I like to imagine it drifting age after age, while the generations fight, sing, love, expire. Now, perhaps, it bumps the very wharpiles of Mycenae, where my fatal voyage began. Now it passes a hairsbreadth from the unknown man or woman to whose heart, of all hearts in the world, it could speak fluentest, most balmly—but they're too preoccupied to reach out to it, and it can't reach out to them. It drifts away, past Heracles's pillars, across Oceanus, nudged by great and little fishes, under strange constellations bobbing, bobbing. Towns and statues fall, gods come and go, new worlds and tongues swim into light, old perish. Then it too must perish, with all things deciphered and undeciphered: men and women, stars and sky.

Will anyone have learnt its name? Will everyone? No matter. Upon this noontime of his wasting day, between the night past and the long night to come, a noon beautiful enough to break the heart, on a lorn fair shore a nameless minstrel

Wrote it.

Modes of Realism
and Elements
of Modern Fiction

Introduction to
Modes of Realism
and Elements
of Modern Fiction

IN MOST CASES of literary usage, "realistic" means "possessed of verisimilitude or lifelikeness," or to put it negatively, containing nothing inherently improbable, vatic, or romantic. A realistic work has no one-eyed giants, flying horses, hermits, or excessively happy endings. As Northrop Frye suggests, by contrast to romance's "implicit mythical patterns," realism emphasizes "content and representation" rather than "the shape of the story." Between the extremes of myth, which pulls a pretended historical world entirely into its shaped aesthetic pattern, and a naturalism whose concern is affairs that could easily be mistaken for fact, the less extreme forms of fiction combine formal symmetries, general statement, and imitations of common experience. Realism falls closer to the mimetic extreme but does not exclude either aesthetic pattern or general statement, which give its lifelikeness organic shape and meaning.

Pattern and statement, however, naturally tend to diminish as mimesis or "verisimilitude" becomes prominent. The inverse relationship between these two tendencies might be described graphically as on page 294. Any given narrative will partake of both components. By giving every character and object a special illustrative point to make, however, archetypal modes and didactic allegory stay close to generalized or universal meaning along the path of "A." Flat or type characters are similar: Stripped of all detail except those recurrent traits that identify them readily, they are forbidden to be influenced by time and change, fact or circumstance. (The more they are allowed to change, the less they cleave to the type.) Characters of greater psychological complexity whose portrayal leans toward realism and whose surroundings are believable images of social and natural forces

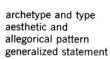

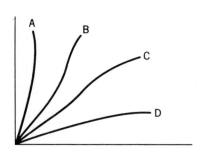

archetype and type
aesthetic and
allegorical pattern
generalized statement

mimetic or factual detail
circumstantiality, verisimilitude

may still represent general theses or aesthetic patterns, but those who lean
very far toward the curve of, say, "C," suggest symbolic dimensions and
general significance only incidentally, making meaning emerge from details
and surfaces. Mimetic characters of this kind tend to be additive and to
follow loosely structured plots of chronological growth. "D" represents a
thorough-going documentary realism without noticeable interference from
plan or idea. A work such as Johnson's fable of the vultures falls close to A
and most modern fiction to B or C. For works of a purer circumstantiality
we would have to look to naturalism or outside the boundaries of fiction
altogether, in biographical narrative and certain kinds of journalism—though
even these of course are far from uninterpreted representations of experience.

Though helpful in making basic distinctions, such classifications of narrative form should obviously not be pushed too far. In many novels, for
instance, the mix is very complex. As Robert Penn Warren remarks of the
"philosophical novelist," he "is one for whom the documentation of the world
is constantly striving to rise to the level of generalizations about value, for
whom the image strives to rise to the symbol, for whom images always fall
into dialectical configuration, for whom the urgency of experience, no matter
how vividly...experience may enchant, is the urgency to know the meaning
of experience." Warren makes use of a polarity similar to that of the
diagram above, but in order to account for the type "the philosophical novel"
he is forced to go beyond diagrammatic simplicity, as we are with nearly
any form of narration that we consider closely. Even allegory often contains
not merely a set of illustrated ideas set in motion as fictional characters but
a historical dimension in which the figure in the fiction represents a real
personage outside it; mimetic details are entangled in the allegorical message. In a similar manner, a character such as Gimpel the fool (in the

story by Isaac Singer) can have highly individualized details and still be typical of certain psychological patterns or fictional types (the scapegoat and the fool in this case). Or again, despite many highly individuating details, the four men in "The Portable Phonograph" and Eve in "Eve's Diary" are placed in situations that cause them to pass beyond the normal boundaries of realism toward symbolic myth. We read their stories as a continuous and subtle tension between myth and lifelikeness, and the nuances of that tension are important to the texture and surface of the story as well as to its thematic significance. No summary of the plot or general theme of a story should ever quite forget its density, the movement of particular incidents and individual sentences, or the complexities of character in excess of what the pattern of the story may require. On the other hand, no reading of a story should merely respond to this or that detail without bringing to bear upon it the entire organization and meaning of the story.

Thus when Northrop Frye distinguishes between mythic pattern and "content and representation" as the main elements of different modes, he should not be taken to suggest that we can always separate them. Realism merely emphasizes more than other modes the limitations of aesthetic pattern and meaning when circumstantiality becomes important. Its growth in the eighteenth century was not a sudden departure from other modes when it tended to become isolated in and consigned to the novel but a shift in emphasis whose points of departure were narrative kinds already well established and congenial to realistic technique. Even if we ignore the roots of realism in Homer, Chaucer's *Canterbury Tales,* fabliaux, northland sagas, and Elizabethan drama, we find the eighteenth-century novel itself drawing upon the past, especially upon picaresque narrative, Elizabethan and seventeenth-century romances (which often have realistic passages), and books of conduct and manners that present models of proper social behavior. (In writing *Pamela,* sometimes considered the first modern novel, Samuel Richardson began with the intent of writing a conduct book for young servants vulnerable to temptations among the higher classes.) A student who approaches modern realism by way of these roots or by way of the two previous sections should notice, then, that although mimetic accuracy dominates it, elements of myth, parable, romance, and satiric fantasy are often amalgamated and blended with it. Satiric novelists such as John Barth, Kurt Vonnegut, Joseph Heller, Samuel Beckett, and other "dark humorists" (whose ancestry is Rabelais, Voltaire, and Swift as well as Defoe, Richardson, and Fielding) combine realism and the incredible. Conversely, the parable and romance. which have able modern practitioners in Kafka, Borges, Conrad, and Faulkner among others, have absorbed some of the techniques of the realist tradition.

When we consider its origins and its contemporary mixture with so many other narrative elements, realism begins to seem less a narrative form in its own right than a dimension of all fictive method. Considered too much in isolation, especially as the center of the novel, it quickly leads to a naive mimetic theory in which the work of art is considered to be a "mirror" of reality; characters become the same as the living, complex creatures that we encounter in everyday life rather than parts of a fictional construction. The very term "realism" fosters confusion between fictional representation and "truth." Whereas ironic modes heighten the incongruity between statement and fact, and myth and romance foster a double awareness of the work as art and the exterior world of normality, realists sometimes set out to make us forget the mode of representation, as though fiction could be a colorless glass through which we perceive reality itself.

Let us therefore beg the question of what "reality" is and how it should appear (if in fact we could reproduce it,) and ask another kind of question about realism, namely what its stylistic and structural techniques are and how these differ from comparable elements in other modes.

First, realism tends to give uniform emphasis to each particular that it presents, and to disguise narrative crescendo and the psychological shape of the story. In point of view, it maintains a detached perspective even when presenting internal worlds, which the reader either judges through externalized behavior or, if given privileged entry to the inner world of dream and thought, samples without interposed interpretation or evaluation from the author. To remove any intrusive sense of shaping art or layers of time that might arouse nostalgia or foreboding, the realistic narrator usually arranges incidents in chronological order, or at least makes clear the place of retrospective views and flashbacks. As Eric Auerbach writes of Homeric realism a major source of the western tradition of realism, the separate elements of a given incident are placed before us in an orderly progression, all of whose causes are readily visible in the phenomena themselves without gaps in knowledge or need for interpretive generalization:

> The separate elements of a phenomenon are most clearly placed in relation to one another; a large number of conjunctions, adverbs, particles, and other syntactical tools, all clearly circumscribed and delicately differentiated in meaning, delimit persons, things, and portions of incidents in respect to one another, and at the same time bring them together in a continuous and ever flexible connection; like the separate phenomena themselves, their relationships—their temporal, local, causal, final, consecutive, comparative, concessive, antithetical, and conditional limitations—are brought to light in perfect fullness; so that a continous rhythmic procession of phenomena passes by, and never is there a form left fragmentary or half-illuminated, never a lacuna, never a gap, never a glimpse of unplumbed depths. (*Mimesis,* p. 4)

As Auerbach's emphasis on grammatical elements reveals, even the most rigorous of realists cannot pretend to render things-as-they-are (whatever they may be) because language is a special kind of representation with built-in sets of relationships—consecutive, comparative, concessive, antithetical, and conditional. Realism edits and orders its objects and necessarily delays our understanding of their full significance as it puts significant events together piece by piece. In this respect realism shares certain traits with romance and myth. But these modes also present more apparently discontinuous worlds, with salient events, strong crescendoes of action, more clearly pronounced psychological patterns, heightened darks and lights, unspecified causes and unprobed motives, dramatic contrasts, and often a multilayered time that makes it impossible for all the contributing elements of a given incident to be known at once. (The landscapes and castles that Lancelot encounters on his grail quest, for instance, are foreboding and fraught with a dark significance that is momentarily unknowable both to Lancelot and the reader.)

Because these stylistic features of romance and realism are so largely a matter of degree, some critics prefer to use comparative stylistic terms to distinguish between them. If we keep in mind a standard of common experience, such terms as "inflationary" and "deflationary" are sometimes helpful to that end. Hardy and Conrad can be said to write novels of tragic inflation in the sense that their characters encounter catastrophes greater than ordinary, in a context of hidden demonic forces. Scripture "inflates" by reminding the reader of a greater story behind the immediate episodes, operating as a concealed but powerful influence upon them. Hemingway is usually a novelist of tragic "deflation" who understates misfortune—sometimes, however, with the inverse effect of inflation by understatement, as when a grievously wounded man appears indifferent to pain. Flaubert is a novelist of comic and ironic deflation who "belittles" the aspirations of his characters by exposing the discrepancies between their dreams and their circumstances. Dickens is a novelist of comic inflation whose characters are often flamboyant caricatures in the manner of such standard types of an earlier period as the *eiron* or self depreciator, the *miles gloriosus* or braggart soldier, the fool, the miser, or the *alazon* or self-deceiver.

As a style and a method of representation, realism not only shapes and selects materials but also shares with romance the capacity to draw the reader into an engrossing world of the imagination. It may seem paradoxical that the greater the sense of psychological and circumstantial reality a work has, sometimes, the more convincing its imaginary world, its aesthetic shape, and its vicarious excitement. But so circumstantial and believable is Defoe's day-by-day portrayal of Robinson Crusoe on his island, for instance, that we are led to forget the "fiction" and see his mimetic progress through practical affairs as virtually our own. Crusoe's existence hovers between a minutely creditable reality and the recurrent dream of a solitary life on a remote island; the realism of husbandry and daily survival becomes the instrument of an archetype and a psychological pattern, the details of which are filled in more meticulously than they would be in romance or myth but without detracting from the sense of romantic adventure. This reinforcement of dream and myth by realistic detail does not invalidate the suggestion we made earlier that each tends to diminish as the other comes forward; it merely suggests in addition that their interaction is often more important than any distinction we may try to maintain between them.

As Ian Watt points out in *The Rise of the Novel,* even the silent and essentially private reading of narrative fiction contributes to realism's paradoxical combination of realistic detail and imagination. Because the printed text of a novel is an impersonal and regulated medium of some size, duration, density, and uniformity of print, it can catalogue a world of objects almost scientifically, extending their duration through serial incidents and great detail, the very successiveness of which draws us further into the suspenseful world of the work. The reader is free to cross-reference one incident with another, to review and reread, and in other ways benefit from the documentary nature of a pretended historical record such as Crusoe's. The printed book itself has all the appearance of factualness formally set before us in the vouched-for sanctuary of print. At the same time, because a printed narrative is so easily entered and believed in, it is all the freer to structure its documented material in the habitual patterns of the creative and inventive mind. Dream and fact lie together so comfortably in the novel that the careers of such heroes and heroines as Moll Flanders, Robinson Crusoe, Tom Jones, Dorothea (in *Middlemarch*), and Becky Sharp (in *Vanity Fair*) may follow curves as perfectly plotted and shaped as those of many a romance figure. Their patterns merely emerge from a more solid density of facts and events, and they are less able to transcend domestic, economic realities and the laws of process and change.

The privacy of our reading contributes to the work's illusion of reality, then, without ruling out the distancing of reality as an aesthetic and often dreamlike experience. In the novel as opposed to the primitive epic, for instance, we do not have a live narrator before us to remind us by his presence and manner that the story is a public entertainment (though some works still close to epic offer a printed equivalent to live address, as in Fielding's "comic epics" *Joseph Andrews* and *Tom Jones*). The difference is perhaps even more evident if we think of the movies. There realism is equally beguiling and capable of making us forget the artifice of cameras, projectors, and techniques of visual association, but other viewers around us sometimes prevent the complete internalizing of the story that a novel manages. Whereas the world of the film, like that of the oral epic, belongs to the public imagination, the novel's world easily becomes the reader's own, at least for a moment. This difference partly explains the fact that until the recent change in our sense of what is public and private, degrees of frankness in realism were denied the film that were permitted in the novel: An explicitness that exceeds public norms of decency may be harbored in the private imagination because nothing we think to ourselves is shocking; but people gathered in a theater are brought to a crisis of acceptance or rejection by the public nature of the situation, in which is threatend the illusion of reality by a breach of decorum.

Thus in fictional representations of normal reality, the privacy of the reading assists the reader's passage across the threshold between the exterior world and the work and enables the work to gratify the imagination through its transcription of plausible events. Factualness, cause and effect progression, and mythic or psychological patterns reinforce each other even as they stand in tension.

So self-sustaining and convincing is the moment-by-moment experience of good realism that it need not present always a finished action—in the sense that a "completion myth," parable, fairy story, or other highly patterned mode does. The "unfinished" effect is a critical and telling dimension of realism, and any attempt to explain it leads us toward the essence of the realistic method. We are sometimes disturbed by unfinished or open-ended stories, but at the same time most of us are willing to accept them if they have given us an insight into some aspect of the subject, developed properly through the details. The conclusion of "The Basement Room," the unresolved dissonance of "Gooseberries" and "A Tree, A Rock, A Cloud," and the comic frustration of the old-fashioned western ruffian at the end of "The Bride Comes to Yellow Sky" are all purposeful minor chord endings. As in so many modern fictionalists, the nature of both narrative sequence and outcome is radically affected by the concept of reality that the story-teller holds. Other realistic stories have more formally completed shapes, but they take them from nature itself, from cycles of growth, decay and death, for instance, that allow a story like "The Jilting of Granny Weatherall" to arrive at a conclusion without violating the open-ended quality of natural process. Still other stories make use of shaped single occurrences such as arrivals and departures, or journeys, as "A Worn Path" does. We usually realize at the point of exit from a realistic work such as "Gimpel the Fool" that it is both a finished fabrication and an image of a reality that continues beyond anyone's control, even the writer's. Though aesthetic pattern and meaning are finished in a sense further events are easily imaginable. The events of the story thus point toward a meaning that *includes the irresolvable nature of complex, historical experience.* Realism is simultaneously a triumph of encompassing understanding and a defeat of maximum form. (This is no less true of films such as Antonioni's *L'Avventura* and Truffaut's *The 400 Blows,* plays like Shakespeare's history plays, and poems like *Paradise Lost* than of prose fiction; every work finds its own kind of compromise between its formal boundaries and projected events that begin before it and continue after.) If the writer of stories, as James remarks, is a watcher at the window of private lives, the reader at the end of a realistic narrative is a Januslike figure whose lingering view inward toward the work reveals the mastery of art even while it commands him to turn away toward a world that art does not control. The act of relating these two visions is very complex, and of all literary forms perhaps realism most insistently demands that we not avoid it—that we not dissociate the world of idea, imagination, and dream from a world of facts. It asks us to take leave of the world outside the work in order to see it more clearly in the mirror of the work, and then to return to it with a new way of interpreting it derived from the perspective of the work. When our understanding of the subject is complete and the work has in fact expended its formative energy, any further concluding of plot strands would merely upset the balance between form and circumstance.

It is the special handling of this balance finally that makes realism a significant narrative method and the following stories interesting examples of that method. In "The Wall," for instance, condemned prisoners attempt to find meaning in their imminent deaths and discover that such an end as their execution renders everything leading to it senseless. At the same time, the story itself makes a finished statement about that absurdity. Whereas in a "complete" fable or myth the interim happening between a decisive beginning and an equally decisive ending are ordered and arranged by the overall purpose that links them, for Pablo Ibbieta death destroys any rationale he might have manufactured to account for his life. The prisoners can only endure the indignities of their own bodily processes, which go on independently of their wills, and their uncontrollable thoughts; and for Pablo the length of that endurance seems finally a matter of indifference: "A few hours, or a few years of waiting are all the same, when you've lost the illusion of being eternal." Events become merely "happenings." Since "no life was of any value," the frenzied political activity on both sides of the Spanish civil war seems equally purposeless.

Several other stories concern the nature of the "real" as well as the problem of formal shape and coherence. Among them are Henry James's "The Real Thing," Chekhov's "Gooseberries," and Barth's "Anonymiad" (in the previous section). The latter mixes pastoral, myth, satire, and other elements as components of a mixture of reality and imagination that the anonymous speaker works upon as he moves from an extreme innocence which mistakes all appearances for realities through disillusioning experience and back to a higher innocence on a paradisal isle. There he is free to dwell in his own imagination but with a certain sophistication that he once lacked. Barth's inventor of written fictions also desires to communicate, however, not merely to write for his own amusement, and this requires of him that he avoid solipsism and discover a sense of reality that can be held in common with at least one other person. He sends the products of the muses forth upon the waters, and when one of them—or some similar product from another hand—returns, he is inspired to write the final story that is the "Anonymiad" before us. The story's concern for the making of stories, the confusion of myth and reality (a recurrent theme of its companion pieces in *Lost in the Funhouse*), and the problem of escaping the self-enclosed constructions of one's own mind are concluded with the ironic realization that the "shape" of the story is given ultimately by the size of the goat parchment one has to scribble on.

A writer who looks into the nature of reality as Barth's hero does is likely also to examine the nature of his art and his own interior idea of reality. The artist of James's "The Real Thing" adds to these problems the special problem of the unique and the typical, and the genuine and the fraudulent. To a painter, the question of how to tell costuming from "the real thing" is inseparable from the problem of style and content. A similar example of the concern for appropriate style is "The Man of the House," in which three sisters, practiced in the comfortable arranging of their lives, make a series of compromises between given conditions and their sense of artfulness and propriety. Unlike Barth and James, Ethel Colburn Mayne does not examine the nature of her own fiction, but she does consider the daily interaction of small fictions and realities in the lives of the three sisters. The last test of their powers of self-deception and their comforting rearrangement of events comes when the cat Timothy dies after spending his life as a substitute for the man of the house who has never appeared for any of them. With an exquisite sense of ritual propriety, Nana arranges his funeral ceremony, converting the distasteful fact of his death into something like a work of art. She is consoled by her success, which is after all a triumph of aesthetic arrangement, and for a moment the three sisters are tempted almost to worship at the shrine of her creation, as "in Egypt, people used to worship cats." But a rough edge intrudes in the rites, and Melicent is not *quite* consolable. Her silence indicates an unwillingness to suspend disbelief and is a qualifying discord in the story's general mellowness.

Chekhov's "Gooseberries" also probes the discrepancy between idyllic dreams and the circumstances with which the dreamer is faced. It is difficult to say who has the best of each, so entangled are they in the story's several layers—the brother Nikolay, for instance, who realizes part of his dream; or Ivan, his critic, who cannot pretend that sour berries are sweet, nor piggish people noble. On one hand, falsehoods that exalt are dearer than "hosts of baser truths." Yet Ivan also sees clearly that the population of provincial Russia lives under a general hypnotism and inertia that prevent them from shaking off their unprogressive slumber. A happy few enjoy the illusion that the miserable are really content, and the rest keep silent. But what Ivan says about these "hosts of baser truths" is not acceptable to his listeners, who do not need to be reminded of them and cannot accept them as final. It is fitting that such a story remain somewhat unresolved because its strands are too finely interwoven and necessarily too "opposed" to unravel: Dream and fact depend upon one another, and we cannot imagine them separate in the context of the story. For instance, the oppressive smell of stale tobacco that pervades the upstairs room and prevents Burkin from dropping into sleep is the kind of untranslatable reality that usually nags Ivan. It represents all the things that one cannot put out of one's mind and that divert attention at times from other tangible and delightful sensations (such as the swim in the mill pond and the beauty of the girl Pelageya). No one in the story quite manages to formulate clearly the relationship between imagined idylls and such thorny facts. The alternation of pleasant and unpleasant sensations, work and relaxation, oppressive and delightful weather, the graciousness and the oppressive power of the nobility will continue.

The keynote of Chekhovian characters is hesitation and irresolution among such contrasts, and "Gooseberries," like Chekhov's major plays, threads its way loosely among a chronology of daily facts and social conditions that bring forward first one and then the other extreme. No intelligence in the story manages to master the combinations. The desire for order and clarity is thus successfully resisted by the givens of the natural and social world until the curtain of sleep finally does fall, postponing the next round of their struggle. Meanwhile, the smell of tobacco will no doubt linger on to greet Burkin again when he awakes.

The unresolvable subjects of realism include not merely the processes of time and change but also the sense frequently of complex societies beyond the hero's control. We often sense these societies as the background of short fiction, but they are perhaps nowhere so subtly woven into the story as in Crane's "The Bride Comes to Yellow Sky." Marshal Potter's taking of a bride is a catalyst of specific social change in Yellow Sky and a symbol of much more. It is also something of an innovation in western pulp literature if we come to the story from the tradition of western myths and see the impact of real time and change on figures freshly removed from the never-never land of fable. Crane places every conventional western scene of the story under the scrutiny of realism and embarasses the Marshal with a new found social consciousness. (The patrons of the train's dining car sit on the edge of sympathetic embarrassment at Potter's stumbling progress into a new time and order.) The town itself is revolutionized by the coming of the bride and all that she implies; she demands an entirely different set of manners—and behind the manners, a new psychology and a new social arrangement. The fumbling Potter is ironically treated so that we realize Crane's ambivalence toward her "improvements" upon western customs: Something of the untamed outdoors is chastened, something of the primitive comradeship of the "boys" is lost in the western hero's abandoning of bachelorhood. On Potter's return the romance of the West shrinks into the constricting facts of the small town, soon (we imagine) to be a large town and eventually an urban center. The outmoded, primitive Scratchy Wilson comes to the edge of the new day, looks in, and turns away in bewilderment.

Crane is adept at measuring myth and reality against each other in this way, both in "The Bride" and his other western fable, "The Blue Hotel." In the latter, however, primitive nature rages with greater force against the lonely institution of the western hotel. In this respect Crane typifies the experiments with realism that so many modern stories have undertaken: the hotel is a remarkable image of men's attempts to establish shelters against forces within themselves and in the landscape outside. The rituals and social forms do not hold, nor, as the conclusion indicates, does the moral will. With similar thematic concerns but opposite conclusions, Eudora Welty's "The Worn Path" protrays a triumph of ritual and moral consciousness over formidable obstacles. The very title of the story signals us that it is a story of process and well-traveled ground. Part of the charm of "The Worn Path" is that it restores the basic physical elements of the path without sacrificing its symbolic value and sense of fabled depth. Miss Welty renders it in so literal and vivid a fashion that we share Phoenix Jackson's physical encounters and at the same time make the path our own indirect, sybolic voyage of discovery. Some of the charm is to doubt due to the central figure herself, who is no knight or Everyman in quest of illumination but a domestic translation of these: She combines the commonplace and the unheroic with the marvelous, "Jackson" with "Phoenix" (the mythic bird of miraculous death and rebirth). The rhythm of the seasons, Phoenix's greetings to each object, and the ceremonies of Christmas are form-giving elements that suggest her mastery of each obstacle as it turns up before her.

Each of these stories in its own way seeks a fruitful blend of fictional types and unique character, aesthetic pattern and mimetic realism, and makes whatever conclusion that blend dictates. Its union of form and content must be read individually finally, but the success of one writer influences another, and the tradition of realism influences our reading of them as contributors to a continuing experiment in realistic narrative method.

The Real Thing

henry james

i

WHEN THE PORTER'S WIFE, who used to answer the house-bell, announced "A gentleman and a lady, sir," I had, as I often had in those days—the wish being father to the thought—an immediate vision of sitters. Sitters my visitors in this case proved to be; but not in the sense I should have preferred. There was nothing at first however to indicate that they mightn't have come for a portrait. The gentleman, a man of fifty, very high and very straight, with a moustache slighlty grizzled and a dark grey walking-coat admirably fitted, both of which I noted professionally— I don't mean as a barber or yet as a tailor—would have struck me as a celebrity if celebrities often were striking. It was a truth of which I had for some time been conscious that a figure with a good deal of frontage was, as one might say, almost never a public institution. A glance at the lady helped to remind me of this paradoxical law: She also looked too distinguished to be a "personality." Moreover one would scarcely come across two variations together.

Neither of the pair immediately spoke—they only prolonged the preliminary gaze suggesting that each wished to give the other a chance. They were visibly shy; they stood there letting me take them in—which, as I afterwards perceived, was the most practical thing they could have done. In this way their embarrassment served their cause. I had seen people painfully reluctant to mention that they desired anything so gross as to be represented on canvas; but the scruples of my new friends appeared almost insurmountable.

Reprinted by courtesy of Alexander R. James.

Yet the gentleman might have said "I should like a portrait of my wife," and the lady might have said "I should like a portrait of my husband." Perhaps they weren't husband and wife—this naturally would make the matter more delicate. Perhaps they wished to be done together—in which case they ought to have brought a third person to break the news.

"We come from Mr. Rivet," the lady finally said with a dim smile that had the effect of a moist sponge passed over a "sunk" piece of painting, as well as of a vague allusion to vanished beauty. She was as tall and straight, in her degree, as her companion, and with ten years less to carry. She looked as sad as a woman could look whose face was not charged with expression; that is her tinted oval mask showed waste as an exposed surface shows friction. The hand of time had played over her freely, but to an effect of elimination. She was slim and stiff, and so well-dressed, in dark blue cloth, with lappets and pockets and buttons, that it was clear she employed the same tailor as her husband. The couple had an indefinable air of prosperous thrift—they evidently got a good deal of luxury for their money. If I was to be one of their luxuries it would behoove me to consider my terms.

"Ah Claude Rivet recommended me?" I echoed; and I added that it was very kind of him, though I could reflect that, as he only painted landscape, this wasn't a sacrifice.

The lady looked very hard at the gentleman, and the gentleman looked round the room. Then staring at the floor a moment and stroking his moustache, he rested his pleasant eyes on me with the remark: "He said you were the right one."

"I try to be, when people want to sit."

"Yes, we should like to," said the lady anxiously.

"Do you mean together?"

My visitors exchanged a glance. "If you could do anything with *me* I suppose it would be double," the gentleman stammered.

"Oh yes, there's naturally a higher charge for two figures than for one."

"We should like to make it pay," the husband confessed.

"That's very good of you," I returned, appreciating so unwonted a sympathy—for I supposed he meant pay the artist.

A sense of strangeness seemed to dawn on the lady. "We mean for the illustrations—Mr. Rivet said you might put one in."

"Put in—an illustration?" I was equally confused.

"Sketch her off, you know," said the gentleman, colouring.

It was only then that I understood the service Claude Rivet had rendered me; he had told them how I worked in black-and-white, for magazines, for storybooks, for sketches of contemporary life, and consequently had copious employment for models. These things were true, but it was not less true—I may confess it now; whether because the aspiration was to lead to everything or to nothing I leave the reader to guess—that I couldn't get the honours, to say nothing of the emoluments, of a great painter of portraits out of my head. My "illustrations" were my pot-boilers; I looked to a different branch of art—far and away the most interesting it had always seemed to me —to perpetuate my fame. There was no shame in looking to it also to make my fortune; but that fortune was by so much further from being made from the moment my visitors wished to be "done" for nothing. I was disappointed; for in the pictorial sense I had immediately *seen* them. I had seized their type—I had already settled what I would do with it. Something that wouldn't absolutely have pleased them, I afterwards reflected.

"Ah you're—you're—a?" I began as soon as I had mastered my surprise. I couldn't bring out the dingy word "models": It seemed so little to fit the case.

"We haven't had much practice," said the lady.

"We've got to *do* something, and we've thought that an artist in your line might perhaps make something of us," her husband threw off. He further mentioned that they didn't know many artists and that they had gone first, on the off-chance—he painted views of course, but sometimes put in figures; perhaps I remembered—to Mr. Rivet, whom they had met a few years before at a place in Norfolk where he was sketching.

"We used to sketch a little ourselves," the lady hinted.

"It's very awkward, but we absolutely *must* do something," her husband went on.

"Of course we're not so *very* young," she admitted with a wan smile.

With the remark that I might as well know something more about them the husband had handed me a card extracted from a neat new pocket-book —their appurtenances were all of the freshest—and inscribed with the words "Major Monarch." Impressive as these words were they didn't carry my knowledge much further; but my visitor presently added: "I've left the army and we've had the misfortune to lose our money. In fact our means are dreadfully small."

"It's awfully trying—a regular strain," said Mrs. Monarch.

They evidently wished to be discreet—to take care not to swagger because they were gentlefolk. I felt them willing to recognise this as something of a drawback, at the same time that I guessed at an underlying sense—their consolation in adversity—that they *had* their points. They certainly had; but these advantages struck me as preponderantly social; such for instance as would help to make a drawing-room look well. However, a drawing-room was always, or ought to be, a picture.

In consequence of his wife's allusion to their age Major Monarch observed: "Naturally it's more for the figure that we thought of going in. We can still hold ourselves up." On the instant I saw that the figure was indeed their strong point. His "naturally" didn't sound vain, but it lighted up the question. "*She* has the best one," he continued, nodding at his wife with a pleasant after-dinner absence of circumlocution. I could only reply, as if we were in fact sitting over our wine, that this didn't prevent his own from being very good; which led him in turn to make answer: "We thought that if you ever have to do people like us we might be something like it. *She* particularly—for a lady in a book, you know."

I was so amused by them that, to get more of it, I did my best to take their point of view; and thought it was an embarrassment to find myself appraising physically, as if they were animals on hire or useful blacks, a pair whom I should have expected to meet only in one of the relations in which criticism is tacit, I looked at Mrs. Monarch judicially enough to be able to exclaim after a moment with conviction: "Oh yes, a lady in a book!" She was singularly like a bad illustration.

"We'll stand up, if you like," said the Major; and he raised himself before me with a really grand air.

I could take his measure at a glance—he was six feet two and a perfect gentleman. It would have paid any club in process of formation and in want of a stamp to engage him at a salary to stand in the principal window. What struck me at once was that in coming to me they had rather missed their vocation; they could surely have been turned to better account for advertising purposes. I couldn't of course see the thing in detail, but I could see them make somebody's fortune—I don't mean their own. There was something in them for a waistcoat-maker, an hotel-keeper or a soap-vendor. I could imagine "We always use it" pinned on their bosoms with the greatest effect; I had a vision of the brilliancy with which they would launch a table d'hôte.

Mrs. Monarch sat still, not from pride but from shyness, and presently her husband said to her: "Get up, my dear, and show how smart you are." She obeyed, but had no need to get up to show it. She walked to the end of the studio and then came back blushing, her fluttered eyes on the partner of her appeal. I was reminded of an incident I had accidentally had a glimpse of in Paris—being with a friend there, a dramatist about to produce a play, when an actress came to him to ask to be entrusted with a part. She went through her paces before him, walked up and down as Mrs. Monarch was doing. Mrs. Monarch did it quite as well, but I abstained from applauding. It was very odd to see such people apply for such poor pay. She looked as if she had ten thousand a year. Her husband had used the word that described her: She was in the London current jargon essentially and typically "smart." Her figure was, in the same order of ideas, conspicuously and irreproachably "good." For a woman of her age her waist was surprisingly small; her elbow moreover had the orthodox crook. She held her head at the conventional angle, but why did she come to *me*? She ought to have tried on jackets at a big shop. I feared my visitors were not only destitute but "artistic"—which would be a great complication. When she sat down again I thanked her, observing that what a draughtsman most valued in his model was the faculty of keeping quiet.

"Oh *she* can keep quiet," said Major Monarch. Then he added jocosely: "I've always kept her quiet."

"I'm not a nasty fidget, am I?" It was going to wring tears from me, I felt, the way she hid her head, ostrich-like, in the other broad bosom.

The owner of this expanse addressed his answer to me. "Perhaps it isn't out of place to mention—because we ought to be quite business-like, oughtn't we?—that when I married her she was known as the Beautiful Statue."

"Oh dear!" said Mrs. Monarch ruefully.

"Of course I should want a certain amount of expression," I rejoined.

"Of *course!*"—and I had never heard such unanimity.

"And then I suppose you know that you'll get awfully tired."

"Oh we *never* get tired!" they eagerly cried.

"Have you had any kind of practice?"

They hesitated—they looked at each other. "We've been photographed—*immensely*," said Mrs. Monarch.

"She means the fellows have asked us themselves," added the Major.

"I see—because you're so good-looking."

"I don't know what they thought, but they were always after us."

"We always got our photographs for nothing," smiled Mrs. Monarch.

"We might have brought some, my dear," her husband remarked.

"I'm not sure we have any left. We've given quantities away," she explained to me.

"With our autographs and that sort of thing," said the Major.

"Are they to be got in the shops?" I enquired as a harmless pleasantry.

"Oh yes, *hers*—they used to be."

"Not now," said Mrs. Monarch with her eyes on the floor.

ii

I could fancy the "sort of thing" they put on the presentation copies of their photographs, and I was sure they wrote a beautiful hand. It was odd how quickly I was sure of everything that concerned them. If they were now so poor as to have to earn shillings and pence they could never have had much of a margin. Their good looks had been their capital, and they had goodhumouredly made the most of the career that this resource marked out for them. It was in their faces, the blankness, the deep intellectual repose of the twenty years of country-house visiting that had given them pleasant intonations. I could see the sunny drawing-rooms, sprinkled with periodicals she didn't read, in which Mrs. Monarch had continuously sat; I could see the wet shrubberies in which she had walked, equipped to admiration for either exercise. I could see the rich covers the Major had helped to shoot and the wonderful garments in which, late at night, he repaired to the smoking-room to talk about them. I could imagine their leggings and waterproofs, their knowing tweeds and rugs, their rolls of sticks and cases of tackle and neat umbrellas; and I could evoke the exact appearance of their servants and the compact variety of their luggage on the platforms of country stations.

They gave small tips, but they were liked; they didn't do anything themselves, but they were welcome. They looked so well everywhere; they gratified the general relish for stature, complexion and "form." They knew it without fatuity or vulgarity, and they respected themselves in consequence. They weren't superficial; they were thorough and kept themselves up—it had been their line. People with such a taste for activity had to have some line. I could feel how even in a dull house they could have been counted on for the joy of life. At present something had happened—it didn't matter what, their little income had grown less, it had grown least—and they had to do something for pocket-money. Their friends could like them, I made out, without liking to support them. There was something about them that represented credit—their clothes, their manners, their type; but if credit is a large empty pocket in which an occasional chink reverberates, the chink at least must be audible. What they wanted of me was to help to make it so. Fortunately they had not children—I soon divined that. They would also perhaps wish our relations to be kept secret: This was why it was "for the figure"—the reproduction of the face would betray them.

I liked them—I felt, quite as their friends must have done—they were so simple; and I had no objection to them if they would suit. But somehow with all their perfections I didn't easily believe in them. After all they were amateurs, and the ruling passion of my life was the detestation of the amateur. Combined with this was another perversity—an innate preference for the represented subject over the real one: The defect of the real one was so apt to be a lack of representation. I like things that appeared; then one was sure. Whether they *were* or not was a subordinate and almost always a profitless question. There were other considerations, the first of which was that I already had two or three recruits in use, notably a young person with big feet, in alpaca, from Kilburn, who for a couple of years had come to me regularly for my illustrations and with whom I was still—perhaps ignobly—satisfied. I frankly explained to my visitors how the case stood, but they had taken more precautions than I supposed. They had reasoned out their opportunity, for Claude Rivet had told them of the projected *édition de luxe* of one of the writers of our day—the rarest of the novelists—who, long neglected by the multitudinous vulgar and dearly prized by the attentive (need I mention Philip Vincent?) had had the happy fortune of seeing, late in life, the dawn and then the full light of a higher criticism; an estimate in which on the part of the public there was something really of expiation. The edition preparing, planned by a publisher of taste, was practically an act of high reparation; the wood-cuts with which it was to be enriched were the homage of English art to one of the most independent representatives of English letters. Major and Mrs. Monarch confessed to me they had hoped I might be able to work *them* into my branch of the enterprise. They knew I was to do the first of the books, "Rutland Ramsay," but I had to make clear to them that my participation in the rest of the affair—this first book was to be a test—must depend on the satisfaction I should give. If this should be limited my employers would drop me with scarce common forms. It was therefore a crisis for me, and naturally I was making special preparations, looking about for new people, should they be necessary, and securing the best types. I admitted however that I should like to settle down to two or three good models who would do for everything.

"Should we have often to—a—put on special clothes?" Mrs. Monarch timidly demanded.

"Dear yes—that's half the business."

"And should we be expected to supply our own costumes?"

"Oh no; I've got a lot of things. A painter's models put on—or put off—anything he likes."

"And you mean—a—the same?"

Mrs. Monarch looked at her at her husband again.

"Oh she was just wondering," he explained, "if the costumes are in *general* use." I had to confess that they were, and I mentioned further that some of them—I had a lot of genuine greasy last-century things—had served their time, a hundred years ago, on living world-stained men and women; on figures not perhaps so far removed, in that vanished world, from *their* type, the Monarchs' *quoi!* of a breeched and bewigged age. "We'll put on anything that *fits*," said the Major.

"Oh I arrange that—they fit in the pictures."

"I'm afraid I should do better for the modern books. I'd come as you like," said Mrs. Monarch.

"She has got a lot of clothes at home: They might do for contemporary life," her husband continued.

"Oh I can fancy scenes in which you'd be quite natural." And indeed I could see the slipshod rearrangements of stale properties—the stories I tried to produce pictures for without the exasperation of reading them—whose sandy tracts the good lady might help to people. But I had to return to the fact that for this sort of work—the daily mechanical grind—I was already equipped: The people I was working with were fully adequate.

"We only thought we might be more like *some* characters," said Mrs. Monarch mildly, getting up.

Her husband also rose; he stood looking at me with a dim wistfulness that was touching in so fine a man. "Wouldn't it be rather a pull sometimes to have—a—to have—?" He hung fire; he wanted me to help him by phrasing what he meant. But I couldn't—I didn't know. So he brought it out awkwardly: "The *real* thing; a gentleman, you know, or a lady." I was quite ready to give a general assent—I admitted that there was a great deal in that. This encouraged Major Monarch to say, following up his appeal with an unacted gulp: "It's awfully hard—we've tried everything." The gulp was communicative; it proved too much for his wife. Before I knew it Mrs. Monarch had dropped again upon a divan and burst into tears. Her husband sat down beside her, holding one of her hands; whereupon she quickly dried her eyes with the other, while I felt embarrassed as she looked up at me. "There isn't a confounded job I haven't applied for—waited for—prayed for. You can fancy we'd be pretty bad first. Secretaryships and that sort of thing? You might as well ask for a peerage. I'd be *anything*—I'm strong; a messenger or a coalheaver. I'd put on a gold-laced cap and open carriage-doors in front of the haberdasher's; I'd hang about a station to carry portmanteaux; I'd be a postman. But they won't *look* at you; there are thousands as good as yourself already on the ground. *Gentlemen,* poor beggars, who've drunk their wine, who've kept their hunters!"

I was as reassuring as I knew how to be, and my visitors were presently on their feet again while, for the experiment, we agreed on an hour. We were discussing it when the door opened and Miss Churm came in with a wet umbrella. Miss Churm had to take the omnibus to Maida Vale and then walk half a mile. She looked a trifle blowsy and slightly splashed. I scarcely ever saw her come in without thinking afresh how odd it was that, being so little in herself, she should yet be so much in others. She was a meagre little Miss Churm, but was such an ample heroine of romance. She was only a freckled cockney, but she could represent everything, from a fine lady to a shepherdess; she had the faculty as she might have had a fine voice or long hair. She couldn't spell and she loved beer, but she had two or three "points," and practice, and a knack, and motherwit, and a whimsical sensibility, and a love of the theatre, and seven sisters, and not an ounce of respect, especially for the *h*. The first thing my visitors saw was that her umbrella was wet, and in their spotless perfection they visibly winced at it. The rain had come on since their arrival.

"I'm all in a soak; there *was* a mess of people in the 'bus. I wish you lived near a stytion," said Miss Churm. I requested her to get ready as quickly as possible, and she passed into the room in which she always changed her dress. But before going out she asked me what she was to get into this time.

"It's the Russian princess, don't you know?" I answered; "the one with the 'golden eyes,' in black velvet, for the long thing in the *Cheapside*."

"Golden eyes? I *say!*" cried Miss Churm, while my companions watched her with intensity as she withdrew. She always arranged herself, when she was late, before I could turn round; and I kept my visitors a little on purpose, so that they might get an idea, from seeing her, what would be expected of themselves. I mentioned that she was quite my notion of an excellent model—she was really very clever.

"Do you think she looks like a Russian princess?" Major Monarch asked with lurking alarm.

"When I make her, yes."

"Oh if you have to *make* her—!" he reasoned, not without point.

"That's the most you can ask. There are so many who are not makeable."

"Well now, *here's* a lady"—and with a persuasive smile he passed his arm into his wife's—"who's already made!"

"Oh I'm not a Russian princess," Mrs. Monarch protested a little coldly. I could see she had known some and didn't like them. There at once was a complication of a kind I never had to fear with Miss Churm.

This young lady came back in black velvet—the gown was rather rusty and very low on her lean shoulders—and with a Japanese fan in her red hands. I reminded her that in the scene I was doing she had to look over some one's head. "I forget whose it is; but it doesn't matter. Just look over a head."

"I'd rather look over a stove," said Miss Churm; and she took her station near the fire. She fell into position, settled herself into a tall attitude, gave a certain backward inclination to her head and a certain forward droop to her fan, and looked, at least to my prejudiced sense, distinguished and charming, foreign and dangerous. We left her looking so while I went downstairs with Major and Mrs. Monarch.

"I believe I could come about as near it as that," said Mrs. Monarch.

"Oh you think she's shabby, but you must allow for the alchemy of art."

However, they went off with an evident increase of comfort founded on their demonstrable advantage in being the real thing. I could fancy them shuddering over Miss Churm. She was very droll about them when I went back, for I told her what they wanted.

"Well, if *she* can sit I'll tyke to book-keeping," said my model.

"She's very ladylike," I replied as an innocent form of aggravation.

"So much the worse for *you*. That means she can't turn round."

"She'll do for the fashionable novels."

"Oh yes, she'll *do* for them!" my model humorously declared. "Ain't they bad enough without her?" I had often sociably denounced them to Miss Churm.

iii

It was for the elucidation of a mystery in one of these works that I first tried Mrs. Monarch. Her husband came with her, to be useful if necessary—it was sufficiently clear that as a general thing he would prefer to come with her. At first I wondered if this were for "propriety's" sake—if he were going to be jealous and meddling. The idea was too tiresome, and if it had been confirmed it would speedily have brought our acquaintance to a close. But I soon saw there was nothing in it and that if he accompanied Mrs. Monarch it was—in addition to the chance of being wanted—simply because he had nothing else to do. When they were separate his occupation was gone and they never *had* been separate. I judged rightly that in their awkward situation their close union was their main comfort and that this union had no weak spot. It was a real marriage, an encouragement to the hesitating, a nut for pessimists to crack. Their address was humble—I remember afterwards thinking it had been the only thing about them that was really professional—and I could fancy the lamentable lodgings in which the Major would have been left alone. He could sit there more or less grimly with his wife—he couldn't sit there anyhow without her.

He had too much tact to try and make himself agreeable when he couldn't be useful; so when I was too absorbed in my work to talk he simply sat and waited. But I liked to hear him talk—it made my work, when not interrupting it, less mechanical, less special. To listen to him was to combine the excitement of going out with the economy of staying at home. There was only one hindrance—that I seemed not to know any of the people this brilliant couple had known. I think he wondered extremely, during the term of our intercourse, whom the deuce I *did* know. He hadn't stray sixpence of an idea to fumble for, so we didn't spin it very fine; we confined ourselves to questions of leather and even of liquor—saddlers and breeches-makers and how to get excellent claret cheap—and matters like "good trains" and the habits of small game. His lore on these last subjects was astonishing—he managed to interweave the station-master with the ornithologist. When he couldn't talk about greater things he could talk cheefully about smaller, and since I couldn't accompany him into reminiscences of the fashionable world he could lower the conversation without a visible effort to my level.

So earnest a desire to please was touching in a man who could so easily have knocked one down. He looked after the fire and had an opinion on the draught of the stove without my asking him, and I could see that he thought many of my arrangements not half knowing. I remember telling him that if I were only rich I'd offer him a salary to come and teach me how to live. Sometimes he gave a random sigh of which the essence might have been: "Give me even such a bare old barrack as *this,* and I'd do something with it!" When I wanted to use him he came alone; which was an illustation of the superior courage of women. His wife could bear her solitary second floor, and she was in general more discreet; showing by various small reserves that she was alive to the propriety of keeping our relations markedly professional—not letting them slide into sociability. She wished it to remain clear that she and the Major were employed, not cultivated, and if she approved of me as a superior, who could be kept in his place, she never thought me quite good enough for an equal.

She sat with great intensity, giving the whole of her mind to it, and was capable of remaining for an hour almost as motionless as before a photographer's lens. I could see she had been photographed often, but somehow the very habit that made her good for that purpose unfitted her for mine. At first I was extremely pleased with her ladylike air, and it was a satisfaction, on coming to follow her lines, to see how good they were and how far they could lead the pencil. But after a little skirmishing I began to find her too insurmountably stiff; do what I would with it my drawing looked like a photograph or a copy of a photograph. Her figure had no variety of expression—she herself had no sense of variety. You may say that this was my business and was only a question of placing her. Yet I placed her in every conceivable position and she managed to obliterate their differences. She was always a lady certainly, and into the bargain was always the same lady. She was the real thing, but always the same thing. There were moments when I rather writhed under the serenity of her confidence that she *was* the real thing. All her dealings with me and all her husband's were an implication that this was lucky for *me*. Meanwhile I found myself trying to invent types that approached her own, instead of making her own transform itself—in the clever way that was not impossible for instance to poor Miss Churm. Arrange as I would and take the precautions I would, she always came out, in my pictures, too tall—landing me in the dilemma of having represented a fascinating woman as seven feet high, which (out of respect perhaps to my own very much scantier inches) was far from my idea of such a personage.

The case was worse with the Major—nothing I could do would keep *him* down, so that he became useful only for the representation of brawny giants. I adored variety and range, I cherished human accidents, the illustrative note; I wanted to characterise closely, and the thing in the world I most hated was the danger of being ridden by a type. I had quarrelled with some of my friends about it; I had parted company with them for maintaining that one *had* to be, and that if the type was beautiful—witness Raphael and Leonardo—the servitude was only a gain. I was neither Leonardo nor Raphael—I might only be a presumptous young modern searcher; but I held that everything was to be sacrificed sooner than character. When they claimed that the obsessional form could easily *be* character I retorted, perhaps superficially, "Whose?" It couldn't be everybody's—it might end in being nobody's.

After I had drawn Mrs. Monarch a dozen times I felt surer even than before that the value of such a model as Miss Churm resided precisely in the fact that she had no positive stamp, combined of course with the other fact that what she did have was a curious and inexplicable talent for imitation. Her usual appearance was like a curtain which she could draw up at request for a capital performance. This performance was simply suggestive; but it was a word to the wise—it was vivid and pretty. Sometimes even I thought it, though she was plain herself, too insipidly pretty; I made it a reproach to her that the figures drawn from her were monotonously (*bête-ment,* as we used to say) graceful. Nothing made her more angry; it was so much her pride to feel she could sit for characters that had nothing in common with each other. She would accuse me at such moments of taking away her "reputytion."

It suffered a certain shrinkage, this queer quantity, from the repeated visits of my new friends. Miss Churm was greatly in demand, never in want of employment, so I had no scruple in putting her off occasionally, to try them more at my ease. It was certainly amusing at first to do the real thing—it was amusing to do Major Monarch's trousers. They *were* the real thing, even if he did come out colossal. It was amusing to do his wife's back hair—it was so mathematically neat—and the particular "smart" tension of her tight stays. She lent herself especially to positions in which the face was somewhat averted or blurred; she abounded in ladylike back views and *profils perdus.* When she stood erect she took naturally one of the attitudes in which court-painters represent queens and princesses; so that I found myself wondering whether, to draw out this accomplishment, I couldn't get the editor of the *Cheapside* to publish a really royal romance, "A Tale of Buckingham Palace." Sometimes however the real thing and the make-believe came into contact; by which I mean that Miss Churm, keeping an appointment or coming to make one on days when I had much work in hand, encountered her invidious rivals. The encounter was not on their part, for they noticed her no more than if she had been the housemaid; not from intentional loftiness, but simply because as yet, professionally, they didn't know how to fraternise, as I could imagine they would have liked—or at least that the Major would. They couldn't talk about the omnibus—they always walked; and they didn't know what else to try—she wasn't interested in good trains or cheap claret. Besides, they must have felt—in the air—that she was amused at them, secretly derisive of their ever knowing how. She wasn't a person to conceal the limits of her faith if she had had a chance to show them. On the other hand Mrs. Monarch didn't think her tidy; for why else did she take pains to say to me—it was going out of the way, for Mrs. Monarch—that she didn't like dirty women?

One day when my young lady happened to be present with my other sitters—she even dropped in, when it was convenient, for a chat—I asked her to be so good as to lend a hand in getting tea, a service with which she was familiar and which was one of a class that, living as I did in a small way, with slender domestic resources, I often appealed to my models to render. They liked to lay hands on my property, to break the sitting, and sometimes the china—it made them feel Bohemian. The next time I saw Miss Churm after this incident she surprised me greatly by making a scene about it—she accused me of having wished to humiliate her. She hadn't resented the outrage at the time, but had seemed obliging and amused, enjoying the comedy of asking Mrs. Monarch, who sat vague and silent, whether she would have cream and sugar, and putting an exaggerated simper into the question. She had tried intonations—as if she too wished to pass for the real thing—till I was afraid my other visitors would take offence.

Oh they were determined not to do this, and their touching patience was the measure of their great need. They would sit by the hour, uncomplaining, till I was ready to use them; they would come back on the chance of being wanted and would walk away cheerfully if it failed. I used to go to the door with them to see in what magnificent order they retreated. I tried to find other employment for them—I introduced them to several artists. But they didn't "take," for reasons I could appreciate, and I became rather anxiously aware that after such disappointments they fell back upon me with a heavier weight. They did me the honour to think me most *their* form. They weren't romantic enough for the painters, and in those days there were few serious workers in black-and-white. Besides, they had an eye to the great job I had mentioned to them—they had secretly set their hearts on supplying the right essence for my pictorial vindication of our fine novelist. They knew that for this undertaking I should want no costume-effects, none of the frippery of past ages—that it was a case in which everything would be contemporary and satirical and presumably genteel. If I could work them into it their future would be assured, for the labour would of course be long and the occupation steady.

One day Mrs. Monarch came without her husband—she explained his absence by his having had to go to the City. While she sat there in her usual relaxed majesty there came at the door a knock which I immediately recognised as the subdued appeal of a model out of work. It was followed by the entance of a young man whom I at once saw to be a foreigner and who proved in fact an Italian acquainted with no English word but my name, which he uttered in a way that made it seem to include all others. I hadn't then visited his country, nor was I proficient in his tongue; but as he was not so meanly constituted—what Italian is?—as to depend only on that member for expression he conveyed to me, in familiar but graceful mimicry, that he was in search of exactly the employment in which the lady before me was engaged. I was not struck with him at first, and while I continued to draw I dropped few signs of interest or encouragement. He stood his ground however—nor importunately, but with a dumb dog-like fidelity in his eyes that amounted to innocent impudence, the manner of a devoted servant—he might have been in the house for years—unjustly suspected. Suddenly it struck me that this very attitude and expression made a picture; whereupon I told him to sit down and wait till I should be free. There was another picture in the way he obeyed me, and I observed as I worked that there were others still in the way he looked wonderingly, with his head thrown back, about the high studio. He might have been crossing himself in Saint Peter's. Before I finished I said to myself "The fellow's a bankrupt orange-monger, but a treature."

When Mrs. Monarch withdrew he passed across the room like a flash to open the door for her, standing there with the rapt pure gaze of the young Dante spellbound by the young Beatrice. As I never insisted, in such situations, on the blankness of the British domestic, I reflected that he had the making of a servant—and I needed one, but couldn't pay him to be only that—as well as of a model; in short I resolved to adopt my bright adventurer if he would agree to officiate in the double capacity. He jumped at my offer, and in the event my rashness—for I had really known nothing about him— wasn't brought home to me. He proved a sympathetic though a desultory ministrant, and had in a wonderful degree the *sentiment de la pose*. It was uncultivated, instinctive, a part of the happy insinct that had guided him to my door and helped him to spell out my name on the card nailed to it. He had had no other introduction to me than a guess, from the shape of my high north window, seen outside, that my place was a studio and that as a studio it would contain an artist. He had wandered to England in search of fortune, like other itinerants, and had embarked, with a partner and a small green handcart, on the sale of penny ices. The ices had melted away and the partner had dissolved in their train. My young man wore tight yellow trousers with reddish stripes and his name was Oronte. He was sallow but fair, and when I put him into some old clothes of my own he looked like an Englishman. He was as good as Miss Churm, who could look, when requested, like an Italian.

iv

I thought Mrs. Monarch's face slightly convulsed when, on her coming back with her husband, she found Oronte installed. It was strange to have to recognise in a scrap of a lazzarone a competitor to her magnificent Major. It was she who scented danger first, for the Major was anecdotically unconscious. But Oronte gave us tea, with a hundred eager confusions—he had never been concerned in so queer a process—and I think she thought better of me for having at last an "establishment." They saw a couple of drawings that I had made of the establishment, and Mrs. Monarch hinted that it never would have struck her he had sat for them. "Now the drawings you make from us, they look exactly like us," she reminded me, smiling in triumph; and I recognised that this was indeed just their defect. When I drew the Monarchs I couldn't anyhow get away from them—get into the character I wanted to represent; and I hadn't the least desire my model should be discoverable in my picture. Miss Churm never was, and Mrs. Monarch thought I hid her, very properly, because she was vulgar; whereas if she was lost it was only as the dead who go to heaven are lost—in the gain of an angel the more.

By this time I had got a certain start with "Rutland Ramsay," the first novel in the great projected series; that is I had produced a dozen drawings, several with the help of the Major and his wife, and I had sent them in for approval. My understanding with the publishers, as I have already hinted, had been that I was to be left to do my work, in this particular case, as I liked, with the whole book committed to me; but my connexion with the rest of the series was only contingent. There were moments when, frankly, it *was* a comfort to have the real thing under one's hand; for there were characters in "Rutland Ramsay" that were very much like it. There were people presumably as erect as the Major and women of as good a fashion as Mrs. Monarch. There was a great deal of country-house life—treated, it is true, in a fine fanciful ironical generalised way—and there was a considerable implication of knickerbockers and kilts. There were certain things I had to settle at the outset; such things for instance as the exact appearance of the hero and the particular bloom and figure of the heroine. The author of course gave me a lead, but there was a margin for interpretation. I took the Monarchs into my confidence, I told them frankly what I was about, I mentioned my embarrassments and alternatives. "Oh take *him*!" Mrs. Monarch murmured sweetly, looking at her husband; and "What could you want better than my wife?" the Major enquired with the comfortable candour that now prevailed between us.

I wasn't obliged to answer these remarks—I was only obliged to place my sitters. I wasn't easy in mind, and I postponed a little timidly perhaps the solving of my question. The book was a large canvas, the other figures were numerous, and I worked off at first some of the episodes in which the hero and the heroine were not concerned. When once I had set *them* up I should have to stick to them—I couldn't make my young man seven feet high in one place and five feet nine in another. I inclined on the whole to the latter measurement, though the Major more than once reminded me that *he* looked about as young as any one. It was indeed quite possible to arrange him, for the figure, so that it would have been difficult to detect his age. After the spontaneous Oronte had been with me a month, and after I had given him to understand several times over that his native exuberance would presently constitute an insurmountable barrier to our further intercourse, I waked to a sense of his heroic capacity. He was only five feet seven, but the remaining inches were latent. I tried him almost secretly at first, for I was really rather afraid of the judgement my other models would pass on such a choice. If they regarded Miss Churm as little better than a snare what would they think of the representation by a person so little the real thing as an Italian street-vendor of a protagonist formed by a public school?

If I went a little in fear of them it wasn't because they bullied me, because they had got an oppressive foothold, but because in their really pathetic decorum and mysteriously permanent newness they counted on me so intensely. I was therefore very glad when Jack Hawley came home: he was always of such good counsel. He painted badly himself, but there was no one like him for putting his finger on the place. He had been absent from England for a year; he had been somewhere—I don't remember where—to get a fresh eye. I was in a good deal of dread of any such organ, but we were old friends; he had been away for months and a sense of emptiness was creeping into my life. I hadn't dodged a missile for a year.

He came back with a fresh eye, but with the same old black velvet blouse, and the first evening he spent in my studio we smoked cigarettes till the small hours. He had done no work himself, he had only got the eye; so the field was clear for the production of my little things. He wanted to see what I had produced for the *Cheapside,* but he was disappointed in the exhibition. That at least seemed the meaning of two or three comprehensive groans which, as he lounged on my big divan, his leg folded under him, looking at my latest drawings, issued from his lips with the smoke of the cigarette.

"What's the matter with you?" I asked.

"What's the matter with *you?*"

"Nothing save that I'm mystified."

"You are indeed. You're quite off the hinge. What's the meaning of this new fad?" And he tossed me, with visible irreverence, a drawing in which I happened to have depicted both my elegant models. I asked if he didn't think it good, and he replied that it struck him as execrable, given the sort of thing I had always represented myself to him as wishing to arrive at; but I let that pass—I was so anxious to see exactly what he meant. The two figures in the picture looked colossal, but I supposed this was *not* what he meant, inasmuch as, for aught he knew to the contrary, I might have been trying for some such effect. I maintained that I was working exactly in the same way as when he last had done me the honour to tell me I might do something some day. "Well, there's a screw loose somewhere," he answered; "wait a bit and I'll discover it." I depended upon him to do so: Where else was the fresh eye? But he produced at last nothing more luminous than "I don't know—I don't like your types." This was lame for a critic who had never consented to discuss with me anything but the question of execution, the direction of strokes and the mystery of values.

"In the drawings you've been looking at I think my types are very handsome."

"Oh they won't do!"

"I've been working with new models."

"I see you have. *They* won't do."

"Are you very sure of that?"

"Absolutely—they're stupid."

"You mean *I* am—for I ought to get round that."

"You *can't*—with such people. Who are they?"

I told him, so far as was necessary, and he concluded heartlessly: "Ce sont des gens qu'il faut mettre à la porte."

"You've never seen them; they're awfully good"—I flew to their defence.

"Not seen them? Why all this recent work of yours drops to pieces with them. It's all I want to see of them."

"No one else has said anything against it—the *Cheapside* people are pleased."

"Every one else is an ass, and the *Cheapside* people the biggest asses of all. Come, don't pretend at this time of day to have pretty illusions about the public, especially about publishers and editors. It's not for *such* animals you work—it's for those who know, *coloro che sanno;* so keep straight for *me* if you can't keep straight for yourself. There was a certain sort of thing you used to try for—and a very good thing it was. But this twaddle isn't *in* it." When I talked with Hawley later about "Rutland Ramsay" and its possible successors he declared that I must get back into my boat again or I should go to the bottom. His voice in short was the voice of warning.

I noted the warning, but I didn't turn my friends out of doors. They bored me a good deal; but the very fact that they bored me admonished me not to sacrifice them—if there was anything to be done with them— simply to irritation. As I look back at this phase they seem to me to have pervaded my life not a little. I have a vision of them as most of the time in my studio, seated against the wall on an old velvet bench to be out of the way, and resembling the while a pair of patient courtiers in a royal ante-chamber. I'm convinced that during the coldest weeks of the winter they held their ground because it saved them fire. Their newness was losing its gloss, and it was impossible not to feel them objects of charity. Whenever Miss Churm arrived they went away, and after I was fairly launched in "Rutland Ramsay" Miss Churm arrived pretty often. They managed to express to me tacitly that they supposed I wanted her for the low life of the book, and I let them suppose it, since they had attempted to study the work—it was lying about the studio—without discovering that it dealt only with the highest circles. They had dipped into the most brilliant of our novelists without deciphering many passages. I still took an hour from them, now and again, in spite of Jack Hawley's warning: it would be time enough to dismiss them, if dismissal should be necessary, when the rigour of the season was over. Hawley had made their acquaintance—he had met them at my fireside—and thought them a ridiculous pair. Learning that he was a painter they tried to approach him, to show him too that they were the real thing; but he looked at them, across the big room, as if they were miles away: They were a compendium of everything he most objected to in the social system of his country. Such people as that, all convention and patent-leather, with ejaculations that stopped conversation, had no business in a studio. A studio was a place to learn to see, and how could you see through a pair of feather-beds?

The main inconvenience I suffered at their hands was that at first I was shy of letting it break upon them that my artful little servant had begun to sit to me for "Rutland Ramsay." They knew I had been odd enough— they were prepared by this time to allow oddity to artists—to pick a foreign vagabond out of the streets when I might have had a person with whiskers and credentials; but it was some time before they learned how high I rated his accomplishments. They found him in an attitude more than once, but they never doubted I was doing him as an organ-grinder. There were several things they never guessed, and one of them was that for a striking scene in the novel, in which a footman briefly figured, it occurred to me to make use of Major Monarch as the menial. I kept putting this off, I didn't like to ask him to don the livery—besides the difficulty of finding a livery to fit him. At last, one day late in the winter, when I was at work on the despised Oronte, who caught one's idea on the wing, and was in the glow of feeling myself go very straight, they came in, the Major and his wife, with their society laugh about nothing (there was less and less to laugh at); came in like country-callers—they always reminded me of that—who have walked across the park after after church and are presently persuaded to stay to luncheon. Luncheon was over, but they could stay to tea—I knew they wanted it. The fit was on me, however, and I couldn't let my ardour cool and my work wait, with the fading daylight, while my model prepared it. So I asked Mrs. Monarch if she would mind laying it out—a request which for an instant brought all the blood to her face. Her eyes were on her husband's for a second, and some mute telegraphy passed between them. Their folly was over the next instant; his cheerful shrewdness put an end to it. So far from pitying their wounded pride, I must add, I was moved to give it as complete a lesson as I could. They bustled about together and got out the cups and saucers and made the kettle boil. I know they felt as if they were waiting on my servant, and when the tea was prepared I said: "He'll have a cup, please—he's tired." Mrs. Monarch brought him one where he stood, and he took it from her as if he had been a gentleman at a party squeezing a crushhat with an elbow.

Then it came over me that she had made a great effort for me—made it with a kind of nobleness—and that I owed her a compensation. Each time I saw her after this I wondered what the compensation could be. I couldn't go on doing the wrong thing to oblige them. Oh it *was* the wrong thing, the stamp of the work for which they sat—Hawley was not the only person to say it now. I sent in a large number of the drawings I had made for "Rutland Ramsay," and I received a warning that was more to the point than Hawley's. The artistic adviser of the house for which I was working was of

opinion that many of my illustrations were not what had been looked for,
Most of these illustrations were the subjects in which the Monarchs had
figured. Without going into the question of what *had* been looked for, I had
to face the fact that at this rate I shouldn't get the other books to do. I
hurled myself in despair on Miss Churm—I put her through all her paces. I
not only adopted Oronte publicly as my hero, but one morning when the
Major looked in to see if didn't require him to finish a *Cheapside* figure for
which he had begun to sit the week before, I told him I had changed my
mind—I'd do the drawing from my man. At this my visitor turned pale and
stood looking at me. "Is *he* your idea of an English gentleman?" he asked.

I was disappointed, I was nervous, I wanted to get on with my work;
so I replied with irritation: "Oh my dear Major—I can't be ruined for
you!"

It was a horrid speech, but he stood another moment—after which, without a word, he quitted the studio. I drew a long breath, for I said to myself
that I shouldn't see him again. I hadn't told him definitely that I was in
danger of having my work rejected, but I was vexed at his not having felt
the catastrophe in the air, read with me the moral of our fruitless collaboration, the lesson that in the deceptive atmosphere of art even the highest
respectability may fail of being plastic.

I didn't owe my friends money, but I did see them again. They reappeared
together three days later, and, given all the other facts, there was something
tragic in that one. It was a clear proof they could find nothing else in life
to do. They had threshed the matter out in a dismal conference—they had
digested the bad news that they were not in for the series. If they weren't
useful to me even for the *Cheapside* their function seemed difficult to determine, and I could only judge at first that they had come, forgivingly, decor-
ously, to take a last leave. This made me rejoice in secret that I had little
leisure for a scene; for I had placed both my other models in position together
and I was pegging away at a drawing from which I hoped to derive glory. It
had been suggested by the passage in which Rutland Ramsay, drawing up a
chair to Artemisia's piano-stool, says extraordinary things to her while she
ostensibly fingers out a difficult piece of music. I had done Miss Churm at
the piano before—it was an attitude in which she knew how to take on an
absolutely poetic grace. I wished the two figures to "compose" together with
intensity, and my little Italian had entered perfectly into my conception.
The pair were vividly before me, the piano had been pulled out; it was a
charming show of blended youth and murmured love, which I had only to
catch and keep. My visitors stood and looked at it, and I was friendly to
them over my shoulder.

They made no response, but I was used to silent company and went on
with my work, only a little disconcerted—even though exhilarated by the
sense that *this* was at least the ideal thing—at not having got rid of them
after all. Presently I heard Mrs. Monarch's sweet voice beside or rather

above me: "I wish her hair were a little better done." I looked up and she was staring with a strange fixedness at Miss Churm, whose back was turned to her. "Do you mind my just touching it?" she went on—a question which made me spring up for an instant as with the instinctive fear that she might do the young lady a harm. But she quieted me with a glance I shall never forget—I confess I should like to have been able to paint *that*—and went for a moment to my model. She spoke to her softly, laying a hand on her shoulder and bending over her; and as the girl, understanding, gratefully assented, she disposed her rough curls, with a few quick passes, in such a way as to make Miss Churm's head twice as charming. It was one of the most heroic personal services I've ever seen rendered. Then Mrs. Monarch turned away with a low sigh and, looking about her as if for something to do, stooped to the floor with a noble humility and picked up a dirty rag that had dropped out of my paint-box.

The Major meanwhile had also been looking for something to do, and, wandering to the other end of the studio, saw before him my breakfast-things neglected, unremoved. "I say, can't I be useful *here?*" he called out to me with an irrepressible quaver. I assented with a laugh that I fear was awkward, and for the next ten minutes, while I worked, I heard the light clatter of china and the tinkle of spoons and glass. Mrs. Monarch assisted her husband—they washed up my crockery, they put it away. They wandered off into my little scullery, and I afterwards found that they had cleaned my knives and that my slender stock of plate had an unprecedented surface. When it came over me, the latent eloquence of what they were doing, I confess that my drawing was blurred for a moment—the picture swam. They had accepted their failure, but they couldn't accept their fate. They had bowed their heads in bewilderment to the perverse and cruel law in virtue of which the real thing could be so much less precious than the unreal; but they didn't want to starve. If my servants were my models, then my models might be my servants. They would reverse the parts—the others would sit for the ladies and gentlemen and *they* would do the work. They would still be in the studio—it was an intense dumb appeal to me not to turn them out. "Take us on," they wanted to say—"we'll do *anything*."

My pencil dropped from my hand; my sitting was spoiled and I got rid of my sitters, who were also evidently rather mystified and awestruck. Then, alone with the Major and his wife I had a most uncomfortable moment. He put their prayer into a single sentence: "I say, you know—just let *us* do for you, can't you?" I couldn't—it was dreadful to see them emptying my slops; but I pretended I could, to oblige them, for about a week. Then I gave them a sum of money to go away, and I never saw them again. I obtained the remaining books, but my friend Hawley repeats that Major and Mrs. Monarch did me a permanent harm, got me into false ways. If it be true I'm content to have paid the price—for the memory.

Gooseberries

anton chekhov

THE WHOLE SKY had been overcast with rain-clouds from early morning; it was a still day, not hot, but heavy, as it is in gray dull weather when the clouds have been hanging over the country for a long while, when one expects rain and it does not come. Ivan Ivanovich, the veterinary surgeon, and Burkin, the high school teacher, were already tired from walking, and the fields seemed to them endless. Far ahead of them they could just see the windmills of the village of Mironositskoe; on the right stretched a row of hillocks which disappeared in the distance behind the village, and they both knew that this was the bank of the river, that there were meadows, green willows, homesteads there, and that if one stood on one of the hillocks one could see from it the same vast plain, telegraph-wires, and a train which in the distance looked like a crawling caterpillar, and that in clear weather one could even see the town. Now, in still weather, when all nature seemed mild and dreamy, Ivan Ivanovich, and Burkin were filled with love of the countryside, and both thought how great, how beautiful a land it was.

"Last time we were in Prokofy's barn," said Burkin, "you were about to tell me a story."

"Yes; I meant to tell you about my brother."

Ivan Ivanovich heaved a deep sigh and lighted a pipe to begin to tell his story, but just at that moment the rain began. And five minutes later heavy rain came down, covering the sky, and it was hard to tell when it would be over. Ivan Ivanovich and Burkin stopped in hesitation; the dogs, already drenched, stood with their tails between their legs gazing at them feelingly.

"We must take shelter somewhere," said Burkin. "Let us go to Alehin's; it's close by."

"Come along."

They turned aside and walked through mown fields, sometimes going straight forward, sometimes turning to the right, till they came out on the road. Soon they saw poplars, a garden, then the red roofs of barns; there was a gleam of the river, and the view opened onto a broad expanse of water with a windmill and a white bathhouse: This was Sofino, where Alehin lived.

The watermill was at work, drowning the sound of the rain; the dam was shaking. Here wet horses with drooping heads were standing near their carts, and men were walking about covered with sacks. It was damp, muddy, and desolate; the water looked cold and malignant. Ivan Ivanovich and Burkin were already conscious of a feeling of wetness, messiness, and discomfort all over; their feet were heavy with mud, and when, crossing the dam, they went up to the barns, they were silent, as though they were angry with one another.

In one of the barns there was the sound of a winnowing machine, the door was open, and clouds of dust were coming from it. In the doorway was standing Alehin himself, a man of forty, tall and stout, with long hair, more like a professor or an artist than a landowner. He had on a white shirt that badly needed washing, a rope for a belt, drawers instead of trousers, and his boots, too, were plastered up with mud and straw. His eyes and nose were black with dust. He recognized Ivan Ivanovich and Burkin, and was apparently much delighted to see them.

"Go into the house, gentlemen," he said, smiling; "I'll come directly, this minute."

It was a big two-storied house. Alehin lived in the lower story, with arched ceilings and little windows, where the bailiffs had once lived; here everything was plain, and there was a smell of rye bread, cheap vodka, and harness. He went upstairs into the best rooms only on rare occasions, when visitors came. Ivan Ivanovich and Burkin were met in the house by a maidservant, a young woman so beautiful that they both stood still and looked at one another.

"You can't imagine how delighted I am to see you, my friends," said Alehin, going into the hall with them." "It is a surprise! Pelageya," he said, addressing the girl, "give our visitors something to change into. And, by the way, I will change too. Only I must first go and wash, for I almost think I have not washed since spring. Wouldn't you like to come into the bathhouse? And meanwhile they will get things ready here."

Beautiful Pelageya, looking so refined and soft, brought them towels and soap, and Alehin went to the bathhouse with his guests.

"It's a long time since I had a wash," he said, undressing." "I have got a nice bathhouse, as you see—my father built it—but I somehow never have time to wash."

He sat down on the steps and soaped his long hair and his neck, and the water round him turned brown.

"Yes, I must say," said Ivan Ivanovich meaningly, looking at his head.

"It's a long time since I washed . . ." said Alehin with embarrassment, giving himself a second soaping, and the water near him turned dark blue, like ink.

Ivan Ivanovich went outside, plunged into the water with a loud splash, and swam in the rain, flinging his arms out wide. He stirred the water into waves which set the white lilies bobbing up and down; he swam to the very middle of the millpond and dived, and came up a minute later in another place, and swam on, and kept on diving, trying to touch bottom.

"Oh, my goodness!" he repeated continually, enjoying himself thoroughly. "Oh, my goodness!" He swam to the mill, talked to the peasants there, then returned and lay on his back in the middle of the pond, turning his face to the rain. Burkin and Alehin were dressed and ready to go, but he still went on swimming and diving. "On, my goodness! . . ." he said. "Oh, Lord, have mercy on me! . . ."

"That's enough!" Burkin shouted to him.

They went back to the house. And only when the lamp was lighted in the big drawing-room upstairs, and Burkin and Ivan Ivanovich, attired in silk dressing-gowns and warm slippers, were sitting in armchairs; and Alehin, washed and combed, in a new coat, was walking about the drawing-room, evidently enjoying the feeling of warmth, cleanliness, dry clothes, and light shoes; and when lovely Pelageya, stepping noiselessly on the carpet and smiling softly, handed tea and jam on a tray—only then Ivan Ivanovich began on his story, and it seemed as though not only Burkin and Alehin were listening, but also the ladies, young and old, and the officers who looked down upon them sternly and calmly from their gold frames.

"There are two of us brothers," he began—"I, Ivan Ivanovich, and my brother, Nikolay Ivanovich, two years younger. I went in for a learned profession and became a veterinary surgeon, while Nikolay sat in a government office from the time he was nineteen. Our father, Chimsha-Himalaisky, was the son of a private, but he himself rose to be an officer and left us a little estate and the rank of nobility. After his death the little estate went in debts and legal expenses; but, anyway, we had spent our childhood running wild in the country. Like peasant children, we passed our days and nights in the fields and the woods, looked after horses, stripped the bark off the trees, fished and so on. . . . And, you know, whoever has once in his life caught perch or has seen the migrating of the thrushes in autumn, watched how they float in flocks over the village on bright, cool days, he will never be a real townsman, and will have a yearning for freedom to the day of his death. My brother was miserabe in the government office. Years passed by, and he went on sitting in the same place, went on writing the same papers and thinking of one and the same thing—how to get into the country. And this yearning by degrees passed into a definite desire, into a dream of buying himself a little farm somewhere on the banks of a river or a lake.

"He was a gentle, good-natured fellow, and I was fond of him, but I never sympathized with this desire to shut himself up for the rest of his life in a little farm of his own. It's the correct thing to say that a man needs no more than six feet of earth. But six feet is what a corpse needs, not a man. And they say, too, now, that if our intellectual classes are attracted to the land and yearn for a farm, it's a good thing. But these farms are just the same as six feet of earth. To retreat from town, from the struggle, from the bustle of life, to retreat and bury oneself in one's farm—it's not life, it's egoism, laziness, it's monasticism of a sort, but monasticism without good works. A man does not need six feet of earth or a farm, but the whole globe, all nature, where he can have room to display all the qualities and peculiarities of his free spirit.

"My brother Nikolay, sitting in his government office, dreamed of how he would eat his own cabbages, which would fill the whole yard with such a savory smell, take his meals on the green grass, sleep in the sun, sit for whole hours on the seat by the gate gazing at the fields and the forest. Gardening books and the agricultural hints in calendars were his delight, his favorite spiritual sustenance; he enjoyed reading newspapers, too, but the only things he read in them were the advertisements of so many acres of arable land and a grass meadow with farmhouses and buildings, a river, a garden, a mill and millponds, for sale. And his imagination pictured the garden-paths, flowers and fruit, starling cotes, the carp in the pond, and all that sort of thing, you know. These imaginary pictures were of different kinds according to the advertisements which he came across, but for some reason in every one of them he always had to have gooseberries. He could not imagine a homestead, he could not picture an idyllic nook, without gooseberries.

" 'Country life has its conveniences," he would sometimes say, 'You sit on the veranda and you drink tea, while your ducks swim on the pond, there is a delicious smell everywhere, and...and the gooseberries are growing."

"He used to draw a map of his property, and in every map there were the same things—(a) house for the family, (b) servants' quarters, (c) kitchen-garden, (d) gooseberry-bushes. He livel parsimoniously, was frugal in food and drink, his clothes were beyond description; he looked like a beggar, but kept on saving and putting money in the bank. He grew fearfully avaricious. I did not like to look at him, and I used to give him something and send him presents for Christmas and Easter, but he used to save that too. Once a man is absorbed by an idea there is no doing anything with him.

"Years passed: He was transferred to another province. He was over forty, and he was still reading the advertisements in the papers and saving up. Then I heard he was married. Still with the same object of buying a farm and having gooseberries, he married an elderly and ugly widow without a trace of feeling for her, simply because she had filthy lucre. He went on living frugally after marrying her, and kept her short of food, while he put her money in the bank in his name.

"Her first husband had been a postmaster, and with him she was accustomed to pies and homemade wines, while with her second husband she did not get enough black bread; she began to pine away with this sort of life, and three years later she gave up her soul to God. And I need hardly say that my brother never for one moment imagined that he was responsible for her health. Money, like vodka, makes a man queer. In our town there was a merchant who, before he died, ordered a plateful of honey and ate up all his money and lottery tickets with the honey, so that no one might get the benefit of it. While I was inspecting cattle at a railway-station a cattle-dealer fell under an engine and had his leg cut off. We carried him into the waiting-room, the blood was flowing—it was a horrible thing—and he kept asking them to look for his leg and was very much worried about it; there were twenty roubles in the boot on the leg that had been cut off, and he was afraid they would be lost."

"That's a story from a different opera," said Burkin.

"After his wife's death," Ivan Ivanovich went on, after thinking for half a minute, "my brother began looking out for an estate for himself. Of course, you may look about for five years and yet end by making a mistake, and buying something quite different from what you have dreamed of. My brother Nikolay bought through an agent a mortgaged estate of three hundred and thirty acres, with a house for the family, with servants' quarters, with a park, but with no orchard, no gooseberry-bushes, and no duck-pond; there was a river, but the water in it was the color of coffee, because on one side of the estate there was a brickyard and on the other a factory for burning bones. But Nikolay Ivanovich did not grieve much; he ordered twenty gooseberry-bushes, planted them, and began living as a country gentleman.

"Last year I went to pay him a visit. I thought I would go and see what it was like. In his letters my brother called his estate 'Chumbaroklov Waste, alias Himalaiskoe.' I reached 'alias Himalaiskoe' in the afternoon. It was hot. Everywhere there were ditches, fences, hedges, fir-trees planted in rows, and there was no knowing how to get to the yard, where to put one's horse. I went up to the house, and was met by a fat red dog that looked like a pig. It wanted to bark, but was too lazy. The cook, a fat, barefooted woman, came out of the kitchen, and she, too, looked like a pig and said that her master was resting. I went in to see my brother. He was sitting up in bed with a quit over his legs; he had grown older, fatter, wrinkled; his cheeks, his nose, and his mouth all stuck out—he looked as though he might begin grunting into the quilt at any moment.

"We embraced each other, and shed tears of joy and of sadness at the thought that we had once been young and now were both grayheaded and near the grave. He dressed, and led me out to show me the estate.

" 'Well, how are you getting on here?' I asked.

" 'Oh, all right, thank God; I am getting on very well.'

"He was no more a poor timid clerk, but a real landowner, a gentleman. He was already accustomed to it, had grown used to it, and liked it. He ate a great deal, went to the bathhouse, was growing stout, was already at law with the village commune and both factories, and was very much offended when the peasants did not call him 'your Honor.' And he concerned himself with the salvation of his soul in a substantial, gentlemanly manner, and performed deeds of charity, not simply, but with an air of consequence. And what deeds of charity! He treated the peasants for every sort of disease with soda and castor oil, and on his name-day had a thanksgiving service in the middle of the village, and then treated the peasants to a gallon of vodka—he thought that was the thing to do. Oh, those horrible gallons of vodka! One day the fat landowner hauls the peasants up before the district captain for trespass, and next day, in honor of a holiday, treats them to a gallon of vodka, and they drink and shout 'Hurrah!' and when they are drunk bow down to his feet. A change of life for the better and being well fed and idle develop in a Russian the most insolent self-conceit. Nikolay Ivanovich, who at one time in the government office was afraid to have any views of his own, now could say nothing that was not gospel truth, and uttered such truths in the tone of a prime minister. 'Education is essential, but for the peasants it is premature.' 'Corporal punishment is harmful as a rule, but in some cases it is necessary and there is nothing to take its place.'

" 'I know the peasants and understand how to treat them,' he would say. 'The peasants like me. I need only to hold up my little finger and the peasants will do anything I like.'

"And all this, observe, was uttered with a wise, benevolent smile. He repeated twenty times over 'We noblemen,' 'I as a noble'; obviously he did not remember that our grandfather was a peasant, and our father a soldier. Even our surname Chimsha-Himalaisky, in reality so incongruous, seemed to him now melodious, distinguished, and very agreeable.

"But the point just now is not he, but myself. I want to tell you about the change that took place in me during the brief hours I spent at his country place. In the evening, when we were drinking tea, the cook put on the table a plateful of gooseberries. They were not bought, but his own gooseberries, gathered for the first time since the bushes were planted. Nikolay Ivanovich laughed and looked for a minute in silence at the gooseberries, with tears in his eyes; he could not speak for excitement. Then he put one gooseberry in his mouth, looked at me with the triumph of a child who has at last received his favorite toy, and said:

" 'How delicious!'

"And he ate them greedily, continually repeating, 'Ah, how delicious! Do taste them!'

"They were sour and unripe, but, as Pushkin says:

> *Dearer to us the falsehood that exalts*
> *Than hosts of baser truths.*

"I saw a happy man whose cherished dream was so obviously fulfilled, who had attained his object in life, who had gained what he wanted, who was satisfied with his fate and himself. There is always, for some reason, an element of sadness mingled with my thoughts of human happiness, and, on this occasion, at the sight of a happy man I was overcome by an oppressive feeling that was close upon despair. It was particularly oppressive at night. A bed was made up for me in the room next to my brother's bedroom, and I could hear that he was awake, and that he kept getting up and going to the plate of gooseberries and taking one. I reflected how many satisfied, happy people there really are! What an overwhelming force it is! You look at life: the insolence and idleness of the strong, the ignorance and brutishness of the weak, incredible poverty all about us, overcrowding, degeneration, drunkenness, hypocrisy, lying...Yet all is calm and stillness in the houses and in the streets; of the fifty thousand living in a town, there is not one who would cry out, who would give vent to his indignation aloud. We see the people going to market for provisions, eating by day, sleeping by night, talking their silly nonsense, getting married, growing old, serenely escorting their dead to the cemetery; but we do not see and we do not hear those who suffer, and what is terrible in life goes on somewhat behind the scenes... Everything is quiet and peaceful, and nothing protests but mute statistics: so many people gone out of their minds, so many gallons of vodka drunk, so many children dead from malnutrition...And this order of things is evidently necessary; evidently the happy man only feels at ease because the unhappy bear their burden in silence, and without that silence happiness would be impossible. It's a case of general hypnotism. There ought to be behind the door of every happy, contented man someone standing with a hammer continually reminding him with a tap that there are unhappy people; that however happy he may be, life will show him her jaws sooner or later, trouble will come for him—disease, poverty, losses, and no one will see or hear, just as now he neither sees nor hears others. But there is no man with a hammer; the happy man lives at his ease, the trivial daily cares faintly agitate him like the wind in the aspen-tree—and all goes well.

"That night I realized that I, too, was happy and contented." Ivan Ivanovich went on, getting up. "I, too, at dinner and at the hunt liked to lay down the law on life and religion, and the way to manage the peasantry. I, too, used to say that science was light, that culture was essential, but for the simple people reading and writing was enough for the time. Freedom is a blessing, I used to say; we can no more do without it than without air, but we must wait a little. Yes, I used to talk like that, and now I ask, 'For what reason are we to wait?" asked Ivan Ivanovich, looking angrily at Burkin. "Why wait, I ask you? What grounds have we for waiting? I shall be told, it can't be done all at once; every idea takes shape in life gradually, in its due time. But who is it says that? Where is the proof that it's right? You will fall back upon the natural order of things, the uniformity of phenomena; but is there order and uniformity in the fact that I, a living, thinking man, stand over a chasm and wait for it to close of itself, or to fill up with mud at the very time when perhaps I might leap over it or build a bridge across it? And again, wait for the sake of what? Wait till there's no strength to live? And meanwhile one must live, and one wants to live!

"I went away from my borther's early in the morning, and ever since then it has been unbearable for me to be among people. I am oppressed by peace and quiet; I am afraid to look at the windows, for there is no spectacle more painful to me now than the sight of a happy family sitting round the table drinking tea. I am old and am not fit for the struggle; I am not even capable of hatred; I can only grieve inwardly, feel irritated and vexed; but at night my head is hot from the rush of ideas, and I cannot sleep.... Ah, if I were young!"

Ivan Ivanovich walked backwards and forwards in excitement, and repeated: "If I were young!"

He suddenly went up to Alehin and began pressing first one of his hands and then the other.

"Pavel Konstantinovich," he said in an imploring voice, "don't be calm and contented, don't let yourself be put to sleep! While you are young, strong, confident, be not weary in well-doing! There is not happiness, and there ought not to be; but if there is a meaning and an object in life, that meaning and object is not our happiness, but something greater and more rational. Do good!"

And all this Ivan Ivanovich said with a pitiful, imploring smile, as though he were asking him a personal favor.

Then all three sat in armchairs at different ends of the drawing-room and were silent. Ivan Ivanovich's story had not satisfied either Burkin or Alehin. When the generals and ladies gazed down from their gilt frames, looking in the dusk as though they were alive, it was dreary to listen to the story of the poor clerk who ate gooseberries. They felt inclined for some reason to talk about elegant people, about women. And their sitting in the drawing-room where everything—the chandeliers in their covers, the armchairs, and the carpet under their feet—reminded them that those very people who were now looking down from their frames had once moved about, sat, drunk tea in this room, and the fact that lovely Pelageya was moving noiselessly about was better than any story.

Alehin was fearfully sleepy; he had got up early, before three o'clock in the morning, to look after his work, and now his eyes were closing; but he was afraid his visitors might tell some interesting story after he had gone, and he lingered on. He did not go into the question whether what Ivan Ivanovich had just said was right and true. His visitors did not talk of groats, nor of hay, nor of tar, but of something that had no direct bearing on his life, and he was glad and wanted them to go on.

"It's bedtime, though," said Burkin, getting up. "Allow me to wish you good night."

Alehin said good night and went downstairs to his own domain, while the visitors remained upstairs. They were both taken for the night to a big room where there stood two old wooden beds decorated with carvings, and in the corner was an ivory crucifix. The big cool beds, which had been made by the lovely Pelageya, smelt agreeably of clean linen.

Ivan Ivanovich undressed in silence and got into bed.

"Lord forgive us sinners!" he said, and put his head under the quilt.

His pipe lying on the table smelt strongly of stale tobacco, and Burkin could not sleep for a long while, and kept wondering where the oppressive smell came from.

The rain was pattering on the windowpanes all night.

The Blue Hotel

stephen crane

i

THE PALACE HOTEL AT FORT ROMPER was painted a light blue, a shade that is on the legs of a kind of heron, causing the bird to declare its position against any background. The Palace Hotel, then, was always screaming and howling in a way that made the dazzling winter landscape of Nebraska seem only a grey swampish hush. It stood alone on the prairie, and when the snow was falling the town two hundred yards away was not visible. But when the traveller alighted at the railway station he was obliged to pass the Palace Hotel before he could come upon the company of low clapboard houses which composed Fort Romper, and it was not to be thought that any traveller could pass the Palace Hotal without looking at it. Pat Scully, the proprietor, had proved himself a master of strategy when he chose his paints. It is true that on clear days, when the great transcontinental expresses, long lines of swaying Pullmans, swept through Fort Romper, passengers were overcome at the sight, and the cult that knows the brown-reds and the subdivisions of the dark greens of the East expressed shame, pity, horror, in a laugh. But to the citizens of this prairie town and to the people who would naturally stop there, Pat Scully had performed a feat. With this opulence and splendour, these creeds, classes, egotisms, that streamed through Romper on the rails day after day, they had no colours in common.

As if the displayed delights of such a blue hotel were not sufficiently enticing, it was Scully's habit to go every morning and evening to meet the

Reprinted by courtesy of Alfred A. Knopf, Inc.

leisurely trains that stopped at Romper and work his seductions upon any man that he might see wavering, gripsack in hand.

One morning, when a snow-crusted engine dragged its long string of freight cars and its one passenger coach to the station, Scully performed the marvel of catching three men. One was a shaky and quickeyed Swede, with a great shining cheap valise; one was a tall bronzed cowboy, who was on his way to a ranch near the Dakota line; one was a little silent man from the East, who didn't look it, and didn't announce it. Scully practically made them prisoners. He was so nimble and merry and kindly that each probably felt it would be the height of brutality to try to escape. They trudged off over the creaking board sidewalks in the wake of the eager little Irishman. He wore a heavy fur cap squeezed tightly down on his head. It caused his two red ears to stick out stiffly, as if they were made of tin.

At last, Scully, elaborately, with boisterous hospitality, conducted them through the portals of the blue hotel. The room which they entered was small. It seemed to be merely a proper temple for an enormous stove, which, in the centre, was humming with godlike violence. At various points on its surface the iron had become luminous and glowed yellow from the heat. Beside the stove Scully's son Johnnie was playing High-Five with an old farmer who had whiskers both grey and sandy. They were quarrelling. Frequently the old farmer turned his face toward a box of sawdust—coloured brown from tobacco juice—that was behind the stove, and spat with an air of great impatience and irritation. With a loud flourish of words Scully destroyed the game of cards, and bustled his son upstairs with part of the baggage of the new guests. He himself conducted them to three basins of the coldest water in the world. The cowboy and the Easterner burnished themselves fiery red with this water, until it seemed to be some kind of metal-polish. The Swede, however, merely dipped his fingers gingerly and with trepidation. It was notable that throughout this series of small ceremonies the three travellers were made to feel that Scully was very benevolent. He was conferring great favours upon them. He handed the towel from one to another with an air of philanthropic impulse.

Afterward they went to the first room, and, sitting about the stove, listened to Scully's officious clamour at his daughters, who were preparing the midday meal. They reflected in the silence of experienced men who tread carefully amid new people. Nevertheless, the old farmer, stationary, invincible in his chair near the warmest part of the stove, turned his face from the sawdust-box frequently and addressed a glowing commonplace to the strangers. Usually he was answered in short but adequate sentences by either the cowboy or the Easterner. The Swede said nothing. He seemed to be occupied in making furtive estimates of each man in the room. One might have thought that he had the sense of silly suspicion which comes to guilt. He resembled a badly frightened man.

Later, at dinner, he spoke a little, addressing his conversation entirely to Scully. He volunteered that he had come from New York, where for ten years he had worked as a tailor. These facts seemed to strike Scully as fascinating, and afterward he volunteered that he had lived at Romper for fourteen years. The Swede asked about the crops and the price of labour. He seemed barely to listen to Scully's extended replies. His eyes continued to rove from man to man.

Finally, with a laugh and a wink, he said that some of these Western communities were very dangerous; and after his statement he straightened his legs under the table, tilted his head, and laughed again, loudly. It was plain that the demonstration had no meaning to the others. They looked at him wondering and in silence.

ii

As the men trooped heavily back into the front room, the two little windows presented views of a turmoiling sea of snow. The huge arms of the wind were making attempts—mighty, circular, futile—to embrace the flakes as they sped. A gate-post like a still man with a blanched face stood aghast amid this profligate fury. In a hearty voice Scully announced the presence of a blizzard. The guests of the blue hotel, lighting their pipes, assented with grunts of lazy masculine contentment. No island of the sea could be exempt in the degree of this little room with its humming stove. Johnnie, son of Scully, in a tone which defined his opinion of his ability as a card-player, challenged the old farmer of both grey and sandy whiskers to a game of High-Five. The farmer agreed with a contemptous and bitter scoff. They sat close to the stove, and squared their knees under a wide board. The cowboy and the Eastener watched the game with interest. The Swede remained near the window, aloof, but with a countenance that showed signs of an inexplicable excitement.

The play of Johnnie and the grey-beard was suddenly ended by another quarrel. The old man arose while casting a look of heated scorn at his adversary. He slowly buttoned his coat, and then stalked with fabulous dignity from the room. In the discreet silence of all the other men the Swede laughted. His laughter rang somehow childish. Men by this time had begun to look at him askance, as if they wished to inquire what ailed him.

A new game was formed jocosely. The cowboy volunteered to become the partner of Johnnie, and they all then turned to ask the Swede to throw in his lot with the little Easterner. He asked some questions about the game, and, learning that it wore many names, and that he had played it when it was under an alias, he accepted the invitation. He strode toward the men nervously, as if he expected to be assaulted. Finally, seated, he gazed from face to face and laughed shrilly. This laugh was so strange that the Easterner

looked up quickly, the cowboy sat intent and with his mouth open, and
Johnnie paused, holding the cards with still fingers.

Afterward there was a short silence. Then Johnnie said, "Well, let's get
at it. Come on now!" They pulled their chairs forward until their knees were
bunched under the board. They began to play, and their interest in the
game caused the others to forget the manner of the Swede.

The cowboy was a board-whacker. Each time that he held superior cards
he whanged them, one by one, with exceeding force, down upon the improvised table, and took the tricks with a glowing air of prowess and pride
that sent thrills of indignation into the hearts of his opponents. A game with
a board-whacker in it is sure to become intense. The countenances of the
Easterner and the Swede were miserable whenever the cowboy thundered
down his aces and kings, while Johnnie, his eyes gleaming with joy, chuckled
and chuckled.

Because of the absorbing play none considered the strange ways of the
Swede. They paid strict heed to the game. Finally, during a lull caused by a
new deal, the Swede suddenly addressed Johnnie: "I suppose there have been
a good many men killed in this room." The jaws of the others dropped and
they looked at him.

"What in hell are you talking about?" said Johnnie.

The Swede laughed again his blatant laugh, full of a kind of false courage and defiance. "Oh, you know what I mean all right," he answered.

"I'm a liar if I do!" Johnnie protested. The card was halted, and the
men stared at the Swede. Johnnie evidently felt that as the son of the
proprietor he should make a direct inquiry. "Now, what might you be
drivin' at, mister?" he asked. The Swede winked at him. It was a wink
full of cunning. His fingers shook on the edge of the board. "Oh, maybe you
think I have been to nowheres. Maybe you think I'm a tenderfoot?"

"I don't know nothin' about you," answered Johnnie, "and I don't give
a damn where you've been. All I got to say is that I don't know what you're
driving at. There hain't never been nobody killed in this room."

The cowboy, who had been steadily gazing at the Swede, then spoke:
"What's wrong with you, mister?"

Apparently it seemed to the Swede that he was formidably menaced.
He shivered and turned white near the corners of his mouth. He sent an
appealing glance in the direction of the little Easterner. During these moments he did not forget to wear his air of advanced pot-valour. "They say
they don't know what I mean," he remarked mockingly to the Easterner.

The latter answered after prolonged and cautious reflection. "I don't
understand you," he said, impassively.

The Swede made a movement then which announced that he thought
he had encountered treachery from the only quarter where he had expected
sympathy, if not help. "Oh, I see you are all against me. I see——"

The cowboy was in a state of deep stupefaction. "Say," he cried, as he tumbled the deck violently down upon the board, "say, what are you gittin' at hey?"

The Swede sprang up with the celerity of a man escaping from a snake on the floor. "I don't want to fight!" he shouted. "I don't want to fight!"

The cowboy stretched his long legs indolently and deliberately. His hands were in his pockets. He spat into the sawdust-box. "Well, who the hell thought you did?" he inquired.

The Swede backed rapidly toward a corner of the room. His hands were out protectingly in front of his chest, but he was making an obvious struggle to control his fright. "Gentlemen," he quavered, "I suppose I am going to be killed before I can leave this house! I suppose I am going to be killed before I can leave this house!" In his eyes was the dying-swan look. Through the windows could be seen the snow turning blue in the shadow of dusk. The wind tore at the house, and some loose thing beat regularly against the clapboards like a spirit tapping.

A door opened, and Scully himself entered. He paused in surprise as he noted the tragic attitude of the Swede. Then he said. "What's the matter here?"

The Swede answered him swiftly and eagerly: "These men are going to kill me."

"Kill you!" ejaculated Scully. "Kill you! What are you talkin'?"

The Swede made the gesture of martyr.

Scully wheeled sternly upon his son. "What is this, Johnnie?"

The lad had grown sullen. "Damned if I know," he answered. "I can't make no sense to it." He began to shuffle the cards, fluttering them together with an angry snap. "He says a good many men have been killed in this room, or somthing like that. And he says he's goin' to be killed here too. I don't know what ails him. He's crazy, I shouldn't wonder."

Scully then looked for explanation to the cowboy, but the cowboy simply shrugged his shoulders.

"Kill you?" said Scully again to the Swede. "Kill you? Man, you're off your nut."

"Oh, I know," burst out the Swede. "I know what will happen. Yes, I'm crazy—yes. Yes, of course, I'm crazy—yes. But I know one thing——" There was a sort of sweat of misery and terror upon his face. "I know I won't get out of here alive."

The cowboy drew a deep breath, as if his mind was passing into the last stages of dissolution. "Well, I'm doggoned," he whispered to himself.

Scully wheeled suddenly and faced his son. "You've been troublin' this man!"

Johnnie's voice was loud with its burden of grievance. "Why, good Gawd, I ain't done nothin' to 'im."

The Swede broke in. "Gentlemen, do not disturb yourselves. I will leave this house. I will go away, because"—he accused them dramatically with his glance—"because I do not want to be killed."

Scully was furious with his son. "Will you tell me what is the matter, you young divil? What's the matter, anyhow? Speak out!"

"Blame it!" cried Johnnie in despair, "don't I tell you I don't know? He—he says we want to kill him, and that's all I know. I can't tell what ails him."

The Swede continued to repeat: "Never mind, Mr. Scully; never mind. I will leave this house. I will go away, because I do not wish to be killed. Yes, of course, I am crazy—yes. But I know one thing! I will go away. I will leave this house. Never mind, Mr. Scully; never mind. I will go away."

"You will not go 'way," said Scully. "You will not go 'way until I hear the reason of this business. If anybody has troubled you I will take care of him. This is my house. You are under my roof, and I will not allow any peaceable man to be troubled here." He cast a terrible eye upon Johnnie, the cowboy, and the Easterner.

"Never mind, Mr. Scully; never mind. I will go away. I do not wish to be killed." The Swede moved toward the door which opened upon the stairs. It was evidently his intention to go at once for his baggage.

"No, no," shouted Scully peremptorily; but the white-faced man slid by him and disappeared. "Now," said Scully severely, "what does this mane?"

Johnnie and the cowboy cried together "Why, we didn't do nothin' to 'im!"

Scully's eyes were cold. "No," he said, "you didn't?"

Johnnie swore a deep oath. "Why, this is the wildest loon I ever see. We didn't do nothin' at all. We were jest sittin' here playin' cards, and he ——"

The father suddenly spoke to the Easterner. "Mr. Blanc," he asked, "what has these boys been doin'?"

The Easterner reflected again. "I didn't see anything wrong at all," he said at last, slowly.

Scully began to howl. "But what does it mane?" He stared ferociously at his son. "I have a mind to lather you for this, me boy."

Johnnie was frantic. "Well, what have I done?" he bawled at the father.

iii

"I think you are tongue-tied," said Scully finally to his son, the cowboy, and the Easterner; and at the end of this scornful sentence he left the room.

Upstairs the Swede was swiftly fastening the straps of his great valise. Once his back happened to be half turned toward the door, and, hearing a noise there, he wheeled and sprang up, uttering a loud cry. Scully's wrinkled visage showed grimly in the light of the small lamp he carried. This yellow effulgence, streaming upward, coloured only his prominent features, and left his eyes, for instance, in mysterious shadow. He resembled a murderer.

"Man! man!" he exclaimed, "have you gone daffy"

"Oh, no! Oh, no!" rejoined the other. "There are people in this world who know pretty nearly as much as you do—understand?"

For a moment they stood gazing at each other. Upon the Swede's deathly pale cheeks were now spots brightly crimson and sharply edged, as if they had been carefully painted. Scully placed the light on the table and sat himself on the edge of the bed. He spoke ruminatively. "By cracky, I never heard of such a thing in my life. It's a complete muddle. I can't, for the soul of me, think how you ever got this idea into your head." Presently he lifted his eyes and asked: "And did you sure think they were going to kill you?"

The Swede scanned the old man as if he wished to see into his mind. "I did," he said at last. He obviously suspected that this answer might precipitate an outbreak. As he pulled on a strap his whole arm shook, the elbow wavering like a bit of paper.

Scully banged his hand impressively on the footboard of the bed. "Why, man, we're goin' to have a line of ilictric street-cars in this town next spring."

" 'A line of electric street-cars,' " repeated the Swede, stupidly.

"And," said Scully, "there's a new railroad goin' to be built down from Broken Arm to here. Not to mintion the four churches and the smashin' big brick schoolhouse. Then there's the big factory, too. Why, in two years Romper'll be a met-tro-*pol*-is."

Having finished the preparation of his baggage, the Swede straightened himself. "Mr. Scully," he said, with sudden hardihood, "how much do I owe you?"

"You don't owe me anythin'," said the old man, angrily.

"Yes, I do," retorted the Swede. He took seventy-five cents from his pocket and tendered it to Scully; but the latter snapped his fingers in disdainful refusal. However, it happened that they both stood gazing in a strange fashion at three silver pieces on the Swede's open palm.

"I'll not take your money," said Scully at last. "Not after what's been goin' on here." Then a plan seemed to strike him. "Here," he cried, picking up his lamp and moving toward the door. "Here! Come with me a minute."

"No," said the Swede, in overwhelming alarm.

"Yes," urged the old man. "Come on! I want you to come and see a picter—just across the hall—in my room."

The Swede must have concluded that his hour was come. His jaw dropped and his teeth showed like a dead man's. He ultimately followed Scully across the corridor, but he had the step of one hung in chains.

Scully flashed the light high on the wall of his chamber. There was revealed a ridiculous photograph of a little girl. She was leaning against a balustrade of gorgeous decoration, and the formidable bang to her hair was prominent. The figure was as graceful as an upright sled-stake, and, withal, it was of the hue of lead. "There," said Scully, tenderly, "that's the picter of my little girl that died. Her name was Carrie. She had the purtiest hair you ever saw! I was that found of her, she ——"

Turning then, he saw that the Swede was not contemplating the picture at all, but, instead, was keeping keen watch on the gloom in the rear.

"Look, man!" cried Scully, heartily. "That's the picter of my little gal that died. Her name was Carrie. And then here's the picter of my oldest boy, Michael. He's a lawyer in Lincoln, an' doin' well. I gave that boy a grand eddication, and I'm glad for it now. He's a fine boy. Look at 'im now. Ain't he bold as blazes, him there in Lincoln, an honoured an' respicted gintleman! An honoured and respicted gintleman," concluded Scully with a flourish. And, so saying, he smote the Swede jovially on the back.

The Swede faintly smiled.

"Now," said the old man, "there's only one more thing." He dropped suddenly to the floor and thrust his head beneath the bed. The Swede could hear his muffled voice. "I'd keep it under me piller if it wasn't for that boy Johnnie. Then there's the old woman —— Where is it now? I never put it twice in the same place. Ah, now come out with you!"

Presently he backed clumsily from under the bed, dragging with him an old coat rolled into a bundle. "I've fetched him," he muttered. Kneeling on the floor, he unrolled the coat and extracted from its heart a large yellow-brown whisky-bottle.

His first manœuvre was to hold the bottle up to the light. Reassured, apparently, that nobody had been tampering with it, he thrust it with a generous movement toward the Swede.

The weak-kneed Swede was about to eagerly clutch this elements of strength, but he suddenly jerked his hand away and cast a look of horror upon Scully.

"Drink," said the old man affectionately. He had risen to his feet, and now stood facing the Swede.

There was a silence. Then again Scully said: "Drink!"

The Swede laughed wildly. He grabbed the bottle, put it to his mouth; and as his lips curled absurdly around the opening and his throat worked, he kept his glance, burning with hatred, upon the old man's face.

iv

After the departure of Scully the three men, with the cardboard still upon their knees, preserved for a long time an astounded silence. Then Johnnie said: "That's the doddangedest Swede I ever see.'

"He ain't no Swede," said the cowboy, scornfully.

"Well, what is he then?" cried Johnnie. "What is he then?"

"It's my opinion," replied the cowboy deliberately, "he's some kind of a Dutchman." It was a venerable custom of the country to entitle as Swedes all light-haired men who spoke with a heavy tongue. In consequence the idea of the cowboy was not without its daring. "Yes, sir," he repeated. "It's my opinion this feller is some kind of a Dutchman."

"Well, he says he's Swede, anyhow," muttered Johnnie, sulkily. He turned to the Easterner: "What do you think, Mr. Blanc?"

"Oh, I don't know," replied the Easterner.

"Well, what do you think makes him act that way?" asked the cowboy.

"Why, he's frightened." The Easterner knocked his pipe against a rim of the stove. "He's clear frightened out of his boots."

"What at?" cried Johnnie and the cowboy together.

The Easterner reflected over his answer.

"What at?" cried the others again.

"Oh, I don't know, but it seems to me this man has been reading dime novels, and he thinks he's right out in the middle of it—the shootin' and stabbin' and all."

"But," said the cowboy, deeply scandalized, "this ain't Wyoming, ner none of them places. This is Nebrasker."

"Yes," added Johnnie, "an' why don't he wait till he gits out *West?*"

The travelled Easterner laughed. "It isn't different there even—not in these days. But he thinks he's right in the middle of hell."

Johnnie and the cowboy mused long.

"It's awful funny," remarked Johnnie at last.

"Yes," said the cowboy. "This is a queer game. I hope we don't get snowed in, because then we'd have to stand this here man bein' around with us all the time. That wouldn't be no good."

"I wish pop would throw him out," said Johnnie.

Presently they heard a loud stamping on the stairs, accompanied by ringing jokes in the voice of old Scully, and laughter, evidently from the Swede. The men around the stove stared vacantly at each other. "Gosh!" said the cowboy. The door flew open, and old Scully, flushed and anecdotal, came into the room. He was jabbering at the Swede, who followed him, laughing bravely. It was the entry of two roisterers from a banquet hall.

"Come now," said Scully sharply to the three seated men, "move up and give us a chance at the stove." The cowboy and the Easterner obediently sidled their chairs to make room for the new-comers. Johnnie, however, simply arranged himself in a more indolent attitude, and then remained motionless.

"Come! Git over, there," said Scully.

"Plenty of room on the other side of the stove," said Johnnie.

"Do you think we want to sit in the draught?'" roared the father.

But the Swede here interposed with a grandeur of confidence. "No, no. Let the boy sit where he likes," he cried in a bullying voice to the father.

"All right! All right!" said Sculy, deferentially. The cowboy and the Easterner exchanged glances of wonder.

The five chairs were formed in a crecent about one side of the stove. The Swede began to talk; he talked arrogantly, profanely, angrily. Johnnie, the cowboy, and the Easterner maintained a morose silence, while old Scully appeared to be receptive and eager, breaking in constantly with sympathetic ejaculations.

Finally the Swede announced that he was thirsty. He moved in his chair, and said that he would go for a drink of water.

"I'll git it for you," cried Scully at once.

"No," said the Swede, contemptuously. "I'll get it for myself." He arose and stalked with the air of an owner off into the executive parts of the hotel.

As soon as the Swede was out of hearing Scully sprang to his feet and whispered intensely to the others: "Upstairs he thought I was tryin' to poison 'im."

"Say," said Johnnie, "this makes me sick. Why don't you throw 'im out in the snow?"

"Why, he's all right now," declared Scully. "It was only that he was from the East, and he thought this was a tough place. That's all. He's all right now."

The cowboy looked with admiration upon the Easterner. "You were straight," he said. "You were on to that there Dutchman."

"Well," said Johnnie to his father, "he may be all right now, but I don't see it. Other time he was scared, but now he's too fresh."

Scully's speech was always a combination of Irish brogue and idiom, Western twang and idiom, and scraps of curiously formal diction taken from the story-books and newspapers. He now hurled a strange mass of language at the head of his son. "What do I keep? What do I keep? What do I keep?" he demanded, in a voice of thunder. He slapped his knee impressively, to indicate that he himself was going to make reply, and that all should heed. "I keep a hotel," he shouted. "A hotel, do you mind? A guest under my roof has sacred privileges. He is to be intimidated by none. Not one word shall he hear that would prijudice him in favour of goin' away. I'll not have it. There's no place in this here town where they can say they iver took in a guest of mine because he was afraid to stay here." He wheeled suddenly upon the cowboy and the Easterner. "Am I right?"

"Yes, Mr. Scully," said the cowboy, "I think you're right."

"Yes, Mr. Scully," said the Easterner, "I think you're right."

v

At six-o'clock supper, the Swede fizzed like a fire-wheel. He sometimes seemed on the point of bursting into riotous song, and in all his madness he was encouraged by old Scully. The Easterner was encased in reserve; the cowboy sat in wide-mouthed amazement, forgetting to eat, while Johnnie wrathily demolished great plates of food. The daughters of the house, when they were obliged to replenish the biscuits, approached as warily as Indians, and, having succeeded in their purpose, fled with ill-concealed trepidation. The Swede domineered the whole feast, he gave it the appearance of a cruel bacchanal. He seemed to have grown suddenly taller; he gazed, brutally disdainful, into every face. His voice rang through the room. Once he jabbed out harpoon-fashion with his fork to pinion a biscuit, the weapon nearly impaled the hand of the Easterner, which had been stretched quietly out for the same biscuit.

After supper, as the men fled toward the other room, the Swede smote Scully ruthlessly on the shoulder. "Well, old boy, that was a good, square meal." Johnnie looked hopefully at his father; he knew that shoulder was tender from an old fall; and, indeed, it appeared for a moment as if Scully was going to flame out over the matter, but in the end he smiled a sickly smile and remained silent. The others understood from his manner that he was admitting his responsibility for the Swede's new view-point.

Johnnie, however, addressed his parent in an aside. "Why don't you license somebody to kick you downstairs?" Scully scowled darkly by way of reply.

When they were gathered about the stove, the Swede insisted on another game of High-Five. Scully gently deprecated the plan at first, but the Swede turned a wolfish glare upon him. The old man subsided, and the Swede canvassed the others. In his tone there was always a great threat. The cowboy and the Easterner both remarked indifferently that they would play. Scully said that he would presently have to go to meet the 6.58 train, and so the Swede turned menacingly upon Johnnie. For a moment their glances crossed like blades, and then Johnnie smiled and said, "Yes, I'll play."

They formed a square, with the little board on their knees. The Easterner and the Swede were again partners. As the play went on, it was noticeable that the cowboy was not board-whacking as usual. Meanwhile, Scully, near the lamp, had put on his spectacles and, with an appearance curiously like an old priest, was reading a newspaper. In time he went out to meet the 6.58 train, and, despite his precautions, a gust of polar wind whirled into the room as he opened the door. Besides scattering the cards, it chilled the players to the marrow. The Swede cursed frightfully. When Scully returned, his entrance disturbed a cosy and friendly scene. The Sweden again cursed. But presently they were once more intent, their heads bent forward and their hands moving swiftly. The Swede had adopted the fashion of board-whacking.

Scully took up his paper and for a long time remained immersed in matters which were extraordinarily remote from him. The lamp burned badly, and once he stopped to adjust the wick. The newspaper, as he turned from page to page, rustled with a slow and comfortable sound. Then suddenly he heard three terrible words: "You are cheatin'!"

Such scenes often prove that there can be little of dramatic import in environment. Any room can present a tragic front; any room can be comic. This little den was now hideous as a torture-chamber. The new faces of the men themselves had changed it upon the instant. The Swede held a huge fist in front of Johnnie's face, while the latter looked steadily over it into the blazing orbs of his accuser. The Easterner had grown pallid; the cowboy's jaw had dropped in that expression of bovine amazement which was one of his important mannerisms. After the three words, the first sound in the room was made by Scully's paper as it floated forgotten to his feet. His spectacles had also fallen from his nose, but by a clutch he had saved them in air. His hand, grasping the spectacles, now remained poised awkwardly and near his shoulder. He stared at the card-players.

Probably the silence was while a second elapsed. Then, if the floor had been suddenly twitched out from under the men they could not have moved quicker. The five had projected themselves headlong toward a common point. It happened that Johnnie, in rising to hurl himself upon the Swede, had stumbled slightly because of his curiously instinctive care for the cards and the board. The loss of the moment allowed time for the arrival of Scully, and also allowed the cowboy time to give the Swede a great push which sent him staggering back. The men found tongue together, and hoarse shouts of rage, appeal, or fear burst from every throat. The cowboy pushed and jostled feverishly at the Swede, and the Easterner and Scully clung wildly to Johnnie; but through the smoky air, above the swaying bodies of the peace-compellers, the eyes of the two warriors ever sought each other in glances of challenge that were at once hot and steely.

Of course the board had been been overturned, and now the whole company of cards was scattered over the floor, where the boots of the men trampled the fat and painted kings and queens as they gazed with their silly eyes at the war that was waging above them.

Scully's voice was dominating the yells. "Stop now! Stop, I say! Stop, now ——"

Johnnie, as he struggled to burst through the rank formed by Scully and the Easterner, was crying, "Well, he says I cheated! He says I cheated! I won't allow no man to say I cheated! If he says I cheated, he's a —— ——!"

The cowboy was telling the Swede, "Quit, now! Quit, d'ye hear ——"

The screams of the Swede never ceased: "He did cheat! I saw him! I saw him ——"

As for the Easterner, he was importuning in a voice that was not heeded: "Wait a moment, can't you? Oh, wait a moment. What's the good of a fight over a game of cards? Wait a moment ——"

In this tumult no complete sentences were clear. "Cheat"—"Quit"— "He says"—these fragments pierced the uproar and rang out sharply. It was remarkable that, whereas Scully undoubtedly made the most noise, he was the least heard of any of the riotous band.

Then suddenly there was a great cessation. It was as if each man had paused for breath; and although the room was still lighted with the anger of men, it could be seen that there was no danger of immediate conflict, and at once Johnnie, shouldering his way forward, almost succeeded in confronting the Swede. "What did you say I cheated for? What did you say I cheated for? I don't cheat, and I won't let no man say I do!"

The Swede said, "I saw you! I saw you!"

"Well," cried Johnnie, "I'll fight any man what says I cheat!"

"No, you won't," said the cowboy. "Not here."

"Ah, be still, can't you?" said Scully, coming between them.

The quiet was sufficient to allow the Easterner's voice to be heard. He was repeating, "Oh, wait a moment, can't you? What's the good of a fight over a game of cards? Wait a moment!"

Johnnie, his red face appearing above his father's shoulder, hailed the Swede again. "Did you say I cheated?"

The Swede showed his teeth. "Yes."

"Then," said Johnnie, "we must fight."

"Yes, fight," roared the Swede. He was like a demoniac. "Yes, fight! I'll show you what kind of a man I am! I'll show you who you want to fight! Maybe you think I can't fight! Maybe you think I can't! I'll show you, you skin, you card-sharp! Yes, you cheated! You cheated! You cheated!"

"Well, let's go at it, then, mister," said Johnnie, coolly.

The cowboy's brow was beaded with sweat from his efforts in intercepting all sorts of raids. He turned in despair to Scully. "What are you goin' to do now?"

A change had come over the Celtic visage of the old man. He now seemed all eagerness; his eyes glowed.

"We'll let them fight," he answered, stalwartly. "I can't put up with it any longer. I've stood this damned Swede till I'm sick. We'll let them fight."

iv

The men prepared to go out of doors. The Easterner was so nervous that he had great difficulty in getting his arms into the sleeves of his new leather coat. As the cowboy drew his fur cap down over his ears his hands trembled. In fact, Johnnie and old Scully were the only ones who displayed no agitation. These preliminaries were conducted without words.

Scully threw open the door. "Well, come on," he said. Instantly a terrific wind caused the flame of the lamp to struggle at its wick, while a puff of black smoke sprang from the chimney-top. The stove was in mid-current of the blast, and its voice swelled to equal the roar of the storm. Some of the scarred and bedabbled cards were caught up from the floor and dashed helplessly against the farther wall. The men lowered their heads and plunged into the tempest as into a sea.

No snow was falling, but great whirls and clouds of flakes, swept up from the ground by the frantic winds, were streaming southward with the speed of bullets. The covered land was blue with the sheen of an unearthly satin, and there was no other hue save where, at the low, black railway station—which seemed incredibly distant—one light gleamed like a tiny jewel. As the men floundered into a thighdeep drift, it was known that the Swede was bawling out something. Scully went to him, put a hand on his shoulder, and projected an ear. "What's that you say?" he shouted.

"I say," bawled the Swede again, "I won't stand much show against this gang. I know you'll all pitch on me."

Scully smote him reproachfully on the arm. "Tut, man!" he yelled. The wind tore the words from Scully's lips and scattered them far alee.

"You are all a gang of ——" boomed the Swede, but the storm also seized the remainder of this sentence.

Immediately turning their backs upon the wind, the men had swung around a corner to the sheltered side of the hotel. It was the function of the little house to preserve here, amid this great devastation of snow, an irregular V-shape of heavily encrusted grass, which crackled beneath the feet. One could imagine the great drifts piled against the windward side. When the party reached the comparative peace of this spot it was found that the Swede was still bellowing.

"Oh, I know what kind of a thing this is! I know you'll all pitch on me. I can't lick you all!"

Scully turned upon him panther-fashion. "You'll not have to whip all of us. You'll have to whip my son Johnnie. An' the man what troubles you durin' that time will have me to dale with."

The arrangements were swiftly made. The two men faced each other, obedient to the harsh commands of Scully, whose face, in the subtly luminous gloom, could be seen set in the austere impersonal lines that are pictured on the countenances of the Roman veterans. The Easterner's teeth were chattering, and he was hopping up and down like a mechanical toy. The cowboy stood rock-like.

The contestants had not stripped off any clothing. Each was in his ordinary attire. Their fists were up, and they eyed each other in a calm that had the elements of leonine cruelty in it.

During this pause, the Easterner's mind, like a film, took lasting impressions of three men—the iron-nerved master of the ceremony; the Swede, pale, motionless, terrible; and Johnnie, serene yet ferocious, brutish yet heroic. The entire prelude had in it a tragedy greater than the tragedy of action, and this aspect was accentuated by the long, mellow cry of the blizzard, as it sped the tumbling and wailing flakes into the black abyss of the south.

"Now!" said Scully.

The two combatants leaped forward and crashed together like bullocks. There was heard the cushioned sound of blows, and of a curse squeezing out from between the tight teeth of one.

As for the spectators, the Easterner's pent-up breath exploded from him with a pop of relief, absolute relief from the tension of the preliminaries. The cowboy bounded into the air with a yowl. Scully was immovable as from supreme amazement and fear at the fury of the fight which he himself had permitted and arranged.

For a time the encounter in the darkness was such a perplexity of flying arms that it presented no more detail than would a swiftly revolving wheel. Occasionally a face, as if illumined by a flash of light, would shine out, ghastly and marked with pink spots. A moment later, the men might have been known as shadows, if it were not for the involuntary utterance of oaths that came from them in whispers.

Suddenly a holocaust of warlike desire caught the cowboy, and he bolted forward with the speed of a broncho. "Go it, Johnnie! go it! Kill him! Kill him!"

Scully confronted him. "Kape back," he said; and by his glance the cowboy could tell that this man was Johnnie's father.

To the Easterner there was a monotony of unchangeable fighting that was an abomination. This confused mingling was eternal to his sense, which was concentrated in a longing for the end, the priceless end. Once the fighters lurched near him, and as he scrambled hastily backward he heard them breathe like men on the rack.

"Kill him, Johnnie! Kill him! Kill him! him!" The cowboy's face was contorted like one of those agony masks in museums.

"Keep still," said Scully, icily.

Then there was a sudden loud grunt, incomplete, cut short, and Johnnie's body swung away from the Swede and fell with sickening heaviness to the grass. The cowboy was barely in time to prevent the mad Swede from finging himself upon his prone adversary. "No, you don't, said the cowboy, interposing an arm. "Wait a second."

Scully was at his son's side. "Johnnie! Johnnie, me boy!" His voice had a quality of melancholy tenderness. "Johnnie! Can you go on with it?" He looked anxiously down into the bloody, pulpy face of his son.

There was a moment of silence, and then Johnnie answered in his ordinary voice, "Yes, I—it—yes."

Assisted by his father he struggled to his feet. "Wait a bit now till you git your wind," said the old man.

A few paces away the cowboy was lecturing the Swede. "No, you don't! Wait a second!"

The Easterner was plucking at Scully's sleeve. Oh, this is enough." he pleaded. "This is enough! Let it go as it stands. This is enough!"

"Bill," said Scully, "git out of the road." The cowboy stepped aside. "Now." The combatants were actuated by a new caution as they advanced toward collision. They glared at each other, and then the Swede aimed a lightening blow that carried with it his entire weight. Johnnie was evidently half stupid from weakness, but he miraculously dodged, and his fist sent the over-balanced Swede sprawling.

The cowboy, Scully, and the Easterner burst into a cheer that was like the chorus of triumphant soldiery, but before its conclusion the Swede had scuffled agilely to his feet and come in berserk abandon at his foe. There was another perplexity of flying arms, and Johnnie's body again swung away and fell, even as a bundle might fall from a roof. The Swede instantly staggered to a little wind-waved tree and leaned upon it, breathing like an engine, while his savage and flame-lit eyes roamed from face to face as the men bent over Johnnie. There was a splendour of isolation in his situation at this time which the Easterner felt once when, lifting his eyes from the man on the ground, he beheld that mysterious and lonely figure, waiting.

"Are you any good yet, Johnnie?" asked Scully in a broken voice.

The son gasped and opened his eyes languidly. After a moment he answered, "No—I ain't—any good—any—more." Then, from shame and bodily ill, he began to weep, the tears furrowing down through the blood-stains on his face. "He was too—too—too heavy for me."

Scully straightened and addressed the waiting figure. "Stranger," he said, evenly, "it's all up with our side." Then his voice changed into that vibrant huskiness which is commonly the tone of the most simple and deadly announcements. "Johnnie is whipped."

Without replying, the victor moved off on the route to the front door of the hotel.

The cowboy was formulating new and unspellable blasphemies. The Easterner was startled to find that they were out in a wind that seemed to come direct from the shadowed arctic floes. He heard again the wail of the snow as it was flung to its grave in the south. He knew now that all this time the cold had been sinking into him deeper and deeper, and he wondered that he had not perished. He felt indifferent to the condition of the vanquished man.

"Johnnie, can you walk?" asked Scully.

"Did I hurt—hurt him any?" asked the son.

"Can you walk, boy? Can you walk?"

Johnnie's voice was suddenly strong. There was a robust impatience in it. "I asked you whether I hurt him any!"

"Yes, yes, Johnnie," answered the cowboy, consolingly; "he's hurt a good deal."

They raised him from the ground, and as soon as he was on his feet he went tottering off, rebuffing all attempts at assistance. When the party rounded the corner they were fairly blinded by the pelting of the snow. It burned their faces like fire. The cowboy carried Johnnie through the drift to the door. As they entered, some cards again rose from the floor and beat against the wall.

The Easterner rushed to the stove. He was so profoundly chilled that he almost dared to embrace the glowing iron. The Swede was not in the room. Johnnie sank into a chair and, folding his arms on his knees, buried his face in them. Scully, warming one foot and then the other at a rim of the stove, muttered to himself with Celtic mournfulness. The cowboy had removed his fur cap, and with a dazed and rueful air he was running one hand through his tousled locks. From overhead they could hear the creaking of boards, as the Swede tramped here and there is his room.

The sad quiet was broken by the sudden flinging open of a door that led toward the kitchen. It was instantly followed by an inrush of women. They precipitated themselves upon Johnnie amid a chorus of lamentation. Before they carried their prey off to the kitchen, there to be bathed and harangued with that mixture of sympathy and abuse which is a feat of their sex, the mother straightened herself and fixed old Scully with an eye of stern reproach. "Shame be upon you, Patrick Scully!" she cried. "Your own son, too. Shame be upon you!"

"There, now! Be quiet, now!" said the old man, weakly.

"Shame be upon you, Patrick Scully!" The girls, rallying to this slogan, sniffed disdainfully in the direction of those trembling accomplices, the cowboy and the Easterner. Presently they bore Johnnie away, and left the three men to dismal reflection.

vii

"I'd like to fight this here Dutchman myself," said the cowboy, breaking a long silence.

Scully wagged his head sadly. "No, that wouldn't do. It wouldn't be right. It wouldn't be right."

"Well, why wouldn't it?" argued the cowboy. "I don't see no harm in it."

"No," answered Scully, with mournful heroism. "It wouldn't be right. It was Johnnie's fight, and now we mustn't whip the man just because he whipped Johnnie."

"Yes, that's true enough," said the cowboy; "but—he better not get fresh with me, because I couldn't stand no more of it."

"You'll not say a word to him," commanded Scully, and even then they heard the tread of the Swede on the stairs. His entrance was made theatric. He swept the door back with a bang and swaggered to the middle of the room. No one looked at him. "Well," he cried, insolently, at Scully, "I s'pose you'll tell me now how much I owe you?"

The old man remained stolid. "You don't owe me nothin'."

"Huh!" said the Swede, "huh! Don't owe 'im nothin'."

The cowboy addressed the Swede. "Stranger, I don't see how you come to be so gay around here."

Old Scully was instantly alert. "Stop!" he shouted, holding his hand forth, fingers upward. "Bill, you shut up!"

The cowboy spat carelessly into the sawdust-box. "I didn't say a word, did I?" he asked.

"Mr. Scully," called the Swede, "how much do I owe you?" It was seen that he was attired for departure, and that he had his valise in his hand.

"You don't owe me nothin'," repeated Scully in the same imperturbable way.

"Huh!" said the Swede. "I guess you're right. I guess if it was any way at all, you'd owe me somethin'. That's what I guess." He turned to the cowboy. " 'Kill him! Kill him! Kill him!' " he mimicked, and then guffawed victoriously. " 'Kill him!' " He was convulsed with ironical humour.

But he might have been jeering the dead. The three men were immovable and silent, staring with glassy eyes at the stove.

The Swede opened the door and passed into the storm, giving one derisive glance backward at the still group.

As soon as the door was closed, Scully and the cowboy leaped to their feet and began to curse. They trampled to and fro, waving their arms and smashing into the air with their fists. "Oh, but that was a hard minute!" wailed Scully. "That was a hard minute! Him there leerin' and scoffin'! One bang at his nose was worth forty dollars to me that minute! How did you stand it, Bill?"

"How did I stand it?" cried the cowboy in a quivering voice. "How did I stand it? Oh!"

The old man burst into a sudden brogue. "I'd like to take that Swade," he wailed, "and hould 'im down on a shtone flure and bate 'im to a jelly wid a shtick!"

The cowboy groaned in sympathy. "I'd like to git him by the neck and ha-ammer him"—he brought his hand down on a chair with a noise like a pistol-shot—"hammer that there Dutchman until he couldn't tell himself from a dead coyote!"

"I'd bate 'im until he ——"

"I'd show *him* some things ——"

And then together they raised a yearning, fanatic cry—"Oh-o-oh! if we only could ——"

"Yes"

"Yes"

"And then I'd ——"

"O-o-oh!"

viii

The Swede, tightly gripping his valise, tacked across the face of the storm as if he carried sails. He was following a line of little naked, grasping trees which, he knew, must mark the way of the road. His face, fresh from the pounding of Johnnie's fists, felt more pleasure than pain in the wind and the driving snow. A number of square shapes loomed upon him finally, and he knew them as the houses of the main body of the town. He found a street and made travel along it, leaning heavily upon the wind whenever, at a corner, a terrific blast caught him.

He might have been in a deserted village. We picture the world as thick with conquering and elate humanity, but here, with the bugles of the tempest pealing, it was hard to imagine a peopled earth. One viewed the existence of man then as a marvel, and conceded a glamour of wonder to these lice which were caused to cling to a whirling, fire-smitten, ice-locked, disease-stricken, space-lost bulb. The conceit of man was explained by this storm to be the very engine of life. One was a coxcomb not to die in it. However, the Swede found a saloon.

In front of it an indomitable red light was burning, and the snowflakes were made blood-colour as they flew through the circumscribed territory of the lamp's shining. The Swede pushed open the door of the saloon and entered. A sanded expanse was before him, and at the end of it four men sat about a table drinking. Down one side of the room extended a radiant bar, and its guardian was leaning upon his elbows listening to the talk of the men at the table. The Swede dropped his valise upon the floor and, smiling fraternally upon the barkeeper, said, "Gimme some whisky, will you?" The man placed a bottle, a whisky-glass, and a glass of ice-thick water upon the bar. The Swede poured himself an abnormal portion of whisky and drank it in three gulps. "Pretty bad night," remarked the bartender, indifferently. He was making the pretension of blindness which is usually a distinction of his class; but it could have been seen that he was furtively studying the half-erased blood-stains on the face of the Swede. "Bad night," he said again.

"Oh, it's good enough for me," replied the Swede, hardily, as he poured himself some more whisky. The barkeeper took his coin and manœuvred it through its reception by the highly nickelled cash-machine. A bell rang; a card labelled "20 cts." had appeared.

"No," continued the Swede, "this isn't too bad weather. It's good enough for me."

"So?" murmured the barkeeper, languidly.

The copious drams made the Swede's eyes swim, and he breathed a trifle heavier. "Yes, I like this weather. I like it. It suits me." It was apparently his design to impart a deep significance to these words.

"So?" murmured the bartender again. He turned to gaze dreamily at the scroll-like birds and bird-like scrolls which had been drawn with soap upon the mirrors in back of the bar.

"Well, I guess I'll take another drink," said the Swede, presently. "Have something?"

"No, thanks; I'm not drinkin'," answered the bartender. Afterward he asked, "How did you hurt your face?"

The Swede immediately began to boast loudly. "Why, in a fight. I thumped the soul out of a man down here at Scully's hotel."

The interest of the four men at the table was at last aroused.

"Who was it?" said one.

"Johnnie Scully," blustered the Swede. "Son of the man what runs it. He will be pretty near dead for some weeks, I can tell you. I made a nice thing of him, I did. He couldn't get up. They carried him in the house. Have a drink?"

Instantly the men in some subtle way encased themselves in reserve. "No, thanks," said one. The group was of curious formation. Two were prominent local business men; one was the district attorney; and one was a professional gambler of the kind known as "square." But a scrutiny of the group would not have enabled an observer to pick the gambler from the men of more reputable pursuits. He was, in fact, a man so delicate in manner, when among people of fair class, and so judicious in his choice of victims, that in the strictly masculine part of the town's life he had come to be explicitly trusted and admired. People called him a thoroughbred. The fear and contempt with which his craft was regarded were undoubtedly the reason why his quiet dignity shone conspicuous above the quiet dignity of men who might be merely hatters, billiard-markers, or grocery clerks. Beyond an occasional unwary traveller who came by rail, this gambler was supposed to prey solely upon reckless and senile farmers, who, when flush with good crops, drove into town in all the pride and confidence of an absolutely invulnerable stupidity. Hearing at times in circuitous fashion of the despoilment of such a farmer, the important men of Romper invariably laughed in contempt of the victim, and if they thought of the wolf at all, it was with a kind of pride at the knowledge that he would never dare think of attacking their wisdom and courage. Besides, it was popular that this gambler had a real wife and two real children in a neat cottage in a suburb, where he led an exemplary home life; and when any one even suggested a discrepancy in his character, the crowd immediately vociferated descriptions of this virtuous family circle. Then men who led exemplary home lives, and men who did not lead exemplary home lives, all subsided in a bunch, remarking that there was nothing more to be said.

However, when a restriction was placed upon him—as, for instance, when a strong clique of members of the new Pollywog Club refused to permit him, even as a spectator, to appear in the rooms of the organization— the candour and gentleness with which he accepted the judgment disarmed many of his foes and made his friends more desperately partisan. He invariably distinguished between himself and a respectable Romper man so quickly and frankly that his manner actually appeared to be a continual broadcast compliment.

And one must not forget to declare the fundamental fact of his entire position in Romper. It is irrefutable that in all affairs outside his business, in all matters that occur eternally and commonly between man and man, this thieving card-player was so generous, so just, so moral, that, in a contest, he could have put to flight the consciences of nine tenths of the citizens of Romper.

And so it happened that he was seated in this saloon with the two prominent local merchants and the district attorney.

The Swede continued to drink raw whisky, meanwhile babbling at the barkeeper and trying to induce him to indulge in potations. "Come on. Have a drink. Come on. What—no? Well, have a little one, then. By gawd, I've whipped a man to-night, and I want to celebrate. I whipped him good, too. Gentlemen," the Swede cried to the men at the table, "have a drink?"

"Ssh!" said the barkeeper.

The group at the table, although furtively attentive, had been pretending to be deep in talk, but now a man lifted his eyes toward the Swede and said, shortly, "Thanks. We don't want any more."

At this reply the Swede ruffled out his chest like a rooster. "Well," he exploded, "it seems I can't get anybody to drink with me in this town. Seems so, don't it? Well!"

"Ssh!" said the barkeeper.

"Say," snarled the Swede, "don't you try to shut me up. I won't have it. I'm a gentleman, and I want people to drink with me. And I want 'em to drink with me now. Now—do you understand?" He rapped the bar with his knuckles.

Years of experience had calloused the bartender. He merely grew sulky. "I hear you," he answered.

"Well," cried the Swede, "listen hard then. See those men over there? Well, they're going to drink with me, and don't you forget it. Now you watch."

"Hi!" yelled the barkeeper, "this won't do!"

"Why won't it?" demanded the Swede. He stalked over to the table, and by chance laid his hand upon the shoulder of the gambler. "How about this?" he asked wrathfully. "I asked you to drink with me."

The gambler simply twisted his head and spoke over his shoulder. "My friend, I don't know you."

"Oh, hell!" answered the Swede, "come and have a drink."

"Now, my boy," advised the gambler, kindly, "take your hand off my shoulder and go 'way and mind your own business." He was a little, slim man, and it seemed strange to hear him use this tone of heroic patronage to the burly Swede. The other men at the table said nothing.

"What! You won't drink with me, you little dude? I'll make you, then! I'll make you!" The Swede had grasped the gambler frenziedly at the throat, and was dragging him from his chair. The other men sprang up. The barkeeper dashed around the corner of his bar. There was a great tumult, and then was seen a long blade in the hand of the gambler. It shot forward, and a human body, this citadel of virtue, wisdom, power, was pierced as easily as if it had been a melon. The Swede fell with a cry of supreme astonishment.

The prominent merchants and the district attorney must have at once tumbled out of the place backward. The bartender found himself hanging limply to the arm of a chair and gazing into the eyes of a murderer.

"Henry," said the latter, as he wiped his knife on one of the towels that hung beneath the bar rail, "you tell 'em where to find me. I'll be home, waiting for 'em." Then he vanished. A moment afterward the barkeeper was in the street dinning through the storm for help and, moreover, companionship.

The corpse of the Swede, alone in the saloon, had its eyes fixed upon a dreadful legend that dwelt atop of the cash-machine: "This registers the amount of your purchase."

ix

Months later, the cowboy was frying pork over the stove of a little ranch near the Dakota line, when there was a quick thud of hoofs outside, and presently the Easterner entered with the letters and the papers.

"Well," said the Easterner at once, "the chap that killed the Swede has got three years. Wasn't much, was it?"

"He has? Three years?" The cowboy poised his pan of pork, while he ruminated upon the news. "Three years. That ain't much."

"No. It was a light sentence," replied the Easterner as he unbuckled his spurs. "Seems there was a good deal of sympathy for him in Romper."

"If the bartender had been any good," observed the cowboy, thoughtfully, "he would have gone in and cracked that there Dutchman on the head with a bottle in the beginnin' of it and stopped all this here murderin'."

"Yes, a thousand things might have happened," said the Easterner, tartly.

The cowboy returned his pan of pork to the fire, but his philosophy continued. "It's funny, ain't it? If he hadn't said Johnnie was cheatin' he'd be alive this minute. He was an awful fool. Game played for fun, too. Not for money. I believe he was crazy."

"I feel sorry for that gambler," said the Easterner.

"Oh, so do I," said the cowboy. "He don't deserve none of it for killin' who he did."

"The Swede might not have been killed if everything had been square."

"Might not have been killed?" exclaimed the cowboy. "Everythin' square? Why, when he said that Johnnie was cheatin' and acted like such a jackass? And then in the saloon he fairly walked up to git hurt?" With these arguments the cowboy browbeat the Easterner and reduced him to rage.

"You're a fool!" cried the Easterner, viciously. "You're a bigger jackass than the Swede by a million majority. Now let me tell you one thing. Let me tell you something. Listen! Johnnie *was* cheating!"

" 'Johnnie'," said the cowboy, blankly. There was a minute of silence, and then he said, robustly, "Why, no. The game was only for fun."

"Fun or not," said the Easterner, "Johnnie was cheating. I saw him. I know it. I saw him. And I refused to stand up and be a man. I let the Swede fight it out alone. And you—you were simply puffing around the place and wanting to fight. And then old Scully himself! We are all in it! This poor gambler isn't even a noun. He is kind of an adverb. Every sin is the result of a collaboration. We, five of us, have collaborated in the murder of this Swede. Usually there are from a dozen to forty women really involved in every murder, but in this case it seems to be only five men—you, I, Johnnie, old Scully; and that fool of an unfortunate gambler came merely as a culmination, the apex of a human movement, and gets all the punishment."

The cowboy, injured and rebellious, cried out blindly into this fog of mysterious theory: "Well, I didn't do anythin', did I?"

The Bride Comes to
Yellow Sky

stephen crane

i

THE GREAT PULLMAN WAS WHIRLING ONWARD with such dignity of motion that a glance from the window seemed simply to prove that the plains of Texas were pouring eastward. Vast flats of green grass, dull-hued spaces of mesquit and catus, little groups of frame houses, woods of light and tender trees, all were sweeping into the east, sweeping over the horizon, a precipice.

A newly married pair had boarded this coach at San Antonio. The man's face was reddened from many days in the wind and sun, and a direct result of his new black clothes was that his brick-colored hands were constantly performing in a most conscious fashion. From time to time he looked down respectfully at his attire. He sat with a hand on each knee, like a man waiting in a barber's shop. The glances he devoted to other passengers were furtive and shy.

The bride was not pretty, nor was she very young. She wore a dress of blue cashmere, with small reservations of velvet here and there, and with steel buttons abounding. She continually twisted her head to regard her puff sleeves, very stiff, straight, and high. They embarrassed her. It was quite apparent that she had cooked, and that she expected to cook, dutifully. The blushes caused by the careless scrutiny of some passengers as she had entered the car were strange to see upon this plain, under-class countenance, which was drawn in placid, almost emotionless lines.

Reprinted by courtesy of Alfred A. Knopf, Inc.

They were evidently very happy. "Ever been in a parlor car before?" he asked, smiling with delight.

"No," she answered; "I never was. It's fine, ain't it?"

"Great! And then after a while we'll go forward to the diner, and get a big lay-out. Finest meal in the world. Charge a dollar."

"Oh, do they?" cried the bride. "Charge a dollar? Why, that's too much —for us—ain't it, Jack?"

"Not this trip, anyhow," he answered bravely. "We're going to go the whole thing."

Later he explained to her about the trains. "You see, it's a thousand miles from one end of Texas to the other; and this train runs right across it, and never stops but four times." He had the pride of an owner. He pointed out to her the dazzling fittings of the coach; and in truth her eyes opened wider as she contemplated the sea-green figured velvet, the shining brass, silver, and glass, the wood that gleamed as darkly brilliant as the surface of a pool of oil. At one end a bronze figure sturdily held a support for a separated chamber, and at convenient places on the ceiling were frescos in olive and silver.

To the minds of the pair, their surroundings reflected the glory of their marriage that morning in San Antonio; this was the environment of their new estate; and the man's face in particular beamed with an elation that made him appear ridiculous to the Negro porter. This individual at times surveyed them from afar with an amused and superior grin. On other occasions he bullied them with skill in ways that did not make it exactly plain to them that they were being bullied. He subtly used all the manners of the most unconquerable kind of snobbery. He oppressed them; but of this oppression they had small knowledge, and they speedily forgot that infrequently a number of travelers covered them with stares of derisive enjoyment. Historically there was supposed to be something infinitely humorous in their situation.

"We are due in Yellow Sky at 3:42," he said, looking tenderly into her eyes.

"Oh, are we?" she said, as if she had not been aware of it. To evince surprise at her husband's statement was part of her wifely amiability. She took from a pocket a little silver watch; and as she held it before her, and stared at it with a frown of attention, the new husband's face shone.

"I bought it in San Anton' from a friend of mine," he told her gleefully.

"It's seventeen minutes past twelve," she said, looking up at him with a kind of shy and clumsy coquetry. A passenger, noting this play, grew excessively sardonic, and winked at himself in one of the numerous mirrors.

At last they went to the dining car. Two rows of Negro waiters, in glowing white suits, surveyed their entrance with the interest, and also the equanimity, of men who had been forewarned. The pair fell to the lot of a waiter who happened to feel pleasure in steering them through their meal. He viewed them with the manner of a fatherly pilot, his countenance radiant with benevolence. The patronage, entwined with the ordinary deference, was not plain to them. And yet, as they returned to their coach, they showed in their faces a sense of escape.

To the left, miles down a long purple slope, was a little ribbon of mist where moved the keening Rio Grande. The train was approaching it at an angle, and the apex was Yellow Sky. Presently it was apparent that, as the distance from Yellow Sky grew shorter, the husband became commensurately restless. His brick-red hands were more insistent in their prominence. Occasionally he was even rather absent-minded and faraway when the bride leaned forward and addressed him.

As a matter of truth, Jack Potter was beginning to find the shadow of a deed weigh upon him like a leaden slab. He, the town marshal of Yellow Sky, a man known, liked, and feared in his corner, a prominent person, had gone to San Antonio to meet a girl he believed he loved, and there, after the usual prayers, had actually induced her to marry him, without consulting Yellow Sky for any part of the transaction. He was now bringing his bride before an innocent and unsuspecting community.

Of course people in Yellow Sky married as it pleased them, in accordance with a general custom; but such was Potter's thought of his duty to his friends, or of their idea of his duty, or of an unspoken form which does not control men in these matters, that he felt he was heinous. He had committed an extraordinary crime. Face to face with this girl in San Antonio, and spurred by his sharp impulse, he had gone headlong over all the social hedges. At San Antonio he was like a man hidden in the dark. A knife to sever any friendly duty, any form, was easy to his hand in that remote city. But the hour of Yellow Sky—the hour of daylight—was approaching.

He knew full well that his marriage was an important thing to his town. It could only be exceeded by the burning of the new hotel. His friends could not forgive him. Frequently he had reflected on the advisability of telling them by telegraph, but a new cowardice had been upon him. He feared to do it. And now the train was hurrying him toward a scene of amazement, glee, and reproach. He glanced out of the window at the line of haze swinging slowly in toward the train.

Yellow Sky had a kind of brass band, which played painfully, to the delight of the populace. He laughed without heart as he thought of it. If the citizens could dream of his prospective arrival with his bride, they would parade the band at the station and escort them, amid cheers and laughing congratulations, to his adobe home.

He resolved that he would use all the devices of speed and plainscraft in marking the journey from the station to his house. Once within that safe citadel, he could issue some sort of vocal bulletin, and then not go among the citizens until they had time to wear off a little of their enthusiasm.

The bride looked anxiously at him. "What's worrying you Jack?"

He laughed again. "I'm not worrying, girl; I'm only thinking of Yellow Sky."

She flushed in comprehension.

A sense of mutual guilt invaded their minds and developed a finer tenderness. They looked at each other with eyes softly aglow. But Potter often laughed the same nervous laugh; the flush upon the bride's face seemed quite permanent.

The traitor to the feelings of Yellow Sky narrowly watched the speeding landscape. "We're nearly there," he said.

Presently the porter came and announced the proximity of Potter's home. He held a brush in his hand, and, with all his airy superiority gone, he brushed Potter's new clothes as the latter slowly turned this way and that way. Potter fumbled out a coin and gave it to the porter, as he had seen others do. It was a heavy and muscle-bound business, as that of a man shoeing his first horse.

The porter took their bag, and as the train began to slow they moved forward to the hooded platform of the car. Presently the two engines and their long string of coaches rushed into the station of Yellow Sky.

"They have to take water here," said Potter, from a constricted throat and in mournful cadence, as one announcing death. Before the train stopped his eye had swept the length of the platform, and he was glad and astonished to see there was none upon it but the station agent, who, with a slightly hurried and anxious air, was walking toward the water tanks. When the train had halted, the porter alighted first, and placed in position a little temporary step.

"Come on, girl," said Potter, hoarsely. As he helped her down they each laughed on a false note. He took the bag from the Negro, and bade his wife cling to his arm. As they slunk rapidly away, his hangdog glance perceived that they were unloading the two trunks, and also that the station agent, far ahead near the baggage car, had turned and was running toward him, making gestures. He laughed, and groaned as he laughed, when he noted the first effect of his marital bliss upon Yellow Sky. He gripped his wife's arm firmly to his side, and they fled. Behind them the porter stood, chuckling fatuously.

ii

The California express on the Southern Railway was due at Yellow Sky in twenty-one minutes. There were six men at the bar of the Weary Gentleman saloon. One was a drummer who talked a great deal and rapidly; three were Texans who did not care to talk at that time; and two were Mexican sheep-herders, who did not talk as a general practice in the Weary Gentleman saloon. The barkeeper's dog lay on the boardwalk that crossed in front of the door. His head was on his paws, and he glanced drowsily here and there with the constant vigilance of a dog that is kicked on occasion. Across the sandy street were some vivid green grass-plots, so wonderful in appearance, amid the sands that burned near them in a blazing sun, that they caused a doubt in the mind. They exactly resembled the grass mats used to represent lawns on the stage. At the cooler end of the railway station, a man without a coat sat in a tilted chair and smoked his pipe. The fresh-cut bank of the Rio Grande circled near the town, and there could be seen beyond it a great plum-colored plain of mesquit.

Save for the busy drummer and his companions in the saloon, Yellow Sky was dozing. The newcomer leaned gracefully upon the bar, and recited many tales with the confidence of a bard who has come upon a new field.

"—and at the moment that the old man fell downstairs with the bureau in his arms, the old woman was coming up with two scuttles of coal, and of course—"

The drummer's tale was interrupted by a young man who suddenly appeared in the open door. He cried: "Scratchy Wilson's drunk, and has turned loose with both hands." The two Mexicans at once set down their glasses and faded out of the rear entrance of the saloon.

The drummer, innocent and jocular, answered: "All right, old man. S'pose he has? Come in and have a drink, anyhow."

But the information had made such an obvious cleft in every skull in the room that the drummer was obliged to see its importance. All had become instantly solemn. "Say," said he, mystified, "what is this?" His three companions made the introductory gesture of eloquent speech; but the young man at the door forestalled them.

"It means, my friend," he answered, as he came into the saloon, "that for the next two hours this town won't be a health resort."

The barkeeper went to the door, and locked and barred it; reaching out of the window, he pulled in heavy wooden shutters, and barred them. Immediately a solemn, chapellike gloom was upon the place. The drummer was looking from one to another.

"But say," he cried, "what is this, anyhow? You don't mean there is going to be a gun fight?"

"Don't know whether there'll be a fight or not," answered one man, grimly, "but there'll be some shootin'—some good shootin'."

The young man who had warned them waved his hand. "Oh, there'll be a fight fast enough, if any one wants it. Anybody can get a fight out there in the street. There's a fight just waiting."

The drummer seemed to be swayed between the interest of a foreigner and a perception of personal danger.

"What did you say his name was?" he asked.

"Scratchy Wilson," they answered in chorus.

"And will he kill anybody? What are you going to do? Does this happen often? Does he rampage around like this once a week or so? Can he break in that door?"

"No; he can't break down that door," replied the barkeeper. "He's tried it three times. But when he comes you'd better lay down on the floor, stranger. He's dead sure to shoot at it, and a bullet may come through."

Thereafter the drummer kept a strict eye upon the door. The time had not yet been called for him to hug the floor, but, as a minor precaution, he sidled near to the wall. "Will he kill anybody?" he said again.

The men laughed low and scornfully at the question.

"He's out to shoot, and he's out for troube. Don't see any good in experimentin' with him."

"But what do you do in a case like this? What do you do?"

A man responded: "Why, he and Jack Potter—"

"But," in chorus the other men interrupted, "Jack Potter's in San Anton'."

"Well, who is he? What's he got to do with it?"

"Oh, he's the town marshal. He goes out and fights Scratchy when he gets on one of these tears."

"Wow!" said the drummer, mopping his brow. "Nice job he's got."

The voices had toned away to mere whisperings. The drummer wished to ask further questions, which were born of an increasing anxiety and bewilderment; but when he attempted them, the men merely looked at him in irritation and motioned him to remain silent. A tense waiting hush was upon them. In the deep shadows of the room their eyes shone as they listened for sounds from the street. One man made three gestures at the barkeeper; and the latter, moving like a ghost, handed him a glass and a bottle. The man poured a full glass of whisky, and set down the bottle noiselessly. He gulped the whisky in a swallow, and turned again toward the door in immovable silence. The drummer saw that the barkeeper, without a sound, had taken a Winchester from beneath the bar. Later he saw this individual beckoning to him, so he tiptoed across the room.

"You better come with me back of the bar."

"No, thanks," said the drummer, perspiring; "I'd rather be where I can make a break for the back door."

Whereupon the man of bottles made a kindly but peremptory gesture. The drummer obeyed it, and, finding himself seated on a box with his head below the level of the bar, balm was laid upon his soul at sight of various zinc and copper fittings that bore a resemblance to armor plate. The barkeeper took a seat comfortably upon an adjacent box.

"You see," he whispered, "this here Scratchy Wilson is a wonder with a gun—a perfect wonder; and when he goes on the war-trail, we hunt our holes—naturally. He's about the last one of the old gang that used to hang out along the river here. He's a terror when he's drunk. When he's sober he's all right—kind of simple—wouldn't hurt a fly—nicest fellow in town. But when he's drunk—whoo!"

There were periods of stillness. "I wish Jack Potter was back from San Anton'," said the barkeeper. "He shot Wilson up once—in the leg—and he would sail in and pull out the kinks in this thing."

Presently they heard from a distance the sound of a shot, followed by three wild yowls. It instantly removed a bond from the men in the darkened saloon. There was a shuffling of feet. They looked at each other. "Here he comes," they said.

iii

A man in a maroon-colored flannel shirt, which had been purchased for purposes of decoration, and made principally by some Jewish women on the East Side of New York, rounded a corner and walked into the middle of the main street of Yellow Sky. In either hand the man held a long, heavy, blue-black revolver. Often he yelled, and these cries rang through a semblance of a deserted village, shrilly flying over the roofs in a volume that seemed to have no relation to the ordinary vocal strength of a man. It was as if the surrounding stillness formed the arch of a tomb over him. These cries of ferocious challenge rang against walls of silence. And his boots had red tops with gilded imprints, of the kind beloved in winter by little sledding boys on the hillsides of New England.

The man's face flamed in a rage begot of whisky. His eyes, rolling, and yet keen for ambush, hunted the still doorways and windows. He walked with the creeping movement of the midnight cat. As it occurred to him, he roared menacing information. The long revolvers in his hands were as easy as straws; they were moved with an electric swiftness. The little fingers of each hand played sometimes in a musician's way. Plain from the low collar of the shirt, the cords of his neck straightened and sank, straightened and sank, as passion moved him. The only sounds were his terrible invitations. The calm adobes preserved their demeanor at the passing of this small thing in the middle of the street.

There was no offer of fight—no offer of fight. The man called to the sky. There were no attractions. He bellowed and fumed and swayed his revolvers here and everywhere.

The dog of the barkeeper of the Weary Gentleman saloon had not appreciated the advance of events. He yet lay dozing in front of his master's door. At sight of the dog, the man paused and raised his revolver humorously. At sight of the man, the dog sprang up and walked diagonally away, with a sullen head, and growling. The man yelled, and the dog broke into a gallop. As it was about to enter an alley, there was a loud noise, a whistling, and something spat the ground directly before it. The dog screamed, and, wheeling in terror, galloped headlong in a new direction. Again there was a noise, a whistling, and sand was kicked viciously before it. Fear-stricken, the dog turned and flurried like an animal in a pen. The man stood laughing, his weapons at his hips.

Ultimately the man was attracted by the closed door of the Weary Gentleman saloon. He went to it and, hammering with a revolver, demanded drink.

The door remaining imperturbable, he picked a bit of paper from the walk, and nailed it to the framework with a knife. He then turned his back contemptuously upon this popular resort and, walking to the opposite side of the street and spinning there on his heel quickly and lithely, fired at the bit of paper. He missed it by a half-inch. He swore at himself, and went away. Later he comfortably fusilladed the windows of his most intimate friend. The man was playing with this town; it was a toy for him.

But still there was no offer of fight. The name of Jack Potter, his ancient antagonist, entered his mind, and he concluded that it would be a glad thing if he should go to Potter's house, and by bombardment induce him to come out and fight. He moved in the direction of his desire, chanting Apache scale-music.

When he arrived at it, Potter's house presented the same still front as had the other adobes. Taking up a strategic position, the man howled a challenge. But this house regarded him as might a great stone god. It gave no sign. After a decent wait, the man howled further challenges, mingling with them wonderful epithets.

Presently there came the spectacle of a man churning himself into deepest rage over the immobility of a house. He fumed at it as the winter wind attacks a prairie cabin in the North. To the distance there should have gone the sound of a tumult like the fighting of two hundred Mexicans. As necessity bade him, he paused for breath or to reload his revolvers.

iv

Potter and his bride walked sheepishly and with speed. Sometimes they laughed together shamefacedly and low.

"Next corner, dear," he said finally.

They put forth the efforts of a pair walking bowed against a strong wind. Potter was about to raise a finger to point the first appearance of the new home when, as they circled the corner, they came face to face with a man in a maroon-colored shirt, who was feverishly pushing cartridges into a large revolver. Upon the instant the man dropped his revolver to the ground and, like lightning, whipped another from its holster. The second weapon was aimed at the bridegroom's chest.

There was a silence. Potter's mouth seemed to be merely a grave for his tongue. He exhibited an instinct to at once loosen his arm from the woman's grip, and he dropped the bag to the sand. As for the bride, her face had gone as yellow as old cloth. She was a slave to hideous rites, gazing at the apparitional snake.

The two men faced each other at a distance of three paces. He of the revolver smiled with a new and quiet ferocity.

"Tried to sneak up on me," he said. "Tried to sneak up on me!" His eyes grew more baleful. As Potter made a slight movement, the man thrust his revolver venomously forward. "No; don't you do it, Jack Potter. Don't you move a finger toward a gun just yet. Don't you move an eyelash. The time has come for me to settle with you, and I'm goin' to do it my own way, and loaf along with no interferin'. So if you don't want a gun bent on you, just mind what I tell you."

Potter looked at his enemy. "I ain't got a gun on me, Scratchy," he said. "Honest, I ain't." He was stiffening and steadying, but yet somewhere at the back of his mind a vision of the Pullman floated: the sea-green figured velvet, the shining brass, silver, and glass, the wood that gleamed as darkly brilliant as the surface of a pool of oil—all the glory of the marriage, the environment of the new estate. "You know I fight when it comes to fighting, Scratchy Wilson; but I ain't got a gun on me. You'll have to do all the shootin' yourself."

His enemy's face went livid. He stepped forward, and lashed his weapon to and fro before Potter's chest. "Don't you tell me you ain't got no gun on you, you whelp. Don't tell me no lie like that. There ain't a man in Texas ever seen you without no gun. Don't take me for no kid." His eyes blazed with light, and his throat worked like a pump.

"I ain't takin' you for no kid," answered Potter. His heels had not moved an inch backward. "I'm takin' you for a damn fool. I tell you I ain't got a gun, and I ain't. If you're goin' to shoot me up, you better begin now; you'll never get a chance like this again."

So much enforced reasoning had told on Wilson's rage; he was calmer. "If you ain't got a gun, why ain't you got a gun?" he sneered. "Been to Sunday school?"

"I ain't got a gun because I've just come from San Anton' with my wife. I'm married," said Potter. "And if I'd thought there was going to be any galoots like you prowling around when I brought my wife home, I'd had a gun, and don't you forget it."

"Married!" said Scratchy, not at all comprehending.

"Yes, married. I'm married," said Potter, distinctly.

"Married?" said Scratchy. Seemingly for the first time, he saw the drooping, drowning woman at the other man's side. "No!" he said. He was like a creature allowed a glimpse of another world. He moved a pace backward, and his arm, with the revolver, dropped to his side. "Is this the lady?" he asked.

"Yes; this is the lady," answered Potter.

There was another period of silence.

"Well," said Wilson at last, slowly, "I s'pose it's all off now."

"It's all off if you say so, Scratchy. You know I didn't make the trouble." Potter lifted his valise.

"Well, I 'low it's off, Jack," said Wilson. He was looking at the ground. "Married!" He was not a student of chivalry; it was merely that in the presence of this foreign condition he was a simple child of the earlier plains. He picked up his starboard revolver, and, placing both weapons in their holsters, he went away. His feet made funnel-shaped tracks in the heavy sand.

The Man
of the House

ethel colburn mayne

WHEN OLD DR. MOUNT DIED, and in a few months Mrs. Mount, the three Miss
Mounts left Nottingham for London. Their father had advised them to do
this when they became "whole orphans," as he said; there would be better
opportunities in London. He meant opportunities in their professions. Melicent, the eldest, was a maternity nurse; Thomasine a masseuse; Constance a
dispenser. Dr. Mount had insisted that his daughters should learn a trade—
not that they would need to live by it, for each would have a little money.
But he held that in another sense all men and women needed an occupation to
"live by"; and he had made up his mind that none of the girls would marry.
He said to Mrs. Mount that Thomasine and Constance talked too much, and
Melicent not enough.

"So, either way, men can't get to know them. If Melicent could speak
at all—" He mused a moment. "That young Brierly. . . . But he's as dumb
as she is, and if possible a little shyer. Affinity may go too far," said Dr.
Mount.

Mrs. Mount was "dumb," like Melicent; but Dr. Mount declared she
wasn't shy, so he had got to know her. She had never got to know *him,* but
that did not matter; one was enough, he said. She looked up when he mentioned "that young Brierly."

"Yes," said Dr. Mount. "He brought her lilies-of-the-valley the other
day, and now she has a bunch of artificial ones in her best hat. Didn't you
notice? *I* did."

Reprinted by permission of the Estate of the late Ethel Colburn Mayne and of
A. P. Watt & Son.

By the time Dr. Mount died Mr. Brierly had married a girl whom he had got to know, through her talking enough and not too much. Melicent was maternity nurse to their two babies, for Mrs. Brierly had no idea that there had ever been the little interlude, and was determined to engage her both times. The Brierlys had no more babies, but Melicent went on seeing a great deal of them and of "her" children.

While they were quite young, the three Miss Mounts had not been glad to learn their trades. They said it was a shame, or Thomasine and Constance did; Melicent said nothing. But as they grew older Thomasine and Constance became interested, and declared that after all it *was* a blessing not to be old maids.

Melicent, who sometimes of course did speak, said once: "Aren't we old maids?"

Thomasine and Constance both cried that indeed they weren't. You weren't old maids when you were business-women.

"At all events," said Constance, "no one *says* you are."

But Thomasine, who was most like their father, saw a little deeper. "That's not it; you really aren't. Old maids are failures; we aren't failures."

"Oh, I see," said Melicent.

They took their house in London in a long, perfectly straight street which at their end preserved a flavour of gentility. The houses in their block had no bay-windows, porticoes, nor red-brick trimmings; they were reticent, not tall for London, with nice first-floor balconies and hall-doors that well repaid attention from the housemaids. Three shallow steps led up to the halldoors; the areas weren't abysses.

They settled down with Nana, their old nurse, and a new youthful "general." Melicent and Thomasine worked up their connections; Constance found a post at once. They were not young, but neither were they old; their little incomes, added to their earnings, gave them ease of mind in money-matters. Very fond of one another, and successes now at their three trades, each brought into the common stock an ever-changing interest which some-times quite developed—Melicent's particularly. She entered more familiary the lives of those for whom she worked than Thomasine or Constance could; but all had anecdotes to make diversion for the others and for Nana.

Nana had her meals with them; they sat together in the evenings. Irene, the new importation, wasn't jealous. She would have thought it awful to be mewed up after dinner in the drawing-room; as for meals, she much pre-ferred hers in the kitchen, where she could eat as she liked and read the story in the *Daily Mirror* while she ate. Every one, in short, was happy, occupied, and sensible.

But there had to be a folly somewhere, and for the Miss Mounts and Nana that was Timothy the cat. He, like Nana, was a bit of the old home; they'd had him thirteen years. He was black, not handsome, of no special breed, although he had a plumy tail. The tail was Orientalism enough for them. "At all events," said Constance, "he can't swallow his fur." He was uncannily clever; he knew every word you said about him; "in another tick he'd speak to you," said Thomasine.

Like all cats, he did precisely as he pleased to the top limit of his powers. The Miss Mounts and Nana asked for nothing better. To claim anything from Timothy would be to make him less than cat. If he wanted to catch mice, he would; they never shut him in the coal-cellar, or withheld his meals to make him hungry. They bought fish for him three times a week; a saucer of milk stood always full in dining-room and kitchen; he drank tea too, and thin bread-and-butter was as much for him as them.

Timothy repaid their devotion. He showed no favouritism; perhaps, they said, he turned a little more to Nana in his illnesses, and the depression of the mating seasons when he saw the real males (for Timothy, as a kitten, had been "attended to") crouch moaning on the garden wall, or leap, still moaning, on the females who allured them. The Miss Mounts were cleareyed in these matters, and they noticed that he did, at such times, turn to Nana— she was always there for him, and they were not. She did not boast; she couldn't but be proud, yet would have been as proud, they knew, in quite another way, if he had taken his poor puzzled head and body to *their* laps, for Nana loved the three Miss Mounts with all her heart.

Melicent said once, in May, that if she had realised she wouldn't have permitted the early attention to Timothy. That was natural, the other two said; Melicent's profession led her to think more than they did about "That." The only thing that puzzled them was how she hadn't realised—for when Timothy was a kitten, she was already a maternity nurse. They asked her, and she didn't answer for a moment; then she said: "Well, I'm the eldest."

Next day she observed, when feeding Timothy at dinner time, that he had never had his chance. "However, we can make it up to *him*, in some ways."

Thomasine and Constance didn't understand. They say that she was nervous, as she always was in May; but even Constance, who was noted for outspokenness, did not ask her what she meant. She never liked to be asked that; she found it difficult enough to say what she did say.

Constance, like Thomasine, talked enormously—Thomasine the faster, but Constance the more lengthily. Nothing stopped her, except her own giggle. She would break off to giggle, but went on again before the other could break in. Thomasine had learnt to speak at the same time, and let the giggle do what it could for her; occasionally Constance noticed, and did stop.

Constance was the youngest, but the plainest. She was low on the ground, like a dachshund; pale, and wore rimless glasses. The blue eyes behind the glasses were well-set and honest. A cousin, whom they didn't like, said Connie's eyes were honest, all for nothing. It was silly—how could eyes or anything be honest all for nothing? but it wounded Constance. "Call her clever! *That* isn't clever, at all events," said Constance and took off her glasses, wiping them with the silk handkerchief she kept expressly for the purpose. The cousin had said too, when Constance first adopted them, that of all futile vanities she thought that rimless glasses were the chief.

"Smart women wear tortoiseshell rims, as dark as possible. Then the glasses are *amusingly* unbecoming. Isn't it clever?"

"All very well for them!" cried Thomasine. "Other people can't afford tortoiseshell."

"Celluloid or horn looks just the same," the cousin said.

"The fashion will soon die, then—always does when cheap imitations begin," retorted Thomasine, who knew quite as much about smart women as the cousin could; and indeed the cousin laughed and said that Thomasine was right. "But I detest the rimless things!"

It was afterwards that she said that about Connie's eyes. Of course it wasn't clever, Melicent agreed. She said so in her timid manner, looking very nice in her grey cloak with the white bonnet, for she had come back from a case, and met the cousin on the doorstep.

"You look like a nun," the cousin cried, "with your great melancholy eyes and your clear brows. *Mille-Saintes!*"

They hated that joke of the cousin's, who declared that "Melicent" came from the French, when the Miss Mounts all knew—for a very learned friend of Dr. Mount's had told them—that it was straight from the Greek, and meant as sweet as honey.

Melicent had come in smiling; the cousin pretended to be fond of her and she *was* as sweet as honey, and liked every one who liked her. But when Constance told her she looked angry, and that comforted poor Constance. who said Melicent was like still waters: "you run deep, I mean." Constance didn't mind being plain, if she *was* plain; she knew she spoke freely enough herself, but it was always kind, at all events, sobbed Constance.

The Mounts indeed were kind. They would lend their telephone to neighbours, and ring for neighbours' cats who mewed at the hall-doors. Once, on a moonlit night, Constance came downstairs when she had taken off her skirt and blouse, and was in her dressing-jacket and flannel petticoat, with her hair plaited. She heard a new outside, and opened the hall-door. Their right-hand neighbour's cat was wanting to get in, so she rang. Before she could escape, the door was opened by a gentleman in evening-dress.

"Wasn't it awful?" said Constance, who slipped into Thomasine's room to tell her. "When I remembered I was in my flannel petticoat and my red dressing-jacket, and my hair tied with a bit of boot-lace—!"

She giggled, and Thomasine said: *"Boot-lace!* Oh, my goodness!"

"I couldn't find a ribbon," Constance said. "At all events, he mayn't have noticed. I only remembered afterwards, the moon was so bright. He thanked me very much, and said 'Come in, puss.' I suppose he didn't know their cat's name is Girlie. Of course he might have thought Girlie would sound queer when I was there alone, if any one had been passing."

She giggled again, but Thomasine was too sleepy to take advantage. Besides, she felt angry with Constance. That soiled red jacket and a *flannel* petticoat (why had she taken off her moirette one?) and boot-lace in her hair! It was to be hoped he wouldn't recognise her if he saw her in the daytime.

Thomasine was very nearly good-looking. Her back was quite good-looking. Men who saw her passing quickly, sometimes looked again. She had pretty feet and ankles, and she dressed them well; her clothes sat smartly. Her face—a pointed oval with great breadth between the eyes—was like a leaf, now withered. Thomasine *had* to dress, for she massaged so many fashionable women. From them she picked up hints; they talked to their maids, or frocks and hats would arrive and be unpacked, and Thomasine in this way saw the first-fruits of the "Paris openings"—that was what you said. Her stories were the most exciting of the stock; there were Ladies So-and-So in them, often.

Nana always went to bed soon after dinner, and the Miss Mounts read or sewed. Thomasine and Constance liked the sewing best, for they could talk; but when Melicent was tired, as she sometimes was, they got their books. Timothy sat on anybody's lap, and whoever had him took him down to the garden the last thing, and waited for him. He came in soon, having no temptation to stay out. Sometimes, though, he cried as he came in. When Thomasine or Constance took him down, she told the others when he cried. Melicent, they thought, did not. He must have done it with her too, but she said nothing, for some reason. He slept in her room; he could have slept in anybody's, but Melicent had a sofa—he liked that.

They called him the man of the house, and said the hat in the hall-rack was his. Thomasine often apologised to him at breakfast for reading the paper first, but pionted out that she would have no other chance till evening while he had the whole day to himself. Timothy listened, blinking his yellow eyes and smiling. He would put out a paw and pat the paper, as if to say he understood and Thomasine might have it.

She was the social favourite. Everything combined for that—profession, clothes, looks, "quickness"; her speciality was quickness. She knew what everybody meant, except sometimes the cousin. Even she could not explain the thing the cousin said to Melicent about her grey-and-white uniform. "So Puritan; and child-beds are so Pagan!"

You expected coarseness from the cousin; but what could she mean by Pagan? The children were always christened. Melicent said so, and the cousin laughed and kissed her. "Oh, *isn't* it Mille-Saintes? she cried; and Thomasine herself confessed that she was puzzled.

One summer, Thomasine had a delightful invitation for the holiday.

Some old friends who had gone to Cornwall asked her there. None of the Miss Mounts had been to Cornwall, which was a nice part, they knew; and the old friends were dear, so Thomasine accepted. She looked well when she went off, in a check coat and a small, dashing hat, and shoes and stockings that surpassed all earlier ones. As she got into the taxi a man passed, and turned to look again. Melicent and Constance, on the steps with Nana and Timothy, thought that she must know him; Constance ran out and asked her, in a whisper. But she said she never had laid eyes on him before. She was blushing a little. "At all events he'll know you again," said Constance, and Thomasine said "Nonsense!"

She drove off then, alert and gay; Timothy kissed a paw to her, and she to him.

Constance soon departed, leaving Melicent at home, for she was out of work. Timothy was with her, in a heavenly mood, rubbing his head, stretching his paws: "Quite a flirtation," said Constance on the steps, more loudly than she should have, but she *was* a madcap sometimes.

She came home that evening to find Melicent in great anxiety. Not about Thomasine, who had wired and had a comfortable journey; but about Timothy. He wouldn't eat, he wouldn't even drink his milk. The one thing he would touch was water. Like most cats, he never cared for water if you poured it out for him; he'd only take it from the bedroom jugs. Melicent had gone into her room and found him trying, but the jug was nearly empty. So she filled it in the bathroom: "He waited all the time, the clever little man!" Then he had drunk till she thought he would never stop; but not a morsel had he eaten.

He lay on Nana's lap. His ears and nose were hot; his eyes looked heavy. "We must have the vet.," said Constance, and she telephoned that instant. But they had to dine before the vet. arrived.

He said that there was nothing much the matter; he would send some pills. "You know how to give them?" It would be queer, said Constance, if she didn't; at all events, she worked at a chemist's.

"He'll be all right," the vet, said, hurrying off. Late as it was, he was going into the country about a horse.

"A horse, of course!" said Constance. "They care about nothing but horses. *I* don't believe they understand cats; at all events, they never do them any good."

The pills came, and she gave Timothy the two ordained. He would sleep in Melicent's room as usual, and if Melicent was going to sit up with him, so would Constance.

Nana was crying. "You mustn't cry," they said. "He'll be himself tomorrow."

"No, he won't," said Nana. "And Miss Thomasine at the Land's End—indeed they may well say it!"

"We'll wire in the morning, if he isn't better," Constance said. "It's a shame it should have happened, when she's only just gone. But we must let her know, at all events, or else she'd never forgive us, if anything happened."

Timothy got worse in the night; they all assembled in Melicent's room, except Irene. In the morning Constance went out, first thing, and wired to Thomasine: "Timothy very ill. Will wire again during day." She telephoned to her chemist to say she couldn't come, because their cat was ill.

The vet. came again, and said that Timothy was dying.

"Last night you said there was nothing the matter!" Constance cried.

"Cats are deceptive," he answered. "The pills did him no harm, you know."

"They didn't do him any good, at all events," said Constance.

Melicent said nothing, but looked like a ghost. Nana said she always knew it. They sat in Melicent's room; they hadn't dared to move him. Irene did the room out gently; she was a good girl.

Timothy lay on the sofa, his head between his outstretched paws. His coat had lost its gloss; his eyes were so dilated now that when you saw them, you might think that he was well—they were so bright. But his little heart . . . his little heart was scarcely beating; he moaned pitifully now and then; he didn't seem to know them. Constance was to give him two more pills; they'd ease his going, the vet. had said. She did it beautifully, but when it was done, she cried a moment. Timothy had moaned when she disturbed him. "I *had* to, little man," she whispered. "Do you think I would if I could help it?" and she pressed his head against her breast; but Nana said: "I wouldn't do that, Miss Constance; he wants all the air he can get"; so they dared only stroke him very softly.

They sat up there till lunch-time; then went one by one to lunch, and then sat there again, just waiting.

About four o'clock he stretched a little, opening his eyes. They weren't bright now, but glazed and wild. He turned them upon Nana. All were kneeling close, but it was Nana that he looked at.

"Little man," she said, and smiled at him; but then she cried: "For God's sake, love, be done with it! Oh, I can't bear his eyes."

Melicent and Constance would have liked to cover their eyes too, for Timothy's were so beseeching and so terrified that they could hardly bear them either. But Melicent said: "He'd feel deserted. *You* do, Constance, if you like"; but Constance said she'd do what she could, at all events. So they knelt, smiling through their tears at Timothy, but now Timothy was gazing at the door as if he wanted to run away from them, and from something else—he even raised himself a little. But he was too weak; he fell back, gazing still and uttered a faint growl, as when he saw a dog.

"May I never again see a dumb creature die!" sobbed Nana. "I'd sooner watch a dozen men and women."

She moaned as Timothy had moaned at first; but Timothy had done with moaning. There was nothing but a feeble panting now; then once more the eyes closed—he stretched a paw forth blindly.

Melicent took it in both hands and kissed it. She couldn't see him any more, her tears were gathering so thick—the little paw that seemed to beg for love to help him through. . . . "Thank God!" said Nana's voice in a few moments; and Melicent knew then that he was dead. She trembled; Constance clasped her hand, and Nana put her arm about them both.

Not long afterwards came Thomasine's wire. She would be with them about seven.

"I *knew* she'd come!" Constance exclaimed. "If only she had been in time!"

But Nana said: "Indeed, I'm thankful one of us was spared it."

Melicent went out of the dining-room where they were having tea—the first meal without him. She came back with him in her arms—quite calm at first, but then she broke down dreadfully. None of them had ever seen her cry like that. Constance and Nana took the little body from her arms, and laid it on the table. His black coat was rough and stiff; the white evening-waistcoat he had kept so beautifully looked all poor and soiled. Their tears fell upon the staring coat; they tried to smoothe it, but it wouldn't smoothe. The cold roughness made them think of rabbits and hares in shops; none of them could ever eat a hare or rabbit.

"Ought we to let her see him?" Constance whispered.

Nana said, "Leave him to me."

They hid their faces.

"Now go out, the two of you, and take a breath of air," continued Nana. "Leave the little love to me."

"You'd never have the strength," said Constance.

"Strength? What strength?" cried Nana.

"It'll be a job, the soil's so stiff."

Nana had a queer look in her eyes, but only said: "Come back in half an hour and see." She pushed them gently out and shut the door.

They went to their own rooms; not out. In half an hour they came back to the dining-room. Nana was there, and on the table still was Timothy. But now there was a white cloth on the table—the best afternoon one, with the Irish crochet border. Timothy was laid on it, his head just raised against a pillow. He was on his side, his front paws lightly crossed, his back limbs turned a little, so that he was not at full length. The plumy tail showed beautifully, the coat no longer stared; it glimmered sleek and dark, and the white waistcoat was like snow. You might have thought he was alive.

"Doesn't he look lovely?" Nana said. "I thought my nice macassar oil would do it. But it was a job."

She seemed consoled by her success, for she was smiling.

"Yes, he looks lovely, Nana," Melicent and Constance said; but into both their minds had crept a fear. He looked just as if he were alive, and Thomasine might think he was.

"I know!" cried Constance, and she hurried out.

Melicent looked after her, then followed eagerly. Nana soon went too, for she must wash her hands. She looked back from the door and said: "I won't be long, my love."

About seven Thomasine arrived. She looked as trim as yesterday, but that she couldn't help, and her white face was anxious. They shook their heads in answer; then got the taxi away quickly, and drew her to the dining-room. She understood at once, for now a white silk scarf of Constance's was tied in a big bow about his neck, and in his front paws lay a little bunch of artificial lilies-of-the-valley, fastened with white satin ribbon; and Thomasine knelt down and hid her face upon the corner of the table.

She couldn't speak for a long time, though she soon raised her head and looked at him. At last she said: "How beautiful he looks!"—and she got up and kissed his head between the ears. They led her away then, and she took off her things and came to dinner, which was in the drawing-room. Irene had made "Nana's pudding," of her own accord, while Nana had been busy. It was not a good attempt, but very nice of her to think of it, they all said kindly.

After dinner—not till then, they had agreed—they told Thomasine about his sudden illness; and on the way to bed, they went into the dining-room again.

"We'll leave a bead of gas for him," said Melicent. "I know cats see in darkness, but—*he* can't."

She covered up her face again, but did not cry this time.

"Yes, a nice bead, at all events," said Constance with a glance at Thomasine and Nana, who both nodded. Melicent would miss him worse than they, at night.

"That ribbon shows up very handsome on his coat," said Nana.

"And the lilies look so sweet," said Thomasine. "Where did you find them?"

Constance turned to Melicent, but Melicent still had her hands over her face.

"Well, come to bed, my dears," said Nana then.

They looked back from the door. By the faint light they saw the gleam of the white cloth and ribbons, and his waistcoat and the lilies.

"Long ago," said Thomasine, "in Egypt, people used to worship cats."

"At all events," said Constance, on the stairs, "we made him happy."

Melicent, who was in front, turned quickly round. She looked as if she meant to speak, but she turned back again and went into her room without a word, and shut the door.

The Basement Room

graham greene

1

WHEN THE FRONT DOOR HAD SHUT THEM OUT and the butler Baines had turned back into the dark heavy hall, Philip began to live. He stood in front of the nursery door, listening until he heard the engine of the taxi die out along the street. His parents were gone for a fortnight's holiday; he was "between nurses," one dismissed and the other not arrived; he was alone in the great Belgravia house with Baines and Mrs. Baines.

He could go anywhere, even through the green baize door to the pantry or down the stairs to the basement living-room. He felt a stranger in his home because he could go into any room and all the rooms were empty.

You could only guess who had once occupied them: the rack of pipes in the smoking-room beside the elephant tusks, the carved wood tobacco jar, in the bedroom the pink hangings and pale perfumes and the three-quarter finished jars of cream which Mrs. Baines had not yet cleared away; the high glaze on the never-opened piano in the drawing-room, the china clock, the china clock, the silly little tables and the silver: but here Mrs. Baines was already busy, pulling down the curtains, covering the chairs in dust-sheets.

"Be off out of here, Master Philip," and she looked at him with her hateful peevish eyes, while she moved round, getting everything in order, meticulous and loveless and doing her duty.

Philip Lane went downstairs and pushed at the baize door; he looked into the pantry, but Baines was not there, then he set foot for the first time on the stairs to the basement. Again he had the sense: this is life. All his seven nursery years vibrated with the strange, the new experience. His crowded busy brain was like a city which feels the earth tremble at a distant earthquake shock. He was apprehensive, but he was happier than he had ever been. Everything was more important than before.

Baines was reading a newspaper in his shirt-sleeves. He said, "Come in, Phil, and make yourself at home. Wait a moment and I'll do the honours," and going to a white cleaned cupboard he brought out a bottle of ginger-beer and half a Dundee cake. "Half-past eleven in the morning," Baines said. "It's opening time, my boy," and he cut the cake and poured out the ginger-beer. He was more genial than Philip had ever known him, more at his ease, a man in his own home.

"Shall I call Mrs. Baines?" Philip asked, and he was glad when Baines said no. She was busy. She liked to be busy, so why interfere with her pleasure?

'A spot of drink at half-past eleven," Baines said, pouring himself out a glass of ginger-beer, "gives an appetite for chop and does no man any harm."

"A chop?" Philip asked.

"Old Coasters," Baines said, "call all food chop."

"But it's not a chop?"

"Well, it might be, you know, cooked with palm oil. And then some paw-paw to follow."

Philip looked out of the basement window at the dry stone yard, the ash-can and the legs going up and down beyond the railings.

"Was it hot there?"

"Ah, you never felt such heat. Not a nice heat, mind, like you get in the park on a day like this. Wet," Baines said, "corruption." He cut himself a slice of cake. "Smelling of rot," Baines said, rolling his eyes round the small basement room, from clean cupboard to clean cupboard, the sense of bareness, of nowhere to hide a man's secrets. With an air of regret for something lost he took a long draught of ginger-beer.

"Why did father live out there?"

"It was his job," Baines said, "same as this is mine now. And it was mine then too. It was a man's job. You wouldn't believe it now, but I've had forty niggers under me, doing what I told them to."

"I married Mrs. Baines."

Philip took the slice of Dundee cake in his hand and munched it round the room. He felt very old, independent and judicial; he was aware that Baines was talking to him as man to man. He never called him Master Philip as Mrs. Baines did, who was servile when she was not authoritative.

Baines had seen the world; he had seen beyond the railings, beyond the tired legs of typists, the Pimlico parade to and from Victoria. He sat there over his ginger pop with the resigned dignity of an exile; Baines didn't complain; he had chosen his fate, and if his fate was Mrs. Baines he had only himself to blame.

But to-day, because the house was almost empty and Mrs. Baines was upstairs and there was nothing to do, he allowed himself a little acidity.

"I'd go back to-morrow if I had the chance."

"Did you ever shoot a nigger?"

"I never had any call to shoot," Baines said. "Of course I carried a gun. But you didn't need to treat them bad. That just made them stupid. Why," Baines said, bowing his thin grey hair with embarrassment over the ginger pop, "I loved some of those damned niggers. I couldn't help loving them. There they'd be laughing, holding hands; they liked to touch each other; it made them feel fine to know the other fellow was round. It didn't mean anything we could understand; two of them would go about all day without loosing hold, grown men; but it wasn't love; it didn't mean anything we could understand."

"Eating between meals," Mrs. Baines said. "What would your mother say, Master Philip?"

She came down the steep stairs to the basement, her hands full of pots of cream and salve, tubes of grease and paste. "You oughtn't to encourage him, Baines," she said, sitting down in a wicker armchair and screwing up her small ill-humoured eyes at the Coty lipstick, Pond's cream, the Leichner rouge and Cyclax powder and Elizabeth Arden astringent.

She threw them one by one into the wastepaper basket. She saved only the cold cream. "Telling the boy stories," she said. "Go along to the nursery, Master Philip, while I get lunch."

Philip climbed the stairs to the baize door. He heard Mrs. Baines's voice like the voice in a nightmare when the small Price light has guttered in the saucer and the curtains move; it was sharp and shrill and full of malice, louder than people ought to speak, exposed.

"Sick to death of your ways, Baines, spoiling the boy. Time you did some work about the house," but he couldn't hear what Baines said in reply. He pushed open the baize door, came up like a small earth animal in his grey flannel shorts into a wash of sunlight on a parquet floor, the gleam of mirrors dusted and polished and beautified by Mrs. Baines.

Something broke downstairs, and Philip sadly mounted the stairs to the nursery. He pitied Baines; it occurred to him how happily they could live together in the empty house if Mrs. Baines were called away. He didn't want to play with his Meccano sets; he wouldn't take out his train or his soldiers; he sat at the table with his chin on his hands: this is life; and suddenly he felt responsible for Baines, as if he were the master of the house and Baines an ageing servant who deserved to be cared for. There was not much one could do; he decided at least to be good.

He was not surprised when Mrs. Baines was agreeable at lunch; he was used to her changes. Now it was "another helping of meat, Master Philip," or "Master Philip, a little more of this nice pudding." It was a pudding he liked, Queen's pudding with a perfect meringue, but he wouldn't eat a second helping lest she might count that a victory. She was the kind of woman who thought that any injustice could be counterbalanced by something good to eat.

She was sour, but she liked making sweet things; one never had to complain of a lack of jam or plums; she ate well herself and added soft sugar to the meringue and the strawberry jam. The half light through the basement window set the motes moving above her pale hair like dust as she sifted the sugar, and Baines crouched over his plate saying nothing.

Again Philip felt responsibility. Baines had looked forward to this, and Baines was disappointed: everything was being spoilt. The sensation of disappointment was one which Philip could share; knowing nothing of love or jealousy or passion he could understand better than anyone this grief, something hoped for not happening, something promised not fulfilled, something exciting turning dull. "Baines," he said, "will you take me for a walk this afternoon?"

"No," Mrs. Baines said, "no. That he won't. Not with all the silver to clean."

"There's fortnight to do it in," Baines said.

"Work first, pleasure afterwards." Mrs. Baines helped herself to some more meringue.

Baines suddenly put down his spoon and fork and pushed his plate away. "Blast," he said.

"Temper," Mrs. Baines said softly, "temper. Don't you go breaking any more things, Baines, and I won't have you swearing in front of the boy. Master Philip, if you've finished you can get down." She skinned the rest of the meringue off the pudding.

"I want to go for a walk," Philip said.

"You'll go and have a rest."

"I will go for a walk."

"Master Philip," Mrs. Baines said. She got up from the table leaving her meringue unfinished, and came towards him, thin, menacing, dusty in the basement room. "Master Philip, you do as you're told." She took him by the arm and squeezed it gently; she watched him with a joyless passionate glitter and above her head the feet of the typists trudged back to the Victoria offices after the lunch interval.

"Why shouldn't I go for a walk?" But he weakened; he was scared and ashamed of being scared. This was life; a strange passion he couldn't understand moving in the basement room. He saw a small pile of broken glass swept into a corner by the waste-paper basket. He looked to Baines for help and only intercepted hate; the sad hopeless hate of something behind bars.

"Why shouldn't I?" he repeated.

"Master Philip," Mrs. Baines said, "you've got to do as you're told. You mustn't think just because your father's away there's nobody here to——"

"You wouldn't dare," Philip cried, and was startled by Baines's low interjection:

"There's nothing she wouldn't dare."

"I hate you," Philip said to Mrs. Baines. He pulled away from her and ran to the door, but she was there before him; she was old, but she was quick.

"Master Philip," she said, "you'll say you're sorry." She stood in front of the door quivering with excitement. "What would your father do if he heard you say that?"

She put a hand out to seize him, dry and white with constant soda, the nails cut to the quick, but he backed away and put the table between them, and suddenly to his surprise she smiled; she became again as servile as she had been arrogant. "Get along with you, Master Philip," she said with glee, "I see I'm going to have my hands full till your father and mother come back."

She left the door unguarded and when he passed her she slapped him playfully. "I've got too much to do to-day to trouble about you. I haven't covered half the chairs," and suddenly even the upper part of the house became unbearable to him as he thought of Mrs. Baines moving round shrouding the sofas, laying out the dust-sheets.

So he wouldn't go upstairs to get his cap but walked straight out across the shining hall into the street, and again, as he looked this way and looked that way, it was life he was in the middle of.

2

It was the pink sugar cakes in the window on a paper doily, the ham, the slab of mauve sausage, the wasps driving like small torpedoes across the pane that caught Philip's attention. His feet were tired by pavements; he had been afraid to cross the road, had simply walked first in one direction, then in the other. He was nearly home now; the square was at the end of the street; this was a shabby outpost of Pimlico, and he smudged the pane with his nose looking for sweets, and saw between the cakes and ham a different Baines. He hardly recognised the bulbous eyes, the bald forehead. It was a happy, bold and buccaneering Baines, even though it was, when you looked closer, a desperate Baines.

Philip had never seen the girl. He remembered Baines had a niece and he thought that this might be her. She was thin and drawn, and she wore a white mackintosh; she meant nothing to Philip; she belonged to a world about which he knew nothing at all. He couldn't make up stories about her, as he could make them up about withered Sir Hubert Reed, the Permanent Secretary, about Mrs. Wince-Dudley who came up once a year from Penstanley in Suffolk with a green umbrella and an enormous black hand-bag, as he could make them up about the upper servants in all the houses where he went to tea and games. She just didn't belong; he thought of mermaids and Undine; but she didn't belong there either, nor to the adventures of Emil, nor the Bastables. She sat there looking at an iced pink cake in the detachment and mystery of the completely disinherited, looking at the half-used pots of powder which Baines had set out on the marble-topped table between them.

Baines was urging, hoping, entreating, commanding, and the girl looked at the tea and the china pots and cried. Baines passed his handkerchief across the table, but she wouldn't wipe her eyes; she screwed it in her palm and let the tears run down, wouldn't do anything, wouldn't speak, would only put up a silent despairing resistance to what she dreaded and wanted and refused to listen to at any price. The two brains battled over the tea-cups loving each other, and there came to Philip outside, beyond the ham and wasps and dusty Pimlico pane, a confused indication of the struggle.

He was inquisitive and he didn't understand and he wanted to know. He went and stood in the doorway to see better, he was less sheltered than he had ever been; other people's lives for the first time touched and pressed and moulded. He would never escape that scene. In a week he had forgotten it, but it conditioned his career, the long austerity of his life; when he was dying he said: "Who is she?"

Baines had won; he was cocky and the girl was happy. She wiped her face, she opened a pot of powder, and their fingers touched across the table. It occurred to Philip that it would be amusing to imitate Mrs. Baines's voice and call "Baines" to him from the door.

It shriveled them; you couldn't describe it in any other way, it made them smaller, they weren't happy any more and they were't bold. Baines was the first to recover and trace the voice, but that didn't make things as they were. The sawdust was spilled out of the afternoon; nothing you did could mend it, and Philip was scared. "I didn't mean. . . ." He wanted to say that he loved Baines, that he had only wanted to laugh at Mrs. Baines. But he had discovered that you couldn't laugh at Mrs. Baines. She wasn't Sir Hubert Reed, who used steel nibs and carried a pen-wiper in his pocket; she wasn't Mrs. Wince-Dudley; she was darkness when the night-light went out in a draught; she was the frozen blocks of earth he had seen one winter in a graveyard when someone said, "They need an electric drill"; she was the flowers gone bad and smelling in the little closet room at Penstanley. There was nothing to laugh about. You had to endure her when she was there and forget about her quickly when she was away, suppress the thought of her, ram it down deep.

Baines said, "It's only Phil," beckoned him in and gave him the pink iced cake the girl hadn't eaten, but the afternoon was broken, the cake was like dry bread in the throat. The girl left them at once; she even forgot to take the powder; like a small blunt icicle in her white mackintosh she stood in the doorway with her back to them, then melted into the afternoon.

"Who is she?" Philip asked. 'Is she your niece?"

"Oh, yes," Baines said, "that's who she is; she's my niece," and poured the last drops of water on to the coarse black leaves in the teapot.

"May as well have another cup," Baines said.

"The cup that cheers," he said hopelessly, watching the bitter black fluid drain out of the spout.

"Have a glass of ginger pop, Phil?"

"I'm sorry. I'm sorry, Baines."

"It's not your fault, Phil. Why, I could believe it wasn't you at all, but her. She creeps in everywhere." He fished two leaves out of his cup and laid them on the back of his hand, a thin soft flake and a hard stalk. He beat them with his hand: "To-day," and the stalk detached itself, "to-morrow, Wednesday, Thursday, Friday, Saturday, Sunday," but the flake wouldn't come, stayed where it was drying under his blows with a resistance you wouldn't believe it to possess. "The tough one wins," Baines said.

He got up and paid the bill and out they went into the street. Baines said, "I don't ask you to say what isn't true. But you needn't mention to Mrs. Baines you met us here."

"Of course not," Philip said, and catching something of Sir Hubert Reed's manner, "I understand, Baines." (But he didn't understand a thing; he was caught up in other people's darkness.)

"It was stupid," Baines said. "So near home, but I hadn't time to think, you see. I'd got to see her."

"Of course, Baines."

"I haven't time to spare," Baines said. "I'm not young. I've got to see that she's all right."

"Of course you have, Baines."

"Mrs. Baines will get it out of you if she can."

"You can trust me, Baines," Philip said in a dry important Reed voice; and then, "Look out. She's at the window watching." And there indeed she was, looking up at them, between the lace curtains, from the basement room, speculating. "Need we go in, Baines?" Philip asked, cold lying heavy on his stomach like too much pudding; he clutched Baines's arm.

"Careful," Baines said softly, "careful."

"But need we go in, Baines? It's early. Take me for a walk in the park."

"Better not."

"But I'm frightened, Baines."

"You haven't any cause," Baines said. "Nothing's going to hurt you. You

just run along upstairs to the nursery. I'll go down by the area and talk to
Mrs. Baines." But even he stood hesitating at the top of the stone steps
pretending not to see her, where she watched between the curtains. "In at
the front door, Phil, and up the stairs."

Philip didn't linger in the hall; he ran, slithering on the parquet Mrs.
Baines had polished, to the stairs. Through the drawing-room doorway on the
first floor he saw the draped chairs; even the china clock on the mantel was
covered like a canary's cage; as he passed it, it chimed the hour, muffled and
secret under the duster. On the nursery table he found his supper laid out: a
glass of milk and a piece of bread and butter, a biscuit, and a little cold
Queen's pudding without the meringue. He had no appetite; he strained his
ears for Mrs. Baines's coming, for the sound of voices, but the basement held
its secrets; the green baize door shut off that world. He drank the milk and
ate the biscuit, but he didn't touch the rest, and presently he could hear the
soft precise footfalls of Mrs. Baines on the stairs: she was a good servant, she
walked softly; she was a determined woman, she walked precisely.

But she wasn't angry when she came in; she was ingratiating as she
opened the night nursery door—"Did you have a good walk, Master
Philip?—pulled down the blinds, laid out his pyjamas, came back to clear
his supper. "I'm glad Baines found you. Your mother wouldn't have liked
your being out alone." She examined the tray. "Not much appetite, have you,
Master Philip? Why don't you try a little of this nice pudding? I'll bring
you up some more jam for it."

"No, no, thank you, Mrs. Baines," Philip said.

"You ought to eat more," Mrs. Baines said. She sniffed round the room
like a dog. "You didn't take any pots out of the waste-paper basket in the
kitchen, did you, Master Philip?"

"No," Philip said.

"Of course you wouldn't. I just wanted to make sure." She patted his
shoulder and her fingers flashed to his lapel; she picked off a tiny crumb of
pink sugar. "Oh, Master Philip," she said, "that's why you haven't any
appetite. You've been buying sweet cakes. That's not what your pocket
money's for."

"But I didn't," Philip said. "I didn't."

She tasted the sugar with the tip of her tongue.

"Don't tell lies to me, Master Philip. I won't stand for it any more than
your father would."

"I didn't, I didn't," Philip said. "They gave it me. I mean Baines," but
she had pounced on the word "they." She had got what she wanted; there
was no doubt about that, even when you didn't know what it was she wanted.
Philip was angry and miserable and disappointed because he hadn't kept
Baines's secret. Baines oughtn't to have trusted him; grown-up people

should keep their own secrets, and yet here was Mrs. Baines immediately entrusting him with another.

"Let me tickle your palm and see if you can keep a secret." But he put his hand behind him; he wouldn't be touched. "It's a secret between us, Master Philip, that I know all about them. I suppose she was having tea with him," she speculated.

"Why shouldn't she?" he said, the responsibility for Baines weighing on his spirit, the idea that he had got to keep her secret when he hadn't kept Baines's making him miserable with the unfairness of life. "She was nice."

"She was nice, was she?" Mrs. Baines said in a bitter voice he wasn't used to.

"And she's his niece."

"So that's what he said," Mrs. Baines struck softly back at him like the clock under the duster. She tried to be jocular. "The old scoundrel. Don't you tell him I know, Master Philip." She stood very still between the table and the door, thinking very hard, planning something. "Promise you won't tell. I'll give you that Meccano set, Master Philip. . . ."

He turned his back on her; he wouldn't promise, but he wouldn't tell. He would have nothing to do with their secrets, the responsibilities they were determined to lay on him. He was only anxious to forget. He had received already a larger dose of life than he had bargained for, and he was scared. "A 2A Meccano set, Master Philip." He never opened his Meccano set again, never built anything, never anything, died, the old dilettante, sixty years late with nothing to show rather than preserve the memory of Mrs. Baines's malicious voice saying good night, her soft determined footfalls on the stars to the basement, going down down.

3

The sun poured in between the curtains and Baines was beating a tattoo on the water-can. "Glory, glory," Baines said. He sat down on the end of the bed and said, "I beg to announce that Mrs. Baines has been called away. Her mother's dying. She won't be back till to-morrow."

"Why did you wake me up so early?" Philip said. He watched Baines with uneasiness; he wasn't going to be drawn in; he'd learnt his lesson. It wasn't right for a man of Baines's age to be so merry. It made a grown person human in the same way that you were human. For if a grown-up could behave so childishly, you were liable too to find yourself in their world. It was enough that it came at you in dreams: the witch at the corner, the man with a knife. So "It's very early," he complained, even though he loved Baines, even though he couldn't help being glad that Baines was happy. He was divided by the fear and the attraction of life.

"I want to make this a long day," Baines said. "This is the best time."
He pulled the curtains back. "It's a bit misty. The cat's been out all night.
There she is, sniffing round the area. They haven't taken in any milk at 59.
Emma's shaking out the mats at 63." He said: "This was what I used to
think about on the Coast: somebody shaking mats and the cat coming home.
I can see it today," Baines said, "just as if I was still in Africa. Most days
you don't notice what you've got. It's good life if you don't weaken." He
put a penny on the washstand. "When you've dressed, Phil, run and get a
Mail from the barrow at the corner. I'll be cooking the sausages."

"Sausages?"

"Sausages," Baines said. "We're going to celebrate to-day. A fair bust."
He celebrated at breakfast, restless, cracking jokes, unaccountably merry
and nervous. It was going to be a long, long day, he kept on coming back
to that: For years he had waited for a long day, he had sweated in the damp
Coast heat, changed shirts, gone down with fever, lain between the blankets
and sweated, all in the hope of this long day, that cat sniffing round the area,
a bit of mist, the mats beaten at 63. He propped the *Mail* in front of the
coffee-pot and read pieces aloud. He said, "Cora Down's been married for the
fourth time." He was amused, but it wasn't his idea of a long day. His long
day was the Park, watching the riders in the Row, seeing Sir Arthur Still-
water pass beyond the rails ("He dined with us once in Bo; up from Free-
town; he was governor there"), lunch at the Corner House for Philip's sake
(he'd have preferred himself a glass of stout and some oysters at the York
bar), the Zoo, the long bus ride home in the last summer light: the leaves in
the Green Park were beginning to turn and the motors nuzzled out of
Berkeley Street with the low sun gently glowing on their wind-screens. Baines
envied no one, not Cora Down, or Sir Arthur Stillwates, or Lord Sandale,
who came out on to the steps of the Army and Navy and then went back
again because he hadn't got anything to do and might as well look at another
paper. "I said don't let me see you touch that black again." Baines had led
a man's life; everyone on top of the bus pricked their ears when he told
Philip all about it.

"Would you have shot him?" Philip asked, and Baines put his head back
and tilted his dark respectable man-servant's hat to a better angle as the
bus swerved round the artillery memorial.

"I wouldn't have thought twice about it. I'd have shot to kill," he
boasted, and the bowed figure went by, the steel helmet, the heavy cloak, the
downturned rifle and the folded hands.

"Have you got the revolver?"

"Of course I've got it," Baines said. "Don't I need it with all the
burglaries there've been?" This was the Baines whom Philip loved: not
Baines singing and carefree, but Baines responsible, Baines behind barriers,
living his man's life.

All the buses streamed out from Victoria like a convoy of aeroplanes to bring Baines home honour. "Forty blacks under me," and there waiting near the area steps was the proper conventional reward, love at lighting-up time.

"It's your niece," Philip said, recognising the white mackintosh, but not the happy sleepy face. She frightened him like an unlucky number, he nearly told Baines what Mrs. Baines had said; but he didn't want to bother, he wanted to leave things alone.

"Why, so it is," Baines said. "I shouldn't wonder if she was going to have a bit of supper with us." But he said they'd play a game, pretend they didn't know her, slip down the area steps, "and here," Baines said, "we are," lay the table, put out the cold sausages, a bottle of beer, a bottle of ginger pop, a flagon of harvest burgundy. "Everyone his own drink," Baines said. "Run upstairs, Phil, and see if there's been a post."

Philip didn't like the empty house at dusk before the lights went on. He hurried. He wanted to be back with Baines. The hall lay there in quiet and shadow prepared to show him something he didn't want to see. Some letters rustled down, and someone knocked. "Open in the name of the Republic." The tumbrils rolled, the head bobbed in the bloody basket. Knock, knock, and the postman's footsteps going away. Philip gathered the letters. The slit in the door was like the grating in a jeweller's window. He remembered the policeman he had seen peer through. He had said to his nurse, "What's he doing?" and when she said, "He's seeing if everything's all right," his brain immediately filled with images of all that might be wrong. He ran to the baize door and the stairs. The girl was already there and Baines was kissing her. She leant breathless against the dresser. "This is Emmy, Phil."

"There's a letter for you, Baines."

"Emmy," Baines said, "it's from her." But he wouldn't open it. "You bet she's coming back."

"We'll have supper, anyway," Emmy said. "She can't harm that."

"You don't know her," Baines said. "Nothing's safe. Damn it," he said, "I was a man once," and he opened the letter.

"Can I start?" Philip asked, but Baines didn't hear; he presented in his stillness and attention an example of the importance grown-up people attached to the written word: you had to write your thanks, not wait and speak them, as if letters couldn't lie. But Philip knew better than that, sprawling his thanks across a page to Aunt Alice who had given him a doll he was too old for. Letters could lie all right, but they made the lie permanent; they lay as evidence against you: they made you meaner than the spoken word.

"She's not coming back till to-morrow night," Baines said. He opened the bottles, he pulled up the chairs, he kissed Emmy again against the dresser.

"You oughtn't to," Emmy said, "with the boy here."

"He's got to learn," Baines said, "like the rest of us," and he helped

Philip to three sausages. He only took one himself; he said he wasn't hungry; but when Emmy said she wasn't hungry either he stood over her and made her eat. He was timid and rough with her; he made her drink the harvest burgundy because he said she needed building up; he wouldn't take no for an answer, but when he touched her his hands were light and clumsy too, as if he was afraid to damage something delicate and didn't know how to handle anything so light.

"This is better than milk and biscuits, eh?"

"Yes," Philip said, but he was scared, scared for Baines as much as for himself. He couldn't help wondering at every bite, at every draught of the ginger pop, what Mrs. Baines would say if she ever learnt of this meal; he couldn't imagine it, there was a depth of bitterness and rage in Mrs. Baines you couldn't sound. He said, "She won't be coming back to-night?" but you could tell by the way they immediately understood him that she wasn't really away at all; she was there in the basement with them, driving them to longer drinks and louder talk, biding her time for the right cutting word. Baines wasn't really happy; he was only watching happiness from close to instead of from far away.

"No," he said, "she'll not be back till late to-morrow." He couldn't keep his eyes off happiness; he'd played around as much as other men, he kept on reverting to the Coast as if to excuse himself for his innocence; he wouldn't have been so innocent if he'd lived his life in London, so innocent when it came to tenderness. "If it was you, Emmy," he said, looking at the white dresser, the scrubbed chairs, "this'd be like a home." Already the room was not quite so harsh; there was a little dust in corners, the silver needed a final polish, the morning's paper lay untidily on a chair. "You'd better go to bed, Phil; it's been a long day."

They didn't leave him to find his own way up through the dark shrouded house; they went with him, turning on lights, touching each other's fingers on the switches; floor after floor they drove the night back; they spoke softly among the covered chairs; they watched him undress, they didn't make him wash or clean his teeth, they saw him into bed and lit his night-light and left his door ajar. He could hear their voices on the stairs, friendly like the guests he heard at dinner-parties when they moved down to the hall, saying good night. They belonged; wherever they were they made a home. He heard a door open and a clock strike, he heard their voices for a long while, so that he felt they were not far away and he was safe. The voices didn't dwindle, they simply went out, and he could be sure that they were still somewhere not far from him, silent together in one of the many empty rooms, growing sleepy together as he grew sleepy after the long day.

He just had time to sigh faintly with satisfaction, because this too perhaps had been life, before he slept and the inevitable terrors of sleep came round him: a man with a tricolour hat beat at the door on His Majesty's

service, a bleeding head lay on the kitchen table in a basket, and the
Siberian wolves crept closer. He was bound hand and foot and couldn't move;
they leapt round him breathing heavily; he opened his eyes and Mrs. Baines
was there, her grey untidy hair in threads over his face, her black hat askew.
A loose hairpin fell on the pillow and one musty thread brushed his mouth.
"Where are they?" she whispered. "Where are they?"

4

Philip watched her in terror. Mrs. Baines was out of breath as if she
had been searching all the empty rooms, looking under loose covers.

With her untidy grey hair and her black dress buttoned to her throat, her
gloves of black cotton, she was so like the witches of his dreams that he didn't
dare to speak. There was a stale smell in her breath.

"She's here," Mrs. Baines said; "you can't deny she's here." Her face was
simultaneously marked with cruelty and misery; she wanted to "do things"
to people, but she suffered all the time. It would have done her good to
scream, but she daren't do that: it would warn them. She came ingratiatingly
back to the bed where Philip lay rigid on his back and whispered, "I haven't
forgotten the Meccano set. You shall have it to-morrow, Master Philip.
We've got secrets together, haven't we? Just tell me where they are."

He couldn't speak. Fear held him as firmly as any nightmare. She said,
"Tell Mrs. Baines, Master Philip. You love your Mrs. Baines, don't you?"
That was too much; he couldn't speak, but he could move his mouth in
terrified denial, wince away from her dusty image.

She whispered, coming closer to him, "Such deceit. I'll tell your father.
I'll settle with you myself when I've found them. You'll smart; I'll see you
smart." Then immediately she was still, listening. A board had creaked on
the floor below, and a moment later, while she stooped listening above his
bed, there came the whispers of two people who were happy and sleepy
together after a long day. The night-light stood beside the mirror and Mrs.
Baines could see bitterly there her own reflection, misery and cruelty wavering in the glass, age and dust and nothing to hope for. She sobbed without
tears, a dry breathless sound; but her cruelty was a kind of pride which
kept her going, it was her best quality, she would have been merely pitiable
without it. She went out of the door on tiptoe, feeling her way across the
landing, going so softly down the stairs that no one behind a shut door
could hear her. Then there was complete silence again; Philip could move;
he raised his knees; he sat up in bed; he wanted to die. It wasn't fair, the
walls were down again between his world and theirs; but this time it was
something worse than merriment that the grown people made him share; a
passion moved in the house he recognized but could not understand.

It wasn't fair, but he owed Baines everything: the Zoo, the ginger pop, the bus ride home. Even the supper called on his loyalty. But he was frightened; he was touching something he touched in dreams: the bleeding head, the wolves, the knock, knock. Life fell on him with savagery: you couldn't blame him if he never faced it again in sixty years. He got out of bed, carefully from habit put on his bedroom slippers, and tiptoed to the door: it wasn't quite dark on the landing below because the curtains had been taken down for the cleaners and the light from the street came in through the tall windows. Mrs. Baines had her hand on the glas door-knob; she was very carefully turning it; he screamed: Baines."

Mrs. Baines turned and saw him cowering in his pyjamas by the banisters; he was helpless, more helpless even than Baines, and cruelty grew at the sight of him and drove her up the stairs. The nightmare was on him again and he couldn't move; he hadn't any more courage left for ever; he'd spend it all, had been allowed no time to let it grow, no years of gradual hardening; he couldn't even scream.

But the first cry had brought Baines out of the best spare bedroom and he moved quicker than Mrs. Baines. She hadn't reached the top of the stairs before he'd caught her round the waist. She drove her black cotton gloves at his face and he bit her hand. He hadn't time to think, he fought her savagely like a stranger, but she fought back with knowledgeable hate. She was going to teach them all and it didn't really matter whom she began with; they had all deceived her; but the old image in the glass was by her side, telling her she must be dignified, she wasn't young enough to yield her dignity; she could beat his face, but she mustn't bite; she could push, but she mustn't kick.

Age and dust and nothing to hope for were her handicaps. She went over the banisters in a flurry of black clothes and fell into the hall; she lay before the front door like a sack of coals which should have gone down the area into the basement. Philip saw; Emmy saw; she sat down suddenly in the doorway of the best spare bedroom with her eyes open as if she were too tired to stand any longer. Baines went slowly down into the hall.

It wasn't hard for Philip to escape; they'd forgotten him completely; he went down the back, the servants' stairs because Mrs. Baines was in the hall; he didn't understand what she was doing lying there; like the startling pictures in a book no one had read to him, the things he didn't understand terrified him. The whole house had been turned over to the grown-up world; he wasn't safe in the night nursery; their passions had flooded it. The only thing he could do was to get away, by the back stair, and up through the area, and never come back. You didn't think of the cold, of the need of food and sleep; for an hour it would seem quite possible to escape from people for ever.

He was wearning pyjamas and bedroom slippers when he came up into the square, but there was no one to see him. It was that hour of the evening in a residential district when everyone is at the theatre or at home. He climbed over the iron railings into the little garden: the plane-trees spread their large pale palms between him and the sky. It might have been an illimitable forest into which he had escaped. He crouched behind a trunk and the wolves retreated; it seemed to him between the little iron seat and the tree-trunk that no one would ever find him again. A kind of embittered happiness and self-pity made him cry; he was lost; there wouldn't be any more secrets to keep; he surrendered responsibility once and for all. Let grown-up people keep to their world and he would keep to his, safe in the small garden between the plane-trees. "In the lost childhood of Judas Christ was betrayed"; you could almost see the small unformed face hardening into the deep dilettante selfishness of age.

Presently the door of 48 opened and Baines looked this way and that; then he signalled with his hand and Emmy came; it was as if they were only just in time for a train, they hadn't a chance of saying good-bye; she went quickly by like a face at a window swept past the platform, pale and unhappy and not wanting to go. Baines went in again and shut the door; the light was lit in the basement, and a policeman walked round the square, looking into the areas. You could tell how many families were at home by the lights behind the first-floor curtains.

Philip explored the garden: It didn't take long: a twenty-yard square of bushes and plane-trees, two iron seats and a gravel path, a padlocked gate at either end, a scuffle of old leaves. But he couldn't stay: Something stirred in the bushes and two illuminated eyes peered out at him like a Siberian wolf, and he thought how terrible it would be if Mrs. Baines found him there. He'd have no time to climb the railings; she'd seize him from behind.

He left the square at the unfashionable end and was immediately among the fish-and-chip shops, the little stationers selling Bagatelle, among the accommodation addresses and the dingy hotels with open doors. There were few people about because the pubs were open, but a blowsy woman carrying a parcel called out to him across the street and the commissionaire outside a cinema would have stopped him if he hadn't crossed the road. He went deeper: you could go farther and lose yourself more completely here than among the plane-trees. On the fringe of the square he was in danger of being stopped and taken back: it was obvious where he belonged: But as he went deeper he lost the marks of his origin. It was a warm night: Any child in those free-living parts might be expected to play truant from bed. He found a kind of camaraderie even among grown-up people; he might have been a neighbour's child as he went quickly by, but they weren't going to tell on him, they'd been young once themselves. He picked up a protective coating of dust from the pavements, of smuts from the trains which passed along the backs in a spray of fire. Once he was caught in a knot of children running away from something or somebody, laughing as they ran; he was whirled with them round a turning and abandoned, with a sticky fruit-drop in his hand.

He couldn't have been more lost; but he hadn't the stamina to keep on. At first he feared that someone would stop him; after an hour he hoped that someone would. He couldn't find his way back, and in any case he was afraid of arriving home alone; he was afraid of Mrs. Baines, more afraid than he had ever been. Baines was his friend, but something had happened which gave Mrs. Baines all the power. He began to loiter on purpose to be noticed, but no one noticed him. Families were having a last breather on the doorsteps, the refuse bins had been put out and bits of cabbage stalks soiled his slippers. The air was full of voices, but he was cut off; these people were strangers and would always now be strangers; they were marked by Mrs. Baines and he shied away from them into a deep class-consciousness. He had been afraid of policemen, but now he wanted one to take him home; even Mrs. Baines could do nothing against a policeman. He sidled past a constable who was directing traffic, but he was too busy to pay him any attention. Philip sat down against a wall and cried.

It hadn't occurred to him that that was the easiest way, that all you had to do was to surrender, to show you were beaten and accept kindness. . . . It was lavished on him at once by two women and a pawnbroker. Another policeman appeared, a young man with a sharp incredulous face. He looked as if he noted everything he saw in pocket-books and drew conclusions. A woman offered to see Philip home, but he didn't trust her: she wasn't a match for Mrs. Baines immobile in the hall. He wouldn't give his address; he said he was afraid to go home. He had his way; he got his protection. "I'll take him to the station," the policeman said, and holding him awkwardly by the hand (he wasn't married; he had his career to make) he led him round the corner, up the stone stairs into the little bare over-heated room where Justice waited.

5

Justice waited behind a wooden counter on a high stool; it wore a heavy moustache; it was kindly and had six children ("three of them nippers like yourself"); it wasn't really interested in Philip, but it pretended to be, it wrote the address down and sent a constable to fetch a glass of milk. But the young constable was interested; he had a nose for things.

"Your home's on the telephone, I suppose," Justice said. "We'll ring them up and say you are safe. They'll fetch you very soon. What's your name, sonny?"

"Philip."

"Your other name?"

"I haven't got another name." He didn't want to be fetched; he wanted to be taken home by someone who would impress even Mrs. Baines. The constable watched him, watched the way he drank the milk, watched him when he winced away from questions.

"What made you run away? Playing truant, eh?"

"I don't know."

"You oughtn't to do it, young fellow. Think how anxious your father and mother will be."

"They are away."

"Well, your nurse."

"I haven't got one."

"Who looks after you, then?" That question went home. Philip saw Mrs. Baines coming up the stairs at him, the heap of black cotton in the hall. He began to cry.

"Now, now, now," the sergeant said. He didn't know what to do; he wished his wife were with him; even a policewoman might have been useful.

"Don't you think it's funny," the constable said, "that there hasn't been an inquiry?"

"They think he's tucked up in bed."

"You are scared, aren't you?" the constable said. "What scared you?"

"I don't know."

"Somebody hurt you?"

"No."

"He's had bad dreams," the sergeant said. "Thought the house was on fire, I expect. I've brought up six of them. Rose is due back. She'll take him home."

"I want to go home with you," Philip said; he tried to smile at the constable, but the deceit was immature and unsuccessful.

"I'd better go," the constable said. "There may be something wrong."

"Nonsense," the sergeant said. "It's a woman's job. Tact is what you need. Here's Rose. Pull up your stockings, Rose. You're a disgrace to the Force. I've got a job of work for you." Rose shambled in: black cotton stocking drooping over her boots, a gawky Girl Guide manner, a hoarse hostile voice. "More tarts, I suppose."

"No, you've got to see this young man home." She looked at him owlishly.

"I won't go with her," Phillip said. He began to cry again. "I don't like her."

"More of that womanly charm, Rose," the sergeant said. The telephone rang on his desk. He lifted the receiver. "What? What's that?" he said. "Number 48? You've got a doctor?" He put his hand over the telephone mouth. "No wonder this nipper wasn't reported," he said. "They've been too busy. An accident. Woman slipped on the stairs."

"Serious?" the constable asked. The sergeant mouthed at him; you didn't mention the word death before a child (didn't he konw? he had six of them), you made noises in the throat, you grimaced, a complicated shorthand for a word of only five letters anyway.

"You'd better go, after all," he said, "and make a report. The doctor's there."

Rose shambled from the stove; pink apply-dapply cheeks, loose stocking. She stuck her hands behind her. Her large morgue-like mouth was full of blackened teeth. "You told me to take him and now just because something interesting...I don't expect justice from a man..."

"Who's at the house?" the constable asked.

"The butler."

"You don't think," the constable said, "he saw..."

"Trust me," the sergeant said, "I've brought up six. I know 'em through and through. You can't teach me anything about children."

"He seemed scared about something."

"Dreams," the sergeant said.

"What name?"

"Baines."

"This Mr. Baines," the constable said to Philip, "you like him, eh? He's good to you?" They were trying to get something out of him; he was suspicious of the whole roomful of them; he said "yes" without conviction because he was afraid at any moment of more responsibilities, more secrets.

"And Mrs. Baines?"

"Yes."

They consulted together by the desk: Rose was hoarsely aggrieved; she was like a female impersonator, she bore her womanhood with an unnatural emphasis even while she scorned it in her creased stockings and her weather-exposed face. The charcoal shifted in the stove; the room was over-heated in the mild late summer evening. A notice on the wall described a body found in the Thames, or rather the body's clothes: wool vest, wool pants, wool shirt with blue stripes, size ten boots, blue serge suit worn at the elbows, fifteen and a half celluloid collar. They couldn't find anything to say about the body, except its measurements, it was just an ordinary body.

"Come along," the constable said. He was interested, he was glad to be going, but he couldn't help being embarrassed by his company, a small boy in pyjamas. His nose smelt something, he didn't know what, but he smarted at the sight of the amusement they caused: the pubs had closed and the streets were full again of men making as long a day of it as they could. He hurried through the less frequented streets, chose the darker pavements, wouldn't loiter, and Philip wanted more and more to loiter, pulling at his hand, dragging with his feet. He dreaded the sight of Mrs. Baines waiting in the hall: he knew now that she was dead. The sergeant's mouthings had conveyed that; but she wasn't buried, she wasn't out of sight; he was going to see a dead person in the hall when the door opened.

The light was on in the basement, and to his relief the constable made for the area steps. Perhaps he wouldn't have to see Mrs. Baines at all. The constable knocked on the door because it was too dark to see the bell, and Baines answered. He stood there in the doorway of the neat bright basement room and you could see the sad complacent plausible sentence he had prepared wither at the sight of Philip; he hadn't expected Philip to return like that in the policeman's company. He had to begin thinking all over again; he wasn't a deceptive man; if it hadn't been for Emmy he would have been quite ready to let the truth lead him where it would.

"Mr. Baines?" the constable asked.

He nodded; he hadn't found the right words; he was daunted by the shrewd knowing face, the sudden appearance of Philip there.

"This little boy from here?"

"Yes," Baines said. Philip could tell that there was a message he was trying to convey, but he shut his mind to it. He loved Baines, but Baines had involved him in secrets, in fears he didn't understand. The glowing morning thought "This is life" had become under Baines's tuition the repugnant memory, "That was life"; the musty hair across the mouth, the breathless cruel tortured inquiry "Where are they," the heap of black cotton tipped into the hall. That was what happened when you loved: you got involved; and Philip extricated himself from life, from love, from Baines with a merciless egotism.

There had been things between them, but he laid them low, as a retreating army cuts the wires, destroys the bridges. In the abandoned country you may leave much that is dear—a morning in the Park, an ice at a corner house, sausages for supper—but more is concerned in the retreat than temporary losses. There are old people who, as the tractors wheel away, implore to be taken, but you can't risk the rearguard for their sake: a whole prolonged retreat from life, from care, from human relationships is involved.

"The doctor's here," Baines said. He nodded at the door, moistened his mouth, kept his eyes on Philip, begging for something like a dog you can't understand. "There's nothing to be done. She slipped on these stone basement stairs. I was in here. I heard her fall." He wouldn't look at the notebooks, at the constable's spidery writing which got a terrible lot on one page.

"Did the boy see anything?"

"He can't have done. I thought he was in bed. Hadn't he better go up? It's a shocking thing. O," Baines said, losing control, "it's a shocking thing for a child."

"She's through there?" the constable asked.

"I haven't moved her an inch," Baines said.

"He'd better then——"

"Go up the area and through the hall," Baines said, and again he begged dumbly like a dog: one more secret, keep this secret, do this for old Baines, he won't ask another.

"Come along," the constable said. "I'll see you up to bed. You're a gentleman; you must come in the proper way through the front door like the master should. Or will you go along with him, Mr. Baines, while I see the doctor?"

"Yes," Baines said, "I'll go." He came across the room to Philip, begging, begging, all the way with his soft old stupid expression: this is Baines, the old Coaster; what about a palm-oil chop, eh?; a man's life; forty niggers; never used a gun; I tell you I couldn't help loving them: it wasn't what we call love, nothing we could understand. The messages flickered out from the last posts at the border, imploring, beseeching, reminding: this is your old friend Baines; what about an eleven's; a glass of ginger-pop won't do you any harm; sausages; a long day. But the wires were cut, the messages just faded out into the enormous vacancy of the neat scrubbed room in which there had never been a place where a man could hide his secrets.

"Come along, Phil, it's bedtime. We'll just go up the steps..." Tap, tap, tap, at the telegraph; you may get through, you can't tell, somebody may mend the right wire. "And in at the front door."

"No," Philip said, "no. I won't go. You can't make me go. I'll fight. I won't see her."

The constable turned on them quickly. "What's that? Why won't you go?"

"She's in the hall," Philip said. "I know she's in the hall. And she's dead. I won't see her."

"You moved her then?" the constable said to Baines. "All the way down here? You've been lying, eh? That means you had to tidy up. . . . Were you alone?"

"Emmy," Philip said, "Emmy." He wasn't going to keep any more secrets: He was going to finish once and for all with everything, with Baines and Mrs. Baines and the grown-up life beyond him; it wasn't his business and never, never again, he decided, would he share their confidences and companionship. "It was all Emmy's fault," he protested with a quaver which reminded Baines that after all he was only a child; it had been hopeless to expect help there; he was a child; he didn't understand what it all meant; he couldn't read this shorthand of terror; he'd had a long day and he was tired out. You could see him dropping asleep where he stood against the dresser, dropping back into the comfortable nursery peace. You couldn't blame him. When he woke in the morning, he'd hardly remember a thing.

"Out with it," the constable said, addressing Baines with professional ferocity, "who is she?" just as the old man sixty years later startled his secretary, his only watcher, asking, "Who is she? Who is she?" dropping lower and lower into death, passing on the way perhaps the image of Baines: Baines hopeless, Baines letting his head drop, Baines "coming clean."

Commentary

plot and setting
in
"the basement room"

Aristotle's concept of plot as the imitation of an action (*praxis*) and the arrangement of incidents apparently assumes that character is the moving force of what happens. Thus, Francis Fergusson speculates that Aristotle means by *praxis* not merely events or happenings but something closer to "purpose" or "spiritual movement." A plot develops out of two or more purposes in alignment or in conflict and may be simple or complex depending on whether it includes a reversal, or "peripety." A reversal plot is complex by virtue of a hidden action behind the apparent direction of the work, a second force invisible to the protagonist that has sufficient strength and importance to turn the movement of the plot around. A central and climactic "discovery" or *anagnorisis* often coincides with the reversal in complex plots and brings new knowledge startling enough to force the protagonist to reconsider the manifest logic of events.

Elaborating upon Aristotle in this regard, commentators on the *Poetics* have suggested various connections between reversal and discovery, which Paul Goodman in *The Structure of Literature* defines as "the emergence of the hidden plot to become part of the unity of time" (p. 25). The protagonist may himself cause the reversal that brings "the destruction of the apparent plot and the succession of the hidden plot," contributing thereby to his own downfall, as Oedipus does, and making the plot ironic as well as complex. The terms "ironic" and "complex" thus refer to a discrepancy between the hero's knowledge at a given moment and the totality of moving forces that cause things to go as they do.

Although they are usually applied to drama, these terms are equally useful in describing fictional plots and novelistic characters, whose "motion" or *praxis* does not differ in essentials from that of either epic or dramatic characters. A novelistic plot, however, often takes a different pace through its opening exposition, complication, rising action, climax, and resolution, and the hero is beset by different obstacles and hindrances to his discovery of what must happen and how he must respond. Such a plot is likely to be more heavily strewn with diversions and less completely governed by the character's will, idea, and passion, and to describe it we must therefore consider several side actions, internal movements, and those much larger movements that fiction encompasses in its collective socil organism. Thus retardation of the hero's progress sometimes comes from an entire society, with its conventions, toboos, negotiable contracts, and institutions, which he finds difficult to comprehend in their entirety. Recoiling from so many obstructions to his will and understanding, he is forced to alter his original psychic motion and is often carried down byways—until in a novel as encompassing as Tolstoy's *War and Peace* or Conrad's *Nostromo* characters touch upon massive accumulations of influence. Recognition, reversal, and irony are all somewhat changed by this enlargement of circumstances, which make a single unmasking very unlikely and cause continued ignorance to be more probable.

Even in long and complex works of prose fiction we can generally locate a unifying movement of some kind, and various genres tend to illustrate typical movements—the *Bildungsroman* a gradual maturing of a youth, for instance; the picaresque, an episodic series of adventures in which a rogue, after many escapades, remains much the same rogue. But the overbalancing of the protagonist's will by a large society and by his own inner variety makes a fictional plot much more plentiful in tributary elements and softens the outlines of the work. As Goethe has someone remark in *Wilhelm Meister*, "in the novel, it is chiefly *sentiments* and *events* that are exhibited; in the drama, it is *characters* and *deeds*. The novel must go slowly forward; and the sentiments of the hero, by some means or another, must restrain the tendency of the whole to unfold itself and to conclude." It must be so because without that restraint novelistic plots would shrink into the single, simple actions of short fiction. "The novel-hero must be suffering, at least he must not in a high degree be active," Goethe adds, because passive suffering provides not only the delay and the complication of plaited strands of action but also the occasions for an elaboration of sentiment.

Any complication in sentiment or delay of the hero's goals is likely to mean an extensive use of interior information. The complex movement of an interior life often enriches fictional character beyond what would be strictly required as the "motion" of a dramatic action. As we will note with respect to character in "Gimpel the Fool" later, fiction paradoxically emphasizes both character and the submergence of character in detailed setting and action. Even in action-oriented fiction like *Robinson Crusoe* we are often given the psychological stages by which a "motion" is set going. Notice in Crusoe's decision to rescue Friday (in the first section), for example, how elaborately Defoe has woven action and Crusoe's development together, giving us a prefiguring dream, numerous occasions on which Crusoe reflects upon his need for a servant, and finally the stages of his reasoning when he makes his decision to intervene. In all of this we can clearly see the event itself developing as a product of combined "motions" and circumstances. This much interior material and such realistic occasions would obviously be difficult to render in either drama or verse narrative.

As we realize from observing our own reflexes, even when we are not resisted we seldom think straight to a given point: The mind combines and amalgamates, associates one thing with another, detours, and proceeds according to its own whims. It is the privilege of the fictionalist to probe that interior career and to know fictional characters somewhat as people know themselves. He thus enables us to trace complexes of sentiment in the context of evolving actions. When interior careers assume prominence and the novel gives them ample opportunity for expression, we have what Paul Goodman calls—without prejudice—a sentimental plot, which is a sequence of occasions for sentiment "leading to abiding attitudes" (*Structure of Literature*, pp. 127 ff.). If character is defined and fixed from the outset as in conventional or flat types, the plot becomes a succession of changes in situation, usually in comic collisions between situation and character type; but if the situation is beyond influence and character striving and evolving, the conflict is so intensified, as often in naturalism, that the protagonist is eventually rendered passive and helpless. The lyric novel brings together an especially dynamic interior world and an exterior society that exists mainly to provide material for assimilation, as in Virginia Woolf's novels, which are concerned less with collisions among dramatic characters than with subjective associations, recollections, and oblique expressions of passion and suffering. As Goodman suggests, these elements in the novel are normally more loosely joined in opening sections than in later sections, after setting and action have made their demands upon the protagonist and forced him to shed inclinations incompatible with them. The modern novel was conceived in part in the passive suffering of Samuel Richardsons's heroines Pamela and Clarissa and in the entanglement of the outcast Moll Flanders in standards and codes which by and large condemn her. Both the first-person narrative of Defoe and the epistolary novel of Richardson were ideally suited to exhibit the intimacies of thought and sentiment as episodes cause them to arise. Even simple plots such as Robinson Crusoe's civilizing of an island are perpetual *adjustments* between an initial character, an environment, and an action that grows out of their organic interaction.

Short fiction presents a slightly different problem in the defining of plot because it has fewer parallel and analogous actions, fewer incidents, and contrasting developments, and less expansion of situation and character than the novel. This difference does not mean, however, that its characters and plots cannot also be complex. In point of fact, the protagonists of the short story frequently undergo significant changes in knowledge, instigated from several directions, and their plots contain all the major devices of complication, delay, climax, plaited strands, and resolution that novelistic plots illustrate. But short fiction is less likely to blur the outlines of its central movement with the kinds of descriptive amplification and social density that a novel offers. In this respect, it remains closer to dramatistic plots, though here again fiction and drama must take slightly different courses because of fiction's possibile interior focus. Most short stories compress their actions into brief narrative representation and give dramatic representation only to key moments. A parable, to take an extreme example, may represent an abiding general state of affairs or general truth, but will do so in a single illustrative situation or incident, offering no more detail than is required to make the point. The moral appended to most fables could be amplified with countless illustrations and parallel situations. "The Portable Phonograph," to take a longer example, represents only the culmination of a long history in the simple meeting of four men and its immediate aftermath; the rest is left to implication. "The Basement Room" (which we will examine in a moment) concerns a critical period of arrested change and merely glances at long-range repercussions. "The Grave" represents a cycle of growth and return, leaving out all the potential "in between" that a novel might have filled in and a play would have had to find a way to dramatize. "Gimpel the Fool" concerns a large span of Gimpel's life but represents only comparatively small samples directly.

Another peculiarity of fictional plots is that our privileged access to complex interior worlds often reveals a simplifying rather than expanding movement in the central character, whose initial inner richness may stand in the way of his performance of what is required of him. (By resorting frequently to non-dramatic soliloquies, Shakespeare sometimes achieves novelistic effects in this regard; Hamlet, for instance, must cast aside scruples, intelligence, and nuances of feeling in order to murder his uncle.) The very demand for such a reduction brings these inner qualities to the surface and tests them. Rather than evolving from motives as the expansion of a psychic action or *praxis*, the plot is more or less imposed by the situation. Some characters, especially in comic plots, undergo this reduction without struggle because they are implicitly created to perform whatever is required of them, as Dicken's Pickwick willingly surrenders whatever complications we might imagine for him in order to be simply Dicken's Pickwick. In most cases, however, a reductive action is "agonizing" because the hindrance that must be overcome is the hero's own character. In still other cases losses and gains are balanced, as in *Paradise Lost* the original potential of Adam and Eve is destroyed but then replaced with a greater destiny.

As we suggested, the brevity of the short story demands a tighter integration of its resources and allows less interior and exterior expansion than longer fiction. But short fiction may still consider the tension between inner motive and constricting environment and treat the passionate or agonizing reduction of dynamic characters in the face of necessity and outside pressure. In "The Basement Room," Philip Lane is such an evolving character whose discoveries have a drastic and largely reductive impact upon him as he proves unable to carry through his initial spiritual motion. The climax of the story is a simultaneous recognition and reversal in which apparent advances in knowledge are turned around and the rest of his life is cast in shadow. The concealment of the counter forces that cause this reversal make the plot of the story both complex and ironic.

Initially, however, the departure of Philip's parents places him on the edge of an exciting change and intensifiies his expectations, as so often happens at the gateway to fictional worlds. Both Philip and the reader embark on courses of investigation. The area of mystery and the place of instruction for Philip's initiation is the basement room, which he enters for the first time, with a sense that "this is life." "All his seven nursery years vibrated with the strange, the new experience. His crowded busy brain was like a city which feels the earth tremble at a distant earthquake shock."

Plots that stem not from one psychic movement but from the joint energy of two or more close associates easily become secret sharer plots, the reciprocity among the characters of which, like those of the love plot, is very close and intense. One character becomes not only a mirror for the other but a dramatic catalyst as well, stimulating change for better or worse. Baines and Philip have aspects of such a relationship, capable of deepening into a joint conspiracy or of breaking apart into a tortuous antagonism. When Philip's parents leave, Baines, with a touch of warm, exotic Africa about him and lingering traces of a will to resist the meticulous and loveless Mrs. Baines, becomes Philip's guide to the world that seems about to open up. Baines himself is still capable of changing, and his desire to change is the moving force of the apparent or primary plot and the key to Philip's own adventure. Mrs. Baines, their mutual antagonist, resembles the forbidding guardian or Terrible Mother, who prevents entry into the treasure of manly experience that Baines promises; she forces the "spiritual movements" of Baines and Philip to interlock tightly because their ways to "live" (as Philip thinks of it) must exclude her. Her threat makes them feel responsible for each other especially Philip for Baines, who deserves "to be cared for" and protected. Eventually, they come also to share the intimation of a violated promise, of a day that looks fair and is blighted, "something exciting turning dull," because of her influence.

The first surprising turn of the story and the clearest preparation for Philip's reversal, however, is a glimpse, upon Mrs. Baines' sudden return to the house at night, of the motives behind her cruelty and her resistance to their betrayal. Having become accustomed to seeing her as the principle of retardation in the plot of Baines and Philip, we discover then that the situation could easily be turned around; her motives are humanly understandable and perhaps even, in an ambivalent way, sympathetic:

> The night-light stood beside the mirror and Mrs. Baines could see bitterly there her own reflection, misery and cruelty wavering in the glass, age and dust and nothing to hope for. She sobbed without tears, a dry, breathless sound; but her cruelty was a kind of pride which kept her going; it was her best quality, she would have been merely pitiable without it.

For the moment, the main plots—Baines' conspiracy and Philip's growth into an understanding of manhood—appear to be *her* obstacles, as she becomes the detective who seeks to expose a hidden plot and salvage a social right. (She should not after all be merely cast aside at the first adventure that strikes the male imagination—so it seems for the moment.) We understand at this point the irreconcilable conflict of two quite different codes, which become internalized in Philip as a psychological tension. Whereas Baines has failed to comprehend or anticipate his wife, she clearly anticipates *him*.

Philip glimpses enough of this complication in the half light (Mrs. Baines is otherwise a creature of concealment, darkness, and nightmare) to compromise his commitment to Baines: The effort to strike back proves to be too great. Their conflict becomes his paralysis.

From Baines' standpoint, the plot is ironic as well as constrictive: The apparent unloosing of controls that gives rein to his conspiracy proves to be a trap, and his relationship with Philip, which would have protected him and given him closeness and intuitive understanding of the kind he has admired in the blacks once under him, betrays him. Their disparity in age and experience and Philip's inability to fend off Mrs. Baines makes them dangerous allies; they have areas hidden from one another. Philip's youth has no safeguards against the complexities of Baines' adult world, and Baines in turn has no way to prevent Philip's betrayal. At the critical moment, communication between them closes off: "The wires were cut, the messages just faded out into the enormous vacancy of the neat scrubbed room in which there had never been a place where a man could hide his secrets." Their relationship is crushed by a social necessity that resists Baines' freedom and Philip's growth as transgressions. (Although he is the champion of masculine freedom, Baines has some stake in this same repression; he thinks of his best moments as those in which he too exercised virtually unrestricted power over forty blacks.) Although ostensibly the reversal of the conspiracy is the accidental murder of Mrs. Baines in the midst of what was to have been a joyful, truant occasion, the real crux of the plot lies in this critical moment, in the failure of understanding between the conspirators. Their *hamartia* or flaw as a pair is now layed bare, and we recognize it as less their failure to understand Mrs. Baines than their failure to recognize the feebleness of their own defenses. Whereas the first incident, the return of Mrs. Baines, destroys Baines' manly stature and pride, which have led him to rebel against marital duty, the second isolates him and renders his case futile. In place of the furies who administer punishment to Greek tragic heroes for "hubris" or pride, Baines is handled by the forces of social retribution—a logical substitute for furies in this realm of domestic realism.

The moment of Baines' ironic reversal is also Philip's. His development is turned back at this point because he cannot grow into a confident, exploratory manhood without understanding the "hidden strands" that adults are to him, and yet to understand them at this premature moment requires a courage that is beyond him. Insofar as he never realizes quite what happens, the plot remains inconclusive for him, but it is complete for the reader in the sense that he knows why Philip will never proceed further. As knowledge fails to pass between Philip and Baines, in its place mere information passes from Philip to the police; and in this difference between the role of the informer and the conspiracy of comrades lies much of the story's meaning. Philip crosses over to a fixed moral order and abandons the vital possibilities implicit in the natural cycle from youth to adulthood.

Though sensational in some respects, the plot of "The Basement Room" is basically realistic as well as complex and ironic: nothing wonderful or improbable happens; the interaction of environment and the three main characters (plus the somewhat shadowy but creditable Emmy) is sufficient to explain the events. The constrictions of realism—like the difference between the secret sharer that Philip sets out to be and the social informant that Philip becomes—are part of the story's significance. Though the departure of Philip's parents appears to set up an adventure beyond ordinary, the potential romance turns out to be very vulnerable. Only a slightly seamy side of the same old story—the triangle and human betrayal—is revealed to him.

As the chief setting of the plot and a silent but impressive influence upon it—almost a tributary action in its own right—the house itself is a central example of this realism. It has previously meant to Philip primarily the nursery, but he leaves that permanently in the course of the story. Its other rooms and their furnishings define graphically his range of possibilities. The upstairs where he normally lives is comparatively isolated from the servants; it is highly formal, dark, and forbidding. (The levels of the house are brought to our attention several times by the sounds that pass among them and by the frequent climbing and descending of stairs, often as someone intrudes upon a private place.) The basement room into which Philip descends resembles the perilous place of heroes who pass into an underworld adventure; but of course it is merely a basement room finally, and the house as a whole proves to be not so much a romantic chamber of gothic horrors as a mirror of the outside world, which multiplies Mrs. Baines in inquisitive inspectors and policewomen. Her spirit lives on, haunting the house and the memory of the aging Philip.

By extending the significance of the action and suggesting parallels in the greater society outside, the house makes another contribution to plot. Settings often fill out the experience of the protagonist, amplifying his situation like a sounding-board and linking the action of the story to a larger, framing history. It stands as a symbol of a times and of the dominating forces that have made it. At the same time, it is an enclosed private world penetrated eventually by outside influences, and thus stands also as a natural symbol for Philip's inner sanctuary. It is violated just as his nursery-mind is wrenched open and he is converted into the man we see years later. Thus it looks both inward and outward and defines the limits of Philip's growth. The final turn of the story is a projection of it and the basement room as compartments of Philip's memory: Having drawn his harbored sensibility into its chambers, the house is in turn encompassed as an enigmatic element of his isolated old age. The plot is completed only by that turn, which is a falling resolution after an intense climax. It is significant that the house is recalled not in a dramatically represented time but a narrated distance and introspective moment in a kind of fade away—as an element in the final twinges of Philip's initial *praxis* and questioning spirit.

Gimpel the Fool

isaac bashevis singer

1

I AM GIMPEL THE FOOL. I don't think myself a fool. One the contrary. But that's what folks call me. They gave me the name while I was still in school. I had seven names in all: imbecile, donkey, flax-head, dope, glump, ninny, and fool. The last name stuck. What did my foolishness consist of? I was easy to take in. They said, "Gimpel, you know the rabbi's wife has been brought to childbed?" So I skipped school. Well, it turned out to be a lie. How was I supposed to know? She hadn't had a big belly. But I never looked at her belly. Was that really so foolish? The gang laughed and hee-hawed, stomped and danced and chanted a good-night prayer. And instead of the raisins they give when a woman's lying in, they stuffed my hand full of goat turds. I was no weakling. If I slapped someone he'd see all the way to Cracow. But I'm really not a slugger by nature. I think to myself: Let it pass. So they take advantage of me.

I was coming home from school and heard a dog barking. I'm not afraid of dogs, but of course I never want to start up with them. One of them may be mad, and if he bites there's not a Tartar in the world who can help you. So I made tracks. Then I looked around and saw the whole market place wild with laughter. It was no dog at all but Wolf-Leib the Thief. How was I supposed to know it was he? It sounded like a howling bitch.

When the pranksters and leg-pullers found that I was easy to fool, every one of them tried his luck with me. "Gimpel, the Czar is coming to Frampol; Gimpel, the moon fell down in Turbeen; Gimpel, little Hodel Furpiece found a treasure behind the bathhouse." And I like a golem believed everyone. In the first place, everything is possible, as it is written in the Wisdom of the Fathers, I've forgotten just how. Second, I had to believe when the whole town came down on me! If I ever dared to say, "Ah, you're kidding!" there was trouble. People got angry. "What do you mean! You want to call everyone a liar?" What was I to do? I believed them, and I hope at least that did them some good.

I was an orphan. My grandfather who brought me up was already bent toward the grave. So they turned me over to a baker, and what a time they gave me there! Every woman or girl who came to bake a batch of noodles had to fool me at least once. "Gimpel, there's a fair in heaven; Gimpel, the rabbi gave birth to a calf in the seventh month; Gimpel, a cow flew over the roof and laid brass eggs." A student from the yeshiva came once to buy a roll, and he said, "You, Gimpel, while you stand here scraping with your baker's shovel the Messiah has come. The dead have arisen." "What do you mean?" I said. "I heard no one blowing the ram's horn!" He said, "Are you deaf?" And all began to cry, "We heard it, we heard!" Then in came Rietze the Candle-dipper and called out in her coarse voice, "Gimpel your father and mother have stood up from the grave. They're looking for you."

To tell the truth, I knew very well that nothing of the sort had happened, but all the same, as folks were talking, I threw on my wool vest and went out. Maybe something had happened. What did I stand to lose by looking? Well, what a cat music went up! And then I took a vow to believe nothing more. But that was no go either. They confused me so that I didn't know the big end from the small.

I went to the rabbi to get some advice. He said, "It is written, better to be a fool all your days than for one hour to be evil. You are not a fool. They are the fools. For he who causes his neighbor to feel shame loses Paradise himself." Nevertheless the rabbi's daughter took me in. As I left the rabbinical court she said, "Have you kissed the wall yet?" I said, "No; what for?" She answered, "It's the law; you've got to do it after every visit." Well, there didn't seem to be any harm in it. And she burst out laughing. It was a fine trick. She put one over on me, all right.

I wanted to go off to another town, but then everyone got busy match-making, and they were after me so they nearly tore my coat tails off. They talked at me and talked until I got water on the ear. She was no chaste maiden, but they told me she was virgin pure. She had a limp, and they said it was deliberate, from coyness. She had a bastard, and they told me the child was her little brother. I cried, "You're wasting your time. I'll never marry that whore." But they said indignantly, "What a way to talk! Aren't you ashamed of yourself? We can take you to the rabbi and have you fined for giving her a bad name." I saw then that I wouldn't escape them so easily and I thought: They're set on making me their butt. But when you're married the husband's the master, and if that's all right with her it's agreeable to me too. Besides, you can't pass through life unscathed, nor expect to.

I went to her clay house, which was built on the sand, and the whole gang, hollering and chorusing, came after me. They acted like bear-baiters. When we came to the well they stopped all the same. They were afraid to start anything with Elka. Her mouth would open as if it were on a hinge, and she had a fierce tongue. I entered the house. Lines were strung from wall to wall and clothes were drying. Barefoot she stood by the tub, doing the wash. She was dressed in a worn hand-me-down of plush. She had her hair put up in braids and pinned across her head. It took my breath away, almost, the reek of it all.

Evidently she knew who I was. She took a look at me and said, "Look who's here! He's come, the drip. Grab a seat."

I told her all; I denied nothing. "Tell me the truth," I said, "are you really a virgin, and is that mischievous Yechiel actually your little brother? Don't be deceitful with me, for I'm an orphan."

"I'm an orphan myself," she answered, "and whoever tries to twist you up, may the end of his nose take a twist. But don't let them think they can take advantage of me. I want a dowry of fifty guilders, and let them take up a collection besides. Otherwise they can kiss my you-know-what." She was very plainspoken. I said, "It's the bride and not the groom who gives a dowry." Then she said, "Don't bargain with me. Either a flat 'yes' or a flat 'no'—Go back where you came from."

I thought: No bread will ever be baked from *this* dough. But ours is not a poor town. They consented to everything and proceeded with the wedding. It so happened that there was a dysentery epidemic at the time. The ceremony was held at the cemetery gates, near the little corpse-washing hut. The fellows got drunk. While the marriage contract was being drawn up I heard the most pious high rabbi ask, "Is the bride a widow or a divorced woman?" And the sexton's wife answered for her, "Both a widow and divorced." It was a black moment for me. But what was I to do, run away from under the marriage canopy?

There was singing and dancing. An old granny danced opposite me, hugging a braided white *chalah*. The master of revels made a "God 'a mercy" in memory of the bride's parents. The schoolboys threw burrs, as on Tishe b'Av fast day. There were a lot of gifts after the sermon: a noodle board, a kneading trough, a bucket, brooms, ladles, household articles galore. Then I took a look and saw two strapping young men carrying a crib. "What do we need this for?" I asked. So they said, "Don't rack your brains about it. It's all right, it'll come in handy." I realized I was going to be rooked. Take it another way though, what did I stand to lose? I reflected: I'll see what comes of it. A whole town can't go altogether crazy.

2

At night I came where my wife lay, but she wouldn't let me in. "Say, look here, is this what they married us for?" I said. And she said, "My monthly has come." "But yesterday they took you to the ritual bath, and that's afterward, isn't it supposed to be?" "Today isn't yesterday," said she, "and yesterday's not today. You can beat it if you don't like it." In short, I waited.

Not four months later she was in childbed. The townsfolk hid their laughter with their knuckles. But what could I do? She suffered intolerable pains and clawed at the walls. "Gimpel," she cried, "I'm going. Forgive me!" The house filled with women. They were boiling pans of water. The screams rose to the welkin.

The thing to do was to go to the House of Prayer to repeat Psalms, and that was what I did.

The townsfolk liked that, all right. I stood in a corner saying Psalms and prayers, and they shook their heads at me. "Pray, pray!" they told me. "Prayer never made any woman pregnant." One of the congregation put a straw to my mouth and said, "Hay for the cows." There was something to that too, by God!

She gave birth to a boy. Friday at the synagogue the sexton stood up before the Ark, pounded on the reading table, and announced, "The wealthy Reb Gimpel invites the congregation to a feast in honor of the birth of a son." The whole House of Prayer rang with laughter. My face was flaming. But there was nothing I could do. After all, I *was* the one responsible for the circumcision honors and rituals.

Half the town came running. You couldn't wedge another soul in. Women brought peppered chick-peas, and there was a keg of beer from the tavern. I ate and drank as much as anyone, and they all congratulated me. Then there was a circumcision, and I named the boy after my father, may he rest in peace. When all were gone and I was left with my wife alone, she thrust her head through the bedcurtain and called me to her.

"Gimpel," said she, "why are you silent? Has you ship gone and sunk?"

"What shall I say?" I answered. "A fine thing you've done to me! If my mother had known of it she'd have died a second time."

She said, "Are you crazy, or what?"

"How can you make such a fool," I said, "of one who should be the lord and master?"

"What's the matter with you?" she said. "What have you taken it into your head to imagine?"

I saw that I must speak bluntly and openly. "Do you think this is the way to use an orphan?" I said. "You have borne a bastard."

She answered, "Drive this foolishness out of your head. The child is yours."

"How can he be mine?" I argued. "He was born seventeen weeks after the wedding."

She told me then that he was premature. I said, "Isn't he a little too premature?" She said, she had had a grandmother who carried just as short a time and she resembled this grandmother of hers as one drop of water does another. She swore to it with such oaths that you would have believed a peasant at the fair if he had used them. To tell the plain truth, I didn't believe her; but when I talked it over next day with the schoolmaster he told me that the very same thing had happened to Adam and Eve. Two they went up to bed, and four they descended.

"There isn't a woman in the world who is not the granddaughter of Eve," he said.

That was how it was; they argued me dumb. But then, who really knows how such things are?

I began to forget my sorrow. I loved the child madly, and he loved me too. As soon as he saw me he'd wave his little hands and want me to pick him up, and when he was colicky I was the only one who could pacify him. I bought him a little bone teething ring and a little gilded cap. He was forever catching the evil eye from someone, and then I had to run to get one of those abracadabras for him that would get him out of it. I worked like an ox. You know how expenses go up when there's an infant in the house. I don't want to lie about it; I didn't dislike Elka either, for that matter. She swore at me and cursed, and I couldn't get enough of her. What strength she had! One of her looks could rob you of the power of speech. And her orations! Pitch and sulphur, that's what they were full of, and yet somehow also full of charm. I adored her every word. She gave me bloody wounds though.

In the evening I brought her a white loaf as well as a dark one, and also poppyseed rolls I baked myself. I thieved because of her and swiped everything I could lay hands on: macaroons, raisins, almonds, cakes. I hope I may be forgiven for stealing from the Saturday pots the women left to warm in the baker's oven. I would take out scraps of meat, a chunk of pudding, a chicken leg or head, a piece of tripe, whatever I could nip quickly. She ate and became fat and handsome.

I had to sleep away from home all during the week, at the bakery. On Friday nights when I got home she always made an excuse of some sort. Either she had heartburn, or a stitch in the side, or hiccups, or headaches. You know what women's excuses are. I had a bitter time of it. It was rough. To add to it, this little brother of hers, and bastard, was growing bigger. He'd put lumps on me, and when I wanted to hit back she'd open her mouth and curse so powerfully I saw a green haze floating before my eyes. Ten times a day she threatened to divorce me. Another man in my place would have taken French leave and disappeared. But I'm the type that bears it and says nothing. What's one to do? Shoulders are from God, and burdens too.

One night there was a calamity in the bakery; the oven burst, and we almost had a fire. There was nothing to do but go home, so I went home. Let me, I thought, also taste the joy of sleeping in bed in mid-week. I didn't want to wake the sleeping mite and tiptoed into the house. Coming in, it seemed to me that I heard not the snoring of one but, as it were, a double snore, one a thin enough snore and the other like the snoring of a slaughtered ox. Oh, I didn't like that! I didn't like it at all. I went up to the bed, and things suddenly turned black. Next to Elka lay a man's form. Another in my place would have made an uproar, and enough noise to rouse the whole town, but the thought occurred to me that I might wake the child. A little thing like that—why frighten a little swallow, I thought. All right then, I went back to the bakery and stretched out on a sack of flour and till morning I never shut an eye. I shivered as if I had had malaria. "Enough of being a donkey," I said to myself. "Gimpel isn't going to be a sucker all his life. There's a limit even to the foolishness of a fool like Gimpel."

In the morning I went to the rabbi to get advice, and it made a great commotion in the town. They sent the beadle for Elka right away. She came, carrying the child. And what do you think she did? She denied it, denied everything, bone and stone! "He's out of his head," she said. "I know nothing of dreams or divinations." They yelled at her, warned her, hammered on the table, but she stuck to her guns: it was a false accusation, she said.

The butchers and the horse-traders took her part. One of the lads from the slaughterhouse came by and said to me, "We've got our eye on you, you're a marked man." Meanwhile the child started to bear down and soiled itself. In the rabbinical court there was an Ark of the Covenant, and they couldn't allow that, so they sent Elka away.

I said to the rabbi, "What shall I do?"

"You must divorce her at once," said he.

"And what if she refuses?" I asked.

He said, "You must serve the divorce. That's all you'll have to do."

I said, "Well, all right, Rabbi. Let me think about it."

"There's nothing to think about," said he. "You mustn't remain under the same roof with her."

"And if I want to see the child?" I asked.

"Let her go, the harlot," said he, "and her brood of bastards with her."

The verdict he gave was that I mustn't even cross her threshold—never again, as long as I should live.

During the day it didn't bother me so much. I thought: It was bound to happen, the abscess had to burst. But at night when I stretched out upon the sacks I felt it all very bitterly. A longing took me, for her and for the child. I wanted to be angry, but that's my misfortune exactly, I don't have it in me to be really angry. In the first place—this was how my thoughts went —there's bound to be a slip sometimes. You can't live without errors.

Probably that lad who was with her led her on and gave her presents and what not, and women are often long on hair and short on sense, and so he got around her. And then since she denies it so, maybe I was only seeing things? Hallucinations do happen. You see a figure or a mannikin or something, but when you come up closer it's nothing, there's not a thing there. And if that's so, I'm doing her an injustice. And when I got so far in my thoughts I started to weep. I sobbed so that I wet the flour where I lay. In the morning I went to the rabbi and told him that I had made a mistake. The rabbi wrote on with his quill, and he said that if that were so he would have to reconsider the whole case. Until he had finished I wasn't to go near my wife, but I might send her bread and money by messenger.

3

Nine months passed before all the rabbis could come to an agreement. Letters went back and forth. I hadn't realized that there could be so much erudition about a matter like this.

Meanwhile Elka gave birth to still another child, a girl this time. On the Sabbath I went to the synagogue and invoked a blessing on her. They called me up to the Torah, and I named the child for my mother-in-law—may she rest in peace. The louts and loudmouths of the town who came into the bakery gave me a going over. All Frampol refreshed its spirits because of my trouble and grief. However, I resolved that I would always believe what I was told. What's the good of *not* believing? Today it's your wife you don't believe; tomorrow it's God Himself you won't take stock in.

By an apprentice who was her neighbor I sent her daily a corn or a wheat loaf, or a piece of pastry, rolls or bagels, or, when I got the chance, a slab of pudding, a slice of honeycake, or wedding strudel—whatever came my way. The apprentice was a goodhearted lad, and more than once he added something on his own. He had formerly annoyed me a lot, plucking my nose and digging me in the ribs, but when he started to be a visitor to my house he became kind and friendly. "Hey, you, Gimpel," he said to me, "you have a very decent little wife and two fine kids. You don't deserve them."

"But the things people say about her," I said.

"Well, they have long tongues," he said, "and nothing to do with them but babble. Ignore it as you ignore the cold of last winter."

One day the rabbi sent for me and said, "Are you certain, Gimpel, that you were wrong about your wife?"

I said, "I'm certain."

"Why, but look here! You yourself saw it."

"It must have been a shadow," I said.

"The shadow of what?"

"Just one of the beams, I think."

"You can go home then. You owe thanks to the Yanover rabbi. He found an obscure reference in Maimonides that favored you."

I seized the rabbi's hand and kissed it.

I wanted to run home immediately. It's no small thing to be separated for so long a time from wife and child. Then I reflected: I'd better go back to work now, and go home in the evening. I said nothing to anyone, although as far as my heart was concerned it was like one of the Holy Days. The women teased and twitted me as they did every day, but my thought was: Go on, with your loose talk. The truth is out, like the oil upon the water. Maimonides says it's right, and therefore it is right!

At night, when I had covered the dough to let it rise, I took my share of bread and a little sack of flour and started homeward. The moon was full and the stars were glistening, something to terrify the soul. I hurried onward, and before me darted a long shadow. It was winter, and a fresh snow had fallen. I had a mind to sing, but it was growing late and I didn't want to wake the householders. Then I felt like whistling, but I remembered that you don't whistle at night because it brings the demons out. So I was silent and walked as fast as I could.

Dogs in the Christian yards barked at me when I passed, but I thought: Bark your teeth out! What are you but mere dogs? Whereas I am a man, the husband of a fine wife, the father of promising children.

As I approached the house my heart started to pound as though it were the heart of a criminal. I felt no fear, but my heart went thump! thump! Well, no drawing back. I quietly lifted the latch and went in. Elka was asleep. I looked at the infant's cradle. The shutter was closed, but the moon forced its way through the cracks. I saw the newborn child's face and loved it as soon as I saw it—immediately—each tiny bone.

Then I came nearer to the bed. And what did I see but the apprentice lying there beside Elka. The moon went out all at once. It was utterly black, and I trembled. My teeth chattered. The bread fell from my hands, and my wife waked and said, "Who is that, ah?"

I muttered, "It's me."

"Gimpel?" she asked. "How come you're here? I thought it was forbidden."

"The rabbi said," I answered and shook as with a fever.

"Listen to me, Gimpel," she said, "go out to the shed and see if the goat's all right. It seems she's been sick." I have forgotten to say that we had a goat. When I heard she was unwell I went into the yard. The nannygoat was a good little creature. I had a nearly human feeling for her.

With hesitant steps I went up to the shed and opened the door. The goat stood there on her four feet. I felt her everywhere, drew her by the horns, examined her udders, and found nothing wrong. She had probably eaten too much bark. "Good night, little goat," I said. "Keep well." And the little beast answered with a "Maa" as though to thank me for the good will.

I went back. The apprentice had vanished.

"Where," I asked, "is the lad?"

"What lad?" my wife answered.

"What do you mean?" I said. "The apprentice. You were sleeping with him."

"The things I have dreamed this night and the night before," she said, "may they come true and lay you low, body and soul! An evil spirit has taken root in you and dazzles your sight." She screamed out, "You hateful creature! You moon calf! You spook! You uncouth man! Get out, or I'll scream all Frampol out of bed!"

Before I could move, her brother sprang out from behind the oven and struck me a blow on the back of the head. I thought he had broken my neck. I felt that something about me was deeply wrong, and I said, "Don't make a scandal. All that's needed now it that people should accuse me of raising spooks and *dybbuks*." For that was what she had meant. "No one will touch bread of my baking."

In short, I somehow calmed her.

"Well," she said, "that's enough. Lie down, and be shattered by wheels."

Next morning I called the apprentice aside. "Listen here, brother!" I said. And so on and so forth. "What do you say?" He stared at me as though I had dropped from the roof or something.

"I swear," he said, "you'd better go to an herb doctor or some healer. I'm afraid you have a screw loose, but I'll hush it up for you." And that's how the thing stood.

To make a long story short, I lived twenty years with my wife. She bore me six children, four daughters and two sons. All kinds of things happened, but I neither saw nor heard. I believed, and that's all. The rabbi recently said to me, "Belief in itself is beneficial. It is written that a good man lives by his faith."

Suddenly my wife took sick. It began with a trifle, a little growth upon the breast. But she evidently was not destined to live long; she had no years. I spent a fortune on her. I have forgotten to say that by this time I had a bakery of my own and in Frampol was considered to be something of a rich man. Daily the healer came, and every witch doctor in the neighborhood was brought. They decided to use leeches, and after that to try cupping. They even called a doctor from Lublin, but it was too late. Before she died she called me to her bed and said, "Forgive me, Gimpel."

I said, "What is there to forgive? You have been a good and faithful wife."

"Woe, Gimpel!" she said. "It was ugly how I deceived you all these years. I want to go clean to my Maker, and so I have to tell you that the children are not yours."

If I had been clouted on the head with a piece of wood it couldn't have bewildered me more.

"Whose are they?" I asked.

"I don't know," she said. "There were a lot...but they're not yours." And as she spoke she tossed her head to the side, her eyes turned glassy, and it was all up with Elka. On her whitened lips there remained a smile.

I imagined that, dead as she was, she was saying, "I deceived Gimpel. That was the meaning of my brief life."

4

One night, when the period of mourning was done, as I lay dreaming on the flour sacks, there came the Spirit of Evil himself and said to me, "Gimpel, why do you sleep?"

I said, "What should I be doing? Eating *kreplach?*"

"The whole world deceives you," he said, "and you ought to deceive the world in your turn."

"How can I deceive all the world?" I asked him.

He answered, "You might accumulate a bucket of urine every day and at night pour it into the dough. Let the sages of Frampol eat filth."

"What about the judgment in the world to come?" I said.

"There is no world to come," he said. "They've sold you a bill of goods and talked you into believing you carried a cat in your belly. What nonsense!"

"Well then," I said, "and is there a God?"

He answered, "There is no God either."

"What," I said, *"is* there, then?"

"A thick mire."

He stood before my eyes with a goatish beard and horn, long-toothed, and with a tail. Hearing such words, I wanted to snatch him by the tail, but I tumbled from the flour sacks and nearly broke a rib. Then it happened that I had to answer the call of nature, and, passing, I saw the risen dough, which seemed to say to me, "Do it!" In brief, I let myself be persuaded.

At dawn the apprentice came. We kneaded the bread, scattered caraway seeds on it, and set it to bake. Then the apprentice went away, and I was left sitting in the little trench by the oven, on a pile of rags. Well, Gimpel, I thought, you've revenged yourself on them for all the shame they've put on you. Outside the frost glittered, but it was warm beside the oven. The flames heated my face. I bent my head and fell into a doze.

I saw in a dream, at once, Elka in her shroud. She called to me, "What have you done, Gimpel?"

I said to her, "It's all your fault," and started to cry.

"You fool!" she said. "You fool! Because I was false is everything false too? I never deceived anyone but myself. I'm paying for it all, Gimpel. They spare you nothing here."

I looked at her face. It was black; I was startled and waked, and remained sitting dumb. I sensed that everything hung in the balance. A false step now and I'd lose Eternal Life. But God gave me His help. I seized the long shovel and took out the loaves, carried them into the yard, and started to dig a hole in the frozen earth.

My apprentice came back as I was doing it. "What are you doing boss?" he said, and grew pale as a corpse.

"I know what I'm doing," I said, and I buried it all before his very eyes.

Then I went home, took my hoard from its hiding place, and divided it among the children. "I saw your mother tonight," I said. "She's turning black, poor thing."

They were so astounded they couldn't speak a word.

"Be well," I said, "and forget that such a one as Gimpel ever existed." I put on my short coat, a pair of boots, took the bag that held my prayer shawl in one hand, my stock in the other, and kissed the *mezzuzah*. When people saw me in the street they were greatly surprised.

"Where are you going?" they said.

I answered, "Into the world." And so I departed from Frampol.

I wandered over the land, and good people did not neglect me. After many years I became old and white; I heard a great deal, many lies and falsehoods, but the longer I lived the more I understood that there were really no lies. Whatever doesn't really happen is dreamed at night. It happens to one if it doesn't happen to another, tomorrow if not today, or a century hence if not next year. What difference can it make? Often I heard tales of which I said, "Now this is a thing that cannot happen." But before a year had elapsed I heard that it actually had come to pass somewhere.

Going from place to place, eating at strange tables, it often happens that I spin yarns—improbable things that could never have happened—about devils, magicians, windmills, and the like. The children run after me, calling, "Grandfather, tell us a story." Sometimes they ask for particular stories, and I try to please them. A fat young boy once said to me, "Grandfather, it's the same story you told us before." The little rogue, he was right.

So it is with dreams too. It is many years since I left Frampol, but as soon as I shut my eyes I am there again. And whom do you think I see? Elka. She is standing by the washtub, as at our first encounter, but her face is shining and her eyes are as radiant as the eyes of a saint, and she speaks outlandish words to me, strange things. When I wake I have forgotten it all. But while the dream lasts I am comforted. She answers all my queries, and what comes out is that all is right. I weep and implore, "Let me be with you." And she consoles me and tells me to be patient. The time is nearer than it is far. Sometimes she strokes and kisses me and weeps upon my face. When I awaken I feel her lips and taste the salt of her tears.

No doubt the world is entirely an imaginary world, but it is only once removed from the true world. At the door of the hovel where I lie, there stands the plank on which the dead are taken away. The gravedigger Jew has his spade ready. The grave waits and the worms are hungry; the shrouds are prepared—I carry them in my beggar's sack. Another *shnorrer* is waiting to inherit my bed of straw. When the time comes I will go joyfully. Whatever may be there, it will be real, without complication, without ridicule, without deception. God be praised: there even Gimpel cannot be deceived.

Commentary

character
and
"gimpel the fool"

In his perceptive analysis of the relationship between character and time in *Character and the Novel,* W. J. Harvey remarks that the sequential course of a hero's life and the duration of his growth have much to do with the parallels that we establish between fiction and "real life"; and certainly when we speak of fiction as imitation it is in characterization that we expect to find its greatest lifelikeness. Especially in long fiction the connection between the reader's world and the story is strengthened by the hero's having a "degree of real psychic existence" like the reader's, as early incidents assume the quality of remembered events. Even in shorter fiction, a growth character fosters a similar identification, so that in observing the changes in him over a significant period of his life we participate in the process of internalizing vicariously, stretching the comparatively brief time of reading toward the duration he lives through. An extended action and a psychic center through which we are engaged in it thus create the illusion of substantial character and "real" life. At the same time, however, we are also detached from fictional characters in a special way. Whereas the connections between this or that aspect of a personality and various elements of a social context remain somewhat random and uncoordinated in life, in fiction they function together in a coherent system of meanings and create a concerted action. We assume perspectives on given characters from a knowledge of that whole, which they themselves are denied. We continually assess a multiplicity of interacting objects, events, and people as the context of judgment.

We are perhaps more aware of the distance between the work and real life in short than in long fiction. Understandably, most of the evolving characters that we find lifelike come from long works such as Stegner's *The Big Rock Candy Moutain,* George Eliot's *Middlemarch,* Tolstoy's *War and Peace,* or from multivolume works like Galsworthy's Forsyte saga. Short fiction does not usually evoke a sense of duration or full social context as the novel does, and of all the kinds of characterization that it might attempt—comic or satiric types who remain resolutely themselves no matter what happens, vaguely etched heroic archetypes, caricatures, realistic figures who respond to a single intense incident, and evolving heroes who accumulate a character over an extended period—the last of these is clearly the most difficult.

The surroundings and circumstances are obviously extremely important to characterization, because the fictionalist habitually uses analogical objects, scenes, action, and circumstances as mirrors of character. Beyond their use as mirrors, these external influences also form an order of their own that is in tension with the psychic makeup of the hero. They, as much as inherent character, determine the nature of a protagonist's growth and the degree to which the work resembles life. If the hero is innocent and the environment calculated to take advantage of him, for instance, the work often portrays his ironic destruction rather than growth, as in Nathanael West's *A Cool Million or, The Dismantling of Lemuel Pitkin,* in which each incident repeats the action of other incidents in altering Lemuel's anatomy for the worse. In realistic and naturalistic works such as Zola's, character tends to be overpowered and thwarted by an unavoidable natural and social context. In works with strong growth characters, the inner self exerts a proportionately more important influence on the action. Most highly mimetic works (*Middlemarch* is a good example) balance the will and energy of the protagonist against an environment that partially shapes his course for him. New sensory facts and social complications combine with an initial predisposition and will to produce a compromise action or a direction of growth that is a constant interaction of psychic and social phenomena. The protagonist is assisted by some elements of his environment and must resist others; some experiences confirm and strengthen what he tends to want to be and do; others force him to "dismantle" his original identity.

Prose fiction more than any other form of narration is suited to this kind of interplay because of its twofold focus on social documentation and interior lives. Perhaps only fiction, in fact, can pass effortlessly back and forth between dreams, imagination, and desire on one hand and the social and natural context of their operation on the other. Kinds of fictional character can be discussed in part as kinds of collision and tension between these.

A matter central to all such collisions is the discrepancy between the tempo of change in the context and the hero's rate of progress, or between the duration and power of the forces the hero confronts and the strength, endurance, and growth of his own predispositions. Psychic development tends to want to follow a certain rate as well as a certain direction, to unfold at a natural educational tempo as the hero takes in an increasing range of experiences and amalgamates everything new with everything established in him. This development is usually resisted or interrupted by external forces that have evolved for much longer than the hero understands at first and have a scope and a diversity that overwhelm any single personal capacity. Fictional plot is thus often a knitting together of several strands or "motions," each of which wants to take its own pace. Few (if any) modern fictional heroes are capable of performing actions critical to their entire cultures, as epic heroes once did: The total action and the total context are much larger than they. At best they are able to strike bargains with their surroundings and assume minor places within them. Consequently, a protagonist's education typically combines an expansion of his awareness and a shrinking of his expected function, as past events, social, moral, and psychological patterns, and nature are imposed on the pattern of his development.

In highly thematic and generalized forms such as the didactic parable, the individual career counts for little in itself; it models a general law, as the particular instance repeats a universal pattern. For the servants of Christ's parable of the talents (in the first section), for instance, the pattern that the man from the far country imposes on them transcends the social laws that they have already learned to accept; the "talents" are not merely pieces of money, they discover, but gifts of divine grace, to be repaid according to the kinds of links individual lives have with God's ultimate purposes. Likewise, the force that commands Abraham to slay his son requires the uprooting of Abraham's customary values (particularly his love for Isaac!); in effect, Abraham is forced to become an archetypal pattern for which his previous character gives him little inclination. In both narratives the expansion of one's psychic makeup requires a reconceiving of the individual will in the light of rather forceful mandates given from above.

Heroes of epic and romance also encounter enduring powers of some scope that make large demands upon them. In *The Iliad* and *The Aeneid* the destruction and founding of civilizations is viewed not merely as a social and military action but as the outgrowth of the quarrels of gods. In *Paradise Lost,* Milton treats the immediate episode of the central story (the Fall in Eden) in the context of a story that begins with the exaltation fo Christ in Heaven preceding Satan's fall and ends with Satan's final defeat at the radical end of history. Adam must be educated by Raphael and Michael in the events of the universe before and after his Fall in order to see the place of his few days in that total story of the universe. In Malory's grail stories, the grail leads the knights of the Round Table away from their customary fellowship, with its relatively limited history, and involves them in a pattern that extends over centuries. Their individual tempos must be fused with a very large destiny and very general pattern that universalizes all its participants. Such a plot or action clearly dominates the ordinary "localities" of character. In Joyce, Hardy, Conrad, Barth, Vonnegut and other modern novelists with mythic or romance leanings, we frequently find several layers and cycles of time reflecting each other and bearing upon the particular course that hero takes. He is forced to negotiate among them.

For most novelists, larger panoramas of time are less important than the close details of a given social mechanism, and these are likely to be shortened to a generation or two. Thus the last chapter of Thackeray's *Vanity Fair*, despite the reference to *Pilgrim's Progress* in the title, ends not with the heroine's discovery of a celestial destiny beyond her customary social affairs but with the novel's typical "Births, Marriages, and Deaths"—or the normal beginnings, middles, and endings of individual careers in a domestic context. The hero's individual predisposition in normative realism—in a world of commonsense realities that most of us accept without serious question—is opposed by "institutions" of one kind or another, which he either learns to accept after some adjustments or which turn him into a partial exile, condemned to keep part of his psychic potential entirely within. Having already managed to endure for some time, these institutions are not greatly disturbed by any single individual; they are usually tighly organized enough to resist foreign intrusions. Consequently, where the hero's forward drive and the makeup of his society collide, in realism, he generally bends more than it does, though the animal energy of a Tom Jones, the ingenuity of a Moll Flanders, and the uncontrollable oddities of Dicken's people are by no means totally subdued by the contexts within which they perform. In traditional realism, individuals and society generaly strike a contractual bargain, usually a marriage arrangement coupled with a middle class inheritance or some confirmed position. The wilder and more extravagant potentials of a given character are thereby set aside and official social recognition is extended to what remains: Identity is at last confirmed, as growth is arrested at an acceptable stage. In other forms, the individual and society continue their hit and run affair, as in the rogue novel, where no convincing reform ever quite finishes the episodic adventures of the hero or heroine. (A reform like that of Moll Flanders usually strikes readers as somewhat at odds with the cumulative character of the outcast.) Frequently in modern fiction, societies and heroes maintain an implacable enmity (as in stories of crime and punishment); or their relationship remains unresolved and cloudy, as in the "open-ended" novel.

The influence of social context on character and action is incontestable in all of these narrative kinds, but it is perhaps clearer in works in which individual character and its context fail to mesh, giving us a constantly interrupted stream of collisions and rival actions rather than a "growth" plot. In *Tristram Shandy* a multitude of intersecting forces prevents both the telling of a straightforward story and a coherent intertwining of Tristram's inner disposition and his surrounding society. The warring animal spirits that pass from his father to him at his begetting, the hobby horses and eccentricities that his relatives and neighbors pursue, the object-strewn physical world, and the strange associations of past and present that his own brain invents cause him to bounce from influence to influence without a sense of meaningful change. As Samuel Richardson remarks in a letter (with obvious irritation), the book has an "unaccountable wildness; whimsical digressions; comical incoherencies; uncommon indecencies; all with an air of novelty." Thus in Stern the usual fictional fabricator who constructs for us a designed unity of parts becomes the "concocter" who puts a hero together out of odd patches and pieces sewed in combinations of unlike elements. Fictive incident, essay, and digression are given approximately equal space, and the novel as a whole (if it is a novel) creates a sense not of duration and evolution but of fragmented time, repeatable static types, and intricate mechanisms of reaction.

At the opposite extreme, in a Henry James novel, for instance, character and society are perfectly meshed and every movement either psychic or social contributes to a single coherent growth. Each character is closely keyed to others who are psychologically open to him; he registers the slightest tremor from outside on the energy and movement of his own interior life. Whereas Tristram is assaulted by the eccentric and the nonsensical, James's characters assimilate whatever comes before them from the enclosed group of the novel. The action of the story is the unfolding of a "destiny" contained in the seeds of what he and his dynamic society of moral and social consciousnesses are.

The story of Gimpel is somewhat closer to Tristam Shandy's career than it is to that of a Jamesian character. It portrays comic collisions between Gimpel and the people of Frampol, who try to steer him into a particular course, and it follows the bumpy path of episodes joined loosely in illustration of his resistance. As a relatively short story, it does not realize every stage of Gimpel's career as fully as a novel might, but it does manage a sense of significant duration and social density. Frampol's wish to force Gimpel into the fixed role of the fool will obviously last as long as he lives there; that role begins in his childhood and extends to middle age, and he still remembers details of it in his old age. In a sense, the town seeks to do to Gimpel what fiction must do with the complex mass of tendencies and possibilities out of which people are made: that is, cut through the tangle, find a telling label or typical gesture, and affix character in it. Gimpel waivers between two possibilities: he can either resign himself to the reading others give him and play the complete fool, thus satisfying society's need for scapegoats; or he can learn from his experience and evolve into someone not limited to foolishness. (Actually, though Frampol scarcely realizes it, he is more sentimental than foolish; others use his emotions as a handle to make him do things that he knows are foolish.)

The first few sentences of the story set up this tension between exterior circumstance and inner life and suggest Gimpel's honesty in confronting it. As is so often the case with novelistic as opposed to epic and romance figures, Gimpel is an outsider, and the clash between his idea of himself and the idea that others have of him reveals once again—as in the life of picaro and criminal figures like Moll Flanders—society's tendency to assign functions to people as its mechanisms require. If fools are necessary to bolster the sense of worth in others, society will create them out of the raw material at hand. As Gimpel discovers, the pressure that society applies to a foolish man to accept its judgment is particularly strong, accompanied as it is by the added inducement of laughter and ridicule ("The gang laughed and hee-hawed, stomped and danced and chanted a good-night prayer").

But Gimpel also reveals increasingly that to play the fool requires one to be a strangely complex and in a sense even a wise man. We realize at the outset that his foolishness is not a product of stupidity so much as of a weak good-heartedness and an inability to adhere to what the evidence clearly indicates. Not realizing the difference between the divine miracles referred to in the sacred script and the foolish wonders he is asked to believe, he rationalizes, "everything is possible, as it is written in the Wisdom of the Fathers." He allows the obvious lies that Frampol fashions for him to displace what are after all very impressive physical facts—the bagels, burrs, glumps and ninnies, buckets, noodles, macroons, louts, loudmouths, and chicken legs of his village life. But to put the most favorable construction on him, he also lives in a world in which cause and effect have richer possibilities than for other people, in which "whatever doesn't really happen" is at least "dreamed at night." His eventual wisdom consists in the openness he finds in all sequences of incident and evidence, which never quite prove to him that they are actually what they seem; even if they are, in the long run no final truth is revealed by that.

Thus he stands in a "wise" defiance of the belittling circumstances of realism. The difference between the fictions of the townspeople and the lies of his dreams and illusions is that their unrealities are created for cynical purposes, his out of charity and the promptings of his simplicity. Their hardheadedness is directed solely toward others and offers no assistance to self-appraisal; his soft-heartedness is directed toward the acceptance of everything that happens or might happen, as part of God's will.

Over the long run of his transformation (the critical moment of which is his revolt and departure from Frampol, his first real act of will), Gimpel therefore adds to the foolish scapegoat something like the believer, whose greatest illusionist and tormenter, he comes to believe, is God himself. Though he never ceases entirely to be the butt of jokes, he becomes in addition the interpreter and teller of stories, capable of analyzing to some extent the ancient problem of illusion and reality. His mastery over that commonplace but very complex problem transcends the pramatic instinct for the cunning use of illusion that the townspeople of Frampol have. Though the comparative brevity of the story makes it impossible for Singer to include all the stages of that transformation, the effect of Gimpel's closing paragraphs is to make us realize that a new potential has been awakened in him by his decision to leave Frampol without taking revenge upon it. In his unsystematic way, he stumbles upon an inner reason for the existence of such fictions as he has always wanted to believe: his trials produce in him a strong desire for some final transformation when the uncomplicated truth will be given to him "without ridicule." When such a time comes, "I will go joyfully," he remarks. Meanwhile, the world of illusion and process will continue to mix dreams and realities inextricably. The facts outside and the dreams within hold him in suspension. Though he can never know exactly where he stands, in compensation he enjoys an increasingly rich world, and his imagination returns even his earlier days to him with some comfort. Elka becomes "as radiant" as a saint and speaks outlandish words to him, which (if our memories serve us correctly) she never did in the real Frampol. We are not certain, however, that the creature of his invention is not closer to the potential Elka than the snippish and truant wife who once tormented him: The imagination collects unrealized possibilities and escapes the comedy of circumstances that twists everyone in his real history.

Gimpel's glance backward to his former life maintains continuity with what he has been, then, but it also suggests has a possible transcendence of mere village fact. In this respect, he becomes typical of every fictional hero who imagines a possible life for himself and different roles for others (whom he automatically makes subordinate characters in his own improved story), and at the same time operates in a world of necessity. The shaping spirit, busily creating conceivable roles for itself, and the realities of its context fight in Gimpel one of the typical battles of narrative realism.

The Wall

jean-paul sartre

THEY PUSHED US into a large white room and my eyes began to blink because the light hurt them. Then I saw a table and four fellows seated at the table, civilians, looking at some papers. The other prisoners were herded together at one end and we were obliged to cross the entire room to join them. There were several I knew, and others who must have been foreigners. The two in front of me were blond with round heads. They looked alike. I imagine they were French. The smaller one kept pulling at his trousers, out of nervousness.

This lasted about three hours. I was dog-tried and my head was empty. But the room was well-heated, which struck me as rather agreeable; we had not stopped shivering for twenty-four hours. The guards led the prisoners in one after another in front of the table. Then the four fellows asked them their names and what they did. Most of the time that was all—or perhaps from time to time they would ask such questions as: "Did you help sabotage the munitions?" or, "Where were you on the morning of the ninth and what were you doing?" They didn't even listen to the replies, or at least they didn't seem to. They just remained silent for a moment and looked straight ahead, then they began to write. They asked Tom if it was true he had served in the International Brigade. Tom couldn't say he hadn't because of the papers they had found in his jacket. They didn't ask Juan anything, but after he told them his name, they wrote for a long while.

"It's my brother José who's the anarchist," Juan said. "You know perfectly well he's not here now. I don't belong to any party. I never did take part in politics." They didn't answer.

Then Juan said, "I didn't do anything. And I'm not going to pay for what the others did."

His lips were trembling. A guard told him to stop talking and led him away. It was my turn.

"Your name is Pablo Ibbieta?"

I said yes.

The fellow looked at his papers and said, "Where is Ramon Gris?"

"I don't know."

"You hid him in your house from the sixth to the nineteenth."

"I did not."

They continued to write for a moment and the guards led me away. In the hall, Tom and Juan were waiting between two guards. We started walking. Tom asked one of the guards, "What's the idea?" "How do you mean?" the guard asked. "Was that just the preliminary questioning, or was that the trial?" "That was the trial," the guard said. "So now what? What are they going to do with us?" The guard answered drily, "The verdict will be told you in your cell."

In reality, our cell was one of the cellars of the hospital. It was terribly cold there because it was very drafty. We had been shivering all night long and it had hardly been any better during the day. I had spent the preceding five days in a cellar in the archbishop's palace, a sort of dungeon that must have dated back to the Middle Ages. There were lots of prisoners and not much room, so they housed them just anywhere. But I was not homesick for my dungeon. I hadn't been cold there, but I had been alone, and that gets to be irritating. In the cellar I had company. Juan didn't say a word; he was afraid, and besides, he was too young to have anything to say. But Tom was a good talker and knew Spanish well.

In the cellar there were a bench and four straw mattresses. When they led us back we sat down and waited in silence. After a while Tom said, "Our goose is cooked."

"I think so too." I said. "But I don't believe they'll do anything to the kid."

Tom said, "They haven't got anything on him. He's the brother of a fellow who's fighting, and that's all."

I looked at Juan. He didn't seem to have heard.

Tom continued, "You know what they do in Saragossa? They lay the guys across the road and then they drive over them with trucks. It was a Moroccan deserter who told us that. They say it's just to save ammunition."

I said, "Well, it doesn't save gasoline."

I was irritated with Tom; he shouldn't have said that.

He went on, "There are officers walking up and down the roads with their hands in their pockets, smoking, and they see that it's done right. Do you think they'd put 'em out of their misery? Like hell they do. They just let 'em holler. Sometimes as long as an hour. The Moroccan said the first time he almost puked."

"I don't believe they do that here," I said, "unless they really are short of ammunition."

The daylight came in through four air vents and a round opening that had been cut in the ceiling, to the left, and which opened directly onto the sky. It was through this hole, which was ordinarily closed by means of a trapdoor, that they unloaded coal into the cellar. Directly under the hole, there was a big pile of coal dust; it had been intended for heating the hospital, but at the beginning of the war they had evacuated the patients and the coal had stayed there unused; it even got rained on from times to time, when they forgot to close the trapdoor.

Tom started to shiver. "God damm it," he said, "I'm shivering. There, it is starting again."

He rose and began to do gymnastic exercises. At each movement, his shirt opened and showed his white, hairy chest. He lay down on his back, lifted his legs in the air and began to do the scissors movement. I watched his big buttocks tremble. Tom was tough, but he had too much fat on him. I kept thinking that soon bullets and bayonet points would sink into that mass of tender flesh as though it were a pat of butter.

I wasn't exactly cold, but I couldn't feel my shoulders or my arms. From time to time, I had the impression that something was missing and I began to look around for my jacket. Then I would suddenly remember they hadn't given me a jacket. It was rather awkward. They had taken our clothes to give them to their own soldiers and had left us only our shirts and these cotton trousers the hospital patients wore in mid-summer. After a moment, Tom got up and sat down beside me, breathless.

"Did you get warmed up?"

"Damn it, no. But I'm all out of breath."

Around eight o'clock in the evening, a Major came in with two falangists.

"What are the names of those three over there?" he asked the guard.

"Steinbock, Ibbieta and Mirbal," said the guard.

The Major put on his glasses and examined his list.

"Steinbock—Steinbock...Here it is. You ares condemned to death. You'll be shot tomorrow morning."

He looked at his list again.

"The other two, also," he said.

"That's not possible," said Juan. "Not me."

The Major looked at him with surprise. "What's your name?"

"Juan Mirbal."

"Well, your name is here," said the Major, "and you're condemned to death."

"I didn't do anything," said Juan.

The Major shrugged his shoulders and turned toward Tom and me.

"You are both Basque?"

"No, nobody's Basque."

He appeared exasperated.

"I was told there were three Basques. I'm not going to waste my time running after them. I suppose you don't want a priest?"

We didn't even answer.

Then he said, "A Belgian doctor will be around in a little while. He has permission to stay with you all night."

He gave a military salute and left.

"What did I tell you?" Tom said. "We're in for something swell."

"Yes," I said. "It's a damned shame for the kid."

I said that to be fair, but I really didn't like the kid. His face was too refined and it was disfigured by fear and suffering, which had twisted all his features. Three days ago, he was just a kid with a kind of affected manner some people like. But now he looked like an aging fairy, and I thought to myself he would never be young again, even if they let him go. It wouldn't have been a bad thing to show him a little pity, but pity makes me sick, and besides, I couldn't stand him. He hadn't said anything more, but he had turned gray. His face and hands were gray. He sat down again and stared, round-eyed, at the ground. Tom was goodhearted and tried to take him by the arm, but the kid drew himself away violently and made an ugly face. "Leave him alone," I said quietly. "Can't you see he's going to start to bawl?" Tom obeyed regretfully. He would have liked to console the kid; that would have kept him occupied and he wouldn't have been tempted to think about himself. But it got on my nerves. I had never thought about death, for the reason that the question had never come up. But now it had come up, and there was nothing else to do but think about it.

Tom started talking. "Say, did you ever bump anybody off?" he asked me. I didn't answer. He started to explain to me that he had bumped off six fellows since August. He hadn't yet realized what we were in for, and I saw clearly he didn't *want* to realize it. I myself hadn't quite taken it in. I wondered if it hurt very much. I thought about the bullets; I imagined their fiery hail going through my body. All that was beside the real question; but I was calm, we had all night in which to realize it. After a while Tom stopped talking and I looked at him out of the corner of my eye. I saw that he, too, had turned gray and that he looked pretty miserable. I said to myself, "It's starting." It was almost dark, a dull light filtered through the air vents across the coal pile and made a big spot under the sky. Through the hole in the ceiling I could already see a star. The night was going to be clear and cold.

The door opened and two guards entered. They were followed by a blond man in a tan uniform. He greeted us.

"I'm the doctor," he said. "I've been authorized to give you any assistance you may require in these painful circumstances."

He had an agreeable, cultivated voice.

I said to him, "What are you going to do here?"

"Whatever you want me to do. I shall do everything in my power to lighten these few hours."

"Why did you come to us? There are lots of others: the hospital's full of them."

"I was sent here," he answered vaguely. "You'd probably like to smoke, wouldn't you?" he added suddenly. "I've got some cigarettes and even some cigars."

He passed around some English cigarettes and some *puros,* but we refused them. I looked him straight in the eye and he appeared uncomfortable.

"You didn't come here out of compassion," I said to him. "In fact, I know who you are. I saw you with some fascists in the barracks yard the day I was arrested."

I was about to continue, when all at once something happened to me which surprised me: The presence of this doctor had suddenly ceased to interest me. Usually, when I've got hold of a man I don't let go. But somehow the desire to speak had left me. I shrugged my shoulders and turned away. A little later, I looked up and saw he was watching me with an air of curiosity. The guards had sat down on one of the mattresses. Pedro, the tall thin one, was twiddling his thumbs, while the other one shook his head occasionally to keep from falling asleep.

"Do you want some light?" Pedro suddenly asked the doctor. The other fellow nodded, "Yes." I think he was not over-intelligent, but doubtless he was not malicious. As I looked at his big, cold, blue eyes, it seemed to me the worst thing about him was his lack of imagination. Pedro went out and came back with an oil lamp which he set on the corner of the bench. It gave a poor light, but it was better than nothing; the night before we had been left in the dark. For a long while I stared at the circle of light the lamp threw on the ceiling. I was fascinated. Then, suddenly, I came to, the light circle paled, and I felt as if I were being crushed under an enormous weight. It wasn't the though of death, and it wasn't fear; it was something anonymous. My cheeks were burning hot and my head ached.

I roused myself and looked at my two companions. Tom had his head in his hands and only the fat, white nape of his neck was visible. Juan was by far the worst off; his mouth was wide open and his nostrils were trembling. The doctor came over to him and touched him on the shoulder, as though to comfort him; but his eyes remained cold. Then I saw the Belgian slide his hand furtively down Juan's arm to his wrist. Indifferent, Juan let himself he handled. Then, as though absent-mindedly, the Belgian laid three fingers over his wrist; at the same time, he drew away somewhat and managed to turn his back to me. But I leaned over backward and saw him take out his watch and look at it a moment before relinquishing the boy's wrist. After a moment, he let the inert hand fall and went and leaned against the wall. Then, as if he had suddenly remembered something very important that had to be noted down immediately, he took a notebook from his pocket and wrote a few lines in it. "The son-of-a-bitch," I thought angrily. "He better not come and feel my pulse; I'll give him a punch in his dirty jaw."

He didn't come near me, but I felt he was looking at me. I raised my head and looked back at him. In an impersonal voice, he said, "Don't you think it's frightfully cold here?"

He looked purple with cold.

"I'm not cold," answered him.

He kept looking at me with a hard expression. Suddenly I understood, and I lifted my hands to my face. I was covered with sweat. Here, in this cellar, in mid-winter, right in a draft, I was sweating. I ran my fingers through my hair, which was stiff with sweat; at the same time, I realized my shirt was damp and sticking to my skin. I had been streaming with perspiration for an hour, at least, and had felt nothing. But this fact hadn't escaped that Belgian swine. He had seen the drops rolling down my face and had said to himself that it showed an almost pathological terror; and he himself had felt normal and proud of it because he was cold. I wanted to get up and go punch his face in, but I had hardly started to make a move before my shame and anger had disappeared. I dropped back onto the bench with indifference.

I was content to rub my neck with my handkerchief because now I felt the sweat dripping from my hair onto the nape of my neck and that was disagreeable. I soon gave up rubbing myself, however, for it didn't do any good; my handkerchief was already wringing wet and I was still sweating. My buttocks, too, were sweating, and my damp trousers stuck to the bench.

Suddenly, Juan said, "You're a doctor, aren't you?"

"Yes," said the Belgian.

"Do people suffer—very long?"

"Oh! When...? No, no," said the Belgian, in a paternal voice, "it's quickly over."

His manner was as reassuring as if he had been answering a paying patient.

"But I...Somebody told me—they often have to fire two volleys."

"Sometimes," said the Belgian, raising his head, "it just happens that the first volley doesn't hit any of the vital organs."

"So then they have to reload their guns and aim all over again?" Juan thought for a moment, then added hoarsely, "But that takes time!"

He was terribly afraid of suffering. He couldn't think about anything else, but that went with his age. As for me, I hardly thought about it any more and it certainly was not fear of suffering that made me perspire.

I rose and walked toward the pile of coal dust. Tom gave a start and looked at me with a look of hate. I irritated him because my shoes squeaked. I wondered if my face was as putty-colored as his. Then I noticed that he, too, was sweating. The sky was magnificent; no light at all came into our dark corner and I had only to lift my head to see the Big Bear. But it didn't look the way it had looked before. Two days ago, from my cell in the archbishop's palace, I could see a big patch of sky and each time of day brought back a different memory. In the morning, when the sky was a deep blue, and light, I thought of beaches along the Atlantic; at noon, I could see the sun, and I remembered a bar in Seville where I used to drink manzanilla and eat anchovies and olives; in the afternoon, I was in the shade, and I though of the deep shadow which covers half of the arena while the other half gleams in the sunlight: it really gave me a pang to see the whole earth reflected in the sky like that. Now, however, no matter how much I looked up in the air, the sky no longer recalled anything. I liked it better that way. I came back and sat down next to Tom. There was a long silence.

Then Tom began to talk in a low voice. He had to keep talking, otherwise he lost his way in his own thoughts. I believe he was talking to me, but he didn't look at me. No doubt he was afraid to look at me, because I was gray and sweating. We were both alike and worse than mirrors for each other. He looked at the Belgian, the only one who was alive.

"Say, do you understand? I don't."

Then I, too, began to talk in a low voice. I was watching the Belgian.

"Understand what? What's the matter?"

"Something's going to happen to us that I don't understand."

There was a strange odor about Tom. It seemed to me that I was more sensitive to odors than ordinarily. With a sneer, I said, "You'll understand, later."

"That's not so sure," he said stubbornly. "I'm willing to be courageous, but at least I ought to know...Listen, they're going to take us out into the courtyard. All right. The fellows will be standing in line in front of us. How many of them will there be?"

"Oh, I don't know. Five, or eight. Not more."

"That's enough. Let's say there'll be eight of them. Somebody will shout 'Shoulder arms!' and I'll see all eight rifles aimed at me. I'm sure I'm going to feel like going through the wall. I'll push against the wall as hard as I can with my back, and the wall won't give in. The way it is in a nightmare. . . . I can imagine all that. Ah, if you only knew how well I can imagine it!"

"Skip it!" I said. "I can imagine it too."

"It must hurt like the devil. You know they aim at your eyes and mouth so as to disfigure you," he added maliciously. "I can feel the wounds already. For the last hour I've been having pains in my head and neck. Not real pains—it's worse still. They're the pains I'll feel tomorrow morning. And after that, then what?"

I understood perfectly well what he meant, but I didn't want to seem to understand. As for the pains, I, too, felt them all through my body, like a lot of little gashes. I couldn't get used to them, but I was like him, I didn't think they were very important.

"After that," I said roughly, "you'll be eating daisies."

He started talking to himself, not taking his eyes off the Belgian, who didn't seem to be listening to him. I knew what he had come for, and that what we were thinking didn't interest him. He had come to look at our bodies, our bodies which were dying alive.

"It's like in a nightmare," said Tom. "You want to think of something, you keep having the impression you've got it, that you're going to understand, and then it slips away from you, it eludes you and it's gone again. I say to myself, afterwards, there won't be anything. But I don't really understand what that means. There are moments when I almost do—and then it's gone again. I start to think of the pains, the bullets, the noise of the shooting. I am a materialist, I swear it; and I'm not going crazy, either. But there's something wrong. I see my own corpse. That's not hard, but it's *I* who see it, with *my* eyes. I'll have to get to the point where I think—where I think I won't see anything more. I won't hear anything more, and the world will go on for the others. We're not made to think that way, Pablo. Believe me, I've already stayed awake all night waiting for something. But this is not the same thing. This will grab us from behind, Pablo, and we won't be ready for it."

"Shut up," I said. "Do you want me to call a father confessor?"

He didn't answer. I had already noticed that he had a tendency to prophesy and call me "Pablo" in a kind of pale voice. I didn't like that very much, but it seems all the Irish are like that. I had a vague impression that he smelled of urine. Actually, I didn't like Tom very much, and I didn't see why, just because we were going to die together, I should like him any better. There are certain fellows with whom it would be different—with Ramon Gris, for instance. But between Tom and Juan, I felt alone. In fact, I liked it better that way. With Ramon I might have grown soft. But I felt terribly hard at that moment, and I wanted to stay hard.

Tom kept on muttering, in a kind of absent-minded way. He was certainly talking to keep from thinking. Naturally, I agreed with him, and I could have said everything he was saying. It's not *natural* to die. And since I was going to die, nothing seemed natural any more: neither the coal pile, nor the bench, nor Pedro's dirty old face. Only it was disagreeable for me to think the same things Tom thought. And I knew perfectly well that all night long, within five minutes of each other, we would keep on thinking things at the same time, sweating or shivering at the same time. I looked at him sideways and, for the first time, he seemed strange to me. He had death written on his face. My pride was wounded. For twenty-four hours I had lived side by side with Tom, I had listened to him, I had talked to him, and I knew we had nothing in common. And now we were as alike as twin brothers, simply because we were going to die together. Tom took my hand without looking at me.

"Pablo, I wonder...I wonder if it's true that we just cease to exist."

I drew my hand away.

"Look between your feet, you dirty dog."

There was a puddle between his feet and water was dripping from his trousers.

"What's the matter?" he said, frightened.

"You're wetting your pants," I said to him.

"It's not true," he said furiously. "I can't be...I don't feel anything."

The Belgian had come closer to him. With an air of false concern, he asked, "Aren't you feeling well?"

Tom didn't answer. The Belgian looked at the puddle without comment.

"I don't know what that it," Tom said savagely, "but I'm not afraid. I swear to you, I'm not afraid."

The Belgian made no answer. Tom rose and went to the corner. He came back, buttoning his fly, and sat down, without a word. The Belgian was taking notes.

We were watching the doctor. Juan was watching him too. All three of us were watching him because he was alive. He had the gestures of a living person, the interests of a living person; he was shivering in this cellar the way living people shiver; he had an obedient, well-fed body. We, on the other hand, didn't feel our bodies any more—not the same way, in any case. I felt like touching my trousers, but I didn't dare to. I looked at the Belgian, well-planted on his two legs, master of his muscles—and able to plan for tomorrow. We were like three shadows deprived of blood; we were watching him and sucking his life like vampires.

Finally he came over to Juan. Was he going to lay his hand on the nape of Juan's neck for some professional reason, or had he obeyed a charitable impulse? If he had acted out of charity, it was the one and only time during the whole night. He fondled Juan's head and the nape of his neck. The kid let him do it, without taking his eyes off him. Then, suddenly, he took hold of the doctor's hand and looked at it in a funny way. He held the Belgian's hand between his own two hands and there was nothing pleasing about them, those two gray paws squeezing that fat red hand. I sensed what was going to happen and Tom must have sensed it, too But all the Belgian saw was emotion, and he smiled paternally. After a moment, the kid lifted the big red paw to his mouth and started to bite it. The Belgian drew back quickly and stumbled toward the wall. For a second, he loooked at us with horror. He must have suddenly understood that we were not men like himself. I began to laugh, and one of the guards started up. The other had fallen asleep with his eyes wide open, showing only the whites.

I felt tired and over-excited at the same time. I didn't want to think any more about was going to happen at dawn—about death. It didn't make sense, and I never got beyond just words, or emptiness. But whenever I tried to think about something else I saw the barrels of rifles aimed at me. I must have lived through my execution twenty times in succession; one time I thought it was the real thing; I must have dozed off for a moment. They were dragging me toward the wall and I was resisting; I was imploring their pardon. I woke with a start and looked at the Belgian. I was afraid I had cried out in my sleep. But he was smoothing his mustache; he hadn't noticed anything. If I had wanted to, I believe I could have slept for a while. I had been awake for the last forty-eight hours, and I was worn out. But I didn't want to lose two hours of life. They would have had to come and wake me at dawn. I would have followed them, drunk with sleep, and I would have gone off without so much as "Gosh!" I didn't want it that way, I didn't want to die like an animal. I wanted to understand. Besides, I was afraid of having nightmares. I got up and began to walk up and down and, so as to think about something else, I began to think about my past life. Memories crowded in on me, helterskelter. Some were good and some were bad—at least that was how I had thought of them *before*. There were faces and happenings. I saw the face of a little *novilero* who had gotten himself horned during the *Feria*, in Valencia. I saw the face of one of my uncles, of Ramon Gris. I remembered all kinds of things that had happened: how I had been on strike for three months in 1926, and had almost died of hunger. I recalled a night I had spent on a beach in Granada; I hadn't eaten for three days, I was nearly wild, I didn't want to give up the sponge. I had to smile. With what eagerness I had run after happiness, and women, and liberty! And to what end? I had wanted to liberate Spain, I admired Py Margall, I had belonged to the anarchist movement, I had spoken at public meetings. I took everything seriously as if I had been immortal.

At that time I had the impression that I had my whole life before me, and I thought to myself, "It's all a goddamned lie." Now it wasn't worth anything because it was finished. I wondered how I had ever been able to go out and have a good time with girls. I wouldn't have lifted my little finger if I had ever imagined that I would die like this. I saw my life before me, finished, closed, like a bag, and yet what was inside was not finshed. For a moment I tried to appraise it. I would have liked to say to myself, "It's been a good life." But it couldn't be appraised, it was only an outline. I had spent my time writing checks on eternity, and had understood nothing. Now, I didn't miss anything. There were a lot of things I might have missed: the taste of manzanilla, for instance, or the swims I used to take in summer in a little creek near Cadiz. But death had taken the charm out of everything.

Suddenly the Belgian had a wonderful idea.

"My friends," he said to us, "if you want me to—and providing the military authorities give their consent—I could undertake to deliver a word or some token from you to your loved ones. . . ."

Tom growled, "I haven't got anybody."

I didn't answer. Tom waited for a moment, then he looked at me with curiosity. "Aren't you going to send any message to Concha?"

"No."

I hated that sort of sentimental conspiracy. Of course, it was my fault, since I had mentioned Concha the night before, and I should have kept my mouth shut. I had been with her for a year. Even as late as last night, I would have cut my arm off with a hatchet just to see her again for five minutes. That was why I had mentioned her. I couldn't help it. Now I didn't care any more about seeing her. I hadn't anything more to say to her. I didn't even want to hold her in my arms. I loathed my body because it had turned gray and was sweating—and I wasn't even sure that I didn't loathe hers too. Concha would cry when she heard about my death; for months she would have no more interest in life. But still it was I who was going to die. I thought of her beautiful, loving eyes. When she looked at me something went from her to me. But I thought to myself that it was all over; if she looked at me *now* her gaze would not leave her eyes, it would not reach out to me. I was alone.

Tom too, was alone, but not the same way. He was seated astride his chair and had begun to look at the bench with a sort of smile, with surprise, even. He reached out his hand and touched the wood cautiously, as though he were afraid of breaking something, then he drew his hand back hurriedly, and shivered. I wouldn't have amused myself touching that bench, if I had been Tom, that was just some more Irish play-acting. But somehow it seemed to me too that the different objects had something funny about them. They seemed to have grown paler, less massive than before. I had only to look at the bench, the lamp or the pile of coal dust to feel I was going to die. Naturally, I couldn't think clearly about my death, but I saw it everywhere, even on the different objects, the way they had withdrawn and kept their distance, tactfully, like people talking at the bedside of a dying person. It was *his own death* Tom had just touched on the bench.

In the state I was in, if they had come and told me I could go home quietly, that my life would be saved, it would have left me cold. A few hours, or a few years of waiting are all the same, when you've lost the illusion of being eternal. Nothing mattered to me any more. In a way, I was calm. But it was a horrible kind of calm—because of my body. My body—I saw with its eyes and I heard with its ears, but it was no longer I. It sweat and trembled independently, and I didn't recognize it any longer. I was obliged to touch it and look at it to know what was happening to it, just as if it had been someone else's body. At times I still felt it, I felt a slipping, a sort of headlong plunging, as in a falling airplane, or else I heard my heart beating. But this didn't give me confidence. In fact, everything that came from my body had something damned dubious about it. Most of the time it was silent, it stayed put and I didn't feel anything other than a sort of heaviness, a loathsome presence against me. I had the impression of being bound to an enormous vermin.

The Belgian took out his watch and looked at it.

"It's half-past three," he said.

The son-of-a-bitch! He must have done it on purpose. Tom jumped up. We hadn't yet realized the time was passing. The night surrounded us like a formless, dark mass; I didn't even remember it had started.

Juan started to shout. Wringing his hands, he implored, "I don't want to die! I don't want to die!"

He ran the whole length of the cellar with his arms in the air, then he dropped down onto one of the mattresses, sobbing. Tom looked at him with dismal eyes and didn't even try to console him any more. The fact was, it was no use; the kid made more noise than we did, but he was less affected, really. He was like a sick person who defends himself against his malady with a high fever. When there's not even any fever left, it's much more serious.

He was crying. I could tell he felt sorry for himself; he was thinking about death. For one second, one single second, I too felt like crying; crying out of pity for myself. But just the contrary happened. I took one look at the kid, saw his thin, sobbing shoulders, and I felt I was inhuman. I couldn't feel pity either for these others or for myself. I said to myself, "I want to die decently."

Tom had gotten up and was standing just under the round opening looking out for the first signs of daylight. I was determined, I wanted to die decently, and I only thought about that. But underneath, ever since the doctor had told us the time, I felt time slipping, flowing by, one drop at a time.

It was still dark when I heard Tom's voice.

"Do you hear them?"

"Yes."

People were walking in the courtyard.

"What the hell are they doing? After all, they can't shoot in the dark."

After a moment, we didn't hear anything more. I said to Tom, "There's the daylight."

Pedro got up yawning, and came and blew out the lamp. He turned to the man beside him. "It's hellish cold."

The cellar had grown gray. We could hear shots at a distance.

"It's about to start," I said to Tom. "That must be in the back courtyard."

Tom asked the doctor too give him a cigarette. I didn't want any; I didn't want either cigarettes or alcohol. From that moment on, the shooting didn't stop.

"Can you take it in?" Tom said.

He started to add something, then he stopped and began to watch the door. The door opened and a lieutenant came in with four soldiers. Tom dropped his cigarette.

"Steinbock?"

Tom didn't answer. Pedro pointed him out.

"Juan Mirbal?"

"He's the one on the mattress."

"Stand up," said the Lieutenant.

Juan didn't move. Two soldiers took hold of him by the armpits and stood him up on his feet. But as soon as they let go of him he fell down.

The soldiers hesitated a moment.

"He's not the first one to get sick," said the Lieutenant. "You'll have to carry him, the two of you. We'll arrange things when we get there." He turned to Tom. "All right, come along."

Tom left between two soldiers. Two other soldiers followed, carrying the kid by his arms and legs. He was not unconscious; his eyes were wide open and tears were rolling down his cheeks. When I started to go out, the Lieutenant stopped me.

"Are you Ibbieta?"

"Yes."

"You wait here. They'll come and get you later on."

They left. The Belgian and the two jailers left too, and I was alone. I didn't understand what had happened to me, but I would have liked it better if they had ended it all right away. I heard the volleys at almost regular intervals; at each one, I shuddered. I felt like howling and tearing my hair. But instead, I gritted my teeth and pushed my hands deep into my pockets, because I wanted to stay decent.

An hour later, they came to fetch me and took me up to the first floor in a little room which smelt of cigar smoke and was so hot it seemed to me suffocating. Here there were two officers sitting in comfortable chairs, smoking, with papers spread out on their knees.

"Your name is Ibbieta?"

"Yes."

"Where is Ramon Gris?"

"I don't know."

The man who questioned me was small and stocky. He had hard eyes behind his glasses.

"Come nearer," he said to me.

I went nearer. He rose and took me by the arms, looking at me in a way calculated to make me go through the floor. At the same time he pinched my arms with all his might. He didn't mean to hurt me; it was quite a game; he wanted to dominate me. He also seemed to think it was necessary to blow his fetid breath right into my face. We stood like that for a moment, only I felt more like laughing than anything else. It takes a lot more than that to intimidate a man who's about to die: it didn't work. He pushed me away violently and sat down again.

"It's your life or his," he said. "You'll be allowed to go free if you tell us where he is."

After all, these two bedizened fellows with their riding crops and boots were just men who were going to die one day. A little later than I, perhaps, but not a great deal. And there they were, looking for names among their papers, running after other men in order to put them in prison or do away with them entirely. They had their opinions on the future of Spain and on other subjects. Their petty activities seemed to me to be offensive and ludicrous. I could no longer put myself in their place. I had the impression they were crazy.

The little fat fellow kept looking at me, tapping his boots with his riding crop. All his gestures were calculated to make him appear like a spirited, ferocious animal.

"Well? Do you understand?"

"I don't know where Gris is," I said. "I thought he was in Madrid."

The other officer lifted his pale hand indolently. This indolence was also calculated. I saw through all their little tricks, and I was dumbfounded that men should still exist who took pleasure in that kind of thing.

"You have fifteen minutes to think it over," he said slowly. "Take him to the linen-room, and bring him back here in fifteen minutes. If he continues to refuse, he'll be executed at once."

They knew what they were doing. I had spent the night waiting. After that, they had made me wait another hour in the cellar, while they shot Tom and Juan, and now they locked me in the linen-room. They must have arranged the whole thing the night before. They figured that sooner or later people's nerves wear out and they hoped to get me that way.

They made a big mistake. In the linen-room I sat down on a ladder because I felt very weak, and I began to think things over. Not their proposition, however. Naturally I knew where Gris was. He was hiding in his cousins' house, about two miles outside the city. I knew, too, that I would not reveal his hiding place, unless they tortured me (but they didn't seem to be considering that). All that was definitely settled and didn't interest me in the least. Only I would have liked to understand the reasons for my own conduct. I would rather die than betray Gris. Why? I no longer liked Ramon Gris. My friendship for him had died shortly before dawn along with my love for Concha, along with my own desire to live. Of course I still admired him—he was hard. But it was not for that reason that I was willing to die in his place; his life was no more valuable than mine. No life was of any value. A man was going to be stood up against a wall and fired at till he dropped dead. It didn't make any difference whether it was I or Gris or somebody else. I knew perfectly well he was more useful to the Spanish cause than I was, but didn't give a God damn about Spain or anarchy, either; nothing had any importance now. And yet, there I was. I could save my skin by betraying Gris and I refused to do it. It seemed more ludicrous to me than anything else; it was stubbornness.

I thought to myself, "Am I hardheaded!" And I was seized with a strange sort of cheerfulness.

They came to fetch me and took me back to the two officers. A rat darted out under our feet and that amused me. I turned to one of the falangists and said to him. "Did you see that rat?"

He made no reply. He was gloomy, and took himself very seriously. As for me, I felt like laughing, but I restrained myself because I was afraid that if I started, I wouldn't be able to stop. The falangist wore mustaches. I kept after him, "You ought to cut off those mustaches, you fool."

I was amused by the fact that he let hair grow all over his face while he was still alive. He gave me a kind of halfhearted kick, and I shut up.

"Well," said the fat officer, "have you thought things over?"

I looked at them with curiosity, like insects of a very rare species.

"I know where he is," I said. "He's hiding in the cemetery. Either in one of the vaults, or in the gravediggers' shack."

I said that just to make fools of them. I wanted to see them get up and fasten their belts and bustle about giving orders.

They jumped to their feet.

"Fine. Moles, go ask Lieutenant Lopez for fifteen men. And as for you," the little fat fellow said to me, "if you've told the truth, I don't go back on my word. But you'll pay for this, if you're pulling our leg."

They left noisily and I waited in peace, still guarded by the falangists. From time to time I smiled at the thought of the face they were going to make. I felt dull and malicious. I could see them lifting up the gravestones, or opening the doors of the vaults one by one. I saw the whole situation as though I were another person: the prisoner determined to play the hero, the solemn falangists with their mustaches and the men in uniform running around among the graves. It was irresistibly funny.

After half an hour, the little fat fellow came back alone. I thought he had come to give the order to execute me. The others must have stayed in the cemetery.

The officer looked at me. He didn't look at all foolish.

"Take him out in the big courtyard with the others," he said. "When military operations are over, a regular tribunal will decide his case."

I thought I must have misunderstood.

"So they're not—they're not going to shoot me?" I asked.

"Not now, in any case. Afterwards, that doesn't concern me."

I still didn't understand.

"But why?" I said to him.

He shrugged his shoulders without replying, and the soldiers led me away. In the big courtyard there were a hundred or so prisoners, women, children and a few old men. I started to walk around the grass plot in the middle. I felt absolutely idiotic. At noon we were fed in the dining hall. Two or three fellows spoke to me. I must have known them, but I didn't answer. I didn't even know where I was.

Toward evening, about ten new prisoners were pushed into the courtyard. I recognized Garcia, the baker.

He said to me, "Lucky dog! I didn't expect to find you alive."

"They condemned me to death," I said, "and then they changed their minds. I don't know why."

"I was arrested at two o'clock," Garcia said.

"What for?"

Garcia took no part in politics.

"I don't know," he said. "They arrest everybody who doesn't think the way they do."

He lowered his voice.

"They got Gris."

I began to tremble.

"When?"

"This morning. He acted like a damned fool. He left his cousins' house Tuesday because of a disagreement. There were any number of fellows who would have hidden him, but he didn't want to be indebted to anybody any more. He said, 'I would have hidden at Ibbieta's, but since they've got him, I'll go hide in the cemetery.'"

"In the cemetery?"

"Yes. It was the god-damnedest thing. Naturally they passed by there this morning; that had to happen. They found him in the gravediggers' shack. They opened fire at him and they finished him off."

"In the cemetery!"

Everything went around in circles, and when I came to I was sitting on the ground. I laughed so hard the tears came to my eyes.

The Jilting
of Granny Weatherall

katherine anne porter

SHE FLICKED HER WRIST NEATLY out of Doctor Harry's pudgy careful fingers and pulled the sheet up to her chin. The brat ought to be in knee breeches. Doctoring around the country with spectacles on his nose! "Get along now, take your schoolbooks and go. There's nothing wrong with me."

Doctor Harry spread a warm paw like a cushion on her forehead where the forked green vein danced and made her eyelids twitch. "Now, now, be a good girl, and we'll have you up in no time."

"That's no way to speak to a woman nearly eighty years old just because she's down. I'd have you respect your elders, young man."

"Well, Missy, excuse me." Doctor Harry patted her cheek. "But I've got to warn you, haven't I? You're a marvel, but you must be careful or you're going to be good and sorry."

"Don't tell me what I'm going to be. I'm on my feet now, morally speaking. It's Cornelia. I had to go to bed to get rid of her."

Her bones felt loose, and floated around in her skin, and Doctor Harry floated like a balloon around the foot of the bed. He floated and pulled down his waistcoat and swung his glasses on a cord. "Well, stay where you are, it certainly can't hurt you."

"Get along and doctor your sick," said Granny Weatherall. "Leave a well woman alone. I'll call for you when I want you.... Where were you forty years ago when I pulled through milk-leg and double pneumonia? You weren't even born. Don't let Cornelia lead you on," she shouted, because

Doctor Harry appeared to float up to the ceiling and out. "I pay my own bills, and I don't throw my money away on nonsense!"

She meant to wave good-by, but it was too much trouble. Her eyes closed of themselves, it was like a dark curtain drawn around the bed. The pillow rose and floated under her, pleasant as a hammock in a light wind. She listened to the leaves rustling outside the window. No, somebody was swishing newspapers: no, Cornelia and Doctor Harry were whispering together. She leaped broad awake, thinking they whispered in her ear.

"She was never like this, *never* like this!" "Well, what can we expect? "Yes, eighty years old. . . ."

Well, and what if she was? She still had ears. It was like Cornelia to whisper around doors. She always kept things secret in such a public way. She was always being tactful and kind. Cornelia was dutiful; that was the trouble with her. Dutiful and good: "So good and dutiful," said Granny, "that I'd like to spank her." She saw herself spanking Cornelia and making a fine job of it.

"What'd you say, Mother?"

Granny felt her face tying up in hard knots.

"Can't a body think, I'd like to know?"

"I thought you might want something."

"I do. I want a lot of things. First off, go away and don't whisper."

She lay and drowsed, hoping in her sleep that the children would keep out and let her rest a minute. It had been a long day. Not that she was tired. It was always pleasant to snatch a minute now and then. There was always so much to be done, let me see: tomorrow.

Tomorrow was far away and there was nothing to trouble about. Things were finished somehow when the time came; thank God there was always a little margin over for peace: then a person could spread out the plan of life and tuck in the edges orderly. It was good to have everything clean and folded away, which the hair brushes and tonic bottles sitting straight on the white embroidered linen: the day started without fuss and the pantry shelves laid out with rows of jelly glasses and brown jugs and white stone-china jars with blue whirligigs and words painted on them: coffee, tea, sugar, ginger, cinnamon, allspice: and the bronze clock with the lion on top nicely dusted off. The dust that lion could collect in twenty-four hours! The box in the attic with all those letters tied up, well, she'd have to go through that tomorrow. All those letters—George's letters and John's letters and her letters to them both—lying around for the children to find afterwards made her uneasy. Yes, that would be tomorrow's business. No use to let them know how silly she had been once.

While she was rummaging around she found death in her mind and it felt clammy and unfamiliar. She had spent so much time preparing for death there was no need for bringing it up again. Let it take care of itself now.

When she was sixty she had felt very old, finished, and went around making farewell trips to see her children and grandchildren, with a secret in her mind: This is the very last of your mother, children! Then she made her will and came down with a long fever. That was all just a notion like a lot of other things, but it was luckly too, for she had once for all got over the idea of dying for a long time. Now she couldn't be worried. She hoped she had better sense now. Her father had lived to be one hundred and two years old and had drunk a noggin of strong hot toddy on his last birthday. He told the reporters it was his daily habit, and he owed his long life to that. He had made quite a scandal and was very pleased about it. She believed she'd just plague Cornelia a little.

"Cornelia! Cornelia!" No footsteps, but a sudden hand on her cheek. "Bless you, where have you been?"

"Here, mother."

"Well, Cornelia, I want a noggin of hot toddy."

"Are you cold, darling?"

"I'm chilly, Cornelia. Lying in bed stops the circulation. I must have told you that a thousand times."

Well, she could just hear Cornelia telling her husband that Mother was getting a little childish and they'd have to humor her. The thing that most annoyed her was that Cornelia thought she was deaf, dumb, and blind. Little hasty glances and tiny gestures tossed around her and over her head saying, "Don't cross her, let her have her way, she's eighty years old," and she sitting there as if she lived in a thin glass cage. Sometimes Granny almost made up her mind to pack up and move back to her own house where nobody could remind her every minute that she was old. Wait, wait, Cornelia, till your own children whisper behind your back!

In her day she had kept a better house and had got more work done. She wasn't too old yet for Lydia to be driving eighty miles for advice when one of the children jumped the track, and Jimmy still dropped in and talked things over: "Now, Mammy, you've a good business head, I want to know what you think of this? . . ." Old. Cornelia couldn't change the furniture around without asking. Little things, little things! They had been so sweet when they were little. Granny wished the old days were back again with the children young and everything to be done over. It had been a hard pull, but not too much for her. When she thought of all the food she had cooked, and all the clothes she had cut and sewed, and all the gardens she had made —well, the children showed it. There they were, made out of her, and they couldn't get away from that. Sometimes she wanted to see John again and point to them and say, Well, I didn't do so badly, did I? But that would have to wait. That was for tomorrow. She used to think of him as a man, but now all the children were older than their father, and he would be a child beside her if she saw him now. It seemed strange and there was something wrong in the idea. Why, he couldn't possibly recognize her. She had fenced in a hundred acres once, digging the post holes herself and clamping the wires with just a negro boy to help. That changed a woman. John would be looking for a young woman with the peaked Spanish comb in her hair and the painted fan. Digging post holes changed a woman. Riding country roads in the winter when women had their babies was another thing: sitting up nights with sick horses and sick negroes and sick children and hardly ever losing one. John, I hardly ever lost one of them! John would see that in a minute, that would be something he could understand, she wouldn't have to explain anything!

It made her feel like rolling up her sleeves and putting the whole place to rights again. No matter if Cornelia was determined to be everywhere at once, there were a great many things left undone on this place. She would start tomorrow and do them. It was good to be strong enough for everything, even if all you made melted and changed and slipped under your hands, so that by the time you finished you almost forgot what you were working for. What was it I set out to do? she asked herself intently, but she could not remember. A fog rose over the valley, she saw it marching across the creek swallowing the trees and moving up the hill like an army of ghosts. Soon it would be at the near edge of the orchard, and then it was time to go in and light the lamps. Come in, children, don't stay out in the night air.

Lighting the lamps had been beautiful. The children huddled up to her and breathed like little calves waiting at the bars in the twilight. Their eyes followed the match and watched the flame rise and settle in a blue curve, then they moved away from her. The lamp was lit, they didn't have to be scared and hang on to mother any more. Never, never, never more. God, for all my life I thank Thee. Without Thee, my God, I could never have done it. Hail, Mary, full of grace.

I want you to pick all the fruit this year and see that nothing is wasted. There's always someone who can use it. Don't let good things rot for want of using. You waste life when you waste good food. Don't let things get lost. It's bitter to lose things. Now, don't let me get to thinking, not when I am tired and taking a little nap before supper. . . .

The pillow rose about her shoulders and pressed against her heart and the memory was being squeezed out of it: oh, push down the pillow, somebody: it would smother her if she tried to hold it. Such a fresh breeze blowing and such a green day with no threats in it. But he had not come, just the same. What does a woman do when she has put on the white veil and set out the white cake for a man and he doesn't come? She tried to remember. No, I swear he never harmed me but in that. He never harmed me but in that. . . and what if he did? There was the day, the day, but a whirl of dark smoke rose and covered it, crept up and over into the bright field where everything was planted so carefully in orderly rows. That was hell, she knew hell when she saw it. For sixty years she had prayed against remembering him and against losing her soul in the deep pit of hell, and now the two things were mingled in one and the thought of him was a smoky cloud from hell that moved and crept in her head when she had just got rid of Doctor Harry and was trying to rest a minute. Wounded vanity, Ellen, said a sharp voice in the top of her mind. Don't let your wounded vanity get the upper hand of you. Plenty of girls get jilted. You were jilted, weren't you? Then stand up to it. Her eyelids wavered and let in streamers of blue-gray light like tissue paper over her eyes. She must get up and pull the shades down or she'd never sleep. She was in bed again and the shades were not down. How could that happen? Better turn over, hide from the light, sleeping in the light gave you nightmares. "Mother, how do you feel now?" and a stinging wetness on her forehead. But I don't like having my face washed in cold water!

Hapsy? George? Lydia? Jimmy? No, Cornelia, and her features were swollen and full of little puddles. "They're coming, darling, they'll all be here soon." Go wash your face, child, you look funny.

Instead of obeying, Cornelia knelt down and put her head on the pillow. She seemed to be talking but there was no sound. "Well, are you tongue-tied? Whose birthday is it? Are you going to give a party?"

Cornelia's mouth moved urgently in strange shapes. "Don't do that, you bother me, daughter."

"Oh, no, Mother. Oh, no. . . ."

Nonsense. It was strange about children. They disputed your every word. "No what, Cornelia?"

"Here's Doctor Harry."

"I won't see that boy again. He just left five minutes ago."

"That was this morning, Mother. It's night now. Here's the nurse."

"This is Doctor Harry, Mrs. Weatherall. I never saw you look so young and happy!"

"Ah, I'll never be young again—but I'd be happy if they'd let me lie in peace and get rested."

She thought she spoke up loudly, but no one answered. A warm weight on her forehead, a warm bracelet on her wrist, and a breeze went on whispering, trying to tell her something. A shuffle of leaves in the everlasting hand of God, He blew on them and they danced and rattled. "Mother, don't mind, we're going to give you a little hypodermic." "Look here, daughter, how do ants get in this bed? I saw sugar ants yesterday." Did you send for Hapsy too?

It was Hapsy she really wanted. She had to go a long way back through a great many rooms to find Hapsy standing with a baby on her arm. She seemed to herself to be Hapsy also, and the baby on Hapsy's arm was Hapsy and himself and herself, all at once, and there was no surprise in the meeting. Then Hapsy melted from within and turned flimsy as gauze and the baby was a gauzy shadow, and Hapsy came up close and said, "I thought you'd never come," and looked at her very searchingly and said, "You haven't changed a bit!" They leaned forward to kiss, when Cornelia began whispering from a long way off, "Oh, is there anything you want to tell me? Is there anything I can do for you?"

Yes, she had changed her mind after sixty years and she would like to see George. I want you to find George. Find him and be sure to tell him I forgot him. I want him to know I had my husband just the same and my children and my house like any other woman. A good house too and a good husband that I loved and fine children out of him. Better than I hoped for even. Tell him I was given back everything he took away and more. Oh, no, oh, God, no, there was something else besides the house and the man and the children. Oh, surely they were not all? What was it? Something not given back. . . . Her breath crowded down under her ribs and grew into a monstrous frightening shape with cutting edges; it bored up into her head, and the agony was unbelievable: Yes, John, get the doctor now, no more talk, my time has come.

When this one was born it should be the last. The last. It should have been born first, for it was the one she had truly wanted. Everything came in good time. Nothing left out, left over. She was strong, in three days she would be as well as ever. Better. A woman needed milk in her to have her full health.

"Mother, do you hear me?"

"I've been telling you—"

"Mother, Father Connolly's here."

"I went to Holy Communion only last week. Tell him I'm not so sinful as all that."

"Father just wants to speak to you."

He could speak as much as he pleased. It was like him to drop in and inquire about her soul as if it were a teething baby, and then stay on for a cup of tea and a round of cards and gossip. He always had a funny story of some sort, usually about an Irishman who made his little mistakes and confessed them, and the point lay in some absurd thing he would blurt out in the confessional showing his struggles between native piety and original sin. Granny felt easy about her soul. Cornelia, where are your manners? Give Father Connolly a chair. She had her secret comfortable understanding with a few favorite saints who cleared a straight road to God for her. All as surely signed and sealed as the papers for the new Forty Acres. Forever. . . heirs and assigns forever. Since the day the wedding cake was not cut, but thrown out and wasted. The whole bottom dropped out of the world, and there she was blind and sweating with nothing under her feet and the walls falling away. His hand had caught her under the breast, she had not fallen, there was the freshly polished floor with the green rug on it, just as before. He had cursed like a sailor's parrot and said, "I'll kill him for you." Don't lay a hand on him, for my sake leave something to God. "Now, Ellen, you must believe what I tell you. . . ."

So there was nothing, nothing to worry about any more, except sometimes in the night one of the children screamed in a nightmare, and they both hustled out shaking and hunting for the matches and calling, "There, wait a minute, here we are!" John, get the doctor now, Hapsy's time has come. But there was Hapsy standing by the bed in a white cap. "Cornelia, tell Hapsy to take off her cap. I can't see her plain."

Her eyes opened very wide and the room stood out like a picture she had seen somewhere. Dark colors with the shadows rising towards the ceiling in long angles. The tall black dresser gleamed with nothing on it but John's picture, enlarged from a little one, with John's eyes very black when they should have been blue. You never saw him, so how do you know how he looked? But the man insisted the copy was perfect, it was very rich and handsome. For a picture, yes, but it's not my husband. The table by the bed had a linen cover and a candle and a crucifix. The light was blue from Cornelia's silk lampshades. No sort of light at all, just frippery. You had to live forty years with kerosene lamps to appreciate honest electricity. She felt very strong and she saw Doctor Harry with a rosy nimbus around him.

"You look like a saint, Doctor Harry, and I vow that's as near as you'll ever come to it."

"She's saying something."

"I heard you, Cornelia. What's all this carrying-on?"

"Father Connolly's saying—"

Cornelia's voice staggered and bumped like a cart in a bad road. It rounded corners and turned back again and arrived nowhere. Granny stepped up in the cart very lightly and reached for the reins, but a man sat beside her and she knew him by his hands, driving the cart. She did not look in his face, for she knew without seeing, but looked instead down the road where the trees leaned over and bowed to each other and a thousand birds were singing a Mass. She felt like singing too, but she put her hand in the bosom of her dress and pulled out a rosary, and Father Connolly murmured Latin in a very solemn voice and tickled her feet. My God, will you stop that nonsense? I'm a married woman. What if he did run away and leave me to face the priest by myself? I found another a whole world better. I wouldn't have exchanged my husband for anybody except St. Michael himself, and you may tell him that for me with a thank you in the bargain.

Light flashed on her closed eyelids, and a deep roaring shook her. Cornelia, is that lightning? I hear thunder. There's going to be a storm. Close all the windows. Call the children in. . . . "Mother, here we are, all of us." "Is that you, Hapsy?" "Oh, no, I'm Lydia. We drove as fast as we could." Their faces drifted above her, drifted away. The rosary fell out of her hands and Lydia put it back. Jimmy tried to help, their hands fumbled together, and Granny closed two fingers around Jimmy's thumb. Beads wouldn't do, it must be something alive. She was so amazed her thoughts ran round and round. So, my dear Lord, this is my death and I wasn't even thinking about it. My children have come to see me die. But I can't it's not time. Oh, I always hated surprises. I wanted to give Cornelia the amethyst set—Cornelia, you're to have the amethyst set, but Hapsy's to wear it when she wants, and, Doctor Harry, do shut up. Nobody sent for you. Oh, my dear Lord, do wait a minute. I meant to do something about the Forty Acres, Jimmy doesn't need it and Lydia will later on, with that worthless husband of hers. I meant to finish the altar cloth and send six bottles of wine to Sister Borgia for her dyspepsia. I want to send six bottles of wine to Sister Borgia, Father Connolly, now don't let me forget.

Cornelia's voice made short turns and tilted over and crashed. "Oh, Mother, oh, Mother, oh, Mother. . . ."

"I'm not going, Cornelia. I'm taken by surprise. I can't go."

You'll see Hapsy again. What about her? "I thought you'd never come." Granny made a long journey outward, looking for Hapsy. What if I don't find her? What then? Her heart sank down, there was no bottom to death, she couldn't come to the end of it. The blue light from Cornelia's lampshade drew into a tiny point in the center of her brain, it flickered and winked like an eye, quietly it fluttered and dwindled. Granny lay curled down within herself, amazed and watchful, staring at the point of light that was herself; her body was now only a deeper mass of shadow in an endless darkness and this darkness would curl around the light and swallow it up. God, give a sign!

For the second time there was no sign. Again no bridegroom and the priest in the house. She could not remember any other sorrow because this grief wiped them all away. Oh, no, there's nothing more cruel than this— I'll never forgive it. She stretched herself with a deep breath and blew out the light.

The Grave

katherine anne porter

THE GRANDFATHER, dead for more than thirty years, had been twice disturbed in his long repose by the constancy and possessiveness of his widow. She removed his bones first to Louisiana and then to Texas as if she had set out to find her own burial place, knowing well she would never return to the places she had left. In Texas she set up a small cemetery in a corner of her first farm, and as the family connection grew, and oddments of relations came over from Kentucky to settle, it contained at last about twenty graves. After the grandmother's death, part of her land was to be sold for the benefit of certain of her children, and the cemetery happened to lie in the part set aside for sale. It was necessary to take up the bodies and bury them again in the family plot in the big new public cemetery, where the grandmother had been buried. At last her husband was to lie beside her for eternity, as she had planned.

The family cemetery had been a pleasant small neglected garden of tangled rose bushes and ragged cedar trees and cypress, the simple flat stones rising out of uncropped sweet-smelling wild grass. The graves were lying open and empty one burning day when Miranda and her brother Paul, who often went together to hunt rabbits and doves, propped their twenty-two Winchester rifles carefully against the rail fence, climbed over and explored among the graves. She was nine years old and he was twelve.

They peered into the pits all shaped alike with such purposeful accuracy, and looking at each other with pleased adventurous eyes, they said in solemn

From THE LEANING TOWER AND OTHER STORIES, copyright, 1944, by Katherine Anne Porter. Reprinted by permission of Harcourt Brace Jovanovich, Inc.

tones: "These were graves!" trying by words to shape a special, suitable emotion in their minds, but they felt nothing except an agreeable thrill of wonder: They were seeing a new sight, doing something they had not done before. In them both there was also a small disappointment at the entire commonplaceness of the actual spectacle. Even if it had once contained a coffin for years upon years, when the coffin was gone a grave was just a hole in the ground. Miranda leaped into the pit that had held her grandfather's bones. Scratching around aimlessly and pleasurably as any young animal, she scooped up a lump of earth and weighed it in her palm. It had a pleasantly sweet, corrupt smell, being mixed with cedar needles and small leaves, and as the crumbs fell apart, she saw a silver dove no larger than a hazel nut, with spread wings and a neat fan-shaped tail. The breast had a deep round hollow in it. Turning it up to the fierce sunlight, she saw that the inside of the hollow was cut in little whorls. She scrambled out, over the pile of loose earth that had fallen back into one end of the grave, calling to Paul that she had found something, he must guess what. . .His head appeared smiling over the rim of another grave. He waved a closed hand at her. "I've got something too!" They ran to compare treasures, making a game of it, so many guesses each, all wrong, and a final showdown with opened palms. Paul had found a thin wide gold ring carved with intricate flowers and leaves. Miranda was smitten at sight of the ring and wished to have it. Paul seemed more impressed by the dove. They made a trade, with some little bickering. After he had got the dove in his hand, Paul said, "Don't you know what this is? This is a screw head for a *coffin!*. . .I'll bet nobody else in the world has one like this!"

Miranda glanced at it without covetousness. She had the gold ring on her thumb; it fitted perfectly. "Maybe we ought to go now," she said, "maybe one of the niggers 'll see us and tell somebody." They knew the land had been sold, the cemetery was no longer theirs, and they felt like trespassers. They climbed back over the fence, slung their rifles loosely under their arms —they had been shooting at targets with various kinds of firearms since they were seven years old—and set out to look for the rabbits and doves or whatever small game might happen along. On these expeditions Miranda always followed at Paul's heels along the path, obeying instructions about handling her gun when going through fences; learning how to stand it up properly so it would not slip and fire unexpectedly; how to wait her time for a shot and not just bang away in the air without looking, spoiling shots for Paul, who really could hit things if given a chance. Now and then, in her excitement at seeing birds whizz up suddenly before her face, or a rabbit leap across her very toes, she lost her head, and almost without sighting she flung her rifle up and pulled the trigger. She hardly ever hit any sort of mark. She had no proper sense of hunting at all. Her brother would be often completely disgusted with her. "You don't care whether you get your bird or not," he said. "That's no way to hunt." Miranda could not understand his indignation. She had seen him smash his hat and yell with fury when he had missed his aim. "What I like about shooting," said Miranda, with exasperating inconsequence, "is pulling the trigger and hearing the noise."

"Then, by golly," said Paul, "whyn't you go back to the range and shoot at bulls-eyes?"

"I'd just as soon," said Miranda, "only like this, we walk around more."

"Well, you just stay behind and stop spoiling my shots," said Paul, who, when he made a kill, wanted to be certain he had made it. Miranda, who alone brought down a bird once in twenty rounds, always claimed as her own any game they got when they fired at the same moment. It was tiresome and unfair and her brother was sick of it.

"Now, the first dove we see, or the first rabbit, is mine," he told her. "And the next will be yours. Remember that and don't get smarty."

"What about snakes?" asked Miranda idly. "Can I have the first snake?"

Waving her thumb gently and watching her gold ring glitter, Miranda lost interest in shooting. She was wearing her summer roughing outfit: dark blue overalls, a light blue shirt, a hired-man's straw hat, and thick brown sandals. Her brother had the same outfit except his was a sober hickory-nut color. Ordinarily Miranda preferred her overalls to any other dress, though it was making rather a scandal in the countryside, for the year was 1903, and in the back country the law of female decorum had teeth in it. Her father had been criticized for letting his girls dress like boys and go careering around astride barebacked horses. Big sister Maria, the really independent and fearless one, in spite of her rather affected ways, rode at a dead run with only a rope knotted around her horse's nose. It was said the motherless family was running down, with the Grandmother no longer there to hold it together. It was known that she had discriminated against her son Harry in her will, and that he was in straits about money. Some of his old neighbors reflected with vicious satisfaction that now he would probably not be so stiffnecked, nor have any more high-stepping horses either. Miranda knew this, though she could not say how. She had met along the road old women of the kind who smoked corn-cob pipes, who had treated her grandmother with most sincere respect. They slanted their gummy old eyes side-ways at the granddaughter and said, "Ain't you ashamed of yoself, Missy? It's aginst the Scriptures to dress like that. Whut yo Pappy thinkin' about," Miranda, with her powerful social sense, which was like a fine set of antennae radiating from every pore of her skin, would feel ashamed because she knew well it was rude and ill-bred to shock anybody, even bad-tempered old crones, though she had faith in her father's judgment and was perfectly comfortable in the clothes. Her father had said, "They're just what you need, and they'll save your dresses for school..." This sounded quite simple and natural to her. She had been brought up in rigorous economy. Wastefulness was vulgar. It was also a sin. These were truths; she had heard them repeated many times and never once disputed.

Now the ring, shining with the serene purity of fine gold on her rather grubby thumb, turned her feelings against her overalls and sockless feet, toes sticking through the thick brown leather straps. She wanted to go back to the farmhouse, take a good cold bath, dust herself with plenty of Maria's violet talcum powder—provided Maria was not present to object, of course—put on the thinnest, most becoming dress she owned, with a big sash, and sit in a wicker chair under the trees...These things were not all she wanted, of course; she had vague stirrings of desire for luxury and a grand way of living which could not take precise form in her imagination but were founded on family legend of past wealth and leisure. These immediate comforts were what she could have, and she wanted them at once. She lagged rather far behind Paul, and once she thought of just turning back without a word and going home. She stopped, thinking that Paul would never do that to her, and so she would have to tell him. When a rabbit leaped, she let Paul have it without dispute. He killed it with one shot.

When she came up with him, he was already kneeling, examining the wound, the rabbit trailing from his hands. "Right through the head," he said complacently, as if he had aimed for it. He took out his sharp, competent bowie knife and started to skin the body. He did it very cleanly and quickly. Uncle Jimbilly knew how to prepare the skins so that Miranda always had fur coats for her dolls, for though she never cared much for her dolls she liked seeing them in fur coats. The children knelt facing each other over the dead animal. Miranda watched admiringly while her brother stripped the skin away as if he were taking off a glove. The flayed flesh emerged dark scarlet, sleek, firm; Miranda with thumb and finger felt the long fine muscles with the silvery flat strips binding them to the joints. Brother lifted the oddly bloated belly. "Look," he said, in a low amazed voice. "It was going to have young ones."

Very carefully he slit the thin flesh from the center ribs to the flanks, and a scarlet bag appeared. He slit again and pulled the bag open, and there lay a bundle of tiny rabbits, each wrapped in a thin scarlet veil. The brother pulled these off and there they were, dark gray, their sleek wet down lying in minute even ripples, like a baby's head just washed, their unbelievably small delicate ears folded close, their little blind faces almost featureless.

Miranda said, "Oh, I want to *see*," under her breath. She looked and looked—excited but not frightened, for she was accustomed to the sight of animals killed in hunting—filled with pity and astonishment and a kind of shocked delight in the wonderful little creatures for their own sakes, they were so pretty. She touched one of them ever so carefully, "Ah, there's blood running over them," she said and began to tremble without knowing why. Yet she wanted most deeply to see and to know. Having seen, she felt at once as if she had known all along. The very memory of her former ignorance faded, she had always known just this. No one had ever told her anything outright, she had been rather unobservant of the animal life around her because she was so accustomed to animals. They seemed simply disorderly and unaccountably rude in their habits, but altogether natural and not very interesting. Her brother had spoken as if he had known about everything all along. He may have seen all this before. He had never said a word to her, but she knew now a part at least of what he knew. She understood a little of the secret, formless intuitions in her own mind and body, which had been clearing up, taking form, so gradually and so steadily she had not realized that she was learning what she had to know. Paul said cautiously, as if he were talking about something forbidden: "They were just about ready to be born." His voice dropped on the last word. "I know," said Miranda, "like kittens. I know, like babies." She was quietly and terribly agitated, standing again with her rifle under her arm, looking down at the bloody heap. "I don't want the skin," she said, "I won't have it." Paul buried the young rabbits again in their mother's body, wrapped the skin around her, carried her to a clump of sage bushes, and hid her away. He came out again at once and said to Miranda, with an eager friendliness, a confidential tone quite unusual in him, as if he were taking her into an important secret on equal terms: "Listen now. Now you listen to me, and don't ever forget. Don't you ever tell a living soul that you saw this. Don't tell a soul. Don't tell Dad because I'll get into trouble. He'll say I'm leading you into things you ought not to do. He's always saying that. So now don't you go and forget and blab out sometime the way you're always doing. . . . Now, that's a secret. Don't you tell."

Miranda never told, she did not even wish to tell anybody. She thought about the whole worrisome affair with confused unhappiness for a few days. Then it sank quietly into her mind and was heaped over by accumulated thousands of impressions, for nearly twenty years. One day she was picking her path among the puddles and crushed refuse of a market street in a strange city of a strange country, when without warning, plain and clear in its true colors as if she looked through a frame upon a scene that had not stirred nor changed since the moment it happened, the episode of that far-off day leaped from its burial place before her mind's eye. She was so reasonlessly horrified she halted suddenly staring, the scene before her eyes dimmed by the vision back of them. An Indian vendor had held up before her a tray of dyed sugar sweets, in the shapes of all kinds of small creatures: birds, baby chicks, baby rabbits, lambs, baby pigs. They were in gay colors and smelled of vanilla, maybe. . . . It was a very hot day and the smell in the market, with its piles of raw flesh and wilting flowers, was like the mingled sweetness and corruption she had smelled that other day in the empty cemetery at home: the day she had remembered always until now vaguely as the time she and her brother had found treasure in the opened graves. Instantly upon this thought the dreadful vision faded, and she saw clearly her brother, whose childhood face she had forgotten, standing again in the blazing sunshine, again twelve years old, a pleased sober smile in his eyes, turning the silver dove over and over in his hands.

Commentary

"the grave"
theme and symbol

"The Grave" provides several excellent examples of the manner in which theme and symbol may reinforce the main development of a story and how a repeated act itself may become symbolic as it collects new significance from parallels. Basically, the story concerns the discovery of treasures in reopened graves and the repossession of the past, as one who moves on and does not return to old places devises ways of carrying the past with him. Thus Miranda's grandmother has twice moved her husband's grave, and Miranda herself discovers that she contains the treasury of her past within her.

To be transportable, the past must be symbolized in some way, and for Miranda and Paul, the first open grave is a discovery of symbols—not a rediscovery because its relics have no special message for them. Our understanding of the silver dove and the gold ring carved intricately with flowers runs ahead of theirs, and we also realize that in their innocent games they strike a contrast between youth and age, vitality and death, and more comprehensively an unknowing acceptance of the surface of the present and a layered, complex time. As they then proceed to hunt live creatures, we see them reenacting what is after all a very common story, growing up and discovering cycles of life and death for the first time. For Miranda, hunting of Paul's sort is no longer the proper game as she begins to understand the stringent rules of a more sophisticated social game in which propriety is defined for young ladies by their elders. The ring on her thumb assumes an added signifiance as a symbol of adult ceremonies, pledged loyalty, marriage, and elegance. These are just beginning to seem important to her, especially the elegance of the ring as a keepsake embodiment of civilization's finest craftsmanship and beauty. Cast in the "serene purity of fine gold," it suggests a tension between art and nature, in contrast to the hunt and to Miranda's own childlike animality. (Her grubby thumb, her overalls, and her sockless feet begin to seem crude to her as she develops "vague stirrings of desire for luxury or a grand way of living.") Gradually and unobtrusively, Miss Porter enriches the meaning of the ring as the focal point of several thematic strands.

As Miranda ponders the ring, Paul lays bare, in another "grave," a stark image of birth and death lying together; and here again the interaction of plot, character, and symbol sharpens the conflict between artifact and nature. The symbols bring into focus this time the difficulty of recapturing life in artifacts like the ring and the dove. The starkness of nature's cycles of life and death should expand for Miranda the meaning of the first grave (though we cannot be sure how much she grasps at this point), because Paul's discovery is also of buried treasure—not a cache of relics but a fragile and precious life whose waste raises both revulsion and wonder. It is apparent that no culture or its artifacts can protect Miranda from the random and starkly physical truths of the animal life that she shares. Somewhat ashamed of their second disinterment, the two of them agree to keep their discovery a secret and close the grave.

Many writers might have been satisfied with this association between life and death, youth and age, and with the implication that whatever culture Miranda grows into and enshrines in the fur clothes and golden rings she dreams of, nature will always prevail: The rabbit incident implicitly passes judgment on all social distinction and manners, and especially upon the narrow sense of propriety that a segment of Miranda's adult society seeks to impose upon her. But for Miss Porter the implicit conflict between the artifacts of the first grave and the womb that generates new life in the second grave is as yet unresolved. She carries the reduplication of action another step, with a third disinterment and a third treasure, as much later Miranda again explores new territory "in a strange city of a strange country."

Miranda's third discovery exists on another plane but is composed of materials similar to those of the first two, and it causes us to reinterpret the earlier episodes. Though the ring and the dove are perfectly shaped and wrought, they do not really share the warm, disorderly life of animal nature—which is as different from them as real doves are from silver coffin ornaments. But the third grave, the treasury of the mind itself where Miranda still carries the past ripe for repossession, unites the past with a living and disorderly present; its symbols contain the past as something available for living reenactment. The past proves capable of enlivening the artifacts themselves and making them objects of a new understanding:

> Instantly upon this thought the dreadful vision faded, and she saw clearly her brother, whose childhood face she had forgotten, standing again in the blazing sunshine, again twelve years old, a pleased sober smile in his eyes, turning the silver dove over and over in his hands.

Where before, the reader's anticipation of the meaning of the objects has run ahead of Miranda's understanding, this recapturing of the past comes very quickly and causes the reader to review the details of the story as she reviews her life, to discover what they mean. Thus we too make a kind of disinterment and discover that the details of the story's treasure that we have set aside are more than a serviceable realism. The last paragraph is composed of reiterated images that collect previous meanings and at the same time round off the story by recapitulating the past on another plane. This recovery of the past is not only accomplished by symbols but concerns them as well. Unlike the raw experience of the children in the hot sun, Miranda's remembered experience is transformed into the stuff of the mind where the sun becomes "illumination." A nature that was formerly inconclusive and unmastered is now re-presented as symbol, and it is in this re-presentation that the apparently irreconcilable differences between symbolic relics and disorderly life are transcended. Miranda's recaptured vision is filled with the glow of a vital past youth and yet shares the permanence and radiance of art. In her memory Paul and the silver dove exist on the same footing.

The scene of Miranda's reopening of the past tells us something further about the cleansing and enlivening influence of memory and its symbols. The Indian marketplace illustrates another war of opposites: On one hand, the day is hot and the market is filled with noises and the smells of raw flesh that recall the mingled sweetness and corruption of the original grave and the slain rabbit. This similarity triggers the association of past and present. But the market also contains artificial shapes, inexpensive sugar artifacts grotesquely out of keeping with the "piles of raw flesh" lying all around. It combines bustling activity and decay, quaint "art," and an unlovely refuse that overwhelms the prettiness of the sugar animals, much as the dead rabbits earlier overpowered Miranda's thought of fur clothes for dolls. The artifact in Paul's hand is rescued both from the confusion of the market and from the artificial prettiness of the sugar animals; its enshrinement in memory makes it distant and elevated above the world of human economy and human waste. What was a "worrisome affair" of "confused unhappiness" years ago becomes orderly in the remembering and yet not deprived of life.

If we follow the rapid sequence of Miranda's sensations in the last paragraph closely—and they are carefully paced in Miss Porter's deft and sensitive prose—we discover not only a recapitulation of the symbols and themes but a similarity between the memory's "cleaning up" of the past and the method of the story. The sensory experience of the scene raises in Miranda a reasonless horror compounded of the original unpleasantness of the child's experience and the greater awareness of the adult in the midst of waste and decay. But as the details assume meaningful parallels with the past they arrange themselves as a coherent scene in a kind of "epiphany" that only symbolic scenes and objects can convey. With the last sentence, as we pass from the cluttered scene of the market into Miranda's interior perspective, meaning is made from the surface of the story, encapsulated in the vital germ of its symbols, which condense and clarify. The "real" world continues to turn; the memory seizes upon not fixed and static images but movement.

But movement itself has become almost ritual in an internal world where the past returns. With a timely repetition of phrases and images, the prose imitates that act of turning and returning and causes the reader to focus upon the symbolic materials of the story's treasury, as Miranda now seizes upon her own layered past.

A Worn Path

eudora welty

IT WAS DECEMBER—a bright frozen day in the early morning. Far out in the country there was an old Negro woman with her head tied in a red rag, coming along a path through the pinewoods. Her name was Phoenix Jackson. She was very old and small and she walked slowly in the dark pine shadows, moving a little from side to side in her steps, with the balanced heaviness and lightness of a pendulum in a grandfather clock. She carried a thin, small cane made from an umbrella, and with this she kept tapping the frozen earth in front of her. This made a grave and persistent noise in the still air, that seemed meditative, like the chirping of a solitary little bird.

She wore a dark striped dress reaching down to her shoetops, and an equally long apron of bleached sugar sacks, with a full pocket; all neat and tidy, but every time she took a step she might have fallen over her shoelaces, which dragged from her unlaced shoes. She looked straight ahead. Her eyes were blue with age. Her skin had a pattern all its own of numberless branching wrinkles and as though a whole little tree stood in the middle of her forehead, but agolden color ran underneath, and the two knobs of her cheeks were illuminated by a yellow burning under the dark. Under the red rag her hair came down on her neck in the frailest of ringlets, still black, and with an odor like copper.

Now and then there was a quivering in the thicket. Old Phoenix said, "Out of my way, all you foxes, owls, beetles, jack rabbits, coons, and wild animals! ... Keep out from under these feet, little bobwhites. ... Keep the big wild hogs out of my path. Don't let none of those come running my direction. I got a long way." Under her small black-freckled hand her cane, limber as a buggy whip, would switch at the brush as if to rouse up any hiding things.

On she went. The woods were deep and still. The sun made the pine needles almost too bright to look at, up where the wind rocked. The cones dropped as light as feathers. Down in the hollow was the mourning dove—it was not too late for him.

The path ran up a hill. "Seem like there is chains about my feet, time I get this far," she said, in the voice of argument old people keep to use with themselves. "Something always take a hold on this hill—pleads I should stay."

After she got to the top she turned and gave a full, severe look behind her where she had come. "Up through pines," she said at length. "Now down through oaks."

Her eyes opened their widest and she started down gently. But before she got to the bottom of the hill a bush caught her dress.

Her fingers were busy and intent, but her skirts were full and long, so that before she could pull them free in one place they were caught in another. It was not possible to allow the dress to tear. "I in the thorny bush," she said. "Thorns, you doing your appointed work. Never want to let folks past—no sir. Old eyes thought you was a pretty little *green* bush."

Finally, trembling all over, she stood free, and after a moment dared to stoop for her cane.

"Sun so high!" she cried, leaning back and looking, while the thick tears went over her eyes. "The time getting all gone here."

At the foot of this hill was a place where a log was laid across the creek. "Now comes the trial," said Phoenix.

Putting her right foot out, she mounted the log and shut her eyes. Lifting her skirt, leveling her cane fiercely before her, like a festival figure in some parade, she began to march across. Then she opened her eyes and she was safe on the other side.

"I wasn't as old as I thought," she said.

But she sat down to rest. She spread her skirts on the bank around her and folded her hands over her knees. Up above her was a tree in a pearly cloud of mistletoe. She did not dare to close her eyes, and when a little boy brought her a little plate with a slice of marble-cake on it she spoke to him. "That would be acceptable," she said. But when she went to take it there was just her own hand in the air.

So she left that tree, and had to go through a barbed-wire fence. There she had to creep and crawl, spreading her knees and stretching her fingers like a baby trying to climb the steps. But she talked loudly to herself: She could not let her dress be torn now, so late in the day, and she could not pay for having her arm or her leg sawed off if she got caught fast where she was.

At last she was safe through the fence and risen up out in the clearing. Big dead trees, like black men with one arm, were standing in the purple stalks of the withered cotton field. There sat a buzzard.

"Who you watching?"

In the furrow she made her way along.

"Glad this not the season for bulls," she said, looking sideways, "and the good Lord made his snakes to curl up and sleep in the winter. A pleasure I don't see no two-headed snake coming around that tree, where it come once. It took a while to get by him, back in the summer."

She passed through the old cotton and went into a field of dead corn. It whispered and shook, and was taller than her head. "Through the maze now." she said, for there was no path.

Then there was something tall, black, and skinny there, moving before her.

At first she took it for a man. It could have been a man dancing in the field. But she stood still and listened, and it did not make a sound. It was as silent as a ghost.

"Ghost," she said sharply, "who be you the ghost of? For I have heard of nary death close by."

But there was no answer, only the ragged dancing in the wind.

She shut her eyes, reached out her hand, and touched a sleeve. She found a coat and inside that an emptiness, cold as ice.

"You scarecrow," she said. Her face lighted. "I ought to be shut up for good," she said with laughter. "My senses is gone. I too old. I the oldest people I ever know. Dance, old scarecrow," she said, "while I dancing with you."

She kicked her foot over the furrow, and with mouth drawn down shook her head once or twice in a little strutting way. Some husks blew down and whirled in streamers about her skirts.

Then she went on, parting her way from side to side with the cane, through the whispering field. At last she came to the end, to a wagon track, where the silver grass blew between the red ruts. The quail were walking around like pullets, seeming all dainty and unseen.

"Walk pretty," she said. "This the easy place. This the easy going."

She followed the track, swaying through the quiet bare fields, through the little strings of trees silver in their dead leaves, past cabins silver from weather, with the doors and windows boarded shut, all like old women under a spell sitting there. "I walking in their sleep," she said, nodding her head vigorously.

In a ravine she went where a spring was silently flowing through a hollow log. Old Phoenix bent and drank. "Sweetgum makes the water sweet," she said, and drank more. "Nobody knows who made this well, for it was here when I was born."

The track crossed a swampy part where the moss hung as white as lace from every limb. "Sleep on, alligators, and blow your bubbles." Then the track went into the road.

Deep, deep the road went down between the high green-colored banks. Overhead the live-oaks met, and it was dark as a cave.

A black dog with a lolling tongue came up out of the weeds by the ditch. She was meditating, and not ready, and when he came at her she only hit him a little with her cane. Over she went in the ditch, like a little puff of milk-weed.

Down there, her senses drifted away. A dream visited her, and she reached her hand up, but nothing reached down and gave her a pull. So she lay there and presently went to talking. "Old woman," she said to herself, "that black dog come up out of the weeds to stall you off, and now there he sitting on his fine tail, smiling at you."

A white man finally came along and found her—a hunter, a young man, with his dog on a chain.

"Well, Granny!" he laughed. "What are you doing there?"

"Lying on my back like a June-bug waiting to be turned over, mister," she said, reaching up her hand.

He lifted her up, gave her a swing in the air, and set her down, "Anything broken, Granny?"

"No sir, them old dead weeds is springy enough," said Phoenix, when she had got her breath. "I thank you for your trouble."

"Where do you live, Granny?" he asked, while the two dogs were growling at each other.

"Away back yonder, sir, behind the ridge. You can't even see it from here."

"On your way home?"

"No, sir, I going to town."

"Why, that's too far! That's as far as I walk when I come out myself, and I get something for my trouble." He patted the stuffed bag he carried, and there hung down a little closed claw. It was one of the bobwhites, with its beak hooked bitterly to show it was dead. "Now you go on home, Granny!"

"I bound to go to town, mister," said Phoenix. "The time come around."

He gave another laugh, filling the whole landscape. "I know you colored people! Wouldn't miss going to town to see Santa Claus!"

But something held Old Phoenix very still. The deep lines in her face went into a fierce and different radiation. Without warning she had seen with her own eyes a flashing nickel fall out of the man's pocket on to the ground.

"How old are you, Granny?" he was saying.

"There is no telling, mister," she said, "no telling."

Then she gave a little cry and clapped her hands, and said, "Git on away from here, dog! Look! Look at that dog!" She laughed as if in admiration. "He ain't scared of nobody. He a big black dog." She whispered, "Sick him!"

"Watch me get rid of that cur," said the man. "Sick him, Pete! Sick him!"

Phoenix heard the dogs fighting and heard the man running and throwing sticks. She even heard a gunshot. But she was slowly bending forward by that time, further and further forward, the lids stretched down over her eyes, as if she were doing this in her sleep. Her chin was lowered almost to her knees. The yellow palm of her had came out from the fold of her apron. Her fingers slid down and along the ground under the piece of money with the grace and care they would have in lifting an egg from under a sitting hen. Then she slowly straightened up, she stood erect, and the nickel was in her apron pocket. A bird flew by. Her lips moved. "God watching me the whole time. I come to stealing."

The man came back, and his own dog panted about them. "Well, I scared him off that time," he said, and then he laughed and lifted his gun and pointed it at Phoenix.

She stood straight and faced him.

"Doesn't the gun scare you?" he said, still pointing it.

"No, sir, I seen plenty go off closer by, in my day, and for less than what I done," she said, holding utterly still.

He smiled, and shouldered the gun. "Well, Granny," he said, "you must be a hundred years old, and scared of nothing. I'd give you a dime if I had any money with me. But you take my advice and stay home, and nothing will happen to you."

"I bound to go on my way, mister," said Phoenix. She inclined her head in the red rag. Then they went in different directions, but she could hear the gun shooting again and again over the hill.

She walked on. The shadows hung from the oak trees to the road like curtains. Then she smelled wood-smoke, and smelled the river, and she saw a steeple and the cabins on their steep steps. Dozens of little black children whirled around her. There ahead was Natchez shining. Bells were ringing. She walked on.

In the paved city it was Christmas time. There were red and green electric lights strung and crisscrossed everywhere, and all turned on in the daytime. Old Phoenix would have been lost if she had not distrusted her eyesight and depended on her feet to know where to take her.

She paused quietly on the sidewalk, where people were passing by. A lady came along in the crowd, carrying an armful of red-, green-, and silver-wrapped presents; she gave off perfume like the red roses in hot summer, and Phoenix stopped her.

"Please, missy, will you lace up my shoe?" She held up her foot.

"What do you want, Grandma?"

"See my shoe," said Phoenix. "Do all right for out in the country, but wouldn't look right to go in a big building."

"Stand still then, Grandma," said the lady. She put her packages down carefully on the sidewalk beside her and laced and tied both shoes tightly.

"Can't lace 'em with a cane," said Phoenix. "Thank you, missy. I doesn't mind asking a nice lady to tie up my shoe when I gets out on the street."

Moving slowly and from side to side, she went into the stone building and into a tower of steps, where she walked up and around and around until her feet knew to stop.

She entered a door, and there she saw nailed up on the wall the document that had been stamped with the gold seal and framed in the gold frame which matched the dream that was hung up in her head.

"Here I be," she said. There was a fixed and ceremonial stiffness over her body.

"A charity case, I suppose," said an attendant who at the desk before her.

But Phoenix only looked above her head. There was sweat on her face; the wrinkles shone like a bright net.

"Speak up, Grandma," the woman said. "What's your name? We must have your history, you know. Have you been here before? What seems to be the trouble with you?"

Old Phoenix only gave a twitch to her face as if a fly were bothering her.

"Are you deaf?" cried the attendant.

But then the nurse came in.

"Oh, that's just old Aunt Phoenix," she said. "She doesn't come for herself—she has a little grandson. She makes these trips just as regular as clockwork. She lives away back off the Old Natchez Trace." She bent down. "Well, Aunt Phoenix, why don't you just take a seat? We won't keep you standing after your long trip." She pointed.

The old woman sat down, bolt upright in the chair.

"Now, how is the boy?" asked the nurse.

Old Phoenix did not speak.

"I said, how is the boy?"

But Phoenix only waited and stared straight ahead, her face very solemn and withdrawn into rigidity.

"Is his throat any better?" asked the nurse. "Aunt Phoenix, don't you hear me? Is your grandson's throat any better since the last time you came for the medicine?"

With her hand on her knees, the old woman waited, silent, erect and motionless, just as if she were in armor.

"You mustn't take up our time this way, Aunt Phoenix," the nurse said.

"Tell us quickly about your grandson, and get it over. He isn't dead, is he?"

At last there came a flicker and then a flame of comprehension across her face, and she spoke.

"My grandson. It was my memory had left me. There I sat and forgot why I made my long trip."

"Forgot?" The nurse frowned. "After you came so far?"

Then Pheonix was like an old woman begging a dignified forgiveness for waking up frightened in the night. "I never did go to school—I was too old at the Surrender," she said in a soft voice. "I'm an old woman without an education. It was my memory fail me. My little grandson, he is just the same, and I forgot it in the coming."

"Throat never heals, does it?" said the nurse, speaking in a loud, sure voice to Old Phoenix. By now she had a card with something written on it, a little list. "Yes. Swallowed lye. When was it—January—two—three years ago—"

Phoenix spoke unasked now. "No, missy, he not dead, he just the same. Every little while his throat begin to close up again, and he not able to swallow. He not get his breath. He not able to help himself. So the time come around, and I go on another trip for the soothing medicine."

"All right. The doctor said as long as you came to get it you could have it," said the nurse. "But it's an obstinate case."

"My little grandson, he sit up there in the house all wrapped up, waiting by himself," Phoenix went on. "We is the only two left in the world. He suffer and it don't seem to put him back at all. He got a sweet look. He going to last. He wear a little patch quilt and peep out, holding his mouth open like a little bird. I remembers so plain now. I not going to forget him again, no, the whole enduring time. I could tell him from all the others in creation."

"All right." The nurse was trying to hush her now. She brought her a bottle of medicine. "Charity," she said, making a check mark in a book.

Old Phoenix held the bottle close to her eyes and then carefully put it into her pocket.

"I thank you," she said.

"It's Christmas time, Grandma," said the attendant. "Could I give you a few pennies out of my purse?"

"Five pennies is a nickel," said Phoenix stiffly.

"Here's a nickel," said the attendant.

Phoenix rose carefully and held out her hand. She received the nickel and then fished the other nickel out of the pocket and laid it beside the new one. She stared at her palm closely, with her head on one side.

Then she gave a tap with her cane on the floor.

"This is what come to me to do," she said. "I going to the store and buy

my child a little windmill they sells, made out of paper. He going to find
it hard to believe there such a thing in the world. I'll march myself back
where he waiting, holding it straight up in this hand."

She lifted her free hand, gave a little nod, turned round, and walked out
of the doctor's office. Then her slow step began on the stairs, going down.

A Tree, A Rock, A Cloud

carson mccullers

IT WAS RAINING THAT MORNING, and still very dark. When the boy reached the streetcar café he had almost finished his route and he went in for a cup of coffee. The place was an all-night café owned by a bitter and stingy man called Leo. After the raw, empty street, the café seemed friendly and bright: Along the counter there were a couple of soldiers, three spinners from the cotton mill, and in a corner a man who sat hunched over with his nose and half his face down in a beer mug. The boy wore a helmet such as aviators wear. When he went into the café he unbuckled the chin strap and raised the right flap up over his pink little ear; often as he drank his coffee someone would speak to him in a friendly way. But this morning Leo did not look into his face and none of the men were talking. He paid and was leaving the café when a voice called out to him:

"Son! Hey Son!"

He turned back and the man in the corner was crooking his finger and nodding to him. He had brought his face out of the beer mug and he seemed suddenly very happy. The man was long and pale, with a big nose and faded orange hair.

"Hey Son!"

The boy went toward him. He was an undersized boy of about twelve, with one shoulder drawn higher than the other because of the weight of the paper sack. His face was shallow, freckled, and, his eyes were round child eyes.

"Yeah Mister?"

The man laid one hand on the paper boy's shoulders, then grasped the boy's chin and turned his face slowly from one side to the other. The boy shrank back uneasily.

"Say! What's the big idea?"

The boy's voice was shrill; inside the café it was suddenly very quiet.

The man said slowly, "I love you."

All along the counter the men laughed. The boy, who had scowled and sidled away, did not know what to do. He looked over the counter at Leo, and Leo watched him with a weary, brittle jeer. The boy tried to laugh also. But the man was serious and sad.

"I did not mean to tease you, Son," he said. "Sit down and have a beer with me. There is something I have to explain."

Cautiously, out of the corner of his eye, the paper boy questioned the men along the counter to see what he should do. But they had gone back to their beer or their breakfast and did not notice him. Leo put a cup of cooffee on the counter and a little jug of cream.

"He is a minor," Leo said.

The paper boy slid himself up onto the stool. His ear beneath the upturned flap of the helmet was very small and red. The man was nodding at him soberly. "It is important," he said. Then he reached in his hip pocket and brought out something which he held up in the palm of his hand for the boy to see.

"Look very carefully," he said.

The boy stared, but there was nothing to look at very carefully. The man held his big, grimy palm a photograph. It was the face of a woman, but blurred, so that only the hat and the dress she was wearing stood out clearly.

"See?" the man asked.

The boy nodded and the man placed another picture in his palm. The woman was standing on a beach in a bathing suit. The suit made her stomach very big, and that was the main thing you noticed.

"Got a good look?" He leaned over closer and finally asked: "You ever seen her before?"

The boy sat motionless, staring slantwise at the man. "Not so I know of."

"Very well." The man blew on the photographs and put them back into his pocket. "That was my wife."

"Dead?" the boy asked.

Slowly the man shook his head. He pursed his lips as though about to whistle and answered in a long-drawn way: "Nuuu—" he said. "I will explain."

The beer on the counter before the man was in a large brown mug. He did not pick it up to drink. Instead he bent down and, putting his face over the rim, he rested there for a moment. Then with both hands he tilted the mug and sipped.

"Some night you'll go to sleep with your big nose in a mug and drown," said Leo. "Prominent transient drowns in beer. That would be a cute death."

The paper boy tried to signal to Leo. While the man was not looking he screwed up his face and worked his mouth to question soundlessly: "Drunk?" But Leo only raised his eyebrow and turned away to put some pink strips of bacon on the grill. The man pushed the mug away from him, straightened himself, and folded his loose crooked hands on the counter. His face was sad as he looked at the paper boy. He did not blink, but from time to time the lids closed down with delicate gravity over his pale green eyes. It was nearing dawn and the boy shifted the weight of the paper sack.

"I am talking about love," the man said. "With me it is a science."

The boy half slid down from the stool. But the man raised his forefinger, and there was something about him that held the boy and would not let him go away.

"Twelve years ago I married the woman in the photograph. She was my wife for one year, nine months, three days, and two nights. I loved her. Yes...." He tightened his blurred, rambling voice and said again: "I loved her. I thought also that she loved me. I was a railroad engineer. She had all home comforts and luxuries. It never crept into my brain that she was not satisfied. But do you know what happened?"

"Mgneeow!" said Leo.

The man did not take his eyes from the boy's face. "She left me. I came in one night and the house was empty and she was gone. She left me."

"With a fellow?" the boy asked.

Gently the man placed his palm down on the counter. "Why naturally, Son. A woman does not run off like that alone."

The café was quiet, the soft rain black and endless in the street outside. Leo pressed down the frying bacon with the prongs of his long fork. "So you have been chasing the floozie for eleven years. You frazzled old rascal!"

For the first time the man glanced at Leo. "Please don't be vulgar. Besides, I was not speaking to you." He turned back to the boy and said in a trusting and secretive undertone. "Let's not pay and attention to him. O.K.?"

The paper boy nodded doubtfully.

"It was like this," the man continued. "I am a person who feels many things. All my life one thing after another has impressed me. Moonlight. The leg of a pretty girl. One thing after another. But the point is that when I had enjoyed anything there was a peculiar sensation as though it was laying around loose in me. Nothing seemed to finish itself up or fit in with the other things. Women? I had my portion of them. The same. Afterwards laying around loose in me. I was a man who had never loved."

Very slowly he closed his eyelids, and the gesture was like a curtain drawn at the end of a scene in a play. When he spoke again his voice was excited and the words came fast—the lobes of his large, loose ears seemed to tremble.

"Then I met this woman. I was fifty-one years old and she always said she was thirty. I met her at a filling station and we were married within three days. And do you know what it was like? I just can't tell you. All I had ever felt was gathered together around this woman. Nothing lay around loose in me any more but was finished up by her."

The man stopped suddenly and stroked his long nose. His voice sank down to a steady and reproachful undertone: "I'm not explaining this right. What happened was this. There were these beautiful feelings and loose little pleasures inside me. And this woman was something like an assembly line for my soul. I run these little pieces of myself through her and I come out complete. Now do you follow me?"

"What was her name?" the boy asked.

"Oh," he said. "I called her Dodo. But that is immaterial."

"Did you try to make her come back?"

The man did not seem to hear. "Under the circumstances you can imagine how I felt when she left me."

Leo took the bacon from the grill and folded two strips of it between a bun. He had a gray face, with slitted eyes and a pinched nose saddled by faint blue shadows. One of the mill workers signaled for more coffee and Leo poured it. He did not give refills on coffee free. The spinner ate breakfast there every morning, but the better Leo knew his customers the stingier he treated them. He nibbled his own bun as though he grudged it to himself.

"And you never got hold of her again?"

The boy did not know what to think of the man, and his child's face was uncertain with mingled curiosity and doubt. He was new on the paper route; it was still strange to him to be out in the town in the black, queer early morning.

"Yes," the man said. "I took a number of steps to get her back. I went around trying to locate her. I went to Tulsa where she had folks. And to Mobile. I went to every town she had ever mentioned to me, and I hunted down every man she had formerly been connected with. Tulsa, Atlanta, Chicago, Cheehaw, Memphis. . . . For the better part of two years I chased around the country trying to lay hold of her."

"But the pair of them had vanished from the face of the earth!" said Leo.

"Don't listen to him," the man said confidentially. "And also just forget those two years. They are not important. What matters is that around the third year a curious thing begun to happen to me."

"What?" the boy asked.

The man leaned down and tilted his mug to take a sip of beer. But as he hovered over the mug his nostrils fluttered slightly; he sniffed the staleness of the beer and did not drink. "Love is a curious thing to begin with. At first I thought only of getting her back. It was a kind of mania. But then as time went on I tried to remember her. But do you know what happened?"

"No," the boy said.

"When I laid myself down on a bed and tried to think about her my mind became a blank. I couldn't see her. I would take out her pictures and look. No good. Nothing doing. A blank. Can you imagine it?"

"Say Mac!" Leo called down the counter. "Can you imagine this bozo's mind a blank!"

Slowly, as though fanning away flies, the man waved his hand. His green eyes were concentrated and fixed on the shallow little face of the paper boy.

"But a sudden piece of glass on a sidewalk. Or a nickel tune in a music box. A shadow on a wall at night. And I would remember. It might happen in a street and I would cry or bang my head against a lamppost. You follow me?"

"A piece of glass. . ." the boy said.

"Anything. I would walk around and I had no power of how and when to remember her. You think you can put up a kind of shield. But remembering don't come to a man face forward—it corners around sideways. I was at the mercy of everything I saw and heard. Suddenly instead of me combing the countryside to find her she begun to chase me around in my very soul. *She* chasing *me,* mind you! And in my soul."

The boy asked finally: "What part of the country were you in then?"

"Ooh," the man groaned. "I was a sick mortal. It was like smallpox. I confess, Son, that I boozed. I fornicated. I committed any sin that suddenly appealed to me. I am loath to confess it but I will do so. When I recall that period it is all curdled in my mind, it was so terrible."

The man leaned his head down and tapped his forehead on the counter. For a few seconds he stayed bowed over in this position, the back of his stringy neck covered with orange furze, his hands with their long warped fingers held palm to palm in an attitude of prayer. Then the man straightened himself; he was smiling and suddenly his face was bright and tremulous and old.

"It was in the fifth year that it happened," he said. "And with it I started my science."

Leo's mouth jerked with a pale, quick grin. "Well none of we boys are getting any younger," he said. Then with sudden anger he balled up a dishcloth he was holding and threw it down hard on the floor. "You draggletailed old Romeo!"

"What happened?" the boy asked.

The old man's voice was high and clear: "Peace," he answered.

"Huh?"

"It is hard to explain scientifically, Son," he said. "I guess the logical explanation is that she and I had fleed around from each other for so long that finally we just got tangled up together and lay down and quit. Peace. A queer and beautiful blankness. It was spring in Portland and the rain came every afternoon. All evening I just stayed there on my bed in the dark. And that is how the science come to me."

The windows in the streetcar were pale blue with light. The two soldiers paid for their beers and opened the door—one of the soldiers combed his hair and wiped off his muddy puttees before they went outside. The three mill workers bent silently over their breakfasts. Leo's clock was ticking on the wall.

"It is this. And listen carefully. I meditated on love and reasoned it out. I realized what is wrong with us. Men fall in love for the first time. And what do they fall in love with?"

The boy's soft mouth was partly open and he did not answer.

"A woman," the old man said. "Without science, with nothing to go by, they undertake the most dangerous and sacred experience in God's earth. They fall in love with a woman. Is that correct, Son?"

"Yeah," the boy said faintly.

"They start at the wrong end of love. They begin at the climax. Can you wonder it is so miserable. Do you know how men should love?"

The old man reached over and grasped the boy by the collar of his leather jacket. He gave him a gentle little shake and his green eyes gazed down unblinking and grave.

"Son, do you know how love should be begun?"

The boy sat small and listening and still. Slowly he shook his head. The old man leaned closer and whispered:

"A tree. A rock. A cloud."

It was still raining outside in the street: a mild, gray, endless rain. The mill whistle blew for the six o'clock shift and the three spinners paid and went away. There was no one in the café but Leo, the old man, and the little paper boy.

"The weather was like this in Portland," he said. "At the time my science was begun. I meditated and I started very cautious. I would pick up something from the street and take it home with me. I bought a goldfish and I concentrated on the goldfish and I loved it. I graduated from one thing to another. Day by day I was getting this technique. On the road from Portland to San Diego——"

"Aw shut up!" screamed Leo suddenly. "Shut up! Shut up!"

The old man still held the collar of the boy's jacket; he was trembling and his face was earnest and bright and wild. "For six years now I have gone around by myself and built up my science. And now I am a master, Son. I can love anything. No longer do I have to think about it even. I see a street full of people and a beautiful light comes in me. I watch a bird in the sky. Or I meet a traveler on the road. Everything, Son. And anybody. All stranger and all loved! Do you realize what a science like mine can mean?"

The boy held himself stiffly, his hands curled tight around the counter edge. Finally he asked: "Did you ever really find that lady?"

"What? What say, Son?"

"I mean," the boy asked timidly. "Have you fallen in love with a woman again?"

The old man loosened his grasp on the boy's collar. He turned away and for the first time his green eyes had a vague and scattered look. He lifted the mug from the counter, drank down the yellow beer. His head was shaking slowly from side to side. Then finally he answered: "No, Son. You see that is the last step in my science. I go cautious. And I am not quite ready yet."

"Well!" said Leo. "Well well well!"

The old man stood in the open doorway. "Remember," he said. Framed there in the gray damp light of the early morning he looked shrunken and seedy and frail. But his smile was bright. "Remember I love you," he said with a last nod. And the door closed quietly behind him.

The boy did not speak for a long time. He pulled down the bangs on his forehead and slid his grimy little forefinger around the rim of his empty cup. Then without looking at Leo he finally asked:

"Was he drunk?"

"No," said Leo shortly.

The boy raised his clear voice higher. "Then was he a dope fiend?"

"No."

The boy looked up at Leo, and his flat little face was desperate, his voice urgent and shrill. "Was he crazy? Do you think he was a lunatic?" The paper boy's voice dropped suddenly with doubt. "Leo? Or not?"

But Leo would not answer him. Leo had run a night café for fourteen years, and he held himself to be a critic of craziness. There were the town characters and also the transients who roamed in from the night. He knew the manias of all of them. But he did not want to satisfy the questions of the waiting child. He tightened his pale face and was silent.

So the boy pulled down the right flap of his helmet and as he turned to leave he made the only comment that seemed safe to him, the only remark that could not be laughed down and despised:

"He sure has done a lot of traveling."

Biographical
and
Critical Sketches

JOHN BARTH (1930–   )

American novelist, writer of short fiction, and essayist. A university teacher, Barth has published a collection of short fiction, *Lost in the Funhouse* (1968) and the novels *The Floating Opera* (1956), *End of the Road* (1958), *The Sot-Weed Factor* (1960), and *Giles Goat-Boy* (1966). The setting for much of his work is Maryland, where he grew up. Barth has been called by one noted critic an "existential comedian," and his works often combine wild comedy, fantasy, and satire in depicting his characters' quests for identity and abiding values in an apparently irrational world.

MAX BEERBOHM (1872–1956)

English satirical essayist, fiction writer, biographer, caricaturist, and drama critic. His works include *A Christmas Garland* (1895; 1912), *Seven Men* (1928), *Around Theaters* (1930), and *Mainly on the Air* (1947). *A Christmas Garland,* from which "Mote in the Middle Distance" is drawn, is a collection of parodies of famous writers.

MIGUEL DE CERVANTES (1547–1616)

Spanish fiction-writer, dramatist, and poet. Cervantes served as a soldier, was a prisoner of pirates for five years, and was twice imprisoned for debt or activities of questionable legality. His short tales, called *Exemplary Novels* (1613), are finished, fast-moving, realistic, and often sharply ironic depictions of everyday people and life. *Don Quixote,* published in two parts (1605 and 1615), is a satiric picaresque novel which among other things mocks the excesses of romantic tales of chivalric knights.

ANTON PAVLOVICH CHEKHOV (1860–1904)

Russian playwright and short story writer. Chekhov's famous plays *The Sea-Gull* (1896), *Three Sisters* (1899), *Uncle Vanya* (1902), and *The Cherry Orchard* (1904) are studies of how changes in nineteenth-century Russian society affected the individual and the family, especially in the middle class (in which Chekhov was born and raised). Chekhov is one of the most important and influential writers of the short story. Like his plays, such stories as "My Life," "Peasants," "The Steppe," and "The Lady with the Dog" combine realism, symbolism, and irony in portraying the drabness and pathos of everyday life.

WALTER VAN TILBURG CLARK (1909–)

American short-story writer and novelist. His novels include *The Ox-Bow Incient* (1940) and *The Track of the Cat* (1949); his stories are collected in *The Watchful Gods* (1950). Clark is often regarded as a regional writer since his subjects are frequently western frontier problems such as survival in the wilderness, violence and justice in a new society, and the conditions of growing up in a small western town.

JOSEPH CONRAD (1857–1924)

Polish-born English novelist and writer of short fiction. Conrad's full name was Teodor Josef Konrad Korzeniowski. He spent much of his early life as a sailor and learned English as his third language after Polish and French. His principal novels are *The Nigger of the "Narcissus"* (1898), *Lord Jim* (1900), *Nostromo* (1904), *The Secret Agent* (1907), *Under Western Eyes* (1911), *Chance* (1913), and *Victory* (1915). In these works and in such shorter pieces of fiction as "Heart of Darkness," "Youth," "Typhoon," and "The Secret Sharer," Conrad often uses the sea and exotic places in evoking a powerfully brooding and mysterious setting against which characters are tested in dangerous situations, suffer isolation, and are caught in perplexing moral dilemmas.

STEPHEN CRANE (1871–1900)

American novelist, short-story writer, poet, war-correspondent and newspaper writer. Crane's novels include *Maggie: A Girl of the Streets* (1892) and *The Red Badge of Courage* (1895). Some of his short stories are "The Open Boat," "The Monster," and "The Whilomville Stories." Crane's writing has been variously described as realistic, symbolic, and impressionistic because his settings are both meticulous in detail and evocative in mood and feeling. To this combination he often adds a biting and pervasive irony.

DANIEL DEFOE (1660–1731)

English novelist, essayist, pamphleteer, and journalist. Defoe came from a middle class background and tried by many forms of writing to earn his living. With Dryden and Swift, Defoe helped mold English prose by the example of his clear, simple, and straightforward style. His focus in his fictional works on everyday life and people, including the less pleasant elements of society represented by its criminals, helped introduce realism into the English novel. Defoe wrote the novels *Robinson Crusoe* (1719), *Captain Singleton* (1720), *Moll Flanders* (1722), *Colonel Jack* (1722), *Roxana, or the Fortunate Mistress* (1724), and a fictional reconstruction of the events of 1665 entitled *Journal of the Plague Year* (1722).

GRAHAM GREENE   (1904–   )

English novelist, short-story writer, essayist and playwright. Greene has divided his longer fictional works into two categories: novels and "entertainments." His "entertainments" are a combination of adventure thriller, psychological study, and exploration of moral and theological issues (particularly those pertinent to Catholicism, the faith to which he was converted). His novels, different primarily because they have fewer popular elements (though they deal with such contemporary topics as the political turmoil in Haiti, Africa, and Vietnam), include *The Man Within* (1929), *Brighton Rock* (1938), *The Power and the Glory* (1940), *The Heart of the Matter* (1948), *The End of the Affair* (1951), *A Burnt-Out Case* (1961), and *Travels with My Aunt* (1970). Greene's short stories have been collected in *21 Stories* (1954), *A Sense of Reality* (1963), and *May We Borrow Your Husband* (1967).

NATHANIEL HAWTHORNE   (1804–1864)

American novelist and short-story writer. Hawthorne's main novels are a blend of symbolism, allegory and the supernatural that he termed "romance." They include *The Scarlet Letter* (1850), *The House of the Seven Gables* (1851), *The Blithedale Romance* (1852), and *The Marble Faun* (1860). His *Twice-Told Tales* (1837) and other collections contain such famous short stories as "My Kinsman, Major Molineux," "The Minister's Black Veil," "The Maypole at Merry Mount," "Rappaccini's Daughter," and "Ethan Brand." In these and in his novels Hawthorne examines central issues in American life and history.

HESIOD   (circa 8th century b.c.)

Greek didactic poet. For many generations along with Homer one of the most famous poets of antiquity, Hesiod composed two main encyclopedic writings, *Works and Days* and *Theogony*. In the former he explains how work came to be a necessity on earth and how to manage a farm properly, while in the latter he gives an account of the origin of the gods and of the world.

HENRY JAMES   (1843–1916)

Expatriated American novelist, short-story writer, critic and essayist. Though born in New York, James increasingly spent more time in Europe, particularly England, to which he officially changed his citizenship the year before his death. His many novels include *Roderick Hudson* (1876), *The American* (1877), *The Portrait of a Lady* (1881), *The Princess Casamassima* (1886), *The Spoils of Poynton* (1897), *What Maisie Knew* (1897), *The Wings of the Dove* (1902), *The Ambassadors* (1903), and *The Golden Bowl* (1904). Some of James's novelettes (a form at which he excelled as did Joseph Conrad) are *Daisy Miller* (1878), *The*

Aspern Papers (1888), and *The Turn of the Screw* (1898), while his celebrated short stories include "A Beast in the Jungle" (1903) and "The Jolly Corner" (1908). James's prolific output includes books of autobiography, criticism, travel and essays as well. A trademark of his fiction is the exploration of the complicated relations between people, the interior world of their thoughts, and their unvoiced perceptions of each other.

SAMUEL JOHNSON (1709–1784)

English essayist, lexicographer, critic and poet. Johnson was one of the central literary figures of the late eighteenth century whose severe good sense, conversational wit, and balanced latinate prose style inspired awe among the public and men of letters alike. His essays (ranging from personal and narrative to philosophical and critical) are collected in the periodicals he published and wrote practically single-handed entitled *The Rambler* (1750–1752) and *The Idler* (1758–1760). Johnson's major work of fiction is *Rasselas* (1759), a philosophical romance and fable suggesting a pessimistic and skeptical wariness about any simple formula for discovering or leading "the good life."

FRANZ KAFKA (1883–1924)

Austrian novelist, short-story writer and fabulist. At his early death few of his works had been published, and many, including all three of his novels, were in manuscript in various stages of completion. His novels, published and edited posthumously by his friend Max Brod, are *The Trial* (1925), *The Castle* (1926) and *Amerika* (1927). Among his better known short stories are "The Judgment," "Metamorphosis," "In the Penal Colony," "The Great Wall of China," and "A Country Doctor." His "parables and paradoxes" are extracted from a wide variety of writings such as journals, letters, novels and stories. Pervaded by the fantastic and by an often difficult symbolism and allegory, Kafka's fiction suggests a world both absurd and paradoxical. It frequently explores the ambivalence of family relationships and the incomprehensibility of the workings of fate and nature.

CARSON MCCULLERS (1917–   )

American novelist and short-story writer. Though she has lived in New York for several years, Carson McCullers was born and raised in the South, which provides the setting for many of her stories. Her novels include *The Heart is a Lonely Hunter* (1940), *Reflections in a Golden Eye* (1941), *The Member of the Wedding* (1946), and *Clock Without Hands* (1961). Her short fiction is collected in *Ballad of the Sad Cafe* (1951), and includes besides the title novelette, "Wunderkind," "The Sojourner," and "The Jockey." Her fiction frequently focuses on grotesque characters and on the grotesque in general, has moody and mysterious settings, and explores loneliness and frustrated love.

SIR THOMAS MALORY (c. 1408–1471)

English fiction-writer and translator. Little is known about his life, though Malory seems to have had a dubious character and to have spent time in prison.

His main composition is *Le Morte d'Arthur* and other prose tales of King Arthur and his court which comprise a unified collection. Whether considered singly or in a group the tales are pre-eminent examples of Arthurian romance—a blend of legend, allegory, fable, adventure story, supernatural settings and events, and codes of chivalry and courtly love.

WILLIAM MARCH   (1893–1954)

American novelist and short-story writer. March is a pseudonym for William March Campbell. He was born in Alabama, the setting of his novel *The Looking Glass* (1943). His short fiction is collected in *The Little Wife* (1935), *Some Like Them Short* (1939), and *Trial Balance* (1945). His main interest is often in the peculiar and sometimes abnormal mentality and perspectives of his characters.

ETHEL COLBURNE MAYNE   (d. 1941)

Irish short-story writer, novelist, critic, biographer, translator, and journalist. An extremely prolific writer, her many works include studies of Byron and Browning, travelogues, biographies of famous women, and articles and reviews for English newspapers and magazines.

KATHERINE ANNE PORTER   (1890–   )

American short-story writer and novelist. Her shorter fiction, often set in the south where she grew up, is mainly collected in *Flowering Judas*   (1930) and *The Learning Tower* (1944). Katherine Anne Porter is a master of what has been called the "lyric" short story, a mode or form that emphasizes acute psychological portrayals of character with a sensitive evocation of feelings, pervasive symbolism, allusiveness, and a suggestive prose style.

FFANCOIS RABELAIS   (1494?–1553)

French fiction-writer. One of the vanguard of the Renaissance, Rabelais was a scholar, humanist, and physician who wrote various works on medicine and made numerous translations of other works in addition to writing *Gargantua and Pantagruel* (published in five parts between 1532 and 1564). This masterpiece is characterized by an extremely candid, boisterous and comic satire, derived in part from the medieval fabliau. Rabelais' prose style, equally exuberant and extravagant, is studded with puns and other verbal devices. He helped to forge such forms as the adventure story, tall tale, mock epic, and mock philosophical treatise.

JEAN-PAUL SARTRE   (1905–   )

French philosopher, novelist, playwright, short-story writer, essayist and critic. Some of Sartre's philosophical writings are *Imagination* (1936), *Emotions* (1939), *Psychology of Imagination* (1940), and the very influential *Being and Nothingness* (1943). Two of his long critical studies are on the famous French writers Baudelaire and Genet. Sartre's novels include *Nausea* (1938), and a trilogy called

The Roads to Freedom. His stories are collected in *The Wall* (1940), and include besides the title story "Intimacy," "Erostatus," "The Room," and "The Childhood of a Leader." Sartre is one of the leading exponents of the philosophy of existentialism, a central tenet of which is that each man is an isolated individual who must confront an absurd and indifferent universe on his own, and many of the ideas of this philosophy are embodied and dramatized in both his fiction and plays.

ISAAC BASHEVIS SINGER (1904–   )

Polish-born short-story writer and novelist. Though living in the United States since his emigration here in 1935, Singer, born and raised an Orthodox Jew, writes in Yiddish (a combination of German and Hebrew), a language slowly becoming extinct. His novels, many of which have appeared serialized in the Yiddish newspaper *Forward,* include *Satan in Goray* (1935), *The Manor* (1955), and *The Estate* (1969). His numerous stories are collected in *Gimpel the Fool* (1957), *The Spinoza of Market Street* (1961), *Short Friday* (1964), *The Seance* (1968) and *A Friend of Kafka* (1970). The subject and setting of Singer's fiction is usually middle European Jewish life and the culture of the ghetto and the rural village—obviously based on the region where Singer was raised. Frequently having elements of the supernatural (demons, magicians and spirits) and the Gothic horror tale, his stories often involve eccentric characters who deal with the problems of daily living, faith, and human relationships in the special circumstances of Singer's usual setting.

WALLACE STEGNER (1909–   )

American novelist, non-fiction writer and short-story writer. Stegner's non-fiction works, studies of American social problems and rural life on the midwestern plains and Canadian border where Stegner was born and raised, include *Mormon Country* (1942), *Beyond the Hundredth Meridian* (1954), and *The Gathering of Zion* (1964). His novels, often dealing with the same problems as his non-fiction and having similar regional settings, include *Remembering Laughter* (1937), *The Big Rock Candy Mountain* (1943), and *All the Little Live Things* (1967). His stories are collected in *Women on the Wall* (1950) and *City of the Living* (1956). *Wolf Willow,* from which "The Question Mark in the Circle" is taken, includes two short stories, "Carrion Spring" and "Genesis" and as a volume experiments with a combination of fiction and non-fictioon. Stegner's fictional works, usually written in an extremely graceful and compact prose style, typically attempt to define frontier experience, often in relation to both earlier and later historical events.

LAURENCE STERNE (1713–1768)

English novelist, journal-writer and letter-writer. Sterne, having had a somewhat parsimonious and itinerate childhood, was educated at Cambridge University and shortly afterwards was ordained a priest, primarily for economic rather than spiritual reasons. Most of his life was spent in ill health, livened primarily by extra-marital flirtation, whimsical behavior, and the fame from his writings. His works include *The Life and Opinions of Tristram Shandy* (1759–1767), *The*

Sermons of Mr. Yorick (1760–1769), and *A Sentimental Journey Through France and Italy* (1768). His novel *Tristram Shandy,* the best known of his works, is famous for its wildly comic digressions, satiric character portraits, satire of celebrated writers and philosophies of the time, and eccentric typographical devices.

JONATHAN SWIFT (1667–1745)

English satirist, poet, pamphleteer, essayist, and letter-writer. Swift was born in Dublin (making him somewhat of an outsider in English society), educated at Trinity College, and ordained a minister. He eventually became Dean of St. Patrick's Cathedral in Dublin. Like his close friend Alexander Pope, Swift was a Tory and a member of the celebrated Scriblerus Club. Shortly before he died, Swift, whose health had never been very goood and had steadily worsened, was declared insane and was confined to his household. Swift's main satires include *A Tale of a Tub* (1704), *The Battle of the Books* (1704), *A Discourse Concerning the Mechanical Operation of the Spirit* (1704), *An Argument against Abolishing Christianity* (1708), *Gulliver's Travels* (1726), and *A Modest Proposal* (1729).

JAMES THURBER (1894–1961)

American humorist, essayist, fabulist, short-story writer, writer of children's books, and cartoonist. Most of Thurber's books, apart from his personal histories *My Life and Hard Times* (1933) and *The Years with Ross* (1958), are anthologies that gather essays, fables, and sketches. These collections include *The Owl in the Attic and Other Perplexities* (1931), *The Seal in the Bedroom and Other Predicaments* (1932), *Fables for Our Times* (1940), *The Thurber Carnival* (1945), and *Further Fables for Our Time* (1956). Thurber's fictional world is often as strange and fantastic as that of his drawings, which are pervaded by the battle between the sexes and inhabited by marauding women and dogs. It also contains stoically repressed and docile men (such as the now celebrated Walter Mitty) who seek to escape from or fend off a comically unpredictable, menacing, and stifling real world.

MARK TWAIN (1835–1910)

American humorist, novelist, short-story writer, essayist, journalist, and lecturer. Mark Twain is a pen name for Samuel Langhorne Clemens. Born and raised in the mid- and southwest, Twain often deals in his works with the rural frontier life in these regions and on the Mississippi River. Twain wrote several travelogues and autobiographical works, often humorous and satirical, including *Roughing It* (1872) and *Life on the Mississippi* (1883). His main novels are *Tom Sawyer* (1876), *Huckleberry Finn* (1884), and *The Tragedy of Pudd'nhead Wilson* (1894). Some of his important stories and sketches are collected in *The Celebrated Jumping Frog of Calaveras County* (1867) and *The Man that Corrupted Hadleyburg* (1900). Twain's stories and other writings are in the tradition of southwestern humor and realism, frequently using the dialect and authentic idioms of regional speech and often containing strong elements of burlesque and satire. In his later works from the middle 1880's onward there is an increasingly strong skepticism and pessimism that weight his writing more and more in favor of satire and polemic rather than comedy and humor.

FRANCOIS VOLTAIRE (1694–1778)

French satirist, philosopher, historian, essayist, poet, and dramatist. Voltaire, a pen name for François Marie Arouet, began his literary career with satires—which were sometimes so successful that he was imprisoned for them. The sharp irony and elevated eloquence present in many of his philosophical and polemic works are even more prominent in his satiric poems. However, it is in fictional works such as *Memnon* (1749), *Micromegas* (1752), and *Candide* (1759)—which are at once philosophical tales and parodies of sentimental romances and adventure stories—that Voltaire truly excels as a satirist. Dealing with large metaphysical issues such as the problem of evil and the nature of man, his works satirize organized religion, inflexible institutions, supersition, authoritarianism, fanaticism, and intolerance.

EUDORA WELTY (1909–)

American short-story writer and novelist. Welty was born in Mississippi, and her fictional works are often studies of small town life in the deep south, marked by keenly portrayed colloquial speech and eccentric or grotesque characters. Her collections of stories include *A Curtain of Green* (1941) and *The Bride of the Innisfallen* (1955). Her novels include *Delta Wedding* (1946) and *Losing Battles* (1970). Like her fellow southern writers Katherine Porter and Carson McCullers, Welty is concerned with the mystery and mythic elements that lie just below the surface of daily living, and with self-knowledge, the hidden inner life, and communication.

NATHANAEL WEST (1904–1940)

American satirical novelist. West, whose real name was Nathan Weinstein, was born and raised in New York, the son of immigrant parents. His observations of American life in the city there and later in Hollywood (where he worked as a screenwriter) provided the basis for the urban settings and the major themes of the four short surrealistic novels he left after he and his wife were killed in an automobile accident in California. In *The Dream Life of Balso Snell* (1931), *Miss Lonelyhearts* (1933), *A Cool Million* (1934), and *The Day of the Locust* (1939), West attacks the simplicity of the Horatio Alger myth and the duplicity of that other favorite mythology, Hollywood, while in general he exposes the horror, lovelessness, cruelty, emptiness, and absurdity of contemporary urban life.

Topical Index